BACK ON COUNTRY

A story of longing for home

Jack Goodluck

Published by

Heart Space Publications
PO Box 1085
Daylesford
Victoria
3460
Australia
Tel +61 450260348
www.heartspacebooks.com
pat@heartspacebooks.com

Published in 2018 at Melbourne

ISBN 978-0-9924939-4-3

First published by Trafford as *Knock 'em Down Moon* ISBN 1-4120-3074-9

Introduction by Jack Goodluck

In the 1970s, for the first time in Australia, a legislation was passed that provided for Aboriginal people to claim ownership of their traditional lands. This coincided with the transfer of mission stations and government settlements to the control of Aboriginal community councils.

This story is about people in the circumstances of that time of change. None of the characters represent any real person, alive or dead. The Wainandas and the Ananardus do not represent any real groups. Their lands are said to be in and near Western Arnhem Land, and therefore they do use some words from a common language of that area. Goose Island, N.T. exists only in this story, as does Malangarri, but nearby Croker Island and South Goulburn Island are real. Two ancient legends, about the moon and an ogre, and the historical stories of a sea monster and of the inter-clan massacres, are public domain stories given to the author while living in Arnhem Land.

None of the characters in positions of public leadership or service represent any real person, living or dead. But the range of attitudes and the kinds of circumstances that are represented here are common in the territory.

Small remnant groups of various clans had, before then, taken refuge on missions and settlements, and had adapted, during three generations, to the ways and laws of mission stations and government settlements. Now the settlement superintendents and most of the missionaries were gone, and the clan remnants were labouring with the enormous responsibility of living together and trying to govern according to foreign notions and foreign structures, such as a community, a town council and public ownership across the clans. Their situations were utterly different from what they had known under the Mission or Settlement regimes or on cattle stations, and were nothing like their own traditional ways of being a lawful and productive network of independent and autonomous nomadic clans.

There was a considerable movement back to ancestral homeland areas with modern facilities that they chose to have, and young Aboriginal adults were needed in those places to cope with modernisation and to teach and lead through modern dangers and confusions. Mani and Helen are fictitious characters, but there are many Territorians in their generation who would understand from experience the predicaments in which they find themselves.

This is about a few characters coping with life and with each other.

There has been a growing awareness that mutual trust between First Australians and would-be helpers is essential to any kind of recovery from present disastrous set-backs.

In his book *The Politics of Suffering* (Melbourne University Press, 2009) Professor Peter Sutton, a long-time fellow worker and student in remote communities, almost despairs of any relief from present sufferings in crumbling communities. Policy-making and interventions will not end destructive trends, and neither will popular liberation movements. The "Reconciliation" that Australia has to achieve is a person-to-person thing, he says (page 209).

My story is about people trying to really relate to each other and to serve the needs of First Australians. Mutual trust, the essential element, is not easy to achieve, and without it the social break-down will continue.

I am a story-teller now, but for five years I conducted staff formation courses for community workers, trainers, jail-guards, adult educators and medical staff, as well as First Australians, at Nungalinya College in Darwin. The Commonwealth Government funded it all, including three month residentials.

We learnt together to be "trusted friendly helpers" to each other and to fringe dwellers of Darwin. Some of our students are still at work, forty-two years on, supporting community development. Sadly, there appears to be no similar staff recruitment and training today.

Jack Goodluck

Back On Country, is a term used by First Nations people that covers; having (their) land restored; life and connection to the land; with self-determination; recognition.

Dedication

In memory of my revered colleague and friend the Reverend Lazarus Lamilami, confirmed as the first indigenous person in northern Australia to be ordained into Christian Ministry. He helped us to understand each other, and made it easy to believe that respecting, serving and loving everyone was really possible. His punch lines made us laugh, even when he was dying – he helped me to see.

I dedicate this book to Peggy May, my inspiration and my partner in all things. Peggy's vibrant spirit with her caring, encouraging approach was essential to all we achieved together. This book would not have been possible without her.

Characters

George Simpson; a head stockman

Harry Simpson; a stockman

Jenny Simpson; wife of Harry

Bar-un-bar-un; local resident of Gugurr

Mr. Charlton; a station owner

Lag-i-ag-a; a stockman from Charlton's

Fred Archer; Director, Liaison Unit

Edward Blyth; Chief Minister of the Northern Territory

Cecil Reeders; Director, Health Department

Andrew Brown; Chief Liaison Officer

Harry Bagent; Aboriginal Liaison Officer and social activist

Gray Bridges; Communication specialist

Olivier (Livvy) Bridges; wife of Gray & educational anthropologist

Old Bil-a-go; a resident of a drinker's camp

Man-i Mang-gil-ul-u; a student teacher and leader to be

Lung-gar-oi; Mani's tribal brother

Bur-ing-al-u; Mani's mother's tribal sister

Jam-ba-gir-ril-a; Wa-i-nan-da Elder (Wainanda – Mainlanders on Goose Is)

Mondi Latu (Rev); Fijian missionary

Lola Latu; wife of Mondi

Jack Foster; town Clerk, Goose Island

Edna Foster; wife of Jack

Helen Cross; a student teacher

Wally Grant; a Bush school principal

Oliver Sutton; Deputy director of education

Lionel Gelles; recorder of rare sounds

Anette Gelles; sister of Lionel

Mr. and Mrs. Lee; old Chinese Territorians

Father Dick Sheean; a Catholic priest

Sister Bernadette; a Catholic nun

Ron Smart; ex-miner, leprosy patient

Stan Armstrong; a black rights activist

Lucy Charlton; a woman from Kununurra

Inspector Donovan; police officer

Na-ma-mu-i-ac; a creature from the sky

Gu-gurr; the man in the moon

Mul-ud-ji; the dog in the moon

Gu-ji-gar-i; a dreamtime ancestor

Pronouncing Aboriginal Characters' Names:

In the list above, the syllables of Aboriginal names are separated by hyphens, this is to help readers to remember to emphasise every syllable.

Vowel sounds:
An "a" is always close to the vowel sound in "h<u>u</u>t" or "ah".
A "u" always sounds like the vowel sound in "p<u>u</u>t", never like "putt" or "true".
A "k" sounds like a soft "g". And "ng" is one sound, as in "si<u>ng</u>".

There are many subtleties in the ancient languages of Australia's indigenous nations, but these simple clues will help English speakers to "hear" the names.

Fictitious:
The only names above that are not fictitious are Gugurr, Muludji and Namamuiac.

Table Of Contents

Prologue
Some years ago, as young men...

Arnhem Land Coast.

George Simpson wrote in the top right corner, then slid the lamp further back, to lure away the flying bugs. A second push just about fixed the problem, and he continued writing:

'Gugurr Creek, Postal Address: Charlton's Private Bag, Malay Bay Landing, via Darwin, Northern Territory.

Dear S. . .'

A light cough from the darkness outside the window-shutter stopped him. Might be a 'possum or something. He waited in the deep stillness, conscious of no sound of anything out there, except a distant crowd of frogs in a swamp, and noticed that, already, sweat from his writing hand had begun to make the edge of the page damp. Laying down the wet pencil on the dressing table that served as his writing desk, he took from his trouser pocket a large red handkerchief. It easily absorbed the sweat that was collecting in his eyebrows and between his fingers and along the low side of both of his forearms. Peering past the glare of the lamp, he studied the face that should have been his. He had seldom looked into a mirror in his years in the Territory, and still wondered if that very tan, work-worn and weather-beaten face, under a nearly white forehead, would ever revert to looking like him when he moved back down south – whenever that might be.

He wiped the pencil dry, folded the handkerchief to have the driest side down on the page under his wrist, and resumed writing.

'Dear Sis.

Hullo down there in that so different world. I wish I could give you some idea of life here. Every time I have been to Gugurr, five times all up now, it has been wonderful. Harry and Jenny are amazing. The other night at a camp fire at the headman's place, Harry read the Easter story to a crowd of about thirty Aboriginal people with a young man interpreting. It was something I'll never forget. And Jenny is a real brick. It's lonely here for a white woman, and always, hot. But this is a very special place, and our big brother is a marvel. This time I have been getting him talking a bit, and I have

written down some more of his ideas on how he works with the local people, and I've done a copy to send with this letter. I'm sure you'll find it interesting to read. I agree with him about what the people here need. They need to feel safe again and respected in their own land, and to find their own ways of sharing their country with us. He calls this "soft-aid", bloody funny name that does not really mean anything. I think they love him here, the native people. Most of them have not been included as traditional land owners because they lived in other parts of the country so they came here anyway, instead of to a government type village. He works for them and with them. He never expects them to work for him. But they seem to want to anyway.
We thought the Wet was finished. I did any way. It's muggy and sweaty tonight after the rain. Today was really hot, with no breeze at all. Then it poured with rain for a few minutes, but since then it has been really sticky.

This climate will never feel normal. I dream about being back down there in the temperate zone. And yet this is an exciting place to be. Here two worlds overlap, the black and the white, and what will be here in years to come hasn't appeared yet. In a way, we are blazing trails for the people who will come after us.

Most of the time everyone is decent and friendly up in these parts, and it's a good life. We're all, the three of us, looking forward to coming down home for Christmas ...'

That cough again. It sounded human this time.

He leaned over to peep through the gap at the side of the propped out shutter.

It was a useless thing to do; he couldn't see out into the semi-darkness, but whoever was out there could see him.

Harry's voice came from the other room. 'It's awright, Barry's come for me.'
   'What's up Barry?'
   'Proba'ly, the old man's died, I reckon. There's no wailing from the camp...'
   'No, you're right there. Might be, later on though. I'll just go and see what's up.'

George held his pencil above the page, waiting to hear if Harry was right: whether or not, in fact, Barry Barunbarun had come to fetch him.

Harry was talking with someone outside now, and George supposed that it must be Barunbarun. This was someone else, and his family too, that he would miss. It was Barunbarun's father who had told him a couple of nights ago, the way this place got the name Gugurr. A man by that name, and his dog, Muludji, walked a dry track in from the sea, in search of water. When nearly dead, the dog smelt underground water. Both man and dog dug until water burst in a whirl-pool, drowning both.

Before they died Gugurr told his dog, 'Come on, we'll send our spirits up to the moon so everyone can see us.' And, today, you can see Gugurr and dog Muludji on the moon, and some people say, 'See, we can keep going even if we die.'

Whoever it was outside, the conversation went on for a couple of minutes. Harry seemed to be weighing up the options of going to the camp or back to bed. Curiosity and concern got the better of George. Now that he was distracted from his letter-writing, he slid clear of the dressing table and made his way outside. It was Barunbarun. Harry was backing away from him, explaining, 'I'll just grab me hat, an' be right with ya, mate'.

'You goin' out then?' George met him.

'Yeah, yeah, mate,' the elder brother stopped to speak with him. 'I thought you'd be sound asleep by now.'

'Nah, I can sleep when I'm gone from 'ere. I'm just scribblin a few lines to Sis. So's yah can get it away in the next mail.'

'Boat unloadin next week!' Harry sounded as if he were reminding himself of things to be done before then.

'Yeah, I know, I want this letter to go on the boat, and I'm sorry we won't be 'ere to help with the unloadin', this time. But it's time to be headin' back. Look, Bro, this might be goodbye.'

'Young Lagi'll be ere with the horses at first light. You gunna be long? Nar, nar... you wouldn't know, I s'pose. But, anyway, if y'are, then...This is it! It's been...you know...'

He faltered, trying to find the right words, and could only feel the sorrow of leaving Harry and Jenny again. Perhaps one day he could stay on here and work with them. Tonight the thought was appealing, but he knew that he had to go back to Charlton's Station where he could earn some real money.

Harry closed the awkward silence. 'Yeah, I well could be late gettin back ere. The old man sent Barunbarun for me. He wants to 'ear the story about Stephen again.'

'Yeah? Like that one, does e?'

'Oh, you know, when Stephen's dyin after they stoned im. An' 'e looks up at heaven and tells the crowd 'e can see Jesus alongside God, an 'e asks God not to blame 'em for what they done to 'im. It's the old man's new dreamin' story, I reckon...since e knew e's dyin. Anyway, Georgie Boy,' He put a hand on his young brother's shoulder. 'It's been tremendous, 'avin you 'ere again. And your little mate, Lagi, 'e's a goer, in't 'e? You'se a both done a power o' work 'ere, and saved me an' the men months on the pick an' shovel. We should ave a workin air-strip by the middle o' the dry, thanks to you two. An it's been great for Jen to 'ave you 'ere, too.

For company.'

To his dismay, George Simpson saw over his brother's shoulder; the words lost as his brother's wife Jenny, was standing in the doorway, backlit by lantern light from the two bedrooms, her arms and legs spread as she leaned a hand on each side of the door frame, with her wonderful female silhouette exposed through her flimsy night dress. '…You're always more than welcome 'ere, Bro,' Harry was saying, and George surprised himself by throwing his arms around him; something he had never done before. Harry returned the hug and patted his affectionate kid brother's back.

'You mind, you look after yourself on the way back up along the coast. Stick near the shore after you cross the river', Harry released him from his arms. 'There's been a bit o' talk about some hostiles camped nearby. From inland up your way.'

'Yeah, we'll play safe, but I'm not too worried about anything 'appening. Between us, I reckon, Lagiaga and me'll be able to convince anyone out there that we're just harmless friends.'

'I'll just get me 'at,' Harry said again and strode over to the doorway, where Jenny was holding something out towards him.

He took his hat, and talked quietly with her. Meanwhile Barry Barunbarun moved towards George Simpson. 'You mob done lot of good 'elp, from work on that airstrip place now,' he said. 'Everyone talk 'bout that work, now.'

'Oh, we're family!' Harry explained. 'We're just family who come to elp,' he made it sound matter-of-fact.

'You go 'long that billabong track, eh?' the local man sounded worried.

'We like to go that way, to camp by the water on the first night.'

'Plenty mosquito there?' Barunbarun asked.

'Yeah, you know that. Always plenty there, but we can use the fire smoke and sleepin nets to keep em off.'

'What about other mosquito with few stingers?'

'What others?'

'Two leg mosquito,' Barunbarun waited for his hearer to recognise and name the subject of his words.

'Two white legs?'

'Not white. Two black leg. Big mob of black mosquito, might be.' George Simpson took the warning, and stepped closer to his informant.

'Thanks, Barry. Don't worry. If we meet any people who want to sting us, we can be friendly and then they can be friendly too.'

'Can't trus that mob. Not from 'ere. They differen' differen', cheeky buggers. They get hot bout them whitefella before. To pay-back. You friendly, but black mosquito still can sting.'

They both turned at the sound of hooves on the track

'Eh!' Barunbarun recognised George Simpson's young travelling mate, Lagiaga, a shortish black man, made taller by his high-heeled riding boots and broad hat. He was leading three horses towards them. 'Ere's your little brother, too early. Ready to ride them 'orses.

Harry Simpson strode back from the house wearing his felt hat, and went aside to briefly rest his arm affectionately around George's shoulders. 'Go with God, Tich.' He spoke softly, using an old favourite name for a little brother. 'Duty calls now and I'm away.'

As he moved off, George called to him, 'See ya later, Gayu!' - a local dialect name for an older brother.

'Watch them mosquito!' Barunbarun cautioned as he passed George Simpson to catch up with Harry. Both men stopped briefly to speak with Lagiaga when he paused with the horses. Harry shook him by the hand, and said something by way of thanks and best wishes for trouble free travelling, then moved on. 'You goin now, eh?' Barunbarun used English, one of the languages he shared with this young fellow from the sunset country.

'You leaving Gugurr now?'

'Yeah, I'll leave Gugurr now,' Lagiaga replied, then added lightly. 'But I might take 'is dog with me.'

The local man turned to go, then burst into laughter. 'Yeeha! Ha! You can't take that dog away, 'e haf ta stay up dere in our moon, this time.'

Lagiaga was grinning as he met George Simpson and handed to him the reins of their pack-carrier, Nugget.

'You're early, mate!'

'Yeah, I can 'elp you load up, Gayu, You had a sleep?'

'No sleep. Too much talk from old men. They say dangers too close. We should go when the moon is down an' before the sun is up.'

The white man from Melbourne took stock. So, it was not just Barunbarun who was concerned about the black mosquitoes. The old men were too. He could not claim to be as wise as they were about safe travelling in the present circumstances. Obviously

Lagiaga was taking them seriously, and so should he.

'I 'aven't started to saddle up yet,' he explained. 'An' I 'ave ta write a little bit more in one jura letter for my sister down south.

Then I can come. I'll tell ya what. You get the croc skins from under the 'ouse. They're all salted and wrapped… an' by the time you've got 'em strapped on Nugget, I'll just about be ready. Okay?'

He turned to look at the house. Lantern light was still showing around the open shutter of his room, but there was no other sign of light in the house. Jenny must have gone back to bed. Before moving in, he turned away and looked at the western sky. His young partner had not moved on. Still he watched George for a moment before he also looked to the west.

The moon was low, and silvering the fluid edges of a passing cloud. Soon it would be behind the trees. Then it would be safer to travel; but they would have to get as far as they could before the sun was up. It was bright now, and they would have no trouble seeing their way around with the horses and skins.

'Irrwadbad mob,' he told George. 'Them stranger mob. They from up that Sun Down Country, I reckon. Irrwadbad story place. We can't trust 'im.'

'Yeah?' George stared at his informant, puzzled to see him still standing there, and talking in terms of a dream-time story from the west when there were better things to do. He had expected him to move on and load Nugget as soon as he could. But then, wasn't he himself too, still standing around. It was time to stop star-gazing, mooning about and get a move on, into the house where his things were, and the unfinished letter to Sis, and where Jenny was too, who he would have to say goodbye to. He was fairly sure that he could do it without making a fool of himself. But he was strangely irritated! What did Lagi Lagiaga mean about the strangers being from Irrwadbad country? That country was important story land for everyone over there in the west, but it was a long time since anyone actually lived there.

'Awright. Let's make a move,' he grunted.

They each went their way, and George stepped lightly into the house and along to his room and finished the letter to Sis.

He then went to the front room door, to say goodbye'.

'I made a cup o' tea for you, and some bread and beef to take with you, Georgie,' Jenny was in the kitchen doorway. Her hair was loose and she was still only wearing that thin nightdress, bare shoulders and arms, bare feet, her pretty, sad little face, and her slim shape still showing. 'Come and have a cuppa and say goodbye.'

'I'll just...' he began with a gesture to suggest that it was his time to roll his swag.

'Please, Georgie,' she pleaded. 'Come and say goodbye to me first.' She took him by the arm and drew him into the kitchen...'I want a hug, too.'

In the filtered moonlight she looked beautiful, and desperate for him to embrace her. His blood stirred and he stopped breathing as if that might calm his pulsing chest.

'Jenny,' he whispered, and his voice sounded to him as enormously guilty as she was for breaking the age-old taboos of looking and closeness, and of naming and touching. New passion surged through his body, and he began to feel capable of doing everything, and increasingly less afraid of the consequences of doing anything.

'You're my family too,' she whispered. 'You gave your brother a hug, and I need hugs more than he does. I always do.'

He pulled her against his throbbing body and held her firmly, surprised at the effect on them both of the touching sensation as his spread hands moved the smooth nightdress fabric over her soft flesh. It was too wonderful to stop, and too...he didn't know what.

'Kiss me goodbye Georgie.' She looked into his face as she whispered, and he bent to put his full lips on hers and taste them.

'Oh, Georgie,' she held him against her more firmly and her open lips towards his mouth. Somewhere outside a wooden door closed sharply and a bolt was shot home.

His head swam as he began to reply with her name. 'Jenni... Irrwadbad!' he gasped.

She froze in his arms. 'What?' she whispered.

Releasing her from his arms, he stepped back. Now he understood why his little mate had spoken about Irrwadbad outside. 'Irrwadbad mob from the Sun Down country,' he had called the strangers lurking out there somewhere in the bush.

Now George remembered that the Irrwadbad dreamtime story, about two brothers and a wife of one of them, was a Western Arnhem Land equivalent of the Adam and Eve story. Unfaithfulness had led to disaster and death to the woman, and to her mother who should have prevented her sin. Lagiaga had not been as worried about where the black mosquito strangers came from as where his Gayu George, was going, into the house with his brother's wife.

'Jen,' he smiled into her face and brushed back loose hair that had fallen forward on her cheek. 'This can't happen, love. You're my dear sister-in-law, and I love you like I love my brother. Let's keep it that way, eh?'

But Jenny seized his hand and pulled him along the passage and into the bedroom.

Lagiaga finished packing things into the saddle bags and waited impatiently for his white fella buddy to reappear from the house.

When George came he approached Lagiaga and held towards him the oilskin bag that held the bread and beef that she had prepared. George glanced at him. How much had he heard, or seen, he wondered?

Lagiaga took it and said, 'you had a hard time to finish your letter to your sister eh?'
   'Yeah, that's right,' George replied as he turned away towards the sky and the pathway out of the place.
   'Buruli!' Lagiaga was pleased, and smiled broadly. 'What d'ya reckon? It's time to go?'

Taking a last look at the house in the moonlight, George Simpson put his foot in the stirrup and swung up into the saddle.

   'Yeah, let's go. You lead us out, all right?'

Nugget was hitched to the saddle of Lagiaga's mount, Pardner, and was apparently contented with carrying the wide load of crocodile skins and camping gear. As the leader mounted up ahead, the three horses, veterans of many long journeys, braced themselves for another dark bush trek. Lagiaga whistled as if he were calling a dog, and looked around the ground behind his horse.

   'Come'n boy!' he called.
   George Simpson glanced about. 'Who're you calling?'
   'We 'afta leave Gugurr now, eh?'
   'Yeah, so what?'
   'But we don't 'afta leave his dog, too!'

This time George got the joke, but without laughing. It was not the first time that young Lagi had clowned about, trying to get a laugh, and last time he did it was when he knew that his gayu was feeling low. Truly, this was developing into a dark morning in more ways than one, but with his little mate at his side things were already beginning to look brighter.

   'Just so long as you keep your flamin' dog away from my horse's legs!' he kept the joke going.

'Yeehee!' the leader hooted. 'Ere we come Billybong!'

He took Nugget and Pardner out towards the track, and George Simpson looked over at the backlit cloud now clearing the moon.

Gugurr and his dog in the moon were settling below the tree-line, and George was glad to still be alive and on the move, cross country, riding high in the saddle again in the land of the living. He patted Dandy, rocked gently once in the saddle, and they moved out to follow the leaders. Straight ahead he could see Nugget's load riding smoothly, and a journey of between one and two weeks, and a future, he was quite certain in his aching heart, in which he would never see this place again.

PART ONE
Signs of Change

Chapter 1
Darwin, many years later

Others out and about in Darwin might be in a swelter, but Fred Archer felt okay. He was determined that the Chief Minister's cronies would see him arrive cool, calm and collected, as usual.

There was definitely a change in the air. The late night rains had been nothing more than end-of-season scattered showers, and there had been no sign for a couple of weeks of another monsoonal trough descending on the coast. It had been a hot and wild four and a half months, since the thundery advent in December of this stormy Wet. The monsoonal deluge had come, repeatedly since then, saturating the world, and, at last, the Wet was into its final movement. The Easter moon was clearly on the wane. Increasingly predictable winds were making afternoon forays from the south-east, with the first of the short, sharp squalls of the Knock-'em-Down Rains. The dragon flies were out and about; sure signs that the true ending of the Wet finally had begun.

Although Archer might be a couple of minutes late, he was bringing home the bacon. The Chief, again, would be pleased with him and confidentiality had been preserved from those who had no right to know.

He would have preferred to go straight into the conference room with the map he had for the Chief, but, there was no avoiding it, he had to do it through the Communication Consultant, and he also needed to run an eye over the Liaison Unit Office as he went through. Still, it didn't really matter either way, he was confident that, when he made his entry alone, the Chief's inner circle would see his special place in the great man's service, and that had to be a good thing.

He looked to the right as he came through the glass door into his Unit's open space, with regret that he could not be so sure of proper respect from the motley crew of assistants he had been given. The Aboriginal Liaison Unit was a unique team of cross-culture operatives that he had to mentor and supervise, but it was a thankless assignment. They didn't appreciate the wisdom and experience that he had to impart. But, whether or not they appreciated it, they were blazing a trail, as pioneers of a new way of operating, and he had been entrusted with their supervision and development.

Only Morris Powell and Sally Forrest, the Darwin City Liaison Officers, who had returned from fostered childhoods in southern and eastern Australia, were at their desks. The women's Aboriginal Liaison Officer, Sally, was on the phone, and Morris was writing, probably filling out the first skimpy draft report of his recent talks with a couple of families about why the Chief Minister would not help them to claim land ownership in a mission area where they had been taken and had spent most of their early childhood years. Three others were absent on field visits, but where was the stirrer?

Might've known, Archer told himself, as he caught sight of the lounging form of the ex-stockman-come-Legal Aid agitator, Harry Bagent, propped against the door jamb of Gray Bridges' office.

Bridges was the big-head consultant who had to process this map for the meeting. Just as well! It looked as if he had nothing else to do. These two misfits were probably arguing about nothing again. He decided again to find a chance to recommend that they get rid of Bagent. He was too full of his own opinions to make a good ALO. Too clever for his own good.

'Have you followed up the talk about Queensland Black Power agents being in town?' he challenged Bagent as he approached to go past him into Bridges' office.

The Aboriginal Liaison Officer turned casually. He was dark brown, medium height, slim but upright and muscular, with close-cut black hair and blue eyes. 'Eh? Oh, yeah. It sounds pretty interestin'. They're gonna 'ave a few meetin's around town this week. I reckon I'll go to 'em meself.'
'Oh, is that so,' the Director of the Liaison Unit was blunt. 'Well, make way now.' He strode on, when Bagent stepped aside, into the office, past its occupant, who waited to hear whatever else it was that had still to be heard. Archer continued,
'Get the written report about these Queensland activists on my desk ASAP, Bagent…if you value your job.'

Because the Unit Director moved to the desk without turning, he missed seeing the obscene gesture that Bagent made. Bridges lingered. He looked cool but a touch formal compared with his brown companion. Paler, too, a lightly tanned Anglo-Australian, with blonde waves, short-sleeved white cotton shirt hanging loose, long light-weight drill trousers and open sided sandals without socks. It was the trousers that created the formal look. The ALO, Bagent wore blue jeans, and his footwear was of the raised heel variety that was favoured by horse-lovers and men who had no intention of stepping lightly on the Earth. Everyone had to notice Harry's comings and goings.

'Well, I think I hear what you're saying, Harry,' Bridges said.

'Yeah, well,' Harry defiantly leaned in through the doorway once more. 'I mean, don't expect me to believe everyone can just shake hands and live together happily ever after. We've had enough o' that oil on troubled waters rubbish. There's no gettin away from the fact that progress can't happen without conflict. Y' know what I mean?'

Archer cut off any response that Bridges was thinking of making. 'This is urgent!' he snapped, looking around so that Bagent could see his annoyance. The insolent grin he received before his mutinous ALO sidled away, convinced him that, given half a chance, he would kick Bagent's backside to hell out of the Aboriginal Liaison Unit, even if current public sentiment was running against being tough with Aborigines.

'The Chief Minister's strategy conference has started,' he told Bridges urgently. He knew that this was so, because the far end of the corridor had been dead quiet as he arrived. The visitors and the Chief were already in the Conference Room.

'I've got this confidential map, and, as the Chief told you, you've got to prepare multiple copies for everyone at the meeting, so I'll leave it with you. Watch you don't leave any spoilt copies layin' around. Treat it as top secret. Right?… Now, I'm going into the meeting. Soon as you've got 'em done come and pass 'em in to me…'

'That's not how it's going to happen, Fred.' Bridges voice was belligerent. 'While you were out, the Chief and I decided that it was better to make use a data projector and to throw it up on the screen. I've set everything up in there; and after I make the image, I'll come in to operate the data-projector.'

'That's hardly necessary!' the Unit Director declared.

'Apparently it is necessary, Fred,' Bridges replied boldly. 'So that you'll remember that I'm not one of your Liaison Officers. Remember? I'm the Chief Minister's Cross-Cultural Communication Consultant. I take my orders directly from the Chief? So that's how it'll be, Fred.'

The Unit Director moved back towards the door impatiently. 'My God, you can be petty Bridges,' he complained. 'I haven't got time to waste here helping you to split more hairs. Just get to it will you. 'Wanting no reply, he rushed into the corridor and along to the Conference Room.

Bridges was frustrated at being robbed of the chance to tell Archer, once and for all, that he would get the job done in his own way and not because the Director of the Aboriginal Liaison Unit told him to do it. Four minutes later he paused at the conference room door to look at the image and the original map in order to tell the top from the bottom, then quietly let himself into the meeting. Fifteen white-shirted

Cabinet Ministers and Heads of Public Service Departments sat around the long table, listening to the thirty-eight year old Chief Minister of the Northern Territory, Edward Blyth. This most brilliant head of government, ever in the Territory, that was according to Archer. Blyth was fondly known to his intimates as Ned.

Archer had found a seat at the far end of the table, and looked at Bridges as he entered and glanced about before going across to a chair that he had earlier placed by the wall close to the data-projector. A glance his way by the Chief Minister, who continued an unscripted inspirational oration about the future of the Northern Territory, told Bridges enough to hold the map before him for the speaker to see. After another glance, the Chief indicated to Bridges to insert the USB memory stick into the computer. At the same time he picked up the remote handset and laser-pointer. When ready, Bridges gave the chief a nod.

As Blyth clicked the remote, a large clear image of the outline map appeared. It was a simplified felt pen drawing of a large area that included the entire length of the Alligator Rivers, East and South, and of the Mary River to the west, and extended from the shore of Van Diemen Gulf in the north to Pine Creek, old worked-out gold and uranium fields in the south. Near the south-eastern corner there was an area shaded in with light strokes. It was a clear image to which Blyth could refer immediately without missing a beat in his improvised address. He put his hand before the map, watching its shadow on the screen, and Bridges withdrew to the chair by the wall. The Chief Minister said one word emphatically as he pointed five outspread fingers at the shaded area in the approximate centre of the map.

'This,' he looked back at them all and went on. 'This area, located in the region beyond the upper catchments of Jim Creek and the South Alligator River has now been recognised as Aboriginal land, belonging, as you all know, to a clan that has made its case and has won in court. It's in an area of rich possibilities and we must support the new owners in realising its potential, and all learn to work together to serve every-one's best interests...'

'Excuse me, Chief Minister,' someone was on his feet, leaning forward on the table and speaking with quiet deference. It was Cecil Reeders, head of the Health Department. He was sitting beside Archer. 'I do apologise for interrupting, but if we are to be discussing political considerations, can you assure us that only people with political or policy-implementation responsibilities are present at this conference?'

'There's no need for concern,' Blyth stopped. 'Oh, Gray! Would you mind? Thank you for your help with the communication technology, but you won't be needed again in this meeting. Would you mind?'

Bridges knew that the question required no answer, especially as Neddy had extended his open hand towards the door. It was simply a polite way of saying, Get lost…you only belong here as a functionary, good for switching on data-projectors, but not to be trusted to hear political discussions. Which was fair enough, but by what kind of logic was the Chief's communication specialist excluded when Archer and a range of public service heavies were included? He didn't look in Fred's direction. He knew that he was smirking happily to see him sent packing. But it did hurt to think that this meeting was probably going to canvass his own original suggestion of a new kind of consultation between government and Aboriginal communities without him even being in the room. Would Fred or the Chief acknowledge his authorship of the idea? Not likely, and most of the time he didn't really mind that, but now, it was hard to take when he thought of some of the other ring-ins, with no better reason than he had for being included in this huddle of the Chief's confidantes.

His proposal to Ned was for another small step towards the government taking a supportive role towards Aboriginal people's self-management of their own affairs. But, he knew that, to some members of this meeting, the suggestion would seem idiotic. If they could have their way they would probably do everything that they could to bluff the newly recognised land owners into opening their country to government exploitation of its minerals and tourist interests. He had heard enough comments to that effect from the Chief himself to make him really nervous about his intentions. If he had been allowed to stay in the meeting he would have at least found out what they were up to. But there was no chance of that now. As he let himself out, he knew that it would be up to him to help to communicate the government's proposals to the indigenous owners, whatever they were. In frustration, he headed for the coffee urn and tried to attempt to concentrate on the preparation of a fuller proposal for the up-coming Territory-wide consultation with a difference.

Bridges left the room in a huff and went outside for privacy. Retrieving his mobile phone from his pocket he called his wife Libby. Upon explaining what had happened, she said "Oh Gray I do love you…but sometimes you need to have more character… you need to fight a bit. But sorry love, I've got to go into a meeting. Can we talk about this tonight?"

Thoughtful, Bridges went back inside to his desk.

When Archer reached the Liaison Unit's open area, Bridges was sitting on a corner of Bagent's desk loosely holding an empty coffee cup. Sally and Morris had turned in their chairs to face Harry and Bridges. The women's ALO was clearly concerned about something.

The Unit Director walked between them. 'I need to see you,' he spoke quite evenly to Bridges as he looked into his face. 'Orders from the Chief. An urgent assignment.'

Without rising Bridges said, 'Anything to do with what Sally's been telling us about?'
'What's that?' Sally's Unit Director asked her directly.
'Oh, well, nothin' really. Only talk I been 'earin' about, from some of 'em at the Women's Centre up at the Uniting Church. They reckon that they're goin' to take their kids to listen to these people who've come 'ere from inter-State.'
'Black Power?' asked Fred.
'I don' know about that. Is that who they are?' Her voice was in neutral. 'What's our job? Do we reco'nise people's rights to make up their own minds about goin' to 'ear 'em, or what?'
'Say nothing,' Fred was in over-drive. 'Don't get involved in talking at all. They're none of our business. Say nothing either way, right?' He turned to look at the door of the Chief LO, next to Bridges' office. The door was slightly ajar. 'Andrew's back, is he?'
'Yeah,' Morris confirmed with a hint of amusement. 'Not very talkative today, 'e just got a cup o' tea, and straight into his office.'
'Will you come into Andrew's for a few minutes?' Archer asked Bridges. 'It concerns the two of you.'

With that, he turned on his heel and went to see Brown. Bagent seized the chance to respond to something that Bridges had been saying earlier. 'Yeah, well, I 'eard what ya said before…but…think about what I was sayin to you too.' His eyes held Bridges. 'We've had enough. If direct action can wake people up, that can't be all bad.'

'Yeah, I take your point, Harry. And I'm sure you're being realistic. Lots o' things point that way,' Bridges was the essence of thoughtful consideration. 'I just happen to see from where I stand a scenario that's not that simple. I mean there are other points of view, mine's one of them…and from where I am, I see direct action as only second best. The way things turn out in the future could depend on whose set of realities we decide to deal with now.'

Harry smiled lightly, 'Do you ever listen to yourself, Gray?' he said. 'You're sufferin' from too many brains, I think. If you go on that way you can always talk yourself out of ever doin' anything about anything. Whatever way you see anything, well, then there's a different way to see it, too, isn't there? So forget it.'

Bridges opened his mouth to reply, but Archer called from the doorway, 'yar right, Gray?'

He had to go, but it annoyed Bridges that Bagent always begrudged him a word or nod, a glance of friendship or cooperation, any sign to put him at ease, to acknowledge that they were allies. Again he was left hanging in limbo, uncertain whether he had been treated as friend or a foe. In the office, Andrew Brown, the Chief Aboriginal Liaison Officer, sat back in his desk chair. Some of the glow that had made his black face shine while Bridges had been talking with him at the coffee urn a few minutes ago had vanished. Both he and the Unit Director who had taken a seat in front of the desk were looking serious.

Bridges dropped into the other chair that faced Brown's desk and asked, 'Has something come up?'

'Yes,' Archer said. 'As I've just mentioned to Andrew, I've been talking with the Chief Minister and he's agreed with me, that you two...'

'Us two, which two?' Bridges responded. Andrew was one of Archer's Aboriginal Liaison Officer Team, nominally at least, the Senior ALO; but Bridges felt bound to make the point once more, in front of Andrew, that he himself was not one of the ALO team but the Cross-Cultural Communication Consultant, and accountable to the Chief Minister alone.

Ignoring his complaint, Archer announced, 'I told the Chief that I would let you know. By all means, check with him if you like. He agrees with me that you and Andrew here are the only two who can handle this sensitive assignment as it should be handled. We want you both to go to Goose Island on the morning flight tomorrow for a specific consultation job.'

Brown leaned further back in his chair tight-lipped. He seemed to be less than pleased with the thought of a flight to Goose. Bridges read the signs of the Senior ALO's reaction, but felt quite differently about it himself. The prospect of visiting the island again delighted him. He had enjoyed his couple of visits there, and, as it happened, his wife, Livvy, would be away at Malangarri in central Arnhem Land for a few days from tomorrow, on an evaluation visit to the community school, something about the effectiveness of bi-lingual education above the infant grades.

Brown raised no objection, and they discussed the assignment for nearly half an hour, all agreeing that it could only be a good thing if two Goose Island men could be persuaded to come to their "Friendly Consultation". Fred emphasised that the contribution of the Aboriginal people to the progress of the Territory was highly valued, and he found an opportunity, as usual, to impress them with the brilliance of the Chief Minister.

Both men listened glassy-eyed with boredom; each in his own way wondered how long the Director of the Liaison Unit could talk without giving them one original thought.

Andrew was making an effort to give full attention to his senior officer. He was sure, for his own reasons, that even when bored, it was necessary for all indigenous people to try hard to fit into the dominant society, a view which he had adopted many years ago. It had paid off in career advancement for him. Bridges' grand obsession was to do anything that would achieve a bit of tunneling through the mountains of ignorance between the positions of culturally deaf powers-that-be in the government and the Aboriginal clans who now bore responsibility for the settlements that used to be run for them, mainly, by the Missions.

Both recognised the importance of the assignment, and the necessity of leaving for the island in the morning, and, when eventually Archer stopped talking, they went to see the booking clerk in the financial section and made arrangements to be on tomorrow's early flight.

Chapter 2
Goose Island

Bridges was home and showered before Livvy climbed the outside stairs with a spring that defied the sultry afternoon. Her final day of preparation for the forthcoming stay at Malangarri had been full of the kind of challenge that she thrived on, and her adrenaline tank was fueled up and ready to go. Brunette, and only four centimeters shorter than Bridges, she was, as usual, managing to look reasonably cool and unflustered. Olivia Bridges always appeared to carry with her an air of confidence and it was infectious among her work colleagues. This had played a real part in her promotion, nearly two years ago, into the position of Educational Anthropologist in the Aboriginal Education section.

Bridges had opened the louvres on both sides of the living room and was ready with a couple of iced drinks. They stretched themselves in cane chairs, enjoying the south-easterly cross breeze, sipping, and sharing the day's doings. She was surprised and interested to hear that she was not the only one going into Arnhem Land in the morning.

Livvy prepared the meal after her shower, with token assistance from Bridges, and after they had eaten, they sat for a while exchanging their plans for the next few days. There were two or three things to rearrange now that both were going away. After the sun was down, they spent a few minutes outside on the decking above the stairs, gazing across northern suburban roof-tops to the sea that was just visible in the moonlight, and catching the breeze on their faces.

Livvy mentioned the outline of her carefully timetabled itinerary, and referred to her new assistant, Helen, a sophisticated single Aboriginal woman, thirty something, who was going with her. She was in a Trainee Teacher placement under Livvy's supervision, because of her special interest in bi-lingual education.

'You sound a bit worried about her.' Bridges put out a feeler.

'Do I?' she was surprised. 'No, not worried. Puzzled, perhaps. She's unusual, beautiful and vivacious, and very outgoing. Not exactly aggressive…more confident and assertive. And yet, this morning she was so subdued, sort of sullen, that it seemed she wasn't happy about our assignment and the flight to Malangarri tomorrow. Then, when I asked her, she was surprised and sparked up, saying that she was looking forward to it.'

'Where's her people's country?' Bridges asked, remembering Andrew's apparent reluctance about the trip to Goose in the morning. .' It had occurred to him that Andrew might have some such reason for not wanting to return to Goose Island.

'I wouldn't know anything about that,' Livvy told him. 'She never talks about such things. But speaking as an Anthropologist, I'd have to say that she appears to be an Arnhem Lander, probably a Western Arnhem Lander, but an atypical one – strong on individuality and weak on social sensitivity. Genetically she's obviously fully Aboriginal, but in cultural orientation she is like an urban person with clear and correct English speech.'

'Do you like her?' Bridges took another tack. Livvy was in no doubt.

'Oh, yes,' she was positive. 'I really do…and I think it's great that in her thirties, she has decided to get teaching qualifications. I'm going to do all I can to support her. I admire her…it's just that…I know it sounds silly…but at times she scares me.'

Bridges rubbed the tense place between her shoulder blades and spoke with assurance, 'Helen's very fortunate to be going out with you, honey… and I think you're both gonna have a ball.'

She accepted the encouragement happily and dropped the subject of the Malangarri visit in order to appear more interested in her man's program than her own.

As they stripped for bed, Livvy said, 'sorry if I offended you earlier on the phone. Just I had so little time'.

Bridges said, 'Oh, you were right with what you said. I do need to have a bit more gumption.'

She smiled at him but said, 'what do you hope the outcomes of your jaunt'll be?'

Livvy was lying on his shoulder under the overhead fan, and whose welcome soft weight on him aroused him. He moved sensuously, but she edged away.

'First things first!' She demanded playfully.

'Oh,' he leaned over her eagerly. 'In that case…It's not the outcomes that come first with me.'

She laughed and squirmed out of kissing range. 'Nor is it with me. But let's just share our hope for outcomes first, then we can get more serious.'

He lay back on his pillow. 'Let me see. Outcomes?' he said, smiling his amusement at Livvy's unswerving practice of talking over their hopes and expectations whenever they were going into a major cross-cultural education venture. Always the outcomes. It was her routine way of planning excursions, and she kept him up to the mark, too. Or was she playing with his mind to see if he were as distracted by her naked body as she hoped he was? Whatever, he decided to play it cool, and answer her routine question in a routine way. 'To get full participation at our new-style consultation,' he said. 'Yes, that's it.'

'Is that all?' she asked, as though there might be more.

'Yes,' he said lightly. 'Yes, that's all. Just to help the Goose Islanders to see the advantages of the consultation, and of being in it.'

'Just that?'

'Yes,' he was more serious. 'That, and helping them to come happily, 'er, willingly. No. More-er-wholeheartedly. Oh, damn it, you know what I mean!'

'Uhu,' she snuggled into his neck. 'I like the Goose Island people.' He responded to her closeness with a kiss and a caressing hand, but his mood was suddenly too cool, and the night seemed to be getting too hot for embraces. He could already feel unpleasant sweat rising where she laid her cheek against his throat.

'I like them too!' he said peevishly. 'I'm looking forward to spending a few days over there!'

'Darling,' she sounded worried, tentative.

'Mmh…' he waited, half knowing what was coming. 'Can you be sure?'

'What, about whether or not I'm being used to manipulate the Goose people to do something they don't really want to do. That's what you mean, isn't it?' He was beginning to sound irritable, and they both noticed it. Why sound irritable if there were no truth in what she was suggesting, about being used for serving a devious purpose?

'Do you think I haven't thought of that?' he said. 'Perhaps Neddy'd likes to think I'll manipulate them, but you know my stand on that sort of thing. My one and only concern is to get people listening effectively to each other. Nothing's changed. I'm as committed to the people's interests as ever…as committed as you are. Do you doubt it?'

'No, of course not,' she said with her fingers in his hair. 'I only wanted to hear you say it again, I suppose.' Then it was her turn to restate her hopes for the Malangarri visit, and Bridges tried to stay focused on her account of the expectations, some additional research data on bi-lingual education, and participatory learning that she and her assistant would do out there. He caught himself not listening, and knew that it was because he was still nettled. Of course he wasn't going to let Neddy use him to play the Goose people for fools. She kissed his mouth and said, 'are we going to say a proper goodnight? Our last chance to for nearly a week…?'

* * *

In the morning, when Livvy dropped Bridges at the Darwin Airport, Brown was already there, having been delivered by a government driver. He was in the act of giving some money and advice to a disheveled old Aboriginal lay-about whom they had often seen hanging around the airport lounge, apparently from a nearby bush camp. There was a "drinking camp" not far away. Bridges had been there once to listen to "the mind of the people", but it had been a futile exercise and he had not bothered to go there again. The camp existed on handouts from relatives coming from and going to homeland settlements through the airport. It seemed likely that this old man was a member of that community.

'Good'ay, Gray, Mrs Bridges,' said Andrew.

The drunk waited, as if to speak to Andrew, but Andrew said to Bridges, 'Excuse me for a second', as he went and whispered something to the old man. The old man glared, but said nothing and he shuffled away.

'Is that Old Bilago?' Bridges asked.

'Yes, that's him,' said Andrew. 'He's up early.'

'Yes, on time for the planes.'

Livvy wished them both a good trip, gave Bridges a quick kiss and she hurried to pick up Helen Cross for the flight to Malangarri. A sharp sense of regret took hold of Bridges because he must spend the next few days with Brown, rather than with Livvy.

'Come on Andrew, we have a plane to catch.'

* * *

Once up in the air and the flight settled, Bridges found himself considering the black white issue.

He and Livvy had often discussed the fact that, even though the Assimilation Policy had been replaced by the Integration Policy, and that was followed by Self-Determination, and now by Self-Management, a rolled back version of Self-Determination, there had been many in career positions of those who were still active in Aboriginal affairs and there were among them unconverted bearers of the colonising attitudes of Assimilation. He knew people as committed now as anyone ever had been to assimilating, rather than to liberating Aboriginal people or supporting their self-management. Archer, the Director of the Aboriginal Liaison Unit himself, gave ample evidence that he was one of these. Not that Fred ever said anything explicitly Assimilationist. In fact he very seldom said anything that would let anyone know where he stood on any issue. Bridges always worried about Fred, as he never let you know whether or not he was really for advancement of

Aboriginal people's interests in the directions that they chose for themselves. He was left with the impression that he was not at all concerned about their interests, so long as his record was clean, his job was done precisely and he was satisfying the Chief Minister.

* * *

When they had been in the air for half an hour, he looked at Andrew's profile as the old man on his right watched the Alligator Rivers country sliding by far below the fuselage. This man sitting beside me has a perfect right to live alone in the YMCA, as he does, and I am just as small-minded and prejudiced as any of the people that I might criticise for squeezing indigenous individuals into stereotyped images of "those people", unless I accept him with his own right to choose, and his own chosen individual style of life.

'Great country down there,' he said near Andrew's ear, leaning across to look at the vast wedge of wilderness lying between the estuaries of the South and the East Alligators.

Andrew nodded. 'True,' he said without turning. 'Great country all right.' There the conversation stopped. Bridges contented himself with gazing at the estuarine mud flats, lush plains and, further ahead and inland, the Arnhem Land Escarpment country, rising to a harsh red plateau and looking almost as though some primordial giant baker had rolled it out when it was still red dough and sliced it irregularly into flat loaves that had risen full and rounded.

Equally incredible was the tiny pimple of rock coming into view to the left, far ahead of them, forcing its way up through the surrounding savannah woodlands near the coastal plains. He recognised it as Tor Rock, and was again reminded of how relative everything was and how dependent on one's point of view. If you were looking at it from off-shore, on high ground near the southern tip of Goose Island, Tor Rock would be prominent on the southern skyline, yet from this altitude it was barely distinguishable from the other patches of red rock standing above the green of the plains and gorges. To the south east, an occasional glint of water showed another river winding through hills and among the scattered patches and peppers of low gums, pandanus palms and, along the muddy rivers and inlets, mangrove trees. Not many tall trees survived here. Few of the spindly eucalypts could withstand the battering of the annual monsoonal storms and the occasional furious attacks of cyclones on parts of this coast. Only around billabongs and in the deep chasms and declines between the rock hills did the trees grow tall. This had not stopped enterprising timber growers from propagating native pines and hardwoods in a few areas, for timber harvesting. Where many trees stood shoulder to shoulder, some were sure to survive the fury of the seasonal cyclones.

Away to the north-east there lay Murganella, the forestry township, visible beside a dark green forest of purpose-grown pines, a timber camp, and the meandering river from which the place took its name.

The eastern sky was blue but hazy around the horizon. Already the evaporation of recent rain was producing a mist. By early afternoon it would form towering piles of white cloud over every land mass, even the smallest green island; and in the late afternoon, or when the temperature dropped at sunset, it would be carried off by the seasonal air currents to fall over land and sea beyond the coast, or precipitate and rain down again on the land from which it came.

He looked around the plane, taking notice of the other passengers. Hang loose, he told himself, taking a deep breath, and deliberately relaxing into the seat. I must be more worried about this assignment than I thought. He wondered about an older Malangarri man chatting to his flying partner. His smoky old eyes and stained teeth flashed his delight as he nodded incessantly about what they were discussing.

'That old chap over there,' Bridges said loudly to Brown's ear, indicating the man from Malangarri, 'I think he's from Malangarri, and I saw him on a visit to the Teacher's College in December?"
'Oh,' Andrew sounded vague. 'That one?' He looked. 'Oh, yes. He's Malcolm's mother's number one brother.'
'Idji?' Bridges affirmed his knowledge of this special relationship. Andrew turned and looked at him blankly.
'Yes,' he said. 'He's his mother's eldest brother.'

This old bloke's really far gone into a white-fella mind-set, thought the cross-cultural consultant. He knows very well that I'm familiar with that relational term for the most important guardian in Manggululu's life. Andrew seems to be determined not to speak in terms of his people's culture!

'Everybody's related on Goose,' said Andrew, turning away as though to return to looking at the distant haze where varied shades of pale blue suggested sea and islands.
'Yes, I know, Andrew,' Bridges didn't need a basic lesson on the all-inclusive kinship system of Aboriginal society. What was Andrew thinking of? Normally he would give Bridges credit for knowing such things. Just what was he thinking about? Definitely pre-occupied, possibly avoiding getting into talking about young Malcolm

Manggululu, the student teacher, better known as Mani, pronounced Munny, who had just returned to visit his family, probably to have talks about the land rights claim. Damn it, thought Bridges, he will talk to me about Mani Manggululu! After all, that's why we're making this trip.

'All related to Mani, then?' he said aloud.

'Yes, yes, that's right,' Brown replied, half turning, but not looking at his staff colleague.

'And all related to you, Andrew?' Bridges' personal thrust got by the other man's guard and touched him. He looked up and stared into the white face for a few seconds before saying, 'yes'.

His voice hung heavy with something. Sadness? His eyes still searched Bridges' face. For what? For some assurance? Some understanding of the nature of the question, the probing into personal areas long guarded against enquiry?

'Yes, and no,' he added turning towards his companion. With a tentative smile, he went on. 'Lot of my family don't like me to live like white people. Lot of them don't want me for family anymore.'

Bridges waited.

'Have you heard the story of Uncle Tom's Cabin, Gray?'

'Oh, that one about the American slaves?' Bridges shammed a naive interest in the question. Already he knew that Andrew was going to talk about the fact that he was widely known as an Uncle Tom.

'What do you reckon, Gray? Uncle Tom was for his own people, or for the slave-owners?'

'Well, I always thought,' Bridges hesitated, realising that he was greatly influenced by modern interpretations of Uncle Tom's faithfulness to his white masters as treachery to his people's cause. 'I never could quite make up my mind,' he said.

'What about you? I mean, er...what do you reckon?'

'I always feel sorry for that old bloke,' Andrew replied. 'He done the best he could for his people. That's what I reckon.'

'Could be right, Andrew,' Bridges found a new surge of sympathy softening his attitude towards his companion. 'Yes, you could very well be right.' Not that he really thought so.

'Not long now,' said the former Goose Islander, glancing back at the coastal scenery, 'All through this way we used to come when we were young fellas.'

'Can you see Goose, yet?' Bridges leaned towards the window.

'I can see it,' Andrew said softly. 'And over that way, more east, you can see Warawi. People over the other side of the plane, they'll be seeing Darch Island and Croker Island and DeCoursey Head. I know all those places from when I was a young bloke. Malay Bay, too. Down that way. Where the Macassans used to meet up with each other from long time ago, before the Balandas (white people) came, hundreds of years, and buy stuff from the trade store.'

Bridges sensed a flood of memories and emotions pouring into Andrew's mind, but could think of nothing appropriate to say about them. He undid his belt and leaned across close to the glass.

'Oh, yes,' he said. 'I see Warawi. Where's Goose? Just back a bit? Could be an island or it could be a cloud.'

'No, it's not just a cloud,' said Andrew. 'It's Goose Island. Best place on this whole coast for getting plenty of Magpie Goose.'

Now that Andrew had begun to open up, Bridges seized the moment, 'We have to get Mani and his grandfather to agree to come to the consultation'. He sat back to re-focus on his mental preparation for the encounter with the young student teacher and his relations.

'Yes,' the older man looked at him reassuringly. 'I know Gray. It might be they'll come, if they want to. If not...I'll try to help them see it's for the best, so they can have a say about land and everything.'

The cross-cultural specialist nodded and dropped into serious reflection, canvassing all the possible ways that he might talk with young Mani and Jambagirrila, the grandfather; rejecting some approaches as manipulative, and others as not positive enough to win a response. He wished that he had taken opportunities to get to know Mani better. On the few occasions on which they had spoken together, at the Aboriginal Teacher Education Centre, he had found the student a bright and alert young man, but stiffer and more serious than most of the others. Perhaps a concealed anger lay there, such as Bagent was beginning to express openly towards whites. What was it Harry had said yesterday? There's going to be no advancement for black Australians without conflict. Was that also what Manggululu believed?

Of course, there was a sense in which Harry was quite right; people can't change for the better the position of a lower socio-economic group without that causing conflict, or at least a sense of competition and threat, among others maintaining a position on the social ladder. But Harry seemed to mean more than that. He spoke as if conflict were a means to an end, a legitimate means of winning advancement, rather than an after-effect of liberation and progress.

Eventually, more than a century later, indigenous Australians were recognised as citizens and assured of the same democratic rights as others, plus, at long last, some overdue respect as the original owners of the land. No longer were they to be treated as the vanquished outsiders of British civilisation, but as the heirs of both the centuries-long European struggle for democracy and the local millennia-long struggle for daily survival in civil relationships with each other, with the land, with the created living world and with the eternal mysteries. Now there was a nationwide ground swell of support for their cause, and deliberate conflict was not necessary. It would be counter-productive.

Yet, the government procrastinates with the amendment of the constitution... This infuriated many...

It indicates that the Australian Federal Government and the various state and territory governments have no real interest in indigenous people rights and concerns for recognition. If there is any one additional reason for the aggravation of the conscious movement, this is the one – that is just the straw that breaks the camel's back...

This was a time for listening to each other, dealing with inherited white racist attitudes and co-operating to serve the needs of all Australians. It was no longer the time for pitched battles; but a time for using all legitimate democratic means of claiming a fair and full life-chance for everyone, especially for those who were behind the racist eight-ball. Creating conflict in this situation could be setting the clock back, when all the conditions already exist for using the legitimate opportunities that are there for all Australians to claim their rightful place in the world, and their rightful equity in Australia, in the land and the nation. But even with this perfect opportunity, the government holds back.

Bridges wondered if the government's real purpose was still the belief that by withholding recognition that there ultimately would be assimilation. Surely not?

Perhaps Mani saw things as Harry did, in terms of advancement through conflict? Time would tell.

There it was, as they flew in below the cloud. The lush darker green of Goose Island's silt plains and forests of native trees, was separated from the brilliant light greens of the Arafura Sea, by the double belt of red cliffs and white sand that ran along its rugged south-western corner. Bridges' nose pressed against the window, delighted at seeing such a beautiful place. Even Brown seemed to be mildly excited as he studied the scene below.

Now that they were in sight of their destination, their assignment became a concrete reality, no longer something to be played with in imagination, but a serious task to be done. It was time to lock into place every principle, value and intention that were essential to the cause that had brought them here; whether for liberation and self-determination or for adjustment to, and advancement into, modern urban society. Bridges knew where he stood, and was clear about what he liked to call his stance. But it was a bit of a worry to have to admit that he was not so sure about where Andrew Brown would stand if the Chief Minister set out to hoodwink and diddle the Goose Islanders.

Chapter 3
Mani Manggululu

Although Mani had worn shoes for much of the last three years, his feet were still hard and left deep tracks in the soft sand as he trod, on the way down to his canoe. The old man, Jambagirrila, lying under his bough shade, rolled on one side to look into the sky for a sight of the inter-island plane that he already had heard in the stillness. Yes, it was coming as expected, but out of sight from the beach this time. He turned to watch his daughter's son march proudly by, fish spear in hand. The young man knew that he was being watched, and waved without turning, calling, 'I will bring you home a big fish, Old Man.'

The end of the Wet Season is a restless time in Arnhem Land. The four months of constricted living close to bough shades and stringy-bark shelters, or, in these more affluent times, for most people, close to an iron and fibro house, is over; and gone is the threat of cyclone and of the fabled "Lightning Man" lurking in mountainous blue and grey thunder-heads. Morning haze and billowing afternoon clouds rise with contented ease up from the mainland horizon and the islands. The coastal people have renewed their covenants with the sea, gleaming green again after months of silver and grey. But sea travelers must stay awake to the possibility of afternoon gales and squalls from the mainland and occasional late cyclones. Water springs out of high coastal rocks and will never be far below the ground's surface in the next few months.

Old men, who have long-gone past participating in hunting expeditions, commission the young to bring a family car or a hired vehicle and drive them to favourite camping spots. To younger men it is a good time to go roaming in the jungles for food or bark or even giant trees to fell and fashion into canoes, or to take the family rambling and "learning" the country. The hunting is not as easy as it will be near the end of the Dry Season, when receding surface water will bring the geese, goannas, pigs, wallabies and buffaloes into shrinking wetlands; but there is good water, and a man may stay long on the hunt. Even those who have lost the habit and the art, since trade stores, wages and social security payments have made hunting no longer necessary, still seem to be affected by the spirit of restlessness at the change of seasons.

Since the dragon flies and the south easterly breezes have returned, the night choruses of the swamp frogs have given way to the shrill mass drumming, in the midday, of armies of cicadas on the hills, newly liberated from seven years underground, and available to mate among the trees. Grasshoppers and other long term residents are also out and about, and, a friendly world is calling all creatures to venture from their sheltered corners into fuller living.

This was a good feeling; the gentle sea air from the bay, his own home bay, cool on one side, except where the brief blue narga cloth was tied about his loins, the mid-morning sun warm on the other.

The sea exhaled like a sleeping giant. He listened to its soft breathing, as of a relentless power in deep slumber. The body of the bay rose, held a moment, and expired in whispering foam around the long beach curve. No-one else was to be seen on the beach. Only a sleeping dog in the shadow of a derelict fishing boat.

This was his bay. Darwin, Batchelor, the Aboriginal Teachers Education Centre, and the world of the know-all white man seemed to belong to another existence.

Changing his thought... take your rest grandfather. Sleep on old sea. I will be at work. I can do what must be done. I will watch over the world. I will be the provider, and bring food this day out of the sea. Food for my people. My grandfather will eat to-night. He will eat well because of me; and so will my brother's "promise girl" because he is away, and her old people, and my youngest mother, Buringalu, and her husband who is too old and weak now to go fishing.

Other places, and other things tried in vain to get into his thoughts, but he turned about, took in the brilliance of the bay, and once more thrust Darwin and the Teacher Training Centre from his mind. Wading in beside the canoe that was floating off the sand again in the high water, he breathed the smell of unseasoned ancient wood, new rope and sea salt and enjoyed the beauty of this special possession, his own canoe. His hand rushed out to touch it, tap it for its wooden sound, grasp it for its strength, and to swing it towards himself for the joy of it being his.

'Canoe,' he said. 'You are beautiful.' Could anyone know this happiness? Yes, it must be like this for Buringalu with her new baby at her breast. He had watched for his youngest mother at her tent door just now, playing with her baby before she put it to her breast. It was a new thing for Buringalu, this happiness. At the Settlement School she had not been so happy, only with the happiness of silly girls, the squealing, giggling excitement of those who fear being more than silly, and will suffer by being what they are. Last month she did not have such happiness, as she walked heavily up the beach carrying water for her white-haired husband. But when her baby had come she had blazed into life, like a fire from the night before when you put on dry grass and your face close to the earth to blow. He had seen it happen before in women. It was their life. It was their secret and untouchable treasure. No man could take it away, and no man could have it. Not in the same way. It could never be the same for him as for Buringalu. She had laboured and brought forth a baby…a new person. He had only helped to bring into being a canoe. This one that he had begun in the last vacation, and his grandfather had completed.

No, not only a canoe! A canoe! A true canoe! From a great jungle tree, a great canoe. Men's hands and a swinging adze had formed it. A canoe of beauty, swiftness and strength; a delight to the eyes of all who saw it, and a powerful vessel for a powerful man. It could never be the same as for a woman. Yet it was enough. You happy, happy women who get babies, if it is more than this!

His gaze skimmed the near waters for unfriendly fins and lurking jelly fish. There were none to be seen, but still he sprang into the canoe before hauling up the anchor rope. It was a new rope from the Trade Store, still stiff. It was a strong rope, as an anchor rope should be; and the anchor rock, whose weight swung up in one hand while the other hand inspected its knotting, was well-tied, as an anchor rock must be.

'Come on, canoe,' he said as he caught sight of one boy who was not at school. Young Madjirri was coming along the beach. Manggululu placed the anchor rock well under the three-cornered seat at the front of the canoe, and neatly coiled the rope on top. He would paddle along the beach to Nabadgardi's place, and wait to see if the boy would show any interest in coming fishing. It was a good back seat, and his feet fitted strongly against the one in front. The paddle cut gently down into the flashing green sea and firmly compelled it to carry the man and his vessel, rising and falling lightly, bow and stern, across the length of the tiny waves.

He sensed a noise inland and raised the blade of his paddle clear of water. Shutting out the noise of the sea, he listened. An urgent purring, different from the electric generator's engine if that were to be carried unexpectedly against the breeze, told of the Land Rover's activities at the station. He waited to be sure.

Yes. It was coming to the beach. 'The Land Rover's coming to visit the beach,' he said, as if the canoe might be interested to know. 'What for this time?' He listened again. Yes, he was certain. It was coming down. 'Let him come,' he went on to the canoe. Let him rush along and butt in on the life of the people with his cheeky orders. Let him try. He can try. Then he can go away again. Soon he'll go away, like the rest of the missionaries who had all those years running this village, and all those short stay government know-alls. I hope he quits soon. He understood why the old people and a few others wanted the missionaries to come back. 'Mission was good,' they say, 'but Gubment too hard. Gubment bring too many Balanda workers, new ones, always new ones…and always they take our jobs off us that we learnt from the Mission. They come and go. But Gayu Jack Foster, true missionary, that bloke, 'e still 'ere.'

But, as for Mani, he had told the other young men, 'Foster and all the other Balandas can all go to hell before they make me take their orders, in my own place!' When will they learn, he wondered; when will my people learn that these Balandas are supposed to be just paid servants of the people?

The Land Rover came into view swerving slightly in sand as it took the turn-off along the back road to the houses. Mani shook his head as he took up his paddling again.

Trust Foster to be in too much hurry to slow down for the turn off, he thought.

What was his hurry this time? Maybe it was Lamara, Ladaga and Bundarai. They were probably sleeping in, after the late night brawl that had flared up after a long sitting around the camp-fire, after they had been hearing Mani's stories about life in Darwin and Bachelor.

'He never walked into my hut again. Not since I told him off and left the building job.' That had been more than three years ago; and Manggululu had clashed with Foster twice after his return from the years in Adelaide. That was one of the main reasons why he had been glad to have more time away, in the college in Bachelor. It was infuriating that, at a time like this, Foster could barge into people's lives, even here in this peaceful beach place if he chose, to hook Mani's frayed temper yet again. 'Why do they let him get away with it? Every one of them will let him barge in and wake them up. They follow him like geese, and will probably do everything he tells them, though nothing more; all for the sake of a quiet life. He thinks he is still a missionary, not an employee of the people. And they let him get away with it.'

Somewhere up there now Foster was doing something, telling someone something about something that should be. They will say, 'yes, yes,' and feel bad when he is gone. They will say, 'this is the law, and we must do what the Balanda tell us. It is still the Mission way, the good way'. But they will know, when he is gone, that it is only the soft way, the money way, sugar, tea and flour way. And the temporary Carpenter, Mechanic, Farmer come Town Clerk will be waiting to teach them again, men who have built houses, to drive a nail with a hammer, and drivers who have brought vehicles to the island by bush roads and rafts, to fill up each morning with, first and most importantly water, then with oil, petrol and air. And their hearts will turn sour because no-one ever listens to them and the bitterness of the New Law has to be swallowed again, and spoil the sweetness of the Old Lore of this place, and the proper Lore of our fathers, and of our people here now.

'Look at him, canoe,' said Mani, noticing young Madjirri standing near the water's edge. 'Glad to be away from the Balanda prison, where children learn to fear the white man's rough ways, and so learn foreign ideas and numbers, instead of the timeless laws of earth, sky and sea, of hunting and food gathering, and the sacred Lore of family duties and right relationship behaviour to all people. It makes me sick to think of being a teacher in a Balanda-run school! They don't care for right relationship behaviour, only for being busy doing useless things and obeying the Balanda bosses.'

Madjirri watched and Manggululu waited, idly paddling off the beach near Nabadgardi's house. The shadow of the Casuarina tree was already off the house, but still much longer than the tree itself, and was imperceptibly moving off the bleached rib bones of a huge turtle the old man's family had enjoyed last year. The Land Rover was on the move again. It came on to the beach with the determined growl of four-wheel driving, bumping across the half-buried logs of the ramp laid over the sand for boat unloading. Foster stopped the vehicle near Madjirri, close to where Mani was paddling; but already the canoe had turned and begun to travel slowly back along the beach. For Mani felt an uncontrollable rush of hostility against this invader, and his angry passion must not be seen. Foster and the boy would not see his angry looks. Steadily he pulled on the oar, crossed over, and pulled again, very slowly.

'Oy!' yelled the staff man. Mani looked over his shoulder as he finished a long, slow stroke, and saw Foster's face under his squatter's broad brim, and an arm that waved him to come ashore.

'We will treat this rude bully as he should be treated,' he told the canoe, and it took the canoe a long time to come back, as he paddled it the long way around the circle, out into the waves and back again into the shore. Foster had left the Land Rover and stepped out after the canoe. He had on his riding boots, khaki shorts and shirt with rolled sleeves and epaulettes. Mani guessed that the Town Clerk had, once more, to double as a stockman and was looking for a couple of other riders to go out with him to round up and bring in a free range steer for a kill to feed the community. He remembered times past when he had helped cut out a steer and bring it to the slaughter yard. It was a worthy job of work for the sons of hunters. But so much bad feeling was standing between them these days, like a heap of garbage to be sorted out, that no-one had much heart for such work anymore. It would be different if all the Balandas would clear off and leave the islanders to do it themselves. Then they'd have a good time riding the range. But as things stood, Foster would be lucky if he could bully one of the riders to go with him today.

Desperate and arrogant, the Town Clerk-cum-stockman continued to wave in the slow paddler, but he must wait until the canoe came in from its long circuit. 'We'll put him off,' said Manggululu. 'His big act of 'I am the great boss' will have to wait and he will be tired of holding his steam for so long.'

'Come on, Muscles! Can't you go any faster than that?' Foster yelled. Madjirri grinned, and Mani made no reply. It was not a real question: it was only an insult and it only sharpens an insult to give it a reply. Instead, Mani brought his canoe to sand further along, so that Foster must walk back further than should have been necessary.

'I came to see if we can talk about your work again, now you're back, Mani,' called Foster; but Mani did not believe him. He knew that Foster was desperate to get anyone to work with him, and had come to call out things in front of the boy, things to make Mani look a fool. He had failed to make him a white man's fool, a copy of busy, mouthy Balandas; he would not succeed in humiliating him now in front of the boy, this tribesman of the coming years.

'You must have been very unhappy, Manny,' called Foster, louder than he needed to, for the boy's sake; it was so that he would hear and see Mani's embarrassment. 'Trying to do teaching work, now you can see that your proper work is here on the station. Your people need you here. I suppose you're glad to be back home, are you, Mani?'

The student decided to let the question pass, but looking straight into the face of the staff man, he rose from the canoe and walked out of the water towards him. He looked searchingly into the tanned face, and asked softly, 'can I do something for you, Mister Foster?'

'You can come and join the work force,' the staff man reacted irritably. Mani shook his head. 'Yes! You can jolly well come and help do some of the work around here,' Foster was getting loud again. 'Either a man is sick or he does a man's work, or he's not a proper man. You people can't keep leaving it all to me.'

The boy, Madjirri, was blank-faced with apprehension. 'It must be you have been working too hard, Mister Foster,' Mani said sarcastically. 'You're getting too hot about nothing. Why don't you take a rest or go back and do the Town Clerk job you get paid for?'

The boy stifled a giggle.

'Yes, I am working too hard, my boy…but I can't say the same about you. Some people have to do the work that others are too lazy to do.'

Not that, Mani softly and silently pleaded, not 'my boy', or else I soon will be too hot and they will see me lose my control about something too little to be a proper trouble.

'It must be that they are doing the wrong work,' he said aloud. 'They better stop that making Balanda lavatories and drains all the time. Just new places for flies to come. And what for do they want to fill the same roads after every Wet?' He was saying too much, but he must finish it now. 'They should build run-off banks or let the holes stay. It won't make food. That's only coming on the boat every month, or huntin it.'

'That's all you think of, isn't it?' snapped the Town Clerk. 'As long as you've got a full belly you don't care a tap whether important work gets done or not. You're not much of an example to the young ones here. You should be ashamed of yourself.'

You should! You should! Again. You should! How dare he, this jumpy, washed-out little foreigner tell him what should be. How would he even know what should be here? His conscience belongs to Down South or to Europe, not to the Bay.

'Mister Foster, I'm sorry, excuse me, but I've got my work to do.' He moved a little closer and spoke in a controlled voice, but with fierce eyes growing larger and whiter. 'You drive along and find some old men if you want to talk. Now I have work to do. The tide won't wait for me. It wouldn't even wait for you, Mister Foster.'

'Don't give me any of your cheek, boy!' Foster barked. Then, more appealingly, he went on. 'There's no need to get nasty. I just hate to see a good boy like you runnin' away from building for your people's future. You're needed here more than at teacher's college. This station's grindin to a halt! And what are you goin to do now, go bushy again, by the look of it. You can do a lot better than that, young fella.'

But Mani had turned to his canoe and was pushing out. The boy watched Mister Foster carefully. He could tell that the Town Clerk was not feeling like joking, but was not sure why.

'Why aren't you in school?' the Balanda demanded, and when there was no reply from the motionless and expressionless Madjirri, he went on, 'get on the back and I'll take you up to the school.' Madjirri did not move except to glance towards Mani for a moment.

'Go on,' the Town Clerk demanded. 'Get on board!' This time the boy did as he was told. Foster strode to the door, climbed into the cabin, revved and began to drive away. As the Land Rover grabbed and lurched forward, the boy decided to jump off straight over the side. The brakes gripped, the vehicle jolted and the irate driver sprang down to the sand again.

'What the devil do you think you're doing, you young idiot?' He was really yelling this time. Mani, in his canoe, turned to discover the cause of the sudden release of the heat that he had kindled in Foster.

When the Mission moved out, and most missionaries had decided not to stay on as employees of the Town Council, why hadn't some of the respectful friends of the people stayed, instead of this know-all, mean-minded old-fashioned missionary? Power had gone to his head. Now he was the great white boss. Just like him to stir up fear in children, and expect children to take growling that adults wouldn't tolerate.

Madjirri had not risen. Instead, he turned his head away, sitting awkwardly where he had landed, both feet and one hand half-buried in the sand.

'How many times have you been told not to get off a moving vehicle? Don't get on again if you can't show that you've got some brains in your head.'

This time as he re-entered the cabin he slammed the door, and took off as fast as he could. Madjirri reached the canoe and Mani leant away to keep the balance as the boy climbed in, while still keeping an eye on the whining Land Rover careering away over the soft sand.

'Here, you have a go!' Mani grinned at Madjirri and passed him the paddle, then moved to sit in the middle of the canoe laughing loudly, 'ha ha ha! Look at the Town Clerk who knows everything and nothing.'

It was a long circuit around the main reefs. Madjirri enjoyed paddling down current while Mani trawled a long heavy line baited with three pieces of red hessian, and taught his outdoor student how to fish in right places at the right time. After two hours at sea they brought home a good catch of the favoured big fish. The two women and four children who met the returning canoe marveled at the skill of the fishermen. Trevally and baramandi, all longer than Madjirri's arm, covered most of the floor between the canoe's seats. The children were eager to get a fish to take home, and Mani quickly began to hand them out with instructions to deliver them to the right people. Jambagirrila's baramandi was there, the biggest, to impress the old ex-fisherman, and a trevally each for his youngest mother, Buringalu, and for his brother's promise girl's family.

'Madjirri is learning to be the fisherman. One day he'll get plenty of fish on his own,' he said, patting the boy's shoulder proudly. 'This is our life,' he said to the boy. 'Don't let the Balandas take it away.' It was a command and a plea.

By the time Mani had distributed fish to his relations, mounted the steep slope behind the beach and come to Jambagirrila's house, a visitor was there who had arrived on the morning plane. It was his idji, his mother's eldest brother, Makkurndil, whose home was in the sunrise country of Malangarri.

This uncle looked like someone who had been staying in Darwin, dressed like a man returning from a city holiday. But this was not where he made his home now. What brought him here? His hair, was beginning to show his arrival at the years of wisdom. Jambagirrila, with obvious pride and glowing pleasure, called as Mani came near.

'See? Idji ere'! Idji came to see his young man. And look at this young man. Fisherman!' He took by the tail the large baramandi that Mani passed to him, proud that his grandson showed him this respect in the presence of his idji.

Strange, thought Mani. I don't mind at all the power of my idji over the course of my life. It is good when my own people want to check up and give direction, but not when foreigners try to do it.

'Plenty fish?' the idji asked his nephew.
'Ee-ee, Idji,' Mani assured him. 'Yes, plenty! Too much fish over that reef. Plenty turtle too, but we let 'im go'.

Mani spoke in English because that was the language that his uncle had elected to use; but when he said turtle, he pronounced it 'duddle' the way his family did. This was a sensitive matter, choosing the language in which to address each other, and he knew that by using English, idji was being considerate to him and his position as a student within the Balanda's education system.

Altogether his idji was fluent in nine native dialects, belonging to two distinct language areas, as well as in English. Had it not been for Mani's involvement in teacher training, his idji probably would have addressed him in their traditional Wainanda mainland language, or the Ananardu tongue of this island, or in the Gundawalidj from further east, which he often now used at Malangarri; then it would have been good manners for Mani to reply in Wainanda. According to the men who taught him to behave in socially appropriate ways – that would have been in strict observance of the code of polite discourse, speak in your own language and listen in the other person's. Mani recognised that his mother's brother was nervous of him, probably because he was getting somewhere in the Balanda culture.

Now these heartless Balandas were the dominators of the people. At times they seemed to control the powers for making the future. How to live with them was a huge and sickening puzzle. He and a few others who had grasped some of the secrets of their power, were expected to go to a college and learn more of their magic, and to teach older and younger generations to understand and use it. But the danger was, as Mani well knew, that some people might think you were a sort of Balanda yourself now. Even worse than that, you might really start to see yourself in that way! Mani was determined that such things would never happen to him. It was for this reason that he was concerned by his idji's way of speaking with him.

To be treated by his idji as if he were now a man of the Balanda culture sickened Mani. Inwardly he rejected the thought, and bitterly regretted what he saw as a sort of fear in his uncle's manner. It was intolerable that this man in whom authority was vested, by the revered Rom, the primordial Lore of the ancestors that had been ceremonially reenacted repeatedly by countless generations, should be intimidated now by his nephew's association with the callous Balandas. Mani felt his whole being mounting a reaction, to rebel against the enormity of this moment; but as quickly as he formed the intention to speak in a traditional language, in favour of respecting his idji's initiative. If his idji chose to speak English, and he did not follow that lead, then he might cause embarrassment or offence. He might appear to be inconsiderate and self-willed, and that would be a shaming thing for both of them.

After a painful moment of tension, he decided to continue in English. Why was it not possible do both things, to be traditional with his own people and also be compliant with his idji? Why were the old men yielding ground to the Balanda culture? Didn't they understand that young people like him could learn to use the outside culture without letting it dominate their lives? The bearers of the eternal Rom and the Madayin rules were growing unsure of themselves. He thought of his father who had died too young, and was angry with him for dying, and with old men of his father's clan who should have authority in his life. There were few, very few, men of the Wainanda mainlanders still alive and leading young ones like himself in the wisdom and laws of the ancestors. Some were city drunks, and some had become assimilated into the Balanda world; and he was, at that moment, angry with them all. Unless they could be shown that it was possible, even today, to be true to the old ways, all the rising generations would be lost. But if they could stand firm, then, he felt sure, the whole coastal society could survive and adapt to new conditions as their ancestors always had done. That was why, he reminded himself, he had been attending ATEC as a sort of culture trader of his people, commissioned by them to bring back needed information and knowledge. He needed to keep reminding himself that there was always a danger that his generation might forget the ways of the Madayin.

'Come and tell me all about college business you been learn,' Makkurndil said.

Jambagirrila waved them closer to each other, to talk together privately. 'Come 'ere,' he indicated the clean sand area beside his fire. 'Sit, sit. You idji an' young man sit 'ere an' 'ave talk.' Then he turned and strode away to his house carrying the baramandi.

Makkurndil and Mani dropped down cross-legged; and the idji adjusted the point of a long log further into the glowing heart of the fire. 'You come 'ome, eh?' he said at last. Still Mani waited, until eventually the old man turned to look at him.
'It's good to come 'ome?' he asked.
'Ee-ee, true, Idji,' Mani was emphatic. 'It's real good to be back 'ere. I always like to come 'ome.'

Makkurndil stared past the fire, towards the sea beyond the nearby pandanus trees. 'Ye-es,' he drawled. 'Good place awright.'

Whatever he had to share with his sister's son, it was clear that he was not going to turn to it in a hurry. Among Balandas, Mani would have expected to come to the point quickly, but with his idji he was prepared to be engaged in indirect discourse until the one who was leading chose the appropriate time to disclose the real purpose of the conversation. It was a matter of great importance among his elders to avoid being direct. Directly disclosing yourself, your opinions or feelings, was seen as a kind of indecent exposure, being too immodestly personal. It could lead into personal comments about one another, and even to directly disagreeing, or confronting another person. Causing offence or animosity threatened the delicate balance of peaceful relationships that were so essential to survival and good order among all the people onwards into the future. Mani had been wondering why, if his idji had been in Darwin, he had not been in touch with him at ATEC to arrange for them to see each other. He was pleased when Makkurndil turned their talk to Darwin.

'More better than Darwin?' he asked. 'You like here better than Darwin?'
'Darwin's ugly!' Mani muttered. 'I don't like to stay too long in that place. I only like to be in Darwin to get a 'plane to come 'ome. Like yesterday. I was in Darwin yesterday.'

Makkurndil smiled because he understood that his nephew was sorry that they had not met in Darwin. Mani's voice betrayed his disappointment. It made the old man smile because he could see that his young man was showing good manners. He still knew that it was good manners to speak without bouncing your words off the other person's chest or questioning him. But it also amused him that Mani's unspoken expression of disappointment showed impatience. They both knew the question that now was in the air. Why had the idji not called his young man in Darwin?

'Looks like good season 'ere,' the idji said, deliberately ignoring the wordless question in order to teach Mani a lesson; not to try to push his idji to talk in a certain way. 'Plenty water in the back billabongs. You seen it yesterday, in the plane?'

'Yeah, I seen it. Good feed everywhere this time. Good time for 'unting, 'ere,' Mani's voice was subdued. He was ready to go wherever Idji led him. 'Big mob geese, and plenty big bush fruit, too.'

'Oh, yeah, always good, 'ere!' Idji's voice sounded as if he were closing that exhausted topic in readiness for moving on. 'Just like Wainanda mainland country.'

'I never been there yet,' Mani picked up what his elder initiated. 'My grandfather tells me lots of stories about his young days there. Good water an' 'untin' down there, in the Gudjigari land, 'e reckons. You went there with Land Rights lawyers and gubment, eh?'

'Oh, ee-ee, that's the really best place,' Idji was staring into the fire and slowly wagging his head, like someone enjoying special memories. He picked up a stick and poked the fire. 'Ee, an' before when I was young fella. We went through all that way. Oh, it's a beautiful country.'

He turned to his nephew. 'Now Bunyi been tellin' me you done a good job in Darwin, talkin' with 'im and those gubment and court people too.'

'Little bit, I been sayin' to them. What my grandfather told me I 'ave to say.'

'You done good, young fella. Now, all our people can't believe we really won against the Balanda gubment in the court. It's a new time for us now.'

'Yeah, it's excitin', eh?' the young man smiled.

'Your old man,' Makkurndil referred to Jamagirrila. ''e been tellin me we gonna sign up the last law papers for that Lands Right next week maybe.'

'Oh, yeah,' Mani agreed tentatively with what his grandfather had said. 'But you know the Balandas! Next week might be next year.'

So they talked for a half an hour. Makkurndil led the conversation around the places, other than this island and his home at Malangarri, where Wainandas live these days, and whether or not they might want to return to live in their ancestral lands sometime in the future, if a homeland settlement is set up over there, in that mainland place. Then he turned to commenting on the coastal places where life was better than inland or in the city, and Mani accepted all that he said, adding here and there a little new information about his discoveries of life in Batchelor and Darwin.

His mentor turned the discussion back to the good conditions to be enjoyed on Goose Island, and spoke of how greatly he had enjoyed his morning fishing excursion with the boy. When the older man paused, staring into the fire and giving the long log a push, Mani sensed that they had arrived back at the centre of their conversation.

'Bit of a grog fight las night, eh? But no more man-woman troubles at this place, like before.'

Makkurndil paused, inviting further agreement. 'Still too many young blokes got no promise girl. That's the trouble,' he added.

'True,' Mani agreed, sensing that, at last, this was it. His idji, who had certain rights and obligations in arranging marriages for his sister's children, had come here today because he had heard in Darwin that Mani had gone home. This was why he had come to visit, so that he could talk to him about having a marriage promise. Perhaps he could give some hope of finding a wife who was straight for him in the old Lore, but who also knew something about how to live in the modern world culture as well as her own.

'Like me. No promise,' he said.

'Yeah, you now,' Makkurndil took the signal that his sister's son was now ready to be led into a consideration of one of the most serious things that could ever happen in his life. 'Some young fellas go to Darwin or Mundaza (Mount Isa) and get a Balanda woman for a wife,' he went on.

Mani was silent for some moments. Why was Idji bringing in Mount Isa, the remote mining town across the Queensland border? The only connection that either of them had with Mount Isa was that Mani's older brother, Dalagain, had gone there about four years ago to ride buck-jumpers in the annual rodeo, and had decided to stay there.

'My brother was in Mundaza', he said.
'I know that,' he was told. 'I been seen 'im last week till yesterday.'
'Ah, you was in Mundaza yesterday?'

The older man looked at the young one, and smiled faintly at the relief he saw there. He nodded once, and said simply, 'that's where I was.'

The unspoken question about the idji's failure to get in touch with Mani before he left Darwin yesterday had, at last, received an unspoken answer. The old man had arrived back in Darwin from Mount Isa after Mani had left on the flight to Goose. This realisation that Idji had gone to Mount Isa to visit Dalagain, and now had come to Goose, out of concern for the happiness and lawfulness of his dead sister's sons, made Mani glad. Family still cared about what happened to him and Dalagain. That was good. Now he was sure that his idji was going to talk about the future and finding a wife; but he was not prepared for what came next.

'Now your brother got Balanda woman', he heard. 'They got married Balanda way in Mundaza Church. 'e didn't tell you, eh? 'e didn't tell no-one, that young bloke. I'm idji for 'im. Who 'e think 'e is? That's not the culture law way. I told 'im off for dirty livin'. Not straight. What about 'is kids now? Where they gonna come in family, eh?'

Mani's mind was drifting into a rising current of emotion. Fragments of remembered past times swept around in a swirl of confused feelings. Promise girl? Dalagain's got a promise, but not Mani. No-one straight for Mani. What will he do, find a white girl? Then he won't want to stay with his people. Dalagain married white? Staying away now. Is that what Idji thinks is going to happen for the younger brother, too? It might happen, but nothing was clear. Still not clear yet. What is Idji talking about? What can I do?

'What about my brother's promise girl?' Mani asked gravely. 'She's waiting for my brother, his promise.'

'That's what I'm asking you.' Idji snatched back the initiative. 'That promise girl is clear now, and, I been talkin 'ere with family. Now I ave to talk to you.'

'Me?'

'Ee-ee, you're the next brother.'

Lilara? She had been nearly old enough to go to Dalagain, her promised man, before he went away. Was she now to be passed on to the next brother? Mani felt a blaze of indignation, but it was quickly quenched by the new prospect that had come to him. Lilara! A few men had been trying to get her interested since her promise man went away, but her mother, or mother's relations, always stayed at her side, and the Minister and his wife, the Fijians, kept watch, to guard her against any hungry men trying any of their funny business. Now, without a promise man, she would find it even harder to keep them at bay. But she would not be without a promise if he was properly understanding what Idji Makkurndil was proposing to him.

'Should be she'll be your promise now. What d'you reckon? Barang? That's okay?'

'Me? 'e told you? Gayu, my brother, 'e told you that?' Mani's voice was thick.

'I told 'im!' Makkurndil declared. 'I'm the idji! That young bloke gone lost. I told im you, young brother can have that promise girl now. 'e knows, that boy. 'e say, You're the idji. You can tell me. So now, I'm telling you, young man. It's time to marry into your own people's life. A good young woman of your own people. Then your family can be 'appy, 'an they can trust you not to go away like your brother and live in the Balanda's world. 'ere is the place to live 'an to get married 'an to work for your people. You 'ear me?''

'What about Lilara and 'er family? What does she say?'

'That's all right,' Makkurndil assured him. 'I talked with her old people, and she was listenin'. We all saw her big eyes, and her smile she tried to turn away and hide. She wants you. So I'm telling you now. She wants you, and she's your promise. What'd you reckon?'

'Yes,' Mani was serious but excited. 'Lilara will be my woman. That's good, and I'm really happy. I came home to my own people and you're 'ere to tell me something that makes me real happy. Now I can be a family person in a straight way. She's good. 'An she's a really beautiful girl. I can't believe what you told me.' He laughed bashfully. 'She wants me, eh? You sure she wants me?'

'Go and be sure yourself,' the old man was smiling now. 'She said it. Now you let 'er tell you. And I reckon you can tell 'er somethin, too.' His tobacco-stained teeth showed in his grin. 'Proper man now! I'll go an 'ave more talk with her family, now you been say. Might be you take 'im girl quick now, before Idji goes away again. I want you to get your wife real quick. You don't need to sit around wastin time. I can tell, she's ready for you. You should be ready, too.'

Without another word, the old man rose and strode off past Jambagirrila's house, heading along the unsealed road of the only street in the settlement. Mani stared at the fire, but imagined Lilara's lovely body moving in the glowing embers and her eyes, big, bright and happy to have him; her lovely face, and the way she looked when she had once turned away shyly and then looked back at him.

Springing to his feet he plunged towards the slope, and bounded downwards along the sandy track to the beach. He continued sprinting around the bay, and only stopped running when he reached the northern rocky tip of the crescent. There he turned and began to walk back, gazing all around, at the sea, the sand, the pandanus palms, the rocks and the sea bird above, whose shadow had crossed the sand in front of him. Was it a sign, this shadow on his track? A warning? Or was it an invitation to life and celebration of the real happiness that had been kept for him until now?

At long last the inner secret, the meaning of his life's riddle, was showing, especially for him. All things were about his happiness, and were new, as though he were seeing them all for the first time. Yes, my bay, yes. I see you, wonderful bird there, dancing in the air. Me, too. I'm dancing. He ran across the beach with hands spread wide, and kicked sand high as he went.

Near the shallow stream of Sulawee Creek cutting across the beach, he strode, kicking sprays with every step, along the water's edge. Where the stream met the aftermath of freshly broken waves running up-current, he stood staring at the bubbling turmoil, and told the disturbed waters to listen to him. Ssh! Ssh, now. D'you know that I'm a man with a woman? Yes! His eyes followed the retreating sea, and he found himself staring passionately at the inviting waves. Suddenly he was aware of how hot he had become from the run; and charged into the next wave as it broke.

'Me! Me and Lilara!' he shouted, galloping into the sea.

'Lilara. Lilara,' he continued, as he ran and delighted with the impact and explosion against his flesh of wave after wave. Lunging forward, he plunged, abandoning himself to the life-force that was flooding over, around and through him. He swam with it, and against it, and played in the powerful, soft embrace of the everlasting sea of life, until he was breathless and ready to rest.

Relieved and calm after riding, weightless, in the heaving bay, he trudged up the sand beside the streaming creek and dropped to his knees, staring out to sea as if somewhere out there he would see clearly what had now happened to him and what he had now become. How long he stayed like that he couldn't tell, but realised that it had been more than a few minutes when he was suddenly aware of the voices of men approaching.

Along the beach towards the settlement he saw the Minister and a Balanda in long trousers, and noticed with regret that they were coming his way. It was beginning to feel like a good thing to hurry back to the village and let people know that he was happy about the new reality of his life, and to find Lilara and ask her, and her people, what they wanted to say about the marriage; and to be, of course, to be, alone with her. With his own promise girl, Lilara! But not to stop and talk with these two; the Balanda visitor and Boonyi Laku, the big Fijian. Not that, not now! At least Mondi Laku, the big Fijian Minister was not a Balanda, more like a local. His own people in the Pacific had put up with Balanda missionaries, too. There was room for more friends like him in Arnhem Land. The only problem that Mani had with Mondi Laku was the way that he always wanted to be up close and personal, and touchy-touchy. That was about the last thing that he wanted just now. Where could he go to avoid the meeting? There was no way of dodging them, and since they might sit down where he was now, making it hard to move away from them, he rose to his feet, and began to walk briskly towards them. Hopefully, they might see that he had set a determined course for home, and let him pass by. This was no time to be fooling around with the social niceties of Balanda and missionary games.

When he was on the other side of the stream he recognised that the Balanda was the Chief Minister's government staff man, Bridges. Not so bad, Mani thought. He is one of the more sensible ones; but that made him more, rather than less, impatient about the inevitable encounter. Talking to the Minister and to Bridges could develop into a long-winded conversation. He and they really did have a lot to say to each other; but why today of all days?

Chapter 4
A way ahead

It was not Bridges' first time on Goose Island, but, it felt as if he were somebody else in a place remote from reality, as he had stepped on to the beach under the midday sun. Fascination with the pale green radiance of New Moon Bay, and the effect of awesome heat rising from the sand as well as beating down from above, threatened him with a kind of light-headedness. Striding past drooping coconut palms, alongside a huge, happy, barefooted Fijian, resplendent in white shirt and grey larva skirt, on a white beach that squeaked to the scuffing of their feet and sandals, Bridges adjusted his hat. Ground vines lay along the high and dry dunes at the top of the beach, with a scattering of broken brown coconut husks, and the sea was slowly and monotonously, rising and falling, running incessantly towards the shore and falling back. The vast still blueness, above long white clusters of mainland clouds, to the south and east seemed at one with the sheen of the sea and the glint of the running arcs of foam fading into the continuous wet curve along two kilometres of white sand. His huge companion beamed and excitedly talked like a newly arrived tourist.

They saw Mani, a black athlete in the distance, with a bright blue narga about his loins, rise to his feet, trudge along the beach in their direction and wade across a shallow stream that ran out through the sand. Although the Lakus had been on Goose Island for four years, Bridges had seen them only at a distance, until today. He had not met them to speak to, and now took the opportunity to make the Minister's acquaintance. As he did, a hope stirred in him that this connection might lead to a useful encounter with Mani. Now it had, and much more easily than he had expected.

'You came back to see the people again,' Mondi Laku had declared, smiling broadly when they had talked on the back of the station truck, coming in from the airstrip, as though Bridges had conferred a great honour on the community, simply by coming to visit someone.

'Yes, it's good to be back at Goose,' Bridges had shouted over the false wind that was coming up over the driver's cabin, tearing at his hair and bending back the pile of springy curls in the Minister's black halo. 'But I'm mainly here to get to know Malcolm Manggululu's family better.'

'That's good,' Mondi Laku had enthused. 'Lovely people. Oh, so you are following the young teacher and learning about his family's life to help with the training? That's really good.'

When the Minister had offered to accompany the Liaison Office visitors to the village, Bridges had accepted gladly, remembering the apparent reluctance of Brown. It could be helpful to have the support of Boonyi Mondi Laku in an approach to Jambagirrila and the others. A visit home to the Manse near the little concrete block church had been necessary, so that Mondi Laku could let his wife know where he would be for the next hour or so in case anyone needed him.

Brown had accepted an invitation to go to Foster's office to continue a conversation about the Town Clerk's opinions of government staffing policy. And Bridges had readily accepted, the Lakus' invitation for them to stay at the Manse. Often a Liaison Officer would stay with an Aboriginal family, but Andrew had made it clear that he intended to avoid that. In Darwin they had arranged, through their office, a booking for a couple of single rooms in the house that served as a visitors' self-care hostel; but it was more pleasant this way, and the Lakes might be persuaded to accept the accommodation allowance grant.

Mondi Laku had begun, excitedly, to tell of the life and times of the Goose Islanders. It was as though he wanted to make up to Bridges for all the long months in which he had been deprived of knowledge of these most important people. Buringalu's baby was an astonishingly progressive and endearing infant; Jambagirrila the most exquisite mixture of quaint naivety and deep human wisdom and experience. Mani was the brightest gem of a gravely burdened and disoriented generation, a treasure for the people, their children and their children's children. Now, as they trudged through the sand, Mondi, still smiling, expressed his concern about some of the young men who had been involved in a fight last night. It was something that had just happened. No-one was to blame. The big changes since the Mission handover were disturbing people; 'too much too fast'. Mining, big money, Town Council business, elections, all clans trying to work together without Mission teams to span the clans, government officials telling them what they have to do, young educated people saying too much to the elders, and alcohol being brought to the island.

Trouble had been brewing for quite a while, and last night, just when a crowd had been enjoying themselves around Jambagirrila's fire, hearing stories from Mani about Batchelor and Darwin, it had flared up.

Three or four who had been drinking in another part of the village and had come along in rowdy fashion; and, among many of the loud things that they had shouted as they pushed in among the people, was the name of Mani's father who had died about five years ago. This public use of a dead person's name had been offensive to all the sober people present. Such a thing was prohibited, but Mani had witnessed plenty of worse behaviour among the drinkers at Bachelor and in Darwin, and although his feelings were hurt by this shaming of the dead, he was not as angered as most of his relations were.

Their Minister had heard the commotion and quickly presented himself on the scene to lend his considerable weight to those who were trying to pull the fighters apart, and calm them down. Bridges marveled at the way Mondi Laku could recount this incident, smiling, and giving the impression that all the combatants were really great young men, just a little overwrought due to circumstances beyond their control. Although it was a flood of information that the Minister wanted him to hear, Bridges was intrigued to get a firsthand account from someone who was neither a Balanda nor an indigenous Arnhem Lander. Since the Mission organisation had been dismantled and government-designed structures put in their place, the different clans were no longer able to have their own clan responsibilities in the work of the station. The Ananardus and Wainandas, as well as the smaller groups from nearby islands and mainland regions, were all frustrated because they were being treated like one community, and supposed to share public ownership and public opinion. And really, in their world there was no such thing as a town community or a "public": there were only autonomous clans.

They belonged to a network in which, back in Mission days, all clans had agreed to work with and for the Mission enterprise. But now Mission no longer ran the settlement and the clan network was being ignored. It was frustrating. Many people would not work with the new Balanda invention, the Town Council. And all this made them blame and shame each other. So it shouldn't be surprising if they get restless and irritable. Anybody would, wouldn't they?

'They need help,' the Minister had said emphatically, 'We're all like children, God's children, and sometimes we need help to find our way back home. I pray for these unhappy children to find their way.'

There was no opportunity for Bridges to initiate any conversation before they approached the athletic young black man in the bright blue narga loin-cloth.

'Hullo, little brother,' Mondi Laku called brightly as they approached each other.

'Ullo, Boonyi,' Mani Manggululu only slowed without stopping, and glanced at the Balanda while he kept moving. 'Mister Bridges, eh?'

'Ah, good'ay, Mani.' Bridges dared to use the name by which the young man had introduced himself when they met at Batchelor College. Mani looked at the two men as they turned and came alongside, all three heading back towards the village. 'So you remember my name all right,' the young local addressed Bridges.

'I see.' The Minister was thrilled that things were immediately going so well. 'You both know each other already. That's very good.'

'Yes,' Bridges told him happily. 'We've had a few good talks down at ATEC in Bachelor, haven't we, Mani?'

'Ee-ee, that's true,' Mani replied. 'I'm sorry, I have to keep going now. People will be waiting for me to get back.'

They assured him that they understood, and that they were pleased to find him on the beach. Mondi Laku explained that Bridges especially wanted to see the young man. 'This is your friend who wants to help you with important things,' he enthused.

Suddenly the Communication Consultant's admiration of the affectionate pastor declined. This was not the way he had intended the encounter to happen. He had imagined himself making a much more casual approach, as he gradually and subtly drew near to the matters he really wanted to discuss.

Mondi Laku's announcement was a clumsy calamity in terms of communication theory! Damn! But it was how things were now, so he just had to make the best of the way the cookie had crumbled.

'Yes, I thought we might have a chance to discuss some ideas together while I'm here,' he covered with a smile. Mani stopped suddenly, and the others, a couple of steps further on, turned to face him.

'What kind of things Mr. Bridges?' he asked deliberately, fixing his eyes on the liaison expert's face.

Bridges realised that his footing was precarious. If Mani became anxious or antagonistic at this point, everything that followed could be a waste of time. He estimated that the man before him had not only the courage to scrutinise every sign his face gave, but the insight to read implications of this event, this beach encounter. Only one day after his arrival to confer with his family about land rights issues or whatever, a government expert in Cross-cultural Communication arrives on the scene, accompanied by the local Pastor, just for a chat? Bridges decided to give credit to the intelligence and sensitivity of Manggululu, and adopt the dangerous tactic of being explicitly candid.

Without hesitation, and matching Mani's intensity, he said, 'you and I are two very important people. We need to help everybody else to understand each other, to keep working together in ways that are fair and right'. Then he waited.

It took several seconds, but the response came. To his relief Bridges found himself addressed with something approaching trust rather than rejection.

'That's true, Mister Bridges,' Mani replied quietly, then smiled and resumed walking, relaxed now, and said loudly, with laughter bubbling through. 'We're a couple of very important blokes, aren't we?'

Mondi Laku had sensed the tension without understanding it, but now relaxed happily at the signs of mutual goodwill.

'It's so good to have you back home, little brother,' he said. 'Is it holiday time at the Teachers' College?'
''No, not term holidays yet, I really came home to talk with my family about things that are going to happen. I don't know if I will go back to teacher training.'
'What's going on, young fella,' Mondi Laku read the excited smile and teased. 'You found a girl? You're not going to get married, are you?

Again Mani stopped. This time his pent up emotion bubbled over in a rush of release, and he let his thoughts turn away from issues that the government expert might be wanting to talk about.

'How did you know?' Mani was laughing. 'Who told you?'
'True?' Mondi Laku had hit the jackpot. He was elated.
'I only found out myself today from my idji.'

Bridges recalled wondering why Makkurndil had been on the flight this morning. Now he thought he knew.

'Idji? Your idji? Yes, that's right!' Mondi Laku had put two and two together. 'Oh, yes! It was your idji I saw. He came on the plane.
'He told you what? You got promise girl, or what?'
'Yeah, yeah. Promise girl.'
'This is wonderful!' the Minister was inspired. 'Where is she? Who? Can you tell us?'
'You know her very well,' Mani told him, still grinning.
'Tell me, then, tell me.'
'She's called Lilara,' Mani told him with a veil of unreality screening his senses. Could it be true?

'O-oooh!' The Fijian was enthralled. 'No-o- o! Tru-u-ue? Oh, my little brother.' He flung his arms around the young man, and as he span him off his feet and danced around the sand, he told him with great jubilation. 'God loves you! You are greatly blessed. My little brother, you have been given a precious gift.'

He put him down gently near the laughing white man, but still did not release him. Holding Mani's face between his huge palms he said softly, 'Mani and Lilara! You will be so happy, and you will make your people, all your people, very happy. God bless you, little brother.' Mani staggered as he was set free, and grinned at Bridges with something akin to embarrassment.

'Yes, er, Mani,' the consultant said. 'Let me, er, congratulate you, all the best.' He grasped Manggululu's hand and shook it firmly.

The grip he had on the task that had brought him to Goose was not nearly so firm. Mani was right there with him, within the grasp of his hand, but he was Manggululu, the indigenous man, about to be embroiled in a new maze of social involvements, of family arrangements and probably married life. How could he hope to get his ear again in the next few days?

'This is a big day for you, Mani,' he said. 'You're going to be a very busy man these next few days.'

'Probly,' Manggululu shrugged. 'I dunno.'

'Oh, you'll be busy all right!' Mondi Laku assured him.

'I was just wondering, Mani,' said Bridges. 'When two important blokes like us are going to have another chance to talk.'

Manggululu looked along the beach towards the settlement, glanced at his shadow. It would soon be at its shortest. He sighed heavily.

'All right,' he said. 'Can we go along to the tamarind tree? It's a good shade. We can have a talk there. But Mr. Bridges, you remember, I came here to talk to my family, not to tell others about my family's business.'

'I respect that Mani,' said Bridges. 'That's just as it should be. But there's one thing that is not as it should be.'

The other two looked puzzled. 'You keep calling me mister. If I can use your personal name, you can use mine, okay?'

'Okay, Mis...Gray.'

'Gray, if that's what you want me to call you. Okay, Gray.' Mondi Laku left them at the tamarind tree after assuring Mani that he would not breathe a word about the coming wedding until after the families had sorted out their agreements and arrangements later in the day. Who could tell, in these changing times, whether or not the old culture law would still be honoured by all parties?

'Just tell me what you want to say,' Mani said, excusing Gray from politely beating around the bush, as they sat on the shaded sand. 'I can't stay long.'

'Okay, here's why I'm here, Bridges told him, and frankly said his piece about the special nature of the forthcoming delegate-led consultation. In return he was assured that Mani was interested in the opportunity that it would give the Arardbis to be heard. It began to appear that he could become one of the most positive advocates of the consultation, but only if he were convinced that it would be a genuine time for the Aboriginal representatives to be the ones holding the initiative, and for the government representatives to be the ones responding to them. Assurance of that would allay many of his fears.

When Bridges repeated that it really would be so, that the Chief Minister had given his word, before witnesses, and it was recorded in official minutes, this was not completely satisfying to Mani.

'So much bad stuff has happened between our people that it's hard to trust any more,' he confided. 'We talk about the Balandas who speak two ways, with a split tongue.'

Bridges could only accept this as reasonable. 'I would feel the same way, if I were in your situation.' he said soberly. 'That's why I take my job seriously, and why I am asking you to work with me for a new day of mutual respect and true listening to one another.'

Mani marked the sand with a stick between his spread feet and drew shapes there for a few thoughtful moments. 'I had to live down south in Adelaide for two years before the penny dropped for me, 'he said, poking at the sand.

'Oh?' Bridges was interested but mystified. 'What penny?'

'How Balandas see life.'

'That'd be lots of different ways, wouldn't it?' Bridges suggested.

'Ee-ee, it would be different for everyone, but there's a same difference of a Balanda way to be in the world. I started to see it. I saw them as people who love this land, but with a sadness deep down inside for another land somewhere else, and for different bad times their ancestors had there. And they had different kinds of mothers and teachers and got beaten and cried when they were little, and starvation and disease in their big stations and towns, and learnt to think about money importance, and being on time, all the time, and stuff like that. And too, I saw that you have many words we never hear, for the deep talks people have to have about trading, and people owing others, and laws and politics, and health and religion, just like we do, words you never hear, Gray. And I saw your people as frightened to stop talking. Sometimes I want to say, It's okay to say nothing. Nothing bad will happen if you just stop talking and think about something that someone else is trying to share with you. There's a fear, a worry in the Balandas I have met, a worry that something terrible will happen if we have to just be who we are without trying to put up masks and tell people stuff all the time. I felt it really; and inside my heart said, Aha! I see you now.'

He looked up and Bridges affirmed his clear statement with a smile. The young man continued. 'Have you ever seen my people's difference like that, Gray?'

'What a good question,' he replied, flicking away a dead creeper leaf from beside his foot. 'To tell you the truth, I don't really know the answer. It's certainly true that we Balandas keep preventing people from responding to us, by interrupting their attempts to respond, and drowning their thoughts under floods of our own talk. How I see your people? I like to think that I respect your people just as they are, but I find them…find you all…mysterious. There is always more to learn about people, isn't there?'

'Yes, there is,' Mani said it definitely as he turned back to the sand and smoothed it as if in preparation for drawing something there. 'And about where they are coming from. I have to go and meet my promise girl and her family Bridges…but first I am gunna to tell you a story. If you and I are important to help our people to hear each other, we better make sure we know who each other is.'

'I agree, and I'm grateful for your willingness to help me understand.'

'Did you know we've only got one Balanda family working for us on Goose now?'

'Yes,' the visiting Balanda assured him. 'I heard about the Engineer and Farmer and…er…Carpenter. All left at the same time, didn't they?'

'All got kicked off the island together, you mean!' Mani enjoyed saying it. 'And it was the Engineer, the Carpenter and the Town Clerk. We kept the Farmer and gave him the Town Clerk's job.

'Jack Foster?' Bridges checked.

'That's 'im,' Mani went on. 'They all thought they could run the natives in their own Balanda ways, different ways. It was white fella politics – two Country Liberal pushers and a Labour stirrer. The people just pulled back. No action, no work, no-one goin to Town Council meetings, till the Gubment asked why, and then they held up the funding so those blokes didn't get paid and they had to go. That was the best thing they ever did for us. But they left the Town Clerk here.'

'Jack Foster? Why did he get to stay?'

'Because he belongs to the old way…the Mission, 'e isn't Gubment and 'e doesn't push party politics. 'e's Mission. And the people trust him, most of 'em do; because, 'e's mission, and like us, 'e doesn't talk about politics, and he does talk about God and spirit. So, now we're left with Jack 'an his missus, and 'e can't handle the whole job, and no-one wants to work with him any more, because he's too bloody bad-tempered. To me 'es like most other Balandas. Doesn't believe in us as real people, and thinks 'es too smart to listen to ignorant natives.'

Bridges waited in a very un-Balanda-like silence, but when Mani continued to drag the stick along a line between two circles in the sand, he asked, 'what's that you're doing?'

'That's us.' Mani re-traced the circle on the left, then did the same to the one on the right. 'And that's the rest of Australia, the Balanda gubment, the mining companies, the banks, the business companies and the tourism…' he paused while he rubbed out with his foot the line he had been strenuously drawing between the circles. 'An across between these two there was the bridge. And the bridge was called the Mission.' He drew a line for the bridge.

'Yes,' Bridges affirmed that he was receiving loud and clear. 'We've heard that's how it was before Livvy and I came north. And then the Mission withdrew.'

'No!' Mani was definite. 'And then the Mission meeting with Arardbi decided to replace the Mission gubment with an elected Town Council. Only Arardbis could vote, and they could vote for Arardbis or any missionary person they wanted on the Town Council. And for the first year or two the old Mission Superintendent would be the Chairman of that Council. Well that was all right. We were all happy to be equal and working side by side on that Mission bridge.' He re-drew the bridge line. 'So they passed a law that all Aboriginal missions and settlements had to be run by elected Town Councils, and they could only vote for Aboriginal people, even for the Chairman job. And the missionaries now all would be the employees of the Town Council.

The gubment would only work with the Town Council, they had to get incorporated, or some bloody thing. Then the government would only fund and work with that Council, not the Mission, and not the clans. Everything would belong to public ownership, like in communist countries, and the mock Town Council had to work with Territory and Canberra gubments and all outside bodies.

That was when everything fell apart and, soon, most of the missionaries left, except for a few like Jack Foster and 'is missus. And the bridge was gone, and the clans couldn't work together, and strangers keep on coming and going, all trying to make us be something they reckon we should be. It's a stupid bloody mess!'

Mani was silent for a moment, then changing the subject said, 'I am very lucky that in these times, I've got a promise girl now who is straight for me. There's lots o' people married wrong now.'

He explained that in the olden days, if there was a shortage of marriageable women, sometimes men would trade for a wife or even steal one from outside the group they lived in, but it was very dangerous. There was a penalty in the ancient Madayin Law for taking someone's wife or promise girl. The penalty was harsh, but it was limited, and clans had accepted its legality for many centuries. But if people went too far with penalties then the other people usually felt that they had to pay them back, an eye for an eye, a life for a life. And just like the Balandas' reprisal attacks, they sometimes went much further than a life for a life. Occasionally, in generations past, pay-back attacks grew into feuds that went on for generations.

'Is that what happened here, when the ..?' Bridges stopped. 'Sorry, your story!'

Without looking up from the sand, Mani continued. 'When the young Ananardu man stole the Wainanda woman, she was straight for him, so his own people reprimanded him for recklessness, but accepted the woman as one of their own. It was too late to try to undo the damage, because the crime had already been committed and already brought a...what do you call it? Incurred a penalty...is crime was 'e stole a woman who was already married straight to someone else, and his life was forfeit. Is that how you say that? It was forfeit?'

'That's it,' Bridges nodded.

'Her life was too, if the offended ones wanted to dish out full payment of their crime. Or they might choose another penalty, such as a wounding, or a promise of another girl, or a payment of something of value. Madayin Law gave them options, but it was a serious code of conduct with real pay-offs, er, consec...quences. It could lead to worry and payback that might be carried on for many years, or even many generations.'

Mani seemed to forget that he was in a hurry to get back to the village, and went on because a Balanda was listening, actually listening, to how life works in this country. He went on to tell that everyone was trained never to break other people's Madayin, but that, of course, it did happen once in a while. Then the people lived in fear of violent attack and, possibly, continued hostile feuding. As a general rule, however, the Madayin was kept, and harsh rules and penalties assured that nobody flirted or fooled around visibly, and when a man and woman were found to be in a wrong relationship they were often executed immediately, and there were no legal grounds for payback penalties after such executions. But the sad truth was that exaggerated paybacks had often destroyed the tranquility of life that the Madayin Lore was supposed to guard. In the case that he was talking about, the Wainandas' Madayin had been broken by wife-stealing, or unloreful relationship, and all that the Ananardus could hope to do was to adjust their life for the anxious business of avoiding the worst kind of penalty that the Wainandas might try to inflict on them, if they had the courage to do it, at whatever time they felt inclined to do it.

'You know about hidden agendas, don't you, Gray?' Mani asked, changing the subject yet again.

'Sure,' said the communications man.

'So do we,' Mani assured him. 'We always knew about things like that. It's not the agenda that Mister Blyth will put on a piece of paper that worries us. It's what's in his heart and mind. That's what we always think about. Our life here, Wainandas and Ananardus living together, is very complicated. We try to work together, to rebuild our relationships in the Madayin law and to keep strong to deal with Balandas. But we don't see Balandas as safe to have dealings with any time, especially not now that some of us are being recognised as land-owners and haven't got the Mission to go between for us. We don't even trust each other's word.'

'I see,' said Bridges, weighing the significance of Mani's amazing revelations.

'Does what I say help you to see other things, too?' Mani waited for Bridges' response.

'Well, yes. It'll take some thinking about,' Bridges began.

'That's because you're a Balanda, Gray,' the story-teller explained. 'For an Arardbi the story says, the people you see living here are not a community. They are old deadly enemies who have to live together in a refugees' camp, so that they can survive in their unfriendly ancestors' country that's been taken over by the invaders from Europe. The story says too, that there is a lot of the old fear and hatred still here between the survivors of the different clans.'

He paused and glanced at Bridges. 'And the story says something about the Balanda who comes here to talk to an old Wainanda man and his grandson about going to represent this Goose Island community at a consultation. It's about you, Gray. You are not talking to the right people. We Wainandas are old enemy mainlanders in the country of the Ananardus, the land-owning clan on the island.'

The Chief Minister's communication expert realised with a shock that it had not occurred to him to direct invitations and messages about the consultation from his department to Nabadgardi, the Ananardu clan leader of the land-owners of Goose. He had arranged for them to go to the Town Council, that hotchpotch group that always had to act for the clans but only carried any weight here if and when the clans wanted them to represent them. His personal visit had been made with a view to concentrating on the two men who appeared to be the most influential, and most likely to persuade others to be interested in the consultation, two Wainanda men, Mani and Jambagirrila, his grandfather.

Mani saw his discomfort and seized the moment to expose what he saw as Bridges' hidden agenda. 'Why has the Balanda come visiting a Wainanda old man and young man? Is it because they are the right people to represent the islanders? No, not that. Is it because they are getting ready to finish the signing off on their mainland homeland ownership papers? Is someone wanting to do something about that?'

'Oh, Mani…Really!' Bridges was embarrassed and offended. 'Believe me. That's not my intention at all…although it might look that way. Perhaps I've let other people use me…but I swear to you, Mani, I only want to give Arardbis and Balandas better chances to listen to each other and to hear each other.'

Mani Manggululu smiled at his squirming companion. 'Me, too Gray. That's what I want to do, too. That's why I took the time to tell you my story from ere. Maybe this is why we're the two important blokes to make a more peaceful country. How can we start to hear? How can we make each hear the other one?'

Bridges looked at his serious young companion and admitted, 'I've learnt some more about that from you just now. Thanks for that. Listen Mani, together we might find ways to do it. Perhaps a thousand and one ways. Whatever'll work.'

Mani nodded and looked away towards the village. 'Ee-ee,' he said absently, 'I hear you Gray. But you have to remember, we still have trouble with trying to trust a Balanda. Why? Because he's a Balanda. We expect him to lie to us, and to take away what's ours. But we are weak and broken, and we don't trust each other. We need real help. We need support to get strong like our people used to be. At least we need the chance to 'ave some sort of supporter like the powerful mission organisations used to be, that let us work in our own clans, and gives us a way to stand together, and is a bridge for us when we talk with Gubment, or mining companies and banks and marketing people. I suppose I'm saying, I dunno about your consultation Gray. I 'hafta ask the question, what difference could it make?'

Bridges nodded uncertainly. 'You've suffered at the hands of plenty of people who speak with split tongues. I'm glad that you told me about these things, and I'm very glad to know that you and your people are wide awake to notice such things. Now listen, I promise you that I'll do all I can to keep the Balanda leaders honest in our consultations. I hope that you will be there to challenge them, too, if they try to trick the people, or to work on their own hidden agendas instead of being open and straight forward. Then, step by step, we might all begin to do what the Arardbis are saying needs to be done.'

They left the shade of the tamarind tree and were strolling back to the settlement when Mani looked up and waved a hand at the nearest buildings. 'It was because the Mission was here that we came here from different places, even enemies, and worked out how to live here as refugees from the white invaders. People told their kids, we are going where the Balandas don't have guns, and they have a good dreaming story, and singing, and pictures to hang on a tree. Now the Mission gave us a self-determination, they call it, and left us clans to face each other and the white invaders. Now we have to be a community, whatever that is, and we have to have a Balanda kind of Town Council, even though, in our way, a council can't decide anything until the clans tell them what to say, and we 'ave all sorts of Balandas coming to run things, and they try to run us. And we have to talk to all the Balanda bosses without the Mission standing alongside us any more to talk to them strongly. 'Nothing is really working the way it should.'

He paused.

'Are you getting a clearer picture, Gray? We might be a bit safer from massacre, and understanding a bit more, but, in other ways, now we are right back where we were with ignorant, bloody-minded Balandas before the Mission came. But weaker. Our clans have been switched off. We're a mob of people whose ancestors slaughtered each other, who have to play a Town Council game, and try huntin' and gatherin the holy dollar, and stand up together to cunning Balanda bastards who want to take whatever is left of our old life in this land. Can you understand why we might feel a bit like sitting ducks?'

They stopped at a junction in the sandy tracks, and looked at each other. Bridges nodded in acknowledgement of all that he had heard; and Mani put the question that had been left in the margin of their conversation until now.

'Tell me Gray, at this consultation, is the Government going to let the Aboriginal people have enough time to go home and listen, to find the mind of their clan people about everything, and to let them have a real say in what is being done in Aboriginal affairs and Aboriginal lands? Or is it just going to play games with us again to make itself look good, then go on doing to us, and our land, and resources, what we don't want?'

Bridges' mind reached out to all the things he knew about Blyth, the government, the economic thrusts that were being mooted and the accepted policies on Aboriginal affairs, and began to grope towards an answer that was true but not destructive to any chance that still existed for mutual trust and open communication.

'It's a good question Mani,' he stalled. 'I guess that's the real bottom line question in all of these things we've been talking about, eh?'

'Yeah,' Mani affirmed, 'it's very nice of Mr. Blyth's government to pay for our plane fares and hotel bills and say a lot of nice things to us. A few years ago I thought that was great. But then I went to the Aboriginal Community College and SAIT, a tertiary college in Adelaide for two years, and that made me see clearer and further. Then I went to the Moral Re-Armament Conference Centre, in a palace in Switzerland, for a few weeks, too. It put everything into an even bigger picture. Now I say, I see the Chief Minister inviting us to tell 'im what we think. That's very polite of 'im to do that. I wonder what 'e thinks 'e's doin'? And 'ow will this 'elp my people to be free in our own land, and 'ave the right to choose our own future? Do you see what I mean?'

'I see it very clearly, Mani,' Bridges assured him, as he digested the surprising facts about Manggululu's exposure to awareness-raising education. It helped to explain his unusually sophisticated way of speaking with a critical appreciation of social circumstances. 'And there are many of us Balandas,' he continued. 'Who also share those concerns about the future of your people. Not just to be polite or kind to your people. Although, that's important, too. But because we are seeing the light at last, about racism and crimes against the human race. We are learning! And we also have begun to see that if we don't succeed in letting your people have what is rightfully yours, land, freedom and a future by your own choice, then we fail as a nation, and Australian democracy is a lie and a joke. We tell ourselves that this nation is the best yet, in terms of giving freedom and human rights to its people…but the benefits of that doesn't seem to reach as far as your people, yet. We need to do better, for the sake of all Australians…all people, in fact.'

'Uhu,' Mani's response sounded like his ultimate concern. 'So, is the Government going to let the Aboriginal people ave a real say about what to do in Aboriginal affairs and Aboriginal lands? What's the Government really intending to do to us this time, Gray? And what about the changing of the constitution to include us? Got anything to say on that?"

The Chief Minister's Cross Cultural Communication Consultant felt ignorant and impotent. He was grave as he replied flatly, 'The short answer is… I don't know Mani. Do we ever know exactly what's in their minds?'

'But you work for the Chief Minister's Department, giving him advice on talking to Aboriginal people?'

'True. But that doesn't mean that I'm consulted about the way the Chief Minister and Cabinet are thinking. No way. Sometimes I think I'm the last one to hear some of the Government's plans. You see I'm not a politician, and I don't get involved in the decision-making processes. In this case, I suggested that we have a new kind of consultation. It was my idea that the agenda should be set by the Aboriginal community reps. And I'm really pleased that Edward Blyth accepted it. It's at least a start, Mani. I don't know any other government, anywhere, that has ever agreed to get its Cabinet Ministers and Departmental Heads together for a consultation with the indigenous people, where the people call the tune and the government leaders have to respond.'

'Yeah, that's good, Gray,' Mani was grave.

'Gray.' Mani was adamant. 'Once we had everything set strong and in place. And we learnt it and lived in it around our family campfires and all across the land. Our life fitted tightly and safely with the land and the sky and each other. We lived in the security of the eternal Rom Lore (ancient law of the land), and the kinship system, and the totem groups, and the Madayin rules of conduct, and the story and song tracks that set our course in ways of water and food across the country, and we had the real places where our ancestors had lived, and were buried, and where we came close to their spirits and learnt their wisdom in the dreaming stories of those places, and our ceremonies that kept straight relationships and straight growing into adulthood, and kept our beliefs and devotions clear, and our education and child-care and... and... everything in its proper place, all in the land, for thousands of years.

'We've lost so much, with nothing to take its place. But while we've got our ancestors' country and some memories and language and songs and stories, then we have somewhere to start again to be who we really are. Our roots are still living in our land. But if our land is taken away, then our life is taken too. We can't keep our ancestors' campfire alight any more. The last sparks of our fire will die, Gray.'

Bridges nodded in silence, stopped walking and looked down at the sand for a long still moment before responding. 'Right. Okay, I'm with you. Thanks. You have said it very clearly, and I can't argue with anything you have said…in fact, I agree with you absolutely. And you must say this to the Government, Mani. Look, it's true that we can never have a guarantee on what politicians will do. We have no way of knowing what they'll make of the meeting. But look at it this way…they are taking a risk, too.'

'We don't have to go at all,' said Mani. 'It's them wanting it.'

'I know,' affirmed Bridges. 'That's right. And they might have their own hidden agenda…and no-one can force you to work for better relations between Arardbis and Balandas.'

'If it's better, we want it.' The young man was more of a potential leader than Bridges had realised. He spoke feelingly. 'But better for who? A government that's greedy for land and minerals, or better for the survival of our people in right relationship to the land and our ancestors' truth?'

They were getting close to the last track up to the settlement, and the consultant pressed for a commitment. 'Will you come Mani?' he asked. 'It'll go ahead, whether or not you come… but it will be a much better meeting if you are there. You are one of the most articulate and confident spokesmen of your people's cause…It's a great chance to say what you want to say, to all the Ministers of the Government. I've sweated to get this chance for you, and for others with something to say. So what do you say, now? Will you be there?'

'Listen,' said Mani quietly. 'You should be talking to my grandfather. He's the one. He'll talk to me and also to the number one Ananardu, Nabadgardi. I'll do what 'e tells me.'

'I'd be very happy to talk to your grandfather,' Bridges was also happy with this sign of approval of going further with his plea for attendance at the consultation. 'But, I feel sure that your grandfather will listen to your story about it all before he makes up his mind. Right?'

They held each other's gaze for a moment before Mani spoke. 'Thanks for being straight with me Gray. But I've got this uncomfortable feeling, like in the old English nursery poem, "Come into my parlour, said the spider to the fly", and it was a funeral parlour.'

'Will you think about it some more, Mani?'

'I'll think about it, and if I get a chance, I'll talk with my grandfather about it. But I think he'll be wanting to talk to me about other things, I mean, about someone else.' He grinned sheepishly.

Bridges extended his hand again. 'I do wish you every happiness in your marriage, Mani…and in everything you do. It was good of you to let me have this talk with you. I'll follow through with your grandfather before I go home, and I'll raise the question with the Chief Minister of inviting representatives from all clans to the consultation. Thanks again for everything.'

They shook hands and Mani strode away, up the track, with his mind already swinging deliriously away from Bridges and politics to the sweet smile of Lilara. And, no doubt to all the people who would be having something to say to him and to her, and to them together, and where it would all take him.

Chapter 5
The Fight

Now that he was alone, Bridges used his toweling hat to wipe the sweat from his head and face. He wanted to be indoors, away from the mounting heat but it had been necessary. He had made a good beginning with Mani.

Whatever else happened now, there was open communication with the bright young Wainanda culture-broker. Bridges decided to continue to take a softly-softly approach to Mani's grandfather when he was no longer busy with family and wedding arrangements, and was available for chatting. He headed up the sandy vehicle track towards the administrative area and the Manse. Where that track was joined by another coming from the village, he saw Mondi Laku and Brown approaching. They had seen him, and were quickening their pace, so that they would arrive at the junction together.

'Hullo, Gray!' The Minister was excited. 'Now you finished your talk with our wonderfully lucky young man. And I can tell you now, and you can tell anyone you like. It will happen…the marriage. I can tell Lola now, and she's going to be very happy. All the old people say yes, and the two beautiful young people will be married.' Brown nodded pleasantly to Bridges.

'Terrific!' Bridges echoed the gladness of the big Fijian. 'Are you going to tie the knot?'

'The knot? Oh, you mean will I marry them?' the Minister was amused, but his voice betrayed some disappointment. 'No. The families have already tied the legal knot by agreeing in front of witnesses. Now it only remains for the young man and the young woman to tie the love knot in the way lovers do. When they are ready they will go away together for a little while, and come back as a husband and a wife."

Bridges looked at Brown who had probably never tied the knot with anyone, and was certainly a loner now. The old man looked embarrassed, as if, perhaps, he were ashamed of his people's primitive marriage procedures.

'Maybe later,' Mondi Laku said wistfully. 'Mani might agree to a Church wedding to ask God's blessing on their union. Lilara is a Christian you know. But today the two families say noo, they must marry the traditional way.'

'Well, I guess that's that,' said Bridges, eager to listen and learn where Andrew had been and what he had been able to accomplish. As they walked he waited. Eventually Mondi stopped talking about the wonderful people he had been with.

'I waited under the possum tucker tree,' Andrew told Bridges, and went on to relate how Jambagirrila had come to him after the talk had finished at Lilara's family's place and taken him down to the shade of a Casuarina tree on the beach.

'Good on you, Andrew,' Bridges was genuinely impressed in the light of his colleague's confession on the plane that he was rejected by most of the people at Goose.

'Oh,' Mondi Laku exclaimed. 'Jambigirrila is a deep well, and a fount of wisdom. He is so happy about the marriage of the two young people.' Andrew spoke whenever the Minister stopped talking. He managed to share some incredibly good news. After talking for a while, chiefly about Mani and the wedding, the Wainandu elder treated Andrew Brown as if there were no obstacle to his acceptance. He had found that the old man was forgiving. Then, as soon as he heard that Andrew had been sent to talk about the gubment meeting with community representatives, he led him along the beach and climbed back up to the chief land-owner, Nabadgardi's house. The two old clan leaders were in good spirits after the marriage agreement, and obviously glad to have another reason to meet and talk together.

The Chief Liaison Officer seemed as calm and quiet as ever. According to him, the conversation had touched on a variety of safe topics and ultimately, turned to the consultation. Jambagirrila had enquired about old relations in Darwin, which was a way of avoiding saying anything about the consultation, and Nabadgardi said something about not many want to work with the Gubment.

There was no further chance to really turn the conversation back to the Government's invitation to meet in Darwin. He had just listened, while they discussed Mani's cleverness and Lilara's goodness. Eventually, Jambagirrila suddenly said to the local land owner, 'Town Council can listen to you. Then they can pick out someone or two to go to talk to the Gubment, true?'

The Ananardu number one land-owner replied agreeably. 'Ee-ee, I can tell 'em. And your gran'son can talk all about that Balanda law way for that meeting. We can listen to 'im.'

Bridges was delighted that Andrew had received such a positive reception although it was clear that neither of the local elders had taken much notice of the assimilated Arardbi's presence. On the way back to Jambagirrila's house the two Wainandus had spoken briefly of their old country on the mainland. Jambagirrila spoke longingly of his father country around Dik Dik River in the area south of Jim Jim Falls.

'We used to be down there together when we was very young,' Andrew explained to Bridges and Mondi. 'And 'e asked me if I'll come with 'im to see the old places again, once more before we die.'

This time Andrew Brown almost smiled, betraying an underlying nervousness. Was it due to the reference to dying, or to his acceptance by Jambagirrila, or fear of what the other old man's intentions were? Or, perhaps, it was something to do with the inner struggle that must arise for him whenever he tried to resume relations with traditional people, having left the tribal life-style so far behind him. Neither Mondi Latu nor Bridges knew what made Andrew look glad; but neither could help noticing that he did, because they had never before seen him display any real emotion.

'Are you going?' Bridges asked.
'Beg pardon?' Andrew seemed surprised by the direct question. 'Oh, to our father country? I don't really know what Jambagirrila is saying to me, yet. But when we can all live back on country I'll be there for sure.'

They arrived at the Manse and found Lola Latu ready to fuss over them all with more iced drinks and a meal of cold pork and salad with chilled watermelon to follow. She was as delighted as Mondi to hear of the forthcoming wedding of their two precious young friends.

'What a pity they won't be married in church,' she said. 'But never mind…we can pray for them on Sunday.'

When the big Fijian had offered words of thanks to the eternal dispenser of human fortunes, for the friends, the events, and the food given in this day, they enjoyed a pleasant meal together in which Mondi turned the conversation back to Andrew's father country. It became clear that Andrew Brown believed that Jambagirrila had been using an indirect method of conversation in which the listener must ask 'what is he getting at? Or why am I being told this? Rather than, what am I being told? It was still not clear why Jambagirrila had talked to Andrew about returning to the country south of Jim Jim. However, they all knew that this was the area that was part of the land claim that Jambagirrila and his nearest relations had won with the help of the Northern Land Council lawyers.

'Do you think the old man wants to go and sit on the land because he thinks someone might still argue about who is the owner, and he will be recognised as the local owner if he is actually occupying the land?' Bridges asked.
'Might be,' said Andrew vaguely.
'I think that the old man just wants to go back home,' said Lola. 'Don't you think so?'

'Don't know. Perhaps,' said Andrew. 'But he is talking to me, too, about going there with him.'

'Can I ask a question about that, Andrew? I don't mean to be personal.'

'Yes, yes, that's all right,' his colleague replied seriously.

'Is he saying something like he wants you to stand with him in claiming his right to the land? To be with him and for him, and not against him?'

'Something like that is what I'm thinking,'

'Aah!' Mondi was fascinated. 'That's very clever of you Gray. Wouldn't it be wonderful to go down into that Jim Jim country with the old man?'

Because everyone seemed to expect Andrew to reply, he spoke with a faint smile. 'I reckon that I might die if I went back there.'

Mondi laughed aloud. 'What? You think you're too much of a city man now and can't live in the bush anymore? I bet you could still hunt and fish as well as anybody.'

* * *

After lunch Mondi excused himself to go to the Workshop to see the men there, and get some odd jobs done, and Lola could hardly wait to go visiting the women of the village to see what everybody else thought about Lilara and Mani. She also hoped that she might spend some time with the bride-to-be. Andrew decided to take time for a siesta and Bridges to write a couple of emails. The first one read:

> 'Hi Olivia. All goes well here. Interesting discussion with Mani, will tell you over a nice cold one. Hope things are well with you? Thinking of you. Love Gray.'

The second was a little longer. To Archer he sent:

> 'Hi Fred. Was warmly received by old and young. Good talk about many important matters but don't trust emails so will tell you in person. No real disagreement. Regards Gray.'

That seemed vague enough but explicit enough that progress was being made he thought.

* * *

Having finished, he popped out to go and see Edna Foster to see what local information he could get. Arriving at her office, and after greeting, said 'it's good news about the young couple'.

'What's that?' Her words were a challenge.

'Oh, haven't you heard?' Bridges was genuinely surprised. 'Mani and Lilara are given to each other in marriage.'

'What?' She was astounded. 'No one told me anything about it, and I'm sure Jack doesn't know. Wait till he hears about this. They really should be a bit more considerate, and let him know what's going on. I worry for him, I really do. He spends every last ounce of energy on these people and they couldn't care less.' she said without looking at him as she typed on her computer.

She snapped, 'if you'll excuse me I haven't got time to sit around talking. I don't want to be rude, but...Do you mind?'

It was no good trying to make further conversation today with either Mani or Jambagirrila, and Bridges decided that Andrew had chosen wisely to take a siesta. There was no telling what late night sittings they might be involved in before they left Goose. Being neither a mad dog nor an Englishman, he felt that he was already a bit overdone by the midday sun and retreated to his room at the Manse, to spread out on his back for an hour or so. For conscience sake, however, he wrote some notes on two conversations, his with Mani, and Andrew's with Jambagirrila, before dozing off.

* * *

'Everybody is so happy for them!' It was Lola Laku. Who was she talking to? He rubbed his face and swung his feet to the floor. How long have I been asleep? He wondered. There was Andrew's soft voice speaking to Lola in the kitchen.

When he emerged with his hair combed and looking as wide awake as he could manage, Lola greeted him. 'Oh, here you are. You had a good sleep? That's good. You need it…travelling around and talking to all the different people. You must be very tired. Sit down, sit down, Gray. You're just in time for a cup of tea. Or do you want a cold drink? You can have both if you like.'

'Tea will be good thanks,' he said. Looking at his watch, 'Half past three…good grief. Don't tell Fred Archer I've been sleeping on the job. You hear now, Andrew, not a word.'

'I won't tell on you, Gray, if you don't tell on me,' Andrew said lightly. The siesta break had obviously helped him relax. Now he seemed more like the old self-assured Andrew. Bridges spent as little time as possible drinking the tea, since he felt obliged to move around and see a few more people to up-date his knowledge of the general community situation. The schoolmaster would be somewhere around and hopefully available for a talk now that the children had gone home. It was possible Bridges might be able to contribute some insights on cross-cultural communication, or pick up some facts about the bi-lingual programme in the school, to share with Livvy when they were back in Darwin.

Something else that hurried him along was the news from Lola that Mani and Lilara were to go before sundown to the Macassan well at the southern end of the bay. They were going by canoe and would probably stay a few days. Any more influence Bridges could have on Mani Manggululu's decision about the consultation might be now limited to a sentence or two.

'Let's go Andrew,' he said.

* * *

They were already too late to speak with the bridegroom. On the beach and hillside several dozen villagers were watching the canoe, now almost a kilometre away, bearing the new couple to their honeymoon campsite. Bridges sat by a casuarina tree and watched his hopes drifting away, and Andrew made his way along the hill in the hope of further conversation with Jambagirrila.

By the time Jack Foster heard about Mani and Lilara they were camped at the southern tip of the Bay, near the Macassan well. Together they gathered poles and paper-bark for their shelter, together they collected oysters from the rocks and wood for their fire, and together they lay on the sand when the huge afternoon clouds were taking on faint evening hues. He leaned across her on his elbow, gazing past the white of her cotton shift, at her dark shoulder, her slender neck that lay turned from him, and the womanly smooth contours of her cheek. He waited for her closed lids to lift.

At last she opened her eyes, with a nervous flicker, and made the effort to look into his face, fearfully at first, but with a smile ready to dawn.

'I'm very glad we are given to each other,' he whispered. 'I hope you are, too. I always liked you.' He smiled into her face. 'We will be very good together, won't we?'

Tight-lipped she managed a brief nod, and when her breath burst from her closed mouth, she tried to suck it back. A glance at his, too close, happy face made her even more nervous, and an uncontrollable excitement brought her smile to the surface, making her turn away.

'You will be mine, and I will be yours,' he whispered. This time he waited, and without turning, she nodded, two rapid, tiny nods.

'Always,' he whispered. She looked at him in awe and suddenly sucked air to end her breathlessness. This thing that was happening was something different from anything she had known until now. It was not like anything real. Always? Each other's always. How awful and how wonderful. This man hovering over her was going to possess her and to give a place to all that was woman in her. At last to be a woman to a man. A woman of a man, her own man…her own…He saw her life surging from deep inner places into her eyes and lips, and he closed the space between them. Their mouths, pressed awkwardly against each other and banished the magic of the moment with the new sensation of timid and clumsy skin in contact. He raised his head and laughed shyly. She laughed too, but their eyes held each other. In a moment the laughter was gone and still they held their intimate gaze.

With a new frankness they explored the other's face for more of the beauty there and the extent of its tenderness, and for echoes of the passion that was beginning to pound through their own bodies. Suddenly, he was kissing her. His greedy lips toured her face, learning of every contour, every twitch of emotion, every show of passion, with a kiss, until their mouths found each other again. Their soft lips clasped and tugged and sucked at each other, and they clung together for a long time: long enough to lose the sense of being separate individuals.

He raised himself from her and tremblingly whispered, 'do you want to take that dress off now?' Her smile was delayed by fear, he noticed, and as he sat back on his heels she relaxed, rolled over to her knees and lifted the white dress over her head. He took it from her raised hands and dropped it behind him. She was naked, and shyly bent forward with her face bowed towards the sand.

'You are very beautiful,' he said. 'Don't move.' Kneeling before her, he untied the narga knot at his hip. The little blue cloth fell from his fingers on the white dress behind him, revealing to her the full readiness of his male body. His fingers found hers, and her eyes were wide with fear and desire as they clung nervously together.

Allowing herself to be drawn into his arms, she leaned against him gently as they rose to their knees, and her lips yielded to his. While they kissed, his hands found her back, and moved with wonderful passion to claim the whole territory as his own. Sensitive of the enormity of claiming another person, he moved with reverent slowness from the high plains of her shoulders down the long central valley of her back, to the friendly round rises of her hips.

Suddenly her arms were about him in a desperate embrace and his hands found gentle curves and hollows where to glide and a new warm softness all over her skin that seemed to want his fingers to stay and play. There on their knees they began first to tremble, then to shake violently. She drew her breath in a quick sob, and he relaxed her from his tight embrace. Sitting back on his haunches, his shaking voice spoke to her anxious eyes.

'What do you say, my beautiful little wife, if we go for a swim?' She nodded, and before he could scramble to his feet, she was running across the sand.

Although she reached the water before him, it was Mani who plunged first. As he did, he grabbed Lilara's hand and pulled her in, screaming. They jumped and plunged, and rushed at each other.

'You too big,' she gasped between bursts of nervous laughter.

'Who me?' he protested. 'Well you push me in, if you like.' And she liked, and fell on him. Over they rolled, through the shallow waves, feeling the sweet intimacy of their bodies in play, breathless with excitement, now unafraid and unashamed.

'My girl,' said Mani, as he lay across her gleaming wet breasts. 'Is it really true that we two are going to be one?'

'Yes,' she whispered, wide-eyed, gasping for breath, and spluttering as a wave ran up their bodies and swirled her dark curls overhead. 'Gamu Laku said we will be one flesh now.'

'Beautiful flesh!' he gasped, bending to kiss each salty wet breast and letting his fingers caress glistening hills and valleys of the sensitive female flesh that was now to be his as well as hers.

'Will we be one flesh now?' he asked, as his legs slid over hers. Anxiously she searched his eyes before nodding once and opening herself to let him enter, and the flare of pleasure that welded their separate beings into one reality consumed their anxieties at losing themselves to someone else. The violent passion for each other's body, that took hold and possessed them, hurled them into each other's flaming desire. It was like something happening independently of their wills, as much an elemental part of Nature's evening play, as was the sea-breeze, the glowing western sky above the island, the slow, pulsating waves of the bay and the gentle writhing of the canoe as it smoothly flowed out and in on its anchor rope beside them.

The sun was already low behind the island when Lilara came back from the Macassan well with a billy-can of water, smiling, and passing her face close to his as he dropped the fire wood he had broken and reached out to touch her with open hands. She laughed as she settled the can on the fire, and glanced across the bay to their home beach. Soon it would be dark, and people at the village would see the light of their fire and rejoice for them in their new love and happiness.

Suddenly, both at the same time, heard a motor and turned to see the community's aluminium boat approaching.

'It's Mr. Foster,' said Lilara, donning her dress. 'And a man. Must be Lunggaroi, I think.'

'What are they coming here for?' said Mani, standing and reaching for his narga to tie about his loins.

'It must be trouble,' replied Lilara.

'They should leave us alone,' said Mani angrily.

'But what if it's your grandfather? What if he's sick?' she said. Mani did not answer and they both sat silently by the fire until the dinghy came to shore; then Mani strode down the sand to meet Foster. The staff man left the dinghy for Lunggaroi to beach while he waded ashore.

'What's your trouble this time, old man?' said Mani boldly.

'Don't give me any more of your cheek,' snapped the staff man. 'Who do you think you are, to run off with your brother's wife?' He glared at Mani in a way that alarmed and puzzled the young man.

'What do you mean?' Mani said. 'She's my wife now. Did my family tell you something different?'

What could have happened to change things? It had been all clear. It was clear now. Lilara was straight for him. Everybody had agreed. There was the message from his brother. What was this Balanda talking about? Didn't he know that Lilara had only been Dalagain's promise? No matter, promised wife or wedded wife, she could still be given. He would not argue with this outrageous, self-appointed master of men and their wives. He would not dignify this arrogance with argument. Foster could go, or take the consequences.

'What do you think we are running here?' asked Foster, using his fighting voice again, and Mani felt his own blood rising warmly to temper him for a clash.

'Do you think this is a lawless camp? If you do, you're sadly mistaken. This is a respectable settlement. It is a town with laws, young fella…and whether you jolly well like it or not, you're breaking the law…'

The nerve of this man. Mani felt his tightly closed mouth twitch and fill with saliva; and struggled to prevent himself from spitting in Foster's face as the intruder continued speaking.

'She must come back with me, and you will be dealt with later.'

'My wife will go with no man but me,' said Mani with a voice that was quiet, but menacing. Let him try, he thought. If he touches her I'll kill him. He's only the Town

Clerk, an employee of the island community, and he is mad. He thinks only his way of life is right, and that he is the law. He has a bad case of Balanda blindness.
'Lilara,' called Foster. 'Come here.' She came obediently, over the sand, but stood by Mani. Lunggaroi also came a step closer.

'She will stay with me!' Mani declared with unambiguous menace in his voice.

Ignoring him, Foster addressed the young woman. 'Lilara, you're a Christian girl. You've tried to be a good girl, and you have been a good girl.' His voice was gentle and encouraging. 'I've been pleased with you. You're doing well. If a few more people around here would come on as well as you have, it would make our job much easier.' His tone became very serious as he went on.

'Now, what you are doing with this man is wrong. It is against the Christian law and the law of the land. Did you know that?' Lilara shook her head and looked down shyly.
'Boonyi and Gamu Laku are happy for us.' She named her church leaders, as evidence of the acceptability of the marriage to people of the Faith.
'They are good people, but they are still learning the way of Jesus,' Foster's words meant that he was sure, but his voice sounded uncertain, even when he went on with a reason why those good people might be mistaken.
'They come from a Pacific Island that is far over in the eastern sea. Their people are far from the land of the Bible, farther away from where God came as a man. The Christian people have come here from the west to teach them and lead them, too. They will learn more about the way of Jesus one day. But I am telling you now ....'

Mani had heard enough nonsense. 'That's bullshit,' he roared. 'You think we're bloody idiots, don't you? They're better Christians than you'll ever be.' Why was Foster so worked up about stopping a straight wedding? It must be some kind of madness.

'Do you want trouble, bad trouble?' Foster addressed his question quietly to Lilara. She looked at Mani.
'Don't listen!' snapped Mani. 'He's mad.'
'Lilara,' said Foster. 'I came today because I thought you might need help to stop yourself from going into a wrong way of life. It won't be only bad for you, though, but bad for this man too.'

He swung his hand towards Mani. 'Do you want the police to come out from Darwin and take your boyfriend away?'

'They won't take me!' Mani said defiantly, but, as he did, betrayed rising nervousness. What if they did come? What could they do? He wondered.

'Mani,' said Lilara softly. 'I don't want trouble for you.'

'That's a good girl!' said Foster. 'You come with me. Don't listen to Mani. He wants to keep you, but he'll be in a lot of trouble. You come now. Just walk down here and hop in the boat.'

To Mani's dismay, she moved off slowly towards the boat. Lunggaroi stood aside to let her pass.

'Lilara,' Mani shouted, 'come back here…wife. Do you run off with every Balanda that tells you to come?'

She stopped with bowed head.

'He is not really your husband girl,' declared Foster. 'Don't listen to him. You don't have to obey him. You must obey the Law. If you care for this young fella, go now. Get in that boat, I'm telling you, or there'll be trouble if you don't. Trouble for him and for you.'

She resumed her walk towards the dinghy.

'Lilara,' shouted Manggululu, but she was already halfway into the dinghy. Lunggaroi was apprehensively watching Mani, but Lilara did not turn back.

'Leave her alone' said Foster. 'Don't try to make her immoral like yourself.'

He strode into the water, saying, 'righto, Lunggaroi, let's get going.' Before they had time to float the dinghy, Mani descended on Foster with all his might and sent the staff man crashing into the sea. The two locked in a fierce struggle in the water.

Foster managed to get his knee up and forced Mani away. The younger man pulled back then sprang forward and caught Foster unprepared, grabbed his enemy's throat with both hands, and forced him backwards into the sea. Foster struggled vigorously, but it was no use. The younger man had the strength of violence gone mad. He pressed his enemy's face under the water and held him down with determined power, crying, 'die you white devil. Die!'

Foster's legs thrashed the water. Lunggaroi gaped with open mouth and Lilara screamed.

'No, no…stop it. Mani. No. Lunggaroi, stop him, quick.' Lunggaroi came to life and plunged at Mani, knocking him over sideways, but still he held Foster's throat in a deadlocked grip. Only the oar that came crashing across his wrists made any difference. Lilara dropped it from above her head, and Mani fell back as if his arms were shattered. He yelled in pain and staggered a few steps out of the water, collapsing on the sand with his face buried in a curled arm. Foster rolled free, scrambled on to his hands and knees, gulping the air and crawling into shallower water.

Mani lay where he had dropped, struggling to regain his breath, his body shaken by powerful sobs. Both Lilara and Lunggaroi began to move towards him, but stopped in embarrassment as his sobbing continued; and, after a glance at each other, turned to Foster. Lilara approached him slowly. He was leaning back on one hand, gulping for air, and massaging his neck. His white face looked ghastly in the fading evening light.

'I'm all right,' he gasped, waving her away impatiently. 'It's that boyfriend of yours, you'd better worry about. He's really in trouble this time. Get him into the canoe.'

He rose and waded, clumsily keeping his balance, to the canoe. He took up its anchor rope, and began to tow it towards the dinghy.

'Lunggaroi,' he croaked, 'tie this on.'

Lilara went to Mani. At the sight of blood on the sand from one of his wrists, she caught her breath. 'Oh, I'm sorry...' At the sound of her voice his sobbing stopped. His breathing stopped. He remained motionless.

'I'm sorry I hit you.' He turned to look at her, his face twisted in terrible rage, but no words came. Instead his eyes filled with bitter tears of shame, and the pain of a violent desire neither to be looked at, nor to see himself. He grabbed his forehead in one hand, and, with tightly-closed eyes, rolled his head and hoarsely gasped, 'go. Go away.'

With an oar Foster brought the dinghy near to Mani, and said, 'get in the canoe'.

At first Mani did not move. He sat there with his elbows resting on his parted knees and his hands clasped in front, staring down at the emptiness between his feet. After a few moments without looking at the others, he rose and walked out to the canoe. He looked Foster in the eye, as he grabbed the rope out of Foster's hands. Turning his back, he towed the canoe for a time before climbing in and paddling away. He was glad to be alone and in his canoe.

Foster said nothing but glared at the retreating back of Mani.

'Oh, canoe,' Mani said, as a tear scalded each eye. 'Oh canoe, canoe.
'What can I do with this madman?'

By the time he reached the station Lilara had left the beach, told by Foster to go. But Foster waited for him. The paddling had settled Mani and his anger subsided. Still his injured feelings gave him consuming pain, compared to which his wrist injuries were minor, painful but unbroken.

'I have decided to be lenient with you, Mani,' Foster said. 'I might be making a bad mistake, but I believe that you can learn a lesson. You have been going a bad way. Today we saw where it can lead you. Do you want to be a murderer?'
'I won't listen. He can't touch me any more,' Mani told the canoe in his thoughts.
'I will take your canoe as a punishment,' said Foster.
I did not hear it. I will not hear. It is a thing he cannot say and I cannot hear…and he's only the Town Clerk. And I must not kill him.
'I hereby confiscate this canoe, which has kept you from coming back to work and led you into bad ways. You have another chance to straighten yourself up, and live as a man should live.'

Mani remained silent and unmoving. 'Do you hear?' asked Foster. Still no reply.
'Get out. You're in the Town Council's canoe.'

No-one saw the war that broke out in the silent Manggululu. 'I am not under his domination…I never will let him control me. But today, now, I must avoid killing him. I must walk away.'

Quickly the conflict was over, and the remnants of his will carried him out of the canoe and slowly away from the beach, with his eyes set on everything and nothing. He looked away, along the beach, far away from the camp. The moon was rising from the east, but it would soon be dark enough to go home unobserved.

Chapter 6
The monster

Andrew Brown's face had begun to open. Almost imperceptibly, like the fraction of a slender, lantern-shaped frangipani bud into petals, his plain exterior now was beginning to display the presence of unexpected color, and an inner glow, pleasing to see in the full light of day. Brown had smiled. After speaking with Mani's grandfather again, he had found Bridges, and smiled as he told of the encounter that had occurred.

Jambagirrila, it appeared, was relaxed and sociable now and Andrew had rightly supposed that it might be a good time to make a new approach.

At the fireside he had found a chance to return to the subject of the Dik Dik country south of Jim Jim on the mainland, where both he and Jambagirrila had lived during their boyhood.

'If ever I go back to that country,' Andrew said, 'I hope I can stand alongside you, old man. And I hope we can always be close to each other in the land of our people, and say "Jambagirrila and his grandson are the right ones to mind it now, to care for the country and teach young ones the mind of the country, because that is the old Law and it also is right in the new Land Rights Law."'

That had greatly pleased Mani's grandfather, and he had almost immediately turned the conversation to the "meeting with Gubment" that was to be held in Darwin. It seemed natural to him to assume that the Balanda, "Mr Britches", would know more about it than old Andrew Brown, the Arardbi playing at being a Balanda; and that had led Andrew to go in search of Bridges, and surprise him with the news that Mani's grandfather wanted to talk with him about the consultation.

After a pleasant evening meal with Andrew and the Lakus, with table talk centering on Lilara and Manggululu, the cross-cultural consultant found himself, in the fading twilight, on his way to an arranged meeting with Jambagirrila. As he neared the house and campfire, he noticed several figures in the small circle of light. A commotion from further along the road had arrested their attention, and all but one began to move off to investigate it. In the camp-fire clearing he found the old man, standing with his back to the fire, staring after the retreating figures, listening to hostile voices that had begun rising to an alarming pitch.

'Them young fella!' Jambagirrila explained to the newcomer. 'They keep make fight on us. We have to fight back on 'im. Can't leave us alone, from that Balanda Lands Right business ere.'

'You've been having some trouble?' Bridges decided not to rush into the many questions that arose at the mention of Land Rights Law. For a long moment the old man stared off into the night, listening intently. Several distinct voices shouted above the general din, and Jambagirrila turned back towards the fire.

'They stop now this time,' he announced. 'Somebody bin call out, Minister comin 'ere for talkin'. Still grumble, them landowner people. But 'e make 'em cool, that one, Boonyi. They always listen im. You want a cuppa tea?'

'Oh, er…yeah, yes, that'd be nice,' said Bridges, eager to be friendly. The old man picked up an enamel mug from the sandy clearing, lifted the billy-can from the embers and poured in some tea. He swirled it around in the mug, and threw it into the darkness. Then he filled the mug and handed it to Bridges.

'You got some sugar dere,' his host told him, pointing to a four gallon tin. Bridges lifted its plastic sheeting lid and felt inside. His sugar-coated fingers found a small round tin. It was empty, and he assumed it was meant to be used as a scoop. Unfortunately the sugar was damp, and he tipped nearly half a tinful into his mug.

'You want more?' Asked Jambagirrila, supplying a stick for stirring.

'No, thank you,' laughed Bridges. 'That's a lot of sugar for me.'

Jambagirrila was again distracted by the proceedings in the outer darkness, where the noise was diminishing but a few isolated voices could be heard, a couple of them nearby on the hillside that led down to the beach.

The enamel mug was so hot that it burnt his lips. In ordinary circumstances he would tip it on the fire or throw it into the long grass; but he was a guest on a diplomatic mission, and must avoid any possible cause of offence. Shifting the mug to the other hand, he decided to finish the thing he had begun.

The old man began to move towards the steep sandy incline saying, "scuse me, Mister Britches! Might be my grandson dere. You stay. You stay. I come back'.

Here we are again, thought Bridges. Patience, patience. One of the most valuable assets of a good communicator. But he allowed himself the satisfaction of impatiently flinging the contents of the mug as far as he could.

As he waited, touching the end of his scalded tongue behind his teeth, he crouched on his haunches by the fire, set down the empty mug and poked at the embers with the stirring stick. A small, glowing block sat precariously on a burning log. It leapt with incandescent energy, breaking the wood of years into the flaming glories of moments. Like an excess of passion, its consuming excitement was transforming it into a momentary wonder of elemental fusion on the way to being a future heap of cold ashes.

'What have we done?' He asked himself. 'Robbing rising generations of fire, and evenings by the fire, has deprived us of a prime source of wonder.'

Before the thermal block quite toppled from its sparkling perch, he touched it with the stick. For an instant it blackened where he touched it, then lurched to the other side and fell, in a final ultra brilliance behind the burning log, into the heart of the fire. The twig in his hand was burning as he withdrew it.

I envy you, old man. His silent thought reached towards the absent Jambagirrila. Wood is for burning. He tossed a tiny branch into the fire. And life is for living. He looked into the darkness beyond the fire, in the way that the old man had taken. You've got troubles, sure enough. Well, that's the way it is.

* * *

All was quiet now, but the humming of pandanus palms in the on-shore evening breeze and the gentle clapping of shallow wind waves as the sea receded down the long beach out there in the darkness. Somewhere in the sky above a gaggle of night fliers were approaching near enough for their honking to carry in the stillness. Magpie geese were sensibly travelling after dark, in the cool of the evening, possibly to the billabong south of the village.

It was the sound of Jambagirrila's voice, as he shouted commands that brought Bridges to his feet. At the brink of the hill looking down he was astonished to see, in the light of the clear moon, a young man, whom he remembered as Lunggaroi, running for his life uphill on one of the tracks. Jambagirrila was standing on another descent beside the reedy soakage of the village spring, shouting commands, but going unheard.

Then Bridges saw the cause of Lunggaroi's flight. It was Mani, back from his honeymoon already, now overtaking Lunggaroi and flinging himself at his back. Over they rolled, off the side of the track and down through the long grass.

Bridges could hear Mani's violent anger roaring at his quarry below, but couldn't understand a word of it. Lunggaroi also shouted with similar velocity. Obviously the physical assault and the fall on the hill had raised his ire, and he was no longer retreating. The watchers above them saw Mani turn and run towards a canoe on the beach.

Lunggaroi rushed into the hut and emerged with a woven palm strip bag between his teeth. He was biting on it and growling ferociously as he ran towards Mani carrying the spear menacingly above his head.

'God Almighty,' exclaimed Bridges, breathlessly accelerating down towards them. 'Are we going to just watch them do each other in?'

The two young men swung into orbit about each other and began rushing to and fro with their weapons repeatedly being raised and swung about alarmingly. Mani was shouting and feinting with the raised sticks, but Lunggaroi could not yell because of the woven bag he held crosswise in his teeth. Instead he growled and kept leaping and weaving and jabbing the spear into empty air as he continued circling his opponent.

'Hey, cool it you blokes,' called Bridges tentatively as he walked up to them, with apparently no effect, except that Mani stopped yelling. Neither of the antagonists stopped moving about, and neither let his eyes leave the other for an instant. Bridges came to a halt, and dodged the back end of the spear as Lunggaroi passed in front of him with a sideward rush and sprang in the air with a fierce growl.

'Now, come on, mate.' said the visitor. 'I'm sure it can't be as bad as all that.' But even as he spoke he knew that he was quite ignorant of how bad it might be, and that he had no idea why he was interfering. 'None of my bloody business, anyway,' he told himself. But the sight of Mani facing that spear with two sticks, and his ability to back off apparently gone, Bridges felt inescapably responsible to do something about the situation.

'You tell that crazy man to go home,' Lunggaroi said as he came to a standstill with the bag in one hand, and the spear in the other.

Flushed with his success, Bridges pressed on. 'Now look, I don't know what you and young Mani have got against each other, but you can work it out quietly, I'm sure. Why don't you put down that spear?'

'You tell 'im put down them sticks' shouted Lunggaroi, throwing away the biting bag and moving around Bridges, ever watchful towards Mani.

'This spear can stop that madman. What for he want to punch my head?'

'Come on, now,' said Bridges, still facing Lunggaroi. 'That spear's dangerous.'

'That's him, dangerous!' Lunggaroi insisted, but still Bridges did not turn to face Mani. It might be because he wanted to remove the threat to his new friend, or because he did not want to embarrass him by confronting him directly, but, he half admitted to himself, the real reason for not turning around was so that he did not have the point of the spear behind him.

'Leave us alone Gray.' Mani spoke calmly. 'We have to settle something, and it's a business between us.'

Bridges turned now, and as he did, ridiculous headlines ran into vision; 'Nosy-Parker Knocked Off For Nothing. Liaison Worker Gives Life in Peace Quest. Bridges bows out.'

'What the hell am I doing here?' he asked himself as realism returned.

'Is this the right way to settle an argument, Mani?' he challenged the young man who moved about before him.

'It's our way,' the angry young man said. 'Don't be like all the other Balandas, Gray. Don't try to take over.'

'I'm not,' said the white man with indignation. 'As soon as you boys put down those sticks and stop threatening to hurt each other.'

'I'll hurt that bloody thief!' Mani suddenly ran a few steps past Bridges and Lunggaroi leapt aside, jabbing at the air as his opponent stopped short of danger; and they began again to circle each other vigorously with simultaneous streams of shouting in clattering dialect. Now Bridges was no longer in their circle. He might as well withdraw for all the effect he was having. They were clearly intent on having a blood-letting or a head-banging, depending on who struck first. Before he had quite resolved to leave them to it, he was touched on the elbow.

''Scuse me, Mister Britches. This my daughter's brother!'

These people must be crazy or something, he thought in despair. Why else would old Jambagirrila, here, think I was wanting to meet someone's daughter's brother right now?

Then he recognised Makkurndil who had been on the plane on the way from Darwin.

'Good'ay,' said Bridges in confusion.

'We can stand over dere, by the tree,' said Jambagirrila, 'an see these two boys shake hands now.'

This I've got to see, thought Bridges skeptically, as he moved over to the nearby Casuarina tree accompanied by Jambagirrila. There they stood in silence and watched the brother of the daughter of Jambagirrila walk between the two circulating antagonists. He looked from one to another and snapped a command, gesturing as he did with both his hands, first raised, then dropped suddenly towards the sand. To Bridges' amazement the two young men stood still and silent. Another gesture, beckoning them to come and stand next to him on either side, was immediately obeyed. Bridges could not believe his eyes, and he told himself again what he had been watching going on out there just now, when he had been trying to calm the fighters. Now the same two men were standing like two chided school-boys, listening to a little old man and obeying him.

Simultaneously they dropped their weapons. Then they were addressed by the old man in a quiet and crackling voice. He spoke for about a minute, and then the impossible happened. Mani and Lunggaroi shook hands.

'Well, I'll be blowed,' gasped Bridges. 'How did he do that?'

Jambagirrila grinned. 'All good now, eh! No more fight. You see dat man, now? 'im my daughter's brother.'

Then light dawned for Bridges, and the old man put into words what he should have already realised. 'You see 'im?' he said. 'I'm what you call uncle these two boys.'
    'They must obey their idji?' Bridges had grasped the clue.
    'Ha...ee -ee, that right way,' laughed Jambagirrila hoarsely. 'Can't stop them boys me. You too, can't stop 'em. But mother brother stop 'em quick. One word. Idji say finish, all finish.'
    'Look,' said Bridges incredulously. 'He's sent them home.' Mani and Lunggaroi had started off, striding towards different parts of the hill. 'Will they leave each other alone now?' he asked.

Jambagirrila pouted and tilted his head thoughtfully. 'Might be,' he said. 'We let my son be quiet in my house now. Must be he got woman trouble. I better see it.'

Bridges assumed he meant his grand-son, Mani. 'Fair enough,' said Bridges, realising that he could hardly expect to get either Mani's or his grandfather's ear for the rest of the evening. Impatience skipped across a flood of questions.

Why was Mani here rather than at the Macassan well with his bride? What went wrong? Was it another imponderable cultural difference?

I suppose, he assured himself, it's not so difficult to see why two young bucks get their blood up at each other. It happens all the time. What had he been thinking of, to allow himself to stick his nose into the fight? Not since schooldays had he done such a thing.

At the Manse, Brown and Lola Laku were just as mystified as Bridges when he told them about the return of Mani and the fight at the beach. But, their hostess assured them, all would soon be sorted out, because Mondi was at the village and would help everyone to be good friends again.

It was late when the Minister finally came home, and he was obviously tired of talking. Briefly he informed them that the row tonight was because there was still restlessness in the village arising from clashes of the previous evening. On top of which, one of the older men who had been getting ready to stake a claim to Lilara, as a second wife, was angry about her marriage to Mani.

'It's a shame,' Lola said. 'Mani's people came here when Jambagirrila was a young man to help to build this place as a mission station.'

Brown nodded. 'I came too,' he said. 'When we were still boys.'

'Yes…there, you see!' Lola was glad to have confirmation of her story.

'That explains something that Jambagirrila said to me,' Bridges told them. 'About the land rights Law causing arguments between the people.' He paused. 'If some of the land-owners here are trying to unseat and kick out long-time influential people like Jambagirrila, then it's important for him to have somewhere else to go. And that means trying to return to old homelands and leaving behind all that they helped to build here'.

'What do they do if they go back to the old homelands?'

'It is very hard for them,' Mondi explained, 'I will spend more time to help them find the true and peaceful way. I am helping them to pray for the guidance of God's Holy Spirit.' He stayed long enough to explain that Jack Foster had misunderstood the wedding of Mani and Lilara, and had stepped in to prevent something immoral happening to Lilara. Foolishly, he had given a punishment to Mani, which he had no right or authority to give, and Lunggaroi had helped him to do it by taking the canoe away to hold it for the Town Council. That was why Mani had attacked Lunggaroi.

'Foster doesn't understand!' Mondi sounded as though he despaired of getting through to the Town Clerk. 'We talk about it, but he thinks I don't understand. He sees the European lifestyle as the Christian way that comes straight from the Bible. And, of course that means all white church workers are right and have to make local people conform to them. So it is the white man's burden, to lift up the local people out of darkness into light. Or that's what he thinks. It's such a pity. The people are grateful that he stayed, like me, as part of the strong Mission way that they really miss. But they are in such danger from us, because they need us. We have to learn the way of the Lord Jesus, "wise as serpents and harmless as doves"?'

'What do you think about the culture and Christianity, Mondi?' asked Bridges.

'Oh, Gray, that's too big to talk about now. But I must say one thing,' said the passionate Minister. 'God, our Father, is the everlasting spirit of love, who looks at our spirit, for the love that is in the deep heart of each person, not at the culture or colour of a person, and God loves what he finds there. Everything else is secondary to that. Culture? It is a way, many different ways, of being in the world. Each culture is a precious and important way of being human. Break it and you break people's way of being who they are. Christianity is a mission to bring a divine light from Jesus to shine on every culture and show the way of love, God's love to all of us. That's my short answer, Gray. I'm sorry. Now I must go with another little message from the great lover of everyone. Please excuse me, my friend.' He smiled and gave Lola a cheek to cheek kiss, saying, 'don't wait up for me.'

Then he nodded a farewell to the two visitors and left the house.

* * *

That night Bridges slept fitfully. His own thoughts were reaching ahead to how things should be in the future. He knew that he was one of only a few who were really working for the emergence of a future racially inclusive society.

When at last he fell exhausted into sleep, he dreamt of a woman clawing at a hill of loose sand and crying 'my baby! My baby! Mani help me. Mani come and help me.'

'Everyone,' an old man cried, and Mani stepped forward with a briefcase. He dragged the case in the sand and drew a deep line from the hole the mother had dug along the hillside moving steadily away from the silent baby and adults.

Bridges woke in confusion. Flinging back the bed sheet and disentangling it from his legs, he sat up, gulping air. A woman's voice was indeed crying, outside the house, announcing some further calamity to the people of Goose Island. By the time he had pulled on his tee-shirt, slacks and sandals and grabbed his hat, the woman had conveyed her message to Lola and Andrew. Already Mondi had left the house and gone to the village again. Lola could hardly speak of the things she had heard, and Andrew looked as if he had seen a ghost.

'What is it?' Bridges asked, seeing the distraught messenger heading away towards Foster's house.

Lola said, 'oh, I don't know what to think!' She was obviously shocked. 'A monster,' Andrew said wide-eyed and wondering. 'A giant creature from the sea.'

'Where?' asked the incredulous Bridges.

'On the sand,' said Andrew.

'There must be some explanation,' said Bridges, and set off at a brisk pace towards the beach. Bridges ran along behind two naked little boys, down the track to the sand, and went around the far end of the crowd. Everybody seemed to be talking at once and looking at something on the sand. Then he saw Mani's uncle, Makkurndil, the one who had stopped the fight. He was loudly talking at top speed.

'Good morning,' Bridges said; and the startled man swung around still talking. He did not miss a beat as he went on now to the visitor.

'We never see this thing. One time might be debbil before. When me young boy. Las' time. But we can know dis. Wat you think? Out that sea, 'ere now. All, dey can't tell this. What you reckon? You know dis one? Can't nobody?'

Bridges looked beyond the man, expecting to see a boat or turtle or some other object from the sea. But there was no such object to be seen. Then he saw it. 'God Almighty!' he gasped. 'What did that?' Before his unbelieving eyes was a footprint, or something resembling a footprint, and it was about forty centimeters long.

'Eee! Ee!' indicated the other man. 'There! There! There!'

As he talked he jabbed a finger at more of the giant prints. Bridges went closer to inspect the depressions. The skeptical imp that he kept in a corner of his mind told him not to be a damned fool; of course, they were ordinary, natural indentations. They just appeared odd, and a closer look would reveal their origins. But a closer look did not. In fact, what he saw baffled him. There was a definite track of prints, but it was impossible to imagine anything that could have made such tracks.

Each print had three long, pointy toes, in places ten to twenty centimeters deep, and had a curious, rough texture.

Bridges got down on his knees beside a very clear print, and peered at it closely. Around him the men grew quiet and drew near. He looked around into the face of the old man peering over his shoulder, and saw a mouth as open and speechless as his own. He looked into the moulded sand again, and sat back on his heels. 'Well, I'll be damned'.

'Wot you see?' enquired the awe-struck elder at his ear.

Bridges reached his fingers into the print and picked up a fragment of feather down. 'You see that?' He held up the specimen to Makkurndil, who twisted around to avoid all contact with it and flung himself backwards in amongst the nearest three or four men. The convulsion spread like an explosion and screaming women and children at the back of the crowd fled in terror. Bridges held the fluffy fragment motionless, and the men moved back close enough to see it without risk of contact… staring at it without a word.

'Feather,' said the white man. The word was picked up and echoed alarmingly through the crowd. Men wagged their heads and sucked or blew through rounded lips, but their wide eyes never left the tiny object that had stimulated such terror.

The long silence was broken only by the sloshing of the waves and murmurs or occasional chattering from the back of the crowd; and, at length, none the wiser, Bridges put his hand down and dropped the fragment back into the deep footprint.

'Mus' be a bird,' said a nearby man, and that started a new wave of excited talk. People pushed to see the row of tracks, but as soon as they broke through, they pushed to get back to avoid being too close.

'What do you think of it, Gray?' Wide-eyed, Mani was at his side. One glance was enough for each of them to know that this was not the time to speak of last night's confrontation.

'I've never seen anything like it before?' said the visitor. 'Have you?'

'Uh -uh!' said Mani with a shake of his head. 'Look, in those other tracks. It looks like the pattern of feathers.'

'You're dead right,' said Bridges. 'I know it. I've been looking at this one. And, no mistake, they are feathers, sure enough.'

'What could it be?' Mani's eyes were wide.

'You tell me,' Bridges challenged. 'I'm new around here, remember?'

Mani looked towards the sea, and pointed. 'You see that?'

The men rushed towards the water, loudly commanding the crowd to keep back and not get too near the weird signs of a mysterious visitation. They engaged in excited discussion of the likely explanations and implications of what they saw; Bridges said to Mani, 'are you trying to tell me that this, whatever it was, came out of the sea?'

'I'm not telling you anything,' Mani replied. 'You can see for yourself.'

'But it can't be. I mean, it couldn't. Could it?' He rubbed the back of his head. 'I'm gonna wake up in a minute. This is too bloody silly to be real.'

'No, it's real,' said Mani gravely. 'It came out of the sea there, and I followed the tracks up.'

'You did?' Bridges stared at his young friend. 'Where'd it go?'

'Up there in the dry sand and along past the houses on the beach.'

'Those just along there?'

'Past all of em, till it got down near the creek.'

'Yeah? Then where?'

Mani swallowed before he answered, and his voice was thin and distorted. 'It went back into the sea.'

'The hell it did!' Bridges challenged.

'It went back into the sea,' Mani repeated dryly.

'This I gotta see,' said Bridges and strode off along the beach with Mani at his heels.

'Up here in the dry sand, see?' The local said.

'But look, that's just unreal.' Bridges had stood beside one of the huge prints and now he stepped as far as he could, well over a metre, and the next print was nearly a metre further on. 'You see the size of the bloody thing?'

What thing? He asked himself. Could he be sure that there was a thing that made such a track? Maybe he was convinced, but, if so, one part of him laughed the idea out of plausibility. He believed the evidence of his eyes, but utterly rejected the only possible explanation of it. Maybe there are life-forms in these warm waters that've died out everywhere else, he thought, but that's not even remotely likely. The indigenous people would be familiar with it if it existed. A giant waterbird? A duck? A goose? The great ghostly Goose of Goose Island? An Aussie Goosie to rival Scotland's Nessie?

All his rational arguments were not convincing, however; and he had to admit that the fear that the people had shown towards "the thing" could, perhaps, be associated with local knowledge. Yet, if so, why was the old man insisting that they had never seen this sort of thing before? Or did he say, not since he was a boy?

So Bridges debated with himself, back and forth, until they reached a place where the tracks turned back towards the sea, and followed the deepening impressions until they disappeared into the flooded sand at the water's edge.

'Mani,' the puzzled Balanda asked thoughtfully. 'How heavy would you say it is?'

'The thing that made these tracks?'

'Yeah.'

'Oh, it's very heavy!'

'Heavy as what? A person?'

'No. Much heavier than a person. You see our tracks?'

The wet sand was firm underfoot and their tracks were only two or three centimeters at the deepest. Just near them "the thing" had made tracks, which went to depths of seven or eight centimeters.

'Must be as heavy as a pony, I think.'

The two men stared at each other, without speaking, and Bridges turned away to look out at the sea. Imagination failed in the attempt to picture what bird-like, pony-sized sea monster might be in the waters of the Bay that could have been prowling about on this beach during the night.

'Do you believe there is something out there that comes out on the beach while everyone's asleep?' the frustrated rational man asked, as they set off to retrace their own steps along the beach.

'Is that what you think?' Mani sounded surprised. 'We can believe all kinds of things. More than Balandas can.'

'That's not answering my question,' Bridges insisted.

'I don't know,' said Mani. 'I don't understand it, but it might be something out there. I s'pose it must be.'

'I hope the people won't spoil the tracks till we work out what made them,' said Bridges.

'We won't walk on the tracks, Gray.' Mani replied. 'Any touching the place of bad spirits can cause terrible things to happen. We always make sure we don't.'

'You think this is a bad spirit?'

Instead of replying, Mani pushed out his bottom lip and tilted his head to one side. Then he said, 'We can't go in the old billabong hole over the other side. One time a staff member threw a wax match in there and big rains came and nearly washed the old mission station away'.

'Eh? You believe that?'

Mani looked down. 'The old men always say it. I wasn't very big then, I don't remember.'

'That billabong has a bad spirit, you say?'

'You've got the idea,' Mani said. 'Just like the Clay Cliffs up north. Never take clay from there, or you'll have so many mosquitoes you'll go crazy.'

Before Bridges left Mani, he expressed his sympathy over the interference in his marriage by Foster. At first Mani reacted with grim-faced silence, then gave his opinion of Foster as an ignorant man who should be removed from the island. Then he simply patted Bridges on the upper arm in a fond brush off, and began talking with the other men, and the mystified Balanda went off to find Foster. The intention had been forming in his mind since Mondi had told him last night about Foster's insufferable interference in Mani's marriage. Surely, not even a man like Foster could seriously think he had the right to do such a thing…and as for his statement to the effect that their marriage was illegal according to Christian and national laws, Mondi was obviously right; it was just so much nonsense. Obviously the puritanical Town Clerk was bending facts to suit his own inclination.

Chapter 7
Help... I can't swim

Whenever he was confronted by traditional Aboriginal dance ceremonies, or other events alien to his cultural outlook, Bridges felt overwhelmed by impenetrable mysteries drifting up darkly from below his mind, banishing his normally bright confidence, and brooding there like a baffling cloud of unknowing. The current community crisis over the visitation from the sea had created a similar sense of unnerving weirdness. It annoyed him that he had no ready explanation, or even a wild guess to offer the locals. But at least it was a conversation starter.

Now that the mystery of the sea monster had arisen, Bridges had an easy way to approach the arrogant Town Clerk of Goose Island. He had been feeling like speaking to him about Mani, but, being honest with himself, he admitted that he also felt the need to get the reaction of a cultural compatriot to the incredible evidence on the beach. Perhaps indigenes could believe things Westerners could not believe. So what if they could? Did that make them right and Westerners wrong? Either way, it didn't matter. Facts were facts, and could only have one true explanation. Whatever made those tracks was not a matter of cultural opinion, but a matter of fact. If he could just get one plausible line of thought, a clue from the past, some local knowledge, or some ideas from someone with mental processes closer to his own, then, he felt sure, he would see the thing as it really was. It must be something obvious, once you got a clue or two. There had to be some missing piece of information that would explain it all. Still he wondered. It was a phenomenon either of the Aboriginal world or of the Balanda world. If it were the first, then the staff people might have no more ideas about it than he did. If it were the second, his mind baulked at this line of thought.

'Perhaps I'm a bit feverish,' he told himself. Then he realised that he hadn't had breakfast, and perhaps he needed to eat soon.

Foster was at breakfast. It was his wife who met Bridges at the door. 'Good morning Mr. Bridges,' she said pleasantly. 'You want to see my husband? Come in, will you?' Apparently he had been right about her abruptness the day before. It was not intentional rudeness, only the snap of an overstressed mind.

'G'day! You're out an' about early. To what do we owe the pleasure of your visit?'
'Will you have a cup of tea?' Edna asked.

'Oh, no! It's not necessary.'

'Go on,' insisted Foster, smiling and pulling out a chair. 'Stop arguin' and do as you're told.'

Bridges did as he was told, and Edna busied herself at the electric stove. 'Not many people have bothered with breakfast yet,' he said. 'The whole village is turned out to see the tracks on the beach.'

'Oh?' Foster bit into a thick slice of toast. 'What tracks?'

'Then you haven't heard?'

'Oh, that'll be what old Molly was goin' on about when she came by,' said the Town Clerk.

'What? What is it?' asked Edna as she put down the teacup and saucer.

'That's what I was hoping you folk could tell me,' Bridges told them.

'I didn't take any notice of it!' Foster sounded irritable. 'Molly's always goin' on about something. She's only ninety cents to the dollar.'

'Well, she had something to go on about this time,' said Bridges. 'A trail of footprints, bigger than any human prints. Coming out of the sea, along the beach and back into the sea.'

Edna gasped and set down the teapot. 'Is that what you saw?'

Foster took a mouthful of tea, pushed away his cup and saucer, stuffed the last piece of toast into his mouth, and let them wait for his comment. Then he said between chews, 'you askin' me what it was?'

'That's right.'

'I'll tell you what it was,' he finished swallowing the remains of the toast. His tongue did a running inspection of his teeth before he went on. 'It's someone trying to drum up a story. You a freelance writer, are you?'

'That's a ridiculous thing to say, Jack. You know I work for the Chief Minister.'

'For a magazine on the side?' Foster was serious. 'We've had a few of them in Arnhem Land in recent years.'

'Oh, Jack! What a thing to say,' his wife chided him. 'Here, have your drink Gray. Where did you see this whatever it is, did you say?'

Bridges relaxed and grinned. 'Don't blame your husband, Edna.'

'I don't blame him, not for a minute. It happens. Nothing quite as blatant and corny as this would be, but it happens. There are newsmen and amateur correspondents who manufacture news. And this is surely like something someone dreamed up.'

'Are you gonna sit there and tell me you're not makin' it up?' asked Foster. 'Or that you didn't have a hand in those tracks or whatever's down there on the beach?'

Bridges drank from the cup. 'That's great, Edna,' he said, smiling at her and telling himself how pleased he was to see her more relaxed, and that, for her sake, he would not allow Foster to get under his skin.

'No Jack,' he went on. 'I didn't have anything to do with it. And I haven't got the slightest idea what did it.'

'I'll get you some toast,' said Edna, full of concern. 'They're pullin' your leg, Bridges,' Foster declared.

Bridges weighed the assertion. It was possible that a community could conspire to fool a visitor. But he dismissed the idea as unthinkable. There was no reason why they should do such a thing, and, even if there had been, they were currently suffering such division that it would be impossible to get everyone to turn out like that, co-operating in a community-wide practical joke. Above all, there was the real fear, the terrified cries of the women and the anxious faces of the men. That was not acting. It was real. Mani's perplexity was real, and so was Makkurndil's.

'If you could see them, you'd know they're not playacting,' he said.
'I'll see them, all right,' Foster said, pushing his chair back as he rose.

He turned to Edna. 'If I'm not back, ring the work bell, will you?'

Bridges gulped down most of his tea. 'Hold it,' he said. 'I'm comin' with you. Thanks Edna. Great. I won't stay for toast, thanks.'

They walked down the road, since, as Foster explained, the Land Rover was at the workshop waiting for an oil change and greasing by one of the trainee mechanics. This gave Bridges a little more time to broach the subject of Mani's marriage and its devastation. He strode alongside Foster, and tried to strike an amiable note. 'You've got an interesting life here, Jack,' he ventured.

'It's interesting,' Foster said blandly. 'Yes it's that. It's interesting.'
'Mani was telling me about his marriage, Jack.'

Foster kept his eyes on the road as he replied. 'How long have you known Mani, Gray?'
'Several months now.'
'I've known him several years.'
'So?'
'So don't try to understand what's too complicated when you don't really know what's goin on.'
'Oh now, come on Jack.'

'I mean it. I can imagine what sort of a sob story he's been tellin ya. But I know what I'm doin'.'

'Do you, Jack?' The sensation he felt was the same as when he had stepped in front of the spear.

'Listen Bridges,' Foster shot a glance at the visitor. 'We've stretched a point to have you here. Don't make yourself unwelcome.'

'Jack! Listen to yourself?' Bridges wished that he was not saying this. 'Do you know what you're doin Jack?'

'Course I do, I tell you!'

'I mean right now. This very minute. In this conversation?'

'What are you drivin' at?'

'At you, Jack. At what you're trying to do to me. You're trying to obligate me, so I'll withhold any criticism I might have of you. You're trying to protect yourself from comment, saying I can't know Mani and you can. Why Jack? Why is it necessary to put up such heavy defences?'

'Don't give me any of your psychoanalysis bunk. Save it for some of your town friends who've nothing better to do with their time than tie themselves up in knots. Sick they are. Save it for them.'

'Jack!' Bridges stopped. 'We're not talkin' about them. We're talkin about you. Listen, Jack, hold it for a minute, will ya?'

Foster stopped and turned to face him. 'We haven't got all day to stand around spoutin fancy theories out here, what do you want?'

'Now listen carefully, Jack, and believe me. I've taken a liking to you and Edna. You're not altogether my style, but God knows, you've got my admiration for your dedication to the people and what you're doin' here. And that's all the more reason to face you up with the truth as I see it.'

Foster did not move a muscle, and Bridges guessed that it was only by such motionlessness that the Town Clerk could trust himself not to react and reveal his inner turmoil.

'I haven't got the time to argue about what you think,' Foster's irritation showed.

'Why did you interfere in Mani's marriage, Jack?'

'Call that a marriage?' Foster snapped.

'It's not what I call it that counts. It's what the Aboriginal cultural community calls a marriage. That's what counts.'

'It's heathenism.'

'Oh, come on, Jack in this day and age...for goodness sake'

Someone was running towards them through the long grass. It was Lunggaroi, probably with news about the footprints on the beach, but why was he so agitated?

To their surprise he called, 'kinoo!' He was pointing to the sea as he lumbered into their presence, panting. He repeated, 'kinoo!'
'Where?' asked Foster.

Lunggaroi haltingly gasped his story. The confiscated canoe had been carried out on the high tide during the night. He might be to blame himself. He thought he had pulled it up far enough, but he had been rushing and had left the anchor rock on board. He had thought that Mani was after him, and he did the beaching in a hurry. Some people were saying that the sea monster took the canoe, but he thought that it could not be true since the monster went off in the other direction. He told Foster that nobody had noticed the canoe missing this morning because there was such a crowd and everyone was looking at the big tracks. Then someone said it went behind rocks.

'I reckon it mus' be that kinnoo went out pas' the Point, roun' them rock out there, in the night time tide…'an now it's turn aroun an' goin down on mainlan' way, this one 'ere now.'

He was able to tell them that it was one of the women on the cliff top at Koopung Creek who spotted it drifting towards the southern tip of the bay.

'Where is it now?' Foster snapped.
'It's there. Still goin' away down that way,' Lunggaroi pointed high towards the south-east, indicating that it was outside the Bay.
'It never rains but pours!' Foster looked at the visitor.
'Well, it's still a running tide,' he said to Lunggaroi. 'We can't let that canoe go. We've gotta give it back to Mani by and by. Come down to the workshop and help me get the aluminium dinghy and outboard motor on the trailer.'

'I'd like to help,' said Bridges.
'Please yourself,' Foster replied as he hurried away.

Ten minutes later, Lunggaroi at the wheel of the Land Rover backed the trailer and boat across the logs and sand, a couple of hundred metres from the cluster of people still lingering by the monstrous foot prints. Bridges lent a hand to unload the boat at the water's edge and put the outboard motor and fuel tin in place. They could see no sign of the canoe.

'Right,' barked Foster, 'let's get goin. The canoe's got a rope on it, hasn't it?'

'Oh, yeah, that anchor rope's there,' Lunggaroi assured him.

'Mind if I come?' Bridges asked, holding the bobbing metal boat as a passing wave tried to carry it up the sand. Lunggaroi got in and adjusted the motor and the rubber tube connection to the fuel tank. 'I can hold ropes, and tow canoes.' Bridges suggested.

'Get in, if you're goin' to…Lunggaroi, you steer. You've got a bit of an idea of where it is.'

'Not me. Wait now,' Lunggaroi said. They followed his gaze and saw Mani standing near them on the sand.

'He's the right one, there now,' said the alarmed Lunggaroi, scrambling over the edge, to make his way, as quickly as the water permitted, to a point further along the beach.

'Well, what are you waiting for?' Shouted Foster. 'Do you want to save the canoe or not?'

Mani shrugged.

'Well, I want to save it,' the staff man shouted. 'And I'm going to need some help.' After another moment's hesitation, Mani came to join them in the boat.

'I'll take the tiller,' Foster announced. 'You two sit on the middle seat and keep the balance.'

That was how they travelled, picking up enough speed to send the spray from the bow to the stern each time they ploughed through a wave. No one spoke; partly because the din of the motor reduced their options to shouting and hand signals, but also because they were awed by the circumstances. Foster and Bridges were acutely aware of the presence of Mani, and of Bridges' accusation that had begun to emerge about the young man's treatment. Mani was sensitive to being confined to the presence of these Balandas, one of whom represented all that he detested about them, and one who had clumsily stepped in to protect him like a brother. These white fellas had been together, talking to one another, when he came along. Could he really trust Gray Bridges? He glanced at the man sitting beside him, looking about the Bay and beach and apparently enjoying the cooling breeze and spray.

Mani gave his mind to the realities that presented themselves to his eyes. The red cliffs gradually drawing nearer, the chop and swell of the sea, the passage around the southern point past Macassan well, where he had spent a brief moment of happiness with a girl whom he now regarded as a betrayer of his trust and love. Near the jutting rocks, past the well, he tried to estimate the boat's drift. The tide was running strongly and any minute now they would get into the swifter current that bypasses the bay during the running tide. It was well-known that it carried everything that had no power to resist it south towards the mainland near DeCoursey Head, and then westwards toward Indonesian waters.

'Can you see it?' shouted Foster. The other two stared ahead without turning, and he shouted again, louder this time, above the motor's din. 'Can you see the canoe anywhere?'

Bridges craned his neck and moved his head from side to side, and Mani stood on the seat. If the sea had been flat, and the sun further up from the east, a canoe would have been visible halfway to the jutting headland, but the flashing of waves in the morning glare was enough to hide it.

'Sit down, you young fool!' Foster shouted. 'Do you want to go overboard?'

Mani ignored his words and pointed as he saw the canoe. That meant that the tide was running faster than he had anticipated. The choppy sea was rough enough to keep the canoe hidden most of the time, and it looked even higher further ahead. Mani swung his extended arm towards the right several times sharply. Foster complied by adjusting the course accordingly, and, as they changed direction, the navigator dropped back to his seat. Bridges gave him a grin and nod of congratulations at being successful in the standing and sitting operation. Mani returned the grin faintly and resumed his watch.

It always worried Foster to come this far from shore. To begin with, he could not swim, then there were the currents. He was mentally kicking himself for not bringing the life-vests from the shed. It meant, more than ever, that it was important to allow for current, tide, wind, swell and wave. He knew about such things, but was not enough of a sailor to be sure that he could always know how to make such allowances. And this wind was offshore, chasing the running tide and cutting across it, a combination he had been told to treat carefully.

'We might be too late!' he bellowed, suddenly anxious about how far they had come and how much further they still had to go. 'If she gets to the point before us we'll lose 'er. The current's too strong past that point. This dinghy's not fit for the open sea on a day like this.'

Bridges half turned to him and nodded, and Mani waved to the right again without either turning or standing. Foster made the adjustment to the right, then corrected to the left slightly as Mani swung out the other arm. Apparently the young man of the coast had some of the old skills of observation, and could see the canoe now without rising. Foster settled to concentrate on watching to catch a glimpse of their target, and gave the throttle handle a couple of quick flick twists in case the motor might not be already running at the top of its power. Within a half a minute he sighted the black form bobbing into view and out again, and, after another five minutes running, they were able to watch the canoe careering up and down waves that were broken by waters emptying from the bay over hidden rocky extensions of the headland. It was daunting to set the bow to clear the hidden hazards and to charge, instead, towards the more violent water where the current met the running tide and was whipped by the off-shore wind. As they nosed down steeply over a wave that rolled under them and left a frightful hollow to be negotiated, all three clutched at their seats to avoid being thrown about, before lurching up suddenly and pitching over the next peak into a series of lesser waves.

Bridges looked at Mani who, though holding on firmly, seemed to be thinking of nothing but the canoe up ahead, then he turned to Foster.

'What do you think!' he shouted in a voice that betrayed nervousness in spite of his efforts to sound unperturbed. 'Are we gonna make it?' He was conscious of the grim ambiguity of his question, but allowed it to stand unqualified, since he really had doubts both ways. Would they reach the canoe while there was still time, and would they get out of this alive? What had they been thinking to set out without life jackets?

'If we get near enough,' Foster shouted, 'one of you grab it, and the other one lean out the other way to keep the balance.'

'Roger,' bellowed Bridges, as Mani nodded and considered perhaps it was not worth it, a canoe against three men's lives. Yes, they would make it, and they all must be ready to co-ordinate their efforts, otherwise anything could happen in these heaving seas. The going was fairly level for a few seconds as they drew near to the canoe, and Mani swung his right arm in an arc suggesting the dinghy be taken that way around to the other end of the canoe. But Foster had already decided to close with the nearest end of the canoe, and aimed straight at it. As they ran in towards it, the swell rose and rolled a series of high and unbroken waves at them. They ran across them diagonally, tossing crazily, and twisting to the left and eastward of the canoe. If they stayed on course they could be in reaching distance within a matter of seconds.

'No!' screamed Mani, spinning to face Foster. 'You can't do it!'

But it was too late. Foster had swung the tiller to bring the boat around towards the near end of the canoe. At top speed they curved along the swell and keeled over in a broadside that just went on as the underside was pushed further up and over by another of the rolling waves. In the split second that it took to capsize, Bridges and Mani were flung into the air, back into the direction from which they had come, and saw Foster falling into the water below them and the boat coming over him. Bridges surfaced near the boat and desperately thrashed through the water to grasp at the silver hull. Foster came up in front of him blurting, trying to yell and sinking before he could. He worked his hands frantically and resurfaced, as the motor spluttered and died, leaving only the dreadful sounds of the wind, the restless sea, and the voice of human fear.

'Help! Help!' Foster cried. 'Help me…I can't swim…help!'

Bridges was so busy trying to reach the dinghy that he was no help to Foster. Though the current and tide were carrying the boat away to the south, the east wind lifted waves that were swamping them and pushing them west towards the shore. He reached Foster with one hand and stretched the other towards the boat. No good. It was too far. He must try again. But before he could, Foster had grabbed him and was trying to pull himself up by his arm and shoulder. Both men went under as Bridges struggled to get his arm free. Foster let go and tried to surface again by flapping his hands. Bridges grabbed the other man's shirt collar as he kicked and came out into air again. Holding hard he struck out with the other hand and kicked furiously. Another wave lifted them away, and he doubled his efforts. They came in nearer, and he gave an all-out effort to reach the edge of the boat. The bow was nearest and almost out of the water. The stern was weighed down by the outboard motor, now silenced. Bridges put his hand under the side, palm upwards and grabbed the edge. It was all he could do to keep his face above water, while he pulled Foster towards the boat.

'Grab it!' he ordered. 'Get your hand under the edge.'

Foster did, but it was no good. He was trying to keep his head and shoulders out of the water, and failed to do so. Instead, he was sinking and panicking. Bridges wanted to tell him to turn his face to the sky and concentrate on just keeping his nose and mouth clear of the water, but the effort had left him gasping and the buffeting waves were constantly making him close his mouth and hoist himself on the edge, where one hand was gripped, and over the top, the other arm was bent across the upturned hull. Seeing Foster's plight, Bridges grabbed him again by the shirt collar and tried to hoist him up on the hull.

'Up, up,' he gasped. 'See 'f ya can…Up! Get up!' Foster put one arm and then the other over the upturned hull and tried to get purchase on one or two of the rounded end-to end ribs of the boat.

It was impossible and he cried, 'oh, my God. Oh, my God! I…I can't'.

'Here,' Bridges tried to shove him towards the lower part of the dinghy, towards the stern. 'Move down. Down. Down there. Lower. Get up on board.'

This time it was low enough for Foster to get some leverage with his hands and elbows. He hoisted on to his stomach and managed to get one knee up. In that position he rested, as did Bridges down beside him in the water, desperately trying to keep his head above water, while they both regained their breath. Bridges looked for Mani, but could not see him. The canoe was on the far side of the dinghy and also out of sight. He assumed that Mani was somewhere around that side. Desperately he edged his way along the edge beneath the water. He passed around the bow and despaired at what he saw. Foster was back in the sea, two metres away from the boat and flapping his arms as he bobbed up and down in the water, gasping and yelling. He was moving away. Behind him was the canoe and it, too, was moving away, fast. Mani was swimming all out after it. Foster was too far away to reach, and Bridges knew that he could not hope to get him back to the boat again. He was all but spent, himself for swimming in such a sea. He needed support himself, and dare not let go his hold. That could only result in him being washed away from the boat, too. He caught the sound of Foster's voice, and knew the words he cried, 'Bridges! Help! Help me!'

But Bridges could do nothing to help. It was every man for himself now. He put his forehead against the side of the boat and clung on for dear life. After a few deep breaths he turned to see what the position was, and was astounded by the sight of Mani making back towards Foster. He had his head down and was swimming with a powerful over-arm stroke. Headway was slow, but sure, and since Foster was being carried towards him it was only a few moments before they touched. Mani snapped commands at Foster, grabbed him with a hand under his chin and pulled him along on his back. Trying to travel back to the boat he soon found that it was too difficult and gave up the effort. Turning towards the rocky shore he struck out with his free hand and began to haul his burden across and down current through rough, but now assisting seas. The loneliness that descended on Bridges at the sight of the departure of his companions was profound. How could he hope to get to shore? It would be impossible to turn the boat over, and, if he did, the motor probably would not start now that it was flooded with sea-water. He decided to climb on to the surging hull. Benefiting from Foster's bad experience, he climbed on to the stern by the propeller column, and took special care not to overbalance. He spread himself face down across the dinghy's steep underside. At least he could breathe and think as he rode the bucking shell.

It was some minutes before Mani got Foster to shore, in which time the boat hardly seemed to change position, while the canoe rushed away into the strait. Bridges could see the others about two hundred metres away, struggling out of the water on to a protected rocky shoulder. Foster looked lifeless. His rescuer was dragging him. What followed looked like efforts to drain Foster's mouth and apply mouth-to-mouth resuscitation. Then Mani sat back for a while. Presently he dragged Foster by the armpits to a place higher on the rock. A few seconds later he ran across the rock and dived into the sea. It cheered Bridges to see that the young rescuer was heading back towards him.

With every heave of the waves the boat threatened to stand on its rear end, and his straddling arms pressed tightly to prevent him from sliding down to the propeller. It was a losing battle, and he found himself slipping with spread legs towards the propeller column and squirming to avoid landing on his crotch. Above him the steep aluminum slope rose steeper, then swayed back, almost to a level position. No sooner had it levelled and he tried to move, than it bucked up again, and brought to his mind films he had seen of ships standing on their end before plunging beneath the waves. It levelled, and this time he did not wait for it to swing up again.

He slid to the right, hooked his left foot up behind the propeller column and lunged forward and to the left. The maneuver was successful and he found himself back on the surging slope and groping for a hold. His arms must now take the pressure to prevent him from getting tossed too far to one side or the other. His legs were on the column and he had begun the struggle to keep them there. This successfully held him in position as he rose and fell with the boat.

When he felt his strength failing, he called up whatever reserves he had and put them into the concentrated work of his chest and arms hard against the boat's sides, and the hostile sea took the opportunity to edge his feet from the column. He crashed helplessly on his crotch and screamed in agony as pain enveloped him and unconsciousness came swamping about his head.

'Gra…Gray! Hang on, Gray! Hang on, Gray!'

He slid sideways into the water and Mani was beside him. Bridges felt his hands being pulled around the propeller column, and hung on.

'Come on Gray. You're okay, man. You're okay, 'ng on…ang on' Mani pushed him in close beside the propeller.
'Now listen Gray. You're okay here for a little while. You hear?' Bridges nodded. 'I'm not goin' to leave you but I've got to go down the anchor rope. It's stuck in

the rocks down there. Just stay, okay?' He moved around the edge of the bucking dinghy and Bridges waited for him to reappear. Nothing seemed real except the pain radiating from his crotch. It threw its waves to the extremities of his body and mind, immobilising all the muscles of his legs and lower trunk. He thanked God he was alive, but suddenly felt violently sick…sea-sick, fear sick and weak sick. He wanted to cry rather than vomit and found himself feebly doing both as consciousness flickered and threatened to go out again. Mani surfaced along the rope, slack now that he had freed the anchor rock from an oyster encrusted crevice about three metres down. Passing along the side again, he put his hand on Bridges' shoulder.

'You all right Gray?' Bridges half looked up to nod, but was overcome with nausea and convulsed again.

'We're moving now Gray,' said Mani assuringly. 'The anchor rock is free and we're on the move. You hear?' Bridges succeeded in nodding. 'Now you listen Gray. You hafta hang on here for a while. I'm goin' around to the front to pull the rope. We'll get it over to the rocks, all right, but you hafta hang on. You hafta do it on your own, awright?'

Bridges looked up. 'Yeah,' he croaked. 'Yeah, I'm....I'm awright.'

Mani frog-kicked, and with his right arm side-stroked while the left towed the boat from a point near the centre of the rope. The trailing anchor rock was far enough below to be out of harm's way.

As soon as he kicked off he knew that it would take everything he had to get to the rocks. He was growing weaker. The waters by the rock shelf where he had landed Foster were sheltered by a steep protrusion of grey rock, and he tried to bring the boat in there. It had gone too far already however, and he was carried on towards the next jutting out-crop. Below him the anchor hit rock or coral and he decided to haul it in. When he had edged around to the stern, Bridges, hugging the column with both arms, looked up at him with and tried to smile.

'How we doin'?' he asked.

Mani heaved on the rope as he gasped, 'Buruli, Goin' good. Only this anchor rock got to come up. Give me a hand, Gray.'

Bridges found that he could relax now and hold on by one arm. They were in calmer waters and, although the boat was still travelling south on the current, it was not tossing now. Together they yanked on the rope, hoisted the anchor rock up against the stern and lifted it into place behind the column.

'Keep it there,' said Mani as he swam away with the rope slipping through his fingers. Bridges responded positively to the direction and found comfort again in knowledge of a task to be done. His hands held the column lightly and he patted the anchor rock occasionally to make sure it wouldn't shift. When Mani's feet touched rock, feeling cautiously for the treacherously sharp edges of coral or oysters, and relieved to touch clear surfaces, he found places to get leverage and pulled strongly on the rope. He leaned back to make use of his weight. Rather than try to pull the boat closer to the high, dry rocks, he hauled in slack rope and piled it on the upturned hull. Then he joined Bridges to push it back towards the sheltered place where he had left Foster.

'Can you touch bottom, Gray?' he called.

Bridges held on firmly, reached down with his feet, tried to touch and failed, then touched, tried to stand and slipped.

'Ye…' he cried with unbounded relief. 'Yes, I can. Huh.' He found a footing on a ledge, and gasped as he stood with head and shoulders clear of the water. 'Thank God! Thank…where…where now?'

'Along this way,' Mani waved towards the quiet waters in the cove, and they half walked, half swam across the submerged rocks.

'Over here now,' Mani gasped, tugging the boat inshore to a sandy bottom no more than a metre under the water. 'We'll turn it over.'

They made three attempts. After the third try Bridges looked at his friend weakly. 'I knew I should 'a' had some breakfast,' he said.

'This time,' said Mani. 'Front up high, both on one side and push up and over. Ready now! One, two, three – muh, muh, muh!' But it was not that time.

'Can we get into shallower water,' said Bridges, and they dragged the boat closer in-shore until the water was below their waists.'

'Same way again,' said Mani. 'One, two, three, muh!' This time it came over and shipped no more than three inches of water. 'In you go,' Mani smiled, and held his side level while Bridges scrambled over into the dingy.

'You see the oars?' Mani asked, still holding on. They were under the seats still, with rowlocks attached, and Bridges quickly pulled them out. While he fitted one rowlock in place, Mani fitted the other and sprang in over the stern.'

'You right?'

'I'll give it a try,' said Bridges, feeling grossly inadequate and followed Main's timing. They moved forward smoothly, and, in spite of the pain, now easing, and the nausea and exhaustion.

Foster was propped up on one elbow in the shade of a higher pile of rocks, when they came into view around the point. Once he was sure of their safety, he sank back feebly, and let himself fade into the sick sleepiness that pulled him down.

When they came ashore Bridges walked painfully up the rock ahead of Mani who stayed to knot the anchor rope in order to shorten the range of the boat while anchored near the rocks.

'How now Jack?' he said softly.

Foster opened his eyes and mouth and gave a faint nod as his eyes dropped shut again. Bridges flopped down beside him, and spread himself face up to the sunshine. When Mani joined them, he lay down alongside them in the same fashion. No-one spoke for some time. Then Mani said, 'We have to wait for the tide turn, before we can row home.'
'The motor,' Bridges began, but Mani shook his head, and they fell silent again.

Without a word, Mani rose and clambered across the high rocks to the south. In that way he came to an old land-slide that ran up several metres to within easy reach of the plateau that topped the red cliffs at that point, and several minutes later, further south along the cliff top, he stood looking across the sea. To the east and the south was the mainland. Tor Rock broke the sky-line to the south, and further away behind it, he could see faintly blue tops of rocky mounds in the Arnhem Land escarpment. But he only had eyes for the sea, searching the waters without picking up any sign of a canoe. By now it would be past the next bay. It might well be as far as Buffalo Landing and turning into the mainland strait.

'Goodbye, canoe!' he murmured. 'I had to let you go.'

A movement behind him made him spin around. It was Bridges, standing there in silence.

'It was my life, Gray,' Mani explained his sorrow. 'That canoe was my life.'

Bridges waited.

'It really was,' Mani went on. 'From this place, where it grew, and with my own hands, and my grandfather's hands, and nobody could take it away from me. They tried. Jack Foster tried to take it, but still it was mine. While I had my canoe I could live without them all, and do good work to keep my people. Now it's gone. Gone. It's gone down that way into the current that will take it around the south end and away to Timor.' He looked off into the distance again. 'Might be it'll go more north to Macassar and wash up on a beach of Macassar. That would be good. It was the Macassan traders who showed our fathers how to make those dugout canoes. They respected our life. They are the only foreigners who ever really respected our life. Old people cried for them. When the Balanda government stopped them from coming every year to trade with us, to live and work along this coast, my people cried. I hope my canoe is found in Maccassar.'

'Mani,' said Bridges hoarsely. 'This is my life.' He put his two hands flat against his chest. 'And I just want to say thanks for letting me keep it.'

'You were alright,' Mani smiled shyly, and looked at the rock and grass between them. 'When I came back, you were hanging on all right, but Foster was goin'. So I went after him first.'

'You saved his life too, brother,' Bridges said. 'But, make no mistake, I was gone when you got to me. I couldn't have stayed with that damned boat another minute… I'm sorry Mani…about the canoe, I mean.'

They eyed each other and Mani turned away in silence, then smiled with a shrug and said, 'A man is more than a canoe Gray. That's what everything's about, all our whole Madayin Law, and some of your Bible too, I think human life surviving and getting saved.'

'I guess you're right Mani,' Bridges said quietly.

They stood for another minute or two staring off towards the south until Mani turned. 'We better go back, I s'pose. Old Jack's a sick bloke.'

'Right,' Bridges replied, and began to hobble back the way he had come.

'You hurt?' Mani asked.

'You bet your life, I hurt!' Bridges exclaimed. 'I hurt here.' He held his cupped hand over his crotch. 'Nearly ruined myself for life on that damned outboard motor.' Mani burst out laughing and Bridges feebly joined in.

'All of them Darwin women are goin' to be a lot safer now, anyway,' Mani chortled.

'Hey, that's enough of that,' Bridges complained. 'I'm a respectable married man, I'll have you know!' He hobbled on exaggeratedly for the sake of the joke. Mani whooped hysterically and flung his arm around Bridges' shoulder, where they laughed all the way back to the rocks above the shelf to Foster.

'You all right now, Mr. Foster?' Mani asked while Bridges was still picking his way down the higher rocks.

Foster looked up from where he sat, gave a grim, silent smile and a flick of his eyelids. He was not all right, but he was alive and he was going to be well.

'You'll be good soon,' Mani said, then turned and walked a few short steps towards the sea. The dinghy swung safely at anchor. 'The boat's all right,' he announced over his shoulder. 'And the oars. The motor won't work, but we can row…only we'll have to wait till the tide turns.'

'You pulled me out?'

Mani turned. 'Eh?' He looked embarrassed. 'Oh, yeah!'

'Thanks,' Foster looked down at his feet and spoke flatly. 'I thought my end had come.'

Mani sat and stared down to the dinghy.

'I owe you my life Mani,' Foster gasped hoarsely. The younger man shook his head.

'No,' he said simply.

'Oh, you're not goin' to argue with me about that are you?'

Foster raised his voice irritably, and was thrown into a fit of coughing by the effort, followed by an attack of retching that left him panting and resting on one elbow while he regained composure.

Mani was looking at him when he turned back.

'I'm not tryin' to argue,' he said. 'You don't owe me your life. Not in the way we people see it. We all owe each other help in times of trouble, especially close relations.'

Foster stared at him.

'You're a big brother to all us people. That's why we all call you that, Gayu.'

Foster stared at him.

'Our big brother was in trouble, and…and I was there.'

Still Foster stared. 'You're a funny bloke Mani. I can't make you out.' He turned to Bridges, who staggered down the rock.

'How ya doin now Jack?' asked the new arrival.

'Comin' on,' Foster replied. 'Thanks to Mani.'

'Oh, we both owe thanks to Mani for fishing us out Jack.' Foster looked up enquiringly.

'It's a fact,' Bridges continued. 'After he got you up here and revived you.'

'Revived me?'

'Yeah, you stopped breathing Jack. This bloke gave you the kiss of life.'

Foster's shocked face was fixed towards the cringing young man's back.

'Oh, yeah, Jack. You were well on your way to the bosom of your fathers when this guy blew you back.'

Noone spoke or moved for a while, then Bridges went on.

'Yeah, well ya see, I was done in, out there. I'd had it. It was hell, 'an I was slippin about like a mad thing. I hung on as long as I could, but it was no use. By God, I never want to go through that again. It was curtains for me, and I knew it, till Mani grabbed me and dragged me ashore. I'm still not clear what happened. The anchor snagged, didn't it Mani?'

'Yeah, that's right,' said Mani, glad to have something impersonal to talk about. He swung his crossed legs around and faced them. 'Down in the oysters.'

'Just as well for us too,' Bridges said. 'Or we'd a' been to hell away down current.'

'Same as the canoe,' said Mani.

'I'm real sorry, about that,' Bridges said.

'The canoe got away, then?' Foster asked weakly. Mani nodded.

'This young guy just about caught up to it,' Bridges informed him.

'An' he could've got it too! Except he decided to come back and get us instead.'

Foster searched his rescuer's face. 'I know how much that canoe meant to you, Mani.'

The young man's black face crumpled and he shook his head, and said simply, 'I had to let it go.'

'How did we go in?' Foster asked. 'We were just goin along and then we went over.'

'Don't ask me,' said Bridges emphatically, 'I'm no sailor…and after today I don't care if I never am.'

Mani looked at them, then down to the rough contours of the rock.

'What do you think, Mani?' Foster asked.

Mani tilted his head and put out his bottom lip, but still made no reply.

'Sea monster?' asked Foster, showing enough return of energy and good humour to do a bit of teasing.

Mani looked up quickly and grinned.

'I tell you,' said Bridges, 'I gave that old monster more than a passing thought when I was flappin about in the water out there.'

'It wasn't the monster,' said Mani. 'We's just turnin too quick from that direction with the waves runnin that same way.'

Bridges glanced at Foster and the Town Clerk's face showed how much he was wishing that he had not heard the last words.

'I...I guess you're right,' Foster said quietly. 'Seems I've still got a lot to learn.'
'Haven't we all?' said Bridges.

Chapter 8
Story Time

When the Arafura Sea ebbs from the islands and mainland beaches near De Coursey Head, along the steamy, green Arnhem Land coast, it runs towards the west. From Half Moon Bay on the east coast of Goose Island, a drifting canoe could be expected to round the southern point, then turn north west and run up the wild mainland coast past the headland and around Croker Island. The course of the runaway canoe on that sea was already as unchangeable as fate. The running sea was indomitable. There was no point in thinking about further efforts to overtake it.

In the couple of hours that they waited for the turn of the tide, the three men talked of the people back at the settlement. They would be getting anxious. All being well, they should be back before any afternoon squally weather arrived. If not, then the people at the station would have good reason to worry about their return trip. One group that would not be worried, according to Jack Foster, were the Council workers. He was sure that they would be happy to sit around doing nothin while they had no supervisor. Bridges gradually involved the recovering Town Clerk in conversation, and took the opportunity to interview him, to discover something about his experiences and motivation. Why did people work as he did, first in Christian missions, and now for the elected Council of a community? He received a few vague statements about having a call to stay with the people, which left him still wondering. The question of the sea monster was not raised again. It was as though they were all in silent agreement that the idea of a sea monster was irrelevant. All that they had been through was enough, without adding monsters. Mani was quiet while the other two talked, until Foster began to reminisce about the events and people of Goose Island. Then he joined in the telling of some of the amusing happenings among locals and staff members.'

'Remember Gumbadjid?' Mani asked ambiguously with a quick glance at the man he had pulled from the sea. It was one of those things that could go either way. They could talk about what an annoying bugger Foster was when he threw his weight around, or they could see the funny side of it. The Town Clerk grinned and took up the story, and together they recounted the scene of a boat unloading a couple of years earlier, when Charley Gumbadjid had reacted violently to Foster, threatening to lay him out, for calling him loudly by name in public. It made no difference that the Town Clerk was simply calling to him to get up on the tractor and back the trailer on the sand. The insult was in the loud public use of a personal name. Foster must have been given a real fright, because, according to Mani, the story of his startled look had often been told as part of an evening's camp-fire entertainment.

'Is that what goes on around the campfires at night?' asked Foster. 'Some of the staff people would get the biggest surprise if they heard our talks at night,' Mani grinned. 'You Balandas really are very funny people.' He fell back and lay on the rock laughing uninhibitedly; and one story led to another until a sort of reverie settled on them. The shade of the tall rocks offered as good a place to rest as they could hope to find anywhere, and since the nearest drinking water ran from rocks just beyond and above the dinghy, an occasional visit to this spring dealt with their thirst, they had no need to go anywhere else until the incoming tide and their oars would provide the power to carry them back to the settlement.

Foster caught Mani staring at him thoughtfully, and the young man gave him a flicker of a smile. Foster replied with a sort of sideways nod. Its meaning was clear.

'You think...' Mani began, then had second thoughts.
'Go on,' said Bridges. 'Do I think what?'
'Nothin.' Mani was apologetic. 'I didn't mean to say anything.'
'Out with it brother', Bridges was suddenly serious.
'All right, it's prob'ly nothing.' said Mani. 'I was just wonderin…you remember out there?'
'What about out there?'
'The anchor stuck, and you came round the boat, and Mister Foster, Gayu here, was gettin carried away, and…all that?'
'Go on.'
'You remember that time?'
'Yes, I remember every moment of it, clearly.'

Bridges stopped suddenly and closed his mouth. In a moment he was on his feet and walking down the rock towards the sea. The boat was swinging stern-most towards him, and he recalled vividly his struggles to hold on to that propeller column for dear life. Then the memory returned with a new and startling clarity. Mani had touched a recall reflex that he had been avoiding, and the horror he now felt told him why. Foster's voice, "…can't swim! Help me!" He had been ready to let Foster drown!

Instead of returning to the others, he walked along the water's edge towards the south. There is something comforting about striding across rocks within the sound of the sea when the mind is distracted. It promises the return of presence, the recollection of all of the whirling and heaving parts, and the recovery of some kind of clarity.

There was no canoe on the sea. The only thing of significance that he saw was a bank of dark cloud. Eventually he looked back down to where the others were still lying in the shade. Mani raised his hand in salute, and Bridges acknowledged with a single, low wave. Did Mani realise what it was that he had caused him to remember? What else could he have been referring to when he spoke about Foster getting carried away? A few minutes later, when he had dropped down next to the others, he crouched on his haunches and waited. The cloud in the south east was not visible from down here.

'I was really sending up my poor old grandfather for having a problem about lacking courage.' He paused. 'I know why now. Mani helped me remember.' He smiled at Mani, and then turned to Foster. 'Jack,' he went on. 'I was goin' to let you go… out there. You slipped off and I was frightened as hell we'd both go down if I came after you. So l...I let you go… and I hung on and buried my head, and the memory of my own cowardice…'

'Oh, come off it', snapped Foster.

'You're no coward,' echoed Mani.

'I'm a good bloke, eh?' Bridges asked in loud mockery.

'Yes, that's right,' the others said in unison, and Foster added, 'if not, you'll do till one comes along.'

'Sorry, Jack. I was more interested in saving my own skin.'

'I didn't want anyone to risk drowning for me,' growled Foster, as if by saying it he absolved all people from the need to have courage in such a situation.

'And I'm sorry I made things so much harder for you, brother,' Bridges told Mani.

'You didn't understand the sea,' Mani excused him.

'I could have tried,' Bridges was gloomy.

'Forget it,' said Mani. 'Anyway, you made us listen to your long story… and then you walked away just when I was going to tell you about my own grandfather's story. You wanna hear it?'

'Sure thing!' said Foster, and when Bridges had propped himself against the overhanging rock that gave them shade.

Mani began. 'You know, my grandfather's people are from the mainland. They're Wainanda people. Well the Ananardu islanders and our Wainanda people ave always got mixed up with each other. Sometimes friendly, sometimes fighting. A long time ago, before the missionaries came to 'ere, and we were still living our own lives in our way, my grandfather, Jambagirrila, you know, 'e was a young man, an' was still livin over there on the mainland, moving about inland, and near the sea with his uncle, and some other Wainanda men. They went to visit some of their clan people who had settled near the coast with a cattle station owner, Mister Charlton, and a hunter, another Balanda bloke, called Smale, but mostly they called him, the Hunter. This Smale bloke always had a bullet-belt, and two revolvers in his holsters. He worked for Mister Charlton.

Sometimes he travelled with pack horses, goin off with a load of crocodile skins, and buffalo horns and green-hide and smoked trepang, you know…the sea-slugs. He always paid people to work for him, with tobacco and flour and stuff, and sometimes even grog. There was plenty of Wainandas ready to work for these things.

Charlton, the cattleman, was kind to the people and married one of the Wainanda women. But the Hunter was a cruel, hard man, and hungry for lots of women. Sometimes, when they wanted to work for Smale, or when they were frightened of him, the Wainandas would lend him their women, to have when 'e wanted. In the old days the men of the tribes didn't do that sort of thing. Not till it wasn't safe to travel in their own country any more. They wanted Charlton's place to stay safe for the families to live there. The Wainandas 'ad seen more of the Balandas than most of the coastal people, and they 'ad learnt how to keep them quiet…you know, always say yes and keep 'em calm.

In that time, my grandfather was trying to get work with the Hunter, Smale, when trouble broke out. Smale got angry about a surcingle, you know, a horse-belt, that was missing, and went looking for it. My grandfather's uncle had seen one of the Wainanda men wearing a surcingle from one of Smale's horses wrapped around for a trousers' belt. He was showin off the belt, you know?

The hunter told my grandfather's uncle, and one of the other men to sit with the bloke who took the belt and give him some tobacco to smoke. They sat down and talked to the man while he smoked his last cigarette. He told them that Smale had been taking his wife, and other women as well without permission. That meant that he had broken our Madayin Law and the penalty payment he was claiming was this belt he had picked up from the ground.

When Smale came along, he told them to hold the man's arms and lift him to his feet. They did this, and they must have thought that Smale was going to talk to him, but straightaway he pulled out a pistol, put it between the man's eyes and pulled the trigger.

'That's to teach you a lesson. You shouldn't take what is not yours.'

My grandfather and his uncle were put in a dinghy by one of the stockmen. The other one who had held the murdered man was there too. They started to row out to

Charlton's supply boat and for some reason my grandfather's uncle got frightened and dived overboard. I suppose he was frightened of being taken on the boat by Balandas. The relations of the murdered man were waiting for the one's that held him, and when my grandfather's uncle arrived at the beach, he was speared to death right at that place. My grandfather saw it, and was glad that he had stayed on the boat. A Balanda stayed with him on the boat, and looked after him, while they were coming over here to Goose Island.'

'Quite a story,' said Bridges thoughtfully.

Mani said, 'not about being frightened but about being stealing. One man gave a punishment for a stealing, but was himself was stealing all the time.'

'What a bastard!' Bridges said bitterly.

'I hope that scoundrel was brought to justice,' growled Foster. 'If that's the sort of thing that went on, it's a wonder your people trust white people at all'.

'We don't?' said Mani. He turned to Foster, who looked embarrassed and confused. 'Sorry, Gayu, but I might as well say what I think. For us, when we think of a Balanda, the story of the men with the horses and guns are not far away, and we are close to our ancestors whose land was taken and whose women were used for sex, and they are reminding us…to be very careful. Don't make them angry.'

Foster stared in mute horror, and the silence extended, like the huge grey cloud that already had come up above the rocks from the south eastern horizon as they spoke, so widespread now that soon it would hide half the sky. Deep shade fell across the rock, and with it, a mood of lost hope. Any light that had made them confident of a new day of positive relations was gone.

'But we can keep on trying,' said Mani encouragingly.

Foster looked up and nodded. Eventually he spoke. 'If the truth be known, I see what you see, Mani. I see the Balandas as a big threat to the Arardbis, too. But not as big a threat as they are to themselves. I've watched the hand-over of the station from the Mission to the local people, and I've seen them backin' away from the new power they've got, power to be in charge of their own affairs on the station. An' what's happenin' is, they're leavin' it to outside contractors to come in and build the houses, and bringin' in staff to do the office work and health and hygiene and the gardens, and the store, and the fishery… Everything. They come for a couple o' years an' leave. An' I'm the meat in the sandwich. How can we work together, if that's the way it is? Town Clerk's just a fancy name for someone stupid enough to try to keep things goin when everyone else gives up tryin. An' you say they see me like that!'

'You don't 'ave to do it all, just because we people are too lazy?'

It was a question as well as a challenge, and Foster tried to explain himself.

'I know that but I cop all the work. Clans had arguments about who'd do what. Nabadgardi's mob are called the land-owners now, and they reckoned they should run things. Then the government said only the elected Town Council can legally decide things, and receive subsidies and grants, and one or two from all the resident clans can be on the council. No-one wants to work with anyone else, and I'm hangin' on here, because I can remember how everyone worked together in Mission days, and local men and women showed they could do all the work that needs to be done. It's heart breakin what's 'appenin. I don't know how much longer I can stay 'an try to hold things together. And you tell me they think of me like that.'

'That's not the only way they see you, Mister Town Clerk.' Mani assured him. 'They remember when the mission gave all the clans a way to work for themselves but together, too… and they see you as the nearest thing to that. They see you and they say, Mission was better than Gubment, an old Foster there, 'e can ride a horse 'an shoot a gun, but he's Mission an 'es our Gayu. You sure you're right about no-one wants to work together in old Mission ways?'

'Not today, I'm not, I'm not sure of anything any more.'

After a short silence he went on. 'Anyway, you blokes 'ave made me think about my own gran' father, and the only thing that comes to mind is one day when I was a little fella visiting him and my gran' mother. I'd been 'avin a good feed o' mulberries off their tree. Grandpa let me eat as many as I liked, and I couldn't get enough. Never did me any harm, 'cept the stains on me hands. I got in a shockin' mess…me hands, that is, with these dark purple stains all over em.' He showed them his hands and rubbed them as if trying to brush away the stains.

'Anyway, old Grandpa, 'e said that 'ed show me how to get the stains off. He told me that there was only one way to do it, crush a red mulberry and rub the juice of it in your hands. It gets it all out, he said. So I crushed a dozen of 'em to get meself clean before me mother and gran' mother saw me that day.' The other two men watched him carefully, but neither spoke.

'I was just thinkin,' he said, breathing heavily from the effort, 'I was just thinkin', how we all seem to find someone or some-thing to crush, like… like a red mulberry, when we want to make ourselves look clean.'

Someone who's got a little bit of fault that's really a weakness of our own, well, they're fair game for us, even when we don't know why we're pickin on em.'

He stopped, breathless, and they sat, unspeaking, while the sound of the breeze about their ears and the slap of the returning tide on the rocks reached them with the news that they could soon set off with the sea assisting. The chance that the capsize had given them to tell each other something from their own lives was ending, and it was time to think about leaving this place and making their way back to the community, which must be wondering what had happened to them.

'Quite a thought, Jack,' said Bridges eventually. 'I do believe you're right you know. It's the things we can't forgive ourselves for, that make us mad when we see them in others.'

'You should come down to our campfires sometimes, Gayu,' Mani told Foster. 'You've got a good story there. Our people would like to talk about that berry tree story, an' what it's saying about how we're treatin' each other.'

'Would you 'ave me?' Foster asked flatly.

'Why don't you come down 'an find out,' suggested Mani.

Foster smiled faintly. 'I just might take you up on that,' he said. 'Look Mani, I had no right to bust into your… your marriage arrangements. None of my business. I… It's just…I don't really know what to say… I'm sorry, I really am. I 'spose I was takin you for another red mulberry. I don't want to talk about it, but when Edna and I got married…well…' He hesitated. 'I've never talked to anyone about this.'

'There's really no need to, Jack,' said Bridges quietly. 'Are you sure you want to?'

'Just between us three, and not for anyone else's ears. It's time I said it to someone,' Foster confided. 'I need to. You see, I love my wife. Edna's, without a doubt, the best person I've ever known. When we first met I was working for her father, an...er...I, well, I wouldn't have given myself any chance with Edna. She was only eighteen, and I was ten years older. But she knew what she wanted, and she got it. One afternoon, when her father was away, I didn't know she was home alone, and I didn't mean to… to be with her. But I was…She got pregnant. We got married. The baby died, and Edna had a terrible time, terrible.' He took a deep breath, looked away to the clearing clouds, then continued. 'She could never have…any...more ba… babies. An' I've never forgiven myself for bringin all this on her like I did…You think you've left it all behind you, but it's still...all still there.'

Mani rose and crossed the rock to crouch beside Foster. 'Thanks for sharing, Jack,' he said. 'I'm glad you told us these things. Now we can see each other a little bit better.'

Foster sobbed openly, and reached out a hand to grasp Mani's. He closed his lips and eyes firmly as he nodded, and received an acceptance for which he had yearned for many years.

Chapter 9
The Black and white bird

Although the tidal current had turned, it was not yet flowing strongly, making the trip back to the settlement painfully slow and exhausting. But thankfully the dark clouds had passed over on high winds, with only a gentle surface breeze, and their return journey was calm and incident free. When Bridges yielded up his oar to Foster, and moved back next to the useless motor, it became clear that neither of them had fully recovered from their ordeal.

Foster was visibly weakened, and Bridges regretted that he was not up to insisting that he be allowed to do more of the rowing. Mani was a little the worse for wear, too but he managed to keep up regular stroking with his oar. The sea became completely calm.

The breeze had dropped altogether, and, although they were fanned by forward rushes, to the rhythm of the oars, they took no comfort from the searing heat of early afternoon. The sea's sheen was undisturbed except for their wake, and an almost imperceptible tidal swell had begun to move in gently all the way to the shore.

For the two Balandas, their frightful experiences in the sea, and their physical discomfort, dulled their enjoyment of what otherwise might have been a pleasurable journey home. As it was, there was a kind of pleasure in deep security and satisfaction. They had lived to tell the story of a brush with death.

Mani was sad about the loss of his canoe. But the sadness was drifting away, too, like a dying refrain behind the exultation that welled up and made him glad to be the strong one who could bring home these two Balanda friends of his people. Not only had he lived through the ordeal, he had made it possible for them to live through it too, and they had come through together, more together now than they had been before; and each man knew himself and his companions in a new way.

Foster lifted his gaze from the stern, where Bridges sat leaning against the useless, tilted outboard motor, and flung his body weight backwards in order to keep up with Mani's stroke.

Bridges lurched back and forth. 'Somethings different,' he spoke loudly so that the rowers could hear him above their own hard breathing. 'We didn't get what we went after,' said Bridges, as the others leaned towards him and lunged back. 'We didn't get the canoe, but we found something else out there.'

The others glanced at him, but kept up a steady rhythm with their oars. 'It's not the same,' he said. 'Between us, I mean. It's a whole different thing to when we were goin' out.'

'We're the same, uh, people,' said Mani pulling on a long shallow stroke.

'But we're different, too,' said Bridges mysteriously. 'You, Mani, you thought that canoe meant everything to you. It was your life, you said. And you didn't exactly love old Jack here. But what you did for him, and for me, when you let your canoe go, is something that will always be there. It's part of you and Jack and me from now on, Mani.'

'Might be,' said Mani with a smile.

'Anyway, uh,' Foster made an effort to join the conversation. 'We can make another canoe.'

'Oh, can we?' Mani sounded indignant. 'So, you think it's easy to make a dug-out canoe?'

'Come on you guys. Don't start fightin' again,' Bridges laughed.

'Anyway,' said Foster, 'What I'm tryin' to say is, will you let me help you make a new canoe?

Mani looked, through two full strokes, at the strong man beside him, survivor of a near drowning. He searched the leathery face. The tired eyes, sad and earnest, but unwavering, the nervous half smile, and the solemn mood that showed in the lines of his brow, all told him what he wanted to know.

Foster was seeing him as a man of some account, and offering himself as a friend. More than that, he also saw beside him a driven man, busily striding through life, trying to do right and save the world, and avoid the pitfalls of temptation on his own vast ocean of loneliness, and the little boy inside him, afraid because his hands were unclean, and in there too, the presence in his heart of stern parents, and, in his deep place, the Christian spirit that made him and his wife stay at Goose Island when other missionaries had withdrawn, so that they could continue to serve the islanders. He knew that he could trust the man that he saw, to treat him as a man, as a person to be honoured and enjoyed in a two-way give-and-take relationship, and be told off or teased and abused when necessary, but never to be reduced to an object that was there to be manipulated or used, and never a red mulberry to be crushed as a sacrifice for someone else's own self-justification.

'We've got no more big trees in the part of the island that's been reconised as our family's borrowed part,' he answered. 'But, might-be we can talk old Nabadgardi's mob into lettin us 'ave one more from the south jungle. If we can, well, we can make another canoe. You really want to 'elp?'

'Yes…I do.'

'Awright, Jack. Buruli, that's good,' Mani grinned. 'You got yourself a job.'

Bridges was surprised to see a magpie goose move overhead.

As the rowers stopped to look at the bird, Mani told them, 'Our people say that the wild birds are always watching us, and when they do something unusual it's probably because they have a message for us.'

As he spoke the goose descended steeply and flew ahead of the boat.

Bridges looked past the black and white rowers and was surprised to see the black and white goose winging along about a metre above the calm level sea only two boat-lengths ahead of them.

'Well, blow me down, that old goose is showin us the way. He must think he's a dolphin.' The other two men paused from rowing.

'Praps 'es tryin to say somethin to us,' Foster suggested half seriously.

'I wonder what it could be?' Amused by the idea, Bridges played along, then while the other two propelled them on towards the waiting people by the coconut palms, he found himself sitting back, unthinkingly humming slowly in time with the rowing, and beginning to sing an old favourite song of longing for inter-racial harmony. 'We shall overco-o-me...Black and white toge...ether, black and white toge...ether. We shall overcome some da-a-a-ay.'

In time they approached the shore and could see the locals waiting by the water's edge, and Bridges announced, 'looks as though we're gonna have a reception committee.'

On the beach, the crowd that had gathered early in the morning, to investigate the weird footprints in the sand, seemed to have reassembled. This time Mondi Laku and Edna Foster had joined the people of the camp, who gasped and cheered as the goose rose from its place ahead of the boat and flew away above the palms. As the boat raced towards the beach, Edna, Mondi and Lunggaroi moved closer to the point of landing. On the last stroke of Mani and Foster's oars, Mondi Laku waded towards the dinghi followed by Lunggaroi, and, together, they heaved it on its way.

'Welcome back to Goose Island,' the Minister clowned. 'You had us all worried.'

'We're all right,' Foster called heartily with a wave of his hand as he lay the oar across the seats and swung his legs over the side to drop down beside the boat. His attempt at heartiness was revealed as a sham when he landed in knee-deep water that was running up the sand, and his buckling knees nearly let him down.

'Whoops-a-daisy,' he bluffed, as he clutched at the side of the boat and pretended to push it further on while he held on through a rush of dizziness. His subterfuge could not deceive the watchful Edna, and she followed the retreating fall-out of a wave down the sand, flapping the water with her rubber thongs at every step.

Lunggaroi hurried to Mani's side of the boat. Nervously he reached out to tug the dinghy, and glanced at his old friend who was his recent enemy. With guilty fear yielding to a stronger concern, he said privately, 'galoo kinoo?'

'Nothing,' replied Mani. 'We never gonna see that kinoo again.'

'Oh, thought. I…' Lunggaroi began. 'It was, it…I put the rock…sorry.' Apprehension flared in his eyes until Mani spoke.

'You wouldn't let that canoe go,' he said. 'That's like our life. You're not going to let that go. Don't worry, cousin, that's an accident.'

'I'll pay,' Lunggaroi said with an enthusiasm multiplied by relief. 'I'll pay what the Madayin says for your canoe.'

'If you want to pay, you can pay me with your work,' said Mani. 'You can help us to get a tree and make another canoe.'

'Yeah, that good way. I can do that,' Lunggaroi smiled happily, and hauled the boat as partner to Mondi Laku. They pulled it clear of the water, while people jumped out of their way, across the dry sand.

'Here do?' asked Mondi.

'Uh-uh, Boonyi. Up the grass, under them coconut,' said Lunggaroi. 'Us blokes left that kinoo too far down before.'

They took the boat all the way to the grassy slope beneath the coconut trees.

'Might as well put it on the trailer now,' said Mondi, and to the delight of the boys and girls who had followed them, he unscrewed the clamps and hoisted the outboard motor clear without a helper.

Dropping the propeller end into a forty four gallon drum nearly full of water, he clamped it to the top edge, then returned to the boat. He rocked it, grabbed the far side and, with a quick movement, stepped beneath it as he hoisted it over his head. With great care and precision he slowly stood tall again with arms outstretched, one massive hand over each rowlock hole, then walked with the upturned aluminum boat held steadily level overhead.

'Yay! Yay! Ya- a-ay', cried the children, jumping and twisting with delight, and their cheers were joined by the gleeful yeehees and excited laughter of the crowd on the beach.

'I'll help it down,' Lunggaroi offered, but the big man insisted on doing it all himself.

'No, no, let me do it,' he grunted as he gently lowered himself to a crouching position and let the inverted bow lightly touch the shiny steel floor of the trailer. By tossing the boat lightly, he was able to slip his hands back towards its stern in several easy movements, let it down in front of him and push it ahead into the trailer.

'Woo-hoo!' they cheered. 'Too strong, Boonyi! That minister really big bloke! Whoo! Strong fella, Boonyi!' Lunggaroi gasped with a huge grin and Bridges was suddenly aware of having, in some sense, been at that point before. Something seemed familiar. This scene belonged with another in his recent past. Was it because he had walked with Mondi by these very trees the day before, to talk with Mani? 'Was that only yesterday?' he marvelled. Perhaps he was reminded of something from another time and place. Something similar. But he had never been anywhere similar. This was a unique event in his experience; and yet, there it was, dejavous, an awareness of...of a place to which he had come, in a pilgrimage of discovery; possibly in one of those complicated, searching and struggling dreams. That was probably it, it recalled an old dream, this scene of a Minister heaving a boat around, single-handedly. Or was it just that this had been a day of larger-than-life experiences? After the monster on the beach and a near death experience, on a danger-filled sea adventure, now here was a super-human missionary.

Mani was walking alongside Edna as she assisted her husband, in spite of his attempts to discourage her. They were heading for the tractor. 'Don't let him drive, Missus Foster,' said the young man. 'Somebody else can do it.'

'Git away with ya!' growled Foster.

'True, Missus Foster. He gotta rest, two, three days. Better you make him rest, Missus Foster,' Mani insisted. 'Cause he got drowned.'

'You what?' Edna Foster was visibly alarmed.

'It's awright, I tell ya,' her husband replied.

'Just the same,' said Bridges, stepping into the conversation. 'I think Mani's right. I shouldn't 'ave let you take over my oar out there, Jack.'

Mani grinned. 'Might be if he didn't, we'd still be been comin at sunset!'

'For sure,' agreed Bridges. 'But seriously, Jack, you've been through an ordeal'.

'We all have,' said Foster.

'Yeah, true, but...' Bridges turned to Mrs. Foster. 'You should know this Edna. We tipped the boat over, and Jack and I've got Mani to thank for our lives.'

The young hero looked nervously from side to side at the sand beside and behind him, in case any of the locals were listening. Lunggaroi had drifted aside to tell the excited children to share the latest sensational report with the village community. A new legend was born, a Minister who could lift a boat on board a truck all by himself. Only the Minister was near enough at that moment to overhear the report of Mani's life-saving achievements.

'No?' Mondi breathed in awe, his eyes were popping, and, for once he was short of words. 'What's this you are telling us? Mani saved your lives?'

'Jack here stopped breathing, and Mani brought him around with the kiss of life,' Bridges told them matter-of-factly.

'Lord save us!' Edna Foster gasped. 'Oh, thank God you're all right. You could've been...' She turned around, clutched Mani and kissed him firmly on the cheek before he had a chance to avoid her. 'God bless you,' she said. Just as quickly she turned back to her husband, cancelled the forming tears with a sniff and demanded to know. 'Why didn't you take the lifejackets?'

'I know, I know!' Foster put up a hand defensively. 'They were in the workshop cupboard, we were in such a rush I never gave 'em a thought. But I can tell ya one thing! I'll never forget 'em again.'

'And little brother was there to save you,' Mondi declared, enfolding Mani to him with one big arm.

Edna clicked her tongue. 'It's not like you to be careless,' she told her husband. 'Well, come on. Get in and we'll get home to bed. Are you all right to drive, Lunggaroi?'

'Ee-ee, me now,' the driver crossed to the driving side.

'You comin up to our place?' Edna asked Bridges for no apparent reason. The enormity of the occasion seemed to require some talking about, and it struck him as reasonable that he be invited to go along.

'Well...' he began, with a glance at Mondi, who looked at him with the usual friendly smile. 'Thank you, Edna, but no,' he said. 'Let me know if there's anything I can do. But I want to walk a bit to get my land legs back, and then I'm going to put my feet up for a while, at my host's place. I'll foot-walk if you don't mind.'

'See you later,' said Foster tiredly.

'What a blessing that you are all here safe and sound,' Mondi Laku took an arm and supported Foster as he made his way to the front of the truck. 'Now you're the one that has to get looked after, Mr. Town Clerk,' he grinned. 'And we all will give God thanks bye and bye for his goodness, and for his servant Mani.'

Shutting the door after they settled into the truck seat alongside Lunggaroi, he told the Fosters, 'I'll come up to see you in a little while.'

Mani had waited to see the truck leave the beach. He watched with Bridges and Boonyi Laku as Lunggaroi backed and turned the trailer across the log ramp in the sand, and headed up the track to the Foster's house.

'I'm not going up that way,' Mani excused himself from their company. 'I dowanna see someone up along the camp road. Not now. I'm going beach way. See you later, Boonyi. Take care, Gray.'

'You too, mate.' Bridges replied, 'And Mani...thanks.'

Mani waved dismissively as he turned and moved across to some of the crowd still waiting to hear his story of this exciting event.

'Are you feeling all right now, Gray?' Mondi asked as they set off up the track.

'Not bad' His voice implied that he was not quite all right. 'A bit of a walk'll do me good'.

'Yah need to rest,' Mondi Laku advised. 'Will you be okay, or do you want me to walk with you? I was on my way to visit a family along here.'

'No, no,' Gray was definite. 'I want to walk and to just think about what's happened'.

'I won't be long,' his host assured him. 'I'll catch up with you probably. Then we can have some food and drink together. I look forward to that. Now you take care, you're a precious friend of the people. They need you to get well. And think of your wife, Olivia. She will want to see you looking well.'

Bridges assured him that he would take it easy and fully intended to retire early. A few minutes later he was ready to break the journey to the Manse and take a spell. He detoured towards the cliff-top fibro shacks, where a large rock offered an ideal place to sit for a while.

* * *

The crowd had dispersed, but the shade of a spindly casuarina tree on the beach below was the chosen play space for four small children and Bridges watched them as he rested. The future generation, he mused. A five or six year old boy threw himself down, rolled over and flipped up again on to his feet. A smaller girl and boy competed to be next to perform this amazing feat, with mixed success, and the remaining, smaller boy, rolled on to his back kicking his legs high and laughing loudly. What will it be like for them and their people when they are twenty years older? Bridges wondered. He'd be retired by then and those little people would be near thirty. What options would they have, and what capacity would they have to use existing opportunities to have a life that they chose for themselves? Would they be sober, steering clear of jail, educated and able to travel, have a steady income, perhaps a family or clan business, a home, healthy wife or husband, and children? Would they be fit and athletic? A friendly community member? Embedded in clan community life? Well-informed, politically literate citizens? At home in the broader society? World citizens, perhaps? Where would they be then? And what difference could anyone from outside the community, like himself, make to their life chances?

They have to do it themselves; take the existing opportunities and build on them. But would it happen? Was it sensible to expect that it would? Could he hope to make a difference to their chances for health and happiness? Perhaps, just a slim chance, was the best answer he could find in his heart and mind. Perhaps not. Our lives touch so lightly and so briefly, but whatever can be done to alleviate the oppressive factors and to increase the means of self-improvement should be done. It is little, but it is all anyone can hope to do, so it is vitally important. A life's work could be a small but indispensable thing, like a canoe on a wide, threatening sea of oppression. Having re-affirmed the value of his vocation to the future prospects of this little community, he promised himself to keep doing whatever he could to level the playing field for the children under the casuarina tree.

Hearing voices, he looked towards the houses. Two chattering ten or eleven year old boys, dressed only in lightweight khaki shorts were approaching with a beautiful, slim teenaged girl in a plain white shift. They approached Bridges. One of the boys put all polite manners aside and asked boldly, 'You seen monster in the sea, eh?'
    'No, we never saw the monster.'

The other boy was ready with the next quickfire question. 'You seen that kinoo, eh?'

Bridges looked from the boys to the girl. She was concerned. Her pretty face was closed, and he felt sure that this was Mani's bride.

    'Hullo,' said Bridges. 'You want to hear about the canoe of Manggululu, do you?'

She stared at him blankly and nodded once. 'usband 'im,' said the first boy, and Bridges raked through his memory's Goose Island resident's file.

    'Er, Manggululu's wife...er...Lara.. Lin...Lilara?' he asked.
    'Yes,' she said shortly and sadly. It was enough to tell Bridges that there was an unbridged distance between the young newlyweds.
    'Well, let me tell you,' he said. 'Your husband is a very brave young man.' He went on to tell her. He told of the great humanity that had let go the canoe, which

was Mani's means of living from Nature, and the courage, strength and skill that had saved two men's lives, the Town Clerk's and his own.

'The three men had to go through deep water and sit together for a long time,' he told them. 'Until the tide turned.' He stared at Lilara, then added with special emphasis, 'and they became friends.'

'Now they good friends?' One of the boys asked quietly.

'Yes,' Bridges said softly, with a smile directed to Lilara alone. She sucked in her breath quickly as her smile flared and threatened to break into a giggle, then turned away to hide her face.

'Now they friends, all them been in the deep water,' said the boy who had first spoken to Bridges. Bridges looked at him and then at Lilara.

'He knows how it is, this boy,' he said, tousling the boy's hair. 'Yes, the men are friends because they went through deep water together' Lilara stared at him, blinking and expressionless, except for a vague perplexity darkening her lovely young face.

'You understand, Lilara?' Bridges asked.

She shook her head briefly and looked down. 'Girls don't know,' said the confident boy.

'The Town Clerk and Mani are friends now? Good friends?' she asked, looking directly at the Balanda. He nodded with his eyebrows held high. She nodded slowly in reply, and a new sense of relief faintly showed in her face.

'When two strong people talk together,' he told her, they get the feeling of coming close and pushing each other. They might get hot. They can hurt each other's feelings. Eh? Sometimes they hurt each other. But when people go into deep water together…'

'Like…' Lilara broke her silence, but hesitated… 'like,' she ventured again, 'one young man and the Town Clerk?' The consultant congratulated himself on being such a good communicator, as he nodded vigorously.

'Yes, as you say,' he assured her. 'Like one young man and the Town Clerk. They went into a new deep place today, and saw each other in different ways. Me too. I was there too, in that dangerous deep water. We were nearly dead, so we saw our life in a new way.'

'They 'ad bigges' bull-fight!' declared the knowledgeable little boy seriously, with wide eyes.

'Who had a fight?' asked Bridges in genuine surprise.

'That one Mani and Town Clerk,' came the confident reply.

Bridges looked away to the sky above the beach, and let the talk of fighting pass him by. The young bride needed to hear something else. He resumed the canoe story. 'In the rough water the boat tipped over and we all fell in. Two Balandas couldn't swim strong. Gayu Foster and me. We were going to die in the sea. But Mani pulled one man out and then the other man out of the water, and on to the big rocks. So now we are like different people. We went through deep dangerous water together, so now see each other different.'

He looked away again, and they waited. 'They will always be friends, now, the young man and the Town Clerk,' he said at length. 'Proper friends. And me, too.'

'I hafta go, now,' Lilara flashed him a nervous smile. She spoke quickly to the boys in a local dialect and walked away. The talkative one said, 'We goin, too. See ya.' Bridges watched them sprinting towards the village.

It was time for him to tackle the next stage of the hike to the Manse, but he was suddenly off balance and lingered, swamped by a wave of terror, as the sea that he had so glibly been speaking about came surging back into consciousness.

The distance to the Manse seemed twice as far as it had before, and the slope of the sandy track made him plod. He was looking forward to having some refreshment, at last, and then some quiet bed rest before the evening meal and conversation with Andrew and the Lakus.

Chapter 10
The new kinoo

Within living memory there had been quite a few giant eucalypts growing among the tropical palms and jungle thickets on the coastal islands. They stood over the tropical bush canopies that sprang and spread in the damp hollows around soaks and springs. Valued for the shade that they provided and because they had known the ancestors of present day islanders and were repositories of stories of past lives, they had become a precious heritage. In ancient times no one would have reason or desire to cut down such a tree, not until the Macassans had come about four and a half centuries ago. It was those friendly traders from the Indonesian islands who had taught local men to fell giant trees and shape the trunks with an adze. They had taught them other things as well, such as what money was for in trading, and its name, rupia. They had introduced them to flour, garnijawa, and sugar, gargu, and to tobacco, bargy, and to the skill of making long pipes for smoking it, and how to dry, in smoke-houses, giant sea slugs, trepang, harvested annually from the shore-line waters for sale in Asian food-houses. They brought alcohol with them, too, and had arrival and departure celebrations with it, but lived quietly and were respected for their civilised behaviour as guests in someone else's land. Until they introduced dugout canoes the only boats that had been made by the locals were flimsy bark vessels.

Inevitably, in over four centuries, the giant trees had been almost completely eliminated from some islands; but, to the credit of the Macassans, they had introduced other kinds of tall trees from their homelands, particularly the tamarinds, which were not valued for timber as much as for their great wide shade and for the sticky little fruit that was popular with traders who were so far from home and its pleasures. But the fact remained that, of the giant native trees that had stood on Goose Island throughout the lives of generations of Nabadgardi's ancestors, only four remained. It was a serious matter for Mani's family to ask the Ananardu people to let them cut down one of these, and nobody would have been surprised if permission had been refused. Then, to everyone's surprise, after only two hours of conversation between Jambagirrila and Nabadgardi a brief gathering was arranged in which Mani spoke to a group of Ananardu about the need for a new canoe, and Nabadgardi admitted that they were responsible for the loss of the Wainanda canoe, because Lunggaroi had carelessly beached it. With a clear consensus, and to everyone's relief, the old man announced that Mani could have a suitable tree and Lunggaroi was required to work with him to produce a new canoe.

Jambagirrila had seemed surprised by Nabadgardi's ready agreement, but when his grandson decided to go immediately to fell the tree, he did not try to stop him. The word had been given, and the tree could be cut. Still Jambagirrila thought that some of the trouble-makers in Nabadgardi's family would grumble and tell their old man that he should not have given the big tree to Mani. Already there had been whispers about their jealousy of Mani over Lilara being given to him for his wife. Let them complain, the word had been given, the Law had been observed, and if they wanted to change their minds then they had better be quick about it, because Mani and his team of helpers intended to fell the great tree, tomorrow morning if possible.

By mid-morning Mani was hard at work with a chain-saw, at the base of the giant tree that grew in the gully forest just south of the settlement. Mondi Laku was at hand, ready to take the heavy saw. Bridges stood nearby, self-consciously unsure if he could be of any use, and trying to copy the stance and manner of Lunggaroi, who was simply standing by while the others worked, yet seemed to be fully engaged in actively watching, participating in the whole event at the feeling level.

'Little bit more,' Mondi shouted above the blare of the saw. The biting chain ripped its way closer to the point of the v-shaped cut that Foster had made in the other side of the trunk by way of a demonstration of how to use the saw, before he left them and went to attend to an urgent pump repair job to ensure that the day's supply of spring water was piped to the tank near the top of Central Hill. Bridges had found Jambagirrila subdued, but quietly agreeable to attending the Darwin consultation. He had left Brown sitting in silence with the old man, his old friend of earlier days, when he went with the others to make a start on a new canoe.

It was a big step that Foster had taken in letting Mani use a valuable piece of Town Council equipment unsupervised. This fact suddenly came to the fore in several minds in the next instant when, with a final 'choomph', the saw stopped.

'Not stuck?' said Mondi in the sudden sound vacuum. Mani pulled and pushed, but there was no movement. After trying to twist it sideways he relaxed.

'Don't let go,' snapped Lunggaroi. 'It can't hold up. Too heavy. Might break 'im.'

As he spoke, he stepped past Mondi and took the weight of the motor end of the saw and Mani stepped back. 'Can we start it with the starter?' he asked.

'No,' said Lunggaroi. 'Not now it's stuck on a straight cut.'

'What can we do?' asked Mondi Laku, looking as helpless as Bridges felt.

'We have to think about what we 'ave to do,' Lunggaroi said flatly. 'Should be we went more further with them vee cuts, then you can just pull it out.'

'You couldn't drive a wedge into the cut to open it, could ya?' asked Bridges tentatively.

'Too heavy,' said Mani, looking up at the towering trunk.

'If it's laying flat, all right. You can put an axe in to open up,' said Lunggaroi. 'This time, standing up, all that tree too heavy.'

'Yeah, I see that now,' Bridges said, feeling foolish.

'Might be, if the wind blows against it, it will lean that way, and open the cut?' ventured Mondi.

'We can't wait till that end of Dry Season wind to get the saw out,' laughed Lunggaroi. Mondi wet his finger and held it up with no result. There apparently was no wind in the gully, and he shrugged his lack of further suggestions.

'We'll just wait,' declared Lunggaroi, getting his thigh in under the end of the motor to take the weight.

'How long we'll wait?' asked Mondi.

'Might be a little while,' replied Lunggaroi confidently.

'What are we waiting for Lunggaroi?' asked Bridges.

'Like some time we have fight or big row,' Lunggaroi explained. 'Sometime might be one man go 'way, over the other side the island or crost the mainland. Bye an' bye 'ell come back when that trouble cool down.'

'You waiting till this trouble cools down?' Mondi asked. Lunggaroi shrugged, and Bridges stepped forward.

'Here, let me give you a rest. I'll hold it for a while.' He took the weight and let Lunggaroi step away. 'I think maybe Lunggaroi's right. When the metal and the wood get hot they swell up, and when they cool down they go thin again. We can wait a bit.'

They all turned at the sound of the Land Rover. It was on the way back from the pump-house at the spring.

'Ah, here comes the Town Clerk,' said Mondi warmly, as though that made the present situation easier to handle.

'Must've got the pump back into action already,' said Bridges, yanking the saw handle upwards and imitating the way he had seen Lunggaroi push his thigh under the weight of the silent motor.

'He too good mechanic, Gayu,' said Lunggaroi, with real admiration for the Town Clerk. The big grey vehicle ground through the grass along the cleared hill-side on the far side of a strung wire fence. Lurching sideways towards them, it rolled to a stop. Foster leapt out, uphill, and let gravity swing the sloping door home with a bang.

'What's goin' on,' he called, striding down to the fence. His leg naturally found the third lowest wire strand and he bobbed through to their side. 'What's up? Y' aven't gone 'an got it stuck ave ya?' He sounded irritable. 'Am I the only person 'round 'ere who can make anything work?' It was more a cry of despair than a boast.
Bridges looked at his friend from the deep waters and said firmly, 'You haven't fixed that pump already, Jack?' He had no desire of getting drawn into stormy seas again today.

'It's all right for the moment,' grunted Foster. 'Give us a look at this 'ere.'

He moved forward to take Bridges' place, but Mani stepped in front of him. The two men stared into each other's face. Mani wore a grimly set mouth, searching eyes, with a covering of running beads of sweat, like Foster's. Lunggaroi put his hand on Mani's arm, and it was allowed to stay there ignored.

'What did you tell me when you went?' Mani asked with quiet displeasure.
'I told you I was leaving that saw in your care,' Foster declared accusingly.
'And now what do you say?' Mani was unshaken.
'It's not what I say…it's what you've done,' Foster corrected.
'Done what?' Mani asked.
'I didn't tell you, you could let Darwin visitors use the bloomin thing.'
'Whoa, whoa, whoa, Jack!' called Bridges. 'Take it easy. I'm not the operator around here. Just these two blokes.' He waved a hand between Lunggaroi and Mani.
'Umph, anyway,' grunted Foster. 'Gimme a look at it.'
'Why, Jack?' Mani asked.
'What do you mean, why?' the Town Clerk snapped. 'So's I can fix the bloomin thing.'
'Why?' Mani asked again.
'What?' Foster looked at him with fresh interest. The other three men stared in silence, waiting. Foster hoisted his belt, pushed in his shirt, and after a long moment, spoke again.
'You got it under control?' he asked, uncertainly. Mani nodded, but kept staring. Foster sniffed and ran a hooked finger down his nose to flick away the sweat. 'Good,' he said quietly. 'Er...what, what are you doin' about it?'
Mani stepped aside and looked towards the saw.

'We're letting it cool down,' he said. Then he added to Bridges, 'you all right?'
'Yeah, yeah, I'm okay,' he replied.
'Here,' said Mondi Laku. 'My turn to hold it.'

He took the weight of the saw motor in one hand. 'You see, Jack, these good fellows here are just helping to hold it up till it's cool and will move again. Foster looked at Mani.

'That your idea?' he asked sternly. Mani pointed at Lunggaroi with his chin.

'His,' he said simply.

'Mmmh,' mused Foster, turning away and walking several steps as he wiped a moist arm across his wet face. 'It should work.'

Mani nodded and replied agreeably. 'Yes, we hope so.' Foster turned and grinned sheepishly. 'Well, I hope so, too.'

He looked up to the high first branches of the giant, then around at them all, shrugged and swung his arms sideways comically as he confessed, 'cause I'm blowed if I know what else to do, if it doesn't.'

It did work. When Mani finally restarted the saw Foster suggested that they risk getting stuck again, and keep cutting forward rather than pulling out, because there was so little distance left to go.

Lunggaroi drove off at Foster's bidding to make sure that the supply tank was filling on Central Hill. He arrived back just in time to see, from the driving seat, the giant fall side-ways along the hillside, taking with it several eucalypt saplings, a hollow grey trunk and a clump of pandanus palms.

'Wow!' shouted Bridges.

'My goodness!' cried Mondi Laku. 'What a thing is this tree.'

'Not a tree, Boonyi,' Mani told him loudly as he set down the saw. 'It's a canoe, can't you see?' A moment later he was walking along its length, bobbing under and stepping over and between branches.

'It will make a good canoe,' he told them after his inspection.

'But there's a lot of hard work waiting here.'

'First job, clean off all dem branch,' said Lunggaroi.

'Right,' replied Mani.

'Right!' echoed Foster, passing out the axes he had brought from the back of the Land Rover. 'What are we waitin' for?'

Half an hour later, when Edna Foster and Lola Laku arrived on foot with refreshments, the branches had been lopped and dragged away, and Mondi was up on the naked trunk in bright sunlight, wearing nothing but short khaki pants, with his legs spread and chips flying from between his feet, as his axe rose and fell. The other men had found a shady place, and while they sat cooling off, were enjoying barracking their pastor, who seemed to gain even more energy from their cheers and laughter. Foster was in the process of yelling something through his laughter when the women came into view around a heap of branches.

'First time I ever saw a horse choppin' wood,' he bellowed.

'No,' yelled Mani. 'It's not a horse; it's a choppin machine. Somebody better switch it off.'

'No, no!' yelled Jack. 'Don't stop it now. It might get stuck'.

'They seem to have all gone crazy!' said Edna Foster.

'Only my man!' corrected Lola Laku. 'Look at him, will you? Who does he think he is?'

Just then Mondi's axe stuck in the trunk. He tugged it a couple of times without moving it.

'It's stuck!' cried Lunggaroi happily.

Bridges lifted his head and called in a comical voice, 'Better we just let it cool down!' That set them all belly-laughing, and Mondi turned to see the cause. For the first time he saw his wife and Edna. Lola looked so beautiful, bare-headed and thong-sandalled, so cool and sweet in her sleeveless white frock, and so fit and fitting in this place that his heart went out to her and her smaller companion. What a welcome sight. Edna's dress was white also, but with strokes of many colours crowded together in gay confusion, and like Lola she wore nothing more than rubber thongs for footwear. The baskets they carried were similar also, the circular kind the local women wove from pandanus strips in the style of the Pacific Islanders. The only feature of difference in their dress was the broad, woven hat Edna wore as a vain endeavour to protect her light complexion from the effects of tropical heat and sunshine.

'Behold,' shouted Mondi. 'Two angels of mercy have come to attend us.' They turned to see the women just as Lola called to her husband, and all rallied with surprised delight at the sight of the company and the baskets they carried.

'What are you doing up there?' Lola called.

'I'm working, wife,' Mondi answered mock-chidingly. 'Don't say you've never seen me working before.'

'Oh, I'm glad you told me,' she replied. 'I'm glad you're not showing off.'

'Showing…Oh, woman,' he feigned offence. 'Don't you know how important work is for man…and even a Minister is a man, you know.'

'I know!' she said with an emphasis that implied many things and was greeted with general laughter.

'Man is supposed to work,' Mondi persevered. 'It's in the Scriptures. "In the sweat of your brow you will eat your bread."'

'Well, we haven't got any bread, only biscuits,' replied his wife. 'So come down from your pulpit and have a cup of tea.'

'I give up,' said the big Fijian, sitting on the trunk and dropping to the ground.

'Why are you all letting him do all the work on his own?' Edna Foster asked as they set down the baskets and sat in the shade.

'He wanted to do it,' replied Foster. 'It's completely unnecessary. We're going to cut it through with the chainsaw in a few minutes. We're all just having a cool off.'

'You mean he's doing all that work for nothing?' asked Edna incredulously.

'For fun,' grunted Bridges painfully.

'For the sake of doing work,' corrected Mondi, recovering his green shirt from a nearby bush.

'Poor Mr. Bridges,' said Lola. 'What have they done to you?'

'I thought I'd like to have a hand in this new canoe of Mani's,' he said, grinning as he came around to a sitting position.

'There, you see,' said Mondi triumphantly. 'Gray is a man too. Not only Fijian Ministers, but even government consultants need to work up sweat before they can be happy to eat their bread.'

The others laughed.

'I've never quite seen it like that, Mondi,' said Bridges.

'This is nice,' Foster told his wife.

'Well, it's a little early for morning tea really,' she replied. 'But you've been out here since daybreak, and we thought you'd be ready for it.'

They all assured her that she was right.

Within as little time as it took Mondi Laku to don his larva skirt and adjust his shirt, the women had produced mugs and filled them with tea from thermos flasks. From one basket Edna took a jar of sugar and another of milk; and Lola produced a tin of homemade biscuits, much to the appreciation of the men.

'Look at your hand!' gasped Edna as Bridges reached into the biscuit tin.

'Oh, it's okay!' he said shyly, and tried to put it out of sight.

'Show me,' demanded Mondi Laku, pulling Bridges' left hand towards him. 'Oh, these hands are not ready for the axe work.'

Bridges' face went even redder, and he tried again to hide his hand and make light of the blistered and broken skin of his third and fourth fingers and the adjacent part of the palms.

Mani looked at the embarrassed man. 'Thanks, Gray for your help.'

'I wanted to do a whole lot more,' said Bridges. 'To tell you the truth I didn't know I'd blistered until the skin broke and the sweat got in. I sure never blistered that easy before.'
'Gettin soft!' chaffed Foster.
'Go on,' countered Edna. 'You know only too well you got blisters yourself in the first couple of months we were in the tropics. It's all the perspiration.' She turned to Bridges, took his hand from Mondi, and looked at it carefully.
'You come up to the dispensary and get something on that broken skin.'
'She's right,' admitted Foster. 'Too many people here have to pull out 'o the work before they should, because they don't follow the simple rule of using an antiseptic for any break in the skin. Scratch a sandfly bite and you open your blood stream to millions of germs. If there's nothin' else handy I dab a bit of Stock'm Tar on. It's good enough for the horses and cattle, so it shouldn't hurt us.'
'Ulcers,' Edna told the Darwinite. 'It's so easy to get an infection. Everything thrives in this humidity. We've got germs the doctors haven't even heard of. Leg ulcers. You should see some of the women we've had here. Scratch, scratch away they do, till they're red raw, and have to be evacuated south. So, you look after yourself,' she told him. Don't you go overdoing it.'
'Not to worry, love,' Foster said. 'Once we've cut the ends off, we'll knock off for the day. The rest of the job'll have to be done with an adze, and I'll leave that to others for the time being.'

He looked at Mani, who rose and stood beside him.

'It's been great to have your help, Jack,' the young man said. 'But I think you should listen to what your wife's saying. We don't want our Town Clerk pullin out before he needs to.'

Foster stared at the young islander in blank silence, the others waited, and Edna and the Lakus all smiled at Mani encouragingly. 'Why don't you drive the ladies back home and take the axes. Just leave us one and the adze. And try and see if you can trust me to take care of the saw.' Foster made a pretence at punching Mani in the abdomen and the young man buckled with a grin.

'I'm not worried about the saw,' said Foster. 'It's only, I wanted to help with the ...., what the heck! Awright, awright. I'll go, if you want to get rid of me.'

'I'll stay on a bit,' said Bridges, in response to Edna's encouragement to join them in the Land Rover. 'I want to see this part o' the job! But thanks a lot for the refreshments. You too Lola. That sure was a life-saver. I promise I'll put some Stockholm Tar or somethin' on this hand in quick time. If it's good enough for Jack and the horses it must be powerful medicine.'

'Awright, awright,' growled Foster from the driver's seat. 'No need to rub it in!'

'No, you don't rub it in!' Mondi called. 'You just spread it on.'

He stayed too, after thanking his wife for the unnecessary reminder that he should be back at the house in time to prepare for a Bible study meeting at Nabadgardi's place.

They saw the Land Rover stop at the road and a woman on foot come over to speak to the driver, apparently to get directions to the place where the tree was undergoing its first stage of transformation into a canoe. As the vehicle moved off and the newcomer came up the gully towards them, they recognised Buringalu, the young clan mother of Mani. She was obviously distressed and had been hurrying.

'Hullo little Sister,' called Mondi, going to hold the wire strands apart while Buringalu climbed through.

''ullo, Boonyi,' she breathed. 'I hafta tok my son.'

'You can talk,' Mani told her.

'Wait there,' said Mondi. 'Come, little sister. You sit here now in the shade. You've been in such a hurry.'

'No, Boonyi. Can't sit,' she said abruptly. 'Afta tok dis boy.'

'It's all right, everyone can 'ear,' Mani told her.

'Big trouble,' she said, her face wreathing with some inner dread. 'Our grandfar, and all family, makin fight over your wife mob. Bi-i-i-g hargue, hargue, hargue.'

'Hand-fighting?' asked Mani anxiously.

'Nothing,' she replied. 'Only talk-fighting. This time shout long time…now all finish up. Everyone gone home now. They say no more tok now.'

'Everything all fixed up?' Mani sounded hopeful.

'Nothing!' she repeated. 'Our grandfar say Lilara no more your wife…'e say dis family got enemy now, your wife mob enemy.'

'Not their old man, he gave me this tree! He asked the people and they were friendly to me. Must be I'll have to come home and talk to him,' said Mani.

'Too late,' Buringalu told him. 'Old men had big tok orready. They got hot this time.'

Lunggaroi stepped forward. 'Those old men told our old men already?' he asked.

'They told em,' she said. 'No more can't Lilara marry my son, they said. Blame you taking that kinoo before.'

'Blame me?' gasped Lunggaroi.

'Just a little bit you,' she assured him. 'All them other trouble things now they bring up.'

'Not that old snake-bite trouble?' asked Mani.'

'That one,' she replied. 'Blaming them mob sending that snake to kill our relation. An all bigges trouble and humbug they tok.'

'What does it mean?' asked Bridges as the others fell silent.

Mondi looked from Bridges to Mani. 'What do you think?' he asked. 'Lilara is my wife,' said Mani, as he walked to the stump of the felled tree. 'It's the Lore.'

Lunggaroi stood behind him. 'But them old men, they the ones who say what is the Lore,' he said.

'They said it. She is my wife,' Mani said quietly but firmly. 'Not this time, now,' said Buringalu.

'Bye and bye,' said Lunggaroi. 'Must be they'll say it again bye 'an bye.'

'Our family got hot. Too hot, 'an now they made a big trouble for you, son,' Buringalu warned. 'You can't tok dat girl. She can't tok, too, to you. Our family make bi-ig trouble.'

Mani raised his fist and hammered it down on the tree stump. Mondi was beside him and wrapped a huge arm around his shoulders. 'You are not on your own, little brother,' he said. 'I am family, too. We two men have to have our say, too.'

Mani looked into the big man's tan face and smiled faintly as he shook his head.

'You remember them other times,' he said. 'This time the old men will be a long time to change their mind.'

'But no night-time fighting, this time,' said Lunggaroi.

'You sure?' asked Mondi.

'Too frightened, Boonyi,' Buringalu assured him. 'Everybody frighten now from that monster on the beach. Can't go out in the dark now.'

'Ah, I see,' he nodded.

Bridges felt useless and came around the stump to let his concern be known. 'What will you do, Mani?'

Mani looked at him, then at the stump. He ran his fingers over the rough edges left by the final rending as the tree fell.

'You know,' he said at length. 'If I'm here, I want my wife, and I want to talk to my cousin.' He turned and put his hand on Lunggaroi's shoulder for a moment. 'Might be...I think.'

They waited to hear what he had decided, and he looked from Mondi to Bridges.

'You know what I think?' he asked them, and went on when they both shook their heads in silence. 'It's going to be a long time before our families are ready to listen to me. I better let it go quiet. I can go back to Darwin. It's better. My wife and me, we don't need to be married yet. Bit later on we can fix it up. They'll all listen when they cool down. Maybe I should go back to the city and follow up all that land business in there for my people, and go back to ATEC and my teacher studies. I can't stay here and argue with them old men.'

They all stared at him blankly for a long moment.

'You going back to Darwin?' Mondi asked with a touch of regret.
'I'll talk to my family,' said Mani. 'If they say yes I'll go.'
'You really want to be a teacher now?' Bridges asked gently.
'Always I wanted to be a teacher,' Mani told him seriously.
'Oh?' Bridges said. 'You could've fooled me.'
'A teacher, but a man too!'
'Gotcha!' said Bridges knowingly, his head nodding.
'I'm thinking,' said the would-be teacher. 'If I keep quiet now and go back to ATEC, bye and bye our families can agree again'.
'Good, good,' Mondi nearly crushed his shoulders. 'Good thinking, little brother. We will be praying for you, and we will keep the families thinking to let you two young people have your happy marriage, won't we cousin?'
'Ee-ee, true,' said Lunggaroi, 'You write letters, 'an we keep tryin to make friendly way 'ere.'
'What you reckon, Gamu?' Mani addressed Buringalu as his tribal mother. She was standing back, listening without any visible response. She shrugged.
'If I go away…' Mani began.
'You should stay,' she said. 'I'm frighten if you go away. Nobody understand. You can understand.'
'The old people understand well, Gamu,' he said. 'They must keep the Lore and help us all to keep the Lore. You'll see they will do what's right.'
'I'm frighten that fighting, 'an dat sea monster,' she insisted.
'But the fighting might be stopped now by the sea monster', said Mondi. 'People are frightened to go out at night. Don't worry, Buringalu, the trouble will cool down and the old men will see that it's good for Lilara to go to Mani.'
'My son should be 'ere,' she said. 'This country, now! This the one. Your own

family country.'

'Not my own father country,' he told her. 'That's down mainland way. We have to keep it, too, so we can go back there…and I have to sign up gubment law way in Darwin. You see? And I have to be a teacher for all the kids growing up with two different laws, and for that work I have to learn more in Darwin and Bachelor, too.'

He watched her until she looked into his face. 'True?' he queried. She shrugged again, this time with a flicker of a smile, still perplexed, but ready now to accept the inevitable. 'If I stay, I'll make the old men angry, and stir up more trouble,' he explained. 'If I go away, you all be good friends to my wife. Just tell her I want her. Talk softly to her, 'an tell her not to worry, 'an to do what the old people tell her, an she can come to me bye an bye.'

'What about this?' Bridges slapped the thick end of the fallen trunk.

'The tree is given, we accepted it, and we hafta go on makin our own kind of life,' said Mani. He turned to Lunggaroi. 'What about it, Cousin? You'll go on with this for making our life, eh?'

'Yeah,' grinned Lunggaroi proudly. 'An' I can get elp from the Minister, 'e one big choppin' machine.'

'True,' exclaimed Mondi happily. 'I'll still be here to help. This is somewhere I can come when my body needs work.'

'So's you can eat your bread in sweat?' teased Bridges.

'Exactly,' agreed Mondi. All of the men had relaxed again, and the pastor spoke encouragingly. 'You'll be proud of the canoe that we make for you, little brother, just as I am proud of you for being a wise young husband and son.'

'If you want some 'elp with the canoe, my grandfather is a very good man for canoe-making,' said Mani. 'You should listen to him.'

'That's good,' Mondi gasped, and turned to Lunggaroi, 'He can come here and tell us what to do, and he can think of his grandson while we make his new canoe.'

'Will you come back to Darwin right away,' Bridges asked Mani.

'If the family say, yes,' he replied. 'Then I'll go quick. I don't want to be near my wife and keepin away from her.'

* * *

A few minutes later Mondi, Bridges and Mani left Lunggaroi proudly swinging an adze at the side of the massive trunk, and Buringalu making her way home on the track to the beach. On the way to the office to see Edna about flight bookings, as they neared Laku's place Mondi suggested that they call in to have a cool drink with him.

'You've got a while to spare,' he said. 'And, if you're leaving here, I've got something I want to show you before you go.'

His eyes twinkled, and, fascinated, they followed him in past the fragrant frangipani tree. 'Here, get a cold drink,' he said swinging open the refrigerator and putting a jug of chilled lime juice and water on the table. 'Glasses there and ice in there.'

While Mani collected three tumblers from a shelf, Bridges manipulated the ice-tray to dislodge blocks into the jug. Mondi was up the stairs and down again before the drinks were ready. He had a large flat parcel under his arm, wrapped in a white linen sheet. After stowing things into the refrigerator he joined his hot friends in quickly disposing of the drinks.

'Now,' he said seriously. 'I want you to understand what I tell you, and I'll be quick.' He smiled and went on. 'When Foster spoke to me about the fighting in the village, he said that the people were like children…and I replied that we are all children, but some are children of light and some are children of darkness.'

Bridges tipped an ice-block into his mouth and wondered what the big man was leading up to with this unusual preamble. He looked at Mani who obviously was just as confused, for he simply pushed his lips together and tilted his head.

'Well,' continued Mondi. 'You poor fellows wonder what I am talking about. I'll tell you.' He picked up the parcel and started to unwrap it. 'When I kept thinking about children of light and children of darkness, I thought if children of light really care about others and they have light, and can see how to help them, then they should do something. So I made these.' He lay the parcel on the table and uncovered the contents – two large flat objects. He lifted one, and left the other on the table. They were covered with feathers. Bridges spat the ice into the tumbler and gaped.
'Mondi!' he gasped. 'Not you?'

In the Minister's hand, and on the table, were a pair of gigantic shoes, a foot and a half long, each with three pointed toes, and covered with hens' feathers. 'The monster'.

'Yes, my brothers,' said Mondi Laku humbly. 'I have to confess that I am the monster of the Bay.'
'You sly ol' dog!' grinned Bridges.
'You mean you…' said Mani seriously.
'We all…Mister Laku! Boonyi! You're deceiving the people.'
'Only for a little while brother,' explained Mondi. 'Only until the trouble cools down. I remembered how many people were hurt last time the fighting started. Bye

and bye I'll get all the old men together and tell them, and we'll all have a laugh, but promise me that you will keep my little secret.'

'Oh, what a man,' Mani laughed at last. 'Our Minister is our sea monster! I can't believe it…you thing.'

'No wonder we couldn't work out what has feathers and lives in the sea,' chuckled Bridges.

'And heavy, like a pony, we said,' laughed Mani. 'Oh, what a man. I didn't think you would play tricks on the people like this.'

'Ah, little brother,' replied the big man smiling warmly. 'You didn't know how I love our people, and want to save them from all evil. Now, you better hurry to make your plane bookings, but, please, don't tell anyone at all. Let me tell them when they are all safe from attacking each other. I want to pick the time when I can give everyone a good laugh about it. Okay?'

'I still can't believe that you made those tracks,' marvelled Bridges. 'Some of 'em were seven or eight feet apart and more.'

'Yes, I know!' said Mondi. 'And it's hard work to get up speed in these things when you are running out of the sea at two o'clock in the morning.'

'Well,' chuckled Bridges. 'Now I've seen everything.'

'We'll keep your secret, Boonyi,' said Mani. He wagged his head. 'Where do you get your ideas from?'

'Oh, little brother,' replied Mondi. 'Where do all good gifts come from? You go now, be quick, or you'll be too late.'

'Did you tell Foster?' Bridges asked.

'Good gracious, no!' said Mondi. 'He would be very worried. He wouldn't believe in doing anything with a trick in it. But don't worry. He doesn't believe in the monster, either. It doesn't matter to him. So…what he doesn't know will not hurt him.'

'Roger, Roger,' grinned Bridges, as they left by the door.

'What do you think of that, Gray,' asked Mani as they set out for the office. 'I think your Minister loves the people more than he loves the truth.'

Bridges laughed.

'You could be right, but he never told us a lie about the monster, you know. He never talked about it at all. He kept away whenever we all talked about it.'

'You're right,' Bridges was still amused. 'What a sneaky one.'

Then he saw it. The connection in the back of his mind when Mondi had single-handedly lifted the boat on to the trailer. It had fitted the empty space in his thoughts that had been waiting for a plausible clue. Why hadn't he seen it earlier? The huge and powerful Fijian fitted the sea monster role as only he could.

The other amazing thing to Bridges was that he felt sure, that Mondi would get away with his trick. After their first shock at his sneakiness, they would forgive him and laugh along with him. Why is it, he wondered, that I feel equally sure that if a Balanda tried to pull such a stunt, it would not be taken with the same good grace?

What did that mean about his perception of the different standing of the two ethnic types had in this part of the world? It was something to do with destroyed trust, resentment about domination, and suspicion about intentions. There was so much at stake in the black and white Australian relationship, so much past treachery and deceit, so many unfulfilled promises and such misunderstanding in even the simplest daily exchanges, that any subterfuge like this one of Mondi's would be seen as ill-meant. He hoped he was wrong, but feared that he was absolutely right. When they reached the office they found that there was no need to worry about bookings for the morning plane to Darwin. Edna was surprised to hear that Mani would possibly be on the morning flight to Darwin, 'Does Jack know that you are going? Oh, I know that he'll be sorry to see you go. He was so glad to have you back here, you know.'

* * *

It was a pleasant evening at Laku's house. Brown had let Lola Laku know that he would stay with Wainanda relations at Jambagirrila's place until bed-time, and Bridges stayed away from there to give his colleague a chance to speak at his own pace and in his own style to the old people about the consultation. At the house no reference was made of the monster, because Lola knew nothing about Mondi's night run on the beach. At bed-time Bridges sincerely thanked his hosts for their kindness to him, and before leaving with Andrew in the morning, left a note of appreciation with his maximum allowance for accommodation payment on the bedside table.

He was glad to have Mani's company as well as Andrew's on the trip home, but this had little to do with Andrew being dull company, since the old man seemed to have a new lease of life. He was able to tell Bridges that Jambagirrila had assured him that Wainanda Goose Islanders were coming to the consultation. Although Nabadgardi had earlier been positive, when Andrew made a second visit he was grimly unresponsive to any mention of the consultation. This meant that, unless local inter-clan relationships improved, they could not expect Ananardus to attend. However, Jambagirrila was hopeful that the present troubles would soon blow over, and he expected that the landowners would want to be represented.

Nabadgardi had given his assurance that if he could not come himself, his grandson would be there to speak for him, and Andrew was fairly sure that he really meant it.

On the plane, Bridges found himself reflecting on recent events. In front of him, Andrew Brown was glued to the window, studying every feature of the mainland coast and distant misty forested hills in the direction of the Wainanda lands… and, across the aisle, Mani stared at the sea, trying to see ahead, searching, perhaps for the canoe, or what route it had followed, or which way around the islands might lead to Maccassar.

Mondi the Monster. No, Bridges reaffirmed his first thought, they would not have taken it as well if he, Bridges, had played the part of the monster from the sea. Why exactly was he so sure of that? Aha, he put his finger on the nub of the thought. It's because I am the real monster from the sea: the mysteriously powerful, inscrutable, and life-threatening Balanda.

PART TWO
Giant Killers

Chapter 11
Windfall

Sunset comes mercifully and swiftly across the Arafura Sea, and relief pours on to the shore and into Darwin's seaside areas, driving out the oppressive regime of afternoon. As day ends, scorched air rises on the buoyancy of its own heat, from headland rocks and sandy shorelines, out of savannah grasslands, dense pockets of rainforest and sluggish muddy creeks. Drier, dustier air lifts from the hard baked structures of the built human environment, and adds to the vast uprising that draws in the flowing tide of cooled ocean air, to infiltrate and over-run the suburbs and city with liberating sea-breezes. Life moves into the open again, freed from the domination of heat, glare and dehydration; and pleasant evening occupations begin restoring a general sense of bodily, mental and spiritual well-being. It is then that many Darwinites realise afresh why they stay in this enervating part of the world. Taking evening leisure on their patios, at the beach or indoors behind open louvres, redeems the dying day, and the cool breath of the evening sea revives their sagging spirits and gives them ease. This is especially so for anyone relaxing in enjoyable company with good conversation and iced drinks. With such pleasant consolations, many locals fancy that they enjoy a rare and magical life-style in a uniquely challenging but rewarding environment. The pleasure of their nights of tropical splendour are addictive enough to bind generations of locals from down south to stay and endure day's oppressive heat, yet again, for another year or two.

This night Bridges was alone. Relaxed and cooling off, but too aware of his need of Livvy's company to take much comfort from being back at home in Darwin. How much would he tell her about his near death experience in the sea? Something factual, but nothing much. Just the bare facts. It was not the first time that he had been home alone, but he had to experience it again to remember how depressingly empty a house can feel.

He thought of the conversations at the office telling Fred and Ned about the various responses they had received, and the implications of these for the planning of the consultation. They had agreed also to let them know of current tensions between the clans as well as attitudes to the whole idea of parleying with the Government. Fred had come into Andrew's office to hear what they had to tell, and they had agreed to complete a joint written report for the Chief Minister tomorrow morning.

They had talked together with Bagent, in one of the most futile conversations Bridges had ever experienced. To Andrew, the coming consultation was a great opportunity and to Harry it was a great confidence trick; and Bridges found himself trying to make clarifying statements that kept coming out ambiguously and triggering reactions from both of his colleagues. They each seemed to think that he was siding with the other's point of view. His own clear position that the consultation should deal candidly but co-operatively with the grievances of the indigenous representatives appeared to make no sense either to Andrew or to Harry.

They had each told him in effect, Andrew politely, and Harry bluntly, that he was trying to have his cake and eat it too. Either there had to be orchestrated co-operation at the consultation, or a no-holds barred conflict. Bridges disagreed, but they had made him sound like an ambivalent fence-sitter. That was when he had found himself trying to handle a conflict with each of them but getting nowhere with either. In fact, he had become impatient with the whole process, and began to doubt the way he expressed his own point of view. He excused himself on the grounds that he had not been feeling particularly well since capsizing in the sea, and then left Andrew and Harry to argue, and went home early. He only wanted to forget about Goose and reporting until tomorrow. At home he had tried to relax as he made a meal and prepared to have an early night.

* * *

The next morning he was a new man, showered, shaved, dressed, fed and with a logical grasp of the time and space available to him. He had returned from the featureless country at the back of his mind to look at the shape of the day that lay ahead, and the actions required by his immediate circumstances. Even without deep peace or inner assurance about his part in the total scheme of things, he could be pragmatic about the things that were at hand. By mid-day he would have copies of a final draft report of the Goose Island dialogues on Archer's desk.

Just as he was about to leave for the office, Livvy called from the Darwin Airport, and at the first sound of her voice the circle of his day's meaning seemed to close. Instantly his okay feeling returned, but at the same time he knew that all was not well. She was in no mood to accept a refusal without feeling let down.

'Can you come and get me Gray?' was all that she said; but he could tell that she was upset. She was asking for comfort and understanding, not just transport.

'Yes, of course,' he said without hesitation, and with the purpose of his life re-opened, but adding, to check his impression of her mood. 'I'm due at the office in a few minutes.'

'Please!' She made it plain.

'Okay, sweetie. Hang on…I'm on my way.' Brown would have a summary of points for report and recommendation when he eventually went to join him. Bridges decided that he would read that first and talk it through with Andrew, then decide whether or not to try to modify it as a joint report or to write his own individual one.

* * *

'Am I glad to see you,' Livvy told him as he came around the back of the car a few minutes later and took her in his arms. Her weight against him affirmed her gladness, and more; she was leaning on him, using his strength. It would be a day for him to offer support rather than to burden Livvy with talk of nearly drowning in the sea.

'Everything okay?' he asked after a soft kiss.

'Everything's a mess,' she said. 'I'm afraid I've made a real botch of things this time.'

'I can't believe that, Liv,' he replied, closing the car boot on her luggage and opening her door. 'Not you.'

'Oh Gray,' she gave him another hug. 'It's so good to have you to talk to. Sometimes I fear all the world's queer except me and thee.'

'And even thee's a little…' he began with a smile. She flashed a faint wry smile.

'You might as well finish it. After the last couple of days, I've begun to doubt my own sanity.'

'Tell me about it,' he said, as they left the car under the house and went upstairs. Over coffee, she told him of the time at Malangarri that had begun well, but developed quickly into an unpleasant episode. She and her assistant, Helen Cross, who was assigned by ATEC to do a three months' special placement with the bi -lingual staff, had been well received by the Malangarri school team, and the first day had been positive and gratifying.

'They are doing wonders with the bi-lingual programme,' she said emphatically. 'Both the expatriate and local teachers are demonstrating the value of our approach. I couldn't be happier about that.'

'So, what happened?' he asked. 'How was Helen?'

'Work-wise?' This was close to the heart of her distress. 'No complaints. She's a very talented teacher and has good understanding of the issues in bi-lingual education. It's not her teaching talent that's in question, it's one of her other talents!'

He listened as she told of the Principal's mounting interest in them both. A man in his mid-forties, Wally Grant had been teaching in Aboriginal communities for about fifteen years. There had been gossip about him and Aboriginal girls from time to time. Apparently he invited Helen around for drinks on the pretense of an email he had received from Darwin for Helen from Father Sheehan of the Catholic Mission in Darwin, and told Helen that she should come to see him in person at her earliest possible convenience on a matter important to her future…Well Helen only returned at dawn this morning.

It had upset Livvy; but she decided to say nothing. Helen and Wally Grant were adults and must be seen to be the responsible ones to judge and choose their own behaviour, and she only had to tolerate it one more day and night before returning to Darwin.

It was an awkward last day, she has such an adolescent way of behaving at times,' she said. 'It's hard to remember that she's a woman in her thirties. I suppose I should have kept right out of it. But I felt responsible for her. She seemed so vulnerable. Anyway, we argued, and she made me feel like an interfering prude! Then she got really dirty. She said, "What's 'a matter Mrs Bridges? A bit narked, are ya? Can't ya stand the competition?"'

'No wonder you're feeling a bit cut up, sweetheart.' Bridges put an arm around her. 'But do you really think you made a mess of things? It sounds to me as though you minded your own business pretty well.'

'I tried to,' she said doubtfully, 'but, really, what business is it of mine if people want to sleep around? Anthropologists are supposed to accept the principle of moral relativity you know. But, you're right. This was unusual behaviour for anyone. I'm not usually a moraliser am I? But I virtually threatened to report Helen, and that would really blot her copy-book. It could ruin her chances with the Department.'

'Oh, do you really think the Department gives a damn who sleeps with who?' he asked.

'Yes, oh, I don't know. Maybe not. The professional ethics, and the image of the staff and the Department… all that is seen as important, I'm sure,' she conceded. 'And it does care about Supervisors' reports and assessments. I could really scotch her chances of being advanced in her training.'

'Is that what you're going to do?'

'Of course not!' she flared, but when he did not reply, sighed and accepted the hand he offered.

'I didn't think so,' he told her. 'What are you going to do darling?' She spent some moments staring at the wall and sipping coffee. 'Helen and I have some repair work to do,' she told him.

'Uhu,' he said. 'That shouldn't be too difficult for you two.' 'I wish I could be as confident as you are,' she replied.

'What about old Grant?' asked Bridges. 'What you've told me about him worries me. Not that I want to play the moralist either, but it's a well-known fact in cross-cultural community service positions that immorality plays hell with positive influence. He's re-enforcing the despised image of the randy Balanda invaders hungry to have all the available women. In the long run what the Department's education programme is doing through people like Wally is self-destructive. He is destroying trust and respect and he's a liability to the developmental programme of the community and the government.'

'Is it really that serious? I mean, whatever else he is, he's committed to bi-lingual and bi-cultural education, which is more than can be said for many principals.'

'It's at least that serious, I'd say,' he told her. 'Woman troubles, as the men say, have always been taken seriously in the old culture. Serious enough to fight wars over.'

'Mmmh, yes, I know. I'll have to think about it. Maybe someone in the Department can straighten him out. But that can wait. I'll have to get back together with Helen straight away.'

Before Bridges left, they decided to have a relaxed meal at the Red Sails Hotel in the evening, and after he had gone, Livvy rang her office and the Mitchell Street Hostel. When the manager checked he reported that Helen had not been back for a couple of days. Livvy considered calling Father Sheehan, at Catholic Mission Headquarters, who had sent Helen the email via Grant, but decided against it. Trying to contact Helen through talking to the Mission staff on the phone seemed too remote, somehow. It would be hard to be informal. What reason could be given for such a contact? If, on the other hand, she happened to call in and find Helen there, that might be easier to handle. That way she could speak with Helen directly.

* * *

Half an hour later, she turned the Land Rover in through the entrance to the Catholic Mission depot, and continued around to the back of a large, warehouse-style building. The roller-door was open, and as she turned in towards the shade, she noted deep inside, stacks of building materials, and pallets of cartons and drums. Someone was in there stacking or packing, and sitting on plastic chairs in the outside shade she recognised Helen Cross and Father Dick Sheehan.

They turned to watch her stop the Rover and get out, then the priest appeared to excuse himself from the young woman who was still talking. He rose and approached the new arrival.

'Ah, good morning. May I help you? I'm sorry, I've forgotten your name,' Father Sheehan sounded welcoming. Livvy noted that he was a tall, slender man in his late thirties, wearing the tropical uniform of a priest, drill trousers, white sports shirt hanging loose, with golden lapel crosses.

'Oh, Father, excuse me for barging into your place. I'm Olivia Bridges.'

'Yes, yes. Of course. And a rare treasure, if I may say so. An anthropologist who is dedicated to the people of the land, and is helping to revolutionise cross-cultural education.'

'Oh, are you sure you've got the right person?' Livvy joked to hide her embarrassment and delight.

'Oh, yes. I'm quite sure. Married to Graedon Bridges, and referred to by people who know as God's gift to the indigenous people and their helpers.'

She smiled self-consciously, 'Well, I will admit to being married to Gray Bridges… Look, Father, I came hoping to catch up with my friend. Helen. She told me she was coming here. I'm sorry if I'm interrupting.'

'Well...er,' the priest looked slightly confused, but was spared the ordeal of deciding whether or not to reveal what might be a confidence when Helen called without rising from her seat in the shade.

'Hi!'

'I'm sorry,' Livvy looked from one to the other. 'I don't want to break in to something private. Can I just...Excuse me, Father, can I just say...'

She stepped towards the entrance. 'Helen we should talk some more?'

'What for?' Helen rose and came forward, appearing genuinely surprised. Something had happened to her. She seemed to be cold or stunned, out of touch with the feelings that had flared between them.

'Well,I...' Livvy hesitated, looking at the priest to see if he would rather she left anything else she had to say until later. Instead he nodded his approval of her continuing. They walked closer, and stood in the shade inside the storage area.

'I just thought I owed you an apology, Helen,' she said. 'I was out of order, reacting to you the way I did, and I don't want it to stand between us.'

At this personal note between the two young women, the priest sidled away into the open building, and called something to a worker inside.

'Is that all?' Helen sounded surprised. 'You could've told me when I came into the office.'

'I didn't know if you would want to come back to work with me. I didn't know if I'd …'

'You don't know me very well, do you, Livvy?' Helen smiled, and Livvy shrugged and smiled.

'That didn't worry me, what you said out at Malangarri. You were right, an' I was wrong… I'm used to being wrong. Doesn't mean I like to be told. I don't. Still, I can't hold grudges. I can't, because I'm like you. I like people too much. Too much for my own good sometimes, eh? But you didn't fool me when you reckoned you might have to put in a bad report on me. Because I know you too well Livvy Bridges. You like people, too much, too, and… and you're fair.'

Livvy felt limp with relief. 'I'm so glad you see it that way, Helen. I'd hate for us to really fall out.'

'Father,' Helen called to the smiling clergyman, who had turned back to hover near, obviously enjoying the spectacle of friendship restored. Helen went on. 'Do you mind if Livvy sits in on our talk? I'd like someone else to help me think about all that, what you've been telling me.' Livvy was surprised and delighted that her strange young assistant wanted her there, but also hesitant and embarrassed.

She didn't want the priest to get the idea that she was hanging around to pry into Helen's private life. Father Sheehan shrugged. 'If that's what you'd like. Just hang on, I'll fetch another chair.'

'There's hardly anyone else I can talk to,' Helen pressed the invitation. 'Nobody of my own. I'm on my own, Mrs. Bridges. Father, there, can talk to me, and a couple of young people I know, but I need to talk to someone who really knows me. Will you stay?'

It did not escape Livvy's notice that a few moments ago, Helen had called her 'Livvy' but now she was reverting to 'Mrs Bridges', and at the same time she was claiming her as someone who really knew her, when a moment ago they had both agreed that she did not know her well at all. Sensing that what she had heard was literally true, and Helen was indeed alone in the world. Livvy could see her young co-worker's inner confusion and uncertainty. Perhaps, by staying, some amends could be made for her earlier unwarranted rejection of the girl because of her sexually adventurous lifestyle. And, in any case, it was a good chance to appropriate the friendly acceptance that Helen was offering her.

'By all means, stay,' said Father Sheehan, turning back to go inside again. Returning with another plastic chair, he beckoned towards the one he had vacated. 'We'll share with you Helen's good news.'

'Go on, Father,' said Helen, when they were all sitting. 'You tell 'er. I still can't believe it. Say it again.'

Explaining to Livvy that the information was to be treated as absolutely confidential, and advising Helen, also, not to talk about it to others until she had finally made up her mind what she thought about it, the priest went on to tell Livvy that a secret benefactor had asked him to make an offer to Helen.

'A lump sum of two million dollars, and an additional one hundred and eighty thousand each year for the rest of her life,' he said profoundly.

'Wha-wha- wa-wa-wa-wait a minute! Do you mean that literally? She...eh? Whooee! Do you mean, like, two million? Did you really say two million bucks?' The anthropologist responded.

'And how much annuity? One hundred and eighty was it? Wow! No wonder you couldn't believe it, Helen...that's wonderful...do you know what this means?'

'What?' Helen looked worried.

'It's enough to go anywhere and get anything you need or want, house, car, anything. And one hundred and eighty thousand a year, that's more than three times my salary. You don't have to worry about anything you need for the rest of your life...'

'But it feels wrong!' Helen said, nervously looking at the priest with a painful expression.

He responded by asking, 'does it worry you that you haven't earnt it?'

'No, that doesn't worry me,' she said, struggling to make sense of her feelings. 'But someone giving you all that money for nothin, someone you don't know, I don't know. It makes me feel...I dunno! Funny, somehow. Sort of taken over... bought. As though they bought me or somethink. You know? It doesn't seem decent! An' I don't want to give 'em power over me. What do I have to do, or give them?'

'Do you know the...er... the secret benefactor, Father?' Livvy asked.

'Oh yes,' he explained. 'I was contacted by the person directly and asked to make the offer to Helen.'

'What does Helen have to do if she accepts it?'

'Nothing, absolutely nothing, except, that is, to agree to accept it, and to use it to live the best and happiest life that she can.'

'It doesn't feel right,' Helen repeated. 'You know how everyone teaches little girls don't accept lollies from strangers? That's how I'm feeling right now.'

'You don't feel you can trust the one who wants to make this gift? I don't blame you,' the priest continued. 'I'm not free to tell you any more than I have, but I can tell you this. I do trust the giver. I have reason to believe that it is a completely genuine offer, with no strings attached…and it's available as soon as you are ready to receive it.'

'I don't want it,' fear was in her face as she looked from one to the other of her hearers. 'Not if I can't see the person. How do I know what I'm gettin into?'

They talked for a few more minutes, with Livvy and Father Sheehan cautioning Helen against making a hasty decision, but without any change in the young woman's troubled state of mind.

'Not if I don't know the person,' she repeated. 'I don't understand why they want to give it to me. It's not like a friend, or something like that… and it's sort of too personal. That sounds silly I know… but I don't belong to anybody else, and I don't want someone to think they can buy me. I'm not one o' those girls who takes money for…for bein' friendly. I don't hold with that…and I don't trust someone who does this sort of thing.'

'Well, it's nice to find someone who doesn't worship the holy dollar,' said the priest.

'What's that?' she was genuinely puzzled.

'Money,' Father Sheehan explained. 'The worship of money, or material wealth, is the number one religion of Australia, you know.'

'I thought it was Aussie Rules football,' said Livvy with a grin.

'I don't have to guess, you come from Melbourne if you thought that.' He chuckled.

'Right!' She laughed along with him; but Helen gave no sign that she was in a laughing mood. It mystified Livvy that, even though she claimed to like people, her young co-worker's basic mistrust of others could be so profound that an unconditional offer of enough money to keep her comfortable for life was causing her extreme anxiety. She liked people, but that was not the same as trusting them.

When Helen asked her directly what she thought she should do, Livvy's first impulse was to tell her to take the gift with both hands, but that would have required a direct reversal of Helen's present thinking, and for the time being, there seemed to be a need to let the whole thing loosen up in her mind. And, in any case, she knew that Helen had to own this decision herself, every step of the way. 'Whatever you think you have to do,' she answered. 'Take whatever time you need to think about it for a while. Just take your time, and I'm sure you'll know what you're going to do.'

'Can I come and talk to you again?' Helen asked the priest.

'Anytime you like, Helen,' he assured her, and they rose and made their way towards Livvy's car. 'Mrs Bridges,' he said. 'May I ask if you have heard of Soft Aid, a particular approach to helping Aboriginal communities?'

'No, I can't say that I have,' she said. 'What's it about?'

'A friend of mine has dedicated himself to its promotion. I thought you might be able to tell me a bit more about it?'

'It's not a term I've heard before.'

'Let's talk about it sometime,' he suggested.

She was glad to agree as Helen joined her in the front seat, and a few minutes later the Land Rover arrived in the side street by the T and G Building in down-town Smith Street, where the Education Department's Consulting Anthropologist had her office, and where a table in one corner served as Helen's temporary desk.

Conversation had ground to a halt, Helen apparently not knowing what to think or say. Unable to tell whether her unusual companion had ceased to think about the offer of great riches, Livvy suggested that she might begin to write her own account of the visit to Malangarri and what they saw happening in bilingual education there.

Helen quietly accepted the assignment, but a half an hour later, when Livvy had completed a summary outline and jottings of what points she wanted to include in her report on Malangarri school. She looked over at Helen and was alarmed to see that her trainee assistant had not typed a word and was just staring at her blank screen.

'Hey, are you all right?' she asked.

Plainly Helen was pre-occupied, and uncomfortable, and Livvy decided to call her back to the present situation as a way of assisting her to handle the distracting thoughts and feelings that must be running wild within her.

'Well, you'd better get on with it,' she said. 'I want your paper before the day is over, for assessment.'

'Get stuffed…'

The forceful reaction found Livvy completely unprepared, and she simply gasped,

'What? What did I do?'

'Oh, go to hell!' Helen looked from the wall to Livvy and saw a confused and hurt woman. 'You know what?' she told her. 'Sometimes you just give me the shits!'

'Oh, come on, Helen,' Livvy began, but on reflection cut short anything further she might have said. Instead she waited.

'I can't work in this place!' Helen declared.

'Look,' Livvy had a bright idea. 'Why don't we do our writing at home at the hostel?'

'What bloody hostel?'

'I thought you moved into the Mitchell Street Hostel.'

'Well, so what? Doesn't mean I 'ave to stay there, does it?'

Her hostile tone hurt Livvy. It had caught her off guard and she found herself breathing deeply to keep her pulse rate down.

'Look Helen,' she put on her best, cool Anthropologist's voice. 'Have I done something to upset you?'

The troubled look that passed over Helen's face reminded Livvy of the conversation at the Catholic Mission. This disturbed girl really had nothing against her. It apparently troubled her to think that Livvy was taking her aggressive reactions to heart, even though, it seemed, at the same time she meant every word that she had said and could not care less about hurting anyone who happened to be within striking distance.

'You found somewhere better to stay, did you?' Livvy asked. She managed to sound like a close friend, reassured and at ease.

'Yeah,' Helen spoke softly, and turned towards Livvy, glancing at her and then away. 'Friend o' mine got a house just over there in the city. Let me stay with him.'

'Ah!' Livvy showed new interest. 'Is he nice?'

The dark girl flashed the large whites of her eyes at Livvy and suddenly laughed like someone much coyer than she really was, as if embarrassed, and yet relieved to have the chance to leave the heaviness of aggression behind.

'I like him,' she admitted.

'Hmmm.' Livvy pressed on playfully. 'And does he like you?'

'What dya reckon?' Helen was reciprocating the playfulness.

'Well, I dunno,' Livvy teased. 'But if he's a normal, healthy male of the human species I reckon he must like you 'cause you must be one of the most beautiful young women he'll ever see.'

'Hey, stop it, will yah!' the embarrassed girl was suddenly in a storm of self-consciousness. 'What d'ya go and say that for?'

'Because it's true,' the older woman told her.

'I don't reckon,' said Helen, rushing for shelter in another topic of conversation. 'Anyway, what're we gonna do about this writing work?'

'Good question,' said Livvy. 'What are we? I've made one suggestion, and you haven't told me what you think of it.' Helen thought for a moment before replying.

'If it's all right with you, I think I will go back to the house. Nothing seems to be coming to me. I think I'll need to think about it.'

'Do that, then,' Livvy said. 'If you get some idea about how you're going to write up the report, have a go at it. If not, don't worry about it. It's not every day you get news like you got today. Tomorrow'll be plenty of time to do the report. Take it easy, and don't forget, you've got my mobile number. If you want to talk about the work, or about your news, don't hesitate to call or SMS me. Okay?'

Helen nodded. 'Okay,' she said. 'Thanks. I still don't know what I'm gonna do. I'm trying not to think about it all. I'll see if I can do some writing a bit later on.'

She sat on the edge of her chair for a few moments staring at her supervisor, before adding, 'You good, Livvy Bridges…thank you.'

'Oho, you can come around and tell Gray if you like. I'm always glad to get a good reference.'

They laughed together and Helen rose to go.

'Now there's an idea!' said Livvy. 'What do you think you'll be doing for dinner this evening?'

'Haven't thought about it.'

Well, Gray and I plan to eat out at the Red Sails Hotel. What about joining us? It's time you and Gray got to know each other better.'

Helen was touched by the invitation, glad to be asked, but not willing to accept. The reasons Livvy was left to guess at, as she was told, 'that's very good of you to ask me, but no thanks. I'll see. I might feel like going out later, but I don't know, though. I'll see my friend and what he wants to do. You never know. I might see you there. You understand, don't you?'

'Yep, no problem' said Livvy. 'We'll catch up a bit later on. Bye for now, Helen. Take care.'

'You too.'

As she watched her trainee moving along the corridor between the cubicles Livvy noticed Oliver Sutton, one of the Deputy Directors coming towards her. As he approached he was looking her way and obviously intended to speak.

'Good'ay Ol,' she said cheerily, pretending to be glad to see him, but wishing that he had not come just at the moment when she had dismissed Helen for the rest of the day.

'Hi, Liv.' He looked her over with undisguised admiration. 'You're looking bronzed and beautiful after your sojourn in the wilderness.' His soft tones carried a mid-England accent, with interesting variations.

Oliver Sutton always appealed to the woman in Livvy. Not that he was sexy in the ordinary sense of the word, but it was clear to her that he found her an attractive woman as well as an interesting colleague; and he always spoke in that soft, intimate way. She supposed that she must find him a little attractive, because it was always an agreeable experience when he looked at her the way that he did. He was not all that good looking, a fit and forty blue-eyed blonde, with a vain line of blonde bristle along his stiff upper lip.

'We had a great trip,' she assured him.
'Found out all you wanted to know?' he asked.
'About the bi-lingual, bi-cultural programme, you mean?' she said. 'Oh yes, we saw some excellent examples of just how effective the programme can be. I'm more than ever convinced that we should continue the double cultural emphasis on into the higher grades.'

He smiled and nodded at her as at an interesting child. 'You're a real enthusiast, aren't you? I admire enthusiasm. If you believe in something, go for it with all you've got, I say. But some of our whizz-bang experiments can cost the budget way out of sight.'

'Whizz-bang?' She suddenly suspected that she was talking to a very objectionable, narrow-minded bigot. 'What experiments? You don't mean bi-lingual education?'

He smiled reassuringly. 'I'm not wanting to knock the project, but we will need to weigh the consequences very carefully of any extra expenditure on perpetuating the native culture through schooling.'

Livvy could hardly believe her ears. She had always known that Olly Sutton was conservative, and very much the conventional bureaucrat, but this was a new revelation to her. He was opposed to allowing education to happen for the indigenous people in their own culture as well as in the imported, dominant European one; and he used the word "native" in a way that she had not heard for years, except on the lips of people with racist leanings.

'Your little programme has nothing to fear from me, dear girl,' he told her; and she chose to let the "little" and the "girl" pass, rather than show that he could nettle her.

'But it's not up to you, is it Oliver,' she asked seriously. 'It's policy. It's some years now since the big battles were fought and won for bi-lingual education. It's not in question any more. Just the implementation of it.'

'Of course,' he said in a dismissive way that infuriated her; as if her opinions were irrelevant and not worth arguing about. He was blatantly indicating his assessment that it would be useless and unnecessary to talk any further with her about the policy, even though he might have plenty more to say.

'Is your charge all right?' He asked. 'The native girl…what's er name? I thought she looked a bit stirred up. Is she? Has anyone been stirring her?'

'She's not feeling particularly well,' Livvy explained shortly.

'I've given her permission to take some work home and do it when she can. No-one's been stirring her. What are you getting at?'

'Beware of softness, Livvy,' he told her. 'I don't think we do these people a favour when we are too soft on em. They've got to learn to live in the real world, the same as the rest of us. They'll take advantage of you, you know.'

'Do you think I'm stirring up Helen to be militant or something, Oliver?' Livvy was out of patience with this arrogant bigot.

'Good heavens, no!' he exclaimed. 'No-one suspects you of that sort of thing. I mean to say, you'd have to be crazy to stick your neck out like that in a sensitive position like yours. And crazy is something that Olivia Bridges quite clearly is not. It's just that it has been confirmed that some urban black stirrers have been brought to town from Brisbane, and it's expected they'll try to hustle people into demonstrations and God knows what sort of carry on...'

'You say it's been confirmed?' She asked. 'Confirmed by whom?'

'Ah, well, yes, it has been confirmed,' he said. 'It's far more than rumour. I've just come from a meeting of the Interdepartmental Committee on Community Health Education…and it was the Director of Health himself, Cecil Reeders, who warned me about it. He is not happy, our Cecil. I think we ought to listen to him…he usually knows what he is talking about on these matters.'

The Director of Health? She was staggered to think the Deputy Director of Education would quote Cecil Reeders, Director of Health, as an authority on fluctuations in the informal politics of urban Aboriginal community organisation. What, she wondered, did the politics of race have to do with health and education departmental leaders?

'Yes,' Sutton said. 'Anyway, we should take fair warning and do what we can, to shield our people from this sort of thing. Your girl for instance, she could get sucked right into this business. They go for the educated ones and work on them to join the cause. I've seen it all before.'

'Oh?' she asked crisply. 'Where?'

'Oh, various places,' he hedged.

'Such as?'

'Oh, well…here and there in this country and some others.'

'I didn't know you had lived in other countries,' she said. 'Apart from England and here, I mean.'

'Oh, good Lord, yes,' he said. 'Indonesia, New Guinea, to name a few.'

'How fascinating that must have been for you,' she said, genuinely impressed. 'Seeing all those places becoming self-governing. But…and here, I suppose, I'm, talking as an Anthropologist. There are vast differences between the socio-political and cultural circumstances of the indigenes of those countries and Australia.'

'You have to think that as an Anthropologist,' he said with a condescending smile. 'But let me tell you, those are academic differences. When it comes down to being brought into a working relationship with civilised society there's not all that much difference. I've seen it…'

'You astound me, Oliver!' She was flabbergasted and decided to bail out of the conversation before she disgraced herself by loudly abusing the Deputy Director. 'I would have thought that all cultural communities of people were different from one another…as different as you and I seem to be in the way we look at cultural matters. But I suppose we'll just have to agree to differ.'

He laughed pleasantly. 'Fair enough,' he said. 'But really, I don't think we disagree with each other deep down. Keep up the good work, Liv, I'll see you around.'

She was glad to see him go, and found her concentration completely shattered.

The Director of Health and a Deputy Director of Education warning people about urban stirrers mobilising indigenes to press for rights. These people! Seen it all before… that's how they work, they go for the educated ones…shield our people… our people. Shield them from their own people? Who was this Oliver Sutton, anyway? She realised for the first time that all she knew about his background she had learnt in the last few minutes. Good God! She was rocked by the thought that, not only this Deputy Director of Education, but the Director of Health, and many others in key development positions were relative newcomers to the Territory, and came from God knew where. The place could be crawling with white racist rejects from the newly independent nations of Asia and Melanesia.

To her great satisfaction, at four thirty, when she left the office she had completed the first draft of her report on the Malingarri visit. Rather than allow the disturbing encounter with Oliver Sutton to throw her off course, she had accepted it as a challenge, and had written an even more positive account of bi-lingual education as it was really happening at the school. She documented every bit of factual evidence of effectiveness that had come to her attention. It pleased her to think that she had been able to turn her anger and frustration into a creative channel. When she reread the manuscript, half-afraid that it would sound subjectively biased, it stood up well as an objective observer's report.

Chapter 12
Who is the drunk?

At home, waiting for Bridges to arrive, Livvy turned off the shower and heard the roaring of rain on the roof. By the time she had slammed shut the east-side louvres the squall had passed over, so she re-opened them, standing barefoot on the polished wooden floor, under the ceiling fan, and slipped into the blue silk happy-house coat that Bridges had insisted on buying for her on their vacation in Singapore two years ago.

This was one of her favourite times of day. Especially when she felt some sense of achievement in what she had done during the day. She always hoped to arrive home before Bridges, never quite sure if the pleasure of anticipating his home-coming was a hang-over of the house-wife syndrome. She was professional enough to apply anthropological insights to herself and admit that she had been deeply conditioned to traditional male-female roles, and was only partially liberated; but it was preferable to her to think that the reason that she enjoyed this little interlude was that it was her own personal and private time, alone, disengaged from all other associations, a time to enjoy what she had become and what she was going to be, and a chance to slip out of her work role and into being the social woman, wife and sweetheart.

It was pleasant to think of dining out at the Red Sails with Bridges after their time apart, very fitting to have a celebration of their reunion. What a good thing it was, their togetherness. She let her mind recall the men she had been relating to in the last few days and congratulated herself again that it was Bridges, and nobody who was anything like any of those others, with whom she was working out her most important social contract.

'So lucky!' she breathed, and over and above all that, to share so closely in each other's vocation. It could not have happened better. She decided to ask Bridges, unless he asked her first, to go for a walk on Rapid Creek beach in the moonlight after they left the Red Sails this evening. But they would not stay late. That would never do. As she thought of the hunger that her body felt for his soft touch and their passion and possession of each other, she let the happy-house coat hang free and the fan's down draft caress her upturned face, breasts and belly.

The sound of the Land Rover announced Bridges entering the street, and the surge of pleasure that she felt brought her back to realism with a foolish flush of modesty and a reflective thought about the things she had to tell her man about her day's doings.

Rather than yield to this impulse, she decided to prove that she was a liberated spirit who could be other than modest and who had no need to talk about her achievements to feel okay. By the time the Land Rover was under the house and Bridges had climbed the side stairs, she was waiting for him inside the door with a drink in each hand and her loosely tied silk cover hanging open most of the way down.

'Gooday lover,' she greeted him seductively as he entered and stopped short at this wonderful sight. The oppressive effects of the afternoon humidity and a day in the office were heavy in his face, but the vision before him had transforming power, and he reciprocated her mood of sensuous fun.

Tossing his brief case into an armchair, he stepped towards her murmuring, 'oh, you doll! You know how to revive a man, don't you? Just what I need'. As he spoke he put out his two hands as though to take her in his arms, but instead all of his fingers closed around the fuller glass she held, and he quickly swallowed the cold liquid, leaving only the ice blocks rattling in the glass.

'Well, I like that!' she feigned exasperation.
'Ah! Me too,' he teased. 'Great drink!' And, before she could swing away, he grabbed her with his empty hand and hugged her to him, muttering aggressively, 'And you're not bad either, come 'ere.'

Her drink spilt over her jolted arm and she squealed. 'Eeeh. Look out you brute! Help! Somebody save me!'

'No-one can hear you, my lovely,' he breathed hoarsely. 'You're mine all mine.'
'And who ...?' He silenced her with a full-mouthed kiss and she yielded to his mastery for a long moment before breaking away, and challenging him. 'What I want to know…you villain, is, if I am yours, all yours, whose are you? Tell the truth now… your life may depend on it.'
'But, of course.' He continued the role-play. 'In that case, I can keep the secret no longer. I am yours all yours.'

She dropped her happy coat to the floor and he scooped her up into his arms and whisked her into the bedroom, where with her squealing, they fell on the bed.

'You know what?' she said gently as he lay over her, smiling into her face.

'What?' he asked contentedly.

In her sweetest voice she confided, 'you smell sweaty.'

'Oh,' he was sobered by the news, but tried to press on in character. 'How does that affect you, sweetheart? I'm told it's nature's own come-on.'

'In that case, I might be unnatural,' she allowed. ''cause I find it quite repulsive. You see, I'm all showered and shiny, ready to go dancing and dining with my husband.'

'Let me see,' he moved back and began to examine her slender golden nakedness.

'Stop!' she cried, buckling herself protectively and diving towards the wardrobe for cover. 'You make me feel undressed.'

'I make you...?' he laughed and came around to where she was already into her panties and poking arms through her bra straps.

'To the shower!' she commanded.

'When I've had a kiss,' he replied.

'It goes much against the grain,' she complained, holding her nose with her elbow in the air, and puckering her lips to be kissed. He kissed her elbow and began stripping for the shower.

'Are we going to talk about our days or not,' he asked, the role-playing forgotten.

'Do you want to?' she asked.

'Not really, he said. 'But we've got a lot of catching up to do sometime.'

They had always shared their daily experiences and given their comments to each other. It was how they developed together their expanding understandings of their cross-cultural support work.

'What about one long German sentence each,' she said. 'Then let's forget work and concentrate on play for the rest of the night.'

'Night?' he queried. 'Don't you mean evening?'

'I meant night!' she grinned.

'Now that's a challenge I'd find hard to let pass,' he smiled happily. She was quite a person, this brilliant educational advisor, who was offering to sum up her day's doings in one long German sentence. 'How did you get on about Helen?' he asked as he tugged at his socks.

Livvy began preparing her compound sentence. 'Helen and I have patched things up, but she couldn't put her mind to her work today, because Father Sheehan told her someone wants to give her two million bucks, and one hundred and eighty thousand a year for the rest of her life. He also asked me if I've heard of Soft Aid to communities, and I think he is rather cute.'

'Some sentence!' he paused naked, by the bathroom door, gaping at her. 'Two million dollars?'

'However,' she continued her carefully constructed sentence. 'My day's endeavours proved very fruitful, in spite of an upsetting encounter with a blatant white racist, in the person of Oliver Sutton, who might be just the tip of a dirty big white-racist iceberg, and I'm really glad we're not going to talk work, and I couldn't think of anything I'd rather be doing than going out to eat with you.'

'Mmmh!' he admired her sentence. 'Quite a day! That's a sentence that deserves thinking about. I'm sure I can't match that, except that last bit, of course. That goes for me too.'

When he emerged from the bathroom with a towel around his loins, she was replacing the ice-block trays to the freezer in the top of the refrigerator. A sharp wind had arisen suddenly, and he noticed that the sky was now overcast. Automatically he began closing the glass window louvres on the eastern side. He was none too soon. Large rain-drops, smacking loudly against the glass, joined with the wind in a roar that made them raise their voices.

'I've squeezed some lemons for lemon ice,' she called.
'I can smell em,' he said. 'Great! Here's my sentence. Are you ready?'

She adjusted the trays and closed the fridge door.

'Not here,' she replied as she picked up two more iced lime drinks from the kitchen bench and passed one to him. She led the way into the lounge room, switched on the two overhead fans, drew drapes across the louvre windows along the southern side, to kill the noise of the 'horizontal rain'. Then they dropped into vinyl covered armchairs on the other side of the room.

'Now,' she stopped to sip. 'What's your day been like?'

Bridges enjoyed a gulp, and then finished off the tall glassful in a couple of seconds. 'Right', he said, 'Pah! I haf bin gombozing a wunderbar Deuschlander, er...long sentence.'

Livvy stopped short of sipping to respond. 'Oh great,' she laughed. 'Is that it? No? Oh, that's good. I hope your sentences are better than your German!'

'I'll ignore that,' he dropped the accent. 'Here we go. After a wonderful, if brief, early morning reunion with my darling wife…'

'I like this sentence already,' she said warmly.

'I spent the rest of the day trying to talk some sense into the Chief Minister and the Aboriginal Liaison Unit, who…'

'You've been talking sense into the Chief Minister?' she gasped.

'Who,' he repeated, 'having heard our positive report of Goose Islanders' readiness to come to the consultation...'

'Oh, I'm glad for you!' She was apologetic. 'I meant to ask this morning how it finally worked out over there.'

'...and, the Chief being greatly disturbed at the news that urban black organisers are about to launch a bit of a rights campaign, starting with a rally tomorrow at the YMCA Amphitheatre, wants me to involve Mani Manggululu in helping to plan our consultation and keep him away from the stirrers...'

'You didn't ...?'

He shrugged. 'How do you explain to politicians and bureaucrats that real human beings like Manggululu are just not going to let themselves be manipulated?'

'Even if real human beings like you wanted to?' she asked with mock apprehension.

'Like me, or him, or the Urban Black agents. Of course, I told him. Well not in so many words, but I let him know that it's not on to manipulate Mani and his people. Of course I did,' he assured her, and he was no longer playing her for laughs. 'They know how I feel. Still they expect me to do whatever can honourably be done to keep the Government's option before him at least as obviously as the other one. They are scared that he will swing over to join the urban protesters and take a lot of tribal people with him.'

'Poor darling.' She kissed his cheek. 'But let's be glad it's you and not someone else.'

'Andrew, too,' he said with a pronounced lack of enthusiasm. 'He and I are both to hang around Mani and get him on side if we can.'

'Well,' she observed, 'yours was quite a sentence, too. It kind of got us talking shop, didn't it? By the way Oliver Sutton also spoke about black stirrers being in town. But we don't want to talk about that tonight.'

'True, Liv,' he agreed light-heartedly. 'Barduwa, now. Finish up. No more work talk today, okay?'

* * *

When they arrived at the Red Sails the sun was already well below the horizon of the Arafura Sea. Beyond the palm tree silhouettes on the esplanade, the faded mango pink sky was split by an upward ray of darkness.

'Isn't it magnificent!' sighed Livvy, looking out to sea.

'Beautiful.' Bridges agreed, revived now that the merciless sun was tucked away for another mild tropical night. It was even more humid after the rain, but the heat had been replaced by the pleasant shades of night.

Once they received their drink, he asked, 'What the hell is Soft Aid? It's been buzzing around in my head ever since you mentioned it. Did you say Dick Sheehan's got an obsession with Soft Aid? What is it? A First Aid Kit? A soft drink? Or what?'

'No, someone he knows, a friend of his, I think he said, has dedicated his life to it. Some kind of helping programme in Aboriginal Communities, apparently. He wanted to know if I had come across it. It's something like a low impact and high success way of helping self-development in communities. I couldn't imagine that something like that exists and we haven't heard of it'

'Sounds fascinating,' he said. 'Sets all sorts of ideas running.'

'Ah, no you don't!" she declared. 'Not tonight, you don't. I demand that you cease thinking immediately.'

'What ...? Wadja say, luv?' He said in his dullest moronic voice.

'That's more like it,' she chuckled.

It was not yet crowded, and the guitarist and drummer were still setting themselves up, while a quiet instrumental medley piped an old Simon and Garfunkel providing an invitingly relaxed character to the place. Bridges leaned over to Livvy sing-whispering to the music, 'like a bridge over troubled wate-e-rr, I will ease your mind.' They skirted the small central dance floor behind the waiter and were well pleased with a table for two under a dim wall lamp.

'This is nice,' Livvy said, looking about at the dozens of couples and several larger parties. The mood was relaxed and quiet.

'It sure beats all the places I've ever been without you,' he told her matter-of-factly, and was gratified by her uncontrolled smile.

A fine bottle of South Australia white wine, a good band, sea food entree and pleasantly presented sushi and side salads, as they chatted but it was not easy for either of them to avoid shop talk, and repeatedly they had to stop in the middle of a half formed word and say, 'forget it', or 'oops!

'Oh Gawd, there's Cec Reeders and his lovely wife,' he said.

'Who?' She turned inconspicuously.

'Cecil Reeders, the Director of the Department of Health.'

'Oh yes,' she said, and went on knowingly. 'Remind me to tell you something about him later.'

'Why not now?' he asked.

'Too much like work,' she grinned. 'But fascinating. I'm sure you'll agree when you hear.'

'I can hardly wait,' he began, but caught sight of someone waving in their direction. 'Do you know those people over there?'

Livvy turned and saw a blonde couple, bronzed and look-alike with long, well-groomed, golden hair to their shoulders and embroidered collarless, open-necked Indian cheese-cloth shirts; casual, but beautiful. Glowing with life, she thought; and overshadowed by their companion, a glamorous black woman, as black as any you would ever see, with flashing white teeth, teased full hair, and a red dress that tied above one shoulder and left the other bare. It was Helen!

Livvy could hardly believe her eyes, but as if she wanted to verify it, Helen sat up with a wide, toothy smile and waved in their direction.

'It's Helen,' she told him, returning the wave and smile. 'I asked her to join us here, but she said that she and her friend might be going somewhere.'

'So it is!' he gasped at the fact. 'You asked her to join us?' His tone carried disapproval.

'Oh, you know? She seemed very much alone.'

'Even so…' he muttered with another glance at the other table and a friendly gesture.

Helen was waving to them again and talking to the others at her table, and Bridges read the signs.

'Oh, no. I'm afraid your young friend is a little the worse for wear,' he said.

Livvy looked again and found Helen still waving. She was also trying to mouth a message and pointing from herself to the blonde couple, who seemed heartily amused by it all.

'Do you mean she's drunk?'

'Well on the way, I'd say,' he was emphatic.

'Like another dance?' He asked her.

'Yes, that would be nice.'

As they moved around Bridges led the way, edging nearer Helen and her friends, 'Let's say hello and move on,' he suggested.

Helen was watching them with a broad smile of appreciation, and clapped their performance as they drew near.

'Good on youse.' she called. 'You're terrific dancers. I didn't … I didn't know you was so good at dancin'. You're terrific! Eh, Livvy, this is my friend, my friends, Lionel, and this 'ere's Annette. Eh, eh, you know what? The priest's gonna fix me up. You know that there thing I told him about. No, I mean that there thing e' told me about, and…and…I told him I can't if I don't know the person. Tomorrow e' said…I can meet 'im, tomorrow night.'

'Great, Helen.' Livvy kept dancing. 'Hi, there.' She greeted the beautiful blonde pair who both smiled more broadly than ever, mouthed, 'i', and raised a hand in listless salute. Bridges returned their greeting.

A slight disturbance at the entrance doors caught their attention as they moved off, after waving again to Helen. Some dancers had stopped to watch an attendant hurry towards the entrance to encounter a drunken, disheveled, white-haired Aboriginal man. The old man appeared agitated, and resisted the pressure on his arm, in an effort to stay inside the doors.

He was looking about as if searching for someone, and they heard him above the music declaring something like, 'Don't tell me. You don't know. Abrignal got Lore too'

A moment later the trouble-maker was bustled through the doorway to the scattered applause of nearby diners.

'I've just remembered where I've seen that old bloke before,' said Bridges. 'Want to sit down?'

Livvy nodded and they picked their way through the other dancers to the table. The incident at the door, or the encounter with Helen, or both, had shaken Livvy, and Bridges realised it. He was also feeling a little disturbed.

'It throws you a bit, doesn't it,' he said. 'Most of the time we can fool ourselves that things are getting better for the indigenous people. But a lot of 'em are still like souls in torment, consigned to the outer darkness, and trying to break back into the campfire circle.'

'Did you say you know him?' she asked.

'Saw him,' he corrected. 'When we arrived at the Airport on the way to Goose. That's the old bloke that Andrew was talking to. He said the old fellow lives in a drinking camp near the airport.'

'Poor old man,' she allowed her genuine sadness to come through. 'He's a long way from home, isn't he?'

'He sure is. In every sense of the word. Do you think he would want us and our help?' he asked.

'Probably not,' she sighed. 'Not if he has any pride left.'

'You know,' Bridges was thoughtful. 'It might sound ridiculous, but I reckon that old guy has got more pride than he knows what to do with. Pride and pain.'

'Did you sense that, too?' she said, smiling sadly. 'He was indignant wasn't he? I wonder what his story is. This should be the age of his greatest influence and importance in his society. That white hair is his badge of wisdom and authority. In earlier times he would have had the young men gathering around him every day to learn about being truly human, and to get their heritage of wisdom from him.'

'Oh, my God.' Bridges had glanced towards Helen's party, now he dropped his gaze to their own table and put a hand to his forehead, as though he wanted to avoid any further sight of what he had seen.

The lights dimmed except for the spot on the singer. The singer swayed as she watched the pianist for her cue.

'Su-mmer-ti-me,' her voice was soft, sweet and high with emotion. She had only sung a few bars when Livvy reached across and grasped Bridges' wrist, gesturing with her head as she looked around. Following her direction he saw, through the semi-darkness, someone with white hair making his way among the tables. It was the same man who had been escorted out before.

'…Oh, your daddy's ri-ich, and your mammy's good lookin…'

The lurching man collided with a table at the edge of the dance floor but staggered on to Helen's table, where he surveyed Helen for a second before he shouted hoarsely, 'You get out! You native girl, dere. You go. Get out now. They make you bad woman, 'ere.'

The music stopped as a buzz of consternation began. Someone called, 'chuck 'im out!' Helen looked from side to side, as if searching for the attendant who could deal with the intruder. Several men, including Bridges, were on their feet but looking about for the bouncer before making any further move.

Suddenly, before any of them were aware he grasped Helen's wrist. Helen, with a cry, tried to get away from the repulsive old assailant, whose voice was amplified as he rasped at her.

'Dis not your life, you think you borned for this? Yah shame yah mother. Get out Get out now.' He tried to haul her away, Bridges and another man, who turned out to be Cecil Reeders restrained him. Then Bridges gently caught Helen in his arms as Cecil Reeders put an armlock round the man and pulled his head back until he released his grip and toppled backwards. The scuffle was over in a few seconds and the bouncer appeared, to take charge of the offender.

'Where were you?' Reeders demanded to know, but without receiving an answer. Instead, the strong-arm man had taken possession of the drunk and was marching him, once more, towards the door. Livvy and Helen's blonde friends, Lionel and Annette, had come around to the sobbing girl. She saw them and took comfort from their presence, then, overcome with rage, she yelled fiercely at the retreating trouble-maker.

'You leave me alone, you stinkin old bastard. Who the 'ell do you think you are? Leave me alone.'

The outburst stunned the room into silence and everyone heard the wretched, ancient voice shout back at her, 'an who do you think you are, too?'

'Thank you…thank you…folks,' the pianist was at the microphone. I've been asked to apologize for this interruption. We're assured that it will not happen again'.

Bridges had gone out through the door, having whispered to Livvy, 'I'll be outside.'

Helen stood up, 'I wanna go home'.

Annette and Lionel looked at each other, and Livvy volunteered, 'we can take Helen if you like? I think I've had enough, and we planned an early night anyway.'

'I'm ready to go,' Annette said softly, giving Lionel the chance to say how he felt about that.
'Well, I'll go and fix up our bill, then let's go,' he said. 'Come back to our place for a drink, will you, Livvy.'
'All right, thank you,' she agreed and received a look of thankful relief from Helen. 'As long as that's all right with Gray. He's outside.
'Wonderful,' said Lionel. 'You can follow us if you like. You don't know my place, do you? It's down Cavenagh Street in the city area, but it's got no number. Easier to follow us.' Outside there was no sign of Bridges. A small group of men were on the footpath, enjoying the mixture of sea air and cigarette smoke, and enduring the efforts of one of their number to convince them all that he knew what he was talking about.
'There 'e is!' Helen mumbled, watching him approach along the footpath twenty to thirty metres away.
'Our car's just over there,' Lionel looked across the road to where a car-park had been made within the grassy verge. 'Yellow Mini. You can't miss us.'

* * *

When Livvy reached Bridges the others were already out of sight in deep shadows over the road, and she quickly explained what was happening. He seemed a little reluctant.

'Do you want to go?' he said. 'It means going into the city and back out again'.
'Oh, I think we'd better, don't you,' she asked. 'Helen's shaken up. I think it'd mean a lot to her. She might think we don't care if we don't go now.'

'I suppose so,' he said, ready to retrace his steps to the car. 'I'm sorry our evening's finished up like this.'

'It's not finished yet, lover,' she took his arm and squeezed.

'Let's not get trapped into staying late,' he said.

'Right,' she replied. 'Let's not. Did you come out looking for the old man?'

'Yes,' he said.

'I thought so,' she waited while he opened the Land Rover's door for her. 'Where is he now?'

'Hop in,' he said softly. 'I'll ring the Red Sails later and fix things there.'

The car reeked of stale, cheap wine and unwashed humanity, and she was startled by a sleepy guttural sound from the back seat.

'Aamf-a-garm-mn.'

'What's…' she turned back as Bridges moved around to the other side,

'Oh, no!' In the back seat, slumped against the side, apparently muttering in his sleep, was the old man who had created the disturbance a few minutes earlier. 'Where are we taking him?' She was incredulous as Bridges moved in behind the wheel.

'I'm sorry, darling,' he explained. 'When I went to speak to the old man he just clung to me and cried. He was distressed and I didn't want just to fob him off. I walked along here with him, and he wouldn't let go. Now he seems to be out like a light.'

'Poor old man,' she looked at the filthy, unkempt figure. 'Where's his camp? Near the airport.'

'Yes, down a bush track. I'm not sure that I could find it in the dark. I suppose he'll have to stay with us till he's fit to go on his way,' she ventured.

'Mmmh,' Bridges was searching for another option. 'We could drop him into the police at Casuarina. They'd let him sleep it off in the cells without booking him, unless someone from Red Sails presses charges.'

'No way!' She hated the idea. 'Here comes the yellow Mini. They're looking for us. Give em a toot.' She reached over and pressed the horn.

He impatiently accepted the awkward situation. The cool voice of reason told him that keeping the old man in their company for the time being, was their best option.

He waved to Annette who was nearest to them as the other car came by, then started up, pulled away and followed along the esplanade.

As they drove, Livvy pondered aloud. 'Why do you think that old man went to Helen? Do you think he knows her?'

'Yeh, was wondering the same thing myself.'

Chapter 13
Gate crasher

As they drove into Daly Street across the railway bridge and entered the city area, Livvy studied the bright moon above the city skyline, and remembered, with sharp regret, her hopes for a moonlit walk along the beach with Bridges. Here they were, instead, with all hope of a romantic stroll on the sand fading fast.

Bridges slowed the Rover to turn into Cavenagh Street, where multi-storeyed office blocks, wholesale and retail stores and modern houses now dominated the broad street along, which the Chinese quarter once had stood. Only a few of the old plain iron and fibro buildings still remained, although many of the descendants of the families who had lived there were still well-known in Darwin, and in every level and sector of society, except among the poor, and the criminal and boozing elements.

Business, professional and political leaders had sprung from the residents of Darwin's Chinatown; they represented a small but respected stable sector of the old Darwin families.

The two cars slowed as they passed a new multi-storey and residentials, with their under-floor voids open to the breeze and screened only by a spindly row of leafy aralia stems, set well back in lawned gardens with frangipanis and poincianas obvious among the trees and shrubs. Bridges pulled the Rover into the kerb in front of the place where Lionel Geddies was already out of the Mini and opening the front door. 'Is he going to be all right here?' Livvy asked, looking around at their sleeping passenger.'

'Sure,' said Bridges, 'It'll just be for a few minutes.'

The lights were on and the airconditioner was picking up speed as they tapped on the fly-wire door and heard the soft voice of Annette call, 'Come in'.

The room they stepped into was stifling, and Lionel was busily opening wooden louvres, below the dado rail; the higher glass ones were already open wide. Helen had obviously gone through to another part of the house.

'Sorry it's so hot,' said Lionel. 'It'll cool down quickly though. Sit down and we'll get a drink. Would you do that, Annie?'

Annette was happy to comply without a word and began to organise drinks for everyone.

'It was too bad what happened at the restaurant,' Lionel said.
'Yeah,' agreed Bridges. 'Pity. I was enjoying the singing.'

Lionel sat on the chair's arm and said, 'What happened wasn't a bit funny. But I propose a toast...to new friends'

'To new friends,' they chorused.

Bridges was impressed with a pair of carved multiple barbed spears crossed on the inner wall of the room, and above their crossover point, a genuine stone axe, complete with bush string binding and beeswax sealing. Its decoration was done in white clay and red and yellow ochre. He wondered about the young man's interest in such things.

'That's a valuable collection you have there on your wall, Lionel,' he began.
'Yes, aren't they beauties,' he replied. 'I'm very proud of them.'
'Are you a collector of Aboriginal artefacts?' Livvy asked.
'No, sound recording is my game; but I couldn't resist those. The old man who made that axe learnt his trade before he had ever seen a white man. I mean, that is the real article...not just an imitation for tourists.'

Helen shuddered as she looked at the object of his pride. 'That there? Doesn't even look like a real axe to me,' she scowled.

'Don't let looks deceive you, Helen, 'Livvy advised. 'With that axe, or one like it, and a hard wood bush chisel, the old people could strip a piece of bark from a tree big enough to make a shelter or a canoe, or smash open a hollow tree to get honey. It was also a fearful weapon in the hands of a fighting man.'
'Ugh!' Helen shuddered and sank back into the chair. 'That's disg... disgusting.'
'You're a recording specialist, you say, Lionel,' Bridges gave a lead to the young man in hope of getting to know him better.
'That's right. Mostly music, but some interviews.'

Helen and Annette looked at each other and smiled briefly.

'He's been recording us,' Helen said.
'That's right,' the quiet young blonde woman confirmed. 'I'm the interviewer, and Helen's been telling her life story.' Suddenly she took fright and covered her mouth with both hands. 'Did I say something I shouldn't? Oh, I'm so...oh...'

'No, it's okay, Annie girl.' Lionel assured her. 'You didn't say anything wrong. Did she, Helen?'

'Course not,' Helen assured her. 'Say what you like. I do.'

Annette seemed relieved, but still anxious and dropped her gaze to the floor just in front of her feet.

'Are you people interested in recording?' the young man asked.

'I've done quite a bit in field research, of course, as an Anthropologist,' Livvy said, and was pleased to see Lionel's new interest in her. He really was a handsome, no, she corrected her impression, a beautiful man.

'That must be terrific!' he said. 'I'd love to do that some time. I think that must be one of the most satisfying things anyone can do!'

Livvy laughed. 'Oh, it's not all exciting. A lot of the time it's just dry, hard work.'

'Yes, I suppose so, but, oh, that's part of the process isn't it? I admire people like you. You are precious, spending your lives preserving the people's stories of themselves and their way of life.'

Bridges thought that the admiration of his wife was getting too passionate too quickly, and cut in with an enquiry that turned the attention away from Livvy and back to Lionel.

'What sort of recording do you specialise in, Lionel?'

'Ah,' the young man rose and moved into a cane chair beneath the spears. 'Anything really, in a manner of speaking. My specialty is high quality recording.'

'For a company, or...?' Bridges pursued the enquiry.

'No, no…or yes, I suppose so, really…but I'm the company,' he grinned.

'Tell us a bit about it?' Livvy asked eagerly, and after a glance at Helen, who was becoming relaxed and laid-back. With Annette now moving to sit on the edge of her chair, with her drink held before her knees by all of her finger-tips, looking nervous and waiting on Lionel's every word as he began to tell them about his work.

He had registered himself as the Hi-Story Recording company. His income was derived mainly from sales of quality recordings for cultural and educational bodies, and rare recordings through music stores and by direct mailing to the public. He secured copyright on forgotten records of special interest, and made high quality recordings of endangered species and also of folk song in various countries. For instance, in such places, as Arnhem Land, and most recently, Katmandu and Timor.

When Bridges and Livvy expressed interest that he had just returned from Asia, he explained that he had been captivated by the news, a year or so earlier, of a cycle of songs that some of the indigenous mountain people sang in preparation for a dangerous ascent. He wanted to record them before they were lost. The burning ambition that motivated his work was to faithfully record the surviving living sounds of pre-industrial forms of human life and culture.

'You asked if I was a collector of artefacts?' he said. 'Well, I have some feeling for that, but all those things will turn to dust one day…and besides, others have done a better job in the museums than I could ever do. I'm interested to have a few pieces around, but audio recording is here to stay, and the sound of a human voice or a hand-carved wooden flute that tells of human feelings, from inside someone's heart.' His eyes widened and he looked inspired by his own words. 'As well as human thoughts and precious words and music that…that has given meaning and pleasure to many lives, still being heard in centuries to come through this work. I mean, even someone's actual voice, from a living moment like our present moment.'

They smiled at the excited young preserver of unusual words and music and people's meaningful moments. They listened encouragingly to hear more about Lionel's novel and original vocation. It appeared that the idea of recording the song cycles of mountaineers of Katmandu had grown into an obsession, and eventually he had made the effort. It had been worthwhile, even though no-one he met in Katmandu could remember a complete cycle of songs, and the custom of singing the songs had almost vanished. This had only seemed to underline the importance of his task. The fact that he had found an old climber who was prepared to sing a half a dozen songs had made the journey worthwhile. On the way home he had interviewed people and recorded folk music in six other countries from India to Timor, and was especially pleased to have captured the sound of a camp-fire group of resistance fighters in East Timor singing their own composition about living in freedom or dying in the hills.

He was silent for a moment, until Annette said, 'tell them, Lionel, Katmandu.'

'Oh, I just get so excited by chances to record the music of human voice or wind instruments,' he enthused. 'Strings and percussion too, but they express the music of the fingers. Voice and wind give us the music of the breath, from inside us.'

'But tell them why you came there, to Katmandu,' Annette insisted. 'As well as to get the music.'

'You sure?' he asked gently.

'Uhu,' she encouraged him.

'I went to bring Annie home,' he confided.

Helen looked across at Annette, and gave her a sleepy smile while Lionel went on with the story of his sister who had gone travelling in search of the secret of inner joy and peace. It was a story not unlike many others they had heard, of experimentation with drugs and sampling exotic religions and erotic sensations. In her lucid years she had sat at the feet of visiting Asian gurus to learn yoga, tai chi and meditation. Then she took a plunge into drugs. And later, started moving on, trying to avoid conflict and friction between people. Soon, she was pursuing a fantastic life in exotic places, and settled in for a while in a group house near Katmandu. She had forgotten why she had gone there and was too weak and confused to begin thinking about leaving there. A year after her arrival Lionel decided the time had come to visit Katmandu.

'It doesn't seem real now,' Annette said with a puzzled frown. 'In fact, there are still times when nothing seems real.'

'So, you two are brother and sister?' Bridges asked.

'Oh, yes. Couldn't you tell?' Lionel was genuinely surprised.

Livvy chimed in, 'yes, of course!'

Bridges admitted, 'no, it hadn't occurred to me until just now. I hadn't really put you down as brother and sister.'

'Must be blind!' grunted Helen. 'They're like the same person.'

Bridges found his interest in the Gellies siblings suddenly kindled and asked, 'and… er Annette, you're helping Lionel in his work, I suppose?'

'Uhu,' she nodded. 'Not that there's much I can do.'

Her brother was not prepared to let that pass. 'Don't sell yourself short, Annie. I keep telling you my work is so much better now that you've joined me. She's a natural interviewer. Everybody loves to talk with Annie.'

Helen shifted into a chair to underline Lionel's statement with an account of the Hi-Story staff visits to the Aboriginal Teachers' Education Centre at Batchelor.

Bridges' recalled a conversation in the Liaison Unit several weeks ago about a memo that someone or other had a permit to record sessions at ATEC on traditional tribal education processes, and Lionel confirmed that it was Hi-Story that had received the permission on the condition that copies of all final recordings were made available without cost to ATEC and the Education Department's bi-lingual staff resource team.

Lionel spoke about the great young people who were training as teachers, including Helen. She took the comment in silence, but waved a "shut up" signal, which was quite at variance with her smile of pleasure. However, the embarrassment was too much when Livvy told the others how fortunate she considered herself to be for having Helen working in a field placement with her.

'Oh, yeah!' the sarcasm was heavy. 'I'm a real help. I don't think.'

Bridges shifted attention away from the self-conscious young woman to enquire if Mani had been one of the people recorded at ATEC.

'Oh, he's lovely!' sighed Annette, with undiluted sentimentality.
'Ask her,' Helen said. 'She knows all about him.'
'Just friends, I think, Helen,' Lionel answered protectively, sensing that his sister was worried about the way her reference to Mani was being interpreted.
'Oh yeah?' Helen persisted clumsily.
'That's what she tells us, but it took her about four days to interview him. Interview's a new word for it. I know you, Annie. You like him, don't you? Come on, now, no fibs! You like him, eh?'

Annette looked at her dark friend shyly and nodded.

'I like him, too, Annette,' said Bridges. 'He's a special person. I've just spent a day or two getting to know him at his home country on Goose Island.'
'He comes here sometimes when he's up in town,' Helen said, still teasing. 'And I don't think he comes to see me or Lionel…'

A voice outside caught their attention. Someone was shouting a challenge and Lionel was on his feet in a second and moving to the front door.

'That sounds like Daniel Lee from next door. He's our landlord. I wonder what's up,' he said. There was someone at the door, and as Lionel opened it, a scruffy man staggered in and fell sprawling on the floor tiles.

Everyone recognised the old man who had devastated the performance at the Red Sails.

'Get out!' screeched Helen, lifting her legs into the chair and covering her face in her arms. 'Leave me alone.'

Mr Lee also appeared in the doorway as Bridges dropped on his knees beside the inert figure.

'You know him?' Mr Lee asked Lionel.

'Yes, yes, it's okay, Mr Lee,' Lionel told the middle-aged asiatic man glaring in at them. 'We'll look after him.'

'Please, look after my house, too,' Mr Lee was serious. 'I just want to be sure that you are safe and my house is safe.'

'I assure you that you don't need to worry, Mr Lee,' Lionel's tone suggested that the other man was being unreasonable. 'I thought that as long as I paid my rent…'

'You pay your rent okay, but I always have a decent place. I don't want this house to get bad name.'

'You don't like Aboriginal people, Mr Lee?'

'I like all kinds of people, Mr Gellies. Native people are okay with me.' The landlord lowered his voice. 'Just asking for a quiet house, that's all, Mr Gellies. Any complaints about what these houses look like…any funny business, and we might get pushed off this street. You understand me, Mr Gellies?'

'I agree that would be a real pity,' Lionel was no longer on the defensive. He tried to be understanding. 'You like this street, Mr Lee?'

'I tell you Mr Gellies, this is my family street. One time this street was all Chinese houses, shops and gardens. My parents and grandparents all grew up along here. Now just me and my wife. Just two houses. What about Land Rights for my people? We've been here for more than a century. Longer than anybody else, except the native people. Don't get me kicked out. Anybody gets me kicked out can look out for bad luck. That's all I can say.'

Lionel's passion for rare historical data was aroused. Leaving Bridges and Livvy to look after the old man he accompanied his landlord down the steps and out to the garden gate, avidly interested in all that he had to say. On the footpath Mrs Lee was waiting in an agitated state. Short, well-formed and middle-aged she would have cut a graceful figure but for her skimpy flat slippers that made her waddle. She turned away towards their house, then stepped aside and turned to wait for her husband. She appeared to be agitated, and ignored Lionel's presence.

'Is he going?' she asked her husband.

'I'll go now,' Lionel assured her, while he continued to look at her husband.

'I'm talking about that old drunken man. Is he supposed to be there? I don't want trouble-makers in our house, that's all. Plenty of quiet people would be glad to rent a house like this.'

Her husband moved closer to speak quietly. 'Don't worry about that. I'll look after this. Mr Gellies wants to speak to me, now. We'll just have a word here, and I will see you when I come in, okay?'

'Goodnight, Mrs Lee,' Lionel called, unanswered, as she shuffled away, and a few minutes later he had assured her husband that he understood and would co-operate wholeheartedly in keeping the good reputation of the Lee houses. He also began negotiations for a recorded interview about the Chinese experience of Darwin.

On arrival back inside, he found only Bridges and the drunken old man there, the latter stretched out and asleep again on a cane settee under the front windows and Bridges watching him from the chair, under the mounted spears and axe, on the other side of the room.

'The girls are in the bedroom, trying to calm Helen,' Bridges' explained. 'I'm sorry about this Lionel.'

'Why, what happened? How did this old chap get here?' Lionel Gellies glanced towards the inner doorway and decided to leave the comforting of Helen to his sister and Livvy.

'Oh, it's my fault…and I do apologise,' Bridges confessed. 'I let him rest in the Rover, then when you folk asked us to follow you here, I just left him there. We were going to let him sleep it off at our place for the night.'

Gellies looked at the other man for a long, searching moment. He smiled as he said, 'You're a good bloke Gray Bridges. Why not let the old guy sleep it off here. Now that he's here he might as well stay.'

'So that you can record him?' Bridges sounded wary.

'Good Lord, no!' Lionel rejected the idea. 'Not unless he decides he has things he wants to tell for the record. I'm not the exploiter of the weak you seem to take me for.'

'Sorry, forget it,' said Bridges. 'It's good of you to offer, but you can't keep him here with Helen living in the house.'

'I'm the chief tenant, and I believe that gives me the right to have the house guests I choose to have. Besides, it might do Helen a bit of good to have this old man of her people here. She has had a hard life and so has he, going by appearances. She might see someone worse off than herself. And he obviously still has a concern and affection for the young generation of his people, such as Helen. I'd like to see her just accept him as he is, and be unafraid.'

'Taking on a second patient are you,' Bridges was beginning to sound sarcastic. 'Look, Lionel, perhaps we are a couple of interfering do-gooders?' said Bridges. 'You'd be taking a risk of provoking Helen to real violence, I think…if you keep Bilago here, I'd think twice about it if I were you.'

'Bilago? Is that his name,' the other man replied. 'I think we could handle the situation. Ours is a house of peace. We like to call it that. Do you have some other good reason why Bilago couldn't just sleep it off here?'
'Not at all,' Bridges sounded relieved. 'It lets us off lightly.'

Livvy reappeared from the inner passageway, walking softly like a mother whose baby is just falling asleep.

'The others are not coming back out,' she told them. 'Helen is lying down, and Annette is telling her a story about the Abominable Snowman. They've decided not to come out while the old chap's still here. Annette persuaded Helen that it would be better that way. What a remarkable relationship those two have.'

Bridges explained to her that Lionel had decided to look after the old man and live with the consequences, and, after he had served them another round of drinks, their host shared with them information which neither of them, as professional people workers, would have told in such circumstances.

'As Helen's friends, perhaps you know that she has a real problem about trusting men at all?' He looked over his shoulder, then continued quietly. They told him that they knew that Helen found people hard to trust, but he said it went further than that. It had happened a few evenings back, that Lionel had been encouraging Annette who was feeling low, and they had spoken in front of Helen about the ongoing effects of several years of drug abuse and what he called 'unbridled experimenting with every kind of pleasure.' That was when Helen had sympathised with Annette and told her own story.

She had told them, matter-of-factly, that when she was fostered to a well-to-do, but childless couple in Perth, the mother used to let the father take his little black daughter for outings. Sometimes they visited men who played with her, and took pictures of her playing with them. And he taught her how to please men, and how to keep secrets.

'Oh, my God!' Livvy gasped, looking towards the bedroom.
'The bastard,' Bridges anger was muted. 'Did they put him away?'
'Unfortunately not. He died, and it turned out that his wife had not wanted a little girl anyway. It had been his idea from the start. Surprise, surprise! So it was that Helen got put away into a southern institution and, eventually, back to the Northern Territory. So, I mean to say, it's no wonder she's confused and doesn't trust men, is it?'

Livvy nodded speechlessly, and looked at Lionel as she qualified his statement. 'She obviously trusts one man. Lionel! She must have felt that she could trust you to hear her story and keep her confidence.'

'Yes, I know!' he was obviously honoured to be the man. 'Oh, you mean perhaps I shouldn't be telling you. Probably you're right, but I thought someone close to her should know when we move on. You won't talk about it to others, will you? And that's why I want to help her to see this old man who's sleeping here, poor old bloke, as another man who won't hurt her.'

Bridges' and Livvy looked at each other in silent comment on the young dreamer, and assured him that they knew how to keep confidences and would do so, then promptly dropped the subject of Helen's past, and prepared to leave.

Livvy excused herself and went along the passage to the door of Annette's room. The door was ajar and she peeped in, ready to say goodnight. Annette was sitting on the bedside with her back to the door and stroking Helen's dense dark curls as she lay across the bed with her head on her blonde friend's lap. Annette was softly crooning something that sounded like, 'sleep my little one, sleep.' Livvy retreated in silence and rejoined the men.

'I suppose you'll be attending the rally at the YMCA tomorrow night?' Lionel asked Bridges' as he saw them to the door.

'Oh, you know about that, do you?' Bridges found it surprising that word of the urban blacks' demonstration had spread so far.

'Yes, we will probably be there.'

Lionel was obviously interested in the forthcoming event. 'The young bloke we were talking about before, who comes here sometimes, Mani? He talks a lot with Annette. They were on the phone today, and she told me that he says he has been invited to be a speaker at the rally.'

'Mani has?' Bridges was aghast. He had visions of Blyth and Archer accusing him of gross disloyalty and incompetence.

* * *

Livvy noticed that he was not pleased with this bit of news, and intuitively knew why; the young Goose Islander that he was supposed to keep involved with the government was doing something with radicals. 'They can't hold you responsible for what Mani Manggululu decides to do,' she said as they reached the car.

'I know that. I'm not worried about that,' He was agitated, and it annoyed her to think that he would let the reference to Mani affect him that way.

'What's eating you, then?' She sounded doubtful.

Bridges steered for home, then answered. 'As a matter of fact, I still can't get over what happened to Helen as a little kid. Doesn't it make you sick?'

Livvy shared his horror. 'I know…imagine how I feel, about being so critical of her for sleeping with the school Principal. My God! She said she was going to please him. That was what her foster father taught her to do, the monster. How does a kid ever leave behind exposure to paedophilia?'

As they turned towards the northern suburbs they talked about the need that anyone with Helen's background must have for absolutely loyal and patient friends. They wondered what sort of therapeutic treatment and care she might have had. Whatever else was true, they agreed that she had done well to be as healthy and whole as she was, and to be continuing her vocational education into her thirties.

Before they arrived home, Livvy felt the need to return to what Lionel had said about tomorrow evening's gathering at the YMCA. 'Darling, what if Mani does choose to go all the way with urban Black Power?' she said. 'Hasn't he got a right to make such a choice if he wants to? They can't expect you to make him do something other than what he wants to do.'

'Oh, come on, Liv!' He was terse. 'Do we have to do this again now?'

'It's all right with me,' she said with an undisguised challenge. 'If you have a reason why you would rather not....'

'Oh, of course I don't! It's just that this was our no shop talk romantic outing… and besides, as I've already explained to you, I'm supposed to be building open and positive communication all round. Now, before I have created any bridges at all, the Queensland activists have already roped him in, while I'm out dining and dancing without even contacting him. I feel such an idiot.'

'Do you think you could have stopped him?'

'Honey!' He was louder. 'You're not listening to me. I'm the one who has been asked to let this key young leader of the tribal people get an unbiased view of all the options…'

She could get mad too! 'Unbiased?' she exclaimed. 'How can you help anyone be unbiased? You're a paid government communicator.'

He took the unfair thrust in angry silence before saying, 'let's drop it, honey. This doesn't seem to be the right time or place.'

They drove on in silence, went upstairs without needing to talk, and, although they embraced tenderly before climbing into bed, something had been lost between them.

They sighed a couple of times to simulate sleepiness and lay awake beside each other for an hour before he leaned over to kiss her and whisper without conviction, 'goodnight, sweetie. It was great to be out with you again.'

She clung to his lips before saying, 'I know you think I'm criticising, or not trusting you, or something, darling. But I'm not meaning to. It's just…well…we're partners as well as lovers. If ever I'm in a situation where the pressure's on to do something unfair to vulnerable people I'd want you to keep my conscience sharp. You know what I mean?'

'Sure, I understand,' he said, and he did, but it still made no difference to the loss of feeling between them.

Eventually her heavy breathing told Bridges that Livvy was asleep, and he was immediately aware of his tenderness for her returning. Why did she have to become his judge like that? It was galling to him, and it chilled his affections for her. Only now that she had gone to sleep and ceased being his self-appointed super-conscience was he aware again of the overflowing passion that was the vital spring of his heart. But she could be so maddening!

Chapter 14
Mystery tour

'One hour South of Darwin, a gateway to the Litchfield National Park,' and make the capital A a lowercase 'a'.

At first glance, the township of Batchelor is one of the most pleasant in the tropical half of Australia. The Rum Jungle Uranium Mine long ago ceased operation; and the mining company that had created this spacious staff town and lush, green parks, gardens, lawns and now soaring eucalypts, massive mangoes, fronded Poinciana flame trees and colourful shrubs, had handed it over for government care. The Education Department had centred its new staff orientations, in-service training and Aboriginal Teacher Education Centre in buildings that once had served a population of miners and support staff. The disused single men's quarters, long barracks-type huts, were gone and now the Centre was located in a contemporary suite of brick buildings connected by walkways and shaded open spaces. The older elevated houses along broad, fenceless streets, were chiefly occupied by various administrative and educational staff personnel, amidst huge, old mango trees, the town surrounded by lush mango and melon farms, 'amidst huge old mango trees, the town surrounded by lush mango and melon farms.

To the students of ATEC, Batchelor was too soft and too far from home to be really pleasant. Everything that they needed was supplied. There was no need to work for survival, all of their energies were available for the hard work of studying, and for whatever recreations they could find to occupy their time in this dreamy, isolated town.

The drive into Darwin took a little less than an hour, but students were not supposed to go to the city whenever they had the inclination. They were encouraged to make their lives in Batchelor.

But the students were often bored as they wanted to socialise and so frequented Darwin, and managed as young people do. For those who desired distraction from loneliness and the puzzling and distressing realities of this remote humid hamlet, liquor was easy to get, through the local club bar, or from considerate individuals.

From time to time, young women who came there to study never returned to their home, but went instead to the home with a male student as his wife. This created grief, anger and hostile criticism of ATEC among the families and elders of the young women.

Nevertheless, it remained in the departmental planners' "too hard" basket, where it had been for several years. Meanwhile, communities were, increasingly, avoiding the problem in their own way, by sending fewer single girls for training as teachers.

Home, for many of the students, was coastal, and they longed for the sea, but Batchelor was too far inland to take walks to the inner reaches of Darwin Harbour at East Arm, the closest shoreline. A few kilometres from the township there was an old lake formed in a large quarry that had been associated with the Rum Jungle uranium mine. Although tests had shown the water to be safe, it was hard for locals to use the diving board without feeling that they were plunging into dead water. What if laboratory tests did show no traces of death-dealing properties? To all appearances this dark water lacked such life as there was in the sea, or in the coastal billabongs that remained when the Dry Season lowered the water table and the rivers abandoned the flood plains. Then, in the billabongs, those vast ponds of dark stillness, huge barramundi, and other great fish continued to thrive, along with water snakes and crocodiles, but not in the Rum Jungle Lake.

Mani Manggululu found life in Batchelor boring. This morning he was more stimulated and alert than usual, as he dressed and prepared to go to breakfast in the dining hall. Only by comparing his Batchelor stay with an enforced period of an ordeal in the wilderness, part of his ancestors' man-making procedures, could he remind himself of the indirect values of enduring the experience, persevering with further exploration of the Balanda culture and the way it operated. As long as he could keep his heart and conscience satisfied about the reason for being there, he could tolerate the situation; which was most of the time. But, occasionally frustration built up to a breaking point, and, once in a while, cast him into a trough of despair and depression. At times he just had to get out of the place and back into touch with people in more realistic social life, including several interesting friends in Darwin.

Today his life was spiced with more interest and challenge than usual. The trip home to Goose Island had given him plenty to think about. Lilara coloured his every waking vision of things, and visited him in dreams. The memory of their love-making filled him with restlessness to be with her again. It was exciting to think of her as his own, the idea of the annulment was unpalatable, and he doubted that he would be able to stay away from her for more than a couple of weeks. He must try to find a place for her to live with good friends in Darwin and get her to come to town.

He couldn't think of their marriage as annulled. He wanted her to be his wife, and she had been given to him within the Law. At the same time, some old yearnings lingered. He was honest enough with himself to admit again that he still had ambitions about living in the whole country, not just the Aboriginal reserve lands. Lilara was a person of the old Lore and culture but ignorant of the modern ways. He wanted more than she could give him, but he also wanted her. It troubled him to think of a whole lifetime with her, but even more sharply he dreaded the thought of being without her a day longer than was absolutely necessary. He could only hope that when she left Goose and joined him in Darwin, they could begin to move closer to each other and journey together in a life in which they could support one another for being modern people of the old culture.

It was maddening that what they had found together had been blown apart already. He could understand why she had hit him with the paddle. It made him feel sick each time he thought about what would have happened if she, or Lunggaroi had not stopped him. Jack Foster would be dead and he would be a murderer waiting for the due processes of the Law to fall on him. She could not have stopped him with her bare hands. He couldn't help smiling in appreciation of her imagination and daring as he thought of the way she had swung the paddle down on his wrists. She had good aim too!

But he was a man and she was a woman. In his parents' generation, a husband would have given her a beating and left it at that, or even just a conclusive slap in the face. As it was, he felt awkward. Perhaps he would come to ignore the impertinence of her action. It was hard to say. In fact, it was hard to say anything about his relationship with Lilara. Being realistic, he had to return repeatedly to the question of what it would do to his future prospects, being married to her. The incident with the paddle had caused him to have second thoughts about the marriage: not simply because she had dared to strike him and interfere with what he was doing, but because it had made him see her not just as a girl to be possessed and enjoyed, but as a person with a mind of her own, a mind that could be contrary to his. He grudgingly conceded her influence had been for the better this time but she was a good, kind and beautiful, but simple-minded mission girl, hardly capable of sharing his multi-cultural and political vision and feeling for life.

He had to get his head around Balanda puzzles and magic and give knowledge of these to his people. Would Lilara be able to keep up with him? Would she appreciate the need for them to find the keys to unlock the Balanda way of seeing the world and producing what was needed without hunting and gathering? The big question about where money comes from had still not been answered to his satisfaction. He had learnt that it was made at a place called the Mint; but that, at that place, the money-makers were forbidden by a law to make all the money that the people wanted.

"How much" was carefully worked out by someone somewhere. This was part of the secret sacred law of The Balanda Culture. The question about "how much" kept rising in every day life. How much to buy. How much to eat. How much someone is worth. Even how much time there is, and how much time it would take to do something, because time apparently is money. How much? He had decided that the how much question was related to the central secret part of the culture.

Another big question is, why? Everything has a why question, and Balanda's get quite excited and agitated about discovering answers to why questions. They love to tell each other answers to such questions, to explain things. They think everything is because of a why. That's why it exists. That's why it is like it is. That's why I'm telling you what I think about things. Why do you think what you think? Why don't you say something? Why did you say something? Do something? It was one thing to learn to understand something mysterious by learning what made it happen, or why it is like it is; but Balandas were stuck in asking why about almost everything. Mani found it boring, but amused himself by asking himself… why? Why must they explain themselves and explain everything by talking about why it is like it is? They seem addicted to the law of cause and effect, but only half aware of what is, and uneducated in laws about how to make and keep honourable relationships, and to behave appropriately or to live together in a community or to survive.

Theirs is a way of talking that is supposed to show that you are clever. It produces a lot of talking, writing and conversation contests to show who knows the most answers to questions. It puzzled Mani when he began to realise that no trusted central body of Balanda knowledge existed as an accessible storehouse of truth and power about living a human life and surviving as a human society. It was understandable to him that the ancient books of the Jews had been so precious to their ancestors for so long, accustomed as he was to the existence of the life-way of the Arardbis, in which individuals were gradually initiated from one degree level to another, into the essential knowledge that had been passed down from their ancestors.

Among the missionaries he had seen this same thing. From them he had got the impression that all Balandas read the Bible to know their Law; and he had expected that colleges and universities would do the same sort of thing... So far he had found no evidence that this was so – on the contrary, in Adelaide, he had found himself among people who were more interested in learning to see what was wrong with ancient knowledge, understanding and wisdom. Why, they seemed to ask, did our ancestors claim to have knowledge? Why did they believe it? We have more knowledge than they ever had, and we can tell you why. So we win the quiz contest against our ancestors…In fact, there seemed to be a Balanda obsession with getting free from ancestors, from laws, from revealed ways of the eternal plan for being human, from each other, and even from being what they really were; like a desire to prove that they could choose to be whatever they chose to be, as if explanation of their own life was something they could make up within themselves. So their life is a private thing that they are making and nothing to do with anybody else. They had private ownership of things and even of themselves. That way strong Balandas could always win every contest with people and with God. They could be furious if any one talked about them, as if they knew anything about them. But they thought it was all right for them to say all sorts of things about others, behind their backs. Like uneducated children, they talked about other people in ways that could cause hostility and feuding.

But why was that childish competition to get high enough to look down on others so important to their life-way? It was a strange, dangerous and mysterious way to exist, and yet it was a way that seemed to empower Balandas to produce food, houses, cars, boats, and all the wonders of communication and transport, and money. But what was their power? Where did they get it from? If it was not to be found in their law and culture, where was it? And what was it? What was the secret force? The magic of the Balandas?

His foundation, and that of all of his people, is a lore and culture that has been passed down from generation to generation for thousands of years. These laws and culture had allowed his people to successfully survive in a hostile country and climate as the longest single-culture land occupation in the history of mankind. But for the Balandas, they cannot offer anything like the foundation that has guided and kept us alive.

But because they did not want to recognise our "lore" or culture as a thing of substance they declared "Terra Nullius", meaning nobody's land, when they invaded our lands. Their "might is definitely right" attitude and inability to recoganise our regulated society was necessary to their want for land, resources and strategic positing.

But be that as it may, one way or another, he would soon be established as a man to be reckoned with in both cultural worlds, the real, but weakened, inner one of his people, and the aggressively dominant and seemingly lawless one of the Balanda system. He would be recognised as a man of tribal importance, a keeper of land, a married man, and a man of the world, speaking English, the global language of many nations, not just the Balandas, and beating them at their own games as Eddie Mabo did. Meanwhile, he must play his part manfully, on behalf of Jambagirrila and the family, to see that the greed of the government for dollars and control would not be successful in taking over and exploiting more of their ancestral homelands.

At times he felt young and exposed to forces that could blow him away like a goose in a cyclone. If only he knew who could be trusted to honour the Lore, the eternal Lore, and to really care about his family's interests, he would be free of much of the anxiety that now was making him so wary and tense. He dare not trust anyone, apart from the old people at home, but they knew nothing about the Balanda social systems, and relied on him to be their informer about such things and to guard their interests.

He knew that he must not completely trust anyone, in the sense of letting them lead his thinking, or even in the sense of leaning on them for support. The only way to be sure that he would not let down his people was to stand on his own feet, carry his own weight, and the burdens of uncertainty and stress that went with his own responsibilities.

Thankfully he could, more or less, rely on the Northern Land Council and its lawyers to press the government all the way through the Law courts to get the full benefit of the Land Rights Act. They had done well in the past three years to secure the recognition of his Wainanda people as land-owners of the Dik Dik country. But it could not be left just to councils to decide what was right. The Land Council had to take land owners' advice, including his and Jambagirrila's; and if the old man had not been able to say that he had been back to live in that ancestral country since fleeing to Goose Island, because of the white man with the gun, and still been able to sing some old songs and tell stories of the old place, their case would have failed. Unfortunately, he could have no confidence that the Land Rights Act would stay in force from one year to another. Opponents of Aboriginal Land Rights already had been trying to discredit the Act and have it repealed, or drastically amended. It was this arbitrary changing of the so-called Law, with every wave of opinion or financial interest among those in power, that was so scandalous to Mani as one educated in the everlasting Rom, lore of the land. What hope was there for justice at the hands of politicians who believed that they could change the Law to suit the personal desires and economic interests of those who were voted in at the most recent election? People who wanted to destroy the Land Rights Act could stand for election to get into the Government! All they had to do was to play the election game better than others and they would be allowed to have power over the Law. Many of these are at the whim of the mining conglomerates and big business. They would try to convince that it is for the development of the north. But really, it is to rape and plunder the north for their desire, and my people and the land are expendable.

It really was confusing, and Mani had learnt to suspect all Balandas of being greedy buggers, more interested in getting what they wanted for themselves than leading the people in living together according to the Law. It seemed incredible that, with all their cleverness and science, the Balandas had never learnt that the Lore was older than the land, and as essential to human survival and proper functioning as it was to the setting and rising of the sun. It was the Lore that gave his family the land and its life, to keep in sacred trust; and it was the Lore that empowered him to defy the greedy invaders and the ingenious schemes by which they gave themselves rights and authorities to justify greed, lust and wanton destruction of the land and its life. Never would he cease to think of himself as part of the life of the land; and if they insisted on destroying that life then they must destroy him with it, as they had already destroyed so many of his people.

So easily he could become bitter towards the Balanda race as a whole as many of his people had. Already he felt a hearty hatred for most of them that threatened to harden into contempt and loathing. But he was fair enough to remind himself of the individual Balandas he knew whom he regarded as 'good blokes', exceptions to the rule. He thought that he could include Gray Bridges among these, and a couple of the training staff at ATEC, and he hoped that he was not mistaken. Either Bridges was a good bloke and trustworthy, or a clever and deceitful enemy of the worst kind, or, then again, perhaps he was a naive fool who was being used by bloody-minded politicians. It was best to play safe, and take no risks with the Communication Consultant of the Chief Minister's Liaison Unit.

The man who was causing Mani real anxiety at the moment was Stan Armstrong from Queensland. Yesterday, when the urban black Australian came to ATEC with Harry Bagent, from the Aboriginal Liaison Unit, Mani had agreed to be a supporting speaker at a rally in the YMCA amphitheater. He had not hesitated to accept the invitation, because it was a good chance to have a public platform, and begin to let Darwin people know how he saw the threat that existed to the position of the people of the land. But he had not been whole-hearted about identifying with the urban activist. In Adelaide he had made a number of close urban Aboriginal friends in his class, and they had helped to radicalise his understanding and raise his social awareness of how things happen in urban society. But he had learnt to avoid getting drawn into things with several of the aggressive agitators in the group. He respected their heroic efforts to equip themselves to do social analysis and to work for justice, freedom and hope. But he felt that he was expected to let himself be recruited to their cause, accept their agenda and see things as they did, and it was no easier to bow to their pressure than it was to the Balandas. Armstrong was an impressive, but not very reassuring, pro-tribal campaigner. Like many urban Australians with Aboriginal ancestry, he had grown up as an inmate of an institution, a government settlement controlled by Balandas.

Now he had come out of the shadow of shame and the sinking sands of shared feebleness in which his depressed minority group had existed for so long. He had stepped into the blazing sunlight of a new enlightenment, on the broad, firm uplands of a liberated humanity, marching up the highway of freedom towards the city of justice. All of this had become possible through the rediscovery of the indigenous side of his heritage, the continuing tribal people, in whom the hope and promise of his indigenous ancestors' dreaming still had a chance to survive and to be honoured as valid and valued down the long road into the infinite future.

Stan Armstrong had told Mani that the greatest conversion day of his life was when he could say with whole-hearted conviction, 'I am an Aborigine!' Since then he had been riding high in a life filled with inexhaustible meaning and purpose. He was a champion of the cause of Black Australia. All that had happened to him, all the humiliation and deprivation, and all the education and socialisation, suddenly had become important assets on the day of his conversion. All through the years in which he had tried to be accepted as a member of the dominant white community, as no different from any white person, he had bitterly resented the hardships and the tedious acculturation that had been his lot, but now it was different. It appeared to him that he was at least as well equipped, through his experiences, to act on behalf of the first nations people of Australia in the encounter with white society, as anyone else in the country, and, therefore, in the world. Enthusiastically he had shared his vision and confidence with Mani, whom he addressed as Malcolm, in their first meeting.

It was that uninhibited self-disclosure that had sounded warnings to Mani. In his own community of origin, no man would have talked about himself in a first encounter, and it might be years before they disclosed as much as Armstrong had made known of himself in the first few minutes. Take care, said the voice of Mani's education, this man is more Balanda than a Balanda. He means well, and he is for us and the Dreaming and the Lore, but perhaps he has only learnt the Balanda business of "I am the one who has the knowledge, and all good will come to you if you follow me." There was a risk in appearing with Armstrong, but to Mani it was a calculated risk, and well worth taking. It would be a way of showing that tribal people were not chained to Balandas, or afraid to take another direction than the one that official guides suggested. It would put them on their mettle to prove their good will to the tribal people; and it would give him and his people more leverage. He had learnt about the use of levers at ATEC and recognised that it was the way the old men had always moved heavy tree trunks; and he had been fascinated at college in Adelaide to hear leverage discussed in a Social Analysis class. He often returned to the idea to be informed by it as to how to behave in situations where he seemed to lack the strength required. A bigger lever, to put his weight on, often had made things move when straight pushing got him nowhere. Armstrong would be his lever this time and the rally at the YMCA a chance to use his weight.

The only danger, was that Armstrong might assume that he could manipulate this new tribal recruit to the campaign for justice for Black Australians. It would be best for them both if Armstrong did not try any such thing. If he did, Mani would keep calm; (he still felt badly about his violent reaction to Foster) but in no way would he let the Queenslander get the idea that he could beat time for him to dance.

* * *

The sausages and fried tomatoes were to his liking, and as he wiped the plate clean with toast, his mobile phone rang.

'Hullo,' said Mani.

Bridges greeted him in that carefully friendly voice that was so encouraging if genuine and so dangerously seductive if an artificial pose.

'G'day, Mani. Hope I didn't get you out of bed, did I? I wanted to catch you before you got busy with other things.'

'No. It's all right, mate,' Mani assured him with a glow of satisfaction at being able to call Bridges 'mate'. It was real: they had shared a near death experience, and had begun to listen to each other. He liked Bridges and wanted to trust him. 'What can I do for you?'

Bridges referred to Jambagirrila. Was that a sign of his cleverness at getting the Arardbi really listening, by involving the name of his revered grandfather? 'I'm remembering that your grandfather told us that he would ask you to be at the consultation with the Government, Mani.'

'Yes.'

'As you know, I'm helping to plan it, and I've got the chance to feed in the ideas of Arardbis, not only for the agenda, but about how the whole thing should be run.'

'Uhu.'

'Well, I was wondering if you're going to be free at all today? I'd like to come down and have a few minutes to get your thoughts on one or two things, and start to get your ideas about this business.'

'Oh, I dunno,' Mani stalled on purpose, to get the other man's reaction. If he came on too strong that would be a sign that the whole thing would be suspect, and he would back off from the meeting.

'I see, 'Bridges sounded ready to be put off for today. 'Okay, if I've caught you on a busy day?'

'No,' Mani listened to what was in Bridges' voice and was satisfied now that this Balanda that he had pulled from the sea would not be too pushy in the proposed interview. 'I think I can make it. Matter of fact, I'm coming up to Darwin this morning.'

'Oh?' Bridges was interested. 'Are you going to have a full programme while you're in town?'

'No. At least, I dunno. I don't think so,' Mani told him, his voice racing a little with excitement about what he was to do in Darwin. 'A friend of mine is going to let me record myself giving a talk. A sort of private rehearsal. I'm giving a talk at the YMCA.'

'At the rally?' Bridges asked, just as if he had not already heard about it.

'That's right,' Mani was glad that Bridges knew about the rally, and waited to get his response to this news.

'I'd been thinking of going along. Now I'm definitely going to be there. You don't mind if I come to hear you, do you?'

'No worries.'

'Remember, Mani?' Bridges queried. 'Out on Goose Island I told you I think you and I are two of the most important individuals around these parts for helping people learn how to live together.'

'Yeah, yeah, I remember,' Mani was smiling, partly because he felt encouraged as well as amused by this Balanda, and partly at the thought that, if Gray Bridges were really a subtle manipulator trying to suck him in, he was very good at it, and really worked hard to get the right responses. The next thing he heard surprised him and made him a little more wary. This government man knew more than one might suppose.

'That friend with the recording equipment, Mani,' Bridges said. 'Do you mean Lionel Gellies?'

'Yes, it is, as a matter of fact,' Mani told him. 'You know 'im?'

'I met him just last night,' Bridges said. 'Look, I was just thinking, could we say a definite time for me to pick you up today, and we could go off to the Vic or the Darwin...'

'Pubs?'

'Yes, is that okay? We could just go to the dining room if you like.'

'Pubs are not my scene, Bridges,' he said. 'Do you know what I mean if I say, I haven't learnt drinking?'

'Yes, I'm familiar with the term.'

Bridges had heard the expression several times in connection with discussions of alcohol related social problems. Among some tribal men, who learnt new degree secrets every few years, drinking alcohol was like an esoteric world for those initiated into it. It was seen as comparable to passing through a ceremonial degree. Once introduced, a man was expected to go all the way into drinking, which in this part of the tropical north was modelled on the brain-blasting benders of the bulk of the Balandas, drinking to get drunk, rather than on any of the restrained styles of other sub-cultural groups, such as the large Chinese and Greek populations. Mani was reminding Bridges that going to a licensed hotel could be taken by other Aboriginal men as a sign that he was now ready to take the plunge into the drinking life.

'What about the park above Lameroo Beach? We can find a shady spot over there.'

'Yeah, good,' Mani agreed, and they arranged that the Land Rover would call at Cavenagh Street at three-thirty.

'By the way, Mani,' Bridges held him on the line. 'Did I say thanks for saving my life?'

Mani grinned. 'Yeh, mate. You did.'

'That's good. I just want you to know I won't forget it.

* * *

Bridges was uninclined to spend the entire morning, and half the afternoon at the office, exposed to the glare of Fred Archer and the Chief Minister. It would not go down very well with them when they expected him to be hotly pursuing Manggululu. He would rather dodge the office and follow up some field work. As he moved away from his desk phone, it rang, and he found himself talking with Father Dick Sheehan.

'Some people's phones get busy early in the morning,' the priest joked. 'I thought you'd never hang up.'

'You've been trying for a while, have you, Dick?' Bridges recognised the voice and the humour. 'Ah, well, some of us have to work from sun-up til sun-down, ya know. No rest for the wicked.'

'Actually I didn't expect you to be at home,' Father Dick told him. 'It was your wife I was wanting to speak to.'

'Is this a confession, Dick?' Bridges teased. 'Do you want to tell me how long this has been going on?'

The priest laughed loudly in appreciation of the easy manner in which Bridges bantered him, refreshingly man to man. 'Rest assured you have nothing to fear from me Gray,' he said. 'This is absolutely the first time I've made any approach to your wife.'

'I'm glad to hear that,' Bridges dared one last bit of game-playing. 'It's a good thing I was around to nip it in the bud.'

Again Sheehan guffawed, and then tried to resume the business of his call, but found himself a trifle embarrassed. 'I'm not sure that I'm game to speak to Livvy now,' he said. 'Actually, there's no reason why I can't share with you…'

'Nonsense,' said Bridges. 'Livvy's getting dressed, I'll…'

'No. Let me share the matter with you, Gray. Quite seriously, I make a rule of dealing with the male member of…'

'You don't have to convince me, Dick.'

'Okay. I know that, but well, your wife was here yesterday with Helen and was taken into confidence on matters relating to Helen's future…'

'I know,' Bridges was absolutely serious now. 'We share most things, and Livvy and I keep each other's confidences with professional confidentiality. I know what you're referring to.'

'Oh, yes…er, good,' the priest was obviously satisfied and went on. 'I am in an awkward situation. Let me fill you in. Our young friend has said that she won't accept an endowment from her would-be benefactor unless she has the chance to meet him. I think she wants to feel that she knows the man and his motives before she takes the gift. I suppose that's natural enough.'

'I guess so,' Bridges wondered how this created such awkwardness for the priest that he needed to consult Livvy.

'Well…the…er benefactor is an unusual man and I'm unsure about letting Helen meet him. I've set it up for this evening, but during the night it has troubled me. I'm no longer sure I'm doing the right thing.'

'How can Livvy help?'

'As a woman, and a close friend of Helen's, and as a student of people, she could give me her opinion, after observing the man who wants to make Helen his heir. Do you think she would consider…'

'Oh, I'm sure she would as long as it fits in with her must-do-list,' Bridges began. 'I'll get her in a tick. But, before I go, can you tell me what you meant by Soft Aid? Livvy said that you were saying something about it yesterday.'

'Oh yes. It's something a friend of mine is working on, an assignment from beyond the grave he calls it. Apparently a dead friend of his had been developing a certain approach to working with Aboriginal communities.'

'Sounds exciting.' said Bridges eagerly. 'I work with communities, and the givers of aid, and policy-makers. Is there any way I could get to talk with this bloke…'

'That could be easily arranged Gray. In fact, if Livvy happens to be free to accompany me this morning, and if you're free yourself, we could all go together and do the two things on the one trip.'

'That would fit in nicely for me,' said Bridges, eagerly snatching at an excuse to avoid the office. 'I'd have to make a couple of phone calls to ensure that other things are getting done. Anyway, look, here's Livvy. I'll just give her the gist of what you've suggested.'

When Livvy heard about the proposed visit to see the mystery man who wanted to secure Helen's financial future, she was hesitant. 'Good morning Father Sheehan. I'd like to help, but I'm just wondering about my work load for this morning.'

'Yes, of course,' he said understandingly. 'I mustn't forget that pastoral care is not really a part of your work. It's just...'

'Well, actually...you know I do feel that I want to help Helen', she considered, 'and besides I do have a duty of care for while she is assigned to work with me.... yes, look, I'm sure it's okay. All right Father, if you think I'd be useful...but it must not take too long.'

'I'm just not sure enough of my own judgement on this one,' he explained. I think it's all right, but then again, I need a second opinion. I appreciate this very much, Livvy....Oh, look,' he added. 'As long as you're coming, you might as well bring your swimming togs.'

'Bathers?' This was a source of amusement, but the arrangements were made and after calls had been put through to their respective offices to indicate that their absences were due to duties elsewhere, they joined Father Sheehan at his office, and set off in his white Holden sedan along Stuart Highway, away from the city.

'I hope you will both be glad you've come along,' said their driver.

* * *

'It's exciting,' said Livvy. 'Not knowing where we are going. A mystery tour.'

'I'm sure I'll be glad I've come!' Bridges assured the priest. 'If, as you say, I meet this Soft Aid fellow. Where exactly is he, Dick?'

The priest drove in silence for a few moments before saying, 'Suppose we just go along with the trip, and let it unfold. It would get complicated if I started trying to explain things in advance. Would you mind if we played a game of mystery touring?'

'That's fine with me,' said Bridges.
'Goody, goody,' Livvy said childishly.

At Berrimah Junction they turned right, off Stuart Highway. Bridges and Livvy looked at each other, each sure that the other had guessed that they were bound for Kormilda College, the post-primary residential for Aboriginal students; but, as they passed its front gates the looks they exchanged were of surprise.

'Have either of you been to the Leprosy Hospital?' Father Sheehan asked.

'No, I haven't,' they both said, suddenly remembering that the East Arm Leprosarium was along this road, almost on the shore of the eastern arm of Darwin Harbour.

'Is this where...?' Bridges began, but Livvy cut him short.

'Uh-uh!' she snapped. 'No questions. This is a mystery tour!'

'Whoops,' Bridges subsided, while the others grinned.

'It's an amazing place,' Dick Sheehan told them. 'It's an official government hospital, with a magnificent staff. Some of the world's best experts serve here. Leprosy sufferers have residential care because they have no access to the treatments in their remote homes but go home often. The community's run by an order of Catholic sisters. Isn't it wonderful to think of the tremendous progress they've made in the control of leprosy?' Most of the treatment is multi drug therapy and most people in urban areas do not even need to come to facilities like this. Treatment usually takes a year or two.

'It's good to hear that they've made good progress' Livvy said.

'I must admit that I'd thought leprosy had been controlled,' admitted Bridges. 'Until we came north.'

'That's because you're of European stock...English ancestry, probably?'

'And French,' Bridges verified.

'Well, there you are, you see. And the same with us Irishmen. We threw it off centuries ago. That doesn't mean that Caucasians can't get leprosy. Most of us are immune to it for some unexplained reason, as I say, but not all. Some people get terribly disfigured as a result of it. Oh, my word...

But here in Australia there are hardly any new cases other than up here in this part of the world with the indigenous people. But it still ravages in places like India, Indonesia and Brazil, with approximately seventy-five cases a day of children diagnosed'.

'Seventy-five a day, poor little darlings,' said Livvy.

'How did the leprosy get here, Dick? Do you know? Was it here when white settlement began?' asked Bridges.

'Oh, no, not at all. But it wasn't the British who brought it in. It is thought to have come across around the 1870s from China when the Pine Creek Gold Rush was on.'

'You mean Chinese lepers were allowed to come into the country?' Livvy seemed horrified at the prospect.

'You see,' the father explained. 'Leprosy has an extremely long incubation period. You could be a carrier for up to twenty years without showing a sign of it. That's why there are still cases in this part of the world'

'Twenty years!' Bridges found that incredible.

'That's right. Do you see how hard it would be to track it down and isolate carriers? A person could have been all over the Territory in that time.'

'And spread the thing wherever he went,' said Bridges.

'Well, not exactly. Research seems to indicate that it is spread by nasal secretions. But believe it or not, it is not as contagious as once thought. Some researchers believe that the spread can be from the nasal passage that muck enters wounds or breaks in the skin. But it also seems that some genes are more susceptible, which means the possibility to contract it is inherited. Therefore, lots of mothers have given it to their children, and bed-mates often both show up with it.'

'Mmmh…you could hardly put a ban on love,' grinned Bridges, taking an elbow bump from Livvy.

'No, to be sure. But it does say something for the advantages of celibacy, doesn't it,' laughed the priest.

'You could have something there,' Livvy chuckled politely.

'Just before we go in, let me assure you of one thing,' Dick Sheehan went on. 'When a case's diagnosed it's only a matter of weeks before the patient's condition can be more or less stabilised. That's if it's caught early enough. Even with bad cases, the right medication makes patients completely safe to be with. You don't have to be Jesus Christ or Francis of Assisi to kiss a so-called leper here. It might be a bit off-putting at first to shake a hand with clawed fingers, or to kiss a face with no nostrils… but it can do you no harm, and often does a lot of good. The biggest problem is people's fear of the thing.'

They drove through an open gate past a house elevated on high stumps, and parked near an open-sided recreation hall.

Dick Sheehan turned to his passengers. 'Got your bathers?'

'Got 'em,' said Bridges, reaching for the bag on the back seat.

Livvy gaped at him idiotically, miming something like, 'Isn't this weird?'

'Mysteriouser and mysteriouser!' he whispered.

Chapter 15
An unusual man

Father Dick Sheehan led his companions along a neat asphalt road, rising past buildings on the left. To the right, the hillside was covered with manicured lawns and, ahead, was topped by weedless gay garden beds and graced by tall spindly Carpentaria palms. Just beyond the nearby pool at the foot of the slope, there was what the Bridges saw as an architectural monstrosity: a fibrous cement sheet imitation of a nineteenth century style stone church with bell-tower.

'The fear has to be eradicated,' Dick Sheehan resumed. 'But it's deeply ingrained. For years, people with leprosy used to be put on an island not far from here, in the East Arm of Darwin Harbour. The supply boat crew didn't even get off when they called there. They'd toss off the supplies and beat a hasty retreat. There was no care programme at all then. You can imagine the fear of being an outcast leper that spread through the country. That's a word that's not used at all today. People are not lepers. They are leprosy patients. For a few years the word 'leprosy' was officially avoided too, in favour of Hanson's Disease. But then, sensibly, the tabu word was brought back, and we are all being re-educated about the new power that we now have over it.'

As they approached the cyclone wire gate, Livvy and Bridges were impressed with the blue tiled chlorinated community swimming pool.

'Hey, that looks great' Bridges exclaimed.

'Now you know why I suggested you bring along your togs,' their guide said with smile.'

'Are you going in?' Bridges asked.

'My very word!' smiled Dick Sheehan. 'This is one of the few things we can do about the fear thing. I take a dip usually after services here. There's no service to-day, but I rang to let the sisters know that we'd be coming. You comin' in? It's okay. I've got standing permission for myself and visitors.'

'It looks too good to refuse,' said Livvy, curious, but ready to go along and be patient enough to let Dick Sheehan take his own time telling the complete story about the connection between the swimming and the fear.

The back door of the chapel was open and the priest suggested that Livvy use the small room there to change in, which she did; and then, she felt naked when she found herself standing on the lawn outside in a rather brief two-piece red swim-suit while the men changed somewhere else. Two patients in wheelchairs were being brought down the concrete path towards the pool, one, an Aboriginal man, steered by a black male orderly and the other, a large man, apparently a white gone brown but now with distinct patches of pink on his face, managing his own chair under the watchful eye of a woman in the unmistakable white dress of a nurse. Livvy went in through the cyclone wire gate and quickly lowered herself into the water.

It was pleasantly cool, but not cold. Turning on her back, she watched the patients and their minder's approach the edge of the pool. The Aboriginal man wore only red and white striped swim shorts, and showed vivid pink scars on the black of his left pectoral muscle and forearm, and on the stumps of four fingers on that hand. His right leg stopped in a rounded point half-way down the shin. He was not old, and had a full head of curly black hair, but his face showed signs of hard times and past suffering. The edge of one nostril was missing and one eye was unmistakably artificial. Behind him the white patient was breathing heavily from the effort of controlling his own chair.

'Good morning Andy,' called Sheehan, crossing the lawn with Bridges towards the new arrivals.

Livvy was relieved to see Bridges and Sheehan in swim shorts, both looking fit, bronzed and handsome. She had suddenly been seized by anxiety and confusion because obviously the patients were lepers ...... he corrected the thought, they were leprosy sufferers; and they apparently had the idea that they were going to swim here, too. She had begun to wonder if they thought that she also had leprosy, and was trying to think of what she might say. It was fine for the priest to say it was all right to swim with them, but it didn't feel all right!

'Good morning, Father,' replied the curly-headed wheelchair traveller as the priest drew near. 'You come for a swim today, eh?'
'I brought a couple of friends to see what a good swimming pool we've got. I can't stay too long today, but I'm glad you could come. I'd like you to meet my friends, Andy. This is Gray Bridges from Darwin, and that's Livvy Bridges already in the water. Couldn't resist it, eh?' The last words he called to Livvy as he caught her attention. 'Livvy, this is Andrew Gumaraj. Gray, Andrew.'

Andy Gumaraj smiled, held out a bony right hand whose fingers were permanently curled. 'Glad to meet yah, Livvy.'

'You too Andrew.' Bridges kept his gaze on the patient's real eye, and found the experience of grasping the curled powerless hand was not particularly unpleasant.

'Oh, hee,' the patient laughed. 'Andrew, you call me? Just Andy.'

Father Sheehan was exchanging a few words with the orderly who stood behind Andrew's chair. 'This is Bill,' he told Bridges. 'Bill's learning all about leprosy to teach people back at his Health Centre in East Arnhem Land.'
'Pleased to meet you, Bill.'

The young man in white shirt and trousers smiled as he said softly, g'day. Pleased to meet you, too.'
'Let's see you get in, Mr Smart,' said the nurse as she stood by the other patient, who was intent on reaching out of the chair to hook his arm around the rail above the steps. When he didn't reply, she sensed a race challenge, and quickly removed her wrap-on white dress, revealing a full figure in a one-piece black bathing suit. Throwing the dress away to the lawn edge, she noticed her patient's arm slip on the rail and swung both hands protectively towards him.
'No, I'm right! In you go,' said her patient. 'I've got it now.'
'I'm sure you have,' she said. 'But I just want to see how well you manage it. You go first.'

Livvy had swum to the edge to be near the men and was anxiously watching Sheehan for a signal. In spite of her determination to stay where she was, she also felt ready to leap out of the pool and run for a hot shower with plenty of soap. The sight of the disfigured old white man with tan and mottled pink skin, standing above the steps on his only foot, unnerved her.
'There was a time when the women did everything I told 'em to,' the old man complained aside to Bridges. 'Now they give me orders.' He turned to the priest. 'G'day, Father. Good to see ya.'
'Gray Bridges and Livvy Bridges,' said the priest. 'Meet Sister Paula and Ron Smart.'
'I reckon it'd be a pleasure to do what Sister Paula asks you to,' said Bridges to Ron Smart awkwardly, with a big grin, trying to ignore the montage of fleshy patches that now comprised the old man's face. The transplant patch across the top of his forehead more or less matched the natural tan of his face, but the swollen strip that ran from top to bottom down the ridge of his nose was a yellowy tan like the skin of pickled pork. Bridges excused himself for such an insulting but unbidden comparison, and concentrated on the obviously courageous character of the man.
'Oh, you'll get on, mate!' the older man exclaimed. 'Picked a great day for a swim, didn't yah?'
'Yeah, it's one out 'o the box,' Bridges concurred. 'Only, I'll be glad when it makes up its mind if it's still the Wet, or if the Knock-em-Downs have really arrived.'

'Beautiful time 'o the year.' the old Territorian declared. 'These are the days that keep us on our toes…those of us who've still got toes…It can be a sleepy old place, here, you know. But then crash, bang, wallop, comes a storm out of nowhere, and we know we're alive again.'

'You could well be right there,' Bridges accepted the older man's opinion.

With the help of the rail, Ron Smart stood taller and balanced on his foot at the third try. As he prepared to dive, Livvy, looking up at him, told herself again that this was the way that people were learning to deal with their fear of leprosy, and she made a mighty effort to be one of those people.

'Getting soft,' the old white man complained, as he leaned on his left hand, and steadied himself with his handless right arm.

'Wanna race?' he half turned to Bridges, who had come to the edge near Livvy to exchange encouraging smiles. Before the younger man could reply or move, his challenger took off. Bridges hit the water a second later, just ahead of Sister Paula.

'You've gotta be quick,' Smart called, rolling on to his back and blurting water.

'Oh, isn't this lovely?' cried the sister.

'You're too quick for me,' Bridges bawled at the other man, and found himself being shoved in the chest by Smart to back up as Sheehan and Andrew Gumaraj landed near them and swam past.

'Road hogs,' called the older man, and set off after them.

'Look at him go.' Bridges called to Livvy and Sister Paula.

'It's wonderful to see,' the Sister said, twisting about in the water as she spoke. 'It's hard to believe he's the same man.'

Livvy's curiosity was fired. 'As?'

'Oh, as the man who was so depressed that he was no longer interested in living. He talks about it openly. I know he wouldn't mind me telling you.'

'No, he certainly doesn't seem to be like that now,' agreed Livvy.

Bridges was picking up their conversation and swam closer. Reading Livvy's uncertainty, he asked, 'you alright sweetie?'

'It really is quite safe,' Sister Paula assured them.

'That's encouraging to hear,' said Bridges. 'It takes a bit of getting used to.'

They floated near each other, chatting, and Livvy relaxed enough to leave the rail again.

'It's largely due to Father Sheehan that Mr. Smart is so different,' the Sister told them as she swam away.

'He seems to be coping all right now, doesn't he?' said Bridges.

Livvy agreed and nodded towards the men at the far end of the pool. 'Do you think he's one of the two we are to meet?' They both looked along the pool and wondered if they had been introduced to the Soft Aid man or Helen's fairy godfather.

The priest was talking privately with Smart at the far end, and they still expected to hear that they had guessed correctly, that he was one or other of the people that they were to meet, when, after a quarter of an hour of swimming and conversation Sheehan led the retreat from the pool. Bridges heaved himself up on to the edge, found his towel and stood side-by-side with Livvy and the priest who were also draping themselves modestly in towels, and watched the two physically incomplete men manage the climb up the steps, with great reliance on the rails. Andrew had only the slightest assistance from Bill, at the top of his climb, but paused to gain strength before making the effort to turn and sit in his chair. The older man struggled up behind him and said with some shortness of breath, 'You're getting too good Andy. Soon be you'll be proper strong man, like me.'

As Sister Paula took hold of Smart's chair, the priest approached. 'Ron,' he said, as the old man dropped into place. 'I told you that I've found someone who's interested to learn about Soft Aid.'

Ron Smart smiled as he turned to his priest, eagerness all over his patchy face.

'You did.' He looked up gratefully. 'Here today, you said he is. So, it must be young Graham over there, is that right?

'Why don't you ask him yourself?'

'Young Gray?' repeated the keen old man. 'What's his line? Teacher or somethink is 'e?'

'He'll tell you.' Father Sheehan stepped aside and waved on towards Bridges. 'I'm going to get dressed and do some quick visits in the wards.'

* * *

From the pool, Livvy and Sister Paula saw Bridges sit on his towel beside Ron Smart's chair and decided that it was time for them to get out, and to leave the two men to enjoy a few minutes of uninterrupted conversation. After some light talk, Bridges began to hear a fascinating story of two Simpson brothers who had worked cattle in Arnhem Land, one of whom was something of a philosopher, missionary and natural encourager of Aboriginal people. They had written of their experiences and their ideas about appropriate ways of aiding the survival and modernisation of Aboriginal society without damaging them or their cultural integrity. They had called their theory Soft Aid. It was a non-destructive way of working to support people's own needs and aspirations. Bridges' mind fastened on the phrase that apparently was central to the Soft Aid approach, "free to decide." It was enough to whet his appetite for more, and he let the disfigured old enthusiast share what it meant to him.

'They opened my eyes, those Simpson boys,' the old man confided. 'We were rogues, you know. All of us white-fellas. We didn't care a dam about any-one else. Some of the things we did to 'em don't bear thinkin about now. But its right through us mob, except for a few truly good characters like the Simpson boys. They saw into the soul of things, I guess. Anyway, I took a long time to see what they saw. Their Soft Aid approach, if it ever catches on, 1 will change all that…And it's the only way I know that the native people of this country can eva have a hope of escaping from the bastardry…s'cuse me French, of white domination.'

Livvy sitting on the pool edge and listening to Sister Paula's account of her work, looked in the direction of Sheehan as he emerged dressed and combed, just in case he gave her a sign that it was time to meet Helen's would-be benefactor, and when he turned away, apparently setting off to make a general visit around the wards. It was pleasant enough in the sunshine, strolling up the hill after a cooling swim, and having a look around the property.

She considered the man that Bridges was speaking to 'a rather unusual man,' the priest had said. What possible connection could there be between the girl and Ron Smart, this aging man with the grossly disfigured face and body and the newly revived spirit? Helen appeared to be, biologically speaking, a fully Aboriginal person, and that ruled out the possibility that Ron Smart might be her natural father.

The sound of an approaching vehicle broke her thoughts, and she made her way around to the road in time to see the priest's car at the top of the hill. It turned and came towards her.

'Thought I'd lost you,' called the driver.
'It's a great place,' said Livvy. 'Sorry you had to come looking for me.'
'Your husband went off to change, and I decided to come for a run along the hillside to see where you were. It's paradise compared with what leprosy sufferers had to put up with all those years ago, out on the island in the harbour, with no staff and only an occasional boat to throw food to them, like they were animals.
'Look at old Ron Smart, will you?'

He turned the car and they began to descend the sealed road past the hospital. The driver tooted and Smart swung up an arm in salute. Bill, the Orderly had come back to push the old man's empty chair up the hill.

'It looks like hard work getting up there on those crutches,' Livvy remarked. 'The old man certainly seems to have plenty of courage.'

'He surely has that,' agreed the priest. At the bottom of the hill Bridges was waiting and climbed in behind Livvy.

'D'you have a good talk?' Livvy asked.

'Fascinating!' Bridges assured her. 'What an interesting old character. And this Soft Aid idea has really grabbed me. It'd need to be looked at closely, but it certainly rings my bells. And it was so good to hear an old bush character like Ron talking in such an enlightened way. He says he has put papers on it together, to hand them to you, Dick. Possibly I might get a look at them some time?'

Several patients were walking along the road and stepped to one side to wave and watch the car leaving.

'Goodbye Father,' called one or two softly. Their priest waved back. So did his passengers.

'Those four are long term. Some need pretty constant attention, and will possibly stay here till they die. Ron Smart, for instance. But even so they go off into town, and other places when they choose.' Dick Sheehan paused thoughtfully. 'That's one man who regrets the way he wasted most of his life doing worthless things. Now he's really numbering his days and using each one.'

When he came here, oh! He's had an amazing life. Found himself on the brink of his existence, up against the loss of everything he'd ever valued. A once proud and selfish, powerful man, now overwhelmed by the futility of this absurd adventure we call life. He tried every way he knew to salvage something of his past existence, to make his old formula for living work, and failed at every point. But he had Leprosy. As far as he was concerned, he was finished, and he more or less accepted it.'

Sheehan looked at his passengers to assure himself that they were interested enough to hear more, then continued. 'What Ron was up against was that bottomless abyss. That abyss of meaninglessness that threatens to suck in all of our illusions like a black hole, and replace our hopes and aspirations with barren despair and dread.'

He looked at them again, and laughed apologetically. 'You'll have to forgive me if I'm a bore. I've just been reading some stuff about the angst, as the Germans call it, anxiety about being. I think it's a very common experience that almost everyone has to go through sooner or later…before we make the discovery that God is being itself.'

'I'd say Ron Smart certainly looks as though he's got over it,' Bridges remarked, opting to stay with what could be seen and heard, rather than getting involved in abstract God-talk.'

'He didn't get over it,' said Sheehan. 'That way of putting it suggests he managed to bypass the threat and come back to things as they were before. I've spent many hours with Ron, and I can tell you, that's far from the truth. In fact, he didn't get over it at all…he got through it. And he came through on the other side of it with a changed perception of reality.'

'I'm intrigued, Father,' Livvy said. 'You are going to tell us whether or not Mr. Smart is Helen's fairy godfather, aren't you.'

'You guessed right,' Dick Sheehan did not really sound surprised.

'Not me,' admitted Bridges. 'That thought came into my mind, but I let it go when Ron turned out to be the Soft Aid man. I thought we were on our way to see the mystery man now.'

'Ron's both of 'em,' said the priest lightly. 'I'll be interested to get your reactions presently. But just to conclude what I was saying about Ron's conversion…let me say this. Do you know the story of Jacob?'

'You mean from the Bible?' Livvy asked.

'That's right.'

'In general,' she said.

'Some of it,' added Bridges.

'The part about Jacob's return to his own home country? To the Jews, the Christians and the Muslims it's a great dream time story.' The priest warmed to his task. 'Jacob had left his own country more or less condemned to death for his villainies. After many years, he comes home, prosperous and hopeful. A scout tells him that his brother's army's approaching. And Jacob reacts by sending his wives, children, animals, and workers on ahead and then goes back to the far side of the river alone. He's up against it, at last. There's no way that he can avoid retribution, the annihilation of all that is his and all that he is.'

The Holden stopped at Stuart Highway and so did the story, until several cars, and a road train had passed by; then they turned and headed towards the city, and the story continued.

'That night, Jacob has no sleep, only wrestling. All night he wrestles a divine visitor. In the morning he has survived, and he is a changed man. He catches up and marches ahead of his people to meet his brother and his destiny. He has found himself as he really is, in the night of wrestling with God, and now faces reality, and prepares to accept the consequences of his own past deeds. But when his brother sees that Jacob is penitent for his treachery, and ready to receive justice, he throws his arms around him and shows him grace. Jacob becomes Israel from that day – a new name to identify the one who wrestled with God.'

'It's a great old story,' Livvy said.

'Yes, it's the beginning of Israel,' said the priest, 'And the root-stock of the greatest parable of Jesus, the one about the father of the prodigal son who comes to the end of his tether in the far country, turns home and finds the father running to meet him with gracious forgiveness. Wrestling Jacob is central to the whole Judeo-Christian-Muslim interpretation of the human predicament. When all his illusions, all his idols, all his schemes, all his power and all his hope are gone, what does a man have left?"

Bridges looked across at the driver, who was obviously waiting for an answer of some kind to his question.

'I'd say he has nothing,' he said, in order to move the conversation along.

'I'd say you're wrong, Gray,' said Sheehan. 'I'd say he has only God. The story of Job spells it out in painful detail, too. When Job lost everything he had God with him in an undeniable and inescapable way. Jacob's story presents the same truth more simply. Jacob found himself wrestling with God in that up against it situation. So did Job, and so did Ron Smart.' The priest stopped talking and left his passengers to cope with the silence. When they failed to respond he added, 'I'm not sure anyone can really encounter God until they have that ultimate sort of up against it experience. It might sound weird and, perhaps cruel, but I sometimes think that leprosy has been Ron's salvation.'

'Is that what led to the big change in his attitudes?' asked Livvy, a little impatiently, growing tired of the imposed seriousness and the silence. She was still waiting for the priest to talk about Helen's situation.

'That's right,' said Dick Sheehan. 'You wouldn't believe what a morose and bitter old cynic he was.'

'There's certainly no way that you could call him that now,' said Bridges.

'No, you're absolutely right!' This time the driver affirmed his passenger. 'At the risk of being a bore, let me just say that I consider that unconverted human nature looks towards itself and hates its own faults. Then, when it turns towards others, it sees its own faults reflected there and hates them again. Given half a chance, it condemns and punishes those faults, or even tries to stamp them out in others.'

'That chimes with my own thinking about human nature,' Bridges agreed.

'And with Karl Jung's, too, I believe,' added Livvy. 'On the way we project our faults on to others.'

'Exactly', Sheehan was pleased that they were in agreement. 'The more we try to justify ourselves the more we condemn and punish others. But converted human nature looks towards God and sees what is good and true and beautiful. It may also see that it is forgiven for its own faults and is accepted and loved in spite of them all. Then, turning to others, it sees the projections of these hopeful things in others. That's how Ron Smart finally recognised the gifts and graces of those two dedicated friends of the Aboriginal people, the Simpson brothers, and their idea of Soft Aid.'

His passengers received this account of Ron's new lease of life in thoughtful silence, and the priest continued. 'It's just a delight seeing him discover the life that he's been refusing to live all these years'.

'That's an interesting way of putting it, Dick,' said Bridges. 'An old friend of mine, an Aboriginal elder actually, said to me recently, "All men've got to live life".'

'He's absolutely right,' said Sheehan enthusiastically. 'It sounds trivial and meaningless to say that we have to live our life, but it's not, you know, it's not. Most people spend years trying to live something else. The greatest gift we can ever be given is our own real life and the grace to be able to live it.'

'Did anyone ever tell you that you are like a tribal elder, Father Dick?' suggested Livvy.

Sheehan smiled. 'I don't think anyone ever did. Am I? Perhaps that's from fifteen years of hob-nobbing with them. How am I like an elder?'

'You're never in a hurry to get to the point are you?' Livvy barged in.

'Which point?' Sheehan asked in mocking voice. 'Oh…about what your reaction to Ron Smart is?'

'Yes, for goodness sake. Do you think Helen will cope with meeting old Ron? Will she be prepared? Will you tell her about him? I mean his appearance?' she asked.

'No. Nothing more than I've already told her…that he is an unusual man. He doesn't want me to say any more. We all have our little problems. Helen won't accept Ron's money until he is someone that she knows and trusts, and Ron wants to be accepted, if possible, just as he is. I'm sure he felt that he was accepted just like that by you folk today. But, the big question is, can Helen accept him like that? He insists on meeting her alone and explaining things to her himself. He's come to terms with the way he is, and he expects her to, also. At any rate, he wants to do it this way. If it turns out to be too hard for Helen to talk with him and learn to trust him, then we go back to square one and take a different approach. What do you think? Is it too much to expect?'

'Oh, wow,' Livvy was reluctant to venture an opinion. 'How do I answer that? She's young, and…'

'Helen can react pretty strongly,' Bridges put in.

'I honestly don't know,' Livvy stalled, and they travelled for a few moments in silence.

As they turned into the Catholic mission grounds she spoke again. 'The worst that could happen is that she would get a shock. It would be better if someone could be there, with her.'

The priest shook his head. 'That's not on. The arrangement is that I will take Ron to a rendezvous address, help him in, leave him to wait for her there alone, and then call back for him an hour later, after I've been to a meeting at the church.'

Livvy was thoughtful, then went on. 'I think she would take it okay, eventually. I just worry about the first reactions. She's so…so impulsive.'

'No lasting bad effects?' asked the priest.

She shook her head. 'I don't think so. I get the feeling that Helen is really a strong person. Mixed up, and not very much together, but still strong, if you know what I mean. So, I think, the deep part of her will take charge of any initial shock. She'll cope.'

They climbed out of the Holden, and Sheehan expressed his gratitude to them. He was glad to know that Livvy's assessment had more or less confirmed his own, and as they strolled to the Land Rover, he confided that now he felt easier in his mind about setting up the unusual rendezvous. The men shook hands, they all said their thanks for a valuable morning and Bridges told Sheehan that he would be in touch.

Before they parted, they all confessed to still having some misgivings about Helen and the strange situation that she was to walk into with her would-be benefactor, and agreed that they would be at the ready to help her cope if it proved to be too hard to bear. Livvy had no expectation of seeing Helen at the office today, but she knew that it would be hard to keep her out of mind for more than a few minutes at a time. Bridges, on the other hand, was determined to stop thinking about her, and leprosy, and Soft Aid, because he must get essential paper-work out of the way and give some focused time to preparation for the consultation and also for a mutually useful talk when he picked up Mani and went down to Lameroo Beach this afternoon.

Chapter 16
The Rally

They travelled towards the central city area in silence, still distracted by their conversation with the unpredictable priest they had left behind, until Livvy broke the silence. 'Well! What did you think of all that?' she asked.

'He knows how to bring a body face to face with reality, doesn't he?' Bridges replied.

'Oh, I tell you what, I was scared silly in that pool when those lepe...leprosy patients rocked up for a swim. I couldn't believe it was happening.'

'I could tell you were slightly phased,' said Bridges. 'I was a bit worried myself. For you down there in the water, I mean. It brings it home to you, though, doesn't it? What's at stake, I mean? Not just how will Helen feel, but what it means to everyone involved with the leprosy scene.'

'I'm amazed that your department has not made more PR out of this,' she said.

He was stunned. 'You do think I'm in the business of making political capital for the government, don't you? When will you get it through your head...'

'Can I help being thick-headed...?' She surprised herself with the strength of her lightning reaction.

'Oh, wait a minute.' Bridges took the Rover to the kerb and stopped it. 'I can't believe this,' he said.

'What?' she snapped. 'Believe what? What are you talking about?' She could hear what was happening. It was in her own voice as well as in his but it had nothing to do with any intentions of hers. It was happening quite independently of her will. He was so annoying sometimes! Why couldn't he see that if he would just let it go and be reasonable, then there really was nothing wrong at all? It was just that they were in a bit of a spin, or at sixes and sevens or something. Why not just leave it and get back to their regular routine, where they should be right now? Right now? It was time for lunch.

'Sandwiches at Myilly Point?' she suggested crisply.

He looked at her fiercely for a second or two before she turned to him and managed to tip her head sideways and raise her eyebrows in question. The smile she intended never surfaced.

'Okay. Suits me.' They stopped and, separately and without conversation, bought a sandwich and cool drink each, then continued in silence towards their picnic spot. Lunch in a small reserve at the end of Myilly Terrace on a headland of the peninsular where Darwin city area was built was one of the most enjoyable customs they had instituted in their shared life. It was not far from either of their offices, and looked across the harbour mouth to a distant line of blue hills. It turned them away from the built urban world, whose systems controlled so much of their waking lives, to the infinities of nature. As they walked to the deep shade of a small tree, the harbour surface flashed constantly with thousands of signals in tribute to the dominion, power and glory of the midday sun.

'Here?' Bridges said obviously trying to relax.

Livvy realized that he was trying to be civil and friendly. He deserved the benefit of the doubt, and she prepared to put the nonsense quarrel behind them and turn away from personal remarks to a safe topic on common ground where they shared positive mutual interest. After all, the annoyance that had unsettled them might be due to a build-up of things in the back of her mind. Maybe Bridges was feeling that way too. There certainly were some unusual things going on.

'You know,' she said, as they settled themselves on the grass and unpacked their sandwiches and cartons of iced drinks, 'Father Dick left too much up in the air. It seems to me, he just touched on things, opened up too many big issues, without us having the chance to deal with them. It's one more disturbing thing to have to cope with. I think that's why I'm a bit…irritable?'

'Is that an apology I hear?' He was smiling, but a shade too victorious for her to yield. She despaired of talking freely with this man who seemed hell-bent on needling her, but replied quietly with her pride intact.

'Not really,' she told him, and bit into a sandwich before adding, 'It's an explanation, if you're interested in trying to understand where I am.'

'Tell me about it, honey.' He settled back on his elbow to hear whatever she had to tell him. It took most of a minute for her to relax and begin to express the underlying unease that she felt. She talked about the reasons why they had gone to East Arm Leprosarium.

'I feel something within me that as yet I can't clearly articulate.' There is something that's happening,' she said. 'I know I'm inclined to be academic at times, but I'm not an academic…I'm a field worker, a practitioner…and if I do say so myself, a dedicated one. I care about people, and all my research is aimed back at the social process, to protect existing life-ways that are under threat, or to contribute to reform. You know what I mean? You've heard it all before.'

His nod told her that he had indeed heard it all before, but was listening and ready to hear it, or anything else, again.

'Don't you feel things, unusual and dangerous things, coming to a head?' she said. 'Like the build up before a thunderstorm?'

'Not really, not like that,' he said. 'But, yes. There are certain things we've been hearing about in these last couple of days that could be heading towards flash points.'

'It's more than that!' she insisted, and proceeded to tell him what more it was. 'We both know that there were stirrings of urban Aboriginal protest in Darwin in the seventies, but what happened to it? Where did it go? It's just gone underground if you ask me. It is still here and now it's stirring and likely to erupt into the open again.'

He resisted the impulse to simply agree with her. Her general comment seemed correct but not discriminating enough. 'Maybe there's a build up of protest, but I don't see a huge storm approaching.'

'Huge storm or not a huge storm', she was seething. 'What's it matter? If you see the build-up, why can't you just say it's so! Is it so hard to accept that I just might be right? Do you or don't you agree with what I'm saying?'

He stared at her before replying with an undefeated calmness.

'First let me say that I can't agree that you sound very reasonable right at the moment. Are you interested in hearing what I think, or just wanting to chew me out?'

'Ooh, you make me mad sometimes, with your superior attitudes!'

'I don't want to be superior! What superior attitudes?'

She expelled the air that she had ready for a powerful come-back, and turned away towards the sea before continuing in a less confrontational way.

'Out at Malangarri one of the Aboriginal teachers...a young man, told me that his people always say they can't understand why the government doesn't keep all its money,' she said. 'And let the people keep all their land. I've heard others say the same.'

'Could be,' he agreed

'No it isn't. Don't you see?' She was excited now. It was becoming clear to her. 'That's it! That's what connects these things all together. At least, it's what's given me this gut feeling that we are nearing a flash-point or...or...a showdown, or something. Things are happening today that didn't before, and the way they happen in the future will depend on how it is all handled right now.'

'There are special times, though, aren't there?' she insisted.

'Like turning points in history. All I'm saying is that, right where we are, things are moving towards a significant turning point and the future of many people are at stake. It's when people have a common desperation to have their needs met that they may eventually consider revolution as a justifiable option.'

'Of course there's another reason why you might have a sense of an impending storm.' He waited to see if she was prepared to hear his comment.

'Oh, don't talk to me about weather patterns. I'm talking about social realities and how I feel, not about the weather!' Her exasperation ran over. 'It's no wonder I feel it's useless talking to you sometimes.'

He couldn't think of anything that he might legitimately say after that. He just looked towards the sea and waited, until Livvy resumed.

Even more exasperated by his eloquent silence, she said, 'I'm so glad Armstrong has come to town!'

To both of them it seemed like the most provocative thing that she could have said at that particular moment, and she wondered why it was so important to her to say it, why the urge to have it said over-rode her concern for having good feeling in their relationship.

'You are?' he said, deliberately speaking quietly. 'I'm happy for you then!' His sarcasm was heavy. 'But please don't expect me to be glad. Armstrong has to do what Armstrong has to do. I just wish he hadn't picked now to do it! These justice issues are vital, but not more important than getting real communication going. He could set back progress in positive relations by ten years or more.'

'He's doing a great service to the whole nation,' she said dogmatically. 'Can't you see that? You can't, can you? I wouldn't expect that you could… and that's what worries me, Gray. Here a man comes to town to challenge us all, to stand up and be counted, for or against the Aboriginal sector of our society. I know I'm for them, Gray… but I'm not sure about you any more. Oh, I know that your sentiments are all their way, but is that enough?

He started to reply but she continued, 'No, don't stop me, darling. Let me say it, it's got to be said. We might find ourselves toeing the line from opposite sides when the crunch comes.'

'Oh, come off it, honey!' he was out of patience. 'Have you ever met this Armstrong guy, or heard anything he has to say? Is he automatically right… the awaited Messiah, or something, just because he's a black agitator?'

'There you see,' she seized her advantage. 'You even use the language of the political reactionaries. How do you know he's an agitator? And what's being a black, as you call him, got to do with anything? What right do you have to condemn him as an agitator? And besides, what if he is an agitator? Someone had better agitate to get this country looking honestly at the social realities, or we're going to drift further and further into white racism and fascism…'

He was insenced, stood up and said, 'I'll drop you off at Smith Street and call for you at four-thirty, okay?' he said, as he headed towards the car.

'Good,' she said flatly.

Give up, he told himself, slipping the car into forward gear and moving out towards Smith Street. Arriving at her drop off point he pulled over.

'Bye,' she said with brisk, cold politeness, springing out, slamming the door behind her and striding across the road.

He took the Rover directly across to Mitchell Street to avoid the midday shoppers in down-town Smith Street, and felt the tension rising as he drove across Knuckey only two blocks from Chan Building and the encounter with his superiors. Suddenly he was struck by a fresh inspiration, like a wind off the sea, and realised again that he had no ultimate need of Archer's or Blyth's approval, nor even Livvy's when it came right down to what was essential. As long as he was consistent with the truth that was in him, did what he saw to be right himself, then he could act with his own approval. Too many people were taking simplistic approaches to the big issues affecting Aboriginal people's futures, and he currently found it hard to line up with any of them. If that meant a fight with Ned and Fred, so be it; and if Livvy thought she could tyrannise him by her moodiness she was welcome to try. Purist anthropologists could be manipulative tyrants, just as surely as politicians could. But he was sure that one of the answers to current dissatisfaction was real, open, consultation, genuine dialogue. That's what I'm committed to, he reminded himself, and, by God, that's what I'll fight for, if they want a fight. People have got to listen to each other, and learn to honour each other, otherwise we might as well all give up. On the road between the broad steps of the Supreme Court building and the small public park along on the opposite side, a dozen or so people were milling about. Apparently there was some sort of commotion in the park. A police officer was trying to move along two men who were in the middle of the road and shouting abuse at each other. One was retaliating as he backed away, but being drowned by the full-throated shouting of the other. It was the old man, Bilago, who was backing off, whom Bridges had last seen on the previous evening, asleep at Lionel Gellies' house. He was obviously in better shape now than he had been then. The other man, who clearly had the better of him in the slanging match, was a young, fair-haired white man in the tropical rig of a white-collar worker, and he was bearing down on the hapless Bilago with a tirade of abuse.

'Don't give me that you lazy old black bludger. We owe you nothing.' Bridges caught the words as he slowed to pass by in the centre of the road.

'Too bloody right!' Bilago was shouting. 'Since that old Captain Cook 'e come up aroun' this way!'

Behind them, a hundred or so people were standing about under the trees, giving attention to someone at a microphone on a low dais. Bridges caught sight of a slogan on a long banner hanging behind the speaker, an Aboriginal man in stockman rig. The words "Land and Liberation" showed in large red capitals on white and black.

'Gray!'

He turned at the sound of his name to see Lionel Gellies and Helen Cross on the opposite footpath, both standing alongside the yellow Mini, illegally parked in front of the Supreme Court. A glance revealed that Lionel was in trouble. Helen seemed to be upset, and the tall blonde man was bending over her, apparently trying to calm her.

Without hesitation Bridges took a quick glance in his mirror and swung the wheel to bring the Rover around behind the Mini. Lionel was looking his way and apparently trying to draw Helen's attention to the new arrival, as though wanting to divert her from whatever was upsetting her.

Bridges scrambled out calling. 'Fancy seeing you here. What's going on?'

'Hi, Gray.' Lionel sounded calm. 'Oh, we came along with Mani to have a listen to Stan Armstrong. I thought I might record him, but I might have to let that go.'

'You came with Mani?' Bridges did not bother to hide his alarm at the news. Wasn't Mani supposed to be coming to the beach for a talk with himself?

'Yes,' said Lionel, 'Mani and…'

'And him!' snapped Helen, thrusting a finger through the air in the general direction of the old man, Bilago, who was in the process of mounting the opposite gutter-kerb, assisted by none other than Bridges' well-groomed colleague, Andrew Brown. 'They better keep that old bastard away from me,' snarled the disturbed girl, shaking feverishly.

Lionel put his arm about her shoulders and spoke quietly. 'Would you like to get in the car Helen?'

'No! I bloody-well wouldn't,' she snapped without shifting. She was beginning to show a fascination with events on the other footpath. The policeman had ushered Bilago's antagonist and the others across the pavement to the crowded lawn area, and was talking quietly with several of the others, both Aboriginal and white, who were arguing loudly.

Lionel went on with his account of bringing Mani to the park. 'As I was saying, Mani came around to see me about something…'

'Right, to record his rehearsal for tonight's speech at the Y, wasn't it?' Bridges asked, in order that Lionel might see him as an intimate friend of Mani's.

'Yes…You know about that, do you?' Lionel appeared pleased.

'Well, Annette stayed home today. She's got a big night coming up tonight, too. So she decided to take it easy today. Which I thought was sensible. Then, Mani was nearly finished recording, when this visitor chap from Queensland, Armstrong, arrived with a local guy. They seemed to know Mani was there.'

'They knew he was there?' Bridges was feeling desperate about getting alongside Mani. 'Where is he now? Mani, I mean.'

'Over there somewhere,' Lionel nodded at the park, then added quietly, 'Helen wanted to come along with him, too. To see what the Aboriginal people have to say for themselves.'

'Till you let that stinkin' old black shit get in the car with me!' Helen barked at him, but made no move to separate herself from his comforting touch.

'Yes, I know,' Lionel sounded sympathetic. 'I'm sorry I did something that upset you Helen. But the poor old man was camped in our front garden. I thought he had left during the night. I really thought I should give him a lift into town.'

'Well, what about me?' she snapped. 'You don't bloody care if it upsets me?'

'Yes I do,' he insisted. 'But I had to think of my sister, too. Do you think it would have been right to leave the old man hanging around our place with Annie in there and not feeling well, and all?'

Helen seemed to see some point in what Lionel was saying, but it no longer held any interest for Bridges, who began to move off, looking from one cluster of people to another in the hope of sighting Mani.

'See you Gray,' Lionel called.

'Yeah, right,' Bridges turned his head to call back as he moved on across the road. 'See you tonight at the Y.'

Nowhere could he see Andrew Brown or Bilago. It appeared that they had gone around to the far side of the crowd, which was larger than it had appeared to be from the oppossite side of the road. Several office girls were nibbling lunches and giggling at a group of male clerks with lusty egos and voices, who were heckling the speaker, a black stockman with limited English but apparently limitless courage. He was proclaiming his opinions fearlessly.

'Aaaarh! Get out with yah!' One of the clerks shouted at him provocatively. 'Your mob had it for forty thousand years, an' you didn't do anything with it. You didn't know how'ta.'

The stockman was clearly aware of the shouting that was aimed at him from several directions, but was deliberately ignoring it, either by design or necessity. If he had replies to offer, he had chosen to keep them to himself. With no attempt at countering the hecklers, he pushed on with determination to get said what he had set out to say.

'Anyway,' he shouted into the microphone. 'Wot I reckon is…first thing us people of the land gotta do, we gotta leave the grog alone…'He stared at a couple of groups of Aboriginal people at the back of the crowd. 'We got plenty trouble, anyway. But we got more if we drink grog. Some people, they, they want us to drink grog. Some they try 'an make us.' He waited while a wave of laughter passed in response to something shouted by one of the clerks. 'Ev'n…ev'n when some of us blokes give it up. When we 'eard the Word of God, 'an we come to be Christian, 'an we say no more grog. Well, dem pub-keepers out in the bush, they say, come on boys, we'll give you free grog. They want us to drink it. They can get the money or even no money sometimes, and we can die and go to 'ell! What do we say? We say, No! No more! Our men can't die. We gotta keep all our men livin' and work together. Women too, they drink grog. It's a shame on them, and their family. Children too, sniffin petrol and killin their brains. Save the people's brains, an' d' women, an d' children, an' d' men. No more grog, only sober people together, an' we can be strong, all d' people, like before.'

The clerks were shouting again, to the amusement of the giggling girls, as Bridges moved around to the back of the dais. He saw Mani talking with a tall athletic Aboriginal man with tan skin, afro hair, dark glasses, black slacks and shirt, and with a black fabric bag on a strap over one shoulder. Behind them he caught sight of Harry Bagent edging his way towards the dais, as the stockman prepared to step down. Bridges's shock, at seeing the young Aboriginal Liaison Officer, Harry, obviously involved in the event, was quickly followed by a heightened sense of doom. Perhaps Livvy was right, a storm was brewing. Whatever else broke loose, when the word reached Archer and Blyth that one of their Liaison Officers was one of Armstrong's cronies, for so it seemed he was, there would be all hell to pay.

Clearly the man in black was none other than the fabled crusader from Queensland,

and he seemed very interested in Mani, as he gestured to show that he wanted the young Goose Islander to move closer to the dais. Mani shifted up in response to the signal, and Bridges quickly strode over to join them.

'G'day,' he said over Mani's shoulder, and the wide eyes that looked around at him were filled with apprehension.

'Oh, g'day, er, Gray,' he relaxed noticeably, and moved sideways to make room. 'Good to see yah!' He smiled and went on. 'Do you know Stan? Ay, Stan. You met Gray? Gray Bridges?'

The black-clad man turned his hidden eyes on the newcomer and leaned towards him with an explanation as he prepared to move away towards the dais.

'Excuse me, won't you?' he addressed Bridges. 'I want to catch Harry's speech. One of our people, he is.'

'One of ours, too,' Bridges said quietly and too late for the Queenslander to hear it. He had already moved and was signaling to Mani to follow. Before Mani could move, Bridges caught him in the crook of his arm and gently restrained him.

'Can I speak to you, Mani?' he said. 'It looks like we won't fit in talking down at the beach later on…'

'Oh? Yeah! This came up,' said Mani looking even more worried. 'We could still go to the beach later on, though.'

Before Bridges could reply the amplifier on a nearby tree blared with Harry's strident voice, distorted from being too near the microphone.

'Yah see? Wha'd I tell yah? This is a day when the black voice of this country is gonna be 'eard. We only got half an hour. The very kind City Council of this city has given us a half an hour to talk to you in our own country. We got a young tribal leader comin up 'ere to speak to youse in a minute…'

Bridges decided not to wait to hear what came next. He knew already who the tribal speaker was. He was looking into his face.

'Listen, Mani,' he spoke loudly and close to the other man's ear to be sure of being heard. 'Why are you getting mixed up with Armstrong's mob? Are they on about the same things as you?'

'I dunno. Probably not,' said Mani with a slightly foolish grin. 'But they give me a chance to say what I want to say.'

'Who do you want to say it to, Mani?'

'I wanna to speak to everybody.'

'Everybody?'
'Everybody who can make things better for my people.'
'The Government?'
'Bye and bye, government, too. Yes.'
'The Chief Minister?'
'Yeah, him too!'
'Come with me, then.'
'What? Where?'

Bridges turned and waved towards Mitchell Street and the government buildings. 'Come down to my office and I'll arrange for you to talk with Edward Blyth today.' He realised as he said it that he had no way of guaranteeing that the Chief Minister would even be in the office today, but he was desperate and was prepared to do everything that he could to keep the channels open between the Goose Islanders and the Government.

'Okay, me boy,' Armstrong grabbed Mani's arm and dragged him. 'You're on!'

Mani stood his ground, pulled his arm free, and stared at the dark glasses that turned towards him. All he said, before moving off with Bridges was, 'who's your boy?'

Armstrong caught up and walked alongside his departing recruit. 'You going then, Malcolm? Okay brother. That's your choice. Just don't let these great white fathers put anything over on you, right?'

'Right, Stanley?' Mani agreed heartily. 'You're right now. I'm gonna let no-one put anything over on me.'
'You're still coming to speak at the rally tonight, aren't you?' Armstrong asked.
'Did I say I was?' Mani asked with what sounded like a challenge.
'You did, yes. That's what you said!' Armstrong declared.
'Well, why are you askin' me?' Mani was blunt, and kept moving towards the footpath.
'Great, bro. See you there. You want me to pick you up?' the black crusader offered.
'No. I'm Arardbi. We foot-walk all the time. See yah.'

Mani came back alongside Bridges just as that unhappy driver remembered where he had parked his car and looked across to the no parking zone by the Supreme Court steps. The Mini had gone, but his Land Rover was still there, the object of serious attention by a policeman with a note pad.

'Oh, no!' he groaned. 'Quick, Mani, my car's over here.' He sprinted across the road, arriving just too late to say anything before the officer had finished marking his pad and was pulling a leaf off it.

'I'm sorry officer,' Bridges was abject. 'That was a sort of emergency. I had no intention of parking here…'

The bronzed face under the peaked cap with its incongruently black and white checkered band, stared at him steadily with the squint of one who had served too many seasons out of doors in inland glare.

'Your car?'

'Yes, it is. I…' Bridges began.

'See your license? You have got a license?'

By this time Mani had arrived, and seemed vaguely amused when Bridges glanced at him.

'Sure, my license is in the glove-box, I…er… hope,' he mumbled as he opened the car and began rummaging. It was there. At least he was saved the humiliation of a lost license. The officer was satisfied after checking the date on the license, 'one hundred eighty-five dollars,' he said drily. 'You can go straight up the court-house steps, and pay along at the office right now or anytime within…'

'But officer I was only here a few…'

'Or,' the droll policeman interrupted. 'If you want to plead diminished responsibility, you can let it come before the magistrate and tell him your story. Now, move along…and read the signs in future.'

Further talk was pointless. Bridges and Mani quietly made their way into the vehicle and drove off to go around the block and back to Chan Building. Bridges was unsure of the legality of a u-turn in that part of the street and took the longer route rather than risk another encounter with the flinty policeman.

Beside him Mani was quietly laughing at his embarrassment; and the more Bridges complained about the unreasonableness of the policeman the more amused was his passenger.

'I can't see that it's as funny as all that!' he said, trying to find a smile.

'Oh, it is Gray. It is!' Mani assured him. 'Anyway,' he tried to stop laughing. 'You can talk to the Chief Minister, eh?"

The embarrassed driver chose not to answer, but took a quick look at his grinning questioner, then asked, 'What are you getting at?'

'Oh, nothin' really,' Mani replied. 'Only it's funny. I think it's funny. You can take me up and talk to the Chief Minister, but you can't say anything to that policeman.'

Bridges wagged his head, looking for the right phrase before saying, 'It's not exactly like that, Mani.'

'Yes,' the young Arardbi insisted. 'It is like that. That is just what it is like, because that is what it is. You know what Gray? That policeman gave me a different feeling. 'e gave me a new hope. I like that policeman, 'es a real law-man.'

'Thanks a lot, mate.'

'No, no, you don't get my meaning,' Mani told him. 'He only did what was the law way. No talk, no argument. No two ways, only one way. Just like a true Arardbi. We do that way. When we know the Lore we do it. Everyone has to come under the Lore. What do you reckon if the Chief Minister parked his car there? Will that policeman give him a ticket, too?'

'That bloke would probably give a ticket to the Queen,' Bridges said emphatically, and set Mani laughing again.

'You see?' the delighted young man said. 'That's what I say. He is a proper Lawman. The Queen is under the same Law. I wish he could talk for us in your conference when the Balandas start to ask questions about our Land Rights. We got lores now, Gray.' He became serious as he went on. 'Lores from the ancestors, and even Balanda Laws, and everyone who knows those Lores knows that we people of the land have to keep our own father country and mother country lands. Everyone knows that. And that policeman made me hope a little bit more they're gonna say the proper Law way if anyone starts to try to push us away from our own country again.'

Bridges was nodding and managed a rudimentary smile as they stopped in the parking area adjacent to Chan Building.

'As I've said before,' he told Mani. 'You and I are two of the most important people alive when it comes to making sure that everyone works together on these things. I don't know what we can expect from the Chief Minister today, but I'm all in favour of people meeting each other, and talking together. That way we come to be real to each other. But I agree with Armstrong. You'll need to be careful that they, we, Balanda heavies, don't try to win you over to our way of thinking, with soft words and hot dinners. You know what I mean? But you want to have your say, and I want the Head of Government of this Territory to hear you. And I want you two men to start to make each other listen. Blyth's got a lot of weight on his side. He won't need any back up from me, and I won't poke my nose into your affairs either. But if you want back-up you give me the nod, because I really want to be sure Blyth hears what you are saying… Right?'

'Yeah, thanks Gray. I'll remember,' said Mani. 'In here, eh?'

'He should be, Mani,' said Bridges. 'He should be. Let's go see.'

Chapter 17
Mani takes his chance

The air inside the Chan Building was cold on Mani's face and arms as he entered the door Bridges held open. He had never been in there before. In fact he would not have been able to say which of the multi-storied buildings at the waterfront end of Mitchell Street housed the Chief Minister's offices. He could have identified the large white bungalow on the hillside above the wharves just beyond the end of the street, being the Government House, and the man whom the Balandas called The Administrator lived there. He was something of a ceremonial elder, who checked to make sure that the laws politicians invented fitted in with the one's that already had been handed down from the ancestors or from the Canberra Government. That building had a clear story, a mayali. It pointed to many things, of which it was itself a part, in the life of the land in this part of the world. But the place he had just entered and whose stairs he now was climbing, with this true or false Balanda friend, had only vague meaning for him. He was climbing into a place of the Number One Mister Talltree of the bossy white society, which, before he had been born, had conquered, and now dominated his people.

Fear rose with every step they mounted. He glanced at Bridges to locate his feelings with someone familiar, and found the other man looking at him.

'Have you ever met Edward Blyth, Mani?'

'No, not really,' Mani replied, feeling easier as he spoke. 'Only heard him on the radio and TV and once when he came to Batchelor College.'

'He's not a bad bloke,' Bridges assured him. 'Sounds tough: and he can be tough, real tough, and often is, with his staff. But he knows how to listen. He'll listen if you state what you have to say strongly and clearly. If you whisper and mumble, and sound weak then he'll treat you like that. But if you present yourself as someone who expects to be heard and respected, he'll hear you and respect you. You know what I mean? Strongly and clearly.'

'Yeah, thanks for saying it, Gray. I know what you mean,'

From the top landing they went through to a large work area.

'My office is along here,' Bridges said. 'I know I don't have to say it again, but remember, make him hear what you think and feel, Mani. Blyth respects strength.'

'That's good!' Mani was scanning the open space coming into view as they went towards the private office area. About a dozen desks occupied the open space, and behind a couple of them sat liaison staff members, silently watching and listening to several other, standing together nearby, intensely involved in conversation.
'Hey, Gray!' One of the group came towards them between the desks. 'You heard about our lunch hour? What's going on? We been talkin', and we all reckon it's not right.'

The speaker was a middle-aged, urban Aboriginal man. Mani had seen him about town, but never met him before.

'What d'you mean about your lunch hour, Albie?' Bridges asked. 'No-one allowed to take the early hour today. They only told us when we come in this mornin'. Whadda you reckon? It's not right, is it? It's this rally in the park. Old Archer just come up to us 'an said that, yah all gotta take late lunch today, and yah godda stay 'ere.'
'And you all stayed?' Bridges sounded critical. 'What could old Fred've done if you all took your usual break?'
'We try to do what we reckon's right if we can. It's caused a stink in 'ere, I can tell yah. There's not much work gittin done.'

Bridges looked about, and noted that all the staff seemed to be present except for Harry Bagent and Andrew Brown.

'I know two who didn't stay," he said.
'Bagent and Uncle Tom,' the other man confirmed. 'Yeah, I know! That's not right, eh? They let Old Uncle Tom Brown go to that rally, so he can see who's playin up and report to his white masters. Well, Bagent just said if 'e can go, so can I. An' 'e went. But us others, we reckoned, well, if we all go an' get the sack what's gonna appen to our work 'ere an' all that.'
'We each hafta do what we hafta do, Albie.' Bridges declared.
'You do what you reckon is right and Harry does, too,' said Bridges. 'Is Archer in, do you know?'
'Yeah, yeah…'es in there with Ned the Head an one 'o them Health Department dandies.'

As he spoke, the door at the end of the corridor opened and Cecil Reeders appeared. The Chief Minister was seeing him out with Archer shadowing him.

'Sure, sure. Right, right. Yeah, yup,' Blyth agreed emphatically with whatever it was that Cecil Reeders was still saying as they drew near. 'Oh, look, Cec...I don't think that at all. No, no, no way. I appreciate your calling. Feel free any time. Right, see you later.'

As he strode by, the Director of the Department of Health looked pleased with himself and smiled as he nodded to Bridges and glanced at the tribal and urban men beside him.

'Any way, Albie,' said Bridges, preparing to move after Blyth. 'Meet Mani Manggululu, from Goose Island.'

Before the two could say a word Bridges had gone.

Bridges called to the Chief Minister before he re-entered his office, 'Mister Blyth!' And as the young Head of Government turned he made the request, 'could I have a word with you, Chief?'

Mani had never heard the Chief Minister referred to as 'Chief', and had not expected ever to hear anyone referred to as a chief. It was centuries since Arardbis had allowed anyone to be a total chief, except for an occasional man of violence who terrorised his locality into submission. He knew that Africans and some others still had chiefs, but he had not realised that Balandas believed in chieftainship. Perhaps it was a game. Maybe Bridges was just trying to make the young politician feel important.

'You been at that rally?' Albie asked the Goose Islander.
'Uh, yeah. I was there for a few minutes.' Mani was preoccupied with what was happening between Bridges and the Chief Minister. The communication expert was being called on to be a good listener. Both the Chief Minister and Archer were agitated and were trying to impress Bridges with the seriousness of something or other.
'I'll have that little bastard's head!' the Chief Minister let himself be heard, and caused a few wide eyes to turn his way. 'Who the hell does he think he's foolin' with? When he comes in tell him to go to buggery… he's sacked!'

This last instruction was addressed to Archer, but loudly enough for everyone to hear.

When Bridges interrupted with a note of caution. 'Do you think that's wise Mister Chief Minister?'

'Wise...or not!' Blyth said. 'He walks today…'
'That might be playing right into their hands?' Bridges continued.
'Whose hands?' Blyth was clearly worried by this suggestion.
'Well, anyone, like the guys running this rally. Anyone who wants our indigenous staff members, who are listening in to all this, to think you have an unfriendly policy… and those who want to discredit the Government and drive a wedge between you and the Aboriginal people,' said Bridges.

'Bloody hell!' was the last thing the listening Liaison Officers heard, as the voices in the passageway dropped to a normal talking level; but they all noticed that Blyth and Archer drew nearer to Bridges and watched his face intently as he spoke to them quietly.

'All right,' the Chief Minister was still in command of the situation, and once more in control of his feelings. 'If that's the way it is, why aren't you down there getting him up here?'

Mani heard these words and wondered if they referred to Bagent, the delinquent Liaison Officer, or himself. He still wondered, when, after another remark from Bridges, Blyth and Archer looked his way. Albie suddenly seemed to become self-conscious and told Mani, as he moved towards his desk, 'Anyway, mate, I'll see you round, okay? Good on ya.'

The talk between the three Balandas dropped to a confidential quietness and Bridges led the way over to Mani.

'Mr Chief Minister,' he said. 'May I present to you Malcolm Manggululu of Goose Island?'

'I'm pleased to meet you at last, Malcolm,' said Blyth, extending his hand to grasp Mani's. 'I've often heard of you, and wished to get to know you. I'm glad you made time to call in. Will you come in for a few minutes?' He was the essence of calm and dignified friendliness, and Mani marvelled at his emotional flexibility and control. Bridges moved to follow them into the room, but Archer stepped in front of him.

'You know what you've gotta do,' said the Unit Director.

'I might be needed in there,' said Bridges on principle. 'You know, cross-cultural communication...er, the Chief told me to stick close to Mani.'

'He doesn't need you now, does he?' the Director told him. 'You'd better go and do what the Chief Minister told you to do. Get Bagent out of that demonstration, and back up here!'

Once more Bridges seethed at the arrogance of Archer, who couldn't accept the fact that the Communication Consultant was directly answerable only to Blyth. But he prepared to move away on principle, as a way of demonstrating his trust in Mani to say what he wanted to say, and a way to keep all of their relationships as relaxed as possible. He was elated. It was a momentous achievement, to have brought the two protagonists together. Ned and Mani were in a situation where a real encounter between them was practically unavoidable. The stage was theirs, and man to man they must improvise their stance and play out this scene free of interference from him or anyone else. There could be a real meeting of minds here today.

Mani hesitated at the door looking for Bridges, reluctant to be left alone with the Head of Government; but Bridges simply raised a clenched fist to the pectoral part of his chest, as he turned away, and withdrew along the corridor. Mani read the hand signal, 'Ned Blyth respects strength.'

'Come in,' said the Chief Minister. 'Take a seat.'

Archer came in, too, closing the door quietly behind him. The door closing gave the young islander some moments of anxiety. They've trapped me in here, he thought. If I need to get out, can I? But he quickly dealt with his fears, telling himself that he was no more trapped than the other two. In fact, he reasoned, if I want to get out of here I can just stand and leave; but these two men had better take care. They are trapped in here with me, too, and where can they run if I start to hit them with the truth? Blyth respects strength...does he? Good. He respects strength: I won't forget it. And what about this other bloke? He glanced at Fred Archer and saw a man waiting for indications of his master's will. Ned Blyth respects strength and Archer is his slave. Blyth does not respect Archer; and Archer will jump when he is told. Mani decided to ignore Archer and deal exclusively with the Chief Minister.

'Come over here. Sit here,' Blyth invited his guest.

'Can I stand up?' Mani stood tall with his feet slightly apart and arms folded loosely across his chest, staring at the Chief Minister, who haltingly moved behind his desk as he spoke.

'Sure Yes...If that's what you want. Stand and grow good, eh?'

'I'm already grown, Mister Blyth,' Mani said firmly with fixed gaze and expressionless face.

'Ha! Right, yes. Of course you are.' The politician made the most of his embarrassment. 'My clumsy words. Just a figure of speech.'

'I'm sorry, Mister Blyth,' Mani told him in the same cold tone. 'I don't know what you're tryen ta say.'

'Well, I'm, er...forget it.' said Blyth. 'Now that you're here. Are you sure you won't sit down?'

'I'm sure, Mister Blyth,' Mani declared. 'Always I try to be sure. But I'll sit down if you sit down.'

The Chief Minister smiled wryly and sat behind his desk. There were two chrome and blue vinyl chairs, one either side of the desk. He indicated one, but Mani sat in the other, so that his back was to the window, and he had the advantage of seeing the other man's face in natural light while his own was shadowed.

Archer moved to the unoccupied chair, and when no sign was given to forbid it, he also sat.

'Look, Malcolm,' the Chief Minister was getting down to serious business. 'You and I both know why you are here, don't we?'

'It's good to hear you say that, Mister Blyth,' Mani was surprised to hear himself speak so boldly, and made a mental effort to hold down his feeling level. 'Because I know why I'm here, and if you know too, then I don't need to tell you.'

'Yes, well, er...' Blyth sensed a criticism and opted for a diplomatic approach, reminding himself that he and his Ministers were going to give an outstanding performance of listening to Aborigines. 'I'd be really interested to hear what you have in mind, Malcolm.' He sat back.

'It might take a long time to tell you my mind, Mister Blyth,' Mani told him. 'Are you sure you really want to know what I think?'

'Of course I do,' Blyth assured him. 'That is to say, if you can tell me what you think about...er, you know, anything you're worried about.'

'Ah!' Mani looked at the floor and then at Blyth. 'Ah, anything, eh? Well, mostly I worry about the war.'

'The war?' Blyth was startled. 'What war?'

'The land war,' Mani stated simply. 'The war that still goes on ever since the first English settlement...even up till now.' Mani continued to stare at the Chief Minister.

'Oh, now, come on, Malcolm,' the head of government reasoned. 'You have protection these days...real land rights.'

'True,' the young man agreed. 'But we always had land rights. Only the Balanda Law was slow to catch up. All the time we had the rights, but still people killed us and took our land. Today it's a bit different, but still people want to be tricky, and take away the new Balanda Law and then take away our land. Used to be they killed us fast, now they work out more ways to kill us slow.'

The Chief Minister leaned forward and vowed, 'You have my solemn promise that my government will not allow anyone to erode the legal rights of your people to land Malcolm. Have no doubts, your people's rights are safe, and will be respected. That's one of the things I want your people to hear clearly at the consultation we'll be having.'

'Ah,' said Mani again. 'I thought Bridges told me you were having a consultation so you could hear what we community people have to say to your Government.'

'Look, Malcolm,' the Chief Minister was beginning to grow tired of the young man's manner. 'Some of us are dedicated to working for the good of your people.'

'Yes, I know that, too, Mister Blyth,' the Goose Islander sat back and sighed before going on. 'And that should be a good thing.' He shook his head and the other men waited for him to complete his comment. But instead he looked at Fred Archer despairingly and shook his head again. Archer glanced from the window to the floor, to his Chief's desk, then the great man's face, which was still turned towards Mani, and back to that young man himself. Archer was a picture of discomfort.

'Can you say a bit more, Malcolm?' the Chief Minister encouraged.

Mani leaned forward. 'I know many people are dedicated to working for the good of the people of the land, my people…That's the trouble.'

'What trouble? What do you mean, Malcolm? Explain it to me, will you?'

'I'm not very good at explainen things, Mister Blyth.' Mani told him. 'That's your way, in your culture. Balanda people are very, very good at explainen and explainen and explainen. In our way, I like to look at what is really there, and say it, not explain it with a lot of opinions, an'…an' more questions.'

'And what do you see? What is there, Malcolm?' the Chief Minister was listening beautifully. It took patience, but he was managing his own reactions masterfully and playing the line out to the Goose Islander with real sensitivity. 'Go ahead, help me to see what you can see is really there.'

Mani shook his head again. This time he smiled as he said, 'I can't help yah to see, Mister Chief Minister. You see it all so much better than me. I'm just an island man, and a student, but you can see the whole Territory.'

'That's probably true…'

'Still I can ask you what you can see…'

'Mani seized the initiative that he'd been offered. 'And I ask you, where does most of the money of the Territory come from?'

'I beg your pardon?' Blyth could not believe that he had heard the young man ask a question about revenue.

'Money…State income, Mister Blyth. Can yah tell me where it comes from?'

'Why…yes…of course,' the Chief Minister of the Territory sat forward with fingers locked on his desk-top. 'Live cattle and beef exports…'

'Not much,' Mani commented. 'Second and third grade beef, and too many poor seasons.'

'Right! That's true. I see you're well-informed,' Blyth shifted in his chair.

'What else?' Mani pursued his quarry.

'Mining.'

'Aha, I thought so, too,' said Mani. 'But still not much, am I right? Comin' up a little bit now with some new uranium mines?'

'Right again,' Blyth agreed. 'Mining could be very big in the Territory. It could bring real prosperity. Economic strength to get all that we need to meet everyone's needs.'

'I spose that's important for people who can't live with what the land and sea gives them in a natural way,' Mani said it as though it was of no importance to him. 'What other revenue bringers, Mister Blyth?'

'Oh, tourism, and a little from agriculture and secondary industries.'

'Very, very little?'

'Very little compared to our total budget needs, but growing.'

'And that's all?' Mani knew that he had created an awkward moment for Blyth. It had been his intention to do so, and it gave him a sense of satisfaction to have achieved his aim.

'Nuthin else, Mister Blyth?'

Blyth sat back and put a couple of fingers up to his cheek as he went on thoughtfully. 'In the strict sense of income from industries, that's just about all… but, of course, much of our revenue is derived from Commonwealth funding. Is that what you're getting at, Malcolm?'

'Yes, sir.' Mani was direct. 'That's what I'm getting at. How much do you get for the Aboriginal Industry?'

'That's a strange way to speak about Aboriginal Affairs, Malcolm?' the Head of Government said. 'You know of course that the programme in the Territory is light years ahead of the other States? This is one of our major commitments, and…'

'And money spinners?' Mani asked innocently.

'Of course funding comes into the Territory from the Commonwealth Government, to finance the health, education, welfare and development programmes amongst Aborigines. It's just as well for your people that it does. There's no way in the world that the Territory could afford to finance such things from its own production.'

Mani stood up suddenly, then said. 'Sorry, can I stretch me legs?' His heart was racing. He turned his back to the desk and walked across to the window. It overlooked the car-park where a tired-looking flame tree stood in a small square garden plot. In four or five months' time, towards the end of the Long Dry, that tree would burst into brilliant new life. It looked weak now, with roots under the tarmac and shining modern cars on every side; but he knew the tenacious life of the tree, and it spoke to him about his position in the room, surrounded by the power of the modern nation. He felt like a dry little tree, but the life that was in him could still show itself. He spoke quietly.

'I always wonder why the government can't keep all that money and just let us keep all our land…Then we could still manage everything ourselves.' He turned towards the desk, and Blyth, who had begun to make scribbled notes, suddenly looked up to find Mani standing directly in front of him with his hands flat on the desk.

Archer had risen and was alongside Mani, about to take hold of his arm, saying, 'just hang on there a moment, young fella!'

'Relax Archer. In fact leave me with Malcolm. I'll talk to you later.' The Chief Minister's words had instant effect, but before the obedient servant could depart, Mani stepped up, grabbed his arm and held him there.

'Can 'e stay?' It was a request to the Chief Minister. 'I would like 'im to listen to what I say.'

Everything stood still for a timeless moment while Archer waited for the word of command, Mani waited for agreement, and Blyth desperately scrabbled his mental tool-box for a rationale that made sense of this unusual circumstance.

'If ...that's what...you want, Malcolm,' the master diplomat said. 'Mister Archer, please sit down and listen.'

The Director of the Chief Minister's Aboriginal Liaison Unit silently resumed his seat and watched the young man who was again leaning on the desk-top and staring into the government leader's face. 'I always wunda about Mister Archer here, and Mister Gray Bridges, and hundreds and hundreds of people who are dedicated to doin good to Aborigines,' the bold young man began. 'We need yah, Mister Archer.' He turned to look at the expressionless public servant. 'An, Mister Blyth, we need yah. All our people respect yah, and respect every government leader and important person. We always respect you. That's our culture way. It's our Lore. And we need you, Mister Blyth. We really do need yah to help us.'

Blyth responded quietly, 'Go on Malcolm. I'm interested to hear what you have to say. It's good to hear you speak as you do. It encourages me. You see, I need you, too, Malcolm. I need you to help this Territory to be the best place in Australia.'

'Is that what yah need us for, Mister Blyth?' Mani took great care in choosing his next words. If Archer and Blyth were going to listen and hear the word of truth it would be now.

'That's something I can't understand. But something I do understand very well is this. You need me and my people to be poor and dependent, sick and ignorant, alcoholic and depressed, because this way we are worth a lot of money to the Territory every year.'

'Oh, you're mistaken....' Blyth tried in vain to cut off the flow of Mani's speech.

'Not just this year, and not just for this Five Year Plan. Yah need special plans to look after our health an' our education, and our welfare, and our town development, and outstation development for many years. If we stand on our own feet, and look after our own selves you'll lose a lot of money that's comin into the Territory every year. You can't afford us to be healthy and self-managing. You can't afford us to live on our own land in our own way. You need us weak and dependent so you can get enough money from Canberra to run your government and build up your Balanda towns and shops and everything, and a good standard of living, or whatever you call it.'

'Who told you all this, Malcolm? I assure you that it is not that way at all!' the Chief Minister insisted. 'Nothing would give us more pleasure than to see Aboriginal Self-Management really happening.'

'And if we tell you to take away all the outsider builders and construction workers and teachers an' shop-keepers an' nurses an' mechanics, an' inspectors an' administrators and town planners and so on, will you take them away, and let our own people have their jobs back that they learnt to do in Mission days?'

'Is that what the people want, Malcolm? I don't hear them asking for that.'

'I'm Arardbi, Mister Blyth. Can yah hear me? And when we ask yah for that will yah listen? And if we say we don' wan' a Local Town Council that does'nt work, under yah Northern Territory Act, but a local government that fits our own clans, an' our own understanding of law and government, too, and that we don't want dozens of politicians and departments and agents flying in and out of our places every week... will you listen? No, you won't because this is the big industry. This is the industry that brings in the supply of money from Canberra to pay all the experts to do good to us people of the land. This brings the money that gets spent in the Territory an' makes the business people and the government people get richer.'

Blyth stared at this remarkable young black man, and weighed his reply. 'What are you really trying to say to me, Malcolm?'

'When I 'eard about Australian Aid to developing countries in a conference in Switzerland that Moral Rearmament invited some of us to, someone said Australia was a developed country, givin' aid money to developing countries so's Australian companies could go in and do projects in those countries, and get developed themselves and bugger the locals.'

'Oh, I don't know...' Blyth began.

'Well Mister Chief Minister, do you know this sir. Yah live in a developed country called Australia, and I live in a broken, developing country also called Australia, and who is watching what's being done to us. A lot of us feel like we are 'elpless little people who're tired of sayin' no, and we are gettin' shafted by big people just for their own pleasure.'

Blyth and Archer had no ready reply. They continued to listen.

'My people didn't want British invasion, and a Balanda government, and Chief Minister, but now you are here we respect you as our top government man of the Territory, and we ask you to 'elp us. But we want you to 'elp us in the way that we won't need yah elp any more. We wanta 'elp ourselves! Let us be free from all the 'elping. It's too much, Mister Blyth. Give us our land and our freedom, and we can 'elp owselves…and we can pick out any different kinds of help we want from Balandas. Give us this chance, Mister Chief Minister. Don't take our land and our self-government away from us. Don't keep on putting programmes and staffs on us, to get Commonwealth money. And don't keep talking us around in circles in consultations and in visits, drowning us in words, and never waiting long enough to hear the mind of the people.'

All were quiet for moment, but almost as if just warming up to the task Mani continued, 'And what about the constitution change…?'[1]

Mani stepped back and stood with his arms by his side, watching the Chief Minister and waiting for his reply. Fred Archer had his face down, but with raised eyes watched the other two men apprehensively.

Slowly Blyth rose and came around the desk to stand face to face with Mani. He put out his hand and smiled.

'I have learnt a lot from you, Malcolm,' he said warmly. 'You're a real thinker and a great advocate for your people. I'm going to be thinking about what you said. You've given me much food for thought. When we all get together at the consultation, I'll be interested to see if the other Aboriginal representatives there are thinking the same way as you. I must listen to everyone, you know. Can I be sure that you will be at the consultation, Malcolm? I hope so, you put the case for your people so well.'

Mani retrieved his hand from the other's warm grasp. 'Prob'ly,' he said. 'But we don't need another consultation, Mister Blyth. We need a chance to have our own life back again. A better chance to live our own life, Mister Blyth, that's what we need. But prob'ly I'll be there.'

'Good! I'll be looking forward to seeing you there,' the Chief Minister told him. 'And, once again, thanks for coming in to see me today. We must get together again soon. I'm sure you have a big future ahead of you, Malcolm. In fact, if you ever think you would like to help us in liaison or community development work, I'm sure we

---

[1]　For the rest of this dialogue relating to constitutional change, see appendix two.

could find a place for you.' He turned to Archer.

'Wouldn't you say so, Mister Archer?'

'Oh, yes,' Fred stood and came forward as he took the cue to be positive and friendly. 'No worries. Plenty of room for a good man.'

Mani stared at the two men incredulously.

'Plenty of room in the Aboriginal Industry, eh? I'm sure there is. But that's not for me. I'm asking you for more freedom, not for more government control of my life. Is it so hard to understand?'

'No, no,' Blyth was trying hard to sound reassuring. 'I see now, yes, of course. That's not the sort of thing you're after at all. Right, we'll be thinking about what you've said. Yes, indeed we will. I just wanted you to know I value your ideas, and believe that you could teach us a thing or two. Keep in touch, Malcolm. Goodbye, and thanks again for coming in. You've shown real grit today. I admire you for it.'

With Archer at his heels, Blyth ushered his visitor out of the room and watched him walk down the corridor.

* * *

'So that's our little Malcolm Manggululu,' he whispered. 'He's quite a boy! Well, at least now we know what we're up against in the Dik Dik land talks, and at the consultation. The main thing is, Archer, he'll be there. And I can beat him at this game.'

'Probably be there, he said,' Archer reminded his chief.

'Probably's not good enough,' Blyth said. 'Keep Bridges on the job. Keep after young Malcolm until the consultation's held. If he stays away so will others, and we want them all there, including his old man. We don't want people to get the impression that we're the kind of people who'd access native lands without first considering their feelings'.

Chapter 18
Understanding at last

It was only 4:28 PM when Bridges stopped the Land Rover in front of the T & G building, but Livvy was already there. As she climbed in he looked for a sign of truce. But he was disappointed. 'Aaaugh!' A sigh this loud usually meant that she was exasperated beyond toleration. 'Can we just drive? Can we talk later?'

'Sure,' he obliged, and drove towards the highway in silence, while she tried to relax. He knew better than to ask what was wrong. She needed time to let things go, or to resolve something or other, or simply to unwind. He could wait. This was a peak hour for traffic outward bound from the city following the four twenty-one conclusion of the public servants' working day. The Land Rover went with the current up Smith Street, turned right into Daly, over the railway bridge, and swung left on to Stuart Highway. As it did, she reached across suddenly and touched his arm. 'Sorry about lunch-time,' she said. He touched her hand briefly, and she went on. 'It's not you. It's just everything. I'm reacting to you because of how everything's building up.'

The humidity seemed to drop ten percent and Bridges found himself able to breathe more easily. The Rover moved beautifully up behind the car in front, its smooth strength a sheer delight.

'What sort of afternoon have you had?' She forced herself to ask, trying to turn away from her own aggravated state of mind.

'Unbelievable!' he said.

'Good unbelievable?' she asked. 'If it's good unbelievable tell me about it. I need something to believe in just at the moment.'

'Some good, some not so good,' he warned.

'Save the not so good,' she told him. 'I've got enough of that to go on with.'

'Well, the good bit is that I got Mani in to see the Chief Minister and they actually talked face to face. Mani told Ned that he wants the government to end the Land War.'

'Good for him!' She was emphatic. 'What did Ned say?'

'I wasn't in there, so I don't know,' Bridges said regretfully. 'But Fred Archer came and raved about it when I brought Harry and Andrew in from a rally at the park. He couldn't help talking about it. He was ropeable! And he really blasted Harry Bagent for going to a lunch-time rally…'

'You left Mani alone with Captain Bligh, Gray?' She was aghast.

'Right!' he was irritated. 'Yes, I left him to it. I didn't intend to, but it was the appropriate thing to do when it happened. I gave Mani some tips and let the two of them deal with each other man-to-man. Mani and I had talked about Ned respecting people who express themselves strongly, and apparently that's just what happened. Fred obviously took some heat. He let it show when he was tearing a strip off Harry. Suddenly he boiled over and started telling us about Mani's high-handedness with Ned.'

Livvy was curious about the rally in the park. 'Armstrong and Co,' he told her. 'A lead-up to the meeting at the 'Y' tonight.' He decided not to tell her about whisking Mani away from the influence of Armstrong; not because he regretted it or because he feared her wrath, but because, now that she was trying to get control of her negative feelings and to be reasonable about his way of seeing things, it was no time to draw battle lines again.

'Old Andrew was sent to observe, and the rest of the Liaison Officers were kept in over lunch hour,' he told her incredulously.

'Kept in!' She exploded. 'What are they? School children? Did they stay?'

'All except for Harry,' he said.

'Good for him.' she declared. 'But how pathetic, Gray, really! You can see why I'm appalled about what's happening, can't you?'

'I'm afraid Harry's in hot water this time,' he told her as they turned into their driveway. They sat for a few minutes with both doors open to the breeze while Bridges recounted Harry's defiance of the order to stay in the office, and his radical speech at the rally, stirring up animosity towards white oppression of black Australians.

'Thank God someone's got the guts to stand up for the people,' she said. 'Oh, Gray. Don't let him stand alone in the Department.'

'Do you think I would?' He was annoyed again. 'We've already talked frankly in front of Fred. I told Harry I didn't want to see him get the boot, but I admired his guts and would stick up for his right to do what he did to get more open communication. Fred as much as told me that two heads can roll as easily as one.'

'Do you think he was serious?' She was more subdued.

'Fred doesn't know how to be anything else but serious,' he said. 'But I don't take him too seriously. I have to work with Fred and the Liaison team, and I know Ned's not as influenced by Fred as he is by others.'

'Such as you?'

'Well, me, yeah. And old Andrew, and probably, Bagent. And then there is young Sally Forrest who as a university qualified ALO is seen to be very smart. They've all got more ideas and opinions of their own than Fred will ever have. He's just Ned's lackey and pet Yes Man. Ned can never be wrong with him.'

'Right, right.' she was savouring a new thought. 'Darling,' she looked at him directly. 'Do you hear what you're saying? If what you say is true, then you and the gutsy ones in liaison work have got a better chance than almost anyone else in the Territory to influence processes that affect policy decisions on Aboriginal affairs.'

He glanced at her. 'That's what I've been trying to tell you for months. I'm neither a politician nor a manipulator. I'm an enabler, Liv. I'm not going to tell anyone how to run any affairs, or what decisions they should make. I'm just going to do whatever I can to see that everyone who has a right to have a say gets heard.'

She sat back thoughtfully. 'But that's what it's all about, isn't it? Wait till you hear what I've got to tell you about my day. We're so far from all getting heard…that it's criminal. If everyone who had the right to have a say was really free to exercise that right, then we would be something like a democracy.'

'I'll drink to that!' he said opening the door. 'Can I pour one for you?' They went into the house and Bridges prepared drinks, while Livvy stripped in preparation for her afternoon shower-bath and appeared in her happy-house-coat.

'You're not going to believe what's been going on at our office today!' she declared.

'Why not?' he joked. 'You believed me.'

'Would you believe ASIO?' she asked, and paused for effect before sipping her drink.

'National Security?' He was genuinely surprised. 'Why? What's ASIO got to do with the N.T. Department of Education?'

'I like you,' she told him. 'You ask such sensible questions. But you seem to have the naive notion that things work how they're supposed to. I tell you, Gray, something's rotten in the State of Capricornia.'

'What happened? ASIO? What makes you think it was ASIO?'

'It was ASIO, I tell you,' she said, dropping into a cane chair. 'In Oliver Sutton's office, for more than an hour. Two security guys, with Oliver Sutton and Cecil Reeders…'

'That's interesting,' said Bridges. 'Cecil Reeders was in talking with the Chief Minister today, too. But who said it was security guys?'

'Bryce Summers,' she replied. 'He'd got wind of tonight's rally at the Y, and put it to his Director at the Department of Aboriginal Affairs that they should put in an appearance at such a public event, to show interest, as a Federal body responsible for

Aboriginal development. When he came out of the office he spotted me, and came over. He told me about it! He was furious, and whispered to me that he was heading for a meeting where some Territory public servants were alerting the ASIO agents to subversive developments in Aboriginal affairs.

'That's what he actually said. Poor old Bryce was nearly spitting chips.' She went on to tell that Bryce Summers had been detained in the room and interrogated for an hour behind a closed door, after which time the men had begun to file out, Bryce first, red in the face and tense. As he came down the office, Oliver Sutton called the other two men back in and closed the door.'

She recounted the furtive way that Summers, the DAA man, had stopped by her cubicle again and expressed his indignation at the way this business was proceeding. When Oliver Sutton's door opened again, Bryce Summers just had time before moving off quickly, to say to her, 'you and Gray are on their check-list.'

'Was he joking?' Bridges asked blankly.

She shook her head slowly. 'Why would he be?' she challenged as she sprang to her feet. 'They've got us listed as possible subversives, stirring mindless natives into revolutionary activity.'

Bridges laughed aloud as he took her in his arms. 'With all the bombings, as carried out by ISIC and other radical groups you would think they have more important things to investigate. They'll be asking for our mobile phones soon so they can data-mine us'

She held him back. 'Do you realise how serious this is,' she complained.

He kissed her ear, before looking into her eyes, still smiling. 'Of course it's serious. And ridiculous. But I don't mind. I'm glad the security men came around and that they've got us listed, because now you believe again that we both really are on the same side, after all.'

'Oh, I don't know what to make of it all,' she was exasperated. 'After Bryce left today I tried thinking about it, and I even began to doubt my sanity. I mean, the business with Helen, and then fighting with you, and now this. I feel so sure of myself, and then I find I'm hopelessly confused.

I'm sorry I gave you a hard time at Myilly Point. But, you do see, don't you? There are things going on. I'm afraid there's going to be real trouble. I mean conflict, violence. Aboriginal people are starting to claim the right to be treated as free citizens, and the reactionaries are ganging up again. It would never do, to have them acting like full-blown human beings.' She paused. 'I shouldn't have blamed you. I don't for one minute think you're like them. Only I've been so disturbed, I mean....where's it all going to end?'

'Don't doubt your own judgement,' he said. 'It's good. I'm convinced you're absolutely right to be concerned. You've got a good feel for what's happening in the social interface between the races. And don't ever stop reminding me not to be too naive.'

'I love you,' she said, and they kissed each other back from the wasteland that had opened between them at lunch-time on Myilly Point. Later, in the shower, Bridges held up in imagination, a picture of approaching violent racial conflict. It looked surrealistic to him. So, yes, it was true that Livvy did have good intuition on social processes, but perhaps she was feeling a bit stressed out or something, and letting feelings exaggerate the danger of conflict, and over-reacting to the news that they were on the list of suspicious people to be kept under surveillance. Under surveillance...what a joke.

* * *

Half an hour later they parked the Rover beside the Travelodge Hotel in the Esplanade, and joined the twenty or so people walking past the parked cars that had overflowed the YMCA car park.

Armstrong would be pleased at the response to his brief publicity campaign. At the glass doors of the foyer they saw Annette and Lionel in conversation. Big brother was obviously encouraging his sister to actually enter the place.

He was hoisting a heavy shoulder bag that Bridges assumed carried recording equipment, into a more comfortable position.

'Hullo, you two,' said Bridges. 'Good to see you again. But we will let you go as I'm sure you need to set up.'
'Yes, thanks,' Lionel agreed.

Bridges and Livvy passed through the outer glass doors into a foyer, where several people were chatting or waiting for someone to arrive.

Chapter 19
The murder

Eighty to a hundred people had already arrived at the YMCA by the time Mani Manggululu came through the inner row of glass doors to the level concourse above the amphitheatre's concrete tiers. He noticed the Gellies and Livvy, then caught sight of Bridges and went across to meet him. Several brown skinned teen-aged girls in close conversation on the central steps, about eight tiers from the top, wore red, yellow and black ribbons across their foreheads and tied at the backs of their heads. The crowd shuffling through the doors was a multi-coloured mixture, mostly black and brown.

People were talking with each other pleasantly and, in most cases, quietly. Few of the men were dressed in public servants' rig, but several passing near to Bridges were; and two of these, whom Livvy recognised as security staffers who had visited the Assistant Director of Education during the day, were talking more intently than the rest. She sidled by them, slowly, trying to overhear what they were saying. Catching a phrase or two…'stockman guy and the fat lady with the red arm band'… She stopped and looked around as if searching down towards the front. Another voice replied confidentially…'other time, too, but…just hangers-on…none of old land ri…ush… agitators and stir…'

'Evening, Mrs Bridges!' The other national security watchman had seen her.

'Oh,' she faked unawareness of their presence. 'Good evening. Have we met?' The second man smiled her way and chimed in.

'Ah, it's a small city. All the nice people get known sooner or later.'

'Is that right?' she said coolly. The first man added his excuse for knowing who she was. 'Some people are so famous that everyone knows them.'

'You surprise me,' she said mysteriously, with an enigmatic smile, and moved on to join Bridges before she had to say anything else to these irritating snoopers. The amphitheatre was still filling fast. Several people were standing on balconies outside hostel residents' rooms and overlooking the rest of the audience. A knot of men, wearing dark trousers or jeans and check or somber coloured shirts, stood about talking together at one side of the entrance. Nearby, a stout woman leaned across two small boys to tap one of the men on the hip, and he replied impatiently with a swing of the broad hat he carried, probably indicating that there was still plenty of room and no need to be panicked into sitting with his family.

Down near the front, on the other side of the central steps, there was a quiet group of tribal Aboriginal people, mainly middle-aged and white-haired, elderly men and women. They seemed ill-at- ease, all silently looking to the front except when one occasionally stole a glance over his or her shoulder and leaned towards someone else to communicate a whispered observation.

'G'day, Gray,' said Mani.

'Hi Mani, good-tar see you, mate,' said Bridges confidentially. 'How'd it go with the Chief Minister, today?'

Mani nodded and smiled. 'You were right,' he said with a grin. 'He listens when you talk strong. I think he listened.'

As they were talking, a young girl nodded to Mani as she was entering the hall. Obviously indigenous, and wearing faded jeans, a white T-shirt, and two red, black, and yellow wrist bands.

Mani said, "Hi Margaret, didn't know you had an interest in this night?"

Bridges stood and waited as she replied, "Yep, of course I do…See yah later.' And she went into the hall.

Mani said to Bridges, "She's from college and is also training to be a teacher".

They were shuffling towards the steps leading down the middle of the tiers, and the Gellies' and Livvy all greeted Mani with friendly smiles. Mani noted Annette Gellies interest in him. She was a strange girl, but very beautiful, perhaps the sort of girl who could open new possibilities for his life. Lionel clearly wanted to sit at the front to do sound recording, but the others all remained together, halfway down on the left, the only place where there was still enough room for four to sit together.

To her delight Annette managed to place herself between Livvy and Mani, who took the aisle seat. In the main, the audience was adult, Mani noticed. Mostly younger and talkative, and generally it consisted of small ethnic clusters of three kinds. Two or three other groups of fully Aboriginal people could be seen, besides the one including the white-haired elders. They were also near the front and quiet. The groups of urban Aboriginal people were bigger, and sat towards the back and sides of the amphitheatre. Nearly all the girls wore red, black and yellow head bands.

One talkative woman wore a head band and another red ribbon around her left upper arm. The rest of the seated audience were Caucasian young adults. They sat in clusters around the central aisle, neither to the back nor to the front, and seemed to have come in twos and threes or alone. Standing near the doors, and on the balconies above, several people were still finding seats, and Bridges and Mani were interested to see Brown pushing into the row in front of them, past the legs of a bulky young white public servant, in Darwin rig, who occupied the aisle position, disturbing his intense concentration on the altogether superfluous task of feeding himself from a packet of potato crisps. Bridges leaned forward to speak to Brown, but before he actually sat down, Andrew saw someone he wanted to speak to near the stage, and went on his way down the steps.

The audience noise level rose, and everyone's attention seemed to focus on what was happening in front of the stage. They saw Brown approach three other men. One was Armstrong, still in his all black outfit, including the sun glasses, which, it was now clear because it was evening, were simply being worn for effect. Harry Bagent and the third man were in casual shirt and jeans, like most other urban Aboriginal men present. They contrasted sharply with Brown's appearance. He was out of his public service rig, and wearing a white shirt hanging over light Grey trousers.

'Look, there's Armstrong,' confided Annette, leaning across towards Mani. He nodded as they strained to hear what was going on. Armstrong was continuing to tap his index finger solidly against Brown's chest as he looked down at him and spoke in a way that suggested that he was putting the old man right. The campaigner from Queensland was in his late twenties, and at least five inches taller than Andrew in his riding boots. His light brown skin was the only thing about him that was other than jet black.

The noise faded and eventually Armstrong stopped lecturing and poking Andrew, turned to the stage, about hip height alongside him, reached out and lay the stand over until the microphone was level with his face, then spoke as if he had reached the climax of an electioneering speech.

'Friends,' he boomed. 'There's a man here who says you should not hear the truth.' The crowd was thunderstruck into silence. 'What 'ee's saying to us 'ere,' the visiting speaker explained in a scathing tone, 'is that you're like children. It's true some are. I see children here. Hi, children. I'm real glad to see you 'ere, even if this old man isn't. But some of you other folk, you know what 'e says? 'e says you're like children, and I mustn't say things that will upset you and be too nasty for your poor little ears to hear.' He propped, poised ready for laughter, and he was not disappointed.

The hungry young man in front of Mani neglected his potato crisps to participate in the audience laughter. Annette began to laugh, but noticed that her companions apparently were not amused, and stopped uncertainly.

'Is this the way it is in Darwin?' Armstrong bellowed into the microphone. 'Are grown up people treated as children 'ere? Do you think that's right? Well, you know what you can do about that.' The chatter that followed was louder, but more scattered now.

'Wait there! Wait a while, friends,' Armstrong pleaded. 'Don't lose your respect for this old-timer, out here. He might be an Uncle Tom, an' he might be a white man's lackey, 'an he might be a traitor to his race. Mind you, I just say he might. I don't know, do I? But you do! And supposin 'e is, well then that's his right. Respect this old man and his right to think as he pleases. I do, and I ask you to, too. But that don't mean we all have to be like 'im, or let the like of 'im tell us what to think, does it? Now I'm goin to hand you over to Harry, Harry Bagent, our chairman for tonight.'

As Harry went around to the stage steps, Brown pressed forward to speak to him, but Armstrong intercepted him and after a few words between them, broke into the rising audience chatter to announce a generous concession he was prepared to make to the older man.

'Friends,' he boomed again. 'This old timer 'ere reckons 'ee's got somethin to say to all you poor little innocents. So I'll tell yah what I'm gunna do. If it's okay with you, Harry?' He turned to the chairman and received a nod of approval. 'We'll give 'im a chance to speak a bit later on, and I'll keep what I've got to say till after 'ee's had is say. Okay? This is an open go tonight. Anyone can speak. That's the idea of it. So everyone can say what they think. So we'll listen to you, Uncle. You can tell us about the way it used to be, then you can sit down an' listen to the way it is now. Right?'

Mani was following this bit of drama closely. He sensed discontent rising in the mingled murmuring and laughter that followed. It was galling to him to see an old tribal elder being ridiculed before a crowd of young people, and yet he found the Queenslander's verbal attack exhilarating. How often he had felt impatient with the old men for not taking a tough stand on things. With an impatient gesture of both hands, Brown went up the steps of the centre aisle amid a stir of excited chatter and laughter. He continued to the top of the steps and stood back beside the entrance doors. Bridges whispered to Livvy, 'I've never seen Andrew so worked up.'

Bagent adjusted the microphone and looked around at his audience, while Armstrong mounted the stage to sit behind the speaker.

'Old Andrew's gamer than I took him to be,' Bridges told Livvy.
'Perhaps someone should talk him out of it,' she replied.

'If he takes the microphone they'll make mincemeat of him.' Bridges looked back at Andrew again.

'I think he's committed himself to speak now. There's too much at stake for him to back down.'

'Well, that's Armstrong, brothers and sisters,' Bagent was at the microphone. 'I'll give you a proper introduction bye an' bye. But you can see we're gonna 'ave a great night 'ere tonight. But first we'll start with a welcome to country. And to do it is Auntie Molly.'

As he said this he indicated with his right arm that Auntie Molly come up to the stage.

Looking like the great grandmother she was, Molly was helped up the steps of the stage. The microphone was adjusted to her short height, and without delay, her firm but gentle voice said, 'This practice gives respect for our land and our customs. The land is our Mother… housing our ancestors…and our people have been honouring this for thousands of years.

And for the children 'ere, I wan yah to understand that a welcome like this one recognises us as the First Australians, and be proud of it. It gives awareness of our culchua and guardianship of the land.'

In a more formal way she continued, 'I would like to acknowledge that this meeting is being held on Aboriginal land and recognises the strength and ability of Aboriginal people in this land.'

The audience respectfully waited until she was helped off the stage and to her seat.

Bagent reclaimed the microphone and after a pause of respect, said, 'Now we gonna 'ave a few songs. Our people 'ave always enjoyed music and song whenever they've got together for important meetins, and we're gonna 'ave some music tonight. Give us that guitar up 'ere, Dave.'

The man called Dave handed up a guitar from the front row, and Bagent put its cord over his head and shoulder, strummed softly and turned one or two keys.

'What we're gonna sing first this 'ere one we all know. So all join in: 'Go tell it on the mountain'. Yah right? Now, let her go!' He strummed strongly and gave a hearty lead to the singing, with good support from the back rows, and others gradually picking up the refrain.

'Go tell it on the mountains, over the hills and everywhere. Go tell it on the mountains, to let my people go.'

After three verses he put up a hand to stop them and continued quietly stroking chords as he introduced the next song.

'This land is my land, this land is your land, from old Tasmania to Melville Island.'

They sang lustily, and most people joined in. Annette began to sing when she saw Livvy and Bridges happily joining in, and was pleased when Mani was quietly singing along. The busy tubby fellow in front of them tapped his fist and nodded his head to the rhythm, but was too busy chewing on a Cherry-Ripe to help with the singing. He turned a chocolatey grin towards Annette who felt encouraged to sing more heartily than ever.

Harry led in two more songs not so well known by the audience, and then a local version of 'Marching Through Georgia' in which they sang *'While we are marching through Darwin.'*

As it was finishing Mani caught Bagent's attention and, without a look at his companions, went down to the stage. Bagent nodded and announced, 'Mani Manggululu of Goose Island, friends, and a group of student teachers from Bachelor, will now favour us with a song.'

Annette was rapturous and repeated the news to her companions, 'Mani's going to sing!' Then, as the man in front turned around, she explained her excitement. 'He's a friend of mine.'

'Oh, yeah,' said the happy young man, nodding as he sucked his sticky fingers. He looked on with added fascination as Mani mounted the stage and several young men and women from ATEC shyly picked their way forward while the audience applauded loudly. A couple of the young women nudged each other and let giggles bubble out as they went on stage. Once in place, facing the audience, they were all seriousness.

'Er...this song,' began Mani, looping Harry's guitar cord over his own head and touching the strings, 'has been written by a young man in Arnhem Land. The words are modern but the tune's old. It's an old island tune. We sing it, some of us younger people, because it tells us that the life of our own ancestors is what we need and what we want today.' He gathered the group of four young men and four young women around him and began to strum. At a nod of his head they joined him.

'Ancestors of our land, I-I-I bring you back to present time.'

The women clapped, the men stamped and Mani slapped the wood of the guitar at the end of the two lines; two beats then another two, then one.

'Walk about living on the life you knew;
New worlds you never dreamed of are in our hand.'

Again they beat out the rhythm, then repeated the four lines and the beating pattern. The staccato movement and the presentation had been dramatic. The applause was spontaneous and enthusiastic. Bagent moved to Mani's side and then to the microphone to announce that the group had another song from the new day song-writers of Arnhem Land.

'This one's got an old-time tune, too,' said Mani as he began to strum, and the group joined in softly with smooth unison singing…*'Journey on, journey on, all of mankind, Future is waiting for you.'*

The cadence rose and fell in each line, and this time, instead of beating a rhythm, they hummed a line at the end of the verse…*'Opportunities, opportunities all in your hand, our mind is limited to foretell.'*

Again they hummed the music that swelled with a great yearning and faded with a little hope.

'All of our own and nature unseen future is waiting for you.'

As the humming died away, the audience broke into enthusiastic applause, led by Armstrong who left his seat to shake hands with Mani, and the others and to talk with them, before they left the stage.'

'Wasn't that tremendous?' said Annette proudly to her friends.
'Really something,' agreed Bridges.
'It was beautiful,' said Livvy. 'I've heard the students sing before, but that was something different.'
'What'd you think of that?' Annette asked the young man in front of her as he sat back opening a can of Fantail Orange.
'Not bad,' he said enthusiastically. 'Not bad at all.'

They all made signs of appreciation to Mani as he rejoined them, and Annette leaned across to say, 'That was wonderful Mani.' As he settled beside her he accepted the words with a smile.

'Well, what'd I tell you brothers and sisters,' said Bagent as the student teachers returned to their seats amid continuing applause. 'This is goin' to be a great night. Anything can happen tonight. Our brother wanted to sing a song, so up he came. You feel at home, too, and be ready to 'ave your say. Thanks Manggululu and gang, brothers and sisters from around the Territory.'

The next song that I want to sing… you will all recoganise, and please join in.

Within a minute all were singing;

Do you come from a land down under?
Where women glow and men plunder?
Can't you hear, can't you hear the thunder?
You better run, you better take cover…
Living in a land down under
Where women glow and men plunder
Can't you hear, can't you hear the thunder?
You better run, you better take cover

When they finished, a tipsy larrikin near the back, shouts, 'what about a Slim Dusty?' causing a mixture of laughter and shooshing from those near him.

'Well, don't you forgit what we're 'ere for,' said Bagent gravely. 'This ain't just a fun sing-song. We sing because we're people who got somethin' in us that's got to get told. You want a Slim Dusty song? I'll give you one. Just one… an' then we're gonna git down to some serious talkin.' He began to strum as he went on. 'This 'ere song's about one o' the men who made Australia the nation it is today. It's the story of undreds of 'ard workin people, too… people pioneering a new kind o civilisation, right 'ere in this country where we are… an' a nation that never even taught 'alf of 'em to read and write… his name was "Trumby".

He fingered the keys and sounded the strings, strummed a jogging introduction reminiscent of Slim Dusty, the Bush's favourite balladeer, and began to sing,

'Now, Trumby was a Ringer, a good one too at that……'

The ballad went on to tell of the misadventure of the Aboriginal Ringer Trumby who met an untimely death by drinking from a water-hole that had been poisoned by Dogger Fry as a means of killing dingoes. The irony of the story was in the fact that Dogger Fry had clearly marked the poisoned waterhole with a written notice… *'Trumby was a good boy, but 'e couldn't read or write…'*

Bagent handed back the guitar and raised his hand to accept the applause for the moving interpretation of a popular outback song. Back at the microphone he said quietly, 'an' that's why we're 'ere tonight. Too many Trumbies are still being' left only 'alf ready to face up to the struggles of life that the white invaders have brought to this country. You might say it's nobody's fault, but that's not true, brothers and sisters. It's the fault of the people who can do somethin about it and don't do it. Now what we want is the chance to do as good as everyone else. That means we need our own country, and our chance to do our kind of thing in our own way. Like all free people.

We want land for all our people in Australia. Land of our own in our own country... Somewhere where we can live in our own way, and not just workin for the Big White Boss all the time. There's been a lot of talk about one Australia wide land rights policy, but when are they gonna do anything about it? We're gettin sick of talk an' promises...An' we want this nation to accept responsibility for the shockin infant death rate amongst our people. Why do they let so many of us die before we even go to school?... Awright, you say, it's not anybody's fault. It might be somethin that just turned out like that. But that's awright...it's the fault of the government of this land if they leave it like that. That's makin 'em die too quick... Most of our population is dead already.

When will this country stop the dyin'?...The first invaders shot us when we were in their way. They don't do that now, but the way things are is still killing us before our time. Our average life span is sixty-nine years. This is eleven years shorter than the whites'... He paused to let the audience think of this, and then continue. 'An' suicide, I looked this up this arvo for you. Reading from a piece of paper; 'For Aboriginal and Torres Strait Islander the highest suicide rate was in the 20-24 age group, with 21.8 deaths per 100,000 population, five times the non-Indigenous female rate for that age group.'

Once again he paused for effect. 'I got that off the Commonwealth of Australia's own website, so mus' be right. But what you godda ask yourselves, why are our people so unhappy with life that they do that? An' it's gunna be like that till when they let us 'ave our own land and freedom to decide our own future an' a bit o' decent health services and education.'

Someone from the back shouted, 'But we give you education. Your kids godda go to school, just like ours do'.

Bagent was not phased. 'Yeah that's right mate, but you godda understand that we learn differently to you white blokes. You white people got books in your houses… yah got TV… an' computors. What this means is that your kids get to school more developed than our kids, so our kids are behind right from the start. Once they get behind, they have self-esteem issues and so just drift further behind.

I tell you, brothers and sisters, I work in one of the government hand-out departments, an' I'm sick an' tired of a system that treats us all as born wrong, and fobs us all off with a few bob an' arithmetic and band-aids.

We want freedom, and we mean to do something about it. Tonight we're gonna ask you to join us in a new movement we call Black, B.L.A.C.K. The letters stand for Black Liberators And Co-operating Kinsmen. We're all kinsmen us blacks. That's something white people can't understand. But we're gonna make 'em understand, an' we're gonna make 'em listen! Thanks for listenin' to me now... Thanks!' The audience response he received was louder than he had earnt with his song – Bagent was pleased.

Annette sat staring in complete bewilderment. In front of her the well-fed young man was slapping his ample thigh along with the applauding crowd while he tilted back a can to drain its contents into his mouth. On one side of her Mani was clapping lightly and on the other Livvy applauded loudly, while Bridges was sitting quiet and still. It disturbed Annette that Bagent had said terrible things about everything that white people were trying to do. He had not one good word to say for what Christian missionaries had been doing over the years and were still doing; at great personal sacrifice. She admired them tremendously for their kindliness and helpfulness.

Livvy was thrilled to find that Bagent was articulate. It was a relief to hear somebody put forceful words of some of the issues that need exposure and reform.

Mani saw her enthusiasm and Bridges' quiet response. It made him aware again that people don't just see things the same way just because they belong to the same race or culture. Bridges must surely see that there was still hope in the situation if indigenous people could stand up and initiate movements for change. It did not matter, ultimately, if they saw the issues with full clarity, and in all their detailed complexity. Probably no-one could do that, anyway. What did matter was that they take up the cause of getting some control of their own lives, that they insist on being taken seriously as players in the power stakes, and get the powers-that-be to support them, instead of controlling them, to work for the reduction of the statistics of failure and decaying lives, and increasing the statistics of survival, health and productive life.

'That young man is going to be an important public speaker one day!' Livvy told Bridges.

'I'm sure you're right,' he replied. 'Harry seems to be growing by the hour. Wait till that guy learns to really put a speech together.'

Livvy tried to think of an apt remark to help Bridges see that he might be mistakenly assuming that what Bagent needed was more formal education, when in reality what he needed was more opportunities to realise his potential, to show what he was really made of. Before she could find the right words, Harry had called them to attention again.

'Now, we had one ol' fella already said 'e wanted to speak tonight, brothers an' sisters. Bye an' bye Brother Armstrong's gunna bring us a word… but right now this is your chance. Y'all know why we're 'ere…an' we want to 'ear from the people what they think. So come right on up 'ere. Who's gunna be first?'

There was an awkward silence followed by an embarrassed stir of movement and whispering. Stan Armstrong rose and spoke to Bagent and Bagent returned to the microphone.

'That's a good idea, Brother Stan. I'm gunna put the microphone down there on the floor in front of the stage, 'cause not many of us are used to gettin up an' speakin to a crowd. But soon it won't be that way, let me tell you, 'cause tonight is just the first public meetin of the Black Liberators And Co-operating Kinsmen. Soon there'll be a whole lot more of you people up 'ere like me tonight. I'm just 'ere to get things started. 'ere, Dave, take this mike. Put 'er over there, mate. Good on yah, brother.'

Bagent sprang down from the stage. 'Awright, now,' he continued. 'It's easy just to come down 'ere an' say a few word. Who'll be first?'

Bagent scanned the audience and saw the arm up of a young woman. 'Margret, would you like to say something'.

It was the same young lady who Mani greeted earlier.

'I've come 'err to tell yah about why we need a treaty in this country….'

Pausing briefly, she looked at her notes. 'The gobberment doe wan us to ave a treaty, but we gunna get one…one day we will git it'.

A roar of approval erupted from the crowd, but soon quietened so they could listen.

'The gubberment reckon's that we not organised enuff to get all the peoples to agree because we too many nations. But we bin have treaties between all the nations for thousands of years… These were not written on paper, which is jus dead trees. Our treaties are written in the land, they are in the rocks and known by our Ancestors… These are our libraries, they are our universities, we doe need paper treaties'….[2]

When she finished she looked at the crowd with a confidence that is not usually given to one so young. For a moment the crowd were just quiet, but as she left the stage, the uproar was loud and long.

---

[2] Publishers note; to read the rest of Margaret's delivery on 'The Treaty' refer to appendix three at the back of the book.

'Who was that?' asked Livvy. 'Wow, she's good.'

Bridges just nodded his head and continued clapping.

Bagent reclaimed the mic, and said, 'I see our old brother, if 'e still is our brother, Mister Andrew Brown. You still want to say somethin, Andrew?'

All eyes were on the old man in spotless white, as he descended the steps with dignity and purpose. Only his hair, caught in the rays of the lights from the balconies, looked whiter than his shirt. He took hold of the microphone and Bagent stepped back to lean against the stage. The elder stared at his audience, turning his head slowly to take in every section of it. Before he spoke there was complete silence.

'Friends,' he said gravely. 'I'm an Aboriginal man, and I am proud to be an Aboriginal man. I am a Wainanda from Western Arnhem mainland country, and I'm not a boy. I've been through all my people's ceremonies.' He looked at his audience as he took a deep breath. 'Long time ago, before some o' your mothers and fathers were born, I was a piccaninny out in that country. It was a good life, but the white man came there. He came to Port Essington and along our country way, on horses we'd never seen before and with guns. Before you were born, a lot of you, we had to run, but the horses were too fast for us. A long, long time before the new settlers, came to Darwin, our old people started to find out that our old life was finished. Our traders and hunters couldn't go over the land that had the cattle on it, or even travel to ceremonies that way anymore.' He stopped and looked around his audience again. There was no movement, and he realised that he could breathe easier and have his say without interruption.
'When they tried to, a lot of them got shot.'

Among the hearers, Mani and Bridges each felt a new respect for the elder, as they watched him reassert his moral leadership in this hostile setting. Still with the art of story-telling, this lapsed elder of the Wainanda just might hold the audience, and possibly even win some sympathy for his point of view.

Bridges found himself fascinated and longing to hear more of Andrew's background. Although he had known that his old colleague originally came from Arnhem Land, it still was hard to believe that he had ever lived a tribal life-style.

'The white man had guns,' Brown continued his story. 'And some of our people died. I saw men shot dead by white men…one man was running away and stuck in a wire fence, and I saw him shot dead, so I just kept runnin'. And I learnt how to hate the white man. At first I was ready to fight 'im, but the elders of my family, and the people, all met together. They had many meetings. This meeting 'ere in Darwin's not the first meeting people ever had to talk about the Balandas and how we can survive with them. We had many, many meetings in those old days… and we decided that we could stop the fighting and learn to be friends, but only one way.

'Some elders told us young blokes we have to work with the Balandas. You see, the Balandas brought more than guns. They brought all the outside world, too. They made our best magic and wisdom look weak and silly. We could get everything we needed without travelling and hunting, if we worked with Balandas and didn't make them too angry. They had new magic to bring in food and money and everything, and we needed to get it, too. We people, we had to decide one way, or the other way, because the Balanda would never go away. Our fathers made 'im go away one time from Port Essin'ton. With spears and fighting-sticks they beat 'im. Same again in another place, cattle station. But 'e come back, more an' more. What we going to do, fight 'im off, an' all die? Everyone die? Or join in and live, and learn to live in the big outside world, speak the Balanda language, learn the Balanda magic and wisdom, and give it to our own people. Some people made war and some people made peace. I made a peace with the Balanda and 'e as taught me many things.

'Now, today...' His voice faltered, and Bridges sensed that by turning from his story of the past to his own present situation, he had tapped feelings that threatened to upset his thoughts.
'Now, today,' he continued. 'I'm still alive, and you people still alive, too. If we talked the way some people talk today, in those old days, we would have made a big war, and we Aboriginal people would all be dead. Is it bad to be alive in the Balanda's world? Is it better to make war and die? Now, today...we ...learnt many things, an' we got many good things, and we learning more, and fitting into the whole world with all people everywhere...'

A harsh female voice near the back cut him off. 'You're run away in the far country, an' got no wife and family! No relations, you black white man.'

A male Aboriginal voice took up the cry. 'You're a coconut, mate! You're dark on the outside and white on the inside.'

Several people murmured in sympathetic disapproval, and a heated exchange threatened to flare in the back rows. This gave Brown the time he needed to get his breath and collect his bounding thoughts for a reply. He firmly took hold of the microphone stand and spoke quietly and hesitatingly...'Yes you speak true, but not because...Balanda ways, an'…fit in…from…other….many have trouble...woman troubles…'

Mani was not the only one who recognised that the old man was losing his nerve. Suddenly everyone was aware that a terrible thing was happening; an old man was trying to speak through weeping, under condemnation for trying to justify himself for having chosen life rather than death, before an audience of young people who had been laughing at him, and who had safely lived in "The Lucky Country" and never had to make that ultimate decision. Why couldn't they see that people like them owed their lives and safety to people like him? Why say he was not a kinsman?

'Now…' the old man mumbled. 'We got plenty good thing. Not my fault, if you not happy 'bout that. An' now Every one gonna' blame Andrew Brown…… helping my people. Some blokes … gettin drunk all 'e time…no more…my people…my people… my fam… only say I'm bad man. That's not true. I'm… not...that way…'

He could not go on, and neither Bagent nor Armstrong seemed to know what to do, for Brown was sobbing quietly into the microphone, and the sound of his sobs were exploding through the amplifiers.

It was Annette who sprang into action. She pushed past Mani who had to jerk back from where he had been leaning forward to catch every word. Five seconds later she was at the microphone beside the old man.

'May I please say something, Andrew?' she asked, and the elder stepped aside still with his head down, to allow her the use of the microphone.

'I just want to say this my dear friends,' she began, with a warmly mellow voice and looking around the startled audience. 'There is a way we may all live together happily. So far the speakers have only talked about the problems of humankind and what humankind can do about these problems. I want to tell you, dear friends, that God has a way to knock down all the middle walls of partition and make us to be one. That way is the way of Jesus, my dear friends. And I stand here tonight, to tell you that Jesus Christ is real. He has come into my heart, and he can come into yours. When we have Christ in our hearts we can love each other, and it doesn't matter what colour or language we are, we are all one in Christ.'

'Hallelujah!' exclaimed a man sitting somewhere close behind Mani. 'God bless ya, sister!'

Annette turned to Brown. 'I'm sure God looks with favour on what Andrew Brown has done for his people, and stamps it with the seal of his approval. Dear Andrew, there is no need to feel upset if people say bad things about you. They even said bad things about our dear Lord, and he will bear all our griefs and sorrows. Everything that is done to help us to be one people, under the Lord, is done as unto him, and to his name be the praise. Let us not speak of anger and of separation, but let us rather speak of love and of being united, and the Lord will be with us, and his way will prevail. I know that we white people have done many wrong things, and we must repent, and ask God to forgive us, but it is not going to make things right if other people stir up bad feelings. That will only lead to more sinning. I felt that I just had to come out here and say this because it was laid on my heart to say it to you. Why not try the way of Jesus?'

'Amen!' called the man behind Mani, and led in a scattered and sporadic round of hand-clapping. Meanwhile, Lionel left his equipment on the front row seat long enough to give his sister a hug and a kiss as she moved from the microphone. She mounted the tier-steps with him in quiet dignity, without looking about her, and continued to the flat area at the top. There she stood back among the men, near the old man, marvelling at what the Lord can achieve through us when we are willing to follow the movement of his Spirit. Sensing that the emotional presentations by Andrew Brown and Annette Gellies had disturbed the audience and distracted them from thinking about the need for change through social action.

Bagent returned to the microphone to refocus the attention of the crowd on the central purpose of the meeting.

'We've 'eard the last two speakers, an' they're entitled to their opinions, but some of us anyway are sick of tryin those ways, an' we're 'ere tonight, because we believe in action that gets results. Now we've got time for one more speaker before I hand over to our visitor from Queensland. Stan Armstrong is waitin up there patiently. But 'e doesn't mind. He wants to know how people 'ere in Darwin feel about the shockin' conditions our people are livin under today. Right you are brother.'

Mani was on his feet and coming forward again. Bagent spoke into the microphone. 'We've heard from Manggululu a couple o' messages in song, now let's listen to what 'es got to say about our real situation today. All yours, brother.'

The young Arnhem Lander stood firmly with his feet spread and his arms folded loosely. 'If that's Christianity, I'm not sure if I understand it properly…You asking us, Miss Gellies to praise injustice, and to sit by and watch humans keep on being unhuman to others because they got power over them? I'm tellin' you, I can't say that's all right, keep goin' that way, great white boss. It's not all right to me. You talk to us about settlin down to be a friendly neighbour, while we're not a free people! You're as bad as that old black man up there with the whitefella heart'.

There was a stir in the audience, and Annette Gellies fell back out of sight among the men near the doors. She was shocked by what she had heard. She felt her heart slip and fall into the deep chasm his words had opened in her soul.

'But that's not all I want to say about it,' he went on, letting his arms hang down at his sides. To Andrew…well…your systems that you cling to are helping to boss us, old man. Someone has to tell you. Can't you see that?…Your system is so good at breaking our young men's spirit in gaols and pushin' our families to the outside… to the rubbish tips of this country, how clever you are at destroying our law, and our living from the land and sea, and tying us down with the sit-down money of your dole. How clever the cops are with an average of one hundred deaths a year in custody of First Nations people… this is seven times higher than the whites. Because our people are being slaughtered in jail…I'll tell you what's criminal in your system, the justice system is, when it comes to First Nation's people. And Mr Brown, what about our children…in what they call juvenile detention… The Prime Minister recently said, it is a disgrace and that we are the laughing stock of the world.

'Talk… always talk, but still the cops pick them up. You are so smart when we want to build up our works and incomes, and you say only if you do it in a white-fella way... So beautiful you let our community life fall away and fall apart, even every Aboriginal person's dreaming and true identity and pride of life?…And anyone who says we are free and equal today is sleepin. Wake up to the reality!

'But we're on the move. People who are a wake-up to how things work, can hear empty words that are said. They can see the white racism in the way things are still gettin done. An anyone who says that it's God's will for us to be getting sucked in and assimilated, to be low class fringe-dwellers of the white-fella world, must be a fool or a liar or both o' them.'

Mani realised that his heart was thumping in his ears, but he had more to say, and the audience was listening with rapt attention. He could see neither Andrew Brown nor Annette Gellies at the back of the standing men. Bridges and Livvy were both transfixed by Mani's radical tirade, not even turning to see what had become of Annette.

Mani turned to Bagent. 'Am I goin on too long?' I'd like to tell a little story if I've got time.'

'I think we should hear it!' said Stan Armstrong, and Bagent motioned to Mani to proceed.

'On North Goulburn Island, over near my own people's country there once lived a giant. His name was Yumbarbar and he was a people-eater…a…what d'ya call 'em… a cannibal. Nobody would go near that jungle, although there was good huntin there, and plenty of wild honey, and yams and all kinds of bush tucker. The people lived in fear, and never felt free to go where they wanted to go in their own country. That's why I think of Yumbarbar when I think about white racism…'

The audience gave a brief but hearty burst of laughter and waited to hear the eloquent young islander finish his speech.

'I'm sorry for Andrew Brown, and people like him. Maybe it was harder in his young days…I don't know. I do know some good men and women died instead of serving the giant white racism. I don't want to hurt you old man, wherever you are, but I want to tell you the truth. You've made life harder for many people who you could have 'elped if you had decided to kill the giant, instead of giving him a throne inside yourself.'

As Mani walked back to his seat, Armstrong and half the audience stood to applaud loudly while others either stared in silence or leaned towards each other and made whatever comment they could about such an unusual presentation. Livvy Bridges released pent-up breath. She glanced around, looking for Annette, then put her hand on Bridges' knee, and turned to search his face for reactions.

'Cer-runch!' he gasped. 'Poor Annette and Andrew.'

'That young fella sure knows how to pack a wallop!' said Livvy. 'Wasn't that incredible! Who said the truth hurts?'

'Gutsy man!' said Bridges, then stood to take Mani's hand as he reached their row, but rather than returning to his seat, or even speaking with Bridges, Mani continued up the steps.

'Annette's goin to be very hurt by that, I'm afraid,' Bridges told Livvy.

'She sure is.'

'She obviously has a hell of a crush on Mani,' said Bridges.

'Oh, darling!' Livvy was suddenly quite alarmed, and peered at Lionel in the first row. He was trying to gather in electric leads and his microphone, but people had risen and were standing in his way.

'Lionel's in a panic, trying to pack up, down there. I'd better go after Annette.'

'I'll come, too,' said Bridges, and they made their way past the tilted back head of the young man in the aisle seat of the next row down as he covered a yawn with a half-opened packet of Minties. Looking towards the front, Bridges saw Lionel's plight and waved. Lionel caught sight of him, waved back and saw Bridges signal his intention of going after Annette. His nodding head and hand assured him that the communication had been received.

There was no sign of Annette in the dense crowd by the doors and Livvy moved directly through into the foyer, while Bridges turned back to see Bagent beginning to speak again. He was on the stage with the microphone, and Bridges heard him say something about 'the moment we've all been waiting for, when Stan Armstrong, from the Queensland branch of B. L. A. C. K., the Black Liberators . . .'

There was no chance for Bridges to hear the rest of the sentence. He moved towards Mani who pushed past the men by the door, and anxiously grabbed his arm.

'Gray!'

'Hi there brother! You were devastating!' he enthused.

'Where's Annette Gellies?' the young Wainanda man asked urgently. A man in public service rig unfolded his arms and pointed towards the doors.

'Come on,' said Bridges. 'Livvy's gone after her,' and added when they were in the foyer. 'You know brother, that kid thinks you are somethin' special. I'm afraid she thinks she's in love with you.'

'Annette Gellies does?' Mani stopped in his tracks.

'I'm as sure as I can be that's the way it is,' said Bridges. 'I sort of hope I'm wrong.'

'Oh, Jesus! I hope you are, too. I don't want to hurt a girl who's away from 'er family an' got a worried mind. My old elder had it comin to 'im.' He gestured back towards the standing men.

'Andrew?'

'Yeah. I didn't want to hurt the poor old bugger. But someone had to say it, an' it just appened to be me. He had to hear the truth one day, Gray. I didn't know I was goin to say it when I got up. It just sort o' came to me and it had to get said.'

They went through the front door and along the footpath to where Livvy was standing in the dim light talking with a girl. It looked like someone taller, and neither man was surprised to find that it was not Annette. They were surprised, however, to find that it was Helen Cross, and that she too, was apparently in some sort of emotional state. Bridges guessed that her encounter with Ron Smart had not been a great success.

'I'm awright,' she was saying to Livvy as they came along. 'I'll be awright. I ran into someone that upset me!'

'Hullo Helen, what's up?' asked Bridges.

'Oh, mind your own bloody business, can't ya!' the girl snapped and rushed on towards the door through which they had just come.

'What's eating her?' Bridges asked. 'I thought she'd still be talkin' with her fairy god-father at Gellies' place.'

'She was supposed to be,' said Livvy.

'She's like that,' Mani told them. 'Her friends never know how she'll be from one minute to the next'.

'Don't I know it? But right now,' said Livvy. 'I'm more concerned about Annette. You were brutally hard on her, young man.'

'Yeah, I know,' Mani admitted. 'It seemed right at the time. But I really didn't mean to 'urt 'er, just help 'er to see 'erself'.

'Well, I think you did that! But I'm worried about whether or not she'll be able to bear what she sees.'

'She shouldn't be out in the streets on her own, either,' said Bridges.

Mani agreed. 'Well, I think she'll either be goin across town to their house, or just over there in the Esplanade Park. Or else she might be walkin around to get her feelings down.'

'She's not along the next street between here and her place in Cavenagh Street. I asked Helen if she had seen her,' said Livvy.

* * *

The Bridges decided to search straight along the dark road as far as Cavenah Street, but Mani ran off along nearby Mitchell Street. She could only be a few hundred yards out of sight, but there was no telling which way she might have gone. It should not take long to find her if she was walking back to the house. Mani moved quickly, peering left and right at each cross street.

Bridges and Livvy walked quickly as far as Cavenagh street, and back in half an hour. They had decided that they would see Annette if she was heading straight home. She would go across to Cavenagh Street, and by hurrying, they must see her on the way to, or still making her way along, that street.

When there was no sign of her, they returned to the YMCA via a side street and along the lawns of the Esplanade Gardens near the dark cliff-top trees. Bridges went on a quick search upstairs, through lounges and along balconies, while Livvy inspected the Ladies' Room. One thing was certain, Annette was not still at the YMCA.

'Well, there's not much more we can do, I suppose,' said Livvy. 'I only hope Mani finds her.'

Bridges left her walking up and down on the footpath outside the front door, anxiously waiting to see Mani returning with the girl. He took out his mobile and made a call.

After five minutes, Bridges came out and slipped his arm through Livvy's. 'I've just been speaking with Father Dick Sheehan,' he said. 'She hasn't gone there, at least not yet…and he can't suggest where she might be. And I told him Helen's arrived here in a state. He's pretty upset about that. Apparently he just made sure that she and Ron Smart had cab fares and decided to leave them to it.'

'What? He didn't even go and introduce them?'

'Incredible, isn't it?' Bridges was amazed. 'I told him about what happened here tonight. You know, a religious crisis for Annette, and he thought it unlikely that she would look to him for help. But he has given her counselling in the past, and will let us know if she turns up. I told him about her and Mani and he agrees it would be a shattering thing for her. But he was mainly worried about old Ron Smart. He had arranged for a taxi to pick him up, and guessed that he would be on his way home to East Arm by now.'

'Well, I hope Mani's found Annette,' Livvy sighed. 'Surely he'll be kind to her this time?' She paused, 'I just hope he doesn't try to be too kind to her.' She looked at Bridges. 'Are you sure she's safe with Mani?'

'Not to worry. He's a pretty serious character, and he's obviously sorry he hurt her. I trust him to keep it cool and easy-going. Frankly, I think he's morally incapable of making a move on her,' he assured her. 'Do you want to drive around town a bit more?'

'I do feel badly about losing her like this. I feel responsible for her.'

'We didn't lose her,' said Bridges. 'She went off without us.'

'Yes, that's right,' she said with some relief. 'After all, if she's old enough to leave home for Katmandu, I guess she's old enough to leave us and to get along on her own for the rest of the evening. Perhaps the best thing we can do is go back in and see how the Black Liberators are getting on.'

Lionel was at the door to meet them, and became panicky when they told him that Annette had not been found. He decided that he must go back to the house and, if she was not there by then, to keep searching. He thanked Livvy and Bridges for their interest and strode away towards the carpark.

Inside, Armstrong was in full cry when they passed through the inner doors, and stood to the left of the men near the top of the centre aisle. Several others had left, but the official looking men were still there. Andrew Brown was nowhere to be seen.

'This'll do,' whispered Livvy, and they stayed to listen to the views of the visitor from Queensland…

'Now, here in the Territory you got it all set out in front of you. Do I have to spell it out for yah? I mean, look at the infant death rate, the eye diseases, family break-ups, an' housing, an dozens of black people in and out o' Berrimah Gaol, bein treated like criminals when really they're the victims of schizophrenia from being stolen when they were babies, or they lost their idea of who they are and where in the Hell they might fit in. An' every time people claim land of their own, which is their legal right, the Territory Government fights them in court, and they do that even though they claim that this country's just an' fair to all the people.'

He began shouting. 'An' I'm throwin down the challenge to youse tonight. Everyone of youse here. I don't care a damn what the colour o' your skin is. If you reckon you got no white racism in you… prove it! I'm givin you the chance to make your decision to get on the side of liberation and a new deal for the first people of the Territory… Today at twelve o'clock, in the lunch hour, we had our first rally in the park opposite the Supreme Court down there in Mitchell Street. There's gonna be more. If you're not a racist you be there! If you believe in liberty for all people you be there!

The time as' come to stand up an' be counted. You whites, be there if you're not racists. You Aboriginal people be there if you're game, if you're ready to say, "Let my people go, and Get your foot off my neck white boss or else you'll be sorry." If we say it, we mean it. Today was just the start. We'll do it again, just carry a few placards and maybe sing a few songs an speak over the microphone to lunch-time passers by…but we'll let the media know an' they'll tell our story, an' we'll be on the move.

Before you leave this place tonight you can register your decision to be in the struggle, to play your part in the cause of liberty and a new deal for the black people of Australia. Thirty dollars and your name in Harry Bagent's Members' Book, and that makes you one of the Black Liberators and Co-operating Kinsmen.

One last word of warning, brothers and sisters. If you are really a coward down under, or if you couldn't stand the sight of blood, you better not come along. Because I might just be that fly that wakes up the sleeping giant…and we might see what we're really up against. Sometimes it goes that way. Sometimes it has to go that way so that people in other places, in other countries, and in this country, can see what really is goin on here. If you got a squeamish stomach, you won't last long in our movement, an' we're in this for keeps.

There's no turnin back. It's right on, till the powers that be in this country learn that it's to their cost if they don't treat the indigenous people with respect, listen to us and hear us, give us equality in human rights and realise that we are a force to be reckoned with, an' we want to lead our own lives, not be led like animals. Harry, you got your books?'

Before Harry could answer, the audience was thrown into a buzz of consternation as two uniformed policemen entered at the top and quickly descended the stairs.

'Hullo, hullo!' said Stan Armstrong in an attempt at sarcastic humour. 'Look who our first two new members are. Come on down brothers, we need your help!'

No-one laughed, but one man near the back called, 'no-one's done anything wrong here!'

One of the policemen went up on to the edge of the stage and spoke with Armstrong and Bagent, while the other officer stood near the microphone and looked back at the audience with a bland face. A few moments later Badgent came to the microphone and told the spellbound crowd, 'listen to what this police officer's got to say to you please.'

The officer stepped forward and spoke in a dry, level voice. 'We have reason to believe that there are one or two people here who need to come along with us for questioning.'

Immediately a hubbub broke out as people expressed their indignation. Livvy turned to Bridges angrily, 'This is outrageous. This is Australia!' But Bridges was waving her to silence as Armstrong returned to the microphone.

'Listen friends, 'Armstrong said. 'This is not what you think it is. I'm sure you won't mind doin' what this officer asks when you hear what he has to tell you.' As they fell quiet the officer began again, still in a level tone.
'I'm sorry to have to inform you that there's been a most unfortunate incident. An unidentified person has been the victim of a brutal attack. The said person has…in fact…been murdered. The, er… crime was committed in a house not far from here. This evening. Only a short time ago.'

Livvy clutched Bridges' arm and they shared each other's unspoken fears as they drew closer together. People looked at each other in horror or disbelief, but few said anything, as the policeman continued, 'is Mr Gellies here?'

Bagent turned and waved towards the empty front seat where Lionel had been. Only his recording equipment was still there.

'Excuse me, officer,' Bridges was on his feet. 'This terrible news you've brought us has created anxiety for a lot of people here. Can you tell us anything about the victim?'

'You'll get a full report through the news media in the morning... Mr Gellies, please come forward if you are here.'

Bridges spoke again. 'It's possible he has gone home in search of his sister who left this meeting some time ago. Some of us are worried about her safety, officer. Can you tell us if you have any knowledge of her situation?'

The policeman suddenly appeared much younger and more human as his voice slipped from its cool formality and shakily ran on with a report of a horror very recently witnessed. 'I can't go into the...the shocking details...It's a complete mess!... I've never seen anything like it... Just unbelievable... He never had a chance.'

Bridges and Livvy were not the only ones to note with relief that the young officer said he, not she.

'The, er...the people next door noticed taxis coming and going. And when they went in they found ...er...rang in to report. We had to go in ...All I can say now,' he steadied his voice. 'Is that the victim was an elderly man with one leg and one hand, and apparently he was murdered with a stone axe. Uh, awful! His head was...It, it happened in the Gellies residence in Cavenagh Street.' Above the sounds of abhorrence and fascination that began pouring from the common voice of the audience, a shrill scream swelled into a wail of horror. Helen Cross was on her feet near the back row with her hands to her head and screaming uncontrollably.

A few people stood and stared at the girl as she continued to shriek in spite of people's attempts to calm her. She was swinging her elbows at the women who attempted to hold her. Others were making for the door in terror, just wanting to get out and away.

Bagent called above the din, 'Don't forget to come and sign up with the Black Liberators and Co-operating Kinsmen before you go home.'

Only a handful seemed interested in joining the movement tonight. The rest were either heading out in haste, buzzing in excited conversation, or transfixed and unable to remove their eyes from the hysterical girl, who although she had not stopped her screaming, had now dropped into her seat and allowed a large black woman with a red, black and yellow head band put an arm about her shoulders.

'What'll we do?' asked Livvy, in obvious confusion. Bridges put an arm around her, as he said, 'would you like to see if there's anything you can do to help Helen?'

'Of course,' she replied with a grimace that told him she was afraid of attempting to handle Helen Cross in her present state. Before Livvy reached her, one of the few white women in the audience had made her way through those who were trying to calm Helen, and now was sitting with her. Livvy recognized her as Sister Bernadette, a progressive Catholic, bareheaded in a light-weight white street frock, whom she had met at several inter-disciplinary seminars on community health and education. Her presence seemed to be having the desired effect of calming Helen. Sliding in beside them, Livvy added her comforting support as people moved away now that Helen's fit of screaming had passed. She was silent but still shaking and gasping.

A few minutes later Livvy gave her a little hug and told her not to worry, but have a good rest at Sister Bernadette's place. Bridges called her Kiddo as he promised to find out what was going on, and told her to take it easy. Before going to their car the Gellies watched as the wide-eyed, and visibly distressed young woman left with Sister Bernadette. Livvy explained that they had known each other for many years, and that Helen had readily agreed to go to the Catholic respite unit in the hostel at the convent complex, where she would be cared for until she had recovered from the ghastly shock that had unnerved her.

Most people had already left, and there was little more that the organisers could do, except to sign up a mother with a headband in the Aboriginal colours who, with her husband, wearing a stockman's hat, and their two little boys, had gone forward to enlist in the new initiative, and to chat about what might happen next.

'I wonder where Annette and Mani are,' Livvy said anxiously. 'It'd be pointless to go looking for them. And I don't suppose we'd be much help if we went poking our nose in at her place now.'

Bridges agreed, but drove the long way around, along the Esplanade to the waterfront, then turned for home along Cavenagh Street. There were a couple of cars outside Gellies and the lights were on. 'Poor old Lionel! But I think we'd better not get involved tonight. What do you think?'

'I agree,' Livvy was tentative. 'It's not our business, and we better not give the impression that it is. Let's wait and contact them in the morning. But what a mess for Annette to cope with, poor kid.'

'Not just Annette,' she reminded him.

'Oh, I know,' he agreed. 'But there's nothing more that we can do about it tonight. It doesn't bear thinking about, really, does it?

'It's hideous,' Livvy declared. 'Who could be so monstrous? After all that poor old Ron Smart had been through, to finish up like this…It's…it's just horrible.'

Chapter 20
Midnight swim

When Mani left Bridges and Livvy at the YMCA he ran along the street for a block and then turned right. If Annette Gellies was upset, he reasoned, she would head for home or somewhere else where she might avoid meeting anyone. That meant that she would be walking either along the parkland or in the streets. Since, according to Helen, she was not on the direct route home to their house in Cavenagh Street, she might be found in the Esplanade parkland or the streets adjacent to it. If not, then he would look in one of the adjoining streets. After sprinting around the nearest block and on to the next street, he turned back towards the parklands and the sea, just in time to see a lone walker turn out of view into the Esplanade.

A few seconds later he overtook her, calling as he came near, 'Annette, don't be frightened. It's me, Mani. Can I come and talk to you?'

She turned around, then resumed her course, walking faster.

'I didn't mean to hurt you, Annette,' he said as he pulled up alongside her.

'Go away,' she muttered without slackening her pace; but, rather than going away, he walked beside her in silence for two blocks, until suddenly, she stopped and fixed him with a fierce look, snapping, 'Go away!'

It was a dark place and he could not see her face. Only the thickness of her voice told him that she had been crying. He waited a while before suggesting, 'You want to go for a cuppa?'

She silently shook her head and sniffed, obviously trying to get better control of her voice before saying any more.

'Well, it's a long way to your place,' he said. 'And a lot further to mine. Where can we go to talk?'

'There's nothing to talk to you about.'

Mani stepped nearer as he said, 'Perhaps you have nothing more to say to me, Annette. I can't blame you. I was a bit rough.'

'A bit?' she exploded, and he was glad to get some sort of response from her. At least she was listening. 'Yes, I'm sorry. I was rough,' he confessed. 'But you should let me tell you how I really do like you and what made me speak the way I did.'

She stolidly resisted his approach, standing with her head turned away, as if she were not interested in anything he had so far said, but waiting for something else.

'I don't think a pretty girl like you should be out in the street at night unprotected,' Mani began, but she interrupted him again.

'You're a fine one to talk about protecting a girl!' Her voice trembled and threatened to fail her. 'I've never been so badly treated all my life!'

He scraped the ground with his foot as he admitted, 'sometimes I'm pretty rough, and…and…er, you and Lionel have been good friends to me 'er in Darwin…'

She took his uneasiness as a form of penitence and softened her resistance towards him.

'Why, Mani?' It came as a cry from her heart, and he was sure that she was weeping. She had turned away from him, gasping in a way that suggested that she neither cared if he heard nor expected an answer. 'Why did you say those terrible things?'

She resumed walking, and, as he walked with her he hesitated between telling her his real reason, namely, that he had felt compelled to speak the truth; and saying something to help her now that she had heard the truth. Instead of doing either he turned the question back to her.

'Why do any of us say things that hurt the people we like?'

'Oh!' she scorned him. 'Don't try to tell me you like me Mani, not after what you've said! In front of all those people.'

He moved ahead and stepped in front of her, to block her path and look into her face, revealed now, red-eyed, in the glow of an overhead street-light. 'Why would I want to hurt you, Annette?' he asked her tenderly.

She dropped her eyes as she replied softly, 'because you hate me.'

'That's not true. And I think you know it. I like you Annette. I like you a lot. And I admire you too. You've done things that most people wouldn't dare to do. Living in foreign countries and all that, and, and, you are one of the nicest young women I've ever seen, or ever heard about.'

She hesitated for a second or two, and when he did not go on, she expressed contemptuous disbelief.

'Ptpph! I don't know why I ever admired you,' she told him. 'You know what? Do you know what, Mani?... I used to think you were an honest and kind person. Now I know that you're neither honest nor kind.' She looked into his face as she said this, and he held her gaze as he replied. 'I'm sorry you think like that because I still like and admire you.'

'Lies, lies, lies!'

'I can't stop you from thinking that way,' he said. 'But I want to stay with you until you're in a safe place; and that's what I'm going to do.'

It had alarmed him to see the sorrow welling up in her face and spilling down her cheeks. Affection and dismay inclined him to take this soft feminine creature in his arms to comfort her, but he dared not. Had his words hit her so hard that something in her was broken, snapped? He had recalled memories of single young people found dead in Darwin hostel rooms after ending their own lives. It had never been understandable to him that anyone could feel so desperately unhappy with living that they could do something to make themselves die. Standing there, looking into that face, it no longer was so hard to understand, and he was not prepared to bear the responsibility for leaving her in despair. He must lessen the pressure on her state of mind, not increase it.

'Can we talk here?' he asked gently.

'No,' she said it abruptly, but then looked about and added,

'It's too public.' On the other side of the Esplanade, the open parklands ran for several hundred metres in either direction. 'We could walk over there,' she said, to his great relief.

'Great, let's do that,' stepping aside to let her pass.

She asked, 'it's all right. Isn't it Mani? It is all right, isn't it?'

'You don't have to worry about me, if that's what you mean, I won't let anyone hurt you. Not me, not anyone.'

Now that Annette had agreed to listen, Mani took the opportunity, as they sat on the grass, to explain that, at the Y, he had been trying to share his idea of what a real Christian was. He acknowledged that she had tried all sorts of religions and lifestyles before she had found a new kind of faith in Christ, and he respected her right to decide her own beliefs, and honoured her as a person who knew so much about religion.

'Perhaps I don't understand your way of looking at things,' he said. 'And perhaps you don't understand my way of looking at things. I'm sorry I said rough things about you and held up your name in front of people in a terrible way. But, Annette, now you are saying rough things about me. You say I am a liar. I don't usually let people get away with calling me a liar. Do you really know that I am a liar? Tell me, Annette, is it part of being a Christian to call me a liar?'

'Oh…I was upset. It seemed true at the time. But, I suppose it was an un-Christian thing to say.'

Mani grinned. 'Careful, Annette. You're not saying you're not a real Christian, are you? I got into trouble for that.'

Annoyed, she raised her voice, 'I don't think that's funny,' but seeing contrition in his lowered gaze, she relented, and tried to smile. 'I suppose I was saying I'm not being a Christian right now, being angry with you…but, oh, Mani, it broke my heart to hear you suggest you hope you will never be a Christian.'

'There are different ways of being a Christian,' he suggested tentatively. 'That was what I meant. I was criticising one way that I see some people being Christians. It wasn't fair of me to use you to say what I did. I'm sorry I put those things on you.'

'Mani…I wish that you did know me. But even more I wish you knew the Lord. There is a difference, between knowing about someone and knowing them, really knowing them, as someone you experience in you…and he knows you, and you love him, and he loves you.'

A car turned into the Esplanade and its light revealed them clearly to each other. Whatever the source of her passion, it had set off a new and positive feeling in her and was obviously driving out her sorrow.

She leaned towards him and stared intently into his face, and he wished that he had not thought about the sexual implications of her words. 'I wish you knew him, Mani,' she breathed. 'Oh, Mani, I have failed you, and I have failed the Lord. I have failed to give a good witness to you. To you who I most wish to find true life, life in all its fullness. Forgive me. Please, Mani, forgive me.'

She began to weep again, and he waited before replying. 'It isn't necessary to apologise to me, Annette,' he told her. 'We all have to do and say the way we think is right at the time. But I wish you would give me the chance to tell you how I feel about it all.'

'Not here,' she said as another car turned into the Esplanade and flooded them with light. Getting to her feet she held out a hand towards him, saying, 'Come. I'll show you a place where we can talk without interruption.'

He took hold of her small, soft hand and walked where she led towards the tree-lined cliff-top overlooking Lameroo Beach. In silence they reached the top of a sealed path that ran into pitch darkness down the cliff face. She moved closer to him in the shadows and bumped against him. She froze and they stopped in the intimate darkness.

'What's up?' he asked.
'It's, it's so dark!' she gasped. 'I can't even see you.'

They could hear the waves whispering on the beach below.

'Don't let that worry you,' he replied. 'I can still see you. I don't mind not bein' seen. That just goes with bein' black. So long as I can see you I know we're still here …an' if you hang on to me you can't get lost... Listen, Annette, you've got no need to be frightened... Come on.'
'Would you keep talking?'
'Sure,' he agreed. 'I was wanting to tell you that I've found out that my people and your people see things in different ways.'
'I suppose I always knew that,' she said, edging down the path and feeling for the rail she knew ran along the outside edge.
'But, I mean,' he tried to make an additional point that he felt sure she did not see. 'In everything we know. It's not just that I've got different ideas, but we know it in a different way. I mean, for instance… take time. Everything that happens, everything that can be experienced, goes on in time, doesn't it? Time is here all the time, isn't it?'
'I suppose so,' she sounded unsure of herself, still groping 'Well,' he continued. 'I've found that you white people all follow the same idea of time as if it is like a long line that started a long time ago, and will end in a long time to come. And we're all moving along the line.'
'Yes, I suppose so,' she repeated, nervously stretching, and grasping the rail, feeling immediately more secure to be in touch with the solid line that had a beginning and an end along the path she was following.
'I don't,' Mani said. 'And neither do my old people, or the Indian people. They think time is like a circle and comes back where it was. Sometimes I think they might be right. Some of our old people talk like great-grandfather times come back, and even you mob sing about the good old Summer time as if it's a time that keeps coming back, and about "ever-circling years". It's a nice idea, isn't it?'
'Really I don't know.' She felt the bend in the rail and said, 'Do be careful, Mani, we have to go down several steps and around a bend to the right. Now we head back

in the other direction for the rest of the way down.'

'There, you see,' he said. 'You can find your way in the dark.' They negotiated the steps and the bend and he resumed his lecture in the dark.

'Not like a straight line, or even a circle… more like a point, that's going nowhere except deeper and deeper. We all just sort of walk through the now time. Everyone does, always. Even the ancestors are in the now, only they're deeper down, underneath our now.'

'I don't know why you are telling me all this,' she said

'Well, you asked me to keep talking in the dark?'

'Hmmh.'

They came to a moonlit section at the end of the path, and she looked at him. 'You're a surprising person, Mani… I didn't know you thought like that about Christianity.'

He laughed, 'no, of course you didn't. How could you? You've never listened to me before.' He helped her down several steps and across a pile of large rocks on to the sand. She hooked her arm through his as they were walking towards the water's edge.

'Tide just turned to go out,' he said as they sat near the waves but on dry sand. When she made no reply he asked, 'What's that wall over there in the water?'

'Lionel said it's the ruins of the old sea baths,' she told him. 'Mani… you must think I'm a blind fool. Next to the way you talk about the Lord I think I'm just, just…'

'You're okay, Annette. You're following the light you've seen. What more can you do?'

'I try… I really try. But I'm just not good enough.'

'Maybe you try too hard to be good.'

'What kind of thing is that to say? You just confuse me, Mani.'

They sat in the sound of the gentle lapping of the waves for a minute or more. The night breeze was drifting from the sea, but here, below the cliff, the air was only faintly stirring.

'What do you mean? If you think there's something wrong with me I want to know.'

Annette,' he said gently. 'You seem afraid that you are wrong. You seem to think you have to be always right and perfect. You ask is there something wrong with you as if you think only people with nothing wrong with them can get saved. Jesus shot that one down in flames. That's prob'ly why they crucified him. It was the do-goodin people who got him in the end! He said sinners were okay, too. If they believed in him an' were sorry, they could get saved, too…die and live again, the proper life God meant them to.'

She stared into the dark sea and the flashing light of the moon as it pursued its endless process of falling and rising again.

'Isn't it beautiful here?' he said, and seeing her nodding added. 'I'm glad you wanted to come here and talk.'

'So am I.' The tiny waves seemed to hold their breath a little longer as the man and woman waited, listening, allowing the night to speak to their feelings.

'I don't know what I've been trying to be,' she said at last.

'Good? Haven't you been trying to be good? And calling it Christian?'

'But shouldn't Christians be good?' She sounded perplexed.

'Shouldn't everyone?' he replied. 'But succeeding in being good by trying is not how it can happen. You tell me if I'm wrong, Annette. We've got this wonderful bloke on Goose Island. He's a missionary from Fiji... he calls me his little brother, and I don't even go to his church much. He helped me to understand that it's not trying to be good, but trying to trust that gets us there. Trust can grow into something more he reckons, faith in God is mostly a matter of trusting, he reckons.'

'Do you believe in Jesus Christ, Mani?'

He looked at the earnest and beautiful face close to his, and said. 'I could give you a long answer about God speaking to people in everything, because God cares about everything, and cares about us, and Christ is a way God is speaking to us up close and personal in our human way... but my short answer is 'yes'. Now can I ask you a question?'

'What?'

'Will you come skinny-dipping?' He saw the shock register as she sat back.

'Really?'

'You never been skinny dippin' before?' he asked.

She put her arms about her knees and looked away.

'Yes, I have,' she admitted with shame. 'But that was before...That was with people who had lost touch with reality. We were trying to be little children again.'

'Anything wrong with that? Except you become as little children.'

'But some of the things they...we...did, little children wouldn't do,' she confessed.

'Sounds like wild people,' he said. 'Tell me...do you trust me? It's such a good thing to find someone to trust, isn't it?'

She turned back to look at him in the moonlight. 'Mani... I want to trust you. But it feels...wicked, now to think of...of undressing with you here.'

'Forget it, then, sorry I shouldn't 'ave suggested it.'

'Why did you?' she asked.

'Well, it wasn't to be naughty with you,' he assured her. 'But I think trusting is more important than keeping rules. Trusting each other to respect each other and play together without doing shameful things. You reckon it's goodness to cover up and be ashamed of your body. My family people are usually too shamed to uncover our thoughts and our feelings in front of other people...You ever heard an Aboriginal person argue in front of a group of people? Only if he's drunk or lost his temper, I bet. Or have you seen a man kiss his wife in public? We think it's rude to let people see our own personal inside feelings. But we don't mind if you see our outside body. That's just the way we got packaged by the Creator.'

'But you're an Aboriginal person and you let your ideas and feelings show in front of others. You certainly did tonight.'

'That's because I'm getting caught in culture tangles. My generation has got a mixture in its life'

'And you think I'm caught in some sort of moral bondage?' she asked.

'I'm not saying that...I was just saying wouldn't it be nice if we could be that free and that trusting?'

Springing to her feet, she giggled. 'I'll race you in!'

'What?' He was taken by surprise and had to cope with the fact that she had accepted his challenge, literally, in order to show how much she trusted him. Or was it something else she wanted? He could not be sure, and found himself suddenly nervous and uncertain about whether or not he trusted her, or himself. Desire for Annette unexpectedly blazed through his body, and he was afraid that he was going to seize her.

Her full white figure was revealed in the half moonlight as her dress was pulled over her head and she quickly dropped her panties and removed her bra.

It was by conscious decision and deliberate exercise of will-power that he remained completely motionless.

'Come on, slowcoach!' she teased and began picking her way across the stones into the water.

'This is my friend, and a sister of a friend,' he told himself firmly. 'She's like a sister to me and a hurt thing. She is so soft and easy to hurt, but she trusts. She trusts me. We are going swimming together, not so that I can have her as my woman, but because she has found that she is free to trust again, and is trusting enough to feel free. If I betray her I am an ogre, and she'll be a victim. As these thoughts were running through his mind, he removed his clothes, gathered up hers with his, and stuffed them under a large undercut rock, in case someone came along.

She was almost invisible in the dark water, but with the silver light of the moon and the ripples that she made as she plunged ahead of him broke up the reflections. Quickly he waded after her, in a rush to overtake her, but she had swum out of sight in the shadow margin beside the low stone wall of the old baths.

'What are you doing?' he called softly, swimming closer.

'Stay there!' She ordered in an equally cautious voice, and began to climb the metre high broken rock wall just as the moon emerged from behind the cloud. In the shadow he moved on his back and watched this exquisite creature gaining her balance and beginning to pick her way along its rough surface in the moonlight. She moved slowly, with her arms extended sideways and singing quietly, 'I'm not ashamed! I'm not ashamed! I'm not ashamed! I'm not asha...oh!'

She stumbled and he called quietly, 'be careful!'

'I'm all right,' she replied, picking her way over the rough section with tentative steps, and then resuming her prancing promenade towards the other end. He kept up with her progress, kicking and waving his hands in a fish-tail fashion. It was amusing to see her so free. So beautiful and so free. To hear her humming, singing and mumbling as she advanced.

He hoped that she would not try to go all the way around the old wall, and turned over to swim ahead of her. When he reached the deep end, he prepared to wait for her on tip-toe. Turning towards her, he froze and held his breath. Yes, he was sure of the sound this time…a car door slamming shut. Above the beach, in the parking area near the top of the cliff path a car had come to rest and at least two people were now outside it, talking to each other. Whoever they were, they could hardly be expected to understand this situation if they were to come down to the beach and see them here. He moved closer in order to warn Annette, but it was unnecessary, she had already taken alarm and was hurrying to climb down. A torchlight flashing across the cliff had alerted her to their approach. It was obviously being carried by someone descending the path.

'Help me!' she whispered. They could hear men's voices as the light continued to bounce along, and as Mani came nearer to ensure that she found a footing, he was glad to have a legitimate reason for closeness, even touching, but also afraid of where this might lead, and the harm that could occur as a consequence. Her foot was down the side and his hands were underneath, letting her down into the water, which was up to his chin as he leaned towards her. She came over the edge quickly and he had to take her weight.

'Careful!' he whispered, taking her with his hands on her soft waist and lifting her away from the rough rock and shell surfaces.

'What can we do?' she gasped, sliding down in front of him and turning to grasp his shoulders in order to support herself.

'Don't worry, just stay still and quiet until they go away,' he whispered, wishing that she would not move at all, and yet desiring very much to move with her. He concentrated his attention on what was happening on the cliff path in an effort to shift his consciousness from the sensation of her naked hip floating against his thigh. He supported her by the elbows and tried to reduce contact to a minimum.

'I'm scared!' she gasped, near his ear – too near. He also was scared, of several things, and was losing the battle to prevent passion for her softness from taking over his body and will. 'What can we do?' she whispered, drawing in towards him, as if for comfort. 'Hold me,' she pleaded.

'I am holding you,' he objected mindlessly. Nothing made much sense any more.

'Properly,' she insisted. 'Close,' and so saying, she put her arms about his body and closed the space between them.

'Oh,' she sighed by his ear with her head on his shoulder.

'You're, you're lovely! You've gone different!' He knew her words referred to the erection that had got out of control and was threatening to control the rest of him.

'Kiss me,' she whispered suddenly.

'Ssh!' he rebuked her, taking fright and moving away without letting go. He transferred his grip to her hands and pulled her along.

'They're on the beach,' he whispered, towing her into a place beside the wall where a rock provided a precarious footing 'What if they find our clothes?' she whispered. He put a finger to her lips, reluctant to relinquish all familiar touch, but glad of the increased distance that made room again for thought and will.

'I hid them pretty good,' he whispered, and, let his hand move over her neck and soggy hair as if this would help him aim his words more directly into her ear. 'Under a rock.'

She leaned over his shoulder, holding him about the neck in like fashion and whispered, 'Isn't this exciting?'

'Shh!'

He watched the light as the men reached the rocky descent on to the sand, and had formed a clear opinion about who they were. His finger tips were on her lips again and she kissed them. With the dying remnants of his will and self-control he managed to whisper the one word that signalled in his mind the supreme reason for exercising every caution in their present situation. 'Police.' She froze and drew back, and they both watched as the two men, now faintly visible in the moonlight, walk along the sand, the torch-bearer leading the way a few yards ahead of the other man.

Suddenly the light flashed wildly then lay still. 'Shit' they heard one say. Someone had apparently fallen over or dropped his torch.

'You awright, Bob?' the other man called. Any other conversation was lost to Mani as he coped with Annette and his passion for her. She was trying to say something but he did not dare let her speak. First with his hand and then with his lips he covered her mouth until the pair on the beach had retreated up the pathway. He held his hand over her mouth until he heard the car doors close again, and the car drive away.
'Want to swim now?' he asked huskily.
'I want to make love with you,' she said boldly.
He kissed her gently before he said, 'are you sure?'
'Oh, yes, dear Mani, I'm sure. I've been sure for a long time.'

To her surprise, he swam a few strokes away, out of the shadow. He was just able to stand alone with the calm sea surging him back and forth as it ran over his shoulder. She swam after him and they embraced and kissed again, but it was impossible to hold a footing with Annette's body as well as his own depending on his stability.

'Let's go back to the beach', and pulled her by one hand as he swam on his back. In shallow water he let her go and lay back on his elbows.
'Isn't this beautiful?' he exclaimed.
'It's lovely!' she confirmed, and pushed herself off from the sand below to float across him with her chin on his chest.

He kissed her on the side of the head and put an arm about her as he said, 'did you ever see what happens to a little tree that is held back and tied down, and then the holding rope is cut?'

'No, I never did!' She grinned as she said it. 'Are you going to give me another lecture? You terrible man! You let me confess my love, and then start lecturing me about trees.'
'But,' he pressed on. 'You do know what happens, don't you? The sapling that was tied down doesn't just stand up straight. It swings right over to the other side.'

She stared at him. He swept a finger down her cheek and around her chin, removing the water running there. She interpreted his silence as a request for her to consider the meaning of his words.

'You think I'm like the little tree?' she ventured. He nodded, and waited.

'I was held back,' she said happily. 'Tied down, in fact; and now…twang! I've gone swinging over.'

'It happens,' he told her. 'It happened to thousands of our people when they got the law letting them drink grog like everyone else. Pow! Right over to killing themselves with booze.'

She stared into his eyes with her mouth open, and he leaned forward to cover her lips with his own; but she pushed him away.

'Do you think I'm bad because I want you to love me, Mani?'

'No, dear, beautiful Annette. If you ask me is it wrong? I have to say, no, it's good and it's true and it's beautiful. It's not wrong…It's right…But I have to ask you too, and you have to say what it is for you. What do you say?'

'About what?' She was confused. 'You just told me it's not wrong, my darling'.

'Listen,' he insisted. 'I said it's not wrong for me. But only you can say if it's right or wrong for you. Remember your culture and mine see things in different ways.'

'But if it's wrong, it's wrong, and if it's right, it's right,' she declared. 'I don't care, Mani. How could it be wrong to be loved by you?…darling, thoughtful Mani. This is ours, our time for love. You told me that now is the only time that is important.' She was overcome with passion and flung herself on him, crying, 'Oh, my darling… I love you.'

Mani was swamped by her assault and came up spluttering to join her in laughing and kissing. 'Come on,' he gasped. 'Let's go up on the beach.' He sprang up, scooped her into his arms and began pushing through the water towards the beach while she clung to him laughing with excitement and nuzzling his neck. 'You should try to take off some weight,' he teased.

'Oh! I'm a dainty little thing, you big brute.'

'Don't tell me that!' he declared. 'You're a lot heavier than my wife!'

He felt her whole body snap, and heard her involuntary cry. She writhed to free herself from his grasp and lunged away from him in the water.

'Your wife?'

'That's right,' he said. 'That's what you need to understand…Annette…In the Lore of my people there's a ceremony lore way that men and women in a special straight group might work out that they could be like husbands and wife to each other. And older men can have more wives. So maybe I could start to work out a straight relationship way to think about something between you and me...'

'Your wife!' she snarled.

'That's right,' he said.

'Why didn't you say you were married!' She was aghast and quickly losing control of her emotions.

He moved towards her. 'Annette, I am allowed to think about more than one wife, if I keep to the straight relationsh...'

'Get away from me! Who sent you? Oh...my God! Forgive me! What have I done? Horrible! Horrible!' She thrashed her arms about as she cried and backed away. 'Why did you come after me and make me filthy again?'

'Oh, no, Annette,' he protested. 'I made you do nothing.'

Suddenly she was seized by a sense of shame and tried to cover her breasts and pubic area with her hands as she crouched and kept backing towards the beach, beginning to sob as she gasped, 'Wicked! Wicked! I am a wicked woman. God have mercy! Forgive me, for I am an unclean woman. Leave me, before I destroy you, too. It's my fault, my own most grievous fault. Oh, I want to die.'

He was alarmed to hear her talking in this unbalanced way. It occurred to him that he might have let her go too far and could be responsible for permanent damage to her fragile mind. He went after her, but she ran up the beach to escape his reach, stumbled on a rock and fell.

He diverted to the place where he had left their clothes, and a few seconds later was dressed and on his way to where she was lying on the sand in a fetal position with arms wrapped around her knees and her face buried while she wept and groaned.

'Annette,' he said gently but firmly. 'Here are your things. Please put them on.'

She sat up quickly and grabbed her dress, using it to screen her body from his sight. 'Go away!' 'This is evil! I've led you into evil! But you tricked me. Satan sent you. Oh, horrible! Horrible! Oh!'

'Stop it', he commanded. 'Now, you shut up that stupid talk! You're not evil. You're a nice girl with a lot of love in you that you want to give to someone. You wanted it to be me...'

'Stop it!' She covered her ears. 'Stop! Stop talking about it!'

He grabbed her wrists and pulled her arms down. 'Listen,' he told her. 'You are a lovely and a loving girl,' she was writhing alarmingly and trying to free her arms. 'Tonight,' he went on. 'You showed some of the love God put in you. It was nice to start to unpack that parcel with you. One day you and your own lover will do that, and it will be good and right.'

She looked at him and sat still. 'Have you finished?'

'Yes, Annette,' he released her. 'Except to say I'm going to walk home with you.'

'Look the other way,' she commanded him. 'I have to get dressed.' It took her three or four minutes to dress. Then, silently she begin to walk towards the cliff path with Mani close behind her.

'Let me take your hand,' he said as they began to pick their way across the rocks on to the path in the deep shade.

'No, no,' she told him lightly. 'You're a married man. Oh, I'm disgusting... But how was I to know if you didn't tell me?...Please don't touch me...I'm not blaming you... I'm the sinful one, but you should have told me.' She led the way up the path with her hand on the rail, but as they strode across the park and around into Knuckey Street, he walked beside her. Once she said to him, 'I wish you would go away. I mustn't be seen walking with a married man.' He ignored her, and they continued for three blocks without a word being spoken. When they reached the corner of Cavenagh Street she told him to go but he thought that he should fulfil his obligation to care for her by seeing her to the door of her house.

'Don't come any further,' she warned. 'Unless you want to bring shame and disgrace on both of us. Go away.'

'All right, if that is what you really want. Goodnight, Annette,' he said with mixed regrets. 'I'm sorry it turned out like this. I only wanted to let you know that I really am your friend.'

'Even friendship can be evil,' she declared. 'I'm sorry I have been an instrument of hell. I hope I can amend my ways and find cleansing grace. I'll pray for you, too.'

'Take it easy, Annette...don't blame yourself so much. Remember we did nothing wrong.'

'Wrong?' she echoed. 'Oh, yes, we did. Very wrong. I'm ashamed to think anyone would ever find out. I couldn't stand it if Lionel did.'

'No-one will find out from me,' he promised, and waited for her reply.

'Goodbye,' she said dully, and walked away along Cavenagh Street towards the house where she lived. There was a light in the front room of Gellies' place and a couple of cars parked across the road, but Mani saw Annette creep around to the back of the house. She obviously wanted to get inside without Lionel and his visitors seeing her.

Someone approached the front steps, then stepped between the garden bushes to peer through the open louvres. Mani thought he recognised the landlord from next door, and this was verified when another figure shuffled towards him, obviously the landlord's wife. Her husband waved her away, and followed her back towards their own place. It annoyed Mani to see this sneaky spying behaviour. But there was no more that he could do here, and, since the College bus would have already gone on to Batchelor, he turned back towards the centre of town where he could find a taxi or phone for one.

PART THREE
Big Man Business

Chapter 21
Who done it?

The cab driver was glad to get a big fare. He was chirpy and sounded as if he might be ready to talk all the way to Batchelor, but Mani rode in the back seat where he could be left alone to think about what had happened to him and Annette.

'And where are we going to?' the driver asked his passenger's image in the mirror.

'Batchelor!' Mani told the back of his head.

'The Batchelor Teacher's College, is it, mate?' The driver checked.

'Yeah,' Mani confirmed. 'I don't want to wake 'em up when we get there. So can you stop before we go right in?'

'Not ay problem!' The driver glanced in the mirrors and swung the cab around to head out of town. 'I know the very spot. Been there many a time.'

'That's good', Mani settled back to try to get straight in his head the weird things that had happened this night.

'Not ay problem,' the driver repeated, sounding hopeful that a conversation might begin to lighten his long dark drive in this sultry midnight hour. 'We always aim to please.'

'That's good,' Mani repeated absently, and added. 'You might have to wake me up when we get there.'

This driver was experienced enough to know when he was being told to shut up. Playfully he replied, 'Roger, wilco!' and fell silent to let his passenger try for a little shut-eye. But this passenger had too much going over in his mind, enough to keep sleep away for hours. His first attempts to think about the events of the evening were swamped by familiar feelings of anger and revulsion that boiled within him yet again. Nothing ever happened the way it should! Oh, Annette, what did you think I was? Oh, bugger it all. Nothing goes right any way.

He stared through the window seeing nothing more interesting than occasional clumps of trees side-lit by the taxi's headlights. Gradually his heart eased, and he thought again about how unfair it was that he could neither live in the old way nor the modern Balanda way. He could only exist as someone jumping from one to the other. And people treated him as some kind of genius who knew all about being both kinds of person. It wasn't like that. Most of the time it was like being in a game of racial football, as the ball! That wasn't the whole story, he knew, but he was tired of the burden of responsibility that had fallen to him. So it was him who had to learn, as his grandfather would say, how the Balanda magic works, and he hated having to be the one who could make the Balandas understand and respect his people's culture. At times he thought he had found a sound way to grasp the magic and the life-style of the Balandas, but then it became more confusing than ever. Tonight he felt as if maybe he had completely failed to understand things at all.

How did he dare say those things to Brown at the YMCA? And what else could he have done in his encounter with this sad, disturbed white girl on the beach? Right now he felt overwhelming doubt about himself. In fact, he was not sure that he could feel any trust or confidence in anyone or anything.

He remembered the way he felt on the sea in his canoe, fishing to feed his people. He longed to live like a man in a canoe. His mind swung back to his lost canoe, and for a while he felt nothing. Nothing but emptiness and heaviness, both at the same time. He looked out for signs along the road, impatient now to be in his bed and asleep.

'Oh no!' the driver was looking at headlights approaching. They were on full beam, and appeared to be veering from left to right and back again! 'You got your belt on?'

'Yeah.' Mani sprang bolt upright. 'What is it?'

'Some o' your mob!' the driver sounded exasperated with Mani's mob, Aboriginal men he supposed. He deliberately maintained speed and steered along the middle of the road.

'There's plenty of room over on the left,' Mani advised.

'That's good! We'll probably need that to dodge 'em.'

'Why don't we pull over and stop until they get past?'

'Because the last time someone tried that, the other car followed them. It ran off the road and into the headlights. No survivors!'

'I heard about it,' Mani recalled. 'Drunks, eh?'

'Suicidal drunks…'ere they come! Now you just shut up, get down low, and cover you face.' Mani filled his lungs and held his breath, preparing to duck down, but transfixed at the glaring lights bearing down on them. At the point when collision seemed inevitable he plunged his face down on his folded arms, and was thrown against the right side of his seat-belt, as the driver swerved violently to the left. A moment later the lights were gone and they had straightened without even running on to the unsealed edge of the highway.

'Whoo!' Mani cried with relief at still being alive. 'Wow! Nice goin'…whoo, thanks mate…Great drivin'.'

'Thank you, kind sir,' the driver managed to sound cool, as if such manoeuvres were all in a day's work. 'We always aim to please.' They were almost at Batchelor, and Mani was anxious to be there now. The incident had made him feel sick. The spectacle of those lethal headlights represented to him the destruction of his people, his self-destructive people. Why couldn't the sober and caring people give leadership and lift the damaged people. Why didn't the old people make them give leadership?' Blaming them or anyone else seemed pointless.

Even what he had said to Annette and Andrew Brown was not necessary, not fair. They were just victims, too, caught up in the chaos of messed up lives and cultures. He tried again to stop thinking about it all, and found himself wondering if it would have been better if he had not met Armstrong and spoken at his rally. Strangely, he felt a sense of relief that he had gone onto the stage and dared to speak his heart and mind, even though now, in the cool darkness of the night, he concluded that he was just as wrong as the people he had criticised. Including Annette. Poor Annette!

* * *

He was aware that it must be long after midnight when he paid the taxi driver at Batchelor. He walked on the lawns and let himself in quietly, but not unheard. Before he could close his bedroom door the leery black face of Joey Barama from the next room appeared.

'Hey, you dirty old man,' rasped the sleepy neighbour. 'It's nearly four o'clock! You been woman 'untin', eh. Dijya get any?'

'What do yah want, Joey?' Mani refused to open the door wide enough for Barama to enter. 'I need to get to sleep.'

'You been with a woman, eh?' Barama persisted.

'Yeah, just sitting on the beach talkin',' Mani began. 'What do want?'

'You dirty old man.' Barama repeated, grinning obscenely, before passing on some serious information. 'The Principal was 'ere, lookin' for yah. Pretty important. They want you for askin' about somethin' or other.'

'Who wants me?' Mani was startled, wondering if it was possible that Annette could have made a complaint against him.

'I dunno, might be police, I reckon,' Barama was serious.

'Did the Principal say police?' Mani asked.

'No,' Barama replied shrewdly. 'Only, I could tell, the way he spoke, mus' be police, I reckon.'

'It's good you told me,' said Mani.

'No worries,' Barama seemed gratified by his neighbour's expression of appreciation. 'You want to talk about it?' Mani preferred not to talk, and Joey Barama withdrew, none the wiser about what woman-hunting or other adventures had cost his fellow student so much sleep.

It was half an hour before Mani got to sleep, and a rapping on the door seemed to begin almost immediately and wouldn't stop. It was the Principal, at half past seven, as Mani discovered when he staggered to the door pulling up his shorts.

'I've got to speak to you,' said a grim-faced Brian Adams, and dumbly Mani let him in. He had a special respect for Mister Adams. He looked like a straight and unbending Mister Talltree, clean-shaven face, short back and sides black hair, slicked back, and neat dark shorts and shoes to contrast with his neat white shirt and socks. But those who had to deal with him soon learnt that there was more to him than appeared on the surface.

'Can I talk with you?' the Principal asked. 'Are you awake enough to talk?'

'Yeah, I think so,' said Mani, sitting on the edge of his bed. 'What's up?'

'Where were you last night?' asked the Principal.

'Why?' Mani's adrenalin had begun pumping, and he found himself suddenly wide awake. 'Why do I have to say where I was?'

Brian Adams came closer and stood before him as he said, 'Because the police were looking for you last night. They rang, and when I checked, Johnny Barama said that other students who had gone up to the rally at the YMCA had returned in the college bus without you. That was at eleven o'clock.'

'But what did they want me for?' Mani was more puzzled than ever. 'They said it was in connection with a murder.' The Principal watched Mani's face as he gave this information.

'Murder?' Mani's genuine surprise gave Brian Adams the assurance he needed that his student was innocent of any involvement with the crime. He pulled up the bed-room chair and gave Mani the bare facts that he had put together from the police visit and the morning radio news. An elderly white man had been murdered with a stone axe in a Darwin house.

'Look Mani,' the Principal said. 'I am confident you had nothing to do with it… but you have to tell the police where you were, and who can vouch for you being there after you left the YMCA. They're coming here to see you this morning. As a matter of fact they're on their way now. So, where were you?'

'Well, I was just…' Mani stopped, remembering Annette's final words before they separated last night. "I'm ashamed to think anyone would find out!" and his reply, "No-one will find out from me".

'I was out walkin',' he offered weakly.

'Oh, you'll have to do a lot better than that, Mani,' Adams warned him, but to no avail. His student had nothing more to tell him.

The next hour seemed quite unreal to Mani. He felt completely stupid as he avoided telling the Principal where he had been in the middle of the night, and even more so when the CIB's Inspector Donovan arrived with a Sergeant Green to ask the same questions. After a quarter of an hour of refusing to answer, Mani was required to enter the police car, in spite of the Principal's objections, and travel to Darwin to be held for investigation at the Darwin Police Station.

As the car was leaving, Adams was called on the public address system to take a 'phone call in the office. It was Bridges, who had been wanting to speak with Mani Manggululu, and been referred to the Principal.

'That's right, Gray,' the Principal agreed with his Darwin caller that it was absurd to try to link Mani with a brutal murder. 'But Mani's going to have to come clean and let them know where he went from the Y, or he's in deep trouble.'

Bridges could not understand why Mani would not tell the police his movements, and said so. 'People make mindless connections, and they're bound to see an association between him and the stone-axe murder, because of his speech at the rally.'

Brian was interested to hear what the speech had been about, and shared Bridges anxiety when he heard of the strong way that Mani had spoken about white racism.

'Oh, 'struth!' he said heavily. 'That's all some of em'll need to pin it on an Aboriginal. He must tell them everything he did.' He paused before saying, 'Gray you don't think there is any chance that Mani is......'

'No way in the world!' Bridges told him, suddenly feeling an uncertainty himself about the whole situation. Even as he assured Adams, his own assurance faltered. What if Mani had gone out and killed the old man? How could he be so sure that it could not have been him who did it? But then Bridges remembered the near strangling of Foster on Goose Island.

When Bridges came off the phone, he found Livvy ready to leave for work, but just as concerned as he was about their young friends who had been swallowed up by the darkness on the previous evening. 'I suppose Annette did come home. Poor Lionel and Annette,' she said. 'They must be in a daze. Fancy having such a terrible thing happen in their house. We could go there on the way to work. And I wonder how Helen is, after her night with the nuns?'

'Perhaps we should give them until lunch time, then call up Sister Bernadette to see how she is,' said Bridges. 'My guess is she'll be fine after having a sleep and a chance to think things over.'

'I hope so.' Livvy did not sound nearly so sure. 'She really went right off, didn't she?'

'Yeah, poor kid.' Bridges' thoughts were swinging to the Cavenagh Street brother and sister and Mani. 'Why don't I drop you off at their place, and you pop in and see how the Gellies are? I've got to get to the office as quick as I can. If Mani's being held for questioning he'll need all the support he can get from the Chief Minister's Liaison people. I've got to get Ned and old Fred on side.'

In spite of a natural repugnance at the thought of visiting the murder house, Livvy agreed to be the one to go there.

* * *

The Chief Minister was already in his office with Fred Archer and a couple of visitors when Bridges arrived, and had been fully briefed already about the murder. But Harry Bagent was the only Liaison Officer who was also making an early start.

'You heard?' Harry asked with his confidence from last night still alive in his face. 'They're holdin' a black on suspicion of murder, and Fred's in with Ned the Head and a couple o' lawyers now. They said I'm to stay out an' tell everyone else to stay out.'

'What are they doin'?' Bridges asked, 'working out how to help Mani?'

'Manggululu, eh?' Bagent whistled. 'That who they're holdin'? What have they got on 'im?'

'Nothing, Harry. Absolutely nothing.' Bridges declared. 'But he'll need some good support if they're to give him a fair go. I want to talk with Ned.'

'Well, 'e don't want o' talk to you, mate...'e said tell everyone to keep out. What a bloody mess!' Bagent was emphatic. 'Just as well us liberators were all at the Y when it happened, or they'd be tryin' to pin it on us. Mani Manggululu, eh!...'e wouldn't've 'ad time to get over there and kill anyone, after 'e left an' before the cops arrived, I don't reckon.'

'I've thought about that, Harry,' said Bridges. 'I'm afraid there was time, all right. It doesn't take long to walk over to Cavenagh Street from the Y. If you ran, it'd only take a few minutes.'

The meeting in the Chief Minister's office continued for half an hour before anyone emerged. By that time all of the Liaison Officers had arrived, including the Chief L.O. Andrew Brown. The old man came in last, five minutes later than official starting time, most unusual for him, and looking as if he had not slept very well. Bridges noticed that Andrew lacked some of his usual shine, and felt sympathetic towards him as he recalled the humiliating condemnation he had suffered during Mani's speech. It obviously had hurt him deeply. He went into Andrew's office and began to express his concern for Mani and the need to win official support for him to get a proper chance to defend himself. Andrew was appalled to hear of Mani's predicament, and committed himself to add weight to Bridges' approach to Fred Archer and the Chief Minister.

'How could they suspect young Manggululu?' Brown said softly, from behind his desk. He looked at Bridges as he said, 'he's got a sharp tongue, and I felt it last night…but he only means to do good. He wouldn't do that kind of thing. Why would he need to kill anybody?'

A group of four white men arrived, all of whom Bridges recognised. The Director of the Health Department, Cecil Reeders, and the Assistant Director of Education, Oliver Sutton, were together with two official-looking men who had been at the YMCA last night. Reeders knocked on the Chief Minister's door and the four were admitted. As they entered Fred Archer emerged. His face was flushed, and he entered Andrew's office with an air of confidentiality. 'Well, this is a fine old tin of worms.' Fred was emphatic, trying, without success, to sound important. 'This is the sort of thing that can set our work back ten years.'

Ignoring the implications of Archer's clichés, Bridges said, 'Fred I'm wondering if the Chief Minister's aware that it is Mani Manggululu who is being held, and if he's prepared to give the young man some official support.'

'The Chief Minister…' Archer snapped, then walked close enough to touch Bridges, before continuing more calmly, '…is aware of far more than you can ever know.'

'Then he will help Mani?' Bridges asked.

'He most certainly will not. Don't you know anything? Do you think a head of a government can just interfere with legal processes when he feels like it?'

'He can let us talk for Mani,' Brown declared, more strongly than Bridges had ever heard him speak. It was truly remarkable that the chastised elder should be coming forward as a champion of the cheeky young man who had publicly criticised him. Again Bridges was confronted by the enigma of Aboriginal personalities.

'I'm afraid he can't do that either,' Archer seemed to get some sort of satisfaction in telling them. 'The Chief Minister has decided that all staff are to stay away from the prisoner…'

'There has been no official arrest…' Bridges began to protest.

'Nevertheless,' Archer went on. 'To stay away. This is a real test for our neutral role as Liaison Personnel. We must not be seen as trying to influence legal outcomes. We are not a legal aid service. And it could reflect poorly on our unit if any of our staff gets too involved with a murder suspect.'

'Oh, come on, Fred!' Bridges was angry. 'This is a classic case where cross-cultural liaison work is needed.'

'No!' said Archer. 'No liaison work, the Chief says.'

Bridges saw that it was pointless to talk further with the Unit Director. He had been given the Chief Minister's orders and he was in an inflexible position. 'We are not a legal aid service,' Archer repeated, 'and we are not a welfare agency. We've got our own work. We'll do that, and we won't do other people's work for them.'

'So we are not allowed to help Aboriginal people now?' It was Brown who put the impertinent question, and the other two men could hardly believe their ears. 'What are we here for then?' he asked, his voice remaining calm and quiet, but newly charged with courage.

'You're here to do as you're told,' Archer told him. 'If Malcolm Manggululu is innocent he'll have the chance to prove it. Meanwhile, we have to get on with our work.' He turned to Bridges. 'It's time the Chief had a bit more paper-work out o' you, on the proposed consultation programme.'

'Right! Relax Fred,' Bridges bridled the obnoxious Unit Director, but decided to stay calm and not get hooked into the usual bickering. 'Fair comment. I'll get it done.' Archer moved towards the door, but turned to speak about something that apparently was too exciting to keep to himself.

'We're gonna have to smarten up this unit. Sometimes I think you people don't appreciate the brilliant leadership that we serve. Right at this moment, while you are grizzling about something that is no concern of ours, our Chief Minister's got it under control. He's getting ready to go himself and talk face to face with the old Wainanda land-owner of that country down Jim Jim way.'

'You mean Jambagirrila from Goose Island?' Bridges asked in astonishment. "The one we were sent out to speak with?'

'That's the one,' Archer told him. 'Mister Blyth's tired of beating around the bush. This is a great man we've got as the head of our government, and he can't wait around until everyone feels happy to move. Today he's going to meet the old man face to face on his land, and they are going to really hear each other.'

'My God!' Bridges gasped, suddenly jolted awake to a sinister side of the Chief Minister that he had never really suspected. Archer looked at him, waiting for an explanation, but Bridges decided not to share with him what was as plain as day. It appalled him to think that while Mani was being detained, the Chief Minister, and

God knew who else, would go and "consult" with Jambagirrila, not about coming to the consultation. That had already been done. Clearly, the present circumstances presented a temptation that could not be resisted, a chance to get an expression of agreement from a number one land-holder. About what? What else? The thing that Ned wanted from the Wainandas was permission to have open access to land for mining and tourism.

It would not be at all surprising if someone took along the necessary documentation to assist the old man to sign away his right to object to anything the government chose to allow on his land. This while his grand-son was in police custody. While staff were directed not to visit him. What other reason could there be why the Chief Minister wanted the unit members to stay away from Mani? The longer it took to get a release, the better it would suit his purpose. Jambagirrila without Mani should be a pushover. If this were the case, then the government might even be advantaged if Mani were to be actually indicted for the murder. Then he would be out of the way for a long time, and unable to influence his grandfather against signing more powerful documents.

Bridges felt sick as he considered the implications of the two circumstances Archer had brought to their attention: that they must leave Mani to handle his own situation as best he could, and that the Chief Minister was arranging a visit of Jambagirrila to his traditional land, and was going there to consult with him while his grandson was locked away.

'When's the Chief going out there, Fred?' Bridges assumed a calm manner.

'Before lunch we'll be in Jabiru, and so will the charter with the elder from Goose Island. From there we'll go south to Gudjigari Rock by four-wheel drive.' He stared at the lesser servants of his Chief. 'I hope you appreciate the Chief's commitment,' he said. 'He is prepared to spend up to three days in the bush with these people, in the cause of good relationships.'

As Archer left them, Andrew's phone rang. The Chief Liaison Officer, Brown, took a call from someone at the Darwin Hospital. Bridges signaled that he was prepared to go and come back later, but Brown waved him into a chair. This suited Bridges because he wanted to stay long enough to shake Brown's hand and express appreciation of the firm approach that he had just taken with Archer.

As he put the phone down Bridges asked, 'someone been in an accident?'

'Yes,' Brown told him. 'The old man, Bilago. He cut open his arm in a fall last night. I'll go and see him bye and bye.'

'Does someone at the hospital let you know when Aboriginal patients come in?' asked Bridges.

'Sometimes.' Brown hesitated. 'But this time the patient asked them to tell me. I try to look after Bilago sometimes.'

'So I've noticed,' Bridges recalled seeing the Chief Liaison Officer caring for Bilago at the Airport and on the edge of the crowd at the demonstration in the park. 'What happened to the old man? Did you say he cut his arm?'

Brown was obviously not at ease talking about the other old man, and spoke haltingly. 'The sister said, he told her a woman pushed him down the front steps of a house, last night.'

'Poor old bloke.' Bridges imagined a scene similar to the one he had witnessed at Red Sails hotel. The old man really was repulsive when he was drunk. On the other hand, the one in front of him was a man to be shown new respect, and he was anxious to do something to acknowledge this.

'Andrew,' he said. 'You're a remarkable man. I liked the way you spoke up to old Fred just now. I don't think I have always shown respect for you as I should have. I want to apologise for that and...' He stood and gave his hand to the older man, who accepted it with a blank expression and shook it warmly.

In the next five minutes Bridges shared his anxiety with Brown about the proposed consultation between the Chief Minister and Jambagirrila, and was delighted to hear the old Liaison Officer say, 'I think you're right, Bridges. That's what the government will try to do. But I will go with the Chief Minister. If he says no, we don't need Aboriginal Liaison Officers, I'll let the newspapers know, and I'll tell him that. I'm the one to go, because I am a Wainanda man, too. I know that country, and I can speak up too, for the people of the land. And I told my old countryman I would stand again with him in that land.'

'Good on you!' Bridges was genuinely thrilled with the fighting spirit of his colleague. Whatever had happened to Uncle Tom? He wondered as he made his way to his own office. It was a sterile little room, and never more so than now. The bark painting of the kangaroo was a pathetic piece of commercial art behind his disgustingly clear desk. Archer was right, he had not turned out much desk-work lately. From the start, he knew that the effort was futile, but he sat at the desk, turned on his PC, and tried to concentrate as he typed some notes with a heading, 'Consultation Strategy Procedures.'

But there were too many thoughts buzzing in his head. For instance, what about Lionel? He was surely going to the house to find Annette. No, the thought of Lionel with his precious stone-axe crashing down on the head of an old stranger really was impossible. By now, Livvy would have spoken with him at the house.

The house. Something about it troubled him. It was a murder house, of course; but there was something else. A thought was begging for his attention. The house had a garden, it had a room with a stone axe on the wall, or a place where it had been, and louvres and flywire door and...!He saw it. It had front steps...The connection was made. The old man Bilago had been pushed down steps by a woman, and a woman had come rushing into the YMCA after fleeing the murder house. Could it be that Helen had knocked Bilago down the steps of the murder house? If so, why? One was now in hospital and the other in care at the Nightcliff Convent, and both had been present at the place where Ron Smart had been murdered! It should be easy enough to visit them. If he could not go to see Mani, then perhaps he could do something else to discover what actually had happened at the Gellies house last night. The next step must be to find out what Livvy had learnt by going to see Lionel and Annette.

* * *

'Hullo darling,' Livvy sounded upset when she answered. 'I'm glad you rang. I've just got in. I was talking with Lionel until a few minutes ago. Gray, Annette's gone missing!'

'Missing?' He was taken completely by surprise by the news. 'Gone missing?'

'That's right,' Livvy assured him. 'When she didn't come in last night, Lionel checked her room and found that she had been back there and taken a travel bag and personal things. After all of our searching for her, she deliberately gave us all the slip, even Lionel... Can you believe that? And she's been so dependent on him to look after her. He's in a mess. He can't handle it, and is close to tears all the time. It's not a pretty sight... What on Earth could have happened to her?'

She went on to say that Lionel suspected foul play and had informed the police. When Livvy left him, the wretched young man was still waiting for Inspector Donovan, the detective in charge of the murder investigation, to arrive to discuss the disappearance.

'It sounds as though they think the murder and the disappearance are linked,' said Bridges.

'What do you think?' she asked.

'It's all so...I don't know what to make of it,' Bridges admitted. After telling Livvy about his own plight of being forbidden to contact Mani at the cells, he shared his idea of a way to make their own investigation. The sooner Mani was cleared of suspicion, the sooner he could support his grandfather in coping with the wily ways of those who had designs on his land. She agreed when he told her of his intention to visit Bilago at the hospital in Casuarina, and she decided to call on Helen at Nightcliff, and then they could meet at Red Sails for lunch and compare notes.

'Sounds good to me,' she said. 'Darling, one other thought…Father Dick.'

'What about him?' Bridges began, then saw her point. 'Oh, yes, of course. The poor guy will be really upset about old Ron being murdered. But you meant something else too, didn't you, like, Dick knows about old Ron Smart's background…?'

'That's right,' she confirmed. 'He would know who else would have any idea that Ron Smart was going to the house.' The sudden return of another thought set off an acutely unpleasant sensation in the pit of Bridges' stomach. If it became public knowledge that he and Livvy had known in advance that the old leprosy sufferer would visit the Cavenagh Street house, and someone pointed out that they were among a small number of people who would have been in the vicinity of the Gellies' house last night, then they could be linked with the approximate time of the killing, the place and the victim. This was the truth, but there was no need to worry Livvy with such negative thoughts. Instead, he shared another significant fact.

'Your old departmental friends were visiting with Ned again this morning, with a couple of well-dressed burlies who were at the rally last night,' he told her confidentially.

'Those ASIO blokes?' she asked, but he cut her off.

'Perhaps we can talk about it when we see each other, sweetie,' he said, and she took his meaning that the phones, even mobiles, were hardly private enough for what they needed to say to each other.

A phone call to the Catholic Mission Office revealed that Father Sheehan would be in near midday, and Bridges left a message to say that he would call in to see him at twelve-thirty. Then he set off to visit someone who, in all probability, had been at the Gellies' house last night.

On the way to the hospital he pondered the fact that the Chief Minister had been consulting in his office with what seemed to be a team of security agents, given to checking up on people, and some other highly placed men. They were being consulted at a time when the Head of Government was planning to move in on a vulnerable old land-owner, and was allowing an honourable young Aboriginal leader to remain in police custody when official advocacy might have gained his speedy release. What were they up to?

Was there a conspiracy to establish the cause of white supremacy while pretending to believe in Aboriginal liberation, self-management and equality before the Law?

Clearly Livvy thought so, but, until now, it had seemed to him to be too far-fetched. Now he was more inclined to believe that, perhaps, he and she both should take care not to let any of the reactionaries get anything on them, such as the knowledge that they were privy to information about Ron Smart's visit to the Gellies' house.

Chapter 22
The Ghost

The Darwin Hospital at Casuarina, modelled on one designed for Canberra, a southern city, looked strangely out of place in this tropical setting.

He found Bilago in a four bed ward. Two of the other beds held sleeping occupants and another was temporarily empty. As he entered, Bilago turned to him as if he had expected a visit, but seemed surprised that the visitor was Bridges. Behind the patient was a stack of pillows and another on the left to support his arm where bandaging protruded past the pulled up sleeve. His groomed white hair and spotless pyjama top contrasted with the usual appearance of the old man. Above the bed a card, over the attending doctor's name bore, the information that the patient was called 'Mr Bilago.'

'Excuse me, sir,' a smiling nurse pushed past Bridges as he approached the bed.

'Here you are!' she said to Bilago, 'a message for you. All right? Do you need anything?' She handed him a note and patted the stack of pillows behind his back. 'Are you all right? Any pain? Want a drink?'

'Jus a liddle dring,' he croaked.

'A drink. All right.' She spoke loudly, but with the soft, sentimental tone of one who wants to comfort. She was young, Bridges noticed. 'I'm sorry I can only let you have orange juice or iced water.'

'Warder,' the thirsty man whispered hoarsely.

'Do you want me to read you what the note says?' she offered. He shook his head, and pointed to the drawer of his bedside cabinet.

'Can I 'ave me glasses?' he looked at her uncertainly. The nurse was glad not only to find the glasses but to take them from their case, unfold them and position them over his ears and nose. Then, with a smile at the waiting visitor, she departed to comfort others. 'You wanna see me?' Bilago asked, surprising Bridges by initiating conversation.

'Yeah, I don't know if you remember me,' said the visitor.

'I remember.' The old patient had removed his spectacles and was wiping them over the folded bed sheet with his free hand. He held them towards the window, breathed on them and rubbed them again on the sheet.

'I remember you around. You Mister Britches. You pick up me when I was drunk.'

'Right,' said Bridges. 'Do you mind if I sit down and have a talk?' Bilago was obviously more interested in reading his note, but he looked up briefly and waved the paper in the general direction of a chair by the other side of the bed. When Bridges had drawn the chair up and sat down, Bilago put the note on the bedsheet in front of him, his freshly shaved, sorrowful, black face a picture of nervous apprehension as he squinted his smoky, blood-shot eyes at the government man.

'Did 'e ask you to come an' see me?' he asked expectantly, lifting the note as he spoke. Bridges read the note that was being offered, and felt more embarrassment that he had not even given a thought to whether or not Andrew Brown might have wanted to travel to the hospital with him. He read.

Sorry you got hurt again. I will come soon. Today I give straight talk to biggest tree. That's all. Andrew.

'Ees a busy bloke, that one,' rasped Bilago. 'Too much work that bloke.'

'Yes, he keeps busy.' Bridges wondered at Bilago knowing that he had some connection with Andrew. 'You know we work together?'

'I know dat!' The old man was blunt, perhaps preoccupied and irritable, with eyes cast down. The devastation of the years showed in his rough, furrowed old face, still quite black, but lacklustre, drained, what Bridges sometimes thought of as pale black.

'No, he didn't ask me to come,' he answered. 'But I decided to come to see you myself. You're right…Andrew's very busy today. He's got an important man to talk…'

'Chief Minister,' Bilago interrupted. 'I know dat! We call 'im Number One Mister Tall Tree. 'Ees the Bigges Tree.' He looked up with the beginnings of a smile. Then he watched his visitor as he went on, 'you wanna talk to me, eh?'

'Really,' Bridges leaned forward over the bed as he spoke. 'I want to listen to you, if you'll give me some of your story, old man.' He waited, steadily watching for a response. The old patient became absolutely serious and tight-lipped. He searched this Balanda's face for a while before reaching for the note. He looked at it again, for a long, silent moment, and laughed with a clattering sound that turned to coughing.

'Yah wanna…. huh, hear my story, eh?… Ol' Bilago?… Hee, ha, huh, huh, huff! I never tol that before. You can't believe that story, mine!'

'You tell me, and I'll believe you,' Bridges vowed with utter seriousness.

'Hmm,' the old man became solemn, laid his hand on his arm and felt the firmness of the bandage under the sleeve at his elbow, then seemed to concentrate on something in the centre of the white sheet that covered his lower body.

The nurse arrived with a bottle of water and a clean glass, and poured him a drink with care. 'There we are!' After she left and after the old man had sipped the water, he looked at his visitor, and spoke in a low voice filled with a new emotion. Was it grief?

'You 'eard that news?' he asked.' 'Ol Balanda got killed las' night?'

'Yes, I heard about that,' Bridges replied. 'How do you know about it?'

'Ere now,' the old man swung his arm towards the earphones lying beside him on the cabinet. 'Radio. I pick up the news ere.' He winced with pain as he adjusted his injured arm.

'Yes, I heard the news,' Bridges repeated and waited to discover why Bilago had raised the subject.

'Bad bissness…' the old man growled, 'e bin all finish now.'

'He sure is finished,' Bridges agreed. 'Did you know the man who was killed, Bilago?' The question seemed to trouble this old man, and it was a few moments before he replied.

'What? You reckon I should know that man, eh?' It was a put-off and Bridges decided not to pursue his enquiry.

'Was just thinking,' he said. 'Yah know Lionel Gellies and people at his house, and I eard that old man got kilt at that place.'

He left it in the air.

'Ee-ee, I know that Gelly, an that 'ouse, all right, and some other people from der. That's true.' The old man stopped again and Bridges decided to be more direct.

'A girl, young Aboriginal woman, came out of the house a bit upset last night. In a big hurry.'

Bilago held his bandaged upper arm with his hand as though in pain. 'She come out like a bloody buffalo an' knock me off that doorstep,' he admitted openly. 'That's how I got this arm cut open. Big stick in the garden somebody lef there pokin up. Stitched up now. Pretty good, too. Nice clean stitchin.'

Bridges was beginning to realise that the man he had been relating to was nothing like the real, unrevealed person on the bed before him. How could he possibly judge whether or not his medical attendant had done nice clean stitching? 'So you were at the house where the old fella got killed?' Bridges asked. Bilago looked at him, and then at the sheet covering his lower body.

'Only outside. I was goin in, but I didn't…she push me off them steps. She didn't try to push me down. No….She jus come bustin out. Jus ran straight through me! I must a been knocked out, I reckon. My arm was bleedin' right down, and I put on pressure with my other hand, and lift it up high to stop the blood…an' start to walk up to the ol' 'ospital. Ol one, cause I was drunk…an' den I membered an' saw a taxi in Smith Street, and dat taxi driver bloke said, 'Get out o' 'ere with your bloody mess. So I give 'im a dollar to ring up the amb…lance, and the amb…lance bloke got me and brought me 'ere. That's true now. That's how I come 'ere dis time. You believe me? I never been goin' in that 'ouse las' night.'

'That's okay, Bilago,' Bridges assured him. 'You don't have to explain anything to me. But I appreciate you telling me. Thank you. I believe what you tell me. Go on with your old story?' He sat back through a long silence and waited while the old man collected his thoughts. The initial signs of response he had made to Bridges' interest in hearing his story, had been in reference to more of his life than just yesterday evening. He had said. 'I never told that before. You can't believe it'. But so far he had not told anything of that unbelievable life story. Bridges waited. He was in no hurry. He dared not be in a hurry. He had no intention of letting impatience be a barrier to communication. As he waited he felt some satisfaction that he had correctly guessed that Helen and Bilago had bumped into each other at the murder house. What connection there was between Bilago and the late Ron Smart was impossible to tell, but Bridges sensed that there was an association of some sort. Why else had this old man begun to talk about the murder victim when he had indicated that he was about to tell his own life story. What was it he had said? 'You know that old bloke who got killed?' Did he, Bilago, know the victim? It seemed likely that he did. Or was his interest simply due to the sensational nature of the news.

'I missed my dreaming!' Bilago announced, searching the Balanda's face for reaction to this tragedy. 'I reckon I must've missed it. But I dunno, maybe I found it. Maybe this is my dreaming, 'ere, now. But I got a new dream las' night. When I was knocked down, an' was bleedin.' He stopped in thoughtful silence for a minute, then continued. 'I was tellin' meself, I'm gonna die ere this time. But I got up to look aroun' there, and I thought I saw a ghost at that 'ouse, an' I fell down again. You know that, Mister Britches? You seen any ghost?'

Bridges shook his head. 'No, I've never seen a ghost.'

'When I'm drunk,' Bilago went on. 'I see lot of things, specly in the night time. Las night a dead man come to see me, when I was layin' there. Down in that garden, an' bleedin like a stuck pig. 'E was just like 'e used to be when we was both young blokes. Use to be 'e was older than me…now I was old but not 'im. I knew im straightaway. This time I seen Gayu George, an' I don't know if I was sleepin. 'E come up and 'e said my name that 'e always used to call me. "Lagi Lagiaga," 'e said.'

I could see I was old, but 'e was still young man…an' I got a fright, you know? I 'aven't 'eard that name for lo-ong time. Not for many, many years…Lagi Lagiaga.'

He paused as he weighed the marvellous fact. 'We used to ride together doin' the stock work on Mister Charlton's cattle station, over near the Iwaidja country, round Port Essi'ton way. An' we caught the crocodiles together, me an' 'im, Gayu George. That bloke taught me plenty things, an' I taught 'im, too.' The storyteller fell silent again, lost for a while in memory…'Las' night e come, an' 'e tol me…' He seemed to recall it now as a vivid reality. "Lagi Lagiaga, you can live."

'Always he keep me safe. Safe from his Balanda people. Ah….I didn't keep 'im safe from my Arargbis.'

He caught his breath suddenly as if blocking a sob. "Don't tell me I died for nothing!" It keep on comin' in my 'ead.

'I was hidin' by the river again, an' I was shit frightened… an' they speared 'im dead. I saw! I saw the spears, an' 'im talking to someone. I knew that way 'e talk, lookin' up like that Stephen Bible man. Forgive them. But I was jus hidin and run away.'

"You can live!" 'e say, by that Gillie 'ouse… an' I got up and started to go to the ospital. That time when I got the taxi. That ghost man, 'e told me, to live now. So I'm tryin', now, if I can live.'

The account had become confused in the old man's mind. Before Bridges could form any idea of whether or not Bilago had anything to do with the murder, he needed more information. Perhaps if the old man kept talking he would give an indication if, when he was shoved by Helen, he had done any more than fall into the garden and struggle up towards Smith Street and the encounter with the taxi driver.

'So you saw a man at that house last night?' Bridges prompted.

'Yeah, I saw that man, my good friend, Gayu George. We call 'im that way, Gayu, we say to that Balanda… Gayu, big brother. We don't say that way 'bout other Balandas.' His gaze moved towards infinite focus, before he added, like a sigh, 'Ah, good bloke.'

'I don't know about him, Bilago,' Bridges said. 'Can you tell me a bit more about your story and that bloke… your Gayu friend?'

'Me? Mister Britches, I can tell you many stories. Many, many…but we be talkin all day an all the night,' Bilago grinned briefly, surprising Bridges with a glimpse of another person in that flickered expression.

'I'm in no big hurry,' Bridges encouraged, making a mental note that he was limited to a maximum of an hour if he were to be on time to meet Livvy at Red Sails. During that hour Bridges heard about Gayu George who had been a stockman and a hunter of crocodiles and buffaloes. It seemed that he was a man of strong moral character, and a friendly disposition. He had given up studying to be a doctor and gone into cattle station work instead, and becoming the Head Stockman on Charlton's station. Bridges tried to recall what he had heard about Charlton, the cattle boss. Charlton, always referred to as Mr Charlton was definitely someone that he had been told about, a cattleman who had operated on the mainland near Cobourg Peninsula for many years.

He tried to keep the outlines of Bilago's memories clearly in his mind, and let the details pass over his head. As the old man had said, he was full of many, many stories. In this way, Bridges learnt that when he was young and known as Lagi Lagiaga, Bilago with a half brother, and a couple of young kinsmen, had gone to the coast to work on the Charlton station. Lagi and his brother and cousin used to talk about the Balanda way of life, and it caused many arguments. They still kept their nick-names for each other. Lagi was called Short Man, his brother was Thin Man and their cousin was Big Man. They needed each other in those changing times. It was hard to think about things on his own, so Short Man Lagi, always stayed with Thin Man and Big Man, or with the friendly Balanda, Head Stockman, Gayu George.

Gayu, the half-doctor, taught Lagi about sickness and medicine in the Balanda way. In those days, most people could not understand it, they thought that disease was only sent by spirits living or dead, but Lagi learnt the germ story and the signs of dangerous and common illnesses. He began to help Gayu George to treat wounds and ailments among the workers and their animals.

'Did you stay there a long time?' Bridges asked, to help the tiring story-teller to move along. Old Bilago gestured towards the bottle of water on his bed-side cabinet and drank what Bridges poured for him before continuing.

'Us young blokes stayed longest time, an' we 'ad good time, too… good life with the cattle an' orses. But somethin' 'appened.'

Here the story-teller became very serious, and slowly related a tragic story of suffering and revenge. After a mustering ride, Lagiaga and other riders were dressing their horses' sore spots with tar.

'One of the stock workers 'ad is trousers held up by a 'orse's belly belt, wrap twice aroun his belly. It was a joke, for funny, and we all 'ad bigges' laughs…'

Bridges could still hear Bilago telling his tale, but he recalled the sound of the sea washing against rocks when Mani had been telling another story '…my grandfather's uncle had seen one of the men wearing a surcingle for a trousers' belt…' Could there be two such stories about a surcingle? Bilago needed even more water before going on to tell about another white worker on the Charlton Station, known as the Hunter. This Balanda had come along, and an old man spoke to him about the surcingle. Instead of laughing about it, the Hunter took a pistol, ordered the man who told him about the belt and Thin Man, to both hold the arms of the man in the surcingle. Then he surprised everyone by shooting the man between the eyes. He told them all that the same thing would happen to 'em if they ever touched any of his things. Mister Charlton said that he would get the police on to the Hunter but he didn't. Instead, he let him leave, and told him never to come back again.

Apparently the tribe's people speared and killed the man who had told the Hunter about the surcingle. They would also have killed Bilago's brother, Thin Man, the other one who had held the murdered man, but Charlton gave horses to him and Big Man, and let them leave with the Hunter, before anyone could stop them. The story stopped at that point, until Bridges prompted the old man by reflecting back what he had heard, 'Your brother and your friend went. Hard for you to go, and hard to stay.'

Old Bilago nodded, and went on to tell that he stayed to work alongside the good Balanda healer, his friend Gayu George. Some time later he went with Gayu to the Gugurr country in the east, where Gayu George's brother, Harry, was helping people build up a village and airstrip and barge landing. They spent a few weeks at the end of the Wet Season visiting and helping the locals with the air-strip construction, and were travelling back to the coast along the Gugurr River when tragedy struck. Bilago recalled that all the coastal people had received messages about the killing of the man in the surcingle on Charlton's station.

They had vowed to avenge the slaying, by taking a Balanda life, a straight pay-back, one-for-one. Bilago knew that they were a danger to his white friend, and tried to protect him by telling the coastal people that they met that Gayu George and the Hunter belonged to two different Balanda clans, and that this Gayu was a good Balanda, like his brother Harry, the missionary whom they all respected. But when they were travelling back west, a group of pay-back men came after Gayu George with spears, and he faced them alone after making Bilago hide by the river. He fired his rifle in the air to silence them. Then he talked to them quietly and threw his weapon on the ground. That was when they speared him, 'I saw 'e died with lot of spears in 'im...'

At that point the story teller fell into a deep silence for several minutes, and Bridges made himself wait beyond his patience, until the old man had finished some "sorry business" in his heart. Bridges was aware of the need to go back to work but instinctively felt he needed to stay and hear the rest of the story.

When he resumed the tale of his early days, Bilago recalled the terrible crisis that he had been plunged into by Gayu George's pay-back execution. He was afraid. He kept out of sight after the killing, and escaped by drifting down-stream to hide nearer the coast. At night he returned to the billabong and found the horses still loaded and waiting. Riding alone all night, he made his way westward along the coast, towards Charlton's place.

Without a wife, close family, or white mentor, the young Wainanda, Short Man Lagiaga, began to panic. The closer he came to Charlton's, the more depressed and anxious he became. He feared showing himself at Charlton's. If he were not marked as a pay-back target because of his brother's part in the surcingle man's murder, he might be blamed for the death of Gayu George Simpson. He dared not return. He was like someone without family. The rest of his story told of long travels, in the Tor Rock country, and around the Alligator Rivers region, and ultimately his acceptance among the Gandarri people at the Pelion Mission Station. His haul of crocodile skins were eventually traded through the Pelion Station Office, and George Simpson's share of the profit was sent to his brother at Gugurr Mission. No-one was likely to hurt him as long as he was on a mission station. Out there, in the bush, the Old Lore and its pay-back system still applied.

For this reason Bilago stayed at Pelion, and seldom ventured into the bush. 'I was 'elpin stock workers, 'an the doctors who came,' the old man explained. Bridges deliberately showed interest in the medical work that Bilago had done there, because to try to rush the process would only short circuit the story-telling. He heard that some missionaries were moved elsewhere, and the station was short-staffed. Bilago supervised sanitation programmes and dog health care, becoming a valued assistant to the resident Nurse, and to visiting doctors and Health Inspectors. They were surprised at how much he had learnt from George Simpson about modern preventive health care. Now he learnt to diagnose and treat some of the most common complaints that afflicted people who came to live in settlements rather than travelling their healthy dreaming trails. He was still at Pelion when word came that the people on Charlton's cattle station were suffering a deadly measles epidemic and needed help. No-one else could be spared from Darwin or the nearby stations, so Bilago returned there in spite of his lingering fears. He went by truck with medical supplies, and took charge of the anti-measles campaign.

Big Man and Thin Man never came back. They were said to be working with the

Balandas, trying to forget their old culture and live like white people. Stories came through that the two men were helping to seize half-caste children of Aboriginal mothers and taking them to children's homes run by white people, but Short Man refused to believe that Thin Man and Big Man could be guilty of such behaviour towards their own people. Big Man's wife, Lura, had not seen her husband since he went with the Hunter. She helped Bilago with the medical work during the measles epidemic, and, since they were both alone, they got together and made a sort of marriage.

At that time it made Bilago furious to learn from Lura that the Hunter had been continuing to call at Charlton's place over the years. He had not brought Thin Man or Big Man there, and nobody had done anything to stop him from coming, because now he worked with the Australian Government, as a Customs Officer and Coast Watcher. He sometimes patrolled the Arnhem Land coast to check up on all the vessels coming in and out of Australian waters. When he called at Charlton's he always wore his gun belt and two pistols. At night he often visited the Aboriginal camp, and used the people's fear of his guns to persuade the men to lend him women. He had taken Lura's mother many times, and eventually he began to take Lura herself.

The next time that he saw the Hunter was when he, himself, and Lura went to Goose Island and helped to deal with a dysentery epidemic there. A message was received from Darwin telling that Big Man, Lura's first husband, was alive and had been seriously injured in a brawl while visiting the Aboriginal camp on an inland cattle station. His condition was critical and worsening. He was in Darwin Hospital, and not expected to live more than a few days at the most; and he had asked if his wife could be brought to him. Lura and Bilago decided that she should go to him if she could, and that was when the Customs ship called at Goose Island to pick her up. On board was the Hunter.

Bilago and the Hunter fought on the beach when the boat came ashore to take Lura on board. Bilago was badly beaten by the Hunter and ashamed that he could not keep Lura from going with this man who had often misused her. She went away with him, and when she did not return, Bilago went to Darwin to find her and learnt that, after her husband, Big Man had died, the Hunter forced her to go with him. She had become his woman, and he had left the Customs work to go prospecting somewhere inland. Once more, Bilago was alone.

This time he found that liquor helped him to forget his sorrow for a while, and he had not had many long spells of sobriety since then. At the time he did most of his drinking in the bush around the edge of Darwin. Now he drank anywhere, openly.

By his telling of the story, suddenly, he seemed exhausted and struggling with a headache or other kind of strain. His smoky eyes were wet with a suggestion of tears.

'I must let you rest, Lagi Lagiaga. May I call you that?' Bridges said. The old man nodded his head and managed a crooked smile.

'Buruli, that's good,' he said. 'That's the name Gayu George always call me. Same as las night. "Lagiaga" 'e say. "Don't say I died for nothin. You can live." "e reckons that. So I can try an' see now if I can live.'

'Can I ask you one more thing before I go Lagi Lagiaga?' said Bridges.

'Ask me,' the old man invited flatly.

'Can you tell me the name of the Hunter?' said Bridges.

Lagiaga lay back into his pillows with closed eyes. 'Yairs,' he drawled. 'I can tell you that.'

He opened his eyes and looked at the young Balanda by his bed, then wiped away more than his tears with his good hands and sniffed, before giving the name.

'People used to call 'im Smale…Artie Smale, the Hunter and the Customs man… but I reckon you and some other people now, you call 'im somethin different.'

'What do we call him?' asked Bridges, feeling unready for any answer that he might receive.

'I reckon you call him Ron Smart,' said Lagiaga.

Chapter 23
Plans are hatched

The smaller dining room at Red Sails Hotel was open for lunch, and when Livvy and Bridges had loaded their plates with salad and cheeses, they sat at a table with a view of the sea.

'I wonder if Annette has turned up yet,' said Bridges.

'I do hope so,' Livvy was clearly anxious. 'I rang Lionel twice this morning. He's a mess. I think I'll call in to see him on my way back to the office.'

The salads were good, and presently they began to pool their information from the visits to Helen and the old man at the hospital. Livvy was still seething over what Bridges had told her about the reactionaries with the Chief Minister, and the designs on Jambagirrila and his land. On the other hand, she was relieved and glad that Bridges was beginning to open his eyes to the realities of racism in high places. They both regarded the official refusal to offer liaison support to Mani as sinister, to say the least.

Then they shared their other discoveries. Bridges was sorry to hear that Helen had gone into some sort of shock condition. 'She just sits there,' said Livvy. Sister Bernadette was trying to interest her in helping with the gardening, but when she showed her a little gardening shovel and fork Helen became frightened and pushed it away. 'I'm afraid she's flipped out, or something.'

'Did she know you?' Bridges asked.

'Yes, I suppose so,' Livvy began. 'At least I don't know really. She just seemed to accept my presence there as natural and looked at me and seemed to be noticing me and what I was saying, but without responding. I couldn't really connect with her. Very depressed, I'd say, but panicky, too. In a real state of depression and anxiety all at the same time.'

'Are they getting her any psychiatric help?' Bridges asked.

'Sister Bernadette's very good,' Livvy assured him. 'She's quite calm about Helen. She's known her since she was a toddler; and she was one of the child-care Sisters who looked after her when she was placed in care after her return from Perth. Yes, and, there's something. Sister Bernadette didn't use Helen's right name when she asked another sister to tell her that she had a visitor.'

'What did she call her?'

'Um, I'm trying to think,' Livvy replied. 'Oh, a short, unusual name, S-S-Slade, Helen Sla......no, not Slade. It was Smale. That's right. Helen Smale she called her. When I repeated the name, Sister corrected herself and said, "I mean Helen Cross, of course." Isn't that funny?' To Bridges it was more than funny. His recent memory echoed with the name Smale, and he had no difficulty recalling where he had heard it.

'Wait till you hear what I've got to tell you,' he said. 'I think there are some connections emerging here that might tell us something. But it's all still a terrible jumble.' He paused, trying to fit together several separate facts that were now available.

'What? Tell me.'

'Guess what the dead man's name was before it was Ron Smart?'

'I don't know. I didn't know he had another name, did I?' She was even more impatient. 'How should I...? Not Smale? Not Ron Smale?'

'No not Ron Smale,' he declared. 'He was Artie Smale, The Hunter. Terror of the North, brutal rapist and slayer of Aboriginal people, and an all-round regular bastard.'

She was astounded and he proceeded to tell her as much as he could of the story of Lagi Lagiaga and his hostile encounters with the Hunter.

'My God.' she gasped. 'Then old Bilago had more than enough motive to kill Ron Smart.'

'Yes, but he didn't do it.' Bridges was confident.

'How can you be so sure?'

'Oh, it stands to reason,' he said. 'He was knocked down the steps by Helen as she ran out, and that's when his arm was gashed open. Now, either Ron Smart had already been killed when Helen ran out, or it happened after that. If before, then Lagi Lagiaga, old Bilago, wouldn't have been coming back to have a look. Not if he'd done it, would he? And Helen obviously didn't know about it until she heard at the YMCA. And if it was done after Helen knocked him down, then Bilago was in no fit state to get up and go inside to murder someone, because he was bleeding, and getting himself to the hospital.'

'Yes, but you've only got his word for that'.

'True,' he conceded. 'But the taxi and ambulance drivers, the casualty staff, and when she's better, Helen herself, can all be asked to verify parts of his story. But mainly I just don't believe the old man I've been talking to killed someone last night. Meanwhile, since you've raised the doubt, I guess we could check the garden for signs. If he fell on a stake it's probably still there, and some evidence of where he landed.'

'But they're holding Mani for the murder!' Livvy let her frustration show. 'If it wasn't the old man, Bilago, then who did it? None of the things we've learnt from these visits gives us a clue about the real murderer.'

'No,' Bridges agreed. 'True, we still haven't got a definite lead on who it is…but perhaps we are getting closer to having one. I don't for a minute think it was Bilago. And I'm sure it wasn't Mani, as sure as I can be. But we at least know that Ron Smart probably has been under sentence of death for many years, according to Aboriginal Lore, and it looks as if he had a family connection with Helen, or someone who gave her the name of Smale, and possibly had other foster placements and names.'

'Can we be sure of all that?'

'I think we can,' he claimed. 'Okay…I'm interpreting the facts, but, what other interpretation fits? There's a story behind Ron Smart's decision to give Helen a fortune. A family connection seems likely.'

'But where does all this get us?'

'I don't know,' Bridges admitted, 'But whatever went on at the Cavenagh Street house last night might be explained if we knew a bit more about Ron Smart and the Aboriginal people's list of grievances against him. Do you suppose Father Dick'll tell us any more than he already has?' Livvy lit up with interest at the thought.

'We can only ask him,' she said. 'Come on, let's go see him.'

* * *

When they arrived at the Catholic Mission Office, Sheehan was there and seemed pleased to see them. 'Come in Gray, Olivia,' he said, getting behind his desk to leave room for their knees when they sat on the plastic chairs that filled most of the available space between cartons and filing cabinets. 'I'm glad you've come. I needed a chance to speak with you. But you first. What was it you wanted to see me about?'

Bridges looked at Livvy then began. 'We wanted to express our sympathy, Dick. It must be a terrible blow to you…Old Ron's death.'

'Yes,' he blinked and nodded in silence, obviously moved by the expression of concern for his well-being. 'It's a shocking business. It's very good of you to come and see me.'

'You've been on our minds, this morning,' Livvy told him. 'It seemed the least we could do was to come and say that we know you must be hurting.'

'I appreciate that very much,' he smiled in a constricted way. He was obviously under great strain.

'There was one other thing, though,' Bridges confessed. 'We want to ask you to help us to understand Ron Smart's situation a bit better. We want to help Mani Manggululu. It's urgent that he be released as soon as possible, and he has no alibi. If we can get a lead on who might have had a reason to hurt old Ron, we think we might be able to get Mani released.'

'How can I help? I would like to help Mani, too.'

'We think that there is some sort of family connection between Ron Smart and Helen Cross,' said Bridges. 'Can you confirm that?'

'No,' the priest was embarrassed. 'I can neither confirm nor deny it. You see, I promised Ron Smart I would never tell anybody anything about why he chose Helen as his beneficiary. As I see it, a person has a right to live down the past and let it be forgotten. If God can forgive and forget our offences we ought to try to do the same.'

'But your information might help save an innocent person from blame....' Bridges began.

'Forgive me, Gray,' Sheehan said carefully but firmly. 'You must leave it to me to make my own judgement of what to do with that information. I can decide for myself whether and when it is necessary to speak in order to help someone.'

'Fair enough, Dick,' Bridges relented. 'Only you might be interested to know that we have discovered that Ron Smart used to be known as Artie Smale, and also as the Hunter, and used to be notorious for atrocities against Aboriginal people.'

'I see,' the priest was obviously shaken by the revelation. 'Furthermore,' Bridges continued. 'We know that when Helen Cross was an infant she was known at the Convent as Helen Smale.'

Sheehan locked his fingers together on the desk and stared at them for some moments before speaking. 'I don't know how you learnt about these things,' he said. 'However, one thing I never agreed to keep private...it might or might not help your investigation. He has left his entire fortune, from deals done on gold and uranium mines, to three beneficiaries in three equal parts...Helen Cross, the Catholic Mission for childcare and research, and a Lucy Charlton of Kununurra, in Western Australia.'

Livvy was suddenly curious and asked impulsively, 'Did he spend some of his time over the WA border then?' Rather than reply, Sheehan smiled at her with his head cocked to one side, as if pleading with her not to ask questions about a closed life story.

'Charlton is another name I know,' said Bridges, wondering if the Kununurra woman were a relative of the old cattle man for whom Lagi Lagiaga and Artie Smale had both worked when they were very young. 'Look, thanks Dick. We understand that you're not free to speak about the old man's background. Be assured that we won't reveal what we know about Helen and Ron having the same name, unless it is to help get someone out of trouble. It's true, a person does have a right to live down the past. And why open up old wounds? But people still living might be hurt, or hurt even more than they already have been, and they need special consideration, too.'

'You mean Helen...of course...as well as Mani,' said the priest. 'Yes, I'm sure you're right. But there's nothing to be gained in revealing all these things to her. Things Ron Smart wanted forgotten.'

'Okay Dick,' Bridges was satisfied that they had gone as far as they could hope to go. 'We'll leave it at that. Lucy Charlton, Kununurra, you say. Interesting! Perhaps that'll be a clue to help us understand the old man. Anyway, thanks again. We must get along.'

'Yes,' Livvy explained to Sheehan. 'We're going to see Lionel Gellies.'

'Uhu,' the priest seemed strangely uninterested in the news, as if he was already distracted by another urgent matter. 'Er, I've been with the police at Mitchell Street. You'll be interested to know that I was allowed to visit Mani Manggululu after they finished with me.'

'Finished with you?' Livvy was indignant.

'Yes, they wanted to know where I was last night. 'They were interested to hear that it was I who arranged for Ron to get to Gellies' place, and to hear also that the Catholic Mission would benefit greatly from Ron's will. I told them that after I had dropped Ron at Gellies' place I spent an hour with a pre-marriage rehearsal at the church. When I returned, to pick him up, the police had already been called in by the landlord who lives next door. It was shocking… ghastly.'

Livvy sympathised. 'I'm sure it must have been, you poor man. And you say that you saw Mani?'

Bridges was interested. 'How is he? Has he given an explanation of his movements last night?'

'He's okay,' the priest said. 'In fact he's very calm. He let me pray with him for God's peace, but I thought he was fairly peaceful as it was. He's got great inner resources, I'd say… but no, he hasn't given an account of his movements last night. It looks bad for him. I mean, going on the reactions of the police. They seem to think he's guilty.'

'Oh,' Livvy gasped. 'They're crazy.'

'Listen, you said you are going to see Lionel Gellies, didn't you?'

Sheehan took another tack. 'You heard that the Gellies girl went missing, I guess?'

They nodded and began to tell their concern, but he interrupted. 'I ought to have told you sooner,' he apologised. 'Her brother rang the station. A police officer came in while I was talking with the detectives. He told them that Lionel Gellies had rung to say to call off the search because his sister was safe. Down the track, at Mataranka, I think it was.'

'Oh, thank God' gasped Livvy. 'Oh, Lionel. He'll be so relieved. Will we still go and see him, darling?'

Bridges nodded and rose. 'There are one or two things I want to look at over at their house…Dick…' He extended his hand. 'I wish you all good things.' The priest took the hand in both of his and replied smilingly.

'And God bless you, too, Gray. I always enjoy meeting up with you and Livvy. Let's keep in touch.'

He gave a hand to Livvy who took it warmly saying, 'let's'.

* * *

At Cavenagh Street, it appeared that the crime scene investigators had finished examinations and photography. There was no sign of them anywhere. Bridges examined the garden beside the steps. The paspalim lawn edges were overgrown and two of the spindly aralia bushes that camouflaged the empty void under the elevated house, were broken down.

Near the steps, he struck a stake with his foot and uncovered it with his hand. It was a piece of aged red hardwood, which had fractured just above ground level. It was sharp and stained at the top. It could have caused Bilago's wound. While they were poking about the overgrown front garden strip, Livvy looked up and caught sight of Mrs Lee in the next garden, peeping between two bushes. She was trying to remain out of sight and moved quickly from view when Livvy turned towards her and waved. Lionel opened his front door.

'Oh, g'day!' he said happily. 'Come in, I've got some good news.'
'So we heard,' Livvy expressed her delight as she hurried up the steps. 'Annette's safe. Isn't that great? You must be relieved.'
'I'm telling you…' He spread his arms in a suggestion of dance that contrasted with the heavy concern in his tired face.
'Bridges is looking about where old Bilago said he fell and hurt himself last night,' she told him. 'Is that all right with you, Lionel?'

Bridges called. 'I'd just like to look under here.' He indicated the space under the house behind the bushes.

'Sure,' Lionel called. 'Can I help?' But there was no help needed, and Lionel led Livvy into the house, while Bridges foraged behind the garden.

The soil was bare, and near the bushes it had been recently disturbed. Dark patches in a depressed pattern on the brown earth looked very much like blood, and were spread over a large area. After about three metres, where the shrub garden ended and afforded a clear exit, the trail went out to the lawn. At the lawn's edge more dry blood indicated that Lagi Lagiaga had made the tracks, had stayed there a while. The confusion of tracks included foot-prints. The prints of a pair of boots or shoes showed clearly in the drier soil at the house edge. Standing alongside them with his feet turned the same way, Bridges found himself peering through the half-opened fibrous cement louvres into the front room, where Lionel and Livvy were sitting on the edges of their cane chairs excitedly discussing Annette's impending arrival.

'Hullo!' Bridges said, causing them both to turn towards him. 'What are you doing?' Livvy laughed.
'Just seeing how public Lionel's lounge room is,' Bridges replied. 'I'll come in.'

The wall where the stone axe had been looked forlorn without it, and the whole place reeked of some kind of industrial antiseptic from the thoroughly effective gory clean-up job, and the cane chair and cushions from below the spears on the wall were nowhere to be seen. Lionel was obviously unnerved to be in this ghastly place and still quite nervous, even though greatly relieved to know that Annette was safe. The shiny wooden floor was spotlessly clean. He told them that, yesterday evening, Annette had apparently been upset about something, and had decided to leave town. She had let herself in the back way, collected some things and then left by the same way.

'Without speaking to you?' Bridges let his amazement show.
'She must have been really very upset,' Lionel said, with a tight upper lip. It apparently hurt to know that his little sister could leave town without him, and without even saying that she was going.
'Lionel was just saying,' said Livvy, 'that some of Annette's clothes and a haversack were gone. When the detectives came it was one of the first things they asked about.'
'That's right!' said Lionel. 'It hadn't occurred to me that she might have left me.' He was struggling to control his feelings. 'I'm looking forward to hearing what went wrong. But the main thing is… she's safe.'

'So, she's coming back to Darwin, is she?' asked Gay.

'Yeah, well, she rang from the roadside shop at Mataranka,' Lionel explained 'Mr Lee is spitting chips about a scandal in his house. But he seems stunned. Or perhaps he's just fascinated.'

'You don't think he could've had anything to do with the murder do you?' Livvy whispered, realising that she was thinking wildly. It was just that the Lees did have easy access.

'Good heavens, no.' The idea was unthinkable for Lionel. 'Mr Lee wants nothing but a quiet life.' He went on. 'Annette was really sorry for causing me worry, and horrified that I'm having to go through something as horrific as this in the house. She told me that she had got a taxi to Katherine late last night, on her own…'

'Taxi to Katherine!' Livvy seemed to doubt what she had heard. 'That's more than a two hour trip.'

'That's right,' Lionel assured her. 'Annette doesn't have much idea of money. Oh, well, as long as she's safe now. At Katherine she got a seat on the Greyhound coach early his morning, to go south to Adelaide. She intended to ring me at a stop further down the track, she said. But she got off the 'bus at Mataranka, because she heard the driver and co-driver talking about a radio announcement about Mani Manggululu being put under arrest on suspicion of murdering someone in our house after leaving the YMCA meeting. One item in Lionel's report appalled them'.

'What? They haven't officially arrested him, have they?' Bridges gasped.

Lionel showed surprise. 'Oh, I thought you would have heard. Mr Lee told me he heard it on the radio. Yes, Mani has been formally arrested on suspicion of murder. They must reckon they've got a case against him.'

This was devastating news, and Bridges told Lionel that he and Livvy had been trying to get a lead while the trail was hot, in order to turn the enquiry away from Mani. He did not bother to explain why it was crucial for Mani to get released as soon as possible and join his grandfather, but Lionel's next few words gave him new hope and another set of possibilities to explore.

'My dear little sister heard the drivers say that there had been reports that Mani had spoken about violently dealing with white racists, and something about killing someone with a stone axe, and then he'd rushed out of the YMCA, and now he was refusing to tell them where he was during the next hour, the time when the murder was committed.'

'Does she think she can say something about that?' Livvy asked.

'Yes, she does,' said Lionel seriously. 'He was on the beach with her.' Again he looked upset, and Livvy put her arm around his shoulder and sat on the chair arm.

'So Mani found her after all,' Bridges was relieved, but could not help wondering why Mani had not told anyone that he had found the upset girl after she had fled from the YMCA.

'Are you worried that Mani might have treated her badly?' Livvy asked.

'I suppose I am,' Lionel admitted.

'Would she be coming back to clear him of suspicion if he had been rough with her? You would be able to tell from her voice on the phone, wouldn't you, if she was scared of him?' said Bridges confidently. 'This is tremendous news….You dear girl, Annette!

Lionel…she must be all right if she's travelling back…I'm sure she'll have a perfectly reasonable explanation for her behaviour…Perhaps she still felt hurt by Mani's rough speech…or…or rejected by him. Seemed to me she has a special feeling for him?'

Lionel glanced at Bridges' face, and seeing that he was quite serious, felt safe in confessing, 'I wondered if it might be something like that. She does like Mani, and her moods are still unpredictable. Perhaps he said he didn't like her, or something. That'd be enough to upset her.'

'So, she's catching the bus home, is she?' asked Livvy.

'No, no…' Lionel informed them, 'she's paying a driver to take her to Katherine, and then she's flying in. She'll be here in two hours time.'

* * *

Two hours later Lionel was at Gateway Two to meet his sister who swung along towards him across the tarmac in jeans and khaki shirt, trying to disguise her heavy tiredness and embarrassment. Inspector Donovan and his sergeant were standing behind Lionel as he embraced Annette, and beside them was Bridges.

'Hi, Annette,' he said, gently touching the arm she had tucked around her brother's back.

'Oh, hullo,' she said, noticing him for the first time.

'Ms Gellies,' said the Inspector, 'I'm Inspector Donovan. I believe you have a statement you would like to make.'

She pulled back from Lionel and faced the detectives solemnly. 'Yes,' she said. 'You've made a mistake about Mani Manggululu. He didn't kill anyone at the time you said he did. He couldn't, he was with me on Lameroo Beach.'

'That's a little hard to believe, Miss Gellies,' the Inspector told her. 'Seeing that you have just flown in from Katherine. Have you got any evidence to prove where you were?'

Annette was embarrassed and glanced at Lionel and then away. For a moment it looked as if she would walk away; but turning back to the Inspector, she told him, 'I acted very foolishly. I threw myself at Mani on the beach, and he…he…didn't respond.' Her face was reddening but she pressed on. 'Then he told me that he was a married man. It…it…made me feel very…very confused, and bad. I thought I couldn't face up to people… to my brother…'

Her brother made a sympathetic sound and put his arm about her again, as she continued. 'I know now how stupid I was. I'm… I'm sorry I made you worry, Lionel.'

'Nonsense,' he said softly. 'I understand. It's all okay, now you're back.'

She continued, returning her attention to the Inspector, 'I've been thinking about who would know we were there. Nobody knew. You see we hid. We…were shy …we went swimming, and we hid in the shadows by the old wall of the sea-baths. But two policemen came on to the beach with torches, and I remember one of them fell over on the rocks, or dropped his torch or something, and the other one called out to him. He called his name. I remember the name…It was Bob. I believe he called, 'Are you all right, Bob?' You see, I thought if I could tell you what I saw and heard from the water, and if you asked Mani, and he could tell you the same things, then you would know that he was there with me, and you would have to let him go, wouldn't you?'

The Inspector looked at her searchingly.

'You have been doing some thinking, haven't you? Hmmm, it wouldn't prove anything, but it would mean that if Malcolm and the police officers concerned agree, and the times match up with the time of the crime, then we would have to admit the case we have against Malcolm Manggululu wouldn't hold water…'

Bridges broke in. 'And you'd have to release him. That's right, isn't it?' The Inspector turned to face Bridges.

'You look pleased about that, Mister Bridges.'
'You couldn't guess how pleased it makes me, Inspector,' smiled Bridges.
'That puzzles me a bit, Mister Bridges,' said the Inspector. 'Because, you see, there were a couple of other people, who left the YMCA about the time that Malcolm Manggululu did, who were seen heading in the direction of the murder house.'

Bridges could hardly believe that he was hearing this allusion to himself and Livvy.

'You couldn't possibly mean that you suspect me or my wife!' he said.

'Let me put it this way. We thought we knew where Malcolm Manggululu went after he left the Y. Now it seems we'll have to think again about that. And while we're doin' that, I'd appreciate it if you and Missus Bridges didn't leave town.'

Lionel and Annette Gellies were staring at Bridges as if trying to see whether or not it were possible that he could be a man of violence. He resented their reaction, and felt anger welling up and threatening to flash at the Inspector.

'I make no promises, Inspector,' said Bridges. 'My work takes me all over the place, and the same is true for my wife. We are both regional field workers.'

'Yes, so I am told.' Donovan seemed pleased with himself as he let the clever government operative know that he had been collecting information about him.

'And you're both champions of Black Power.'

'Is that what they say?' Bridges was dismissive. 'They've given you a garbled version of the facts, Inspector. You've been talking to biased observers.'

'It may be so,' Inspector Donovan admitted. 'Let's just say it would go down better for you if you'd co-operate with our investigation by staying in Darwin.

'Now, Ms Gellies, I'll need to get you to come along with me and make an official statement... All right?'

Before Lionel and Annette climbed into their Mini to follow the detectives' car, Bridges asked Lionel to tell Mani to come to the Liaison Unit office as soon as he was released, if he cared about his grandfather and their ancestral land.

When they had gone, he rang Livvy, who was involved in a hopeless struggle to concentrate on critically reviewing the text of a new bi-lingual reader for grade fours. She was relieved to get his call, and delighted to hear that Mani would probably be released within the hour, but alarmed to hear that the Bridges had been advised that they should stay in Darwin in case the Inspector wanted them for questioning. Before she could get too vocal about this preposterous turn of events, Bridges put to her a new proposal.

'You remember Lucy Charlton?' he asked, and when she hesitated, he reminded her. 'The other beneficiary in Ron Smart's will that Dick Sheehan spoke about. I can't help thinking that if we could talk to her we would open up the story of the old man's past. Helen can't tell us, Dick Sheehan won't tell us, and Lagi Lagiaga has told as much as he is going to. You know... honey, how you were saying that you could feel the build up of a violent situation and I poohooed it? Well, now, I'm saying I realise that the violent situation built up a long time ago. It's been here all the time. We live and move in it. Old Ron was a part of it, and I feel concerned that whoever killed him is part of it, too.'

'What are you getting at, about Lucy Charlton?…She's in Western Australia, isn't she? Kununurra?' Father Dick asked.'

Bridges answers, 'That's right…Before they try arresting us, or something equally silly, what would you think of flying across to Kununurra, finding Lucy Charlton, telling her what's happened, and bringing her back here?'

'Me? Why?' she was staggered. 'Why would she come back here? The police will probably bring her if she's needed. Or, if not, she'll be contacted about the will, anyway…'

'True,' said Bridges. 'But it matters who sees her first. The timing's vital. We might find ourselves officially grounded soon.'

Before he could add any more, she had intuitively taken in the situation and made her decision. 'I've always wanted to see Kununurra…Tomorrow? In the morning? I'll have to take a sickie or maybe two. Wait till Oliver Sutton gets wind of this! He'll think we're organising a revolution, or something!'

'I love you,' said Bridges. 'I can't go there myself, because I'll be away in Mani's father country with him, if all goes well. I'll book two charter planes now with Capricorn Charters. One to Kununurra and one to Jabiru. Just as well you're a well-paid specialist, isn't it? The Liaison Unit can probably pay for Mani and me. And listen, sweetie, the Chief Minister always takes a satalite radio telephone unit on trips like this as there is no mobile signal. You can call me out there, from Kununurra, on Satalite Radio Katherine. Ned always has ten o'clock scheds. That's ten o'clock on Central Standard Time, of course. That way we can talk about what you've discovered.'

'If anything!' she said realistically.

'Right,' he said. 'But Kununurra's a small town, and if Lucy Charlton's there I'm sure you'll find her…and she'll talk with you. Who wouldn't be glad to talk with you? The Chief Minister plans to be out in the bush for two or three days, so here's hoping we're in time to get support to old Jambagirrila before they brow-beat him into signing his rights away.'

'I suppose all this is necessary,' she said.

'We could live to regret it,' he answered, 'If we don't take the chance to get the full story behind this murder of Helen's fairy god-father, we could be in hot water ourselves, with no room to move. The detectives are still suspicious of Mani, and of anyone, including us, who were anywhere near Cavenagh Street last night or had anything to do with Ron Smart or the Gellies.'

'Ow!' she was alarmed. 'Yeah! When you put it like that…Well, if we have to, I guess we can do this'.

Bridges reinforced the picture he had given. 'What Lucy Charlton was to Ron Smart, and what she knows about him, could throw light on the whole gory business. It might be a wild-goose chase, sweetie…or it might make all the difference to getting at the truth.'

'Well,' she said emphatically, 'anything'd be better than waiting to see if they want to run us in, or hanging around hoping everyone will play fair to Mani and his grandfather.'

'Them's my sentiments exactly,' he agreed. 'So I'll book the charters for first light in the morning, and just hope Mani'll be released by then. I'm expecting he'll be prepared to come with me to the Gujigari Rock country.'

* * *

When Mani Manggululu arrived at the Liaison Unit offices after his release, Harry Bagent rushed him with the news of Brown's conversion away from the Uncle Tom way, but it only seemed to worry and confuse the stressed young man. Bridges arrived to find his office occupied by Bagent and Manggululu. He put his hand on Mani's arm and said, 'you all right, mate? Boy, am I glad to see you.'

Mani glanced around at him blankly and nodded before turning back to take charge of a mug of coffee that Bagent had just set up for him. Bagent grinned at Bridges and told him that the urn was hot if he'd like to get his own.

When Bridges returned the two men were sitting on the two visitors' chairs. He sat on the corner of his desk and listened. Mani was already taking the chance to unload his feelings to Bagent and relate his experiences in the city cells.

'She's a beautiful person,' he said, referring to Annette's action that had led to him being freed from arrest and prison. 'But so soft and frightened inside, like a bird.' He looked directly at Bagent and then Bridges as he said, 'I wouldn't do anything to 'urt her, you know. I had to tell er I was sorry about my words at the YMCA, if they hurt er. You know?'

They talked about the repeated interrogations that he had been through and his determination not to say that he had gone to the beach with Annette, unless she said it first, in order not to shame her. 'It was good of her to come back… an' very brave, too, for er.'

They learnt that once Inspector Donovan had been satisfied that Mani's silence was because he had given his word not to speak about the night swimming at Lameroo Beach with Annette, he was ready to release him. A check with the police officer who stumbled on the beach had given positive evidence that Mani and Annette had been where they said they were at the time they each claimed.

The Inspector had said to Mani, 'you can go for now, young man. Perhaps I owe you an apology, but we can't be completely sure yet that you didn't have time to run from one place to another. For now, you're free to go.'

Mani recalled that he had thanked the Inspector, saying something like, 'I know you had to hold me for questioning. You were just doin your job. But now I'm in the clear, are you goin' to stop the newspaper from puttin our names in the paper?' He told them that Miss Gellies shouldn't be shamed in any way by them for what she had done, in coming back to help the police investigation. To which Inspector Donovan had replied that he would do what he could. He had stayed at the station long enough for a brief conversation with Annette and her brother.

That was when Lionel had given him Bridges' message about calling at the office. Lionel also told him that he and Annette had made a decision to pack up and go south as soon as the Inspector approved of them leaving Darwin. They were going to find different quarters today, because they didn't want to sleep another night in the murder house. Then Mani and Annette had approached each other and said together. 'Thanks.'

That had made them both laugh nervously, and they had stood there, trying to find something else to say. Annette's words had come first. 'I think… perhaps …we helped each other to find some freedom.'

He had said that he hoped that was true, and thanked her again for her brave action. 'I'll always think of you as a really special friend, who's very strong and brave.' Then he had wished her a happy life, and the same for Lionel, and left the police station to walk down Mitchell Street to Bridges' office.

'It's just as well that clumsy copper tripped over on the beach,' Bagent grinned, and they all laughed.

'I still can't get it into my head properly,' Mani confided. 'I slept all right in the cell, after I got to sleep. But I sort of feel as if I'm not properly awake now. I got into all that trouble just because I went looking for Annette Gellies and found her and saw her back to her house…'

'Did you go inside?' Bridges asked.

'No, we just talked at the corner, and I watched her go in her back way,' he went on. 'Then I finish up in gaol because they reckon I bashed an old bloke to death, who I never even heard of…with Lionel's stone axe.'

Bridges told him how worried and angry they, he, Andrew Brown and Harry had been at the Chief Minister's attitude to it all. Then he went on to tell Mani plainly of Edward Blyth's decision to take the opportunity while he was in custody, to fly to Jabiru, and meet old man Jambagirrila there in order to go overland with him to the Dik Dik country. It was clear to them all that the plan was to give the old land-holder a good time in the old country and then to persuade him, while Mani couldn't be there to help him understand what was happening, to give them something like a signed personal approval of whatever access rights they wanted, for mining, tourism or anything else.

This news served as a wake-up alarm for Mani. 'The Chief Minister wouldn't do that, would he?' he was appalled.

'Give 'im 'alf a chance, mate! And yeah,' Harry told him. Bridges spoke about Andrew Brown's strong stand, and his threat that, unless Ned took him along as Liaison Officer, he would blow the whistle on his sneaky game.

'Would your grandfather go over to Jabiru and out to the old country, just because Ned told 'im to?' Bagent asked'.

'He'd go,' said Mani. 'I know he wants to see all that place again, Dik Dik River country and Gujigari Rock. A couple 'o days ago 'e was sayin 'e wanted to go back there one day with Andrew Brown. Now, this means 'es got his chance to go. And e'll take someone from Goose Island with him for back up. I don't know who e'll take. It should be me. We 'aven't got many people with strong voices any more.'

Bagent was able to bring them up-to-date with Edward Blyth's actions. Eventually the Chief Minister had agreed to Andrew Brown joining his party, but decided to take Fred Archer and a "couple of other dudes" along as well. They were well away from Darwin by now, probably already on the ground at Jabiru airstrip. Bagent told them, 'When I asked Andrew, what's Freddo Archer goin' for?' the old man said, 'don't you understand, young fella? Mister Ned, Bigges' Tree's, taking him along to keep this old man busy, while 'imself is busy with the other old man.'

'Jus what I was thinkin myself,' Mani said. 'Just as well the old man woke up to im, eh? But I should be out there, too.'

'So you will be,' Bridges assured him. 'I've booked a charter for you and me both. All right?'

'Too right! Let's go!' Mani was on his feet.

'We have to be patient, mate. Dawn departure's the earliest we could get,' Bridges explained, 'In the morning we'll fly out, grab a four wheel drive at Jabiru and still catch up with them fairly early tomorrow. Okay?'

'Yeah,' Mani was dubious, but brightened. 'If that's the soonest we can go. You comin', too, eh?

'I wouldn't miss it for anything,' Bridges said lightly.

'Hey, that's good, mate,' Mani gave the Balanda a smile. 'You've been busy, eh? Good on ya!'

They made a move to leave, and Bagent watched them go. 'Lucky buggers!' he grunted.

Chapter 24
Gujigari Rock

Mani and Bridges were the only two passengers in the six-seater Cessna charter that rose over Darwin's waking northern suburbs and turned east south east towards the coastal flood plains and the distant escarpment country. It was only five days ago that Bridges was beginning that other early flight, with Andrew Brown, to visit Mani on Goose Island; and he recalled now his negative feeling about going on a field-work trip with the Senior Aboriginal Liaison Officer. This time Andrew Brown had gone ahead, at his own insistence, as the Chief Minister's advisor. It amused Bridges to imagine Andrew's new tough line with Ned Blyth, and the surprised look on the face of that shrewd politician at finding himself dealing with a real human being, an elder of the Wainandas, whose country was under threat. It seemed incredible that Brown actually had initiated a confrontation with the Chief Minister.

Mani had bought a toothbrush and a few items of clothing, and accepted the invitation to spend the night at Bridges and Livvy's place before taking the charter at dawn. They had tried to make it an early night in preparation for whatever ordeal might lay ahead, but there was so much to talk about, and then to think about in the darkness, that sleep had evaded each of them for hours.

Now Bridges' mind kept turning to Livvy in the other Cessna, en route to Kununurra. It had departed Darwin about twenty minutes before this flight. Livvy had been excited to be travelling west for a change, crossing into another state. It was a calm morning, ideal for flying, and at this time of day she could be confident that it would be a smooth flight all the way to Kununurra; but the trip back could be bumpy if the sun was high and unseen thermal elevators lifted them suddenly to new heights without warning.

* * *

Being the only passenger on a chartered flight made her feel special, and sitting up beside the pilot even more so. He was a quiet, good-looking young guy, in light khaki gear and a black and tan cloth cap. Neither of them bothered with names. It was too early in the day to feel sociable; and he seemed as happy to just keep his mind on his job as she was to admire the lights of Berrimah receding under the wing and the large dark expanse away to the right side that told the location of the bush and the East Arm of Darwin Harbour.

Slowly she moved her conscious thoughts up through her mental gears, in preparation for making this a real journey of discovery. It had to be done, but the why question was still a bit of a puzzle. It had been a shock to hear that they were on a list of people who had opportunity to murder Ron Smart; but she was glad that Bridges could now see that she was not as fanciful as he had thought, about official reactions to enlightened people who believed in the need for change. In spite of the anxiety she felt over the shadow of suspicion that was drifting their way, and some minor irritation about Bridges only half explaining why she was setting off to locate Lucy Charlton, she found the adventure exhilarating. Bridges had known what she was talking about when she told him that this was another mystery tour for her. She had not the slightest idea where to begin looking in Kununurra, or what Lucy Charlton would look like. Her only clues were that Lucy was probably in the town, likely to be middle aged or older, and that she was the only person besides Helen who had been named as a beneficiary of Ron Smart's fortune.

As the Cessna rose to its travelling altitude, the widening sky and earth revealed more of the coming day. She watched in fascination as the land below emerged from the shade of night. There was a vast area of unspoiled wilderness beneath them, and Livvy hoped that it would always be so.

All too soon she recognised the broad estuary of the mighty Victoria River and began to prepare her mind for an encounter with an unknown woman whom Bridges expected her to bring to Darwin. Before she had any clear idea of how she might persuade the mystery woman to join her on the charter's return flight, she sighted, away to the south, the vast waterways of the Ord River and Lake Argyle. When they wheeled to make a landing approach, she looked down on a small tropically green town that was the haystack in which it was her job to find the needle – Lucy Charlton. It seemed like quite a task, and she thought it highly unlikely that she would have anything to report to Bridges in time for the radio sched at ten o'clock this morning.

The tarmac was already steamy as she double checked that the pilot knew to wait for her in the terminal building no matter how long she took to find the person she had to see. She found her way inside and approached the reception counter. A busy young woman looked up with a smile.

'Goodday. How can I help you?' she said without rising.

'Hi,' Livvy returned the smile and, in her needy-pleady voice, shared her problem. 'I don't suppose you'd know where to start looking for a lady called Lucy Charlton?

'As a matter of fact,' the receptionist was clearly pleased to be able to help. 'I'm almost sure Lucy'll be at the hospital this morning. She helps with morning routines.'

The smiling receptionist sat back now, wagging the pen that she was holding ready for resuming her desk work when this momentary need was met. 'She's a regular volunteer up there. Everyone in Kununurra knows Lucy.'

'Great.' Livvy smiled. 'Will I need a cab?'

'It's not far. If you want to walk.'

When she had taken in the directions, Livvy set out on foot, with a new confidence that she just might have something for Bridges in time for the sched.

* * *

Meanwhile, in front of Bridges, in the south-easterly bound Cessna, Mani sat alongside the pilot, holding the route map before his face, as much to shield the glare of the rising sun and its reflections on distant rivers and wetlands as for any information it could give him.

Bridges knew that, when they reached their destination, it could be awkward for him to face the Chief Minister, or Fred Archer for that matter. He had brought along food and sleeping gear for himself and Mani, and intended to set up in or near the Chief Minister's camp at Dik Dik Waters near Gujigari Rock.

'Look at that!' Mani shouted to Bridges as they banked for landing and looked down through the side window at bared red earth and a grey pile of buildings and plant.

'The Ranger Uranium Mine!' Bridges informed him.

'Yes I know. It's a big shame really. Why can't they leave the spirits of the land alone?'

There was no-one at the airstrip, and it took twenty minutes of waiting around before their taxi arrived, and another ten minutes to find the car hire service and to take out a Land Rover. It was only available on a weekly basis and Bridges decided that his work budget could afford the cost of a week's hire.

They didn't stay to look over the town of Jabiru. It seemed to be a bright little sun-soaked mining town, built in several separate sections, with air-conditioned bungalows, its own small artificial lake, apparently far enough away from the Ranger Mine site for residents to be able to relax and forget about the hazards that people tend to associate with uranium harvesting.

Gujigari Rock was a long way further south than Jabiru. They were able to follow a made track south-easterly for about fifty kilometres until they forded Jim Jim Creek, then they took a bush-track left around a hill and continued south through elephant grasslands. The track became, in places, almost indistinguishable in the grassy wilderness, and in some places they could see nothing but the roof-high grass all around.

Bridges had brought an ordinance map of the area from the Liaison Unit office, to support his GPS. The map showing Dik Dik Waters, was clearly marked with a red circle. It was not the general direction that was difficult to determine, but each turn along the way. Here a clearing between trees, or a bent sapling, there a tyre track through a nearly dry creek-bed, or running across a rocky flat. The GPS kept cutting out, so much of it was guess work. In the vast areas where the Wet Season growth had sprung up on the plains, it was easy to follow the track, because very recently another vehicle had laid a trail through the grass.

At the wheel, Mani said with a smile, 'I'm following in my grandfather's tracks. Nobody else would be able to see the way to go with these long grasses…they'd be frightened of running into somethin. My grandfather showed them the way.'

Bridges looked at the young driver. He was in his element, literally steering them into his ancestors' homeland.

'Have you been down this way often, Mani?'

'Never,' the young Wainanada said as he steered around a high-sided green corridor, and craned his neck upwards to see the grass tops bending over towards them. 'Hey, look at these grasses'.

'Huge, aren't they?'

'Whoo!' Mani was impressed. 'You can say that again. And not only that, see how the tops are hangin over? That's the real start of the knockin down, eh? In a few days these grasses are goin to be knocked flat by the storms'.

'The old men told me we have to try to stay out of the bad heat and storms so we don't get bein knocked flat like these high grasses every year.'

Bridges was fascinated. 'Were they talking about heat from the sun…'

'No, from you mob!' Mani said it matter-of-factly. 'That's why we moved into the safe places, after so many were knocked flat. That's how we lost touch with our roots …you see. For years and years our people only lived on missions and settlements and collected rations, and then wages, to keep out of trouble with the Balandas who roamed the lands with horses and guns, so they wouldn't kill us off completely. We gave up our life for a long time. We didn't dare to try to come home, not even to sing and dance our ceremonies in the right places. The old people always told us all about our ancestors 'ere, but I never came 'ere ever before… this place where all my life's dreaming is in the ground with my people's spirits.'

'Now your family are the recognised owners of the Gudjigari country!' Bridges affirmed.

'Yeah,' Mani said quietly. 'Sounds crazy donit? That's why I'm glad to be cummen down 'ere. So I can see what it is and meet my ancestors 'ere…yah know, sort of meet 'em. An I can't believe it that my grandfather is in 'ere and Mister Biggest Balanda Talltree is here to soften him up and get power off of him to still use this land for the Balandas.'

'There's still time to have your say, mate,'

'Hope so,' Mani slowed the Land Rover to push the bonnet and windscreen through a swathe of high grass that had bent across the track.

'Because me and my grandfather are not goin to fall over and let them walk all over us. Ah, yes…' The young man drove in silence for a while, deep in thought, holding the vehicle to a long track across a plain. 'He came down 'ere sometimes when he was young… my father.'

'Still alive?' asked Bridges.

Mani shook his head. 'Him and four other blokes got drunk on stuff they made out of the duplicator fluid at Goose Island school. Three died. He was one who died. After that's when one other bloke took my mother for his wife. 'E was right in our Law to 'ave 'er, but he couldn't be a father to me. I only knew one father. That bloke was crazy and drunk all the time. Gamu, my mother, she died in the Darwin hospital after he beat her up. After that 'e was locked up an' never came back. I was only a little kid, and I always stuck to my grandfather, you know?'

'I'm sure you and your grandfather mean a great deal to each other,' said Bridges.

'Yep…we do. 'E hasn't got many close people from his young years, just distant relatives and my idji at Malingarri, and me and my brother an' some of our cousins. Most of 'em are dead and some are prodigal sons.'

'That's an interesting expression. Why do you refer to people as prodigal sons?' Bridges asked.

'Old men mostly. They used to talk that way when everyone was tryin to follow the Mission way.' Mani paused as they came out of the long grass and began to rattle over raw edges of rock strata before descending a shaley slope to a near-level river-bed where centuries of Wet Season flooding had rounded rock chips and created deep piles of pebbles. He stopped the Rover and climbed out. Bridges opened his door, but Mani called to him.

'It's okay. They went this way,' he declared and remounted to take them the safe way around the loose stones, sand and water holes.

'Prodigal sons,' prompted Bridges as they mounted the bank on the other side and set off along a track through the trees where grass was sparse.

'Old Bilago,' Mani said. 'They call him a prodigal son, and Andrew Brown, too. Those two old men both left their people and went the Balanda way. They are like that young bloke who went to live in the far country.'

Something in what Mani was saying had offended Bridges' sense of the fitness of things. 'Oh,' he said. 'I couldn't say Old Bilago has gone the Balanda way. He's tried not to go the way of my people, but found it too hard to keep his own life going straight. I've been talking to him at the hospital and listening to his life story. His real name is Lagi Lagiaga.'

'I know that.'

'Then you probably know that he was a medical worker at Goose Island and other places, and he did a lot for his own people and refused to go along with the Balandas who tried to take control of them.'

'Oh...I haven't heard much, really. Our people don't talk much about him and Andrew Brown. They just say they're prodigal sons, gone away from their people.'

The two old men called prodigals, were very different in their life-styles, these occupied Bridges' thoughts until the sight of high rock country, through the trees brought him back to present realities.

'Nearly there, I think,' he said.

'How are you feeling about speaking with the Chief Minister and your grandfather?'

'Just the same'.

'Just the same as what?' Bridges was amused at this vaguary.

'Just the same as always...I will remember my grandfather is a very wise man who has the right to know all about our own people's life, but needs me to understand some Balanda ways and to put his thoughts in a way the Balandas can understand. And I will remember,' he grinned, 'that Mister Blyth respects people who speak up strong.'

'Good for you!' said Bridges, and returned to thoughts of the two old prodigal sons, Bilago and Andrew Brown as youngsters, moving about in this country, sometimes hunting with their fathers, learning to throw spears, sometimes meeting parties of the white invaders and eventually moving north and having to adapt to the society of the newcomers as maladjusted marginal men, in order to survive. 'They went through some rough times together, some of your old men'.

'Oh yeah, I know,' Mani agreed.

'Now old Andrew looks after old Bilago around Darwin,' said Bridges.

'That's our way, if two men are brothers, even just the same father, it's like they are being the same person. They have to look after each other if they can.'

'What? They're brothers?' Bridges felt foolish. It made sense of so many things, and it had not occurred to him before…same father.

The note from Andrew to Bilago in the hospital now took on a new significance. One brother could not visit the other because he must stay and deal with the Chief Minister. Brown had been torn between going to his derelict brother in distress and fighting for a fair deal for his people. This time his commitment to the cause of justice had the priority. It made sense of other things as well.

'Do you know that the old man who was murdered used to work up through this country and further north?' he asked Mani.

'Around here? Did he?'

'He hunted feral cattle and crocodiles and sometimes he hunted people, black people,' said Bridges. 'Then, a bit later on, he became a Customs Officer and patrolled up and down the coast…'

'Customer Officer!' The reference to customs in Andrew's note delivered to the hospital made sense, at last. He saw a connection that he had missed before. The note was not referring to news about tribal customs, but to a custom's man. 'Hear news about customs…The Customs Officer! The old white hunter was dead. That was the news – Customs had been murdered.'

* * *

They drove on sand between a lofty wall of grey and pink rock on their left, and, away on the right, a bank of brown sand, which obviously had been deposited there when the river had flooded recently and left behind a chain of water-holes. Beyond all of this there was a narrow channel and a steadily flowing tree-lined river, probably the Dik Dik.

'Look up there!' Bridges exclaimed as they came around the end of the cliff and drove into a broad open space.

Steep slopes of smooth red rock towered high above the valley on the left. It appeared that this was the near edge of the foot of a high range connected with red rock country now becoming visible in the distance, above the riverside trees straight ahead. The height of the range was impossible to estimate, but the near vertical steeps of the nearby cliffs suggested that what was hidden above these towering faces must be exceptionally high. If this was Gudjigari, then it was much more than a rock, and probably much higher than anything that could be seen from down on this valley floor. Bridges guessed that what he was seeing was Gudjigari Rock. Piles of gigantic boulders formed the first major ascent, with, above that, a cluster of green treetops rising out of a hidden fertile decline; and behind the trees loomed monoliths, such as comprised the main facade of the great Arnhem Land Escarpment for many kilometres through this region. At the bottom of the first monolithic cliff-face, a mammoth pile of breakaway layers had accumulated over many centuries, forming a formidable barrier; and far below, heaped high from ground level, the overflow of falling boulders had piled high and wide above the grassy plain.

Mani was bending low to take glances through the windscreen up and to the left. Something caught his attention near the top, beyond the first great monolith. Where another, darker, hard rock had found a place between the mountainous loaves and created a craggy shelf. Where this prominent projection rose above the shoulder of the nearer loaf it was silhouetted against the morning sky. Something was moving up there.

'There! Hey!' Mani gasped. 'What's that?' Clearly silhouetted against the blue brilliance of the morning sky, beyond one of the lesser tors, clambering over a crumbled shoulder of the mountain, there appeared to be an animal, or, more likely… two people. It was a pair of climbers.
'My God!' gasped Bridges. 'That bloke with the hat and the bag.'

Mani brought the Land Rover to an abrupt stop, so that they could have a better view of the climbers.

'It could be Mister Blyth, couldn't it?' Mani was amazed. 'But what would 'e be doing up there?'
'It is, you know!' Bridges' mind could not accept the appearance of things. He squinted and shielded his eyes, but nothing altered the ways things appeared. Still it took a major effort to believe that the Chief Minister would go mountain-climbing with the sun already more than half-way to its zenith. What could have happened to bring on this fit of reckless energy?
'Who's the other bloke? Do you know?' he asked Mani. 'Looks like someone I know, but can't place 'im.'

Mani swung open the door and stood for a better view. 'One bloke. Just wearing a narga cloth, and carrying a stick. I don't know him. Must be they're showing the sacred sites to the Balandas, or something.'

'I can only see the two of them,' said Bridges.

About five hundred metres further on they drove into the campsite. The site fell away towards a thick cluster of trees, taller than most they had passed along the way, revealing glimpses of the narrow Dik Dik River. The camp had been pitched on a flatter part of the falling land, where the trees offered shade, and far enough away from the river to avoid some of the mosquitoes. Although a tarpaulin was stretched between trees to provide shade, there were no tents. Clearly, the campers were not expecting rain.

The demise of the Wet could lull people into a false sense of the Dry having arrived, but the Knock'em down Rains were just beginning to strike in their late afternoon onslaughts. In spite of this, the campers apparently had decided to risk sleeping out, and each bed-roll or sleeping-bag was either completely in the open, or, in the case of three of them, under individual mosquito nets, each tied to four vertical sticks.

A large Land Cruiser stood nearby in the shade of a clump of gum trees, and a billy-can hung over the edge of a smoldering fire. As they rolled to a halt just beyond the Cruiser and its covered trailer, Bridges noticed the satalite radio unit in the open troop-carrying area at the back of the vehicle, with its aerial wire thrown up over a high branch of a tall gum tree. He glanced at his watch as his mind turned to Livvy's endeavours in Kununurra. It was ten to ten. She would hardly have had time to begin her investigation, but there was a slim possibility that she would put through a call this morning while the set was switched on for the regular sched. He would stay nearby, just in case. Everyone was out of camp, but as Bridges and Mani climbed from the Rover, they saw someone carrying a bucket from the direction of the river. Bridges recognised Reggie Collins, the Chief Minister's Driver and Travel-Organiser.

'G'day Reg,' called Bridges. 'They got you workin' hard?'

'Too right, mate,' said the powerfully built young man. He looked at home here, in his blue shirt and jeans. 'But the money's good!' He was a good-natured, easy-going functionary, who knew his place. Characteristically, he asked no questions about the arrival of the two newcomers. Instead he greeted Mani with a friendly, 'How ya goin mate? Awright?'

Turning to wave towards the smoking remains of the fire, he said, 'the water's been boiled. We'll build 'er up, an' make a fresh cupper. Whadaya say?'

'Sounds good to me...Ta. Where is everybody?' Bridges asked.

'Some of 'em's comin' now, over there.' Reggie Collins pointed towards the Rock. Coming through the grass towards them were two men, one in jeans, white shirt and blue towelling hat, the other in a Grey shirt, khaki shorts and a broad felt.

'That wasn't Ned we saw up on the rock, was it?' Bridges asked as Reggie put his wash-up bucket on a box in the shade of the vehicle.

'Certainly was,' Reggie looked up smiling and light-hearted but refraining from the frivolous comments that obviously occurred to him.

Bridges asked, 'who else? We saw two blokes up there.'

'Who do you reckon?' asked Reggie. 'Your old mate, o' course. From work. The old bloke.'

'Who? Andrew Brown?' Bridges could not believe it. 'But he was only dressed in...'

'It's him I tell ya, mate. Gorn native again, I think.' Reggie glanced at Mani and added, 'like, you know, no offence.' And went off to gather some sticks to get the billy boiling.

Mani strolled with Bridges towards the approaching men. The experienced bushman in the broad hat felt turned out to be Jack Foster of Goose Island.

'D' you see who's come as your grandfather's back-up man from Goose?'

Bridges said to Mani, 'yeah, brilliant, eh?'

Mani grinned. 'I don't know what old Jack could tell anyone about this country.'

The other man was a lawyer, a legal counsellor, Charles Godfrey, who was often called in by the Chief Minister. He was one who advised Edward Blyth on ways to oppose undesirable land claims. Bridges had been called on twice to guide Charles Godfrey on how to be respectful in cross-cultural communication.

'Well, don't ya see some queer sights in the bush when y 'aven't got a gun?' called Foster. Mani glanced at Bridges and read his smile as meaning that Foster was making some sort of stupid joke, and really meant something like, 'hullo, it's good to see you.' His old impatience with Foster, and with the whole race of Balandas, flared for a moment. Why couldn't they just say what they meant and be what they were, without jokes about shooten people and making everything something that it isn't? But quickly his pleasure at seeing the man whom he had pulled from the sea resurfaced, and he called to him.

'Goodday, Jack! You got a tourist guide job now?' He nodded to the other man as Bridges introduced them.

'More like a part-time minder!' Foster made it sound like a joke.

'Where's the Chief gone to?' asked Bridges.

'Heading for the top, as usual!' Charles Godfrey quipped, but his face showed alarm looking towards the top of Gujigari Rock.

'That's not the only way he's gorn, if yah ask me,' Foster added disrespectfully. 'Gorn in the head, too. I'd say! A man's gotta be balmy to go climin' up there in the middle of the day.'

'Is my grandfather here?' Mani asked.

''e went up there first,' said Foster. 'es been up there all night...because 'e had the sense to do the climb when the sun was well over late yesterday afternoon. Something about the Old Lore...It's a long story. He talked about it a lot yesterday, and went up to be alone with his ancestor's all night'.

Mani looked at his grandfather's minder, then, in awed silence, towards the mountains.

'Don't look at me, mate. I tried to talk 'im out of it. Then I tried to go with 'im. Youd o' thought I'd insulted 'im or something. He put me in my place quick-smart. He let me know I haven't got the right degrees to enter the sacred mountain. So all I could do was say, scuse me, beg your pardon. And watch 'im go off on his own.'

'So, why are Ned and Andrew going up?' asked Bridges. 'Are you frightened something's happened to Mani's grandfather?'

'He's awight,' Mani said. 'He can go up there and be safe.'

Foster shrugged. 'I'm blessed if I know...leading them towards the shade of the nearest tree. 'They talked a lot together yesterday, the two men, the Chief Minister and Mani's grandfather. Andrew Brown was busy as the two-way interpreter. I sat in on the conversation for a time, but then, the three of 'em left the rest of us here and walked right around the river bend down there. Old Jambagirrila took along a calico bag, sort of extra large size pillow case, that had in it his secret dillybag and sacred feathered stick. I haven't seen them myself, but he explained to me, before we came, what he had. He said he was going to show them to the Chief Minister when they were alone.'

'That's a great honour. Isn't it, Mani?'

Mani was interested to hear of the private showing. 'Oh, yes.' He was emphatic. 'Speci'ly if my grandfather held the dilly-bag...er, the sacred Madayin bag, open so the other person can see into the inside. That's opening up the secret Lore for the other one to see. If someone looks into that bag without a permission he should be put to death. I wouldn't look at it. I haven't got a permission.'

'Sounds a slightly harsh penalty for just looking at something,' said Charles Godfrey.

'Yes,' Mani agreed. 'It is. Like Old Testament times. If someone touched the sacred box with the Ten Commandments in it, that Ark of the Covenant, they lost their life. It's the same thing in our old Lore. People have to respect it because it is… really is…the Lore. Our old men would know. The sacred bag will have the proper secret feathers and things, and only the right land keeper's can have it.'

'So, compared with our modern Australian Law, would you say that, it's like the owner's title to the land?' Bridges asked, with a look at the listening lawyer.

'I dunno,' said Mani. 'More like a permission and a lore of who is the right one who must always keep and look after this part of the land for the ancestors and for the children coming up.'

Foster glanced over his shoulder along the way that he and Charles Godfrey had come, as if he was looking for someone; and Bridges' vague awareness that somebody was missing turned to realisation that Archer was supposed to be here. He turned and saw nobody in the direction in which Foster was looking.

'Where's Fred Archer?' he asked.

'He's in a bit of a flap about Blyth going up the mountain,' said Foster. 'Reckons he should've gone, too, to look after the Chief Minister…but he was told to stay put. It's only for men of high degree, climbing to the top. Archer seemed a bit put out. He thought he should be able to go if Andrew did…but Andrew said it was disrespectful to the Law, and the Boss said "stay".'

Charles Godfrey joined the conversation. 'I thought Fred said he'd be back here in time for the radio sched…'

'Well, 'e betta get a move on.' It was Reggie Collins who had come near enough to hear and was passing by. 'There's a fresh billy of tea there if anybody wants a cup. I'm just goin t' turn on the radio now. Any messages out?'

'Might be one in for me, through Katherine satellite radio, mate,' said Bridges.

'Probably come on after the sched,' Reggie spoke from experience. 'You be around?'

'Yeah, I'll get a cupper and be right with you,' Bridges assured him.

As they filled mugs and sipped the contents in the shade, Foster continued his account of the Chief Minister's decision to climb the Rock. Apparently a big impression had been made on his way of looking at the two Laws, the modern Australian one and the ancient 'Rom' commandments from the sky, and practical lores flowing from them. By the campfire he had spoken in ways that showed that he was impressed with Jambagirrila's belief in the sacredness of lore, and hinted that he might have regrets that he had sometimes led the charge in court against Aboriginal land claims.

Looking across the fire at Charles Godfrey, he had said, 'if I…as Head of Government… am ready to take seriously the tribal Lore, and willing to go to the traditional place where the Law-men made their judgements, then perhaps the old man will be happier to come our way.' Godfrey confirmed Foster's account of the Chief Minister's desire to go up the mountain. He had assured them that the old man had told him that there were good water holes on the way, and the trail over rock to the top of the mountain was worn smooth by many generations of the ancestors' feet, but was only for men of high degree to climb.

Blyth had said that he was inclined to the idea of going alone to meet with Jambagirrila after he had been with his ancestors up there, and would now be ready to make up his mind what to do about the land. Andrew Brown, who had been away at the river bend for most of the night, while Ned had spoken with the others at the campfire, talked with his Chief in the morning, and heard of his wish that he might make the climb.

That was how it happened that Brown had offered, either as an elder of high degree or as the Chief Liaison Officer, or both, to escort the Head of Government to the special men's business place at the top of Gujigari. He was dressed only in a narga loin-cloth, and he had insisted that no-one but he could accompany the Chief Minister. It was against the ancient Lore. Blyth had agreed that no-one else was qualified to go with them.

Mani who had listened in silence while these facts were passed on to him and Bridges, by Foster and Godfrey, now shared his anxiety with Bridges. 'The Chief Minister is in a very big danger,' he said.

Before Bridges could ask what he meant, a crackling voice that clattered from the satalite radio caught their interest, and was followed by Reggie acknowledging reception inside the back of the Land Cruiser. 'Roger, Roger,' they heard. 'Standing by.'

He leaned out of the back and called, 'Bridges to Bridges. There's a call booked from Kununurra for the end of the sched.'

Bridges was surprised and delighted. 'Roger Roger Reggie!' he called happily, and turned to Mani. 'I'm going to have to go and talk with Livvy. She's been searching for someone who might help us.'

Mani stared at him. 'Help who?' he said.

'Let's wait and see,' Bridges told him. 'But I can tell you this much, mate…the Chief Minister's not the only one that's in danger.'

Chapter 25
Sacred Lore

It was a surprise that Livvy could have anything to report so soon. Bridges' pulse quickened as he anticipated her call on the Kununurra radio telephone. Could it be bad news? Perhaps something had gone wrong, an accident? No, who but Livvy could be calling? She was safe, and she could have information that would be of interest to him. He left Mani talking with Foster about what sort of mood his grandfather had been in before setting off to climb the mountain, and made his way towards the Land Cruiser to take Livvy's call. Glancing sideways, he caught sight of Archer half jogging, half stumbling across the plain. Apparently he also was heading for the radio. He would now be within hearing distance and picking up the jumble of static, and voices that just then ended with the familiar abrupt voice sound that could only be. 'Over!'

Now Collins was speaking again with some urgency. 'Roger, Roger, DHQ. Negative. Negative. Chief Minister is not present. Repeat. Chief Minister is not present. Mister Blyth is out of the camp. Over.'

'Roger,' came the scratchy reply. 'Please put on Fred Archer. Inspector Donovan is here to speak about one of their staff members…'

A wave of raw fear exploded over Bridges' thoughts and scattered them. What did the caller say? Surely this was not happening! Inspector Donovan? Speak about a staff member? Himself? A quick glance revealed that Archer would arrive at the vehicle, breathless and sweaty, within half a minute. The wild thought came of trying to take the call himself as a staff person, but what he wanted to avoid was Inspector Donovan finding out that he was here. It would look bad, since he had been told not to leave town, and it could lead to the police swooping in to carry him away before he had done what he had come to do. He must not be heard on the radio, or let the Inspector hear that he was present. In the same instant that he rejected the thought of speaking to DHQ he leaned in towards Collins, and seeing that the operator's thumb was off the transmit button, said quickly, 'Reg, mate. A favour…A bloody big favour. Don't let Darwin know I'm here. I need to have today to clear my name. The police want me. A big mistake. Trust me, mate!'

For a full second the two men stared into each other's eyes before Collins said, 'Roger… wilco!' Darwin was calling again, 'DHQ calling 8CM. DHQ calling 8CM.

How do you read me? Over.' Reggie rolled an index finger back and forth across the tuning knob as he replied, ending his call with, 'having trouble receiving you. Negative, negative, negative!'

Archer staggered to a halt beside Bridges, looking ghastly. His red face was running with sweat, and brown rivulets. 'What, the…' he began to speak between gasp. 'Wha…tha…'ell, a…you doin…ere?

'It's a long story, Fred,' Bridges tried to divert him from the radio. 'You need a drink. Come and get one, and I'll tell you all about it.'

'Go to buggery!' Acher swung past, to get near the radio. A voice was saying, s impera…ve that…spea…Archer…Brown…out staff…memb…a…ing. Over'

'Can't you get…any better than…!' Archer was impatient to communicate with Darwin. 'Give me the damn…thing!' He depressed the button and called, '8CM to DHQ. 8CM to DHQ. Are you receiving me…?'

Reggie carefully adjusted the tuning, and Darwin could only receive scraps of the transmission. Archer suddenly turned on the operator. 'Get me through!' he shouted. 'The Chief Minister's life is in danger and you sit there fiddling around like a schoolboy.'

Reggie complied, and within seconds Darwin had come in loud and clear. 'There she is.'

Archer made the most of the temporary good reception to get across his message to the effect that the Chief Minister had gone into the barren heights of Gujigari Rock in spite of warnings from staff of the dangers of climbing in the heat of the day. A helicopter rescue might be necessary if no word had been received of the Chief Minister's safety by tomorrow's sched. And he wanted it to go on record that the Chief Minister was climbing without staff by his own direction, and against the advice of his senior staff.

When he finished, and released the button, he was exasperated to hear a Darwin operator tell him, 'Negative, negative. You and Inspector Donovan were speaking over each other. Stand by 8CM.'

Fred Archer swore loudly and yielded the hand-piece to Collins, who was still being attentive to the equipment as though it might stop functioning properly. Archer was apparently ignorant of the ways of satalite phones and Collins was exploiting his ignorance in order to comply with Bridges' plea.

'8CM,' Inspector Donovan came on again. 'Now hear this. Someone out there, inform the Chief Minister that the CIB wants to bring in for questioning one of his staff in connection with the stone-axe murder…'

Reggie was ready to switch the tuner, but when he glanced at Bridges he picked up the signal that he wanted to hear the full message. It was clear that Bridges was happy with receiving the facts even though that meant letting Archer know them. It was only the outward information that he wanted blocked.

'We intend...pick up Mister Graedon Bridges...Missus Olivia Bridges and hol... em for questioning, until th...satisfy us as to their whereabou...the time of the stone axe murder...'

It had been said! Again Bridges' senses lurched into unreality. Archer was gaping at him and Reggie had suddenly become very grave.

'We....do not...ant to...ause embarrass...t...o the Chief Minister...o we are giving him th...notice of our intentions,' the Inspector went on. 'We will…keep it quie...s... long as we can. That's all we ca...romise. Please help, if possible, to locate Mister Bridges. No-one here seems...know where he is. Please comply. Over?'

'Give me that microphone!' demanded Archer. Reggie complied, but as he did he let the handpiece slip, grabbing it by the cord, and, when Fred ducked to catch it, taking the opportunity to twist the tuning knob a quarter turn.

'Ullo.' Archer had the microphone to his mouth, and was not taking his eyes off Bridges, who simply stood there shaking his head and trying to smile at the absurdity of the situation.

'This is Archer. Hullo DHQ. He's right here in front of me. Come and get him, and, for God's sake…!'

Bridges realised that Archer was panicking.

'No good, Fred,' Reggie was telling him. 'She's gorn again, mate. Must be a terrible lot of interference today.'

'Damn the interference!' Fred sprang up into the vehicle. 'Get out of the way… let me do it.' He lunged against Reggie Collins, reaching for the tuning knob. Before he could do anything with it, Bridges leaned forward and unplugged the microphone.

'What the hell are you doing?' Archer drew back in a show of physical fear.

'Oh, come on Fred. It's me, mate,' Bridges said.

'You're interfering with official police business!' Archer accused him. 'How the hell do I know what else criminal you'd do?'

'You don't, Fred,' Bridges said. 'But I'll just have to ask you to trust me.'

That was apparently asking too much. Archer grabbed the microphone and began to struggle with Bridges for its possession. Foster, Charles Godfrey and Mani

Manggululu were standing under the tarpaulin shade, drinking their tea and chatting. Foster noticed the disturbance at the Land Cruiser and he and Mani hurried across to see if they could assist in any way, and were just in time to catch hold of Archer to prevent him from crashing to the ground as Bridges yanked him by the arm. 'What's up?' said Foster, taking Archer's weight

'Oh, good on ya, blokes,' Bridges gasped. 'I'll explain it all later. Fred here is very upset. He thinks I'm a crook. Get him a drink, and get him out o' my sight for a while, will you?'

Foster was glad to oblige, and virtually dragged the protesting Unit Director towards the shade, humouring him as they went, 'Yes, yes, Fred. You'll be all right, mate. Just calm down, boy. Steady now. I told yah you shouldn't go out in this country without a hat. You've had a touch o' the sun, mate. That's what's up with you. A bit of the old sun-stroke!'

Archer gave up all resistance and went along with Foster but reluctantly, continuing loudly to threaten dire consequences that would flow when the Chief Minister learnt what they had done to him.

The way was now clear to resume normal radio communications, and Reggie was in action with the microphone and tuner. 'I hope I'm not gonna regret this.' he said. 'You didn't tell me they wanted you for bloody murder!'

'It's all a mistake, Reg.' Bridges insisted. 'They know Livvy and I were near the murder site about the time the old man was killed, and they're linking us in with the house of people we know there. They've got nothing on us. Old Fred'll be all right. He's in his element'.

They picked up the Darwin station in time to hear to stand by for the call booked from Kununurra through Katherine. 'Over to you,' said Reggie. 'This your missus callin' you? You want me to buzz off?'

'Stay where you are,' Bridges said. 'The more you know about us now the better. Then, when a woman's voice asked if 8CM were there, he replied, 'Roger, 8CM standing by.' A moment later, Livvy's voice came through with some of its tonal qualities gone and excitement added.
'Hullo, Gray? That doesn't sound like you! I hope you can hear me, honey. Lucy Charlton kindly agreed to come and speak to you…She's here now…Over.'
'Loud and clear, Liv,' he said. 'You amaze me. Well done. Hullo… to you, too… Lucy Charlton. Thank you for coming to talk with me… Over.'

After a few seconds delay, Livvy resumed, 'Roger that, darling. Bridges, listen. Lucy's very upset about Ron Smart. She knew him when he was called Artie Smale. She hadn't heard that he was dead. And she says she's ready to come to Darwin with me today...Wait a minute. That right Lucy?...Yes, I know, but tomorrow might be too late to stop some bad trouble. Yes, yes…that's, oh …oh great. You sure about that? Thank you Lucy. That's great…. Gray? No, that's okay. Lucy could make it today. If it's really important. What do you say? Over.'

Bridges hardly knew what to think. His temperature and pulse both seemed to be uncomfortably high. The truck was stuffy in spite of the open back. The scuffle with Archer and the unreality of speaking to Livvy and an unseen, unknown woman in another state about things too complex to explain, made normal rational analysis difficult. It was so unusual for him to be unable to think clearly that it distressed him, and he felt something approaching panic. 'Uh, Liv, darling. Look. That's great...' He struggled to rein in galloping thoughts.

'Sweetie…things are, er…in Darwin, they're getting complicated. It's… er, it's better if you come here. Wait, can I speak to Lucy Charlton? You did say she's there, right? Let me speak to Lucy Charlton, Liv.'

'Yes, she's here, Gray. She's right with me and I think she'll speak to you. Just a minute... yes, Gray. Here's Lucy Charlton. Go ahead Lucy.'

After a short silence, slowly a clear, flat female voice said, ''ullo. This is Lucy 'ere… Lucy Charlton, uh, over to you.'

Bridges took a deep breath. His first thoughts about Lucy Charlton had been confirmed by the voice, she was old and she was Aboriginal. He breathed deeply again, drawing relief and inspiration from the sound of the unseen mystery woman from Ron Smart's past. Her voice cut through his confusion of doubts and questions, helping to restore lucid thinking and direction. Taking a moment to recall stories of Bilago and the dead man, he went on. He might need to compromise his principles as a communicator to get this stranger to agree to what he needed her to do.

'Hullo, Lucy. I'm sorry you've got bad news about Artie Smale. Thank you for coming to the phone, Lucy…I hope we can meet each other soon. I want to meet you. You don't know me, but I hope Livvy has told you about me. I need your help, Lucy…because you knew Artie Smale. Are you hearing me all right, Lucy…and can I go on? Over.'

Again he waited several seconds before the reply. '…ullo. Yes, I did. I knew Artie. Go on if you like. It's awright with me. Over to you.'

Bridges' confidence and clarity were returning. 'I need you to come and help me and my government bosses to know the true story of what happened to Artie Smale and other people. Over.'

She took the bait. 'What people?' she asked. Now was the sensitive moment when experiences of the old days had to be recalled, and he spoke appreciatively and positively of days gone by.

'I need to hear more about the adventures and the hard struggles of Big Man and Lura, and Thin Man and Short Man. I know they lived their young lives when life was hard and dangerous. Many people don't understand them. Will you help us to understand? Over.'

The delay was so long that he feared that he had lost her, but when she spoke she was still receptive. 'Roger that. You're right. I knew them people…They was bad days, awright. But some things we not s'posed to talk about, and some people…I don't think I can talk to you about them old times.'

This was what he had feared, and now decided to take a risk and assume that he had some knowledge that she would be desperate to hear once she realised that it was available. Speaking caringly and carefully he said, 'I'm sorry you can't come and help us, Lucy. You could really help us, more than you think. And, one other thing, I thought you might be interested to hear about Lura's baby girl. I could tell you a lot about her. I know what happened to her…You might like to hear what I can tell you.'

There was no delay this time. 'You know about Lura's girl? What about her? Can you just tell me about her now?'

He felt mean, but had discovered what he wanted to know. She was in a position to give vital information which he needed her to deliver before official witnesses, and he must ensure that she came and gave it in this situation, at Gudjigari rather than in Darwin.

'It's not good to talk about these private things on the satalite phone,' he told her. 'Please come with Livvy. She'll pay for a charter plane and bring you to Jabiru airstrip.' Livvy came on with travel information.

'Gray, the plane is waiting over here to take me to Darwin. Hang on a minute. Okay. Okay Gray. Lucy says… yes… she will come to Jabiru. Whoo!...Yeah…okay. We'll be there. Where do we go when we get there?'

'I'll be there, too,' said Bridges excitedly. 'I'll meet you at Jabiru airstrip.

I reckon, three or four…er, Kununurra to Stuart Highway, and then to Jabiru. Darling, I love you, I'll be there in three hours' time. Tell Lucy I'm real glad she's coming… she's very kind. Great work, Sweetie. See you when you land at Jabiru. See you then Lucy… Over.'

'Roger, Roger,' Livvy closed off. 'Jabiru in three hours. Over and out.'

After further words of gratitude to Reggie, Bridges joined the others in the shade of the tarpaulin. Archer was sitting on a four gallon drum, and glaring in the direction of one object after another, without stopping to face any of the other men present.

'Look, Fred,' Bridges began abjectly. 'I owe you an apology and an explanation.'

Fred looked at Bridges and vented his rage with words that he had apparently been rehearsing for this moment.

'I want nothing more to do with you until my lawyers are ready to deal with you. You've got more than one offence to answer for! Who do you think you are? I know exactly what you owe me, and I won't be satisfied until you've paid in full.'

Bridges sighed. 'Look Fred. Are you sure you wouldn't rather talk about this, and try to understand each other's situation a bit better?…No? All right. Please yourself. That's fine with me. Stew in your own juice, mate.' This seemed to have no effect on Archer, and Bridges added a parting word of consideration, 'Oh, come on! Hang loose, Fred.'

The other three men had been sitting along a log in the shade. Now Charles Godfrey moved away to the fire, presumably in search of more tea; and Foster sat watching as Mani walked over to speak with Bridges.

'I'm getting worried, Gray,' he said. 'Jack's been telling me about the talks they had yesterday. I don't think Mister Blyth understands he's in a real danger.'

Bridges glanced towards Archer and decided that it would be better if that unhappy man was left to his own resources. It would be confusion to let him in on this business. 'Let's get Jack and go for a walk,' Bridges said, looking towards a shady tree.

Mani signalled to his grandfather's back-up man, who joined them to walk down to the riverside. 'Mani's been telling me his fears for Ned's safety,' Bridges told Foster. 'Because he heard what you've been saying about the old men's talk yesterday afternoon.'

'Yeah, I knew I was out o' my depth,' Foster responded. 'I'm supposed to be here to give back-up to Jambagirrila, but I'm not an initiated man, so 'e didn't want me when they went down to the river. It was a private retreat. So I couldn't be with 'em but Andrew Brown could, when they showed Mister Blyth the sacred old feathered stick in the linen bag. I've not been allowed to see it…'

Mani cut in. 'What!… It's only for men of a high degree. It's forbidden for anyone else to look at it. That's the thing that worries me.'

They walked in silence for a few seconds before Bridges replied to Foster. 'You were worried that Ned talked about their conversation after Mani's grandfather went up the mountain? That it?'

'Yes, but not just that he talked about that,' Foster explained. 'I noticed old Andrew Brown was very quiet and didn't seem all that pleased that Ned was telling us all about old men's business. Not that I really know much about this sort o' thing. No, it's just that, puttin two and two together, I think the Chief Minister could be climbin into a heap of trouble up there.'

'Jack's right,' Mani affirmed. 'He should be worried. Mister Blyth's in a big danger.'

They came to a shady place near the water and out of sight of the camp, and Bridges asked Mani and Foster to take him quickly through their reasons for believing that Blyth was in danger.

Floster explained that Jambagirrila and Andrew Brown had taken the Chief Minister for a walk around this river bend, and had given a private viewing of secret symbols of the Lore. They were the ancient icons of the eternal Lore and of custodianship of this part of the country. They took them from the big calico bag that Jambagirrila kept them in at home on Goose Island.

'The old man insisted on bringing the bag with him,' the backup man told them. 'I had no idea what for. But now, it seems from what Manny says, that the one who rightly holds these symbols is traditionally recognised as the keeper of the Dik Dik lands all around this place here.' He swung his arms towards all the surrounding country, then added, 'as well as up there'. He looked up and nodded at the soaring pile of weather-rounded massive red rocks on the near face of Gudjigari, vast and hiding more than half of the eastern side of the clear blue sky. Mani and Bridges anxiously followed his gaze, and what they saw, this near edge of the Arnhem Land Escarpment, filled them with a sense of a vast primordial landscape beyond, a mysterious world as awesome and dreadful as the surface of the moon.

'Later in the day,' Foster continued. 'The old man told me to let everyone else know that he had to go up into the mountains. He had to go alone, he said, to find wisdom or something on the top of the Rock, and to be with the spirit of Gujigari, the Lore-giver for this place, and with all of his ancestors, whose spirits are living up there. He might sleep there for one or two nights, he said. In the place where only men of high degree are allowed to go. Does that sound right, Mani?'

'Yes. It does.' Mani confirmed. 'That sounds like what my grandfather would say.'

Feeling responsible for the old man's safety, Foster had prepared to go with him; and Andrew Brown thought that he was going too. 'But when it came to it,' Jack told them, 'Jambagirrila insisted on going into the mountain on his own, leaving Brown with the Balandas, to talk with them about cultural things.'

The Chief Minister had been annoyed to be deserted by the old man. He had more important things to do in Darwin than to sit down waiting for an old man to go up and down a mountain.

It was Brown's silent presence, in the evening by the campfire that had first worried Foster. Everyone else listened while the Chief Minister told about his viewing of the secret sacred objects, and of the way that his feelings had been stirred by the walk with Jambagirrila and Brown. The private viewing of the traditionally legal symbols of ownership had touched him deeply, but left him with an even stronger sense of cultural distance and religious mystery, rather than with a clearer understanding.

Floster had been conscious of Andrew silently listening, probably monitoring Blyth's statements, as Foster had begun to do himself. The Chief Minister had begun to reveal a confidential conversation with elders about secret sacred things. Foster had watched Brown slip away from the campfire circle, while Blyth was still talking importantly about himself and the elders, just as if he had forgotten that his Chief Liaison Officer was one of them and sitting there. Brown had gone away alone, in the direction of the river-bend.

Fortunately, according to Foster, last evening, although Ned had been indiscreet in saying anything at all about the confidential conversations by the billabong, he had stopped short of telling anything about what he had been told or shown. But that was last night.

This morning over an early mug of tea, when Foster had broached the subject of Blyth's words last night, Brown had told him that he was worried about something that the Chief Minister had said. It was when Blyth, in response to a question about the old Lore, had told Charles Godfrey that, so far, he had seen nothing to say that Jambagirrila and his people had any existing traditional right to ban others from entering the Dik Dik lands. At that time, Foster had thought of the Chief Minister's words as just clumsy, but since Mani's arrival, they had talked together about it, and he had begun to take much more seriously what Brown had been telling him.

'What's the danger you see, Mani?' asked Bridges.

'Mister Blyth said 'e saw nothing,' Mani explained. 'I checked up with Jack, and that's the word 'e used, "nothing". True, Jack?'

'Yeah, that's what he said,' Foster confirmed. 'Nothing. He said he'd seen nothing to show Jambagirrila's rights to the land.'

'Okay. So?' Bridges could see no clear significance in the fact.

'Just this, Gray,' Mani said with quiet gravity, as though even to speak of such things was presumptuous. 'My people learn that the Rom is everlasting and the Madayin Lore was handed down at the beginning of history...'

Here he paused. 'You see...when Mister Blyth said he saw nothing to show that my grandfather had land rights here, he'd already seen the Lore and the loreful sign of ownership. In the sacred bag, and in the showing of the bag by the right man.' He and Bridges stared at each.

'And he called it nothing,' said Mani. Bridges spoke slowly, 'And you think...'

'Doesn't matter what I think,' Mani cut in. 'But Andrew Brown, 'e was there, and 'e tried to tell the Chief Minister, but no-one was listening to 'im.'

'My God!' Bridges began to share his young friend's alarm. 'What are you saying, Mani?

'In our old way, the Chief Minister committed a capital offence. After he looked into the Lore of the ancestors e said, "I 'ave seen nothing. Nothing"'.

The young Wainanda looked at each of the Balandas. 'To us that's like trying to break that sacred bag. People call that sort of thing "Striking at the heart of the Lore...to destroy it". To the old Jews it would be like trying to smash the Ark of the Covenant...Do you hear what I'm saying?...'e is under sentence of death if any traditional tribal elder heard him say he saw "Nothing".'

'But, is Blyth in any real danger, Mani?' Bridges asked,

Foster was solemn as he cut in. 'It was Andrew Brown who was talking to the Chief Minister when he decided to go up there. I wondered at the time why he was so willing to do that, I mean, take a Balanda out in this heat, to climb a mountain that's a secret sacred place. And.. and...why he stripped down to his traditional narga.'

They all paused, staring at each other, then Jambagirrila's back-up man continued, obviously now out of his depth, as he recalled what had happened earlier in the day, added, 'thinkin' about it now, it's almost as if Andrew manipulated Blyth into doing this hare-brained climb!'

'The way I see it, is this,' Mani began with great care and hesitation. 'If it was still last week, and Mister Blyth said those things, and Andrew heard him, I don't think there'd be any danger. But now Andrew's different. Reggie said he thinks Andrew's gone native again. I don't like those words but what if 'e really has, Gray, all the way? Then Mister Blyth might be asked to pay the price for is crimes and for is people's atrocities. What if Andrew's ready, for the first time in his life, to do a pay back on the destroyers of our own people's Lore? An 'es starting with the one who came 'ere to put pressure on a land-owner, and said last night… the Lore is nothing?'

This was too much to think about rationally. Bridges walked away a few paces and looked up again at Gujigari Rock, with the realisation that there was nothing that he could do about whatever might happen up there. It was already time for him to leave for Jabiru airstrip.

'Let's get this straight, mate,' he said as he came over and stared into his young Arardbi friend's face. 'I know you're serious about what you just said. You are deadly serious, aren't you?

'Too right, I am, Gray…I can't joke about this…The Lore's a life and death business for us people.'

'You have no doubts about what you think Andrew has on his mind?'

'I 'ave doubts about what Old Man Andrew and my grandfather are thinkin, an' what they'll do to the Chief Minister. I can't know what they're gonna do. But I've got no doubts in my mind that it's possible they'll make the Balandas' Mister Talltree take the full penalty for his crime. I'm sure it's possible.'

'But the Chief Minister didn't mean to destroy the Lore,' Bridges suggested.

Mani held his gaze as if the silence said it all.

'Didn't 'e, Gray? But, any way, even if 'e didn't …' Mani still had not finished presenting his case against the accused. 'Do you remember the Bible story about the bloke 'elping to carry the Ark of the Covenant with the Ten Commandments inside it?'

'No I can't say I do. What happened?'

'He dropped dead when he touched it!'

'But that was not the same as someone killing him...'

'Doesn't matter, Gray,' Mani was beginning to sound impatient, 'this way or that way. Who cares about if it is our way or the Jews' way. It's the same thing. Attackers of the lore can give up their right to live...then and now. You might not think like that, an' I might not think like that, but it don't matter. It's a lore against stopping destruction of what's sacred. What matters is if my grandfather, and if Old Man Andrew Brown think like that...You hear me, Gray?'

'Fair enough... So you're pretty sure that it's possible that they could kill the Chief Minister?'

Mani stared at the questioner. 'They might,' he said quietly, as if, now that they were being taken seriously, he was weighing the implications of his words. 'And if they do, they will be keeping the Lore. They will be acting legally, as legally as they can.'

He looked from Bridges to Foster and back again, his face registering a new sense of alarm. 'I really think they might do it.'

'Look, Jack...Mani, I have to dash back to Jabiru now to pick up my Livvy and someone else. What can we do to protect Blyth? If the old men execute the Chief Minister of the Northern Territory there'll be all hell to pay.'

They fell silent and, for no reason at all, gazed across the still water of the lily pond that had been left beside the river bank after the seasonal floodwaters of the stormy Wet Season. This had been a wild part of a powerful river, and, before the end of the long Dry, would probably be reduced to a few small ponds. Now the air was heavy with the rich smell of uncovered mud and lily leaves floated on a tranquil pond. Bridges felt the weight of the stillness, and longed for a flowing stream of effective action. He waited in imposed patience, for Mani's response.

'This is the place where my grandfather hid in the lilies and breathed through a mouthful of rushes when he was still very young and the Hunter's gang rode up and shot everyone on the bank.'
'O God, Mani! Don't tell me that!' Bridges was appalled. 'Here?'
'In a billabong of this river,' Mani revised his statement. 'Could be this one.'
'That does it!' Foster grunted. 'Pay-back time. They've got the boss of the Balanda clan now, and they can make him pay for the massacre right here.'
'Ee.. I've eard about the massacre 'ere all my life,' Mani said. 'Now I can almost see that boy with his 'ead down, out there in the lilies...under the water, breating through reed grasses. Now 'es the old man up on the top of the mountain just 'ere, and number one land owner, talkin' to our ancestor's spirits.' He wagged his head incredulously.
'I'm glad he hid in the lilies,' said Bridge absently.

'So am I,' Mani managed a smile. 'Or I wouldn't be 'ere now.'

'Look, Mani,' Bridges was tense. 'I've got to get going to Jabiru. I'll explain why later on…but they're going to help us sort out the murder business. So, I can't do anything to protect Edward Blyth. But, I'll tell you this, if the old men execute him, we can forget about consultations and respectful co-operation for many years to come. You tell me, what can we do here, to protect the Chief Minister?'

Foster cut in. 'I spose I could go up an' have a few words with 'em. After all, I came to help Jambagirrila in communicating with the Balanda Chief.' He looked at Jambagirrila's grandson, who shook his head.

'That would only add one more Balanda offence, Jack. You'd be trespassing, too, in the secret sacred men's business place,' Mani explained. They all realised that it was down to Mani to take any possible action to rescue Mister Biggest Tree of the Balandas from the consequences of his own ignorance. Silently, he stared at the young man, as they all faced the facts. In the silence that fell over them, they all turned to look up towards the heights of Gudjugari, each knowing that Mani was the only person with any chance of making a difference to Edward Blyth's predicament.

'Well, I suppose I better go and see what I can do about it,' Mani said flatly.

'Will you?' Bridges was uncertain. 'I mean… can you? Is it okay in your Lore?'

'No, it's not okay,' Mani said gloomily. 'I'm not an initiated elder. But you tell me, who else is going to go up there and stop something? Something that could just make the trouble get worse between our people?'

'Can you be sure that you could find where Jambigirrila will be camped?' Bridges asked.

'Yeh, I'm sure. Right near the top is an open space where trees grow, where only men of high degree are allowed to tread. That's the ceremony ground for the big manhood ceremony of the elders. I've heard all about it.'

Foster was appalled. 'And what about Blyth? Could he go into that open space safely?'

Mani shrugged. 'He better be careful,' he said. 'He thinks he's a man of high degree because he's a Balanda leader. But he hasn't been through the big man business, the senior degree ceremonies. Might be my grandfather will say, he's a Balanda and he doesn't understand things like this, and let him off.'

'Your grandfather and Andrew Brown surely won't hurt you, will they?' Bridges asked.

'Hope not,' the young man said, 'b'cause I know that Lore, I would be in a biggest trouble. Might be they're already coming down. Or my grandfather might meet them other blokes at one of the waterholes, or in a shade, and I might find them there.'

'So you'll go, will you? Will you, Mani?' Bridges looked at the young man who had so recently confronted the Chief Minister, and also Andrew Brown for being a deserter to his race, and who was now preparing to face the old man again in the hope of protecting the number one Balanda from the due processes of the ancient Lore of the land.

'Nobody else here would understand our old men and this place,' Mani said.

'Are you sure you understand Andrew Brown?' Bridges asked pointedly.

'No,' Mani admitted. 'I know I hurt his feelings badly at the YMCA, and I'll be careful not to get him mad with me. Is that what you mean?'

'That's exactly what I mean,' said Bridges.

'Thanks Gray.' He put his left hand flat on Bridges' chest.

Bridges reciprocated, saying, 'strength to you friend'.

'Thanks to you, too, Jack.' Mani made the same gesture of respectful affection to the Town Clerk of his home community. Foster took his right hand in his own.

'You take care up there. You can make more sense of what's goin on in this business than the rest of us can, but I don't like to see you takin on the dangerous bit. Softly, softly this time, mate. Take it easy. We don't want to see any harm come to you...or to Ned.'

'And thanks,' Mani insisted. 'To both of you for coming 'ere to the water and being 'ere while we listened to each other. Now I can see more clearer ...This is Old Lore business, an' I afta do this one. My old men would be really angry if anyone else came up there.'

'Well, good luck to both of yah. I'll just hold the fort 'ere, then,' Foster put his hands in his pockets and nodded his head.

'Whatever else you do, Jack,' Bridges urged him. 'Stay close to Reggie and make sure he doesn't let old Fred, or anyone, tell the police where I am. Not today. Okay?'

'Sounds a bit shady, but, yeah, right. I'll do what I can... Now, you two, take care. All right? I spose you've both got water for your time on the track?'

Bridges looked towards the hired Land Rover.

'Well,' he began feebly. 'To tell you the truth... I'm not sure. Thanks for the reminder...'

Foster couldn't bear to listen. 'Don't tell me...you didn't check the Rover's water tank on the way down?'

It was not so much a question as a humiliating indictment. Mani grinned at Bridges' discomfort, and Foster pressed the blade of his criticism deeper. 'That's how it happens...how people "a perish". It's a big, unforgiving country out here, and it can't be much comfort when you're doin' a perish, to say, "I thought someone else would've filled up my water tank for me."'

Bridges knew that he didn't have a leg to stand on. 'You're right. It's the driver's job.' Without another word he strode away to examine the tank that was built into the rear end of the vehicle he was to drive.

Foster turned on Mani. 'I don't know what you've got to grin about.' He grated, 'you ought to know better...'

Mani smiled confidently, 'I do know better. I did check that Land Rover tank. It's more than half full. But I knew better than that, too. I knew it was end of the rain season and the ground is full of all the water that has been coming from the sky and running into cool places where it can stay. There's plenty there if you know where to look for it, and I know all the signs.'

'Good for you,' Foster approved. 'But you better take a waterbag up into that mountain.'

'Did my grandfather carry water up there?' The question was a challenge. 'Or Andrew Brown...and Mister Blyth?'

Fosters' answer was that they had taken none, but then, two of them were elders who had lived in this country as young men, and would know how to look after themselves up there, whereas Mani had never been here before. To which the young Wainanda answered, with complete assurance that he also knew how to look after himself. The old men had taken no water into the mountain because they knew where to find three permanent rock pools. Just as Gudjagari had left it for them. He also knew where these spring-filled rock holes were to be found. He could describe the places because he had heard the detailed dreaming story of this place from his grandfather many times, He also had a mental picture of the ceremonial ground on top of the mountain, laid out exactly in the way that the creator spirit, Namamuiak had shown the first people when he had come from the Milky Way. Nearly as big as a football ground, it caught the water in the Wet that would fill the hidden mountain springs for dryer times.

Foster scratched his chin as he considered this way of being sure of your water supplies for a journey, then he relaxed and trusted his young friend's ability to look after himself.

* * *

Twenty minutes later Bridges stopped the Land Rover and looked back at the rugged skyline where, on their way into camp, when he and Mani had stopped here, they had seen Blyth and Brown silhouetted on that ridge.

Now it was Mani, the lone climber, who stood waving in his direction. Bridges returned the wave, and waited for any further signal, before engaging the clutch. Crossing low rock surfaces made smooth by primordial Wet Season torrents that had sculpted the massive high stone country into escarpment cliffs and chasms, he turned the Land Rover towards the tall, falling grass plains beyond the next bank, to resume the urgent task of staying on track back to Jabiru.

Chapter 26
The force the of Lore

So this is the track made smooth by thousands of elders in past centuries, thought Mani, and these are the rocks that Bridges sees from below, that look just as rough to him as they did when we watched Mister Blyth and Andrew Brown climbing here. Now I'm here, passing over these sacred paths. My grandfather is up there, where his grandfather and many of his grandfathers' grandfathers have been. In the days before the old travelling life was destroyed. But this is still the same place, the life is still here and it's our sacred touching place. Gujigari is still here. And I am daring to be here. Can I dare to go all the way? Gujigari, I respect you, but I am being bold, not cheeky, and I'm coming up for my people and for peace in our country.'

The way was easy to follow from boulder to boulder, and over the shelves and declines in Gujigari Rock. It was really a mountain on the edge of the vast escarpment, with a track winding around crags and rising across rocky slopes.

As Bridges' Land Rover disappeared around a bend, Mani turned back to the track, sprang across a ridge of rock and found, on the other side, the first water-hole. In a hollow below him there was a deep pool in a crevice as wide as a double arm span. Overhanging rock gave almost constant shade, and a water-mark down a vertical rockface above the surface glistened with trickling water, revealing the presence of a hidden spring. He marvelled at the providence that made water stores within rocks, even in dry seasons, slowly discharging into a deep cool place where it could support life.

Solemnly Mani approached the pool to stoop and drink from a cupped hand as he was sure his grandfather had done, and many thirsting individuals in the long procession of those who now belonged to the eternal communion of immortal humanity on the other side of this physical plain we call life. Were they watching now? He looked up from the water at the brooding, shadowy characterisations in rock of the eternal mysteries, and knew that, whether there were ever any way to prove it or not, as the Balandas love to do, there was a reality beyond testing, more than physical, undeniable. It was reality itself; and he was part of it, willing to be in it and of it. There was no doubt in his mind that, in this same way his ancestors were also participants in the same reality; and in this present moment, alone as he was in body, he was as much in their company as if he could see them with his eyes.

Gujigari, who had given his name to this rock mountain in days gone by was probably a man like himself, feeling the hard heat that now burnt his feet uncomfortably as he continued to climb and edge around narrow shelves that faced the sun, with his heart pounding.

Strangely, he found himself climbing for Jambagirrila, his grandfather, and for Gujigari, his ancient ancestor, way-finder, law-giver, ceremony-maker and fore-father. For them he pressed on and up, drawing on their strength and wisdom. He mounted steep rises and stretched across dangerous gaps, continuing in strict conformity to the visible signs of the track, confident that, to diverge could be disastrous.

It was like this in the men's "inside" dances. Dancing not for fun and entertainment, as they did in many of the outside events with the women and children, but to be the men that they were, together in the dance with all the men from whom they came and who danced with them, whose lives they shared and lived to fulfil. This was the way his people had come in unison each man using his strength to regulate his personal desire and self-serving in order to move together as one body, one life, in one lore, in what had been laid down as the way to survive, not just physically to stay alive, but to be living properly, surviving as truly human, together and for each other. Climbing here on the rock of Gudjigari was the same as dancing the ceremonies and singing the song cycles of the Lore.

A man of the Gujigari dreaming was alone with the spirits and in the midst of a shining green and ochre-red world spreading below him to far horizons. Here, it was for him to manage, for he was man, and, from time immemorial, he had been made responsible to look after life in this magnificent realm, properly, according to the Law for survival and for being truly human. The days when murderous Balandas had begun to wipe out the people who traded and hunted along the seasonal story trails and made spiritual pilgrimage across this country, were gone. Hopefully they were gone forever, and he had survived to return to his ancestors' sacred tracks. His breathlessness stilled and his heart beat faded as, for one simple moment, everything seemed to become one perfect and permanent reality.

He filled his lungs to capacity, and cried at top pitch of his calling voice, 'Gu -u-ujigari! Gu-u- ujigari! Gu- u-u- jigari! I have co-o-ome! I have co-o-ome! I have coo- ome ho-o-ome!' The effort left him breathless, and he felt slightly ridiculous, but only briefly, for a deep sense of peace and satisfaction welled up within him. It was true, Yumbarbar was dead to the world, and Gujigari was alive to the spirit, and Mani was free to go abroad in the world unafraid. The spirit of white racism would never dominate him. He would always remain a responsible man of the living generation, to fulfil the purpose of human life with personal integrity and cultural consistency. He ran at the smooth, rising stone steps ahead of him and leapt up and over them in an ecstasy of confidence.

* * *

Bridges, twenty-three kilometres to the north, had just driven the Land Rover into a dry creek-bed and rolled to a standstill while he looked for the marks of where they had emerged, not much more than four hours earlier, from the high grass on the other side. Sensing how easily he could get lost if he let present concerns divert his concentration from the business of staying on track, he got out and back-tracked on foot to the centre of the creek-bed. There he saw where they had run off the track in the morning by taking the shortest way over the rocks. Just five metres to the left, the track emerging from the long grass was clearly visible. A glance at his watch and an estimation that he had come about a third of the way, made him anxious to move on quickly. At this rate he could hope to be back by about four thirty or five at the latest, as long as the charter from Kununurra was already at Jabiru when he got there. Sunset across the western plains would be at about seven o'clock: it always was, this far north, give or take a few minutes. There was still plenty of time for what he wanted to do today, but he must keep moving.

* * *

At the second water-hole Mani had the luxury of a rest. He was feeling the heat now, aware that he had become soft in his urban existence. Somewhere ahead, not far above him now, he must face the most important people he could imagine ever having to deal with, the chief protagonists of the two cultural systems of his life, Jambagirrila, his grandfather, and Edward Blyth, his Chief Minister. With them was that enigmatic man, Andrew Brown, whom he had so very recently humiliated in front of a crowd of people.

As a man of the Gujigari dreaming he wanted to be loreful and selfless, but what did that mean in this case? Long ago, when Gujigari had made the track on the rock, and the track through life, the human saga had been simpler, not easier, but less complicated. Survival had demanded constant vigilance and some hard, brutally hard, decisions; but then the Balandas had not arrived, and had not terrorised the people.

In fact, when Gujigari first climbed the rock, in all probability, the nations and cultures of the Balandas had not even been formed in Europe.

The song he had performed with the group at the YMCA returned and he let himself hum the first few lines. Looking up at the towering rock face he sang.

'Ancestors of our land, I bring you back to present time, Walkabout, living on the life you knew…New worlds you never dreamed of are in our hands.'

In this isolated place, he must relate to his grandfather, and, first and last, be respectful to him and his wisdom.

Of two things he could be quite sure. The first was that he would know beyond doubt when he came to the entrance to the sacred valley, just beyond the third pool and through the narrow rock passage. The second certainty was that he would be doing something criminal if he entered there. At the beginning of his climb he had hoped that he might meet the other three climbers somewhere below the final water-hole.

There it was now, beneath a darkening sky, down there, below the place where he was pushing between the smooth surfaces of two boulders flanking the track. Before and below him, across a rock-strewn bank of red soil, lay a stone basin holding a shallow sliver of water. Green grass grew on the side of the red bank nearest the pool. It was not the way that he had imagined the last water-hole, and neither was the gap through the rocks immediately visible beside the pool as he had expected it to be, just a further pile of mountainous rock. The water was sweet, and he took the opportunity to drink his fill.

Around the last large boulder he saw the base of the gap. The moment had come for decision, and he stopped to weigh the possibilities. Until this last moment, he had been clinging to the hope that he might not have to enter the sacred valley to meet the others. It was bad enough that he was here, on the Rock, at all, but to actually walk in through the gap, no longer just a thought, but a real possibility, would be a suicidal blasphemy. It was a reckless thing, which went against Mani's careful nature, like jumping from a high cliff on to a heap of leaves, with small hope of avoiding physical destruction.

He looked up the cliff-face and saw that it appeared possible, if he went to the right, that, without passing through the gap, he might, on this side, climb all the way to the top. His grandfather had not told him that the Lore forbade that. He looked up. The red rock no longer glowed with sunlight up there. It was dull and brown and foreboding against the stony grey of the tumbling edges of the cloud-front. Perhaps if he were up there he might look into the sacred valley. He felt that he must try that, before deliberately flouting the ancient Lore; and lost no more time thinking about it. Hot and tired as he was, he still found it easy to scale the fallen rocks and get to the top of the ridge, from where he encountered rough undulating terrain, in places lightly timbered, and rocky out-cropped strata that ran on towards higher ridges half a kilometre away.

Turning left, towards the low area beyond the gap, he began to make his way across weather-smoothed rocks, down into a steep incline and up the other side, over a crumbling rock-fall and on to a grassy ridge. Now he could see the far side of the valley. In fact, a few seconds later he could see almost all the peaks in the broken top of the whole rugged ring that surrounded this most sacred place of the Gujigari dreaming. It was not huge. At the top of the surrounding ridges it was approximately the size and shape of a football oval, sloped down to a level, fertile area in the centre.

He decided to move down towards the grassy level ground that filled the central plain now partly obscured by the dark dull foliage of several nearby trees. Taking care to make no noise as he left behind him the high rocky outcrops, he began clambering down the slope. The level fertile ground around and beyond the trees appeared to be open and grassy, and he kept watch for signs of the three men as he descended.

He stopped and listened. There again…someone chanting, quite nearby, further to the left and below him. Taking extra care to remain concealed, he moved across the hillside, leaving the rocks behind and using shrubs and trees for cover as he travelled closer to the trees below. The singing was slightly familiar, probably a Wainanda song, but it was not his grandfather's voice. He was close to the singer now, being level with the top of a bright green gum tree, one among several dozen growing close together. Perhaps he would not be able to see the singer from up here on the hill.

Another ancient rockfall, including a number of large split boulders had to be clambered over, and coming out on the far side, he drew back suddenly, because below him he now saw, not just one, but all three men near the shade of the green gums. One man was lying flat on a fallen tree trunk in the sunshine. It must be Blyth! After a momentary rest, to get his breath and collect his thoughts, Mani edged along the boulder where he cowered.

His heart was racing, and breathing was becoming difficult. Looking up, the sight of the dark, churning cloud bank moving over him seemed unnatural. If only it would rain now. Is this really happening? Must I do something unreal? He wrestled again with the seriousness of the circumstances in which he found himself. They were as bad as he had feared they might be, and he had walked into the thick of them. It was frightening. He stared up at the bosom of the sky and sucked air desperately. It must be done, he knew. And he knew that the writhing cloud mass was racing northwards.

Only its edges would pass over them, as it clung to its given course above the margin of the great escarpment. No relief from heaven would pour down on him, to wash away the terrible reality of this moment.

He crept from his rock cover, forward and down towards the plain, slowly, behind several of the smaller rocks. Carefully he searched along them until he found a gap, near the level of the plain, through which he saw again the group below. It was a frightful sight.

The man lying flat in the sunshine was, indeed, the Balanda, Edward Blyth, and the reason he was lying there, on his back, was that his arms were opened wide and tied along a branch of a fallen limb. The situation was obviously serious, because Blyth was struggling, in vain, to free himself, and his uncovered white body was pink with sunburn, his shirt apparently having been torn up to make ties for his arms. Mani could not imagine how the two old men had managed to tie down the young Balanda chief; certainly not by overpowering him. They must have out manoeuvred him, tied him down before he realised they had any sinister intentions, perhaps as a demonstration of some old ceremonial practice. That would be their way. They would trick the trickster. Mani's mind was racing. If they were deadly serious, then the Chief Minister really was in mortal danger.

By the same line of thought he could see that his own life might be ended if he appeared at this point to interfere. Jambagirrila would not disregard the Lore, much as he loved him, and Mani would not disobey his grandfather, much as he dreaded what the consequences might be for everyone if the Chief Minister died here. He must do what he could now to prevent a total disaster for his people. It was the people that mattered. Hadn't his grandfather always told him so?

'Gently', he told himself. 'Gently and obediently I must respect the Lore, but also I must disobey the Lore.' There was no other way. Just to obey the Lore was to forget what the Lore was for; the survival and greater life of the whole people. What was that that English word?… Expendable! Jesus showed us how to be expendable for the people. Yes, that was what I must be now. He told himself confidently. Now I have to be expendable for the people.'

He wished for the opportunity to tell his grandfather. Perhaps it would come later. In imagination he rehearsed that moment. 'For the people, grandfather. Please understand me.' He stood tall and prepared to move.

'I'm coming down grandfather,' he whispered. 'Please listen to me.'

The singer continued, loud and nasal with a passion of zeal, in a vigorous version of an ancient lyric. It was Andrew Brown, chanting with a descending cadence, repeatedly beginning loud and fading away to a breathless murmur. Then the whole pattern repeated itself again, and, as Mani listened, he picked up a word and a phrase that referred to the eagle and the kangaroo. The words were Wainanda, but he knew not the song.

Andrew's back was to Mani and, for the moment, there was a chance to move without being seen by him. As the singer repeated his chant, sitting cross-legged on the ground, and having no music sticks with him, he rhythmically slapped both knees with his open hands. The other old man, his grandfather, was also sitting in the same customary way, but facing the hillside as he worked away at making something. With a hard object, possibly a stone chip, Jambagirrila was shaving a long stick, apparently creating a smooth roundness. When the old man put the tool firmly against one end of the stick and held it there for examination, Mani's fears rose again. His grandfather was making a stone-tipped spear! He watched the old man pick up a length of string, probably native rope from inside bark that had been rolled on his thigh. The craftsman began to lash the stone chip into place as a spear-head.

The victim tied to the tree limb was struggling to raise his head. Blyth tried to call towards the old men, but his voice was so feeble and constricted that Mani heard no words. The Chief Minister was already suffering terribly, and the signs were that every moment was taking them closer to a major tragedy for everyone. Mani stepped into the open and began a slow descent to the plain focusing on the thought that he must display reverence and then plead respectfully with his grandfather and Andrew for mercy for the Chief Minister of the Northern Territory and himself and all of the people.

Before he had gone more than a few steps in the open, Jambagirrila caught sight of him and, with a cry, sprang to his feet. He was wearing only a white narga loin cloth. A gargled shout issued from his throat as he thrust the unfinished spear into the air. Andrew Brown stopped singing and quickly rose to his feet. His narga was a piece of maroon coloured fabric tied at the hips. As he yelled at Mani he held both fists in the air. At that moment Mani felt more awestruck than at any other time in his life. It was as if thunder suddenly rumbled in his head and flashed like lightning down through his guts. Andrew Brown, whom he had chastised so recently as a deserter and traitor, obviously was threatening him for his un-Aboriginal behaviour; and his grandfather was sealing the threat with full throated wrath. Still the young man went on towards the elders, and still they continued their loud harangue.

When he reached the level grass he walked a few paces closer to them and their victim, turned slowly and sat down with his back towards them. He was shaking uncontrollably and sweat was dripping from his forehead as he sat, head bowed, and waited. In less than half a minute Andrew became silent and Jambagirrila had reduced his shouting to almost a normal voice level, but continued to harangue the young trespasser. From the start they had called him names like 'stranger', 'dirty destroyer of the people', 'big-headed breaker of the Lore', 'killer of the truth', 'enemy of the ancestors', 'snake with a split tongue'.

They yelled at him to go from this sacred place at once if he valued his life, and that it was the Lore that no one should look at this place and live, except those who had received the permission through the big men's business, the higher degree of Gujigari, in the way of the people since the beginning of this place. Mani sat with bowed head, and waited, until the elders had finished their condemnations.

Nobody moved or spoke, the time as motionless as the air, as silent as death, except a few stray rain spots adding to the inescapable collision of ancient forces. Motionless, all three felt the terrifying weight of the immovable past bearing down on this unacceptable, yet inescapable moment. Jambagirrila slowly rubbed the rain spots along his fore-arms, not wet enough to smear the ochre dried there, then rose and strode over to his grandson. He firmly said, in the language of the Wainanda, 'you are son of my daughter, but I disown you…You disgrace your people and bring shame to your family. The spirits of the dead will not let you rest for this insult to our sacred Lore. This is the way that came to Gujigari with the first visitors from heaven, and you...you, I taught you everything from a little boy until now....You shame Gujigari, and your grandfather, and your people, you break the Lore and the truth from the sky. You will be put out forever, and now you can get ready to face your punishment'. For a moment there was silence until Jambagirrila continued, 'You will not go unpunished just because you are flesh of my flesh. You have made my heart dead inside me, and I cast you off for your filthy behaviour!'

Mani had been listening with his head bowed in respect and was appalled to hear these words from his grandfather, but took some comfort from the sound of the voice in which his rebuke was delivered. It was more a voice of sorrow than of anger.

The old man was strongly pronouncing the verdict of the ancestors' Lore inspite of his affection for his beloved descendant. He stood tall as Brown came and stood beside him. Mani could see their feet, but dared not look up as Brown spoke. His voice was quiet and caring but tough.

'Why are you here?' he demanded in English. It was a Balanda-type question, about why, not one that his grandfather would ask. Together with the English words it meant that Brown was relating to him as one modern man to another, and appealing that, as men of the wider world, they might make an effort to understand each other. Mani looked up, expecting to see the old man he had confronted at the YMCA now looking slightly different, his transformed attitudes showing in his expression. What he saw shocked him. The face and upper body of the man standing over him were streaked with red ochre, and his wild white mop was dotted with red patches. Could this possibly be Andrew Brown? Jambagirrila was similarly marked and his hair stood out in wild array, also showing red among the white.

They waited. Mani found nothing inside him capable of lifting the weight of his voice and pushing it out into the open. Eventually, as a substitute for speech, he moved on to his knees and then even lower and prostrated himself before the elders with his face in the grass.

'Stand up!' Brown was firm, without being hostile. Mani rose to his feet. 'You, who gave me the straight word in Darwin, what do you have to say for yourself now?' Brown quietly brought home his challenge.
'God help me, and Gujigari, survive and be free,' mumbled Mani.
'What are you saying? Speak up if you want to be heard,' Brown said firmly.

Mani slowly responded in English. 'The everlasting Rom is good, and Madayin and all sacred ceremonies are important, and must be respected. All that my grandfather taught me I believe and I respect. I honour my grandfather, and all my people and the Rom of the ancestors, and of heaven above. I believe, and I honour our great ancestor, Gujigari, and I tremble to follow his track, and to ask for mercy for the crime of entering this ceremony place. I am a maggot and I deserve nothing, but I ask to be spared.'

'You broke the Lore!' Jambagirrila shouted.
'Why should you be spared?' Brown asked.
'The Madayin life is good…the Rom lore is forever,' Mani chanted. 'I am no good… I have done many wrong things. There is no reason to spare me, except that you are wise and merciful. I beg for your mercy to spare my life and hear me.'

Brown was confused and looked towards Jambagirrila, who said quietly, 'he is guilty. No matter if you say anything. Still guilty.'

Mani spoke again. 'It's true. I have come here against the Lore that my grandfather taught me. But I beg you to let me speak.'

His grandfather turned his head away and Brown nodded as he said, 'speak if you have anything to say about this business.'

Mani signalled that he would like to sit if it were permitted, and led the way to the shade. Jambagirrila walked behind. As they drew near the fallen limb and Edward Blyth, Mani looked over at that wretched man. His arms appeared to have been tied down with bush rope and later secured with the torn fabric as well. The victim had stopped struggling and was watching as the three men came near.

'Malcolm,' he gasped. 'Malcolm, am I glad to see...' His voice cracked and broken trailed away, lost in a dry throat.

'Sit here,' Brown gave the order, and Mani complied, squatting cross-legged, facing Blyth, about eight paces away.

Brown sat as close as two paces in front of Mani, and a little to the left, and Jambagirrila came and sat to the left side and slightly behind the other elder. After a minute or more of silence, Mani began his account of why he was deliberately trespassing in this forbidden place.

'For many years I have dreamt of coming here to go on with the elders of my people into the secrets of the Lore. I was ready to wait, and to hope it might happen. I can wait until the proper time. Always I want to do the proper way.' He paused and looked at the other two sitting facing him, then at Blyth who seemed to be trying to hear what was being said.

'Today I have come to be with my grandfather and...er, another elder whom I respect, and with...with our Chief Minister of....of our gobberment. All these men are very important people in my life. I am only a young person, and I do silly things... but today I had to come to show respect for my elders, my leaders, and, er...my Balanda leader, too.'

He waited in silence, until Brown said, 'you did not wait outside. Are you already an elder?'

'No,' Mani said it softly but held Brown's gaze.

'Are you ready to die?' Brown asked it simply, and Mani answered just as simply, 'No.'

After a long silence, Brown said, 'you are not yet an elder and you are not ready to die. One more thing can happen here. Are you ready to go through the big man business?'

The young man could hardly dare to believe that he was hearing an invitation to consider passing through a higher degree, but Brown's next words confirmed it.

'Some of us have gone wrong. Gone off the way.' Mani looked at the ground and nodded. 'Wasted our years. Not many elders now...Not many ceremonies...You are one young man staying on the proper way, till now. Should....we should, help you, put you in the proper business way, this time.' He rubbed his chest, removing the red ochre from three horizontal scars as thick as ropes laid across his skin. 'Are you ready to bleed to leave behind the young man and to be the old man?'

Mani thought quickly and tried to still his racing heart by breathing deeply. 'Gujigari is my lore-giver, and I am ready to follow his way, all the way.'

Brown turned to talk with Jambagirrila for several minutes, before addressing Mani again, saying, 'you talk about this Balanda big man, who has struck at the Madayin. We know this man. We have worked with him for years. He is not a bad man, but he is like all the Balanda destroyers. They know nothing about our Rom, our life and our land, and they don't care...they call it "Nothing"...So they treat it as nothing... This time he has come into a sacred place...'

'With you,' Mani added. 'Forgive me. I am a young fool, but I know you brought him here. Is he to blame for that?'

Confusion was visible in Brown's quiet stillness, before he replied, 'he came to destroy, to take and destroy, as his people have always come.'

'Are we like the Balandas?' Mani's impulse to speak had taken charge. He concentrated as hard as he could, but still allowed himself to say, 'they killed us because we couldn't be like them, and do we kill them now because they can't be like us?'

'Shut your mouth!' Brown commanded. 'We have let the people and the way of the Rom be destroyed for too long. Many people have been hurt. You said it yourself!' He softened as he spoke again. 'And you spoke the truth. We have been too soft. We have been slaves. Now we will keep the Lore...This time a Balanda boss can't wipe it away or make us afraid. Here, in this sacred place, he will feel the force of the Lore of this land.'

Mani persisted, 'Realise, that if you kill this Tall Tree that it will bring many Balandas to this place...it will never be the same again."

Jambagirrila rose slowly and crossed to look closely and thoughtfully at the bound man, then came towards his grandson, and eventually spoke to Andrew. 'One brother can bleed for the other one.'

Brown rose to his feet and raised a fist in the direction of Blyth. 'Let him pay for all their sins against us,' he declared.

Jambagirrila stood beside him and proclaimed, 'It is the Lore!... If my grandson will take the Balanda for a brother he can bleed for him.'

'Do you want that?' Brown stared at Mani as he cried in loud anger. 'Is that what you want, for this lore-breaker who is planning still to take control our lands?'

They waited while Mani looked across at Blyth, then closed his eyes, and chanted several times at a whisper, 'God help me, and Gujigari, survive and be free.'

'Yes,' said the young Wainanda man. 'I'll take him for my brother.'

While Brown moved away a few paces and began to sing through a cycle of songs, Jambagirrila removed the stone chip and took the wooden spear shaft to a nearby rocky outcrop to form a fine point by the process of heavily rubbing it against a rocky ledge.

Eventually they assembled alongside Blyth, who was barely aware of them, and overcome with physical distress and fear. With loud, solemn dignity, Brown asked Mani before all the seen and unseen witnesses, 'do you take this man for your brother in the Lore?'

Mani looked at the ground and waited for his racing heart to let his voice pass through. After another deep breath he felt his body relax with the knowledge that hope had returned. He had been accepted as respectful by Brown and, now, his grandfather, and Brown was opening a life-giving track for him to take. He looked at the pathetic, gasping man tied down to the tree limb.

'This is my brother,' he said. 'I am his brother, and what anyone does to him, it's the same as doing it to me. Because we are brothers.'

Jambagirrila called in a loud ceremonial voice, 'he is the brother! His blood for his brother's life!' He began rhythmical tapping of a stone against the spear shaft, and dancing some staccato stamping steps, while Brown resumed singing loudly and passionately, invoking a spiritual imperative that was beyond both his anger and his understanding.

Raw righteousness cried aloud in the song from his agitated heart, and tumbled in strict rhythmic descent down, down, down to a mumbling petition for a vindication of the lore of all life. Blyth was wide-eyed with anxiety as he lay there at the mercy of these awesome primordial human beings.

As it seemed that the song would finish, Brown held the shoulders of the young man who sat on the grass, his right knee bent, exposing the soft inside muscle. Jambagirrila stopped dancing, poised the sharpened shaft over the exposed muscle, before thrusting. Mani's scream was not drowned by the loud crack of thunder at the very moment of thrust. It rumbled for a full thirty seconds.

Down below, the men in the camp heard the rumble and looked towards the sacred mountain, yet not a cloud was to be seen in the deep blue sky.

At the time of impact, Brown resumed the song, which blended with the rumbling, as did the husky roar of horror that tore itself from Blyth's parched throat.

The shaft passed through Mani's thigh into the earth. Jambagirrila, looked skyward, listening to the rumble, and acknowledging the Ancestors, before jerking out the spear. He resumed his tapping and stamping in time with Brown's song as he turned away from the grandson whom he had punished and danced towards the singer. Mani's leg was bleeding freely and he put a finger over the bottom of the wound to stop the flow. Blood welled and ran across the inside of his thigh, and the pain was real. Jambagirrila was glad to see the blood of his grandson, seep into and feed the sacred earth.

For Mani, it was a relief to find that the pain was bearable; and a great relief to have passed the physical courage test. It was done! Surely now the old men would release Blyth, and there would be no killing, and no nationwide reaction against his people, and the Lore of the ancestors had been satisfied.

'Malcolm,' the Chief Minister croaked, 'what's going on? Are you all right, Malcolm?'

'I'm okay, Mister Blyth,' Mani assured him, speaking rapidly through closed teeth. 'It's a custom. You broke the Old Lore twice, two capital offences, but now you don't have to pay the penalty.'

'You mean, because…' Blyth struggled for voice as well as words. 'Because you got…'

'Don't worry about it Mister Blyth. We're going to get out of here all right,' he grunted.

The old men were still singing and had dance walked over to a fire where Brown scooped up ash, apparently to help stem the blood flow.

'I think my grandfather and Andrew will let you go now, Mister Blyth. But they will probably keep me here, to go through a ceremony, to make me an elder.' He paused and grimaced as the pain threatened to overflow him. I...I...should...n't be here if I am not an...elder. It's their way to let me live, too. You see?' He could not be sure if the Chief Minister saw these things at all.

The old men were continuing to sing at the fireside, and had begun to dance back again towards him. He must finish what he needed to tell the Chief Minister.

'Mister Blyth, don't blame my people,' Mani pleaded. 'We've all got our...own Lores.' The Chief Minister shook his head feebly, then nodded once.

The parched voice said, 'say no more. I heard you speak to the old men, about our two Lores. You're right. There're two Lores in the land. My God, Mani! What a way to find out.'

'I can stay here with my old men,' Mani said. 'If they let you go, you'll be all right. Go slow. Remember, there's three waterholes, going down. Rest at each one until you're not thirsty. Keep out of the hot sun if you can'.

'No rain, clear sky,' Mani's grandfather informed them, pointing his chin towards Brown who was beginning a nasal chant while he threw something into the fire, held his spear aloft towards the clear blue sky and boldly danced back and forth. 'Old man Gudjigari bin sent the rain away so we can send you away, too, Mister Tallest Tree. Now you go down the mountain and you be careful now.' 'You've had too much sunshine for a white bloke,' Mani said sympathetically. When you get down there tell Gray Bridges I'm okay.'

'Gray Bridges?' Blyth was surprised to hear that his communication specialist had come to the rock country.

'Yeah, he came to bring me. 'E is really the one that saved yar life. When I got out of gaol. I thought you were going to trap my grandfather in your Lore, with a signing of a paper.'

Blyth looked away, then turned his face towards the nearest tree's base. 'Look over there,' he said. There was a tan satchel lying at the foot of the tree.

'Your bag?' asked Mani, and as the Chief Minister nodded, he realised the significance of what had been pointed out. 'With the paper and...uh, the pen, to trap my grandfather....uh....' The pain threatened to swamp his thinking. 'Uh! To let you take power over....this family country?'

Edward Blyth sighed deeply and tried to say, 'not really to take it, Malcolm. Just to get permission to do what we like with it and...' But the effort was too much, the words sounded absurd, he let the statement fade away unfinished.

'Don't worry about it, Mister Blyth.' the young man advised. 'You can't help being a sly bastard…you're a Balanda.' Anything else that they had to say to each other must wait. The elders had returned. Brown untied the arm-bands, set Blyth free, and assisted him to his feet. The two men, who had looked at each other so often in the corridors and offices of the Chief Minister's Department, each now searched for the real person before him.

The elder spoke, 'now you know a little bit more what it's like for people when they get caught in other people's Lore. Go now, Mister Chief Minister, get out of this sacred place, and be glad that our Lore, and this young man gave you back your life. Go on! Git out of this sacred place…and never come back 'ere again.'

'Andrew…' the half-naked, pink and white man wheezed painfully.
'Go, Mister Bigges' Tree,' Brown commanded. 'There's nothing more for you to say here. Go back to your Balanda books an' dollars an' guns. Go back to the land of your own Law.'

With a glance at Jambagirrila, and a look of concern for Mani, who nodded, the freed trespasser recovered his brief case and haltingly began his journey back to the camp below. At every step he winced with pain, from the effects of lying in bonds on the tree and the deep abrasions to both of his arms, caused by struggling on the rough bough. The burnt areas of his skin were less trouble to him than his sore and watering eyes, and his throbbing headache.

Nausea told him that the effects of sun-stroke were beginning to take hold. Before he passed into the narrow passage that formed the exit to the arena, the singing began again. He struggled to a vantage point on a rock about seven metres above the level of the grass. From there he could see the men he had left behind. To his horror, he saw Malcolm Manggululu spread across the same branch on which he himself had been tied. His punctured leg had been bound and he was tied down with the same bonds as he had been. While Brown continued to sing, Jambagirrila hovered over the young man's chest with an implement, a rock chip perhaps. The song continued as the elder made a stroke over his grandson's chest, from one side to the other, and blood began to appear, brilliant on black skin in the sunlight. More confused than ever, and cursing his own impotence to do anything for Manggululu, Blyth set himself the ultimate aim of letting the men down in the camp know as soon as possible what was happening.

Focussing on the immediate goal of reaching the first water-hole, he carefully made his way down again towards the grass, and picked up once more the track of Gujigari leading towards the gap.

Chapter 27
The Woman from the west

Bridges arrived as the Cessna was taxiing towards the covered waiting area, and pulled in alongside, ready for a quick transfer of the two passengers from Kununurra. Livvy looked radiant as she climbed down the Cessna steps in her light-weight pink outfit with tapered slacks and short-sleeved top. She turned to offer a hand to her short, white-haired co-passenger, Lucy Charlton, neat in a sleeveless blue shift. The old woman was cautious about placing the soles of her low heeled black shoes on the steps, but, once on the ground, it was clear that she still was a strong, vital woman, erect and slender, with plenty of spring in her step. The meeting was doubly exciting for Bridges. Being with Livvy out here would be exciting at any time, but it was even more so now because of her successful assignment. Added to that, the tussle with Fred Archer and his own deliberate prevention of information of their whereabouts being reported to the police, had heightened his sense of urgency, and now Lucy Charlton was here and available as an informant who might shed light on vital facts from the past. He was betting on the fact that he had knowledge that she wanted, which gave him bargaining power and influence, enough to have persuaded her to make the journey.

'Gray,' Livvy took up the introducer's role.
'This is Lucy Charlton, Gray…and Lucy…this is my man, Gray Bridges.'

Lucy stared at Bridges and he smiled at her, 'I can't tell you how pleased I am to meet you,' he told her.

'Ullo,' she said. 'Thanks for the long aeroplane ride. But what's it all about? What for did I have to come all the way over to 'ere, so you can tell me somethin?'

Rather than reply clearly Bridges looked up at the massive cloud moving in above them, and suggested, 'perhaps we'd better get your bags and get on the road. That cloud looks as if it means business.'

The old woman glanced at the cloud, then watched Livvy collect their two bags and speak with their pilot who would be returning directly to Darwin. That done, she turned to Bridges who took the bags and moved towards the Land-Rover. She suggested that Lucy sit in the front beside Bridges, but that was not acceptable.

'I doe wanna separate a husband and wife,' she said ambiguously, but conveying a clear sense of social duty to keep her place. Livvy sat in the back with her, which suited Bridges because it made it easier for him to avoid speaking about his reasons for asking Livvy to bring Lucy from Kununurra.

'Was it a good flight over?' He asked loudly as they turned on to the road south.

'Yes,' Livvy said. 'But I've had enough flying for today. What do you think, Lucy? Was it a good flight for you?'

'Oh, yeah. I always like to go up there, you know. You can see so much country… But it's always scary, too. I was really frightened, you know? Specially when we was comin in straight at this big cloud up 'ere. Oh, no! I was thinkin. Not that! It was so big, and dark, and I thought we don't know what's in there. I want to get down out of 'ere!'

'The pilot wants to miss it, too,' Livvy told them. 'He was just telling me he has to get refueled quick and get off, to stay ahead of that cloud front, and beat it in to Darwin, or he could get tossed around. He said that the clouds and air currents are unpredictable up there. Last week, he said, he felt as if a giant hand grabbed the plane and swung it across the sky. He didn't know what direction he was flying when he regained control.'

'We don't know what goes on in the sky,' the old woman asserted confidently. 'We 'ave to show respect for all that up there…But, one thing I know…I hope I won't be in it next time that his plane gets grabbed and turned around.'

'Me, too!' Bridges joined in. 'But I can promise you that we'll have a smooth ride in this all the way to Gudjigari. As he spoke, a goanna ran in front of the wheels and he swerved to miss it, flinging the two women side-ways, held in place only by their seat-belts.

'Whoa! Steady up!' Livvy cried.

Lucy heaved herself upright on the seat, and asked with cheek, 'Does 'e break all of 'is promises as quick as that one?'

They all laughed and Bridges was abject. 'Oh, I'm sorry. A goanna shot across and I just dodged it instinctively. I promise I won't dodge next time.'

'Well, thank heavens for that!' Livvy exclaimed.

'Next time, if you can run over the goanna,' Lucy sounded only half serious. 'We can take 'it down to our campfire for supper tonight.'

'You might be so lucky,' Bridges replied, and Livvy chimed in, 'Just a small helping for me, please. I like the tail meat!'

The joke was exhausted, and to end the silence that followed, Bridges said, 'let's wait until it's the right time, after we get there. Then I can explain why we are all here. I have to keep my mind on the road.'

'Good idea!' Livvy piped up. 'And on the goannas, too! But the joke really was exhausted and neither of the others responded. Lucy fell silent and occupied herself in looking at country they passed. Livvy grew restless with so much silence, and leaned forward to report that at the Kununurra Airport she had been given simple directions as to where she would find Lucy. It had been easy then for her to ring through and stand by the hospital radiophone for the Katherine ten o'clock sched, and after the sched with Bridges, for Lucy to arrange time off the hospital volunteer roster, pack an overnight bag and head straight for the Airport. Bridges was appreciative of all that they had done, and thanked them both for making such a huge effort.

'It's very important to me,' he said. 'But also for both of you ladies. It will all become clear later on. Please be patient and trust me until then.'

All he told them about the situation at Gudjigari was that Edward Blyth had gone up the mountain with elders. As they approached Gujigari, the women marvelled at the high rocky country, and Bridges noted that it was a new region to Lucy Charlton. Apparently none of her own personal history had occurred in this area.

* * *

At the camp, Foster had the tea billy boiling in anticipation of their arrival. Charles Godfrey had gone fishing for baramandi in the river, Archer had left, without a word, for Gujigari Rock, to continue his watch for the Chief Minister's return, and Reggie Collins was getting to his feet after a siesta in the shade of the tarpaulin.

'Oh good, this'll be lovely. Just what I need,' Lucy Charlton said as she took the mug of tea that Jack handed her after they had been introduced by Bridges. She declined the camp stool, choosing to sit cross-legged on the ground, modestly flicking her dress as she went down, to cover her legs. Livvy was glad to have a camp stool, and coffee rather than tea; but she had no sooner settled and taken her first sip before she noticed someone approaching.

'Who's this coming?' she asked generally, looking towards the Rock.

'Ullo, ullo!' said Foster. 'What's eating Freddie the Flintstone this time?' Archer was striding towards them in a great flurry, but nobody moved to meet him. Everyone except the two new arrivals assumed that he probably was fussing about nothing in particular and everything in general, but this impression was dramatically changed by his first words.

'Quick! Mister Blyth! Up at the water-hole, up there. He's half dead. Needs help, several people to carry him down. I couldn't do it. He can't walk properly. He's nearly dead, I tell you…Who's going to help?'

'All the men,' Foster declared. 'If we have to carry him down we'll need to relieve each other. How far up is he, Fred? Reggie, what about gettin old Charlie down there at the river, and followin on? Gray an' me can get started.'

Reggie Collins broke out his first aid box and prepared to collect Charles Godfrey from the billabong, but waited to hear any plans the others had. Archer was explaining that the waterhole could be reached in about fifteen minutes of climbing over a steep and rough track.

'I better come along, too,' said Lucy Charlton. 'I'm a nurse, like…I done a lot of nursin.'

'Let's all go,' said Livvy, and there was instant agreement. Having learnt from Archer that Blyth was half-naked, sunburnt and suffering from exposure, but apparently not from any breaks, cuts or bites, Lucy made sure that someone brought along sunburn lotion and clothing, including a hat. Reggie undertook to gather these and bring them to the water-hole.

'I'll jus get me towel,' Lucy crossed to her blue canvas carry-all, and, with a towel tucked under her arm, walked with Livvy after Bridges, Foster and Archer.

Foster was the first up the rocks and over to the rock pool, with Bridges not far behind. They found Blyth barely conscious, leaning against rocks near the deep pool beneath the protective overhang. From where he sat, he could reach a hand in and get water to drink or to splash his red and blistering skin. The fact that there were no signs of water on him, or spilt nearby, revealed his weakness. It was some minutes since he had made any effort to make use of the available water.

'Struth, mate!' gasped Foster. 'What's appened to you?' Blyth raised his head, and opened his eyes as if to do so were a difficult and painful operation.

He lifted a hand feebly and managed to whisper, 'good to see you.'

'Hullo there, Ned,' said Bridges abandoning all formality as inappropriate in such a setting. 'You're gonna be all right now, old son. There's a bunch of blokes here to give you a lift down to the camp. You've had a bad dose of the sun, haven't you?'

By way of reply Blyth let his eyelids drop and rolled his head to one side in an attempt at nodding, but when Jack held a mug of water to his lips he was able to drink and took half the contents before stopping. Before he had finished the mugful Livvy and Lucy arrived.

'You poor ol' boy,' said Lucy, crouching beside him. 'You're sick with the exposure. Do you understand what I'm sayin to yah?'

'Yes,' he whispered.

'Good,' she said encouragingly. 'That's real good. You're gonna be awright. What's your name, can you tell me? An' where do you live?'

'I'm Edward Blyth…and I live in Darwin.'

'Good boy, Edward,' she said. 'Don't you worry about nothin now. You been real worried, I bet, and feelin sick in the head and the stomach. That's from all that burnin and from the shock of it in your nerves. You know what I mean? But you'll be awright now. We gonna take good care of you. First, before we shift you, we gonna get you real cool in this beautiful water 'ere.' She looked up at Foster and Bridges. 'What about if you men pour water on Edward here? All over him. Plenty of cold water to cool him down. Awright?'

'Sure,' said Bridges, who had not brought a mug, but accepted the towel that Lucy passed to him. Foster had already begun to pour water from the mug along Blyth's pink legs. With the towel twisted, Bridges was able to wring water on to the patient's head and shoulders and down his chest and arms.

As he did so, a buffeting wind blasted through the rocks above them but not at the water-hole. Reggie and Godfrey arrived with the clothes and blankets dry. Godfrey was alarmed at the sight of the Chief Minister and dropped on a knee beside him.

'Mister Chief Minister!' Godfrey gasped. 'What have they done to you?' Blyth opened his mouth to reply just as Bridges released a mug of water down his face.

Blyth spluttered and blew the water over Godfrey while Reggie chuckled and said, half publicly, 'I bet that's the first time you poured cold water on something the Chief Minister said, Bridges.'

Foster cackled and Bridges smiled his appreciation, but the only other person who managed to smile in these grave circumstances was the patient. Blyth lifted his eyes towards Bridges and gasped, 'not the last time, eh, Gray?'

This pathetic man was a contrast to the Ned who had come from Darwin. Bridges wondered what could have happened to cause the change.

Where were the elders? And what had they done to him? And what had become of Mani, who had gone up to watch out for the Chief Minister's safety? He hesitated in his cooling task, and Livvy stepped in to take over. He let her take the wet towel and stepped back. Looking along the streaming rocks in the direction of the upward track, he tried to imagine Mani's present situation until his attention was brought back to the pool-side by Godfrey kneeling by the Chief Minister and saying confidentially, 'sir, the brief case?'

Ned leaned feebly to one side and indicated with a hand that the case was behind him, and Godfrey leaned in closer as he asked, 'the signature, sir... Did the old chap sign on the dotted line?'

Fury broke loose within Bridges and he was afraid for a moment that he might do violence to the Chief Minister and his lawyer. He had been right all the time. Blyth had decided to brow-beat and manipulate the old land claimant into signing away his rights while his grandson, the modernised member of the landowning group, was detained in the cells in Darwin. Blyth's reply calmed Bridges' wrath and brought him a measure of gratification.

The Chief Minister stared at Charles Godfrey strangely and whispered hoarsely, 'I can't....begin to explain...the old man put...my...life on the line...too. Malcolm... Mani ...came...saved me....from his Lore Two Laws Godfrey...there's another Lore at work here! Someone else got punished for me. I got pardoned, Godfrey. Can that happen, Godfrey?'

The lawyer wagged his head slowly and drew breath, but when he spoke it was simply to say, 'take it easy, Ned. We can sort all that out later. Just hang loose'.

Lucy, who had been standing back surveying the scene, stepped forward, addressing Reggie, 'Now, Mister, can we put them dry clothes on 'im...very gentle like, so as not ta hurt the skin or break any blisters. Then we'll wet them, too, and he'll be ready to travel.' She and Reggie managed the drawing on of the shirt and trousers. Archer and Foster took Blyth's weight. When the process was completed, Jack and Livvy resumed the cooling operation with mug and towel.

Archer stayed close to Blyth, anxiously watching him and glancing at the others, particularly Livvy and Bridges.

Lucy said, 'I'm thinking, we better wait a bit longer, before we take Edward down.' She addressed her remarks to Livvy, but loud enough for everyone to hear. 'E's nice and cool 'ere, now. 'Ell be feelin a bit more like travellin a bit later on, and the sun'll be gettin down a bit.'

Bridges walked back from the overhanging rocks and looked at the higher rugged sky-line. The track appeared to go up and around the towering block above them, and he found himself wondering again about Mani, Jambagirrila and Andrew Brown. What could have happened when Blyth was further up the Rock? Looking back he saw Archer whispering to Blyth, whose face was contracted with pain. Before Bridges could move forward Livvy reacted, 'Mister Archer, I don't think we should worry Mister Blyth with problems right now!'

Archer was quick to reply, 'no, I bet you don't!'

Not being one to accept such loaded comments without reply, Livvy firmly said, 'I don't know what you're inferring, Mister Archer, but I do know that this is a sick man. Have you ever had sun-stroke, Mister Archer? Have a little consideration and move away! You'll have plenty of chances to talk later on.'

Blyth nodded in silence, his eyes still closed; and Archer begrudgingly moved off, and sat down against the rock in the shade. Foster and Livvy stopped wetting the patient's saturated clothes, and sat back against a nearby rock in compliance with Lucy's advice that they wait.

Only Bridges was standing in the central open space, and Lucy rose and came over to speak to him. ''Es gonna be all right. Doesn't seem to know much about looking after 'imself out 'ere in the bush. 'E must be a town boy, is he?'

Bridges realised that the nurse from Western Australia had no idea that she had been treating the Chief Minister of the Northern Territory, and smiled as he replied. 'Yes, you could say that, Lucy. You've done a great job of nursing there.'

'Oh, not just me,' she protested. 'Everybody's bin 'elpin'. Edward's got some good friends.' Bridges was about to reply something to the effect that it was good to have friends at a time like this, when he lifted his eyes again in the direction of the towering rocks above them, and gasped at what he saw, causing Lucy to look up and to freeze with shock.

Above them, looking down, were three Aboriginal men, two clad only in narga cloths, their bodies streaked with wet red ochre. One had rough bandaging around his chest and thigh. He was being supported, on either side, by the other two.

'Here they are!' breathed Bridges, recognising Jambagirrila, Brown and Mani. 'My God! What's happened?'
'Who are they?' Lucy was awestruck.

Bridges leaned towards the small woman beside him and said quietly, 'I want you to tell me, Lucy. When they come down here, I'm going to ask you to give me the name of any man that you can recognise.'

'Me?' She was startled, and stared at him. 'How can I? I don't even know 'em!'

'We'll see,' said Bridges darting away. He moved closer to the others, calling as he went past to the upward track, 'Going up to give a hand to bring down someone else who's been hurt.'

Before he reached the steeper part of the track, Brown wailed loudly and turned his cry into a song of falling cadences that faded away. Looking up, Bridges and others watching from below, saw Andrew hold his spear aloft, pointing to the sky. It was then that Mani was seen.

Mani was in great pain, and his head hung down. He could barely stand, and the old men, lacking most of their body and hair paint now, were holding his weight. The blood-soaked bandages were of torn shirt fabric. Wet blood showed in several places on Mani's chest bandages, and Bridges grew alarmed for his safety.

'Let me take him,' he offered, but the elders treated his offer with contempt.

'We can bring 'im!' declared Jambagirrila.

'Shouldn't he be resting?' Bridges objected. 'He can't stop bleeding while he's climbing about on the rocks.'

'True, Gray,' Brown spoke. Bridges looked twice to be sure that this ancient tribesman was really the Chief Liaison Officer. 'We should let him rest two days after that ceremony cut, but us old men can't look after him all on our own.

'Got no medicine man, now!' said Jambagirrila. 'Should we...we have few blokes, and medicine man bloke. We got none, us old blokes. Not thinkin straight way. We put ashes in the bloody cuts, but not nough. Still lot of blood. We got fright, now from my young granfader son bleed too much. Goin bring 'im down for Balanda medicine, for cuts, we bin say. Now we nearly down. So you look out, young fella. We finish this last business right way.'

Bridges hurried back to the group and only half-satisfied their questions and quizzical stares. 'Listen everyone. Three men are coming down. One of them has been hurt, and the other two are bringing him down to get proper treatment. He has had chest cuts and is bleeding. So Reggie, the old men need some antiseptic and bandages mate. Now, listen to this, please. I ask you for your absolute co-operation. This is very important to me and some others here.'

Blyth had rallied and was listening intently to Bridges. Archer had risen to his feet apprehensively, and everyone else was giving full attention. Livvy was still puzzled, but sensed that her assignment and Lucy's presence were associated in some significant way with whatever Bridges was about to reveal.

'Please, don't anybody say the name of any of the three men when they come down. Some of you know them very well... but nobody say any names... please. Except Lucy.' He looked at the woman from the West, who was obviously worried by the suggestion.

'I dunno so much about that!'

'Please Lucy... believe me, it's important. Afterwards we can have more talk, you and me. Then I can tell you about Lura's baby...but first, please, do this for me.'

'I'll have ta see first.' she protested. When she did see, as the old men assisting Mani, Mani came into sight around the rock and stumbled towards them, she shrank back shyly by Livvy's shoulder and remained still and tight-lipped.

Foster came forward as if to take care of Mani, but Jambagirrila glared at him and said, 'this is my work, Mister Town Clerk.'

Carefully the elders lowered Mani at the pool's edge near Blyth. Jambagirrila and the Chief Minister faced each other, and the old man said, 'you got down 'ere, awright, 'eh, young fella? Bye an' bye, tomorrow, you'll see, you'll be too strong.'

The unrecognisable Chief Liaison Officer knelt by the Chief Minister, and both stared into each other's face. Neither spoke, but when the Chief Minister nodded in understanding, Brown rose and followed Jambagirrila to the water. Bridges led Lucy, who was inclined to hold back, and needed gentle pressure on her elbow to keep her coming. They stood near Mani, who had become the object of Livvy's and Foster's concern. Foster put a mug of water to his young friend's lips, whilst Livvy held his head.

'Mister Blyth! Friends!' Bridges spoke loudly and clearly. 'I call on you to witness what Lucy Charlton has to say.' Everybody turned to watch. Even the elders, scooping and drinking beside the pool, turned to see what was happening and rose to their feet.

Archer suddenly stepped between Bridges and the Chief Minister, obviously irritated by this deviant behaviour. 'Chief Minister, do you want to put a stop to this nonsense?'

When Blyth slowly shook his head, Archer persisted. 'But these people are ignorant. They have no authority, and they are not permitted to take part in discussing how we deal with Aboriginal problems, sir.'

Blyth murmured, 'listen to him.'

'But the police are looking for Bridges...'.

'Listen Mister.' Lucy had stepped forward, to face Archer. 'Don't you know, there's no such thing as Aboriginal problems? There's only people problems!'

'Is that so?' he replied contemptuously, as he turned away.

Bridges resumed. 'Lucy,' he said in a full, public voice, facing the annoyed woman who glanced again at the back of Archer's head.

'You have seen three men arrive here. If you know any of these men please tell us now.' She looked at him seriously and briefly glanced over towards the Aboriginal men. 'If there is one of these men that you remember, please tell us his name or point to him.'

Everybody waited, but Lucy Charlton would not even raise her eyes. Bridges remained patient, but insisted softly, 'Lucy, look up...Look at these men, Lucy.' She raised her head enough to look at Mani, who, seemed to be feeling some relief. He looked at her, and their eyes met.

'Look also at the other men, Lucy,' Bridges told her. Slowly she looked towards Jambagirrila and Brown for two or three seconds before dropping her gaze again.

'Well, Lucy,' Bridges asked quietly. 'Do you know any of these men?"

She glanced up again towards the elders, then turned to Bridges and whispered, 'one ol' man, there.'

Livvy and Bridges glanced at each other, she wondering if this were the purpose of her excursion into Western Australia, and he beginning to feel triumphant. 'Can you tell us, or show us, Lucy?' he asked with subdued excitement.

'This one now,' Lucy Charlton walked across to Jambagirrila and said, 'you remember measles and dysentery epidemics at Goose ilan long time before. I was there, old man, and you was too, eh? No flour bag hair that time, eh?'

Jambagirrila suddenly recognised the woman addressing him and opened his eyes widely in surprise. 'Ah, ee-ee. You the one now! Proper nurse woman! Everybody been 'ad runnin stomach. Ooh, too much! Now, you ne been dere for longest time. I know you.'

Bridges was still waiting. 'Lucy,' he asked. 'Can you tell me the name of one of these men?' She moved closer to Mani's grandfather. 'This one, now,' she said. 'Is Goose ilan' man, people call Jambagirrila, eh? That's right?' Her question was to the old man.

'Ee-ee,' he managed a tired smile. 'You got 'im right. An' I know you. Bin long time before nurse. You come on the iland, with doctors. That true?'

'That's right, too.' she told him. 'I'm that same one.'

'That's all?' Bridges asked Lucy.

'That's all,' she said, and turned to walk away a few paces. Bridges shrugged and looked surprised.

'Are you quite finished, Mister Bridges?' asked Charles Godfrey. 'If so, can you please explain what all the court-room drama is about?'

Bridges looked foolish, and mumbled words to the effect that he seemed to have made a mistake. Reggie was grinning as though it was a great amusement to see a big build-up to a fizzling anticlimax, and the old men returned their attention to the pool as if they were ready to drink again.

Leaving Foster to tend to Mani, Livvy followed Bridges as he walked away from the others. She put her arm through his as she overtook him and asked, 'wasn't that the outcome that you had in mind?' He pouted and slowly shook his head.

To cheer his spirits she found something positive to say. 'You've won Lucy's confidence.'

He was surprised. 'Why? What makes you say that?' he asked.

'Well,' Livvy delivered her expert anthropologist's opinion. 'She went right up to an elder and spoke his personal name in public. You were asking a lot of her, darling. But, for you, she did it. She knew you expected it of her.'

'Mmmh,' he sounded dubious. 'I think she's chasing the bait I dangled before her. But, yes, I do see what you're saying. That was asking a lot...Hang on! ...Hang on a minute!... Brothers!'

The final word was an excited exclamation and startled Livvy. 'What a donkey I've been. Some cross-cultural specialist I am! You're right! Respect! The avoidance rules, quick!'

He strode back to join the others, calling, 'Excuse me, everybody! I'm sorry to be a nuisance, but could we all listen again to what Lucy has to tell us.'

They all complied, some with reluctance, except Archer, who announced, 'oh, this is ridiculous.'

Lucy once more was uncomfortable to be placed in the position of information-giver about present company. Bridges faced her again, saying, 'Lucy, you have been very kind to this clumsy Balanda. I'm sorry if I embarrassed you before. Please forgive me for that. Just let me ask you something else, Lucy. When you were young, you had a tribal husband didn't you?'

'Yes…I did,' she said cautiously.

'And a second one after your first one went away, right?'

'Yes, that's right.' She sounded worried by this line of questioning. 'Your second husband and his brother used to live around here when they were young fellas?'

'Eh?... I spose. Yeh that's right. They did. Somewhere round 'ere?'

'And you can't say their real names, I know, Lucy. But those two young fellas had public names, didn't they? Names that all the people could say. True?'

'Er, like, the name everyone can say, eh? Yes, that's true. They did had, what yah call'em? Nick-names,' she agreed anxiously.

'And Lucy, you can't say your second husband's brother's name, can you? Or look at him, face to face, or speak to him, or point to him? That's not the right way to behave is it?'

She was hesitant, but agreed. 'That's right.'

'I thought that was how it was,' he said. 'So I wouldn't ask you to say his proper name, Lucy,' he assured her. 'Or to look at him, or to speak to him. That wouldn't be right at all…I know that.'

He paused then said, 'Just tell us what were the nick-names that all the people used to call your second husband and his brother? I know it's okay to say them, isn't it? Just their nick-names?'

She hesitated for a considerable time before speaking, and when she spoke, her face was down and her voice seemed to vaporise before it left her throat. It was impossible to hear what she said.

'It's very good of you to tell us, Lucy,' Bridges encouraged her. 'But I need to hear you. We can just wait here and be quiet for a while. And if you can do it, when you feel ready to tell us, please say it loud enough for me to hear. What were the nick-names that everyone could say for your second husband and his brother?'

He moved away, and the old woman lifted her face high enough to see where he was going. He positioned himself between Charles Godfrey and Edward Blyth who were following events to the best of their ability. There he waited. Thirty seconds lapsed, and there was no sound from Lucy. Another fifteen seconds, and some of the people started to shuffle, but Foster shooshed them. Another thirty, forty, fifty seconds elapsed. For all it was nerve-wracking.

Mani was still preoccupied, dealing with his own pain and nausea. And now in the silence, Livvy, hovering near, was alarmed to hear his groans. She scooped a mugful of water and went to his side to support him while he drank. 'Hang in there Mani.' She whispered as she raised Mani's head and shoulders enough to let him drink. Every movement was painful, but Mani was grateful, drinking the cupful before being gently lowered again. Lucy watched anxiously, but still said nothing.

Another period passed, until finally she cleared her throat, and looked at her questioner, with her head tilted to one side, hiding her face from people on the same side as the three Aboriginal men. She glanced at Bridges twice and moved her lips, but it was not until the third try that the words came.

'My second 'usband was usually called Short...Short Man. An', an' his brother, they alwus called him Thin Man.'

'Thanks Lucy,' Bridges smiled, then added quietly. 'Is he here today, Lucy? Your husband's brother? Is Thin Man with us now at this rock hole?'

'Eh?'

'Is he here now?' He waited.

'Yes,' she said. Bridges looked at the Chief Minister, then at Mani, who was too busy battling pain to heed the proceedings, and at Livvy, Jack, Reggie, Archer and Charles Godfrey, to be sure that they were all listening before releasing Lucy from the dialogue.

'You've been very helpful, Lucy. Thank you very much. I don't need to ask you anything more. Thank you so much.'

Livvy came forward to put her arm about Lucy, and said to Bridges. 'What's this all about, honey? I can't see where it gets us.'

'You will, Liv. Just be patient a bit longer,' he said as he turned towards Charles Godfrey, near the Chief Minister.

'Charles,' he said. 'You're the lawyer. Having heard the evidence, tell us, who is Thin Man?'

'Eh?... er,' the lawyer began. 'Let's see, er, Thin Man is her husband's brother. He is someone here. She can't say his personal name, and she has already said the name of one old man. Er, over here, was it Jambagirrila? Yes that's it. And, let's see. Thin Man, her brother-in-law, has to be young Malcolm, there...which is unlikely, to say the least, because of his youthfulness, or er, or, Andrew Brown.'

He looked at Andrew standing alongside Jambagirrila and affirmed his conclusion. 'Um... yes... that's it. Andrew Brown is Thin Man.'

Bridges went up to Brown and said, 'Andrew, old friend, you hear what's being said. Is it true? You're the one who used to be known as Thin Man?'

The old man's serious face showed no emotion as he said, 'yes. That's me. That's the name my people used to call me. My brother they sometimes called Short Man, but me they always called Thin Man. That's when we were young fellas.'

'Around this country, here?' Bridges asked.

'Oh, yes,' Andrew replied, 'ere and further up, South and East Alligator Rivers country and in the saltwater lands, and the coast, and the islands. All through they used to call me that. Long time ago… They did that. They called me Thin Man.'

'Before Artie Smale took you away from your people?'

'You've got it right, Bridges. Big Man and me.' Brown admitted. 'We followed 'im, and I came to be like 'im, an enemy of my people.'

'And your brother, Short Man, he wouldn't go with you and Artie Smale…?'

'No, he wouldn't come with us. Just me and Big Man. We went with the Hunter. My brother wouldn't come.'

'Your brother, Lagi Lagiaga, who was husband to Lura, after her first husband went away and died?'

Brown dropped his gaze and gave no reply. 'It's all right, Andrew,' Bridges assured him. 'You don't have to tell me. I already know Artie Smale took Lura away from your brother, and he took you away from your people. Didn't he, Andrew?'

Still Brown remained silent. 'And you became a black Balanda for Artie Smale, didn't you, Andrew?' Brown turned a stern face on his Balanda colleague, and spoke firmly.

'Yes!' he declared. 'I was afraid of that two-gun man an' I went with 'im, an' I followed 'im into the way of all the Balandas. I was frightened, but not just for myself, for all my people. An 'e showed me how to be a Balanda, an' get on, an' 'ave a good Balanda kind of life.'

'So that's why you killed him, Andrew? After you went out from the YMCA when you heard this young fella', he looked towards Mani. 'Heard him tell that Mayanaj story, and over to the Cavanagh street house, and killed the Hunter.'

Without hesitating, Andrew, the Thin Man, replied in an even, matter-of-fact voice, 'Yes…Gray, that's why. Prob'ly I'm as bad as 'im …but when I was young, 'e frightened me with the guns, and I went along. I was blind. I couldn't see what 'e turned me into.' He stopped and turned slowly towards Jambagirrila.

That old man nodded and Thin Man went on with his story. 'At the YMCA, Manggululu, this young bloke over 'ere, 'e spoke the truth in the story about Mayanaj…'e cut my heart open and made me look inside. When I saw it, I had to do something. I didn't mean to 'urt anyone, you know? I just went over to that Cavanagh

Street 'ouse, because I knew my brother, my brother Short Man, 'ad been around there the night before, and might be goin' back there. I went there to say to 'im, I'm sorry brother, I was wrong all the way, an' you were right.

But I only saw someone else sittin' there on his own, sittin under that stone axe, waitin' for his punishment. First thing, I thought 'e was the old cannibal Yumbarbar! An' it was all the same. Just as bad. One killer or the other one. For my people and for me, I just walked up and while 'e looked at me, I took the axe off the wall an' killed 'im straight away. The one who should 'ave died a long time ago for all his crimes against my people. I killed that ogre who I used to 'elp to destroy my people's life….'e was the white racist who made me into a white racist like 'im. But I didn't see it that way till I saw it when this young fella gave me those 'ard words.'

Bridges looked at Lucy Charlton. She was in Livvy's arms, her eyes and mouth wide, obviously shocked and distressed but unable to turn away. 'Short man!' she gasped. ''e said Short Man in Cavanah Street at night.'

But Bridges spoke again. 'Andrew,' he said. 'When everyone hears your full story I think they'll understand what made you kill Artie Smale.'

'We'll see about that!' mumbled Archer, without drawing a reply from anyone.

'Might be,' Brown briefly tilted his head to one side. His gaze rested on the Chief Minister, who was, with difficulty, following the present conversation and now awkwardly rolled himself on to an elbow and tried to raise his head. 'The due process of law must...be followed,' he said huskily. He looked directly at Brown. The Wainanda elder met his gaze and after a long silence, nodded in agreement.

Blyth continued. 'But we always must listen well...hear all the facts, and… and both of the laws of this land.' He turned to look at Mani, who at the sound of Blyth's voice near him, had begun listening. 'And, be ready to make allowances, exceptions to the law...'

The effort appeared to have exhausted him, and he fell back with closed eyes. Brown returned to his exchange with Bridges. 'So, Gray, you heard about Thin Man and Big Man and Artie Smale, eh?'

'Yes, and Short Man, too. All you young blokes. From your brother, at the hospital. He told me.'

A strangled cry broke from Lucy Charlton, and Livvy again held her tight, saying, 'what is it, honey?'

'Is 'e talkin about Thin Man's brother? What brother? Not 'im! Did 'e say 'es alive? What brother?' Lucy was very upset. 'In the 'ospital, what brother is in the 'ospital?'

'Short Man, Lucy,' Bridges told her. 'You used to know him as Lagi Lagiaga, Lucy. But today people call him Bilago.'

Suddenly the high crags around them rang with a hideous wailing that seemed to come from more than this one, small, distressed old woman and from far deeper than her throat. Neither a scream, nor a howl, but something containing both, reverberated terrifyingly about the mountain. Uncontrolled waves of full-throated shrieking continued unabated until they took on the rhythm of chanting, only dying away to quiet weeping after Livvy walked with the shocked old woman to the edge of the rock ledge. Everybody else waited, speaking to each other quietly and allowing Lucy time to re-compose her feelings. Eventually the old woman's attention was caught by Livvy's arm through her own, and she returned to the present situation and her patients, and was suddenly concerned about the upsetting effects of her commotion on them all.

Bridges joined the two women and talked quietly for a few minutes, during which time the distressed woman came to terms with the fact that her second husband, Lagi, had not died on Goose Island as she had been told, or anywhere else, and was in fact still living in Darwin.

'I thought 'e told me the truth, Artie Smale…'e told me my 'usband died long time ago on Goose Island. All that time. All them years 'e was there livin somewhere an' I didn't know!'

Foster was eager for action and called for attention. 'These men need 'elp to get down off this mountain. Come on, let's get to it.'

Bridges asked Lucy, as the nurse in the situation, if she thought that it was time to move Blyth and Mani down to the camp, and she took charge of operations. To the whole group she apologised.

'I'm real sorry I made that big fuss. I got of a lot of shock…that's all.' Her emotions threatened to disrupt her speech again. 'I 'ope I didn't give youse all too much of a fright. I'm all right now. What about we get these boys down to camp and dress their wounds and burns properly. Now, whose gonna carry them?'

Her face wreathed with emotional pain again, and she shook her head vigorously to clear her thoughts.

'Lagi's alive,' she gasped. 'An' all this time, I never knew.'

Foster and Bridges headed towards Mani, but were met by Jambagirrila and Brown, who blocked their progress. Brown spoke.

'This is for we elders. This young man is in our hands for proper Big Man business ceremony. We take him all the way!'

'Fair enough, mate,' said Foster. With great care for Mani, whose pain was obvious, Brown supported him on one side and Jambagirrila on the other, and began to move towards the downward track. Reggie stopped in front of them and asked, 'Give us 'im 'ere. I can carry 'im.' Their silent stares were sufficient answer, and the travel organiser backed away. He had more success offering his services to help carry the Chief Minister. Spreading the blanket that he had brought up from the camp and with Foster and Charles Godfrey assisting, he managed to lift Blyth on to it. Archer was hovering near, bewildered, silent and alone.

At a signal from Reggie, he joined the other three in rolling the blanket edges. 'By God,' he mumbled to no one in particular. 'Heads are going to roll,' adding as they lifted together. 'Mark my words!'

More interested in the inert and unprotesting Head of Government, Reggie gave the order as they moved ahead. 'Nice and easy…as we go. Take it slow and steady.'

As the second party passed, Bridges overtook Livvy walking with Lucy, who was still visibly upset. He held Livvy's arm, and she reciprocated, but with a look of exasperation.

'Why didn't you tell me what was going on?' she asked quietly. Bridges smiled and leaned towards her.

'I want to thank you, Lucy, for flying over to here,' he said. 'You probably don't know how grateful I am. You see, the police in Darwin are looking for Livvy and me. They think we might have killed the old man in the Cavenagh Street house.' Livvy was flabbergasted.

'What? Oh, you're kidding! Looking for us?'

'It came over the radio sched this morning,' he told her. 'So…you see, Lucy, we needed someone who knew about Andrew's connection with the old man. I had guessed what Andrew did, but that wasn't good enough. Now he told us all, in front of all these witnesses. So the police can forget about blaming other people. Thanks to you.'

Livvy shook her head in wonderment at her secretive husband. He had told her only part of his thinking. 'How did you guess Andrew did it,' she cut in. Lucy turned to watch him, and both of the women waited for his answer.

'It was something that Bilago said when I was visiting him in the hospital, and something that Andrew said in the office,' he told them. 'Bilago told me about Big

Man and Thin Man going with the Hunter, Artie Smale…and about Smale when he was a Customs Officer, taking someone called Lura away for himself, from Bilago, after a big fight on the beach at Goose Island.'

The old woman closed her eyes and mouth as she nodded, and Bridges continued. 'He also told me that Artie Smale was the one we knew as Ron Smart. That set me thinking about what they all meant to each other. And I remembered that, in the office, Brown had said that Mani Manggululu didn't kill the old man. Then he added these strange words…he said, 'Mani didn't need to kill anyone.'

Didn't need to! It was a strange idea. A need to kill! I began to ask myself who did need to kill the Hunter-come-Customs man? Need to. And why would Andrew Brown have such a thought? Later on it occurred to me that maybe it was someone who saw his own guiltiness in that old murdered man, someone who had a need to crush a red mulberry to get rid of his own stains.'

Lucy frowned, and Livvy said, 'explain it later, honey. It doesn't make much sense right now.' She turned to Lucy.

'So, Lucy,' she began tentatively. 'You used to be Lura?'
'That's right,' the old nurse confided. 'The old man who got killed, 'e give me my name, Lucy, and Charlton from the old cattle station manager's family name, and 'e took me to Kununurra to live. That was after I 'ad me baby girl and 'e sent 'er away, an' then 'e told me she died, too. I always thought I lost 'er father, as well as er.' She began to weep again.
'Her father?' Bridges looked for confirmation. 'Lagi Lagiaga?'

The distressed old woman nodded. 'Why did Artie Smale do such a cruel thing to me? To us, to a family of us. I never did anything to 'urt him. Never. Even if I thought about shootin 'im with is own gun, I never did it, or even tried to. But I can't feel sorry that 'es dead now, or about what Thin Man done to 'im.....' She stifled her sobbing and looked at Bridges. 'Well, are you goin' to tell me about what appened to my little girl or not?'

'Perhaps we'd better get back to the camp first,' he stalled.
'Tell me…now!' she demanded. 'What do you want to say about my little dead baby?'

He relented. 'Okay Lura. Come and sit in the shade,' he said, and when the three of them were seated on a rock ledge, he said gently, 'I've got another big surprise for you, Lura'.

'Your baby went to the Catholic sisters in Darwin, and she's still alive today. Yes,

yes. Let me finish. She works with Livvy, in the Education Department, and she's our friend. We call her, Helen…and she's a beautiful young woman who thinks she has no mother or father.'

'Both still alive.' Lucy Charlton's heart was swamped by another wave of sorrow. 'Artie Smale always told me they was dead and gone. You sure my baby's still alive?' Livvy put an arm behind her shoulder, stroking her back comfortingly.

'Yes, that's what he said,' Livvy affirmed. 'If he's right, I know her very well. She lives in Darwin, and I work alongside her. She's learning to be a fine teacher in Aboriginal community schools.'

The sad old woman leaned against her and looked up into her face. 'Is it true?' She was obviously mystified by the simple fact that her daughter was a living person, and had been alive somewhere all through the long years of mourning. She dissolved into weeping on Livvy's shoulder, pausing only long enough to say, 'we 'haf'ta look after them boys 'ere tonight. They not ready to travel today.'

Walking with her, Livvy and Bridges assured Lura that they would all have a night of rest before the drive to Jabiru airstrip.

'I can't 'ardly believe all the things that are appenin to me,' she told them. 'Now I know why 'e made me go west with 'im, and change my name, and why 'e changed 'is too. So I wouldn't find out 'e was a leper or that my real 'usband and baby was still alive, 'e was a cruel…cruel man.'

Livvy agreed, 'it's a wonder someone didn't stop him a long time ago. But,' her voice softened. 'We heard from Father Sheehan that he came to God and had a real change of heart in his old age. He wanted to help you and Helen with gifts of money from the fortune he made from his mining deals.' Lura looked at her, but kept walking. When she spoke, her voice suggested that she was not impressed by Ron Smart's bequests.

'What's the good o' money without the people you love?' she said, her voice resonant with outrage and resentment. But her next words were indistinct and tentative. 'Can I see 'er?'

Livvy held the little old mother's arm firmly as she told her, 'Helen's been upset, and she's not very well, but I'm sure she'll be ready to meet her Mummy for the first time.'

'You can see her in Darwin,' Bridges added. 'You can see them both there, Lura… Helen and Short Man…Lagi Lagiaga.'

* * *

When Reggie succeeded in getting through on the hourly sched, Bridges spoke with Inspector Donovan. 'Inspector,' he began happily. 'I believe you've been looking for me. I'm sorry, but we had to make a little excursion. It was necessary in order to clear up a lot of wrong suspicions. We've had a large group of witnesses out here listening to the confession of the man who killed Ron Smart. We are all returning to Darwin in the morning.'

The Inspector asked for details, then told them to expect a helicopter to pick up the self-confessed killer, Andrew Brown, and the patients, Edward Blyth and Mani Manggululu. The Inspector would come himself leaving Darwin at first light.

'If things are as you say,' he said with only a hint of resentment that his suspects had run down the real perpetrator, then you've done well, and I congratulate you. I'll see you first thing in the morning. Over.'

* * *

It was a quiet camp after dark. Livvy and Reggie assisted the tired but over-excited old nurse, in watching over the Chief Minister and Mani, both of whom slept deeply.

Foster and Bridges settled by the fire with the two tribal elders, and heard more of Brown's story in explanation of his violent action in the house in Cavenagh Street. 'I tell you the truth…I didn't know I was going to kill the Hunter,' he told them. 'It was a surprise to see him there. I wanted my brother. I wanted to tell him I was sorry I left him and went with the Hunter to live with the Balandas all those years ago. There 'e was… the Hunter, and I was there, too. And I knew what 'e was like, because I knew what I was like. Only him and me there. But somewhere close by I could feel the man who took his horse's surcingle and was shot in the head when I was holding him. And all the people he killed or hurt, and the women he used everywhere he went, and I knew that I had come to him this time for them, to be their payback man. And I 'ad to kill 'im, or I would always be like 'im, meself. So I did it. I 'ad to do it.'

Bridges broke the silence that followed. 'Fair-minded people will understand, Andrew.' The killer of the Hunter silently continued to stare into the embers like someone pondering imponderable things.

* * *

The following morning the Land Cruiser's trailer and the Rover were packed and ready before the arrival of the helicopter bringing Inspector Donovan. Reggie made the bookings by radio for a Heron charter to pick up the rest of them from Jabiru airstrip at eleven o'clock. When the chopper had noisily completed a circle above them, the pilot decided that the clearing by the billabong was his best option and gentled the machine down to rest on the grass beside their campsite. Reggie met Inspector Donovan and brought him to his chief. The Inspector spoke briefly with the sore and sorry Chief Minister, then formally arrested and handcuffed Andrew Brown and ordered him aboard the aircraft.

It was a painfully slow business for both Blyth and Mani to climb aboard and settle into the back seats with the guilty elder, and, at the insistence of the Chief Minister, Andrew Brown's handcuffs were removed. There was no room for their nurse to travel with them, so Lura asked if the helicopter might be put down in the Darwin Hospital helipad, and that the medical sched operator be asked to alert the hospital authorities.

He told her that he would sort it out on the radio once they were airborne. As soon as the helicopter cleared the trees and set course for Darwin, the remaining campers climbed into the Land Rovers and took the track for the Jabiru airstrip.

The Bridges had two overnight guests at their place. Jambagirrila was required to stay in Darwin for the investigation of his part in the ordeal suffered by the Chief Minister, and Foster had come along for support and to give further evidence as requested by Inspector Donovan before returning to Goose Island. It suited him fine to have a day or two in town to do some purchasing of Goose Island community requisites. In Darwin, Lura chose to stay at the Nomad Hostel, one of a chain catering especially for indigenous people's style and comfort. She had agreed to make further statements to the police, and, more importantly to her, she would meet her resurrected husband and daughter. She declined the invitation to also stay at Bridges' house, saying that she was used to being on her own and needed to be quiet.

Livvy and Bridges were awake for hours, wondering about the people whose lives had been destroyed or damaged by Artie Smale, alias Ron Smart, and the way that he had tried to make very belated compensation by doling out large helpings of money. They were concerned for Helen's precarious state of mind, now that Livvy had arranged that, first thing in the morning, she would be present to help to smooth the way for the meeting between Lagi Lagiaga and his long lost love, Helen's mother, Lura, and then to stand by as they met their daughter. What an emotional upheaval all three of them were in for. What had Lura said? 'What's the good of money if you haven't got the people you love?'

Now there was a new chance to have each other, but could they be expected to manage recovery of such long term heart breaks? Could they hope to restore the bonds that were broken so long ago? They were not the same people any more? What if they did renew bonds, would they decide to take the money that Artie Smale had left to them? And how would it all affect Helen? Eventually, when Livvy said that they must get to sleep, Bridges still felt the need to say something about his work colleague, Andrew Brown. His apparently successful adjustment as the assimilated Aboriginal, for something like forty years, had worked for him until he heard a story applied to him that made him look at his treachery to his people and to his own Aboriginal identity.

'But why did he need to kill Ron Smart?' Livvy said sadly. 'It was all so long ago, and the old villain had become a gentle godly person trying to do all the right things.'

Bridges tried to frame a reply, but sleep-deprivation was beginning, at last to outweigh the adrenalin effects of an eventful couple of days. Questions still drifted up, but trying to answer them reasonably was another thing, perhaps better left until morning.

'I believe that it wasn't long ago at all, for Andrew. It was all still happening, there and then. He was, up until then, following, still following Artie Smale, and dis…. hon….shaming his people, so he had to…was trying to…wash the stains…Wash his hands…'

Chapter 28
Tears of joy

In the morning Bridges rang the hospital and learnt that Mani and Blyth would probably not be discharged for a day or two, then decided to be the one to break the news to Lagi Lagiaga about his brother and his long lost love.

When the old man came on the phone, he spoke in a spirited way, and Bridges wondered what had happened for him. To his surprise, Lagi Lagiaga already knew about the things that had happened on Gudjigari Rock yesterday. Bridges supposed that Brown, from prison, or on his way there, had been able to pass a message along the local indigenous grapevine.

Lagiaga's voice seemed livelier and yet more broken than it had been during Bridges' recent visit to his bed-side.

'I reckon this mus' be another dream I'm 'avin, eh?' he told Bridges but gladly accepted the offer of transport. Bridges explained that he himself was committed to taking Mani's grandfather, Jambagirrila, for two visits...one to Andrew Brown at Berrimah Gaol, and one to his grandson, Mani, in the hospital.

When Livvy arrived at Nomad Hostel with her passenger, Lagi Lagiaga, at her suggestion, he waited in the lounge, while she went to Lura's room. It was a quiet meeting. Lagiaga, clean-shaven, in a laundered white shirt and black trousers, with his damp white hair combed down, sat on the edge of a lounge chair and waited while Livvy went to fetch Lura.

He glanced up briefly at the white-haired old woman in a blue dress who entered ahead of Livvy, then down at the floor before she, in turn, looked at him and then away. She sat in a chair about four metres from him, to his right; and Livvy sat beside her on her right, without speaking. After a long silence while their mutual nervousness passed, the two old people looked towards each other and their eyes met. A faint chuckle escaped Lura's lips.

Lagi, who had been holding his breath to stifle a sob, coughed to clear his throat, and said lightly, 'ullo, old woman.'

'Ullo, old man.'

They smiled, and she added, 'or should I say, good mornen docta.'

He smiled and nodded as he replied 'good mornin', to yah, too, Nurse. Yah all right?'

'Ee-ee,' she assured him. 'Buruli. You?'
'Ee-ee,' he grinned. 'This time, today, I'm very well, nurse.'

The silence that followed was theirs now, and Livvy edged forward to make her departure. 'I might go now,' she told them, and, as they listened, she spoke of the possibility of them both visiting their daughter with her this afternoon, if they wanted to do that. Father Sheehan had agreed to pave the way with the Sisters for her to bring them to visit Helen.

They had no hesitation in letting her know that they wanted to make the visit, but both were clearly daunted by the prospect of being together with their unknown daughter.

* * *

Bridges, Jambagirrila and Jack Foster drove to the gaol, but only the Arardbi elder was permitted to visit, and that only after Bridges had put the case for making an exception to the regulations for Brown's "relation from out of town". The two Balandas took the chance while they waited for Jambagirrila's return, to review the events of the few days since they had helped to fell a tree on Goose Island. That reminded Foster that he had decided to do some of the shaping of Mani's canoe, but only if they got a new adze. Today he would see if he could get one in town.

When Jambagirrila returned they drove back to the house to pick up Livvy and deliver her to the Catholic Mission Office. When Bridges dropped her at the entrance, the Mission property felt more familiar than it had the first time that she had come there looking for Helen Cross. As Bridges turned around for the run to the shops, Dick Sheehan came out to meet Livvy. He waved a response in reply to Bridges's hand signal.

'Well, look who it is!' he exclaimed to his visitor. 'What an amazing piece of work. You two are really unstoppable. Finding Lucy Charlton and clearing up the mystery of old Ron's murder…all in one day.'
'Save your praise for Gray, Father,' she advised, 'I didn't know what was going on.'
'All the same,' he said as they belted up. 'Well done to both of you.'
'You're the one who deserves the thanks for putting us on the trail of Lura!' she insisted

'Whatever,' he said absently as he scanned the road and headed out towards the northern suburbs. 'The Sister's expecting us, and is confident that Helen will be ready to talk and listen. How are you feeling about telling her the news?' His uncertain tone invited Livvy to reassure him that this was the right way to proceed.

'Good…yes,' she said. 'It feels right to me. Helen has the right to know A.S.A.P. that she has parents.' As they moved into top gear on Stuart Highway, he thanked her for agreeing to travel to the hostel with him and to discuss along the way how they might prepare Helen for the meeting.

Each assured the other that even though it would be a shock for her, it was the sort of positive surprise that could be expected to counter the shock of horror from the brutal murder of the man who had wanted to give her a fortune. It had to be a good thing to know that she had a family.

Father Sheehan went on to convey to Livvy his second reason for wanting to talk to her at this time. It concerned the man he still called Ron Smart, and a proposal arising from his will, relating to Soft Aid, the Simpson brothers' supportive style of working with indigenous people.

Of a large sum that Ron had left for disposal by the Catholic Church, five hundred thousand dollars had been designated as a scholarship and research fund for a suitably qualified person or persons selected by the priest, to do research and compare current practice with George and Harry Simpson's concept of Soft Aid for Aboriginal community development.

One fact that had stuck in Ron's mind was that George Simpson, whom he had actually met when they both worked as stockmen and hunters for Charlton's, had gone to help his brother, and an Aboriginal clan to build an airstrip on remote clan land in the bush.

Ron Smart had marvelled that the two brothers cared so much for the people of the land and their way of life that they would labour like that for them. They had seen so clearly, while he, in his years in the north, had been mentally blind, and it seemed to be a source of great significance and sorrow to him that it was when George was preparing to return to Charltons and the cattle work, after working on the airstrip, that he had been speared to death by a pay-back party of that region. He had been executed for something a violent Balanda had done back in the cattle country. Livvy felt sure that Dick Sheehan knew that the "violent Balanda" was none other than Ron Smart himself; but neither of them cared to speak of this awful truth just now.

Old Ron had become obsessed with the Simpsons and their dream of better ways to serve the indigenous people. It was after reading their papers that he had decided that the Simpson brothers had been the sort of men that he wished he had been. After talks with his priest, he had decided that the research grant was the next best thing. He wanted someone with the required skill and interest to take up the brothers' ideas and help to get them accepted as the ways things should be done. All to be done and dedicated to "the memory of Harry and George Simpson, true friends of the people of Arnhem Land."

Father Sheehan believed that he knew two people who were highly suitable to receive the research grant if they were prepared to give two or three years to field research as well as critically examining and expanding what the Simpsons had envisaged in their writings. They were Olivia and Gray Bridges.

Livvy was embarrassed, although not completely surprised that this announcement was the end point of the priest's report. All that she could say was,

'Oh, really? Do you really think so? That's very kind of you. But we just work in our own narrow areas of expertise.'

'Nonsense,' Sheehan retorted. I'm not being kind. I'm in no position to be kind. I have a sacred trust to be responsible for the last will of a desperate old man. And, tell me, who isn't limited in looking at a subject like this. At least you know how to listen to people respectfully, and gather their wisdom. Will you share what I've said with Gray? And we'll fix a time to sit down and go into it seriously?'

'Oh, what can I say?' She showed her excitement at the prospects that were already occurring to her. 'I certainly will. What a wonderful chance that would be to do something worthwhile. But we'd want to run it by some of our friends. It might be offensive to them if we accepted the grant money from old Ron, the Hunter. We'd need to talk it over.'

'Of course…I understand. That had occurred to me, too. But, anyway, talk it over with Gray, today if possible, and I will too. I'm anxious to know what you both think of this marvellous opportunity.' It had been a useful conversation, but now they had run out of talking time.

* * *

At the Convent, Sister Bernadette was waiting for them, and left Livvy in a small sitting room scribbling notes about a new insight that had just presented itself to her. It was about the importance of culture-honouring initiatives in education. Yes, yes! She wrote. Soft Aid! Including indigenous cultural realities and living language. It would be exciting to at least read the ideas that had been penned by the Simpson brothers.

Meanwhile, Father Sheehan spent time with Helen Cross. When Sister Bernadette returned she assured Livvy that Helen was in a good frame of mind, having recovered well from the shock that had left her so devastated.

'The good Father is such a comfort,' said the Sister. 'He spoke so nicely with her, and then had a prayer for the Lord's blessing. He asked me to tell her about her coming to the children's settlement when she was a toddler. She didn't remember anything about those early days. She was only a little tot, then. But she remembers the years that followed at the settlement out on the island, until she came back into Darwin. Such a bright girl, she is, too, the poor dear. Will you come and see her now, Missus Bridges? I believe you want to tell her about her relatives. Father seems to think it's the right thing to do, but I don't know, I must say. He has put certain things to her very positively, and I was delighted to hear her say that she would like to travel and learn music and singing so that she could be a music teacher.'

Livvy showed that she was suitably impressed with this news, then joined Helen and the priest, sitting outside in the back garden shade with a breeze. Helen looked well, and as she answered Livvy's 'hi', with a bright 'ullo', it was clear that she was feeling well again.

'Dear Helen, 'she thought,' no wonder her heart goes up and down so easily: she learnt her first life responses through some very serious ups and downs.'

'Father reckons you've met my mother,' Helen sounded excited, but still doubting. She frowned as she glanced at the priest to check his reaction.

'She's a lovely person,' Livvy assured her. 'I did, I met her, and I like her very much. She's surprised to learn that she still has a daughter. She thought you were taken down south and died when you were a baby.'

'Really? You mean it?... I can't believe it's true,' said Helen.

'Have you told Helen what we've learnt about how she came to be sent to the children's homes, Father?' asked Livvy.

'Not about the family connections,' said Sheehan. Turning to Helen he asked,

'Do you want to hear what happened to your mother and your father? Are you ready to hear that sort of thing?'

'Of course I am,' she replied impulsively. 'Everythink!'

For the next few minutes Sheehan sat back and let Livvy tell her young colleague what Bridges had been able to put together of the story of her family, from Lagi's early days in Gujigari country and Lura's on Charlton's Cattle Station, through the coming of Artie Smale and his deliberate prevention of Lura's return to Lagi after the baby was born – and the lies he told about the father dying and the child being sent south for good, and probably dead; then about the same Artie Smale becoming someone else and leaving hundreds of thousands of dollars, from his successful mining enterprises, to Lura and also to her daughter, Helen.

'Him?' Helen was alarmed again at the thought of the murdered man. 'I thought his name was Smart!'

As simply as she could, Livvy explained about him taking a new name after being stricken by leprosy, and his conversion to faith in his old age, and the decision to try to do something creative and worthwhile before he died. To Helen it all sounded unreal, but she wanted to hear more, needing answers to many questions.

She was still too horrified to speak directly about the murder, but had to know who had killed this wicked step-father who had rejected her as a baby and now had given her a fortune. Livvy explained who Andrew Brown was; her uncle, her natural father's brother, who had gone along with the racist crimes of Artie Smale and finally committed murder to try to get rid of his shame, and who was now in Berrimah Gaol, awaiting trial. She told Helen about Brown going to Lionel and Annette Gellies' place looking for his brother, Bilago, probably the man who fell down the steps, when Helen ran out of the house.

'Oh, that disgusting old no-oper.' Helen recalled. 'He didn't fall. I pushed 'im. I had seen that other 'orrible old man and I just took off. I didn't mean to hurt the poor ol' bugger, though…Is 'e all right? 'es not dead too, is 'e?'

Eventually they had come to what Livvy found was the most difficult part of the story to reveal to Helen. Time was running out. Helen's parents' taxi would not be far away now. She had mentioned Bilago, but it obviously had not occurred to Helen that he might be her father.

'Helen,' she said tenderly. 'You deserve the chance to make a happy life on your own…or with your parents…'
'Parents?' Helen had picked up the lead. 'You mean my mother.'
'I mean your parents, love, I've also met your daddy.'
'He's alive?' Helen asked, looking to the priest for verification. He simply nodded in a natural and relaxed way, and left it to Livvy to make the revelations. Rather than answer directly, Livvy opted for the indirect approach.
'Tell me, Helen,' she said. 'A man's loved ones are taken away from him, his father and mother, and his family country were all gone, his first wife and his second wife, too. You know what the man did?'

'Went and found them?' she suggested.

'Ah, but it was a few years ago, when he would have had no money, no wages, no boat, no plane fares. And if he was told that they were dead anyway, what would he do?'

'He'd probly cry, and, I dunno, go out and get drunk,' she said it boldly, but with an uncertain shrug.

'And then?' Livvy persisted.

'I dunno.' Helen was getting impatient. 'What are you askin' me all this for? If 'es like a lot of other people, then, well, maybe he'd keep on gettin drunk.

'Well, my dear,' Livvy told her. 'You should be able to understand how Doctor Lagi gave up trying to live his life of service to sick people and became a town drunk in Darwin.'

The two women stared at each other in silence, until awareness dawned and flooded Helen with horror. Her face distorted in revulsion.

'Not that disgusting ol' lay-about who's been 'angin around me?'

'Old Bilago is Lagi Lagiaga, Darling',' Livvy told her gently. 'Your daddy.'

After a wide-mouthed breathless moment, Helen's face crumpled and she began to sob uncontrollably in Livvy's arms.

Sister Bernadette reappeared, alarmed at Helen's upset state, to give Livvy the news that Mister Bridges' car had arrived, and that he and his passenger, the Goose Island elder, had decided to wait in the garden to talk with her. Livvy had no more time to be subtle. Dick Sheehan nodded, and she continued. She had to find out, now, how Helen felt about matters as they were, by asking her plainly.

'Helen, do you feel up to meeting a couple more visitors?'

'Who?' she asked. 'Your husband and that old man?' Livvy shook her head and waited. Helen clamped her hands over her mouth, and gaped wide-eyed at her informant. 'Not them? Not those two you told me are my…my…'

There was no need to finish the question, and Livvy nodded.

'Yes, darling,' she told her. 'Your mum and dad are on their way here to see you, if you're willing to meet them.'

'We could suggest that they come back tomorrow,' suggested Livvy.

'Uh.. no, no,' Helen was breathless with apprehension. 'Just let me get ready.' She said huskily. 'If they come before I'm back, just ask them to wait a little while. I want to…go and…comb my hair.'

Before she could leave the room, Livvy took her in her arms again. Helen was trembling violently, her wide eyes and tense face fearful, and Livvy firmly held her for a moment. 'Your hair is beautiful and I'm sure you'll do just fine'.

Helen gasped. 'Thanks!' but still went to her room.

'Do you think she's all right?' Livvy asked the Sister, who had reappeared, and priest.

Father Sheehan simply nodded, and Sister Bernadette said, 'I must say, she seems to be taking it all very well, in spite of the tears.'

Livvy went to meet Bridges and Jambagirrila, and walked with them over the drive to the shady front lawn. Sister Bernadette had said that she would keep watch and fetch Helen when her folks arrived. Meanwhile, Sheehan decided that his presence during the reunion would serve no good purpose, and went away to fulfil other pastoral duties in the hostel. Livvy joined Bridges and Jambagirrila in sitting on the grass in the deep shade of a huge mango tree and explained to them that Helen was getting ready to meet her parents.

As Jambagirrila was eager to hear what was to happen and told them, 'me too. I want to come 'ere to meet that father. We was boys learnin to 'unt together, an' we went through man-make cheremony…Other sing-song an' proper cheremony. Everything us young blokes, together. Other time 'e bin 'elp me with that runnin' stomach epidemic, all over Goose Island, long time before. Ah, too bad 'e bin loss is missus an' 'is kid.' He grinned. 'Should be 'es appy bloke now they find together, eh?'

They all agreed that it was a good thing that the family was being reunited after so long, and also that it was not going to be an easy time for them. From his shaded observation point on the lawn, the old Wainanda man turned to studying the tree and the sky, the grass, the garden beds, the shrubs and the behaviour of several passing birds.

The old man produced a folded sheet or two of writing paper, and told them matter-of-factly, 'my countryman give me jura paper in the lock-up. You can copy it for me, then we gonna give it to Lagi Lagiaga, might be nother day. Tomorra. This for 'im. From 'im, Andrew Brown. It's a sorry paper, for 'im…an' for all our own people. He say make copy, an' show our people. 'ere you, and Balandas, too, 'e say, you too, got to look at dis one, too.'

'What's in the note?' Livvy asked, and Jambagirrila handed it to Bridges. 'Let's see,' said Bridges, running his eyes over it. 'Old Andrew wants us all to read it. I think it's a way to let everyone see how he feels now. It's addressed to his brother Lagi Lagiaga, but, according to what he said to you, old man, it's intended for everyone else as well.' He held the paper before Livvy and they both began to read it. It was written in Andrew's cramped but neat style.

Bridges smiled. 'I bet the gaol staff didn't see their prisoner pass a note to a visitor. It's a real no-no because of the security risk.'

'Ah, well,' Livvy grinned. 'It's too late now. But it's a very personal letter isn't it? Are you sure we should be reading it.'

'That's what he told Jambagirrila. Make copies, show the Balanda and all, as well as his brother.' Bridges went over and returned the note to Jambagirrila, so that he might show it to Mani when they reached the hospital, expressing his appreciation of the message, and promising to make copies and let plenty of people see it.

A taxi slowed in the driveway. It pulled in near the hostel's front door, and the old couple who emerged from it seemed to be still feeling quite shy of each other, but glad to be together again after a virtual life-time of separation. Livvy went forward to meet them at the taxi and brought them across to the shade of the mango tree, where Jambagirrila had risen and was approaching Lura. Bridges stood back in the shade and watched, as Jambagirrila approached the old arrivals.

'Ah, you still 'ere, ol' time Goose Ilan' Nurse, eh?' Jambagirrila gave Lura a smile, and nodded once. 'You done good job. Makin' us people better....'

'You awright?' she asked.

'Ee-ee, I'm awright. Little bit tired old man. I'm awright. You look after everyone good way. Buruli. That's good,' Jambagirrila spoke quietly, keeping his eyes on Lura. Then, deliberately, he turned to Lagi Lagiaga, companion of his youth, tireless health worker, who had danced and sung alongside him in ceremonies and celebrations, and also had attended him during a life threatening epidemic on the island. In appearance here now a broken, run-down remnant of the person he had been. 'You awright, Short Man?' he greeted him carefully.

'Ay!' With a shock, Lagi Lagiaga recognised a friend from the past. 'You 'ere, ol' man. Ho, what about you dance...now?' He weakly feinted a set of dance steps and flung his arms upwards. 'Can you go up an' legs over now?'

'No more turn over. Too old...dis bloke now,' Jambagirrila reached out his arms and enfolded Lagi, who responded with a similar body hug. They patted and stroked each other's backs, looked into each other's eyes, then each buried his face on the other's shoulder and began to weep loudly with floods of tears and body shuddering sobs. This passionate outpouring seemed as if it might continue for some time and

Lura and the Bridges slowly retreated to the far side of the tree shade, and turned away. They all looked at each other with a relaxed smile. This was a time to just wait, for the abatement of the old men's sorrow for the loss of so much and the coming back of so much, especially for a found daughter and a restored family.

Livvy explained to Lura that Helen was nervous and getting herself ready for their meeting. Sister Bernadette would be with her now, and she might appear at any moment. 'She's not the only one who's nervous,' Lura confided. 'I might just go for a little walk myself.'

She set off slowly across the lawn to stroll around a circular bed of brightly red and green croton shrubs. Left alone, the Bridgeses turned to their own agenda.

'What did Father Dick want to talk over with you?' Bridges asked.

'Aha!' she said it with the air of an authority on mysterious matters. 'How would you like to be given a special assignment to go and talk with Aboriginal communities and look into the ideas and best practices available, and write a book that guides the giving of supports for indigenous people?'

'Sounds all right to me,' he said, without enthusiasm. 'But I'm not thinking about any other projects until we've done what we can to help Andrew through his trial, and until we bring off a real set of consultations between the government and the people.'

'Fair enough,' she concurred. 'If it all goes the way you hope, it could be a good new beginning. But what will be necessary, I wonder, to move on from there in a positive way. You don't want to have a brilliant flash in the pan consultation series and then everyone going back to the old depressing frustrations, do you?'

He shook his head. 'I can't think about this now, Liv. Step by step, side by side and softly, softly'll be the way to go, I reckon.'

'Ah,' she said. 'That sounds like Soft Aid, to me.'

'Oh,' he saw the drift of her thinking. 'Soft Aid? Sure, of course I'm interested, honey. But another time, okay?'

He nodded towards the hostel door. Livvy saw Sister Bernadette holding the screen door open for Helen. Turning, Livvy moved towards Lura, calling loudly enough for the old men to hear, 'Lura…Helen's here!' Helen was frowning nervously as Livvy joined her.

Jambagirrila, aware that it was time for Lagi Lagiaga to meet his daughter, stood back, patted his reclaimed friend's shoulders and told him, 'Now we can visit and talk more. You should come back on the island. We all member you dere. We don't forget you 'elped us like a doctor.' Lagi nodded. They wiped away their tears, and Jambagirrila moved towards Bridges, while his old friend, Lagi, turned to see the beautiful young woman walking slowly towards her long lost mother.

Lagi seemed powerless to move towards Helen, who was now, after such a long time, truly his daughter. He simply watched as Lura went by him to meet the full-grown woman who was once her baby. Helen averted her eyes from side to side, stealing glances at the advancing woman and the waiting old man.

Could he really be the same old down-and-out nuisance who had been pestering her? Who had told her that she was 'shamin' 'er mother'. This one looked altogether different. As she stopped before the little old lady, her pounding heart restricted her voice and the words that her mind had been practicing.

'Ullo, Mother!'

Chapter 29
Chaos in the hospital

After a short drive from the Catholic Hostel to the Darwin Hospital, Bridges pointed Jambagirrila towards Mani's four-bed ward, with the promise that he would join him there soon, then found his own way upstairs to Blyth's private ward. The door was standing ajar and he peeped in to see the Chief apparently asleep on raised pillows. Both of his arms were bandaged where he had suffered abrasions during efforts to free himself on Gujigari Rock. His face still showed signs of severe sunburn and white powdered patches of broken skin. Bridges watched for a moment and was considering whether or not to leave, when the patient opened his eyes and spoke.

'Oh, Gray!.. Thanks for coming…I'm glad you're here. You and I need to do some talking. Come in, come in.'

Bridges aproached the foot of the bed, 'how are you now, Chief?'

'I've been better…But let me tell you, I'm not, I, it…it's...this is….'

He paused, took a deep breath and began again. 'Sorry, I'm a bit groggy still. I've been to the edge and, and looked over'.

'I had it all worked out, you know. I mean, I've always been so sure of everything… You know? No doubts…everything under control. Know what I mean? Then I stepped outside our little square, out there, and... kerwhump! Nothing's the same out there. It's all relative, Gray.

'We're all relative, how we see things…relative to our own little cultural square. We're in a cultural square, of our own, just like everyone else. I never saw it. But there's more to it, Gray…There's more to it, isn't there?'

'You've had a shock.' Bridges reflected back on what he could understand from Ned's disjointed account of what was on his mind.

'You can say that again, and it's goin' to take some thinking about, I can tell you. I went from being the one in control to a helpless victim of... of something else. Something I didn't see coming, never knew existed, something different. But it was real. Suddenly it was very real to me, Gray. I ran into it. That was it! End of the road. And they had a right.

'That's what gets me. That's the killer! By all I believe and understand about law, Gray. They had a right to do what they did. For them it was loreful. They were justified. They were, and, and I wasn't…Up there, I was the criminal… I've got no come-back to their way of seeing things, or how they treated me. I can see it myself. They had a right. They were right, Gray. Their case against me was strange, outside my understanding…but there was another case, against me. I saw it, if they didn't. I was wrong, Gray…Doing wrong. It, isn't…it isn't easy to say anything clear about it. Have you seen Mani Manggululu?'

Bridges shook his head. It was obvious that Ned was going to keep talking.

'He's down on the next floor. I asked if he could be wheeled in up here, and the staff agreed, but guess what? He refused to be moved. Said he's in a good place, and that I'm welcome to come there if I would like to. Gray, that boy saved my life.'

'I'm not surprised,' Bridges replied. 'Mine, too. He seems to make a habit of it. Just the Aboriginal thing to do, he reckons, helping each other to survive.'

'Whatever it is, he and I have a lot of unfinished business. Fred Archer has been in and I sent him down to arrange for my bed to be shifted into Mani's ward. If the mountain won't come to Mohammed, then he must go…' He closed his eyes and lay back on the pillow.

'You take it easy, Chief.' Bridges cautioned.

'I'm okay,' he nodded without opening his eyes. 'I should be back at work tomorrow, maybe.'

'Perhaps you and Mani are goin' to start the consultation while you're still in here,' Bridges joked encouragingly.

'That's what I want to talk to you about,' he looked at Bridges. 'But I want to talk with Mani first. Meantime, think about this, Gray. Cabinet and permanent secretaries having training sessions with you and Mani, not so that we can con the Aboriginal people, but to follow their traditional protocols, and really hear one another. Get ready to go to places where the people are…where they still keep their own Lore. Staying long enough to really listen and hear. Getting the local people's priorities for their own re-structuring and development, in their own cultural square, where they live. Do you see what I mean?…What do you say?'

Bridges smiled. 'Chief, with respect, I'd say that that's the most sensible thing I've ever heard you say about consulting with the First Nations people.'

'Yes, well,' Blyth seemed suddenly tired. 'We'll talk about some way to do it, a bit later on. All right?'

Fred Archer appeared in the doorway. 'I'm sorry it's taken me so long, sir.' He looked at Blyth, ignoring Bridges. 'I have the young Goose Islander making his way down the passage. There was a rumpus downstairs. The old witch-doctor fella from Dik Dik, who assaulted you and threatened your life, came barging in. He shouldn't be on the loose...the man's a menace!'

'It's Mani's grandfather, Jambagirrila. He regrets hurting you and Mani,' Bridges explained. 'And he's grateful to you, Chief, for persuading the police to let him remain free pending the investigation into what happened on the rock. He's come in with me to visit his grandson, that's all.'

Without looking at Bridges, Archer went on addressing the Chief Minister. 'That's not all, sir.' he declared. 'The old fella's been terrorising the doctors. Abusing them in lingo for the way they are caring for the young fella. I'd like your permission to call in the police. If I don't the staff probably will if he keeps it up. He should be restrained…in any case, after his assault on you. He's gotta be stopped.'

Blyth hoisted himself up to a full sitting position. 'Oh, give me a break Fred…I don't need all this right now…I've got a lousy head-ache. So put a sock in it and get lost.'

'But this old fella's dangerous and still on the loose, and arguing with the doctors. I told his grandson that I had made the arrangements with your doctor for you to visit him down in his ward. Then he had the cheek to say that he'd changed his mind, and because you were prepared to come to his ward, he was now prepared to come up here. So he's here now. If you ask me, he doesn't know his own mind.'

'Fred,' the Chief Minister was out of patience. He pointed to the door. 'I can handle it from here.'

'Yes, sir,' Archer was agitated by the arrival of the wheelchair. 'I just wanted to let you know and check if it was still acceptable to you to have this unstable person coming into your ward with the old witch-doctor hovering around him.' He put a hand in front of Mani Manggululu to stop his progress in the chair with a Sister providing the motive power. Bridges crossed to meet Mani who seemed close to exhaustion. White chest bandaging showed under the flimsy white dressing gown he wore.

At the sight of Bridges he managed a grin.

'Ow yah goin' mate? Good?'

'Yeah, I'm awright!' the young patient cracked hardy. 'Plenty o' good tucker, and nice nurses.' he smiled up in the direction of the Sister, but she was pre-occupied with people loudly approaching along the corridor.

'What now?' Blyth gasped.

'I'll put a stop to it, sir,' Archer went into the corridor to meet two people striding towards the ward, loudly haranguing each other in a running argument. Mani turned the wheels of his chair and the sister pushed him to the bedside.

Blyth looked at him seriously and told him, 'I would have come down to where you were, Mani.'

'Yeah, I was pleased to hear that, Mister Blyth. But you're not well, and you're our number one Northern Territory man, so I should come to you. I brought something that my grandfather gave me. It's from Andrew Brown. I think you might be interested to read it.'

Blyth looked at Mani for a long moment, then said softly, 'Mani, thanks. Thanks for everything. For coming up the mountain and putting your own life on the line, and... et me finish...and for giving me a new chance at life without the old master-race blind-fold.'

Mani stared at him with blank scepticism. 'Read this note from the other ol' elder in the gaol,' Mani urged him. 'E really wants to say something to everybody, 'e wrote it for is old brother, but 'e told my grandfather that he wants to say the same thing to everyone. 'E said show it to us and give copies to the Balanda chiefs or anyone else.'

After quickly reading Andrew Brown's note, the Chief Minister asked with genuine concern, 'how is Andrew? Who else has seen him?'

'Gray went with my grandfather to see him in the gaol.' Bridges nodded as Mani continued, 'But only my grandfather saw him. That's when the old man gave my grandfather that note. He wants to tell everyone what happened. I don't think 'e ever wanted to hurt anyone in is 'ole life. Do you think 'es goin to get charged with murder?'

'Yes, I think so,' the Chief Minister said. 'There'll have to be a trial. I can't interfere with that process. But I'll do what I can to make sure Andrew has adequate defence...'

Blyth heard loud voices and saw the Sister exit towards the commotion. He added quickly, 'Mani, someone should let your grandfather know that he broke the Law by bringing a prisoner's written message out of the gaol?'

'Did 'e?' Mani looked at the Balanda blankly. 'Which Law?'

Blyth failed to raise a smile, but nodded, 'Touché!' he whispered as the Sister reappeared with a couple of noisy quarrellers, Jambagirrila and an agitated doctor in whites. The elder hurried to the side of his grandon.

'See here this,' he said irritably, looking at the irate doctor. He pointed to Mani's chest where the bulky bandaging showed within the neck line area of the dressing gown. The Duty Sister caught a stern look from the doctor and tried to bring an appropriate sense of order and calm to her patient's private ward.

'All right everybody!' she said bravely. 'Outside please. Let's remember that Mister Blyth is very unwell and needing quiet rest.'

Apart from a little shuffling backwards, her order had no effect. Jambagirrila was primarily concerned with the other patient, his grandson. 'An' this young fella, too… 'e gotta get look after him!'

He turned to Blyth for the first time since entering the ward. 'Sorry Mister Ply. You getting better now from all that lore business? I 'afta tell these stupid people they can't kill the big man person.'

The doctor strode forward to explain something to the head of government. 'I'm terribly sorry. You'll have to excuse us, Mister Blyth. I'll clear this ward. This is what we have to put up with on a fairly regular basis from some of these people. Unfortunately they have neither the language nor the intelligence to grasp what's happening here, and there's nothing we can do about it.' He turned to the irate elder saying, 'come on old man. You fella make 'im big trouble. More better you keep quiet now. These fellas too sick. No more talk-talk. You go quick fella now.'

'Mani,' the Chief Minister requested. 'Do you know what your grandfather's worried about?'

'Sure,' Mani said as he turned to the doctor. 'Doctor, you fella savvee English?' he asked sarcastically, but did not wait for an answer. 'No? Oh, well, don't worry. I'll keep it as simple as I can. You see, I got the wounds across my chest as ceremonial cuts. They're real flesh cuts, but not bone deep. They were treated with wood ash to stop the bleeding, keep them open and clean, and to start up a way for thick scars to grow here for a few weeks. It's a very ancient treatment. Your staff here are saying they'll clear out all the ashes and germs and trim up all the rough edges of the cut. They'll stitch up the wounds and try to heal them without any scars. An' my grandfather's saying they're trying to take away my senior man status and the Lore of our land.'

The doctor half folded his arms and stuck two fingers in his cheek while everyone waited.

'Doctor,' Blyth spoke. 'Doctor, isn't there a way that the hospital staff can co-operate with the patient and the elders on this matter? I take it that the scarring is important to the senior status conferred on the patient in the recent Big Man ceremony. Is that so, Mani?'

'Ee -ee, yes! That's right. It's a great importance to me for the rest of my life, and my relationships with all my people. It's like a doctor's degree or a lawyer's, or an ordination of a Minister, but it's not just a paper certificate that you're spoiling, if you stop the scars, it's the real person.'

'Well,' the doctor addressed the Chief Minister carefully. 'If I had only known about this earlier, then perhaps we could have saved all the fuss and bother.' Mani looked at Bridges and rolled his eyes upwards. Bridges nodded. The doctor continued. 'It's possible that we could devise a medically sound way of dressing the wound while allowing for the traditional process of intentional scarring to continue...'

'Wonderful,' Blyth sounded tired. 'I really would like to be quiet now, if you all wouldn't mind going. But I just need to talk with Fred and Gray and Mani before you go. I'm sorry. Then I must sleep, or I'll be in trouble…won't I Sister?'

Without smiling, the Sister nodded; and the doctor, rather than simply accepting the Chief Minister's dismissal, took his pulse and asked about level of pain, while the Sister adjusted the pillows and took away the near empty water-jug, with a promise to return it refilled. Before leaving she appealed to them all, 'Now, I want you gentlemen out of here in five minutes.'

Mani spoke quietly to his grandfather, who seemed relieved at what he heard and followed the doctor into the corridor to speak for a few moments and shake hands. After the doctor left, the old man moved back past the three who were waiting to hear what the Chief Minister had to say to them, to the bed-side where he could speak to the patient.

'You awright now, Minister Chief? We couldn't 'elp it to punish you in that Lore? You know that?'

Blyth nodded, 'I know.' he said simply. 'Don't worry any more about it.'

'I don't worry,' Jambagirrila spoke confidently. 'Tell me something, you can 'elp me now? If you can? Old man Andrew Brown in gaol now, locked up. But I need to see 'im, visit at that place every day. Can't come every day they reckon, one gaol bloke. Now I haf'to go there and bring Andrew Brown's brother. They 'ave talk and see each other, too. They the important one for each one, you know? You can 'elp me? I'll tell them gaol blokes you can tell them that. That'll be all right?'

'Jambagirrila,' the distressed patient stared at the old man who looked and sounded nothing like the tribal ceremonial chief who had threatened him on

Gudjigari Rock, and replied. 'If you have any trouble with them tell them to phone me here. I'll talk to them for you, to let you take in Andrew's brother, all right?'

'That's good,' the old Wainanda was grateful. 'Now you get well. 'N'other day, if you wanna climb my rock place, you can ask me, and I can take you up there right way, awright.' They nodded at each other. 'But don't go up dere your own self, see?' he cautioned. 'Only you can come dere with me, when you ask me right way. You hear me?'

'I give you my word, old man,' Blyth held the old man's gaze. 'You can trust me now. I'll ask for your permission.'

'Ee-ee, that's the right way now. True way…that's good! You get strong now.' The elder turned away, stopping by Mani's chair long enough to say that he would wait in the corridor; then he took up position in the doorway, watching and waiting while the Chief Minister consulted his three advisers, Fred Archer, Gray Bridges and Mani Manggululu.

The Chief beckoned for Archer to stand back and Bridges to wheel Mani closer and step away. Heavy-eyed, with the raking voice of near exhaustion, he bent nearer, looked into Mani's face and spoke in a whisper. 'I think they were going to kill me."

'Yes,' Mani whispered in reply. 'They were.'

'They were really going to kill me?"

'It was the Lore,' Mani explained. 'The old Lore has never died, and they were back home in their own land and in their own Lore.'

'Mani, I saw what they did to you.'

'That was the Lore, too.'

'You gave me back my life. I…I… thought my life was just beginning, and then, it was ending; and… and…I realise now… that I've always been …too busy to get serious….about really living my life.'

Mani waited in silence without turning away. They held each other's gaze, and Blyth struggled to expel the single word, 'thanks!'

Mani dropped his gaze and shook his head, but Blyth was not finished. 'Thank you, Mani, for what you did for me, and… and for giving me another chance… to get it right…my life. I'll always be in your debt. Please believe me. I won't forget what I owe to you.'

He lay back on the pillow and rested for a moment, eyes closed, before turning towards the other two men. They came near as Mani wheeled back to make room and whinced from the painful effects of the effort.

'Listen to me,' the Chief Minister addressed his staffers. 'I want the Liaison Unit to ...uh, prepare a letter to all Aboriginal communities... and homeland centres.... about gatherings with government leaders...in every region of the Territory. In their own homelands, if possible. You hear me? Work out ...uh, suggestions for places, and times. Listen to our Aboriginal Liaison Officers and to Mani, and his people, while you do this. See that they tell you how to... to prepare to have local consultations, about the...er, mind of the people. For new policy making, and for ways to serve... their real neads and aspirations. No more bastardisation...uh...'

He faultered.

'We've got to be more civilised and...u...find ways to be...uh...together and respect, trust each other...er...take the pressure off people...' His voice faded, but he tried to hoist himself on one elbow to complete his directive. 'And begin the circular letters, with my own...personal apology...to them all. These are the sort of words I want all the people to hear.

He read from the note in his hand. 'In my life, I having enjoyed the...good things... that were taken away from you. I have always looked down on you, and I have been one of the people always ready to... give you blame and...advice, about what to do, and...handouts, but I never excepted anything...from you. I never waited to hear you, or listened to you...with respect. For all this I'm now really sorry. Forgive me. All that is finished now. Please give me another chance, to be your respectful friend, as well is your brother...er...no... Just put there, as your.... Chief Minister.

'Ee-ee,' Mani affirmed. 'Chief Minister for all the Territorians, eh?'
'I hope so, Mani.' Blyth said. 'Come back when you're feeling up to it, please, Mani. I really want to get to know you better, and to see what you think about so many things...Okay?'

Mani nodded his agreement, took the note and passed it to Bridges, as Blyth continued. 'And Fred and Gray, we must listen to Mani's people and see what we can....come up with for on-location consultations, okay?'

He winced as if in pain. 'I think I have to go to sleep. I'll see you all later. You'd better go now.' Bridges and Archer reluctantly accepted that they had been dismissed, and withdrew without a word. Mani lingered long enough to bring a clenched fist up to his bandaged chest in signal to his watching fellow patient. Blyth nodded in acknowledgement of the message. 'Be strong.'

As the Chief Minister's Cross-Cultural Communication Consultant and the Director of the Aboriginal Liaison Office went out of the ward past old Jambagirrila watching and waiting by the door for his grandson, Bridges said, 'looks like you and I've got an interesting joint project ahead of us, Fred.' But Archer simply snorted and continued into the corridor, glancing around in case the great man was calling him back. The Chief was apparently sleeping already, as well he might, after the injuries and insults that he had suffered at the hands of ratbags and radicals…

Avoiding all notice of Manggululu in his chair, now being pushed by his delinquent grandfather, Archer deliberately strode away from them all. Mani looked up at Bridges as they came abreast of each other. They gazed at one another as friends with much to share, that must be left until another time.

'Take it easy there, mate! Bridges said. 'You should be getting full rest, too, you know!'

'Yeah, I, will now, mate,' the patient suddenly appeared to be very tired and uncomfortable, and slumped back in the chair to let his grandfather take him to where he would be surrounded by the care that he needed. The Sister was approaching with a fresh jug of iced water, and although they were out of her ward in under the time she had allowed them, she clearly was still not pleased with these unruly invaders.

Bridges phone rang but before he answered he said, 'Sorry Sister, we've been giving you a hard time. Then, as he answered his phone he indicated to Mani, 'Just a second, Bridges here, but please hold…" He then looked back at Mani. 'You take care and I'll see you later.' Mani simply nodded, and closed his eyes. Then to Jambagirrila, 'you all right, old man? Jack Foster coming with a taxi, eh?'

'Ee-ee, you got it right. I'll be 'ere for that taxi car. I gotta look after my granson. See 'im awright…' the worried elder said. He continued as Bridges backed away listening. 'Bye an' bye I can take my proper big man 'ome to that island. All them other people, they can see, and they can say it's buruli now…'e can stay there with his wife, an' look after us people there.'

Mani turned towards Bridges, opening his eyes and rolling them upwards briefly in the direction of his grandfather. He flipped a hand over open palm up, a silent comment about the scenario that his grandfather had just announced for his future career on Goose Island.

Bridges read its meaning. 'Who knows how it will turn out? I must seriously consider my grandfather and my wife and people.' Bridges gave him the Be Strong sign, and both nodded their positive understanding, as he walked out of the ward and answered into his phone, 'Sorry about that'

'Gray, it's Livvy, listen please. I'm still at the hostel with Helen and…and her new parents….'

'How's it all going?' he asked.

'Yeah, going well, I think, all things considered,' Livvy sounded uncertain. 'Helen and Lura are so ready for this. I'm sure, when they get over the strangeness of it all, they're going to be just fine. But Helen's scared of the old man, her daddy. After what happened the other night, it's no wonder, is it? But he's being a quiet old darling. He can see that she's really not ready to get close to him. And, here's why I'm calling you now. Helen wants to go to the Nomad Hostel just with Lura, and that's where her daddy, Bilago…what's his name, Lagi?'

'Yeah, Lagi Lagiaga,'

'As you know….where he's staying, too,' she explained. 'He has said to me, and I think he's right, that it's too soon for him to travel in the same car as Helen. He said, the same car as his daughter. As me daughter,' he said. 'And I got all choked up. Oh, Gray he's a sensitive old man. He doesn't want to worry her any more. So, is there any chance for you to come back this way and drive him to their hostel?'

'Is Dick Sheehan still there?' he asked.

'Yes, he must be in here somewhere,' she reasoned. 'His car is still outside. But I thought, since the old man already knows you…I told him you might be coming back here, and asked if he'd like to travel with you, and he was pleased with that suggestion. I hope you…'

'No, no! It's not a problem,' Bridges assured her. 'I'll see you in a few minutes.'

* * *

In the hospital car park he stared ahead at the build up of dark cloud in the south east. There was no doubting the season. Within the hour they would be deluged, and on the plains, the man-high spear grass would bend a little lower as it was pounded by another onslaught.

Chapter 30
The end, or new beginning?

When Bridges drove up the drive of the Catholic Hostel grounds, Livvy came out to meet him, he parked a few metres from the hostel entrance. Across the driveway on the central lawn, sitting alone, cross-legged under the big mango tree, was Lagi. Bridges gave him a low wave, and the old man answered with a side-tilted bow of his head.

'Thanks for coming, Gray,' Livvy was obviously relieved but visibly concerned. She waved to the old man under the tree, and went on without waiting for any response. And continued, 'we're ready to move off, if you don't mind letting us have the car.'

'This car?' said Bridges.

'Yes, sweetie. I thought you wouldn't mind if we took it. It means I can do a quick call in at the office. Then I can come and pick you up after you take the old man back to their hostel, okay?'

Bridges marvelled again at her nerve! Would he mind? 'And what will we do for a car?' he asked lightly.

'I've called a taxi for you'.

'For me?' There was no hiding his irritation. He hated being organised in his absence. 'Where? Here?'

'That's right, you and Lagi Lagiaga.' Livvy seemed to think it was the only reasonable thing to do. 'I was sure you wouldn't mind. Father Dick's still here problem-solving with the staff. And he wants to talk with you about something. He wondered if you would call in for two or three minutes.'

Sister Bernadette was holding open the screen door for Lura and Helen to come through, and Bridges could see that there was no time to argue. 'Okay,' he affirmed. 'So I'll go see the priest. How long is it before the taxi comes?'

She looked at her watch, 'Twenty minutes. I hope you don't mind. I had to do something because you weren't here to talk to about it.'

Of course he didn't mind, not much, not now that she acknowledged that he had a right to mind.

'What is it Dick Sheehan wants to talk about? Soft Aid, is it?'

'I think so. That's what he tried to talk to me about. But it wasn't possible in the time. He's keen to get us thinking about it.'

'What did you tell him?'

'I told him I'd think about it.'

'Didn't you tell him I'd think about it too.'

'I don't speak for you, darling. You know that.'

'Okay, okay,' Bridges let it go. 'I'll go in and see him...but I'm not going to discuss the ins and outs of Soft Aid with him today.'

'Two or three minutes he said! That's all he wants. Two or three minutes of your time,' Livvy reminded him quietly, as the three women from the hostel approached them.

Bridges was moderatly irritated by Sheehan's imposition, because he had a clear responsibility now to stay with Lagi Lagiaga, who was waiting for the taxi that would soon be here for them both.

'Okay, I'll pop in and see him. You'll be needing these,' he handed her the car keys.

'And you'd better take this,' she took from her handbag the envelope containing sheets from George Simpson's notes that she had received from the priest. 'I've scan read it, but I'll have to read it carefully later on to take it in.'

'Right!' he agreed with finality, as they turned to greet the women. Helen's hair was caught up by the gusting wind, and she swung about to save her hair-do.

'Aaargh!' she complained. 'I hate this wind! It makes me cold!'

'Oh, it's not cold,' Sister Bernadette disagreed, as she smiled at the Bridges. 'I wish it would really cool things down. It'd be lovely if it did.'

'Well, it's cold to me!' Helen insisted, rubbing her upper arms with her hands.

'This wind's my friend,' her mother, Lura confided. 'She comes to visit me every year. They say it's Knock- em-Down time, but it's never knocked me down, yet. It brings me good messages. The storms are over, and the easy dry days are coming back. We got good days coming now, daughter. I'm gonna look after you, my little girl.'

As she said the last three words she stood closer to the tall young woman and looked up into her face with a restrained grin. Helen's miserable pose vanished as she broke into a laugh and gently held her mother by the shoulders. 'I'm going to look after you, little mother, you mean.'

'Oh, that's so sweet!' Livvy said. 'You two look just right together.'

Lura glanced across to her old husband sitting in the shade, and signalled with a hand flat on her chest. He was watching and replied with a similar movement. Clearly he was content to wait for Bridges and the taxi to take him to their hostel after the women left.

'He really is the best person that I 'ave ever met,' Lura looked at Livvy as she spoke, but it was clear that she was saying this for Helen to hear. 'A truly good man…an' a good man is 'ard to find, eh?'

'That's the truth, and there's a fact,' Sister Bernadette was quick to concur.

'Yes, I'll agree with that, too,' Livvy smiled at Bridges, with the old lady noticing.

'Livvy,' she said softly. 'Don't ever let anyone make you sail away from your good man…'

'Wild horses couldn't get me away from him, Lucy,' Livvy assured her.

'That's the way it should be,' the old woman declared. 'I'm glad for you. But I'm not Lucy, darlin'. I'm Lura. Always I've been Lura, but I was made a prisoner in somethin' different. Now I can be in my own life again, an' I can be who I always was. So now I'm goin' to be always Lura, you know?'

'Yes, Lura. I know what you mean. And I wish the real Lura real happiness.' Livvy turned towards Lura's daughter, her own volatile fellow-worker, quiet now but fascinated with every word and action of the little old woman she only called Mother. 'And you too, Helen, and your fa...your family, to have great happiness together.'

Helen slipped her hand into the hook of her mother's arm, and, turning away from the Bridges, she spoke softly. 'Mother.'

Lura placed her hand gently over her daughter's, and waited.

'Mother, I am happy, really happy to have you 'ere after all those years without yah. I…I know we are going to...to be good friends. But I am still mixed up. I'm not a very good person…'

'You are my precious girl and you're good to me…'

'But I can't talk to 'im ...yet. Please don't think I hate him, Mother. I believe yah e's good, but he's been hurt by bad men. That's why he's…'

'Broken, girl, that's what 'e is, a broken man. But we'll love 'im and care for 'im. And we'll pray for 'im. And you'll see, 'e'll mend and be as good as ever 'e was. I know 'e will. But 'e'll need us, Darlin. We'll all need each other now.'

Bridges came near to say goodbye. 'Excuse me, ladies. You'll have lots of things to talk about now, but I'd like you to keep on thinking of us as being available to be called on as your friends. Right now, I'm going over to see Lagiaga, and inside, to talk with Father Sheehan. So I'll wish you both all the best.'

He turned to Livvy. 'And I'll see you over at the Nomad Hostel when you get back there, after you've been to town…yes?'

'Yep, I won't keep you waiting,' she promised.'

As he walked across the driveway to the old man under the tree, he turned and called back to the mother and daughter. 'Have a happy life now!'

Sister Bernadette saw the three women into the car, and backed away, ready to hurry inside as soon as they left. With the breeze, the deep shade and the darkening sky it was almost pleasantly cool where Lagiaga was sitting on the lawn.

'G'day!' Bridges dropped down beside the old man. 'Buruli?'
'Ee-ee! Good, Gayu! You, too?' The greeting shocked Bridges. Lagi had not called him Gayu, Big Brother, before. It was strange that he would use the Gayu term of deference now, especially because his smile displayed an unusual excitement. Bridges put it down to the uniquely exciting events occurring in the old man's life. They had never talked about a kinship agreement between them to warrant this use of the status title, Gayu; and they had hardly begun to get to know each other.

It was troubling to suppose that perhaps the old man was simply deferring to the Balanda as someone of a superior race. That would be doubly unacceptable. This Balanda would never be older than Lagi. If anyone was the older brother here it was the Wainanda man. He was looking past Bridges at the women settling into the car, and watched until Livvy drove by and gave a wave. The passengers were both in the back, and looked without waving. Suddenly Lagi rose to his feet and quickly shuffled across the lawn, past the tree's wide trunk, to watch the car all the way to the exit. Once it was out of sight he returned and sat precisely where he had been before.

'Now,' said Bridges. 'We're goin' to wait here for a taxi. Is that right?'
'Yes, e'll be 'ere bye an' bye.'
'About a quarter of an hour, I think,' Bridges told him.
'Oh, yeah. That's all right, eh? We can go that way to that other station.'
'To the Nomad Hostel?' Bridges checked.
'Yeah,' Lagi looked at him vaguely. 'That's the one. That other 'ostel.'
Bridges drew from his shirt pocket two folded papers, one from Father Sheehan, and the other from Andrew Brown. It had occurred to him that he shouldn't just leave this old man sitting here alone and neglected, while he himself was away talking

with the priest. He recalled now that, in the hospital, he had heard from Lagi about the great relationship that he had enjoyed with George Simpson, whose ghost had visited him at the scene of the murder.

The two page letter that Livvy had given him, written by a Simpson brother, might be of interest to the old man now. It also occurred to Bridges that, if he didn't take it inside with him, then he wouldn't get drawn in today by Dick Sheehan, to discussing detailed stuff that might be in the paper. He unfolded it and glanced over the contents. As far as he could see, it was a bit of plain common sense about positive human relationships.

'Brother,' he said, reciprocating the closeness that had been shown to him by the old man. 'This here is two pages with words from someone I think you might know.'

The old man was immediately interested. 'Have you got your glasses with you?'

'I got 'em,' he removed them from his shirt pocket, and carefully put them on, while Bridges explained to him, 'This other one is from your brother, Thin Man, at the lock-up.'

'Whoa!' Lagi was amazed. 'Two letters for me, 'eh. Whoo! Soon I'll wear out my glasses, an' have ta get another one…Me brother, eh? I can read is letter, then I have ta go to see 'im after.'

'Don't make yourself too tired today, old man,' Bridges cautioned. 'Maybe tomorrow you can go to see him, eh? Today you've got a wife and daughter to be thinking about.'

'That's right.' Lagi sounded glad to agree, but looked as if he might begin to weep, then laughed instead.

'I'm too busy bloke today, eh? I have ta clean my glasses and read my letters. An' talk to my family, too. Too busy.'

'You are, old man, with family business.' Bridges affirmed. 'You really are. Now I have to go and see someone in there.' He looked towards the hostel entrance. 'And then I'll come back before the taxi gets here, okay?'

Lagi was more interested to get the papers in his hand, and simply nodded his head and muttered, 'mmmh!' as he took them.

'I'll be as quick as I can,' Bridges promised as he turned towards the entrance porch across the driveway. The screen door opened easily, and the front door had been left ajar by Sister Bernadette. He entered and was met by the Sister coming to the doorway of the reception lounge on the right.

'I wonder if you would mind, Mister Bridges?' she asked politely. 'Just coming in here for a moment. I know Father wants to share something with you, but I need to share something too.' He followed her in, wondering what was on her mind. She seemed slightly nervous.

'I won't keep you,' she assured him, half-closing the door for privacy, and turning to address him.

'I just want to explain that Father Sheehan would have come out to see you himself, but he's involved in helping two of our community members to understand each other. As you know, our dear Helen has been disturbed, and she's upset one of our older community members, and, there's been a difference of opinion with someone else… and things get said. Well, so it goes. Otherwise Father would have come out to see you.'

Bridges imagined the possible repercussions from Helen's unpredictably explosive temperament and vulgar vocabulary in a nunnery! 'Say no more, Sister,' he sensed that she, herself, was shaken by the staff crisis, whatever it was. 'I'm sure Helen has been very fortunate to have such caring support from you and your sisters,' he assured her.

She smiled lightly and whispered, 'Thank you. Would you come this way, please?' At the end of the long carpeted passage she asked Bridges to wait as she opened an office door and entered. A moment later Father Dick Sheehan appeared.

'Ah, Gray! Thank you for coming. I did want to speak to you today.' He stood close, and stared into Bridges' face. 'Listen, Gray! Let me get right to the point. The resources are there. The money required for a couple of people to evaluate the whole approach of our society to assisting genuine Aboriginal advancement! It's there! It's a given! Someone is going to have that grant to spend on doing that job. I've prayed about it, and I have to tell you that there is no-one with better qualifications and experience for this assignment than you and Olivia.

'I really want to hear you say that you will do it! It could do so much for the future well-being of all of our indigenous people. What do you say, Gray?'

'Well, Dick. I appreciate your confidence, but, after the last couple of days, I'm thinking that maybe Livvy and I should be staying where we are able to keep the politicians and bureaucrats honest.'

'You can't!' the priest was dogmatic. 'If they are honest they'll be honest, and if they're dishonest, they'll be dishonest whether or not you are there to watch them. Face it, Gray! Your future direction must be decided without hitching your wagon to the present masters of the status quo! Who else do you know who is going to be able to use the Soft Aid concept as a measuring stick for all kinds of existing programmes of development?'

'Dick, listen, mate…'

'Gray, forget about being alongside the politicians. After all, who else would be better able to get alongside the people who are the victims of current bumbling attempts to serve indigenous people and their communities?'

'I don't know, Dick,' Bridges confessed. 'But I'm sure that they're out there somewhere!'

'You may believe that, but I don't!' the priest was emphatic. 'You and Livvy can truly listen. You could discover and raise awareness of the people's perception of the way things are being done. It's become very clear to me that we have right here the right people for the job, as well as the resources to enable it to happen.' He paused, waiting.

'What do you say, Gray?'

'Oh, I'll have to read some more about Soft Aid and talk through all the ramifications of taking such a leap…'

'Yes, Gray. You do that, then take the exciting leap into bringing light and newness. Don't settle for a safe, secure pozzie as a functionary for the keepers of the status quo.'

* * *

Lagi Lagiaga stared at the two letters that Bridges had left with him. In his hands, the pair of unfolded pages seemed old. One of them had begun to turn yellow at the edges, and felt as if it might break if he handled it roughly. The old writing, in pencil, was like something from a dead person, and he hesitated to read it. There was no way that he would knowingly do anything to offend the dead. He had put this letter down on the grass before him, and waited respectfully and nervously. Then he read the one on new paper, from Andrew the Thin Man.

It was a good letter. Always Thin Man wrote good letters to him. This one was different, and he could not hold back the tears that flowed from the dusty dry place inside him.

I have always looked down on you, and I have been one of the people always ready to give you blame and advice, about what to do, and hand-outs, but I never accepted anything from you, and never waited to hear you, or listened to you with respect. For all this I am now really sorry. Forgive me. All that is finished now. Please give me another chance, to be your respectful friend, as well as your brother.

It was some minutes before he turned back to the faded pages on the grass in front of him. Gently, he picked them up, and noticed a pencilled heading, which he read, 'Extract of letter from George Simpson, at Gugurr'.

'Oh, Gayu! My Gayu!' he gasped, and put the pages back on the grass in front of his folded legs. A letter? It was a letter. At Gugurr, he could hear him again, even now. 'I have to finish writing a letter to my sister...' He moved back from it. 'Gayu, you come to me again! That night-time before, when I fell down an' cut my arm. Now again! I'm still 'ere now, you see. This is me, still livin' my life now, Gayu. You didn't die for nothin', when you saved me at Gugurr country!'

The rising breeze moved the paper and he lurched forward to grab it before it blew away. Listening, behind the sound of the wind in the trees...he held his breath...here were horses coming. Walking horses. Dandy was there, Gayu's horse with his smart stepping. He knew that sound on the track. 'You're early, mate!'

He blinked in confusion at the sound of Gayu George Simpson's voice...and the clear breathing of approaching horses. There was a strong scent in the air. Pardner and Nugget! They were there, too. He knew their smell! And he looked about him.

'Early? No way. I mus' be very late...this time. Very late!'
'You're early, mate!'
'Yeah, I can 'elp you. I'm ere now, Gayu. I was hidin' by the river. They never found me. You made me hide, an' I'm still alive, now.' Looking about him he saw no sign of Gayu or the horses, but was still aware of their presence. After a few moments of silence, he leaned forward and picked up the pages with the written words of Gayu George.

'We still got long way to go!' he said. 'I can look at your 'and-writin'? That won't 'urt me.' He looked around. The sky was darkening, and the wind was picking up. Grasping the paper in one hand to stop it from blowing away, and bringing it close to see it clearly, he read his Gayu's words. It made him catch his breath and hold back the cry that tried to escape from his heart. 'Hoh, my good friend. You didn't die for nothin'. I can 'ear you, an' I can listen you. Tell me now, what you want to say to me?' He tried to focus on the page before him, then tucked it under his leg while he pulled out the front tail of his shirt, breathed on the lenses of his glasses and rubbed them clean with the shirt, then he replaced them and began to read what was in front of him from George Simpson.

So Sis, here is my strategy for what it's worth. I want to tell the world the way Harry works here, and that us Australians, black and white and in between, can live side by side and get on, and have a society that includes all of us as real people. It is all about how people treat people. This is how I see what Harry calls the Soft Aid approach. It's the most sensible way of helping people to help themselves. Much better than the usual way of putting people under pressure to be something that they're not, in grand social engineering schemes, to civilise them, or subsidise them, or even to Christianise them. The Soft Aid way has more saving grace in it than any high-handed programme of assimilation or indoctrination. Sez who? Sez me! Any way, I've written down my version of it, here. I am leaving this for Jenny to post off with the next boat. Lagi Lagiaga is outside loading our pack-horse, right now. We decided to leave early. By daybreak we'll be well along the track. So, as soon as I finish this letter we'll be on our way. I can't believe our time at Gugurr is all over, but I suppose all good things come to an end. See you in Melbourne for Christmas, dear Sis.

Your loving brother, George (See Enclosed 1).

Turning to the second page, Lagi gently flattened it between the palms of his hands before beginning to read.

'Simpo's Soft Aid Strategy…

… Lagi held the paper closer, to examine what had appeared to be mere scribble.

Someone had written there in light, spidery letters, 'God forgive me.'

Who had read this and prayed to be forgiven?…Could it be the Hunter's hand-writing? Might be…He removed his glasses and turned his head to listen. Confused…there was a sound of voices… were they real …there wasn't much time left.

Same way for taxis or horses. You have to get ready at the right time. He held his breath and listened. There was that voice again…'You 'ad a sleep?'

'No. We should go quick.' Who was asking? Was it Gayu George?

He rose to his feet and slowly walked again to the tree trunk and around it. He glanced about the garden and drive-way…No-one was there, and the voices and horses had faded away…There was no car or taxi out this way.

Nothing yet. No horses, and no taxi. 'I 'aven't started to saddle up yet.' He became anxious about both the voice and what it was telling him. It was a worry. It always was.

There was no two ways about it, he was in trouble…as he had been ever since the attack…He must be careful. There was danger all around this place, too. The wind gusted alarmingly as the old man turned back towards the house. No-one in sight. But they could be hiding anywhere….Under the house? Was the voice in the wind?… Or did they want the croc skins from under there? 'You get the croc skins from under the house,' the voice continued. 'By the time you've strapped 'em on Nugget, I'll be ready. Croc skins? …Gayu might die!... And me…Me now! I might die today, too!' He felt Gayu there…

Lagi looked about him and up at the sky. He saw the mass of dark cloud racing overhead above the mounting wind, and as the dying moon cleared, it was brilliant for a moment. Afternoon seemed to have turned as dark as night, and over the driveway, lantern light was still showing around the open shuttered window, but there was no other sign of light in the rest of the house. He carefully started across the driveway to look about, and in through the windows. Now the voices wouldn't shut up! 'No sleep this night… Old men say…danger, strangers too close. Go quick before sun up.'

It seemed real enough to take seriously. He hurried to the house with a blustery tail wind at his back. The moon was suddenly bright again, in spite of the wild, dark sky.

…You look out! You look out for Irrwadbad. Keep away from that woman bad business…Gayu George…You look out!'

The front door opened and Bridges emerged in a hurry, and was surprised to see that old Lagi had moved across the driveway and apparently had been looking through the windows….

'I'm all clear now,' Bridges announced. 'If you're ready, brother, let's move out!
'You ready?' the old man seemed to be hesitant about leaving. 'You already finished that jura letter for your sister?'

Bridges stared at him, and a blast of cooler air heightened the chilly feeling that arose at being caught in a strange role-change, being taken as someone somewhere else. No telling what it might be like for an alcoholic who goes cold turkey.

Perhaps the reference to the letter applied to something in the house rather than the papers that he had left with the old man. Stepping forward to touch the two-paged letter he held in his hand, Bridges asked Lagi, 'have you finished reading this letter?' The old man, puzzled and speechless, looked at the jura and then at Bridges.

Bridges broke the silence, and left George Simpson's letter in Lagi's hand for the time being, cancelling the need for an answer to his question.

'Thanks for waiting while I was doing my work,' he said.
'You, too Gayu George!' Lagiaga insisted. 'You waited for do your good work, to write for your family jura letter.'

Bridges glanced at the old man. Convinced now of his confusion about what was really happening, he decided to move slowly, and relate to things that were real to his companion. 'How is your sore arm today?' he asked.

Feeling the bandaged area under his shirt-sleeve, the old man replied, 'I dunno... Pretty good, I reckon. It's buruli.' He stared at Bridges as if discovering something new there, then asked, 'You saw that sister girl, eh? All finished now? You finished with that sister?'

Bridges sensed that the old man was hoping, with an unexplained fervour, for a positive answer. Hanging on the answer that would come? He saw the simple truth as the only helpful reply. 'Yes, brother. All finished here now! I said goodbye to Sister and the priest. All finished.'

This appeared to give Lagi a great sense of relief. Stepping in front of Bridges, he looked him in the face and asked, 'You buruli...now?'

'Yeah, I'm okay, Gayu,' Bridges decided that it was time he acknowledged who really was elder brother here. 'I'm feeling good. What about you, Gayu? You all right?'

Lagi grinned. 'I'm really happy!' he announced. 'What d'ya reckon? It's time to go?'

As he spoke, the taxi swung into the driveway, it's headlights on full, highlighting the first drops of the downpour.

'Oh, that's good timing!' Bridges declared. 'They stepped back as they were caught by the first shower of the squalling rain in the covered entrance porch. Lagi folded George Simpson's letter, and put it carefully into his shirt pocket with his brother's letter from prison.

'Oy!' he backed further from the intrusive rain. 'Mister Britches, I can't read this jura now. Too much thinkin bout somethin else! What about I keep it, an' you an' me can look at it tomorru? That be awright? What you reckon, Mister Britches? We can talk 'bout this one tomorru?'

'Sure thing,' Bridges was delighted. Not only was he pleased to see that Lagi was lucid again, no longer confusing him with someone else he called Gayu George, but, also, he was the same clearheaded, co-operative informant who had been so helpful when he was a patient in the hospital. Suddenly a thought ignited in the centre of his gut, and he looked at the old man with a shock of recognition. In less time than it took the taxi to come to the end of the drive, Bridges was seized by an exciting scenario for his immediate future.

On a good day this old man beside him could probably provide the tough wisdom of experience to any discussion about giving support to Aboriginal people and groups, and he knew the Simpsons. This was the same man whose memories had put Bridges on the scent of his brother, Thin Man, and of why he might have killed old Ron Smart. He had chosen to stay with his own people when plenty of his contemporaries were throwing in their lot with the Balanda conquerors, and he had suffered for his choices, and yet, at the same time, he had become literate and a community health worker.

Today, for a while, Lagi had lapsed into a delusionary episode, and no wonder; but, years ago, he had survived frontier violence and had been a cross-cultural worker guiding and treating people through deadly epidemics. He had also survived the devastation of becoming a broken no-account, alcoholic pariah, and lived into old age. One day, possibly as soon as tomorrow, together, they might begin to open up the past again, and get clear the Simpsons' way of working with people.

Just as the taxi pulled up, the peak downpour fell on them like a wind-driven waterfall! Lagiaga went for the near side back door as Bridges dashed around to the other side, and they both scrambled into the back seat and shut out the flood.

'Thanks, driver!' Bridges staged a merry voice. 'You've got impeccable timing!'
'Thank you, kind sir,' the driver replied. 'We always try to please!' He looked at them in the mirror. 'A-a-nd where are we to?'

Bridges glanced at Lagi, remembering who he had been and who he was now.

When the old man hesitated, Bridges asked. 'Where do you want to go now, Gayu?'

His fellow traveller grinned at the joke that he was anybody's gayu, but raised his voice as he leaned back and sat tall to tell the driver, 'I wanna go an' see my wife an' daughter! You can take us to that Nomad Hostel, okay?'

'Not ay problem!' the driver told them as he glanced at his mirrors and set course for down town Darwin. Although the wipers were useless against the torrents that blasted across the wind-screen, and the reflected headlights glared back from the streaming rain but did nothing to improve the failing light on the road ahead, the passengers relaxed, and left it to the driver, the man of experience, to get them to their destination.
'I just want to say, Lagi,' Bridges turned to the man beside him. 'I really am sorry that I've been making you wait all the time, while I went to talk to other people.'
'Don' worry 'bout keepin me waitin,' Lagi told him. 'I been waitin' all my life.'
"And what are you waiting for now Lagi?"
"Who me?" he was amuzed. "Ah…we might get a fair go one day…Now some clever Arardbi young blokes being a go-between an' you watch 'im…'e might be anything that boy. They might listen to 'im.

"You mean Mani Manggululu," Bridges asked.

"That's the one now! 'e can be…a what yah call 'im? A gon…saltnt! That what I reckon. All the guberments and job bosses…or missions…everyone, what is the right way to fix us proppa law ways 'an 'elping us for all the people? Ah…listen to 'em, an' that one young bloke for consultant. That's it…I reckon."

Bridges smiled in agreement, 'Sounds good to me Lagi,' he said, as his phone rang.

It was Livvy calling, Gray told her, 'I was just thinking of calling you. How are you three ladies getting on?'

'All good', she replied. 'But darling, we were wondering if you could get a bed for the night at Lagiaga's hostel, and let Helen and her mum stay the night here at our place; and we could start to get to know each other tomorrow? What do you say?'

Gray hesitated, amazed again at Livvie's daring ideas, and Lagi spoke for him, 'Yo, you can come to my place, I'll show you the way…'

The End?

Appendix one

From Mani's speech in the YMCA, the ancient story of Yumbarbar…

'On North Goulburn Island, over near my own people's country there once lived a giant. His name was Yumbarbar. He lived alone in the jungle and he was a people-eater…a…what do yah call 'em…a cannibal. Nobody would go near that jungle, although there was good hunting there, and plenty of wild honey, and yams and all kinds of bush tucker. The people lived in fear, and never felt free to go where they wanted to go in their own country. That's why I think of Yumbarbar when I think about white racism.

There was one of the men called Mayanaj. He was a shaman kind of bloke, a healer and guide. They all knew he was a man of peace, who never made a fight with anyone…but he could heal people and sometimes he stopped fights and helped people to be friends. One day he decided that he would go into the jungle. No-one had been there for a long time, and he thought he would see if it was still dangerous to go collecting honey, and the inside bark for making rope. He took with him a woven bag and a stone axe for cutting the outer bark.

When he was getting near to where the giant was lying asleep, a fly landed on Mayanaj…to get his sweat. It travelled on him until he was close to Yumbarbar, who was sleeping behind the bushes. Then it flew on to the giant.

Straightway 'e woke up. He knew that something had brought this fly, and 'e sprang up saying, 'A man is coming and waking me up from my sleep.' He saw Mayanaj, and laughed as he bent over and grabbed two very big fighting-sticks shouting,

'Here you are, little man, I will fight you fair.' Just like people throw Aborigine's money today and say now, Come and compete with the strong people. Yumbarbar threw the big stick to Mayanaj and nearly knocked him over. It fell to the ground and when the man bent over to pick it up, Yumbarbar hit him across the back with the other one and knocked him flat.

Mayanaj told himself, 'This is the finish for me.' But he would not believe that, and jumped up as quick as he could and grabbed the fighting-stick. He could just swing it, but before he could use it, the giant laughed again and said, 'this time little man, I'm going to finish you off,' and hit Mayanaj across the back again and knocked him flat.

'This time I'm really finished,' thought Mayanaj, but still he wouldn't believe it, and jumped up again. He knew that there was not much he could do to beat the giant and save his life.

Already Yumbarbar was standing over him with his feet wide apart and was lifting the fighting-stick above is head. Mayanaj could only think of one thing to do and he did it. He swung the big fighting-stick as hard as he could up between the giant's legs.

It was a direct hit in his balls, and the people back in the camp heard Yumbarbar's yell of pain. Down he fell with a great crash, and Mayanaj, who never used violence, very quickly pulled his stone axe from his belt and bashed in the giant's head. One good hit killed Yumbarbar, and Mayanaj turned and ran away from this terrible thing that he had done.

When he arrived back at the camp all the people wanted him to tell what had happened, but he couldn't speak. He vomited because of the horrible thing that had happened, and he lay down exhausted and slept.

'Next day the people wouldn't believe his story, so he took them to the place where Yumbarbar's body was. They could hardly believe it even when they saw it, but then they began to sing and dance right there. 'Now, we have to tell the people of the coast the story of Mayanaj and how he set us free from the giant,' they said. 'So that they will believe us we will take out one of Yumbarbar's big yellow eyes, and show it in a new ceremony. And since that time, two men can take the eye of Yumbarbar and sing and dance and tell the story in many places. And still today the people of the islands and coast sing and tell the story.

'It's a story for us people here tonight, too. "White racism" is the name of the giant we got to kill…but not just in someone else. In ourselves first of all. That's where the jungle is, the jungle where white racism makes us afraid to go in…is inside us! I say we got to kill that white racism in ourself…and that doesn't mean we got to be violent against other people. But it means no-one can expect me to put up with anything that is keepin' that white racism going. If I get the chance, you know where I'm goin' to hit that white racism whenever I see it? Where it hurts the most'.

Appendix two

The dialogue continued between Mani and The Chief Minister Blyth in The minister's office…

Mani continued. 'But since the first constitution and the Australian Commonwealth was created, you 'ave been telling us that we are a part of the Australian way. But the actions show another way, yet you tell us we are free to do as we please. And I guess we could be, but only if we lose our identity as a race. But if we keep our identity, then we are discriminated against and marginalised. So the questions is…why doesn't your government be straight and truthful for once, and tell it like it is? That is…that you really want us to assimilate, thereby losing our identity as a race and culture'.

Mani finished off by asking, 'are yah really serious about helping our people now?'

'Yes I am,' said Blyth, 'and will do anything within my power and within the law that can further your cause.'

'That would be good, but it's about time, that someone up the ladder helped our people. First there was invasion. Then there was colonisation, and still there is colonisation. We don't want to be colonised anymore. And we also don't want that assimilation policy…So what's next?'

'Do you mean a change in the constitution?' asked Blyth.

'Yep. We people of this land are the only original people of any of the colonised countries that weren't respected with a treaty. And even in 1901 when the constitution was created we were of so little value to the Commonwealth that we were not even mentioned'.

'Yes, but that all will change, and the government is looking at ways to incorporate indigenous people into it…'

'Mr Minister, In 1988 Prime Minister Hawk said that constitutional recognition would 'appen within his time. But it didn't appen, and it didn't take long before his people said it would take at least ten years. And then later Prime Minister John Howard recognised that there was long overdue recognition that this nation is on stolen land… but still nothing happened. The Australian government has the opportunity to put that right but they drag their heels with all sorts of reasons.'

Blyth interjected. 'It's a complex matter…'

But Mani interrupted. 'I reckon the main reasons why the so called "Commonwealth" excluded us in 1901 was because it was believed that any official recognition of my people could lead to claims for rights, or compensation for land taken since European invasion…and nothing has changed'…He allowed Blyth to make a comment.

The Chief Minister, was conciliatory when he said, 'neither the government or the politicians can change the Constitution. It can only be changed after a referendum, and then our highest court, the High Court, has the final say on interpreting the Constitution.' He waited for Mani to reply, but when he didn't he continued. 'Look, we know that currently, Aboriginal and Torres Strait Islanders are still not recognised or specifically mentioned in the Constitution, but if you give us a chance…'

Again Mani jumped in, and baited his hook, 'was there another reason for the constitution?'

'Yes…I…guess so…it was to unite all the people of this country and all the separate colonies into one, for one people…'

'But we weren't considered people, would that be correct?' Mani offered. 'Would it be true that not only is the constitution to be all the laws, it's s'posed to show a nation's values of itself?'

Knowing he was being made to look a fool, Blyth stuttered, '…I…I guess so…'

'Yah guess so? You can't be serious. As you agree with me, that the constitution is supposed to give the nations values, it must be right then that it represents what the people of this country want?'

Blyth had no choice but to mutter, 'of course'.

'Then do the Australian people care enough about us or not…enough to vote in a referendum?'

'I should think so.'

'Then why the 'ell does the government not get out of the way and let the people have their say. Then we will know. All the government has to do is to organise a refrerendum and get on with it. But they don't as they know, like in 1901, by recoganising us that there will be changes, compensation, and a final end to the hidden agenda of assimilation.'

'Mani, I agree with you…you are correct. But…but one of the issues is the way the constitution was worded, the preamble, and a change of this nature creates complications. Believe me, an expert panel is…'

'Well there can't be real reconciliation until we are reco'nised. Nor can there be proper social justice if we remain nameless in the constitution. But bugga that, we will be seen and 'eard…so the disadvantage and marginalisation will stop'

Blyth tried again. 'Over recent decades the various governments have tried to understand and meet the issues of Aboriginal and Torres Strait Islander disadvantages. Even now the government is talking about a Royal Commission to support the process. But Mani, it does take time.'

'We don't need another Royal Commission. The Australian's don't need another Royal Commission…everyone knows of the plight of our people. They know that our peoples are dyen…they're dyen in jail, they dyen of diabetes they dyen of substance abuse…they suiciden…of bordom because they be with no land and got nothing to do. Everyone knows of the abuse our kids get when in jail. Just look out the window an' you'll see what's going on… Australians don't want more discussion papers…We have the right to self-determination…that's international law. So, no more reports, no more do-gooders coming to help us. Give us the right to self-determination and we will tell you how we want you to support us…'

Appendix three

From discussion at the YMCA with Margaret…re a treaty… (refer page 234)

'I've come err to tell yah about why we need a treaty…'

Pausing briefly, she looked at her notes. 'The government don't want us to 'ave a treaty, but we gunna get one… one day we will get it'.

A roar of approval erupted from the crowd, but soon quietened so they could listen.

'The government reckons that we not organised enough to get all the peoples to agree because we too many nations. But we bin have treaties between all the nations for thousands of years…These were not written on paper, which is jus' dead trees. Our treaties are written in the land, they are in the rocks and known by our Ancestors.

Another cheer went up for the young lady. 'What we want in a treaty is us deciding what we want because we know. This would come from the grassroots… from youse, from all the people of all the tribes of all the nations. There could be many treaties, as there are many nations but we would make them one.

Once done, it must also be acceptable to all Australians, white Australians and new Australians that come from other countries…and it is only by doin' that then we can grow as a strong nation in togetherness.'

More cheers.

'Many reckon that the treaty and the Constitution are part of the same job. Some believe that the treaty needs to be done first, as it's with the treaty that the Constitution should be changed for us. But then there are others who reckon that the treaty will take long time, and so the Constitutional recognition should come first.

What we need is some sort of Aboriginal assembly, which is representative of all of the different mobs of this country that they call Australia.

And when it is ready it will be submitted to the government for acceptance, and then legislation, and also part of the Constitution. Our treaty must also 'ave international recognition. An in that treaty we want to 'ave the right of self-determination.

But in spite of lots of calls for a treaty between us the Commonwealth Government has resisted. A typical thing they say is that a nation does not make treaties with itself…but we not part of that. They came and took from us, and now we want proper 'elp from them. We want to start with a treaty…A treaty is a statement of recognition and respect… that we is in the land, an' the land is in us…it…it is where our understanding of life is'.

Once again the audience cheered and clapped their understanding. Margaret took the opportunity to have another look at her notes, and then concluded.

'A treaty is also a lot about the need of leadership, our leadership by us. Treaty is not about taking power off the people or the Government. It's about partnerships. A treaty sets all Australians free of that so called terra nullius lie, where all people of this land feel it's wrong…

Simpo's Rules for Trusted Helpers

1. Become trusted friends by being respectful, honest and attentive; and stand by to give help when it is wanted.

2. Never make people answerable to their helpers: they are in charge of their own affairs, and also might be ruled by kinship lores and roles.

3. See help as a put down, unless it's given by family, or people who owe us, or our trusted friends.

4. Never forget that what is suitable can only be decided by the people themselves.

5. And don't forget, responsibility can't be given: it grows up in us as we work for what we have decided to work for.

6. Insist on self-planning because: whoever owns the plan will end up owning the work too.

7. Beware of helping just because you get a lot out of it, it's addictive, and it can be crippling to those you help.

8. Be just, not charitable: offer aid where there is need, and honestly tell what conditions apply.

9. Listen when people state their own conditions on which they are ready to let anyone give them aid.

10. Look for growth in self-management, not for compliance with big helpers, for the sake of more handouts.

11. Believe that; with acceptable help, any free people can still cope, through management by clans or family or teams.

12. That's it in a nutshell. And this I believe.

Signed,

George Simpson

About Jack Goodluck
(by Pat Grayson)

It was Dr Marcus Bach who wrote; *that where our talent meets the needs of the world, that is where God wants us to be.*

Jack Goodluck became an ordained Methodist Minister in 1960. Not wanting to be a "normal" suburban minister, Jack went to Arnhem Land from Melbourne with his wife Peggy and their children, to serve the children and staff of the Croker Island children's Village at Minjilang. It was here that he set out to diminish the devastating effects of widespread prejudice and discrimination towards First Nation's People. This was about the time when men first walked on the moon.

He helped First Nations People for over forty years. Jack was part of a team who initiated and started the Nungalinya College (1974) for adult theological studies, community development, communication skills, and leadership development.

For Jack though, it all had started when his Aunty took him to the museum in Hobart where he saw the skeleton of "Truganini" who at the time was believed to be the last full blooded Aboriginal person in Tasmania. Although he was only eight years old, "little" Jack felt the injustice of the massacres of the time. From that day onwards, Jack was on a path dedicated to First Nations People.

Once, Jack was asked if he was an activist. 'No, no I am more of a support function for the people'. The list of initiatives that Jack instigated on behalf of the First Nations people is long and of credit to him. Jack though, in his humility would rather that they not be mentioned. But certainly what is obvious from his life of dedication is that Jack Goodluck has a love for the original people of this land.

Jack at the time of publishing this book is eighty-nine years of age, his beloved Peggy passed away over two years ago. But Jack is not alone, as there are children, grandchildren, and great grandchildren, who love and support him on a daily basis. But Jack is also happily occupied with memories of a long and satisfying life, knowing that his talents were where God wanted them to be.

Acknowledgement

Song, *Down Under*, sung by Men at Work,

Songwriters: Colin James Hay / Ronald Graham Strykert

Down Under lyrics © EMI Music Publishing, Sony/ATV Music Publishing LLCS

Song Lyrics "Ancestors of Our Land, I Bring You Back to Present Time" by Galarrwuy Yunupingu

Glossary

Knock em Down rains – Northern Territory weather pattern

Sorry business – mourning and working out troubles together

Rom Law (lore) – Lore as handed down from the Dreaming

Madayin – as per Rom Law

Men's business – secret man's place, for worship/learning

Woman's business – secret woman's place, for worship/learning

Namamuiak – creator spirit

Wainandas – fictitious people of the story

Buruli – good

Jura – writing

Drinking camp – placing of inebriation

Dilly bag – a woven grass bag

Territorians – people from the Northern Territory

Assimilation Policy – a policy to "fit" indigenous people into mainstream society.

The Wet – the annual rains and monsoon

Balanda – all white people, based on Hollander's

Macassans – early traders coming from the East Indies/Indonesia

Idji – Uncle (of sorts) and is the most powerful male in an indigenous boy's life